I0675544

Veil of Secrets

A novel of the Seven Deadly Veils, Book Four

Diana Marik

Veil of Shadows
The Blue Veil, a novella
Veil of Mists
Veil of Darkness
Veil of Secrets

Coming Soon:

Veil of Destiny

Praise for Diana Marik's Veilverse

Veil of Darkness

"The chemistry between Miranda and Remare is extraordinary. Marik holds nothing back in this action-packed romance, which delivers all of the danger, darkness and sensuality that readers crave; this is one series not to be missed." TOP PICK! —RT Book Reviews

"Smoking hot chemistry! A wonderful suspense and action novel complete with a sizzling romance. Very addicting!" —L.M. Reigel Reviews

"Another fantastic read in this series. An amazing journey. The characters come to life on the pages pulling you into their world." —PNR/UF Book Lover's Haven

Veil of Mists

"I am obsessed with this series. Diana Marik has created a high intensity series that grabs you and doesn't let go." —Lisa Reigel Reviews

"Danger and deception know no bounds in this riveting second installment of the *Seven Deadly Veils* series. Complex liaisons deliver the action and suspense paranormal fans crave. The passion and sensuality exceed expectations." —RT Book Reviews

"Completely captivating! I LOVE this series and can't get enough of RRRemare. So much happening in this book...deception at its finest! Just when you think you have it figured out, everything changes. Definitely couldn't put this book down and one hell of a ride." —Paranormal/Urban Fantasy Book Lovers Haven

The Blue Veil

"Marik's compelling delivery commands readers' attention; the easy, seamless passion and intensity between characters

is a welcome companion to a perfect balance of action and suspense."
—RT Book Reviews

"The characters are edgy and intriguing. The plot is suspenseful and sexy. I'm drawn into this series and fascinated by this world that Ms. Marik has created."
—Comfy Chair Books

"I am so Team Remare. This novella just keeps us hooked."
—Sik Reviews

"Just one word...Remare. Love that dark and dangerous vampire."
—Paranormal/Urban Fantasy Book Lover's Haven

Veil of Shadows

"The suspense is as dramatic and intense as the action, and paired with Marik's steamy sex scenes, will leave readers satisfied on many levels. Off-the-chart chemistry."
4 STARS HOT—RT Book Reviews

"I flipping LOVED this book. I was drawn immediately to the main characters of *Veil of Shadows*. The characters are edgy, sexy, and intriguing. Her writing style drew me in and kept me fascinated; the suspense kept me on the edge waiting to see what would happen next. *Veil of Shadows* is fast paced and action packed. I highly recommend this book to fans of paranormal romance and romantic urban fantasy."
—Comfy Chair Books

"Ms. Marik has made this new paranormal world come alive and leave me begging for more."
—Sik Reviews

"I absolutely LOVED it! With so many awesome characters, can't decide who I love the most! Refreshing story that completely captivated me. I simply couldn't put it down until the last page."
—PNR/UF Book Lover's Haven

Dedication

For R—You were right!

Acknowledgments

I wish to thank all my readers who've sent me incredible words of encouragement and affection. And to my fans in the Mark's Mortals Fan Club—you guys make me smile.

Special acknowledgment to my editor, Jessica Bimberg—Lady Awesome, who inspires me to excel in creating memorable characters and stories that captivate and delight. And to my cover artist, Kris Norris for the wonderful book covers she designs for me. You guys rock!

Chapter One

"Stop trying to seduce me."

In the vastness of his subterranean archives, Lord Valadon's chuckle sounded smug even to his own ears. "Would I really have to try?" His heart warmed at Miranda's lopsided smile. Frequently, he wondered what he would have to do to win her favor. He could release his pheromones—the allure many vampires used to entice others but denied having. He'd considered it, but she would be highly offended if she realized what he'd done. And that was not who he was. Although, it may have been. A long time ago.

Best not to upset his *Elemental*—especially one with incredible powers. He'd seen what she'd done to one of his Elite Torians. Irina had provoked her into a fight she couldn't win. Miranda had retaliated, using her gifts to blast Irina hard enough against the wall that bones had been broken. He'd never forgotten how her eyes turned black and wondered if Miranda even knew the scope and depth of her abilities. He certainly was curious and contemplated if drinking Remare's blood was somehow enhancing her burgeoning skills.

When Miranda tried to remove the blindfold, he said, "No. Leave it on. Only a few more. Now, open your mouth."

She complied, then offered him a distinctly feminine moan. "Mmm, that's even better than the last one. Creamy, smooth and decadent. I love it."

"Ah, but which one was your favorite?"

Miranda took a deep breath and exhaled. "The first was a mix of orange and apricot coated with milk chocolate. The second morsel had honey and almonds, but the last one," she sighed as if in heavenly bliss, "was blackberry mixed with...pomegranate covered in dark chocolate. Delicious."

"Very good." He removed the blindfold.

"You're going to make me fat with all these chocolate tastings."

"Well, I figured, since your name is on the sweets, you should be the first to sample them."

"I like that you're combining fruits. It gives the taste a certain complexity. I still can't believe you named your chocolate shop, 'Crescent's Chocolates', after me."

"You were the one who gave me the idea, if you remember correctly. The first time I brought you to ValCorp."

"I remember. You were a perfect gentleman when you gave me the tour of ValCorp. You wanted to build a restaurant, and I suggested the chocolatier. I didn't think you took me seriously, though."

"I take everything you say seriously." Valadon glanced over the archives containing his extensive collection of books and paintings. He'd been helping her research the origins of the Human Order of Light, a powerful hate group whose goal was the extermination of his race. For a human, she read uncannily fast and was instrumental in finding ancestral information of some of the HOL's more prominent members. "You've helped me much in researching possible associates of Peralt. Have I been remiss in thanking you for all the time you've given to this project?"

"Not at all. And, as always, you are more than generous in compensation."

He smiled at the genuine warmth in her whiskey-colored eyes. The red striations more pronounced than what he'd remembered. "I try to be." Rarely did he allow himself the deep-rooted pleasure he experienced when in her presence. But Miranda Crescent was unique among women, and she had burrowed deep into his heart.

Unfortunately, she had fallen in love with his second, Remare. It had been difficult adjusting to that reality, but he'd accepted her choice. It was better to have her friendship and loyalty than her ire. In truth, he had two of the strongest allies any high-lord vampire could ever hope to have. He'd be a fool not to realize their worth. Though, not long ago, he'd acted stupidly and nearly lost that which was most precious to him.

He glanced up at the life-size portrait of his deceased sister, Bianca. She would have chastised him for how poorly he'd handled the situation. But that was now past. "Do you want to get out of here for a little while? We've been at it for hours. I think we need a break."

"Sure. What did you have in mind?"

He mentally contacted his butler, Escher, to have a parcel of food prepared for his trip. "Let's go for a ride. I could use some fresh air, and you could, too." He stood. "Give me a few minutes to get ready then meet me upstairs. There's something I want to discuss with you, and I'd rather not do it here."

After Valadon left, Miranda inhaled his wonderful ocean scent that lingered in the air. With his startling green eyes that housed a wealth of knowledge and sculpted good looks the angels must have envied, the High Lord was one of the handsomest and most compelling men to walk the planet. His imposing height alone commanded respect, but it was his deep melodic voice that sometimes sent shivers down her spine.

She gazed down at the books they'd been perusing and felt a pang of guilt. Although she enjoyed helping the High Lord research his enemies, she'd had another reason for agreeing to his more than generous proposal to work in the archives: her origins. As an *Elemental*, she had abilities beyond her scope of reason, powers that scared her as they continually evolved. Peralt was one of the few who had theories about the nature of her kind. He'd given detailed descriptions of the four major elements.

The Undines were the first group he discussed. They had control over the water: oceans, rivers, any water source. Next were the Sylvestris, who had considerable influence with air. Then, there were the Gnomes, who could manipulate the earth. But the last one was the one that intrigued her the most: Vulcanus, those who could invoke fire and use it at will. Miranda glanced down at her hand. She'd had uncanny ability with fire since she was a child. And her powers only seemed to be growing—a fact that both terrified and exhilarated her.

All incredible powers and, in the wrong hands, exceedingly dangerous. Peralt had once thought people like her were spirits, but then later wrote he believed they were descendants of angels. Miranda worried about his theories. She rose and paced. She knew all too well there were good and evil angels. She wondered if there was something to Peralt's cogitations. The human race would have been at a decidedly vulnerable disadvantage if not for those with special abilities. There were all sorts of suppositions that the powers that be had the angels visit earth and mate with humans to give them special attributes to deal with all the hardships they would encounter as their species evolved.

And the rarest of all *Elementals* were the Chameleons, the most powerful of them all. Those individuals who possessed talents in all four areas. Miranda was one of them, and so was her mentor, Guy de Montglat, although her abilities greatly paled compared to his. A fact she could never divulge to anyone. People feared what they didn't understand. During the time of the Inquisition, many innocent people were killed, burned at the stake or suffered other forms of heinous torture simply because they were *Other*.

Only a few close friends knew of her gifts, and she planned to keep it that way. It may take her years of research to find the origins of her kind, but she would keep at it for as long as it took to find the answers she so desperately desired. She instinctively knew there was more information out there, more than Peralt or Montglat had imparted. Somewhere. It was the not knowing that grated. Peralt had mentioned two other authors she'd yet to track down. But she knew, one day, she would.

Shaking off her reveries, she packed up her research and went in search of Valadon. She definitely needed some fresh air to clear her head.

Chapter Two

"My God, when you said 'a ride', I thought you meant your limo," Miranda gushed excitedly. Sure, she'd seen the tourist helicopters plenty of times circling Manhattan, but she never imagined she'd actually ride in one. She spoke loudly to be heard over the whirring of the chopper blades. "Where are we going?"

After donning his aviator glasses, Valadon fastened his seat belt and checked his instrument panel. He grinned at her. "It's a surprise."

His deep, resonant voice never failed to thrill her. As the High Lord of New York City, Valadon was one of the most powerful vampires in the world, wealthy beyond imagination, a force to be reckoned with.

And, at one time, he'd been in love with her.

Pretty heady stuff for an art authenticator. But then, she was hardly what anyone would call normal.

"I bet." Even though the glass of the helicopter was tinted, she kept her sunglasses on to avoid the brightness. She clicked her seat belt and held onto the head gear. "Since when do you know how to fly?"

"Since before you were born. I'm quite capable, I assure you. I've had my pilot's license for decades. We can speak through the head sets, but I'd prefer we speak mentally."

He knew she didn't like invasions into her mind, but when he asked permission, it was more of a request than a violation. *"Okay."*

As they lifted off, she spotted one of his Elite Torians, Tristan, running toward them. Valadon smiled and saluted him.

"Aren't you supposed to have your Torians with you at all times?" In the past his enemies had tried to assassinate him, but he'd out maneuvered them. For that, she was immensely grateful, even though some had suffered terrible deaths. Twelve hundred years old, Valadon was highly intelligent and cunning. Humility, a word not in his vocabulary. Valadon could be incredibly charming, generous, and gracious.

But he could also be arrogant, dictatorial, and ruthless. And, because of that, she was cautious whenever she found herself alone with him.

"I'm their king. I don't answer to them or anyone else. At least, not in my own territory."

Miranda sighed. Choosing not to comment, she marveled at her city. No other place held such profound joy for her. She'd grown up here; this was her home. She almost laughed out loud at the pleasure of seeing New York from above. *"Look, there's the Empire State Building."*

She knew she sounded like a child in her exhilaration, but her giddiness would not abate. *"So, this is what Central Park looks like from above. It's fantastic!"* She shook her head at the sheer awesomeness of the magnificent park. They flew over the carousel, the seals in the zoo, and then Bethesda Fountain where the angel stood erect. Not far from there was her home away from home. Miranda pointed below. *"That's where Werehaven is. Lizandra would get a kick out of this if she knew I was flying over."*

"I'm sure she would. When I first moved here, this was all wildlands. I watched as the engineers developed the park. It was something to behold."

Miranda exhaled as they neared The Cloisters, the museum at the northern most part of Manhattan. Remare had promised to take her there. She hoped someday he would. *"How far out are we going?"*

"Not too much longer. I have some land in the Catskill Mountains. I need the city for my work, but I wanted a place where my Torians and I could go when we needed time away."

She eyed the insulated bag Escher had handed him before they took off. *"I take it dinner is included."*

"Yes, I hope you like Mediterranean food. Escher was preparing lamb kebobs. I told him to pack a few for us."

Miranda grinned. She knew Valadon was aware of her favorites. She glanced down as they passed the Merchant Marine Academy and the Tappan Zee Bridge. Even though it was spring and daylight was longer, she considered the travel time. *"It'll be dark by the time we get back."*

"Most likely. Manhattan lit up at night is exceptional."

It sure was. She and Orion, her roommate and former 'fiancé', sometimes had dinner in Brooklyn just to take in the beauty of the New York City skyline as the sun set.

When they reached the Catskill region, she admired the countryside. *"It's lovely up here."*

"I agree." He pointed to the top of one of the mountains. *"That's my home over there."*

Miranda checked out the modern lodge with the many plate glass windows as Valadon set down the chopper in the parking lot adjacent to the house. She removed the head gear. "Beautiful home."

He removed his, as well. "I wish I had more time to come up here." After sending a quick text, presumably to Aiden, who was his acting second until Remare returned, he replaced the phone in his jacket pocket. After making his way around the helicopter, he helped her out of the cockpit.

She inhaled the cool, crisp air deep into her lungs. "The air is so much cleaner, fresher up here."

"I think it's warm enough to dine outdoors, but if it is too cold for you, we can go inside."

"No. It's fine. I'd love to see the view."

He brought her to the edge of his land where there was an alcove shaded by the willow trees. The view of the other mountains was spectacular. It reminded her of the time she spent petroglyph exploring in the New Mexico wilderness. "It's peaceful up here. Relaxing."

Kneeling, he laid out a blanket on the ground and unpacked the bag. When he sat beside her, he removed his glasses. Miranda knew as a Blueblood, a purebred vampire, the High Lord had light sensitivity and preferred the shade. Valadon had the most amazing green eyes. She'd seem them turn gray when his mood turned turbulent. But, when he was content, they shone like emeralds. "Would you like some wine?"

"Love some." Miranda accepted the offered glass. After taking a sip, she felt herself unwinding. "This place is amazing. It's such a reprieve from the city."

"I looked at several properties but liked this one best. It reminded me of my family's estate outside Paris. We had many orchards and vineyards. I used to go riding in the woods." He seemed reflective. "It was a good life."

"You were lucky."

"Yes. I was." He opened one of the cartons, and the aroma of cooked meat, spiced just right, hit her.

"Oh my God, that smells wonderful."

"Let's eat."

After dinner, wine and chocolate covered strawberries, they moved closer to the ledge overlooking the area. "I'm glad you came with me up here. There are things I wanted to discuss with you in private and didn't want to be interrupted."

"You have my full attention." As an empath, she could sense emotions, and the High Lord was radiating several.

"My marriage will be occurring soon, and I wanted you to be aware of some of the particulars."

"You couldn't find an out?" Miranda knew his marriage
had been arranged by their supreme ruler in France, Queen
Magritte.

"Trust me, I've never endeavored more to find a solution.
I had my legal advisors working overtime to find a loophole,
anything that would thwart the situation. We failed to find
one." He exhaled. "However, there are a few bright spots."

"I don't get it." Miranda shook her head in frustration. "I
really don't. I spoke with Morel and Victor. They explained
the notion of arranged marriages, but I still don't understand.
I even did some research. It's the most antiquated...custom
I've ever heard of."

"That may be. But, in some parts of the world, it is still a
practiced tradition."

"Trap is more like it," Miranda muttered. "In some
villages, rival clans would kidnap women and force them into
marriages as if they were chattel. In others, the father would
have to bribe the groom's family with goats, cows and crops."

"And, in certain areas, marriages were arranged to keep
warring clans from wiping each other out. It was an
instrument of peace. Still is."

She narrowed her eyes. "I also read that aristocrats used
to arrange marriages to preserve their beloved wealth inside
their limited circle of friends and to keep their bloodlines
pure."

"There are those who still believe in those traditions."

"It's ridiculous." Miranda was outraged for him. She
hated the idea of anyone, male or female, being forced to
marry someone they didn't want. "Ludicrous."

"Perhaps, but as a Blueblood, I'm bound by certain laws
of the Vampire Nation." He seemed to be regarding her. "I'm
moved you care so much, but do not fret. I don't intend to
stay married for long. Vivienna has never been known for her

fidelity. Sooner or later, she'll make a mistake. And I'll be waiting."

Miranda groaned. Of all the loathsome people the VN could have chosen for Valadon, Vivienna was the worst. She'd met the Madame Lord in Paris. After she had slit Orion's throat for a minor infraction of vampire protocol. And, if that wasn't bad enough, she had tortured Miranda by piercing her flesh in a perverted game of *Truth or Dare*. "Good luck. I think you're going to need it with her."

"I don't rely on luck. Information is what's important to me, and I have agents in her court and in other places. Trust me to know what I'm doing." He exhaled. "Magritte has long wanted me to marry another Blueblood. I have resisted the idea. Vampires don't marry often; we prefer to take companions or consorts."

Miranda remembered Felicity, her mentor and friend, had introduced Blu as her companion. "How come?"

"Many human marriages fail over such short periods. Imagine if you lived as long as we do. People change with time. They evolve often in ways their partners do not."

"Morel and Cyra were happy. They were together for centuries. And Aiden and Bree seem pretty solid."

"Yes, they are. And I'm glad for them." He closed his eyes as if he were recalling a memory. "Most of the women in our High Court sought to marry for wealth or status. Love was not a considered option." His expression was downcast. "There was one who I wished to marry. Very badly. She had no interest in politics. She enjoyed adventure, reading tales and poetry. I never felt more content than when I was with her. I've met few women since who possess her spirit."

Miranda knew of whom he spoke. "Marlena de Avignon."

"Gabriel told you of her?"

"Yes. He showed me her painting in the archives."

"Did he tell you he was her descendant?"

Miranda nodded.

"There's another reason I'm complying with Magritte's request. Marlena had a child. My child, a son. Magritte knows his whereabouts but refuses to inform me until I marry."

"Are you certain? It could be a ploy."

"Magritte would not negotiate with me unless she had something tangible to bargain with. She always enjoyed possessing the upper hand."

Miranda's spine straightened as a memory surfaced. "Valadon, remember when I was in Vivienna's home? I saw a painting of a young boy resembling you. I asked you after I returned to New York if he could be your son."

"And I told you Vivienna was too old to bear a child. Besides, I was always careful with the women I had relations with. Vampires can sense when a woman is ovulating and avoid intercourse at such times. However, my brother was not so cautious. Even when I tried to advise him to reconsider his libertine ways, he showed little concern. He fathered several children he refused to acknowledge as his. I made sure they were taken care of properly."

"You think the portrait I saw was one of Brandon's?"

"Most likely. Our features are nearly identical, except for his black hair. He was known for his dalliances with members of the High Court."

Miranda remembered well Valadon's treacherous brother who'd kidnapped her and tortured her in a cell beneath Valadon House. He'd shown little restraint, then, as well.

"Enough talk of the past. I think there's another raven-haired vampire you'd rather discuss."

Miranda's face brightened. "Remare."

"Yes. I've missed him almost as much as you. Aiden has made a fine second." Valadon began collecting their things and placed them in the insulated bag. "But he's not Remare."

No, Miranda thought. No one was. And no one warmed her heart as much or as deeply.

"I have good news. He may be returning sooner than planned."

Miranda's heart began to race. It had been months since she'd seen her lover. "When?"

Chapter Three

"Jesus! Is there anything more beautiful than that?" As they approached the city, Miranda pointed to the Manhattan skyline with its myriad of lights.

"It truly is a magnificent sight," Valadon agreed, *"but I might be able to think of a thing or two that holds more fascination for me."*

When they approached ValCorp, Miranda gestured to his waiting Torians. *"I think they have a bone to pick with you."*

"Strong possibility." Valadon grinned then set the helicopter down on top of ValCorp's roof and nodded at his Torians who stood with their arms crossed and expressions of strong disapproval on their faces. Aiden looked like he was ready to pop a blood vessel, and Tristan appeared equally frustrated, standing erect with his rifle slung over his shoulder. His sentinels had every right to be annoyed with him. He'd broken his own protocol by leaving the compound without any notice to his own people.

But, since he was their king, he didn't let it bother him overly much.

Aiden was the first to approach by opening his door. "We tried to get in touch with you."

"It wasn't necessary." He'd read their texts. "Should I arrange transportation for you?"

"No need." Miranda's grin widened. "I brought my Jeep."

He'd known, for some time, Remare had bought her the car. At first, he'd been a little hurt she'd refused his Jaguar, but in retrospect, the Jeep suited her.

As they walked to the elevator that would take them down to ValCorp's subterranean levels, his Torians remained ever vigilant. After one stern look from him, they'd maintained their silence. When the elevator dinged at the garage level, he took Miranda's hand and kissed her knuckles. "Thank you for spending the evening with me. I enjoyed our conversation."

"Likewise." She made her way to her car as the elevator doors closed.

Aiden spoke softly. "We were concerned for your welfare."

When Tristan tried to speak, Valadon raised a hand. "I'm going to rest for a few hours."

Aiden checked his tablet. "There are a couple of matters requiring your attention."

When the elevator doors opened next, they strode down the corridor. "If there's nothing crucial demanding my *immediate* response, it can wait."

As they neared his rooms, Valadon knew he owed them some sort of explanation. "I know I broke procedure. But even a *king*, on occasion, needs time to himself." He stressed his status so there would be no further discussion on the topic. Meeting their eyes, he nodded to them as they bowed, and then closed his door and locked it.

He tossed his jacket over a chair then removed his tie. Eyeing the bar, he poured himself a glass of blood wine. After savoring a few sips, he lay down on his bed. With his upcoming wedding, there would be few moments of peace like the one he shared with Miranda.

She had told him he'd been lucky to have been born an aristocrat. Rather than admit to certain truths, he'd let her believe he'd led a life of leisure. And, for many years, he'd been content. He sighed. Until he was sent to their High Court to learn political détente and commerce. And training.

What training it had been, indeed. Exhaling, he relaxed back into his pillows and remembered when he'd been a young vampire and chosen to learn the art of seduction from the most exquisite female vampire he'd ever met.

Magritte's eyes had lit on him, and immediately, she'd chosen him for her personal pupil. The other aristocrats had congratulated him on landing the most beautiful and talented mentor. She was an elder who rarely chose trainees anymore, preferring the duties of the High Council. In his arrogance, he felt proud he'd won her favor.

What they'd failed to mention was how calculating and vindictive the *Mistress of Games* could be.

Older than most of the others because his father's business concerns required him to be home, he thought there was little about the carnal arts he hadn't already learned for himself. But nothing had prepared him for the voluptuous appetites of the ruling class. After sipping his wine and placing it on his bedside table, he closed his eyes and allowed old memories to surface.

Old France, Northern Territory, 1200 AD

As the horses and carriages neared Mont Helaire, Valadon's breath caught as he eyed the grand palace. His father's Neo-classical estate, elegant with its intricately designed gardens and Greek statues, afforded a warm welcome to visitors. But the home of the High Court, hidden deep in the forest, inspired awe and a sliver of fear to those who ventured near. The Gothic architecture with the gargoyles and armed sentries atop the massive stone structure was a testament to the powerful vampires who lived there.

Valadon breathed deep as he descended from the carriage. He was met by an elegantly dressed man of slender build. "Welcome to Mont Helaire. I am Fabian. I've been sent to greet you."

"Valadon, a pleasure to meet you."

Fabian instructed the servants to unload and handle his belongings and led him inside the castle. The massive oak doors were carved with sigils and runes, the walls decorated with different banners of the ruling courts. The interior, with its textured drapes, exquisitely carved furniture and tapestries depicting battle scenes of the ancient Greek gods, mesmerized him. Whoever lived here had no inhibitions about violence and bloodshed.

The spectacular chandeliers, glimmering with the flames of hundreds of candles, cast illumination over the vast hall. The marble floors and columns shone brightly; the massive fireplace with the twin stone lions was unlike anything he'd seen before.

The court vampires dressed in fashions made from the finest silks and were far more sophisticated than what he'd been accustomed to. Valadon thought it was heaven.

"Who is that stunning creature standing by the door?"

"Magritte, that is Lord Valadon's eldest son." Caltrone added, "His father is a wealthy entrepreneur who has contributed generously to our court."

"Handsome, is he not?"

"Young, almost four hundred years." Caltrone sneered as he studied him. "He has potential."

"Really, Caltrone," Magritte laughed, "if I didn't know better, I'd say you were jealous, but you have too much confidence for that meek emotion. He's magnificent. Have Fabian introduce us."

"As you wish."

Valadon smirked. He knew he'd been blessed with appealing features since birth. For as long as he could remember, women had always been attracted to him. Although the intriguing couple were across the room, he could hear their whispers plainly enough. His senses warned they were much older than him.

And far more powerful.

When Fabian approached him and asked him to follow, he complied.

"Our esteemed High Council member, Magritte." Fabian bowed. "Monsieur Valadon."

Valadon paid no interest to the rest of what Fabian was saying, his eyes captivated by the alluring blonde with translucent skin and eyes of deepest blue. He'd met many lovely women in his travels, but none compared with Magritte. She was beyond beautiful, a flawless diamond. Perfect. His heart beat faster. "A pleasure to meet you." He kissed her hand and glanced up at her.

"It will be." She smiled back at him. "It most certainly will be. They tell me you wish to learn commerce?"

"Yes, my father told me of your libraries. I would very much like to see them. If they are anything like the rest of your home, I'm sure they will be magnificent."

"You will find much here which will exceed your expectations. Come, let me show you." She led him through the marble columns and down a hall lined with several portraits of the elders—the ruling members of the Council and original owners of Mont Helaire. At the end of the corridor, she opened the massive oak doors. He followed her inside and nearly gasped at the vast expanse of books, maps and scrolls.

Nothing he'd heard prepared him for the grandeur of the room. He'd read about the great libraries of Alexandria and wondered if they were anything like this oasis. Aisles upon aisles of books and parchments lined exquisitely carved, ebony bookcases. Objects d' art graced the tables and shelves. At the front of each aisle stood Greek and Roman statues. On the ceiling was a huge painting of a stormy sea and the god, Poseidon, protecting those who paid homage to him, as ships made their way into the harbor.

Magritte whispered close to his ear. "Your studies here will include more than books." Her scent of gardenias intoxicated him.

He turned to face his hostess. The attraction between them stirred his libido. "I was made aware of my responsibilities and obligations."

"Good. Then, let's begin." Magritte led him away from the library and up a marble staircase leading to a suite of rooms. "These will be your quarters for the duration of your time spent with us."

His rooms were no less elegant than the major hall. Exquisite drapes and tapestries lined the walls, and the huge poster bed was an invitation to sin. Valadon strove to suppress his hunger for her, tried to hold back his fangs from lengthening, but Magritte's beauty and her allure were unlike anything he'd ever encountered. He wanted desperately to touch her, to feel her naked body wrapped around his, but sensed he was being tested. "Your hospitality is greatly appreciated."

"You're a handsome man, Valadon. Your attractiveness will serve you well in our courts." Her eyes seemed to be glowing. "If you learn to use it to advantage."

He couldn't resist raising one hand to touch a strand of her hair. "And will you be the one teaching me?" Desire gnawed at his insides, and unless he was very much mistaken, Magritte was feeling the same.

"Yes, among others." She sounded amused as she glided toward the door. "Rest for tonight. Tomorrow will be soon enough for any of your questions. I'll have a meal sent up for you."

He wondered if her quick retreat was due to her own hunger for him. He would make that determination soon enough, he promised himself.

The next day, Magritte had summoned him to her rooms; Fabian accompanied him to meet his tutor. Last night's meal had been a young woman from one of the villages the elders had a treaty with. She had been most gracious in sharing her blood with him and would have bestowed more if he'd so requested. But he thought it wise to wait for Magritte.

After Fabian knocked and heard the permission to enter, he opened the door for Valadon and left. Magritte's chambers were fit for a queen. Her large poster bed had deep purple drapes tied back with strings of gold. The furnishings were the finest gold could buy. A lush fireplace radiated heat into the room. Several attendants, holding fine fabrics, waited around her.

Magritte laughed. "You look surprised. Your clothes are adequate for a merchant's son. But, here at court, you must dress accordingly."

She no sooner said that, then the tailors pulled him farther into the room and began removing his clothes and measuring him. The silks and other fabrics were of the richest textures.

"With his verdant eyes, I wish to see him in green and blue tunics." She seemed to be studying him. "And make one with black and gold. Yes, I think those colors will suit him best."

He bowed. "I appreciate your generosity." His father had instructed him in manners and the expression of gratitude the elders expected from their guests.

"I believe you will reciprocate with other gifts. The woman who served you last night is the daughter of one of our human associates. You must learn our ways in dealing with the humans and others if you are to hold power."

When the tailors and seamstresses left, he said, "I was sent here for that very purpose."

"Politics and finance are crucial to our well-being, but seduction is also important. You will learn many successful business ventures are sealed in the bedroom."

"My father procured the services of women in my village to instruct me. I assure you, I've been well-taught."

She glided toward him and held him spellbound. His body seemed to have a mind of its own in reacting to hers. Her beauty was intoxicating. And her scent played havoc with his senses. "Not by me."

She was using her allure to entice and stimulate. He knew this, and still, he wanted her. Desperately. He'd never been with a woman this powerful, and the idea excited him. Erotic images filled his head. His heart beat strongly in his chest, but his ego would not permit him to fall at her feet.

"You have reserve." She breathed in his ear, her voice a siren's song. "That's good. You will need refinement to succeed in the courts. There is much for you to learn."

"When do we start?"

"So eager. And, yet, not quite ready." She circled him. "You will follow a strict regimen of study in the mornings." She ran her hands over his shoulders and arms. "In the afternoons, you will work to develop your body to perfection." She smiled seductively. "And, in the evenings, you will learn the art of pleasure."

He wanted to show her how much he already knew but resisted the demanding urge. He would follow her instructions. For now.

The days and nights at Mont Helaire went quickly by as he settled into his routine. Valadon rubbed his hands. They healed quickly from the heavy lifting of weights resembling anvils. He had thought himself in reasonable shape but learned the females of the court preferred athletic bodies, so he participated in weight lifting, shot putting, and other sports calculated to perfect his body. He could feel the differences as well as see the enhanced muscle tone in his chest and limbs. He was growing stronger and enjoyed the sensation of knowing others would succumb to him.

At night, when he met with Magritte, she showed him techniques of body posture designed to entice. Along with the cultured clothing, she had his hair cut and styled in the most becoming ways. He spent long periods of time perfecting poses for optimum appeal. He learned how to use his eyes to encourage and attract. Later, he mastered control over the tones in his voice for maximum effect.

In a few months' time, he'd become one of the most sought-after vampires in the court. But, still, Magritte refused his attentions. Then, one night, she brought one of the female vampires into his bedroom and took her seat to watch his performance with the woman.

Although he'd witnessed some lascivious natures at his father's parties, Valadon did not like the idea of an audience, nor did he appreciate being told who to fuck. But, if he was going to win Magritte's favor, he would comply with her request. The knowledge he was accumulating on finance in the libraries was too valuable to dismiss.

"If you don't enjoy it, your paramours will sense your dislike, and that may impede your business transactions. Remember, our security is predicated on how well we maintain relations with all the wealthy courts. There are those who would see our destruction. Only the powerful endure. We must be able to safeguard what is most precious to us. Money buys allies and armies. Our safety is paramount."

"I will do all that is expected of me." He'd been told repeatedly how security was imperative to their survival. Especially in light of the fact some of the lesser courts had been raided by Rogues; blood had been spilled and lives lost.

"Before you can adequately give pleasure, you must experience it. Let her teach you. Anise is one of our finest court ladies. She has far more experience than you."

Valadon tried to relax and willed his body to react to Anise's touches. Indeed, she was talented as she caressed, stroked and licked his body. Magritte wanted a performance, he would give her one. One she would not be so quick to forget.

"Do not come too soon, savor the passion, enjoy it. Let her show you how to prolong the pleasure."

And so it went on for many more months until Magritte was satisfied with his abilities. In truth, he had learned much during his stay at Mont Helaire—some of it pleasurable, some of it painful. A few of the visitors to the castle of the High Court referred to it as Mont Lair.

He soon learned to call it Mont Hell.

"I will not return to Castle Durand!" Valadon's temper had been strained. "If you value my service, you will not send me back there!"

"I told you there are those among us, as well as the humans, who enjoy a little pain with their pleasure." Magritte exhaled. "You never had difficulty with it before."

"A little." His voice dripped venom. "What Durand does to those women I would not consider 'a little'. He abuses them in most horrific ways." He held his stomach at the nauseating memory. "The young one, my God, she was barely more than a child."

"Yes, Durand does like his diversions." Magritte's irritation with him surfaced. "You think I approve of such perversions? You think I haven't had to endure the insults and abuses of those more powerful than us? I have! Far more than you could ever imagine. Leash your emotions! They will not serve you well." She purred in his ear, a combination of sweetness and acid. "School your face, Valadon, and learn to accept there are others who derive pleasure from the weakness of others. If Durand or any of the others become aware this is a vulnerability of yours, they will use it to their benefit." Her voiced hardened. "Do you understand me?"

His breaths evened out. "She was a child." It was one thing to use vampiric abilities with other vampires. Each had different levels of allure, knew what it was, and recognized the sensory enhancement. Magritte had once enveloped him in a cloud of desire so strong she'd sent him to his knees and nearly had him begging for her touch. The Mistress of Games enjoyed her distractions. He'd learned to erect his own defenses. But to force a human, or even a weaker vampire, to want, to accelerate their craving with no way of defending themselves was tantamount to rape. He wouldn't do it.

"There are children all over the world who suffer worse. You were raised with privilege, surrounded by those who loved you and kept you protected. You have no knowledge of the starvation, diseases and other calamities that befall the young." Her voice was acidic. "As uncomfortable as it is for you to accept this, there are far, far worse things that happen to the weak. Always remember: strength is admired, weakness is exploited."

He'd been there long enough to know power was what drove the council members. They needed gold to maintain their resources, their armies. Gold kept their negotiations with the human politicians and religious leaders in check. Gold bought them power. Valadon didn't desire power as much as he coveted his own territory. Freedom from the High Court in a place far away from the machinations of the council members. He would need to amass a fortune if he was to grasp that level of autonomy. "I will not return to his castle."

"Perhaps not." She smiled. "I hear Monsieur Tremaine says your skill in swordsmanship has improved. Tomorrow, you will meet the son of a war general from Rome. They say he is one of the best in technique and in speed. Prove you can defend yourself against any nobles who would challenge you, and I'll send you to the court of a more judicious lord. One you

will approve of." She waited a beat. *"To be his financial advisor."*

Valadon couldn't hide his anticipation. Magritte believed she knew what he coveted most. He'd learned early enough to mask his preferences and dislikes. The courtiers were too wise in discerning a person's passions; knowledge was power, if not a weapon, in the courts. He'd come to Mont Helaire to learn economics and was eager to attain a high-ranking position. He dreamed one day of becoming the High Court's Minister of Finance. But, first, he would prove himself worthy. *"What's this swordsman's name?"*

"Remare."

Chapter Four

Remare was tired after his long flight from Vancouver to Madame Lord Dione's Court in Montreal. Even though his private jet had every amenity, the plane ride had been anything but pleasant with several incidents of turbulence. Conducting business for Valadon and Dione had been extensive but, thankfully, was now complete. As he walked down the hall to his room, all he wanted was to sleep, but maybe a long soak in a warm bath would be soothing.

He was not expecting the sight awaiting him. Nor was it welcome. Throwing his coat over a chair, he glowered at the nude woman with the curly blonde hair and aquamarine eyes in his bed.

"Selena, don't you ever give up?" He removed his suit jacket and undid his tie. "You should be with people your own age." Her elven features and feisty demeanor would attract any of the young men in the court. If it weren't for her irreverent attitude and Neo-Gothic taste in clothing. He suspected her odd fashion choices she wore at formal events were designed to get a rise out of her grandmother, Dione. "Why don't you visit Nick? His room is just down the hall."

"Ugh, all he cares about are his studies." She rolled her eyes. "Boring! He's no fun at all," she teased unrepentantly, "but you are."

"I'm far too old for you." Exhaling, he heard the fatigue in his voice. Selena was about Nick's age and had been trying to get into Remare's pants for some time now. He removed his shoes and sat beside her on the bed. "Now, why don't you tell me what you're really after? If it was only sex, you would have satisfied your urges elsewhere by now."

"Don't you find me attractive?" she asked with a hint of hurt in her voice.

He sighed. Maybe if he was nine hundred years younger. "You're very attractive, but as I've told you before, I have a woman who patiently waits for me back in New York."

"It's been months." She giggled. "I'm sure she'd understand if you got a little."

"Oh, I doubt that." Miranda would wear his balls for earrings if he ever touched another. And, since he was rather fond of his stones, he had no intention of ever succumbing to Selena's charms. "Now, give. Why are you so determined to seduce me?"

She pouted. "Grandmama is so unfair. She wants me to continue studies at McGill. I told her the best fashion houses are in New York City, but she refuses to listen to my requests."

Finally, he was beginning to develop some insight into her rebellious nature. "I'm sure Montreal has many fine universities to further your studies."

"They don't have the Fashion Institute of Technology." Securing the sheet over her breasts, she snuggled closer to him and put her arm around his shoulders. "And they don't have Cesare. I was hoping you'd help me obtain an internship with ValCorp's head designer." Selena pouted. "Pretty please?"

"Dione is Madame Lord. Her word is final where her progeny is concerned."

"Ugh! She doesn't understand me." Frustration laced her words. "I was hoping you would talk to her. Convince her I'd be perfectly safe in New York."

Remare reached for Selena's robe. "That is a discussion you must have with her." When he lifted the material, a book fell to the floor. He handed her the garment and sat again at the edge of the bed. "What's this?"

She fastened the tie to her robe and sat near him. Her Wonder Woman socks peeking out from the edges of her robe. "It's my portfolio. At least some of it." She turned a few pages. "It's the designs I've been working on."

Remare wasn't an expert, but he knew enough of Cesare's and his subordinates' work to recognize quality when he saw it. "These are very good."

"I know," she said without the least bit of humility. "My teachers have always said I had a certain flair to my work."

"They're beautiful."

"Remare, would you please talk to Dione for me? Please? Ever since I was a little girl, I dreamed of going to F.I.T. And to work under Cesare..." She squealed with the enthusiasm of youth.

He was amused at her zeal and offbeat sense of humor. "If I agree to speak with Dione, will you promise to stop with your flirtatious behavior?"

"You will?!" She sounded as surprised at the notion as he was.

"Yes, but if she says no, you must abide by her wishes."

More squealing rang his ears as she spirited up and hugged him. "Thank you, thank you. It means the world to me." She kissed him quickly then grabbed her book and made for the door.

"I know she may still say no, but the fact that you're willing to intercede." She winked at him. "It means a lot to me."

He nodded to her as she left. Laying his head back on the pillows, he wondered how he got himself into these fixes. But, right now, all he wanted was a warm bath and a glass of wine. It had been months since he'd seen Miranda, his lover, his mate. But she was much more to him. Wife didn't ring true, and consort was too formal. He smiled; life partner fit best.

Pouring a glass of Cabernet, he let the tub fill with warm water. After undressing, he immersed himself and imagined Miranda's body enveloping his own. Since he'd left New York, he'd been taking increasingly hot baths until he was nearly boiling his skin. But nothing compared with the warmth of being with Miranda or the heat they generated when their bodies were intertwined.

Valadon had forbidden any *direct* contact, but that didn't stop Morel from sending pictures of Miranda working intently in the archives or having dinner with Rosalyn. He'd studied the images often when he was alone. His friend kept him apprised of his partner's activities and well-being. He'd find a way to thank Morel when he returned.

Sipping his wine, he glanced at the twenty-four-karat gold ID bracelet she'd had Morel send to him. *'Always and Forever—Miranda"* was engraved on the inside. He rarely took the thing off. It warmed his heart every time he touched the links.

Closing his eyes, he found comfort in his memories of the times they'd shared together. During the day, he kept busy, but in the darkest part of the night, when it seemed as if the cold was seeping into his bones, making him ache for her soft caresses, he'd reach for her. He imagined her smiling face, and his heart sped up. He remembered the time when they'd left Nick in the Mid-town apartment after he'd hidden Nick's and his lover's clothes in a wastebasket. She had laughed so much he'd had to hold her upright in the elevator. Her laughter was music to his ears, and he relished the sound of it.

Another memory of them on his boat surfaced as they stood together and gazed at The Statue of Liberty. He could still feel the cool, clean air of the Hudson as he held Miranda close, her hair the scent of orange blossoms. Even now, he could still recall her scent. Those moments and others like them were precious to him.

He sighed as he finished the last of his wine. The one thing she had asked of him was to take a boat trip up to The Cloisters. He would do that for her.

And he'd make it a day to remember.

***

The assassin studied the blue prints of the main room where the reception was to be held. He liked knowing what materials were used in the building's construction when deciding which tools were necessary. All exits had been identified. His escape route carefully planned out. He scrutinized the layout of the room. He would have preferred an aerial shot from a safe distance away, but his employer requested an inside hit. More challenging, but not impossible for a man with his skill set and years of experience.

A sniper during the war in Afghanistan, he found the lucrative benefits of being a contract killer more to his liking. He checked his Swiss account. It showed a marked increase and would again when the job was done. "Almost enough to retire on." He scoffed. Retirement didn't beckon him the way it did others. He liked the thrill of the hunt, thrived on it.

He memorized the photos of his target. From the erect spine and set of the jaw, this one demanded attention and was used to giving orders. There was a steeliness in the eyes that conveyed absolute authority. Instilled fear, but also respect. A strong-willed person who commanded others and didn't tolerate insubordination very well.

Many friends, many enemies—the price of sovereignty. He ran a finger down the target's face. Attractive, yet arrogant. He scoffed. Most monarchs were. "You don't like it much when your orders get disobeyed. Well, you certainly pissed off someone."

He smirked at the nickname he'd garnered in his years as a hit man. They called him *The Ghost,* because seconds after the hit, he ghosted. Left no identifying marks, no signatures of any kind. Unlike others in his line of work, he didn't rely solely on one weapon to get the job done. He was proficient in a variety of armaments.

This new device intrigued him as he examined the mechanism on his recently acquired weapon. Normally, he used his high-powered rifle when on assignment. But, since the hit was scheduled for a wedding in the well-guarded ValCorp building where metal-detectors would be in force, alternate weaponry was necessary. His employer was very specific about where and when the target was to be eliminated. Only after the vows were spoken would he fire the bullet-shaped dart.

In truth, the mechanism reminded him of a miniature crossbow. All component parts carefully imbedded in a cylinder small enough it could pass as a thick fountain pen. However, instead of a cartridge, the contents were far more deadly. The dart had three main coils that, once fired into the back of the neck, would wrap around the spinal cord of the victim. The target then would have barely moments before being terminated.

Any attempt to dislodge the bullet would result in severing the spine. Instant death. He knew because he'd practiced enough times with the weapon to know the velocity, distance and angle of trajectory necessary to complete his mission.

By the time anyone realized the target had been hit, he was history.

A ghost in the wind.

Chapter Five

"I don't get it! I really don't. I mean, I understand, historically, why they had arranged marriages. I just can't fathom their mindset." Perched atop the rock formation of Summit Rock in Central Park, Miranda and several female werewolves of Black Star Clan basked in the late afternoon sun. It had been an unusually warm spring day, and everyone wanted to take in some rays. Curious, she imagined how they'd all look at night in wolf form lounging about.

When a cool breeze brushed over them, Miranda leaned her back into the stone, relishing the warmth the boulders emanated. She loved the spring; it was as if the earth was renewing itself, and all the trees and foliage in the park were greener, more vibrant.

"What's to understand?" Lizandra, Queen of the Weres, lowered her sunglasses so she could see her. "They had to ensure the survival of the races; they did what they had to."

"Goats! Friggen goats! Clan leaders would bribe the prospective husbands with goats and other livestock, as if having daughters was a curse instead of a blessing. Something to be gotten rid of as soon as possible."

"You're just pissed because Valadon is getting married soon."

"I am!" Outrage laced Miranda's voice. "No one should be forced into a marriage. It's barbaric."

"What does the vamp king say about it?" Tia asked as she rolled on to her side.

"He's doing what he has to." Miranda didn't tell them Valadon had his legal team looking for a loophole in the agreement Valadon had signed to gain his independence from the vampires' High Court in France.

"Valadon is not a foolish man." Liz applied more sunscreen to her arms. "If he goes through with it, I'm sure he has his reasons. If not, he'll find a way to end it."

"I hope so. Of all people to marry. Vivienna is such a bitch."

"The one who slashed Orion's throat." Liz grinned like a wolf before it pounces on a succulent dinner. "If he gave the order, I would do away with his little problem."

All the Weres echoed their approval.

"And I'd help." Maxine sat up. "I still can't believe she did that to Orion. I'd love to take a bite out of her hide."

"I'm trying to wrap my mind around it." Miranda pressed her fists to her head. "It's just not computing. I used to believe people married because they loved the person, not because of a truce between Houses or courts."

"Girlfriend, you are naïve." Liz huffed. "People marry for all kinds of reasons. Like the song said, 'What's love got to do with it?'"

Miranda asked, "Why else would anyone want to get married?"

"There are lots of reasons. Some marry for money." Liz shrugged. "Financial security is a big deal with some." She waggled her eyebrows. "With others, it's because the sex is really good."

Humored, Miranda shook her head when the she-wolves growled in sensual appreciation as they peered down at the male Weres working below on their construction projects. High in the distance, she saw Felicity's eagles flying by. A sure sign of spring. The birds had disappeared this past winter, presumably to a warmer climate, and she was glad they'd returned to their nest in St. Patrick's Cathedral.

"Kids. Some women want kids badly enough they marry someone they think will be a good father." Max's eyes slanted toward Liz. "Some people feel pressured, obligated to live up to family customs. Don't want to disappoint the parents. They settle."

"Social status. The wealthy don't like their offspring marrying outside their social station." Tia feigned shock. "God forbid their blood gets polluted!"

"Companionship," Sasha offered as she gazed down at Gavin and the other males who were working up a sweat. They were building an extension to the gazebo, so on rainy days, no one got soaked. Not far from him, Cyrus was plowing the lawn to make room for a three-tiered barbeque pit where the Weres could hang out and party when they wanted a break from being indoors too much at Werehaven. "No one wants to grow old alone."

Miranda considered what they were saying. She'd never really thought about it. She'd just assumed most people married for love. "I suppose."

Sasha asked, "Do you think you'll ever get married, Miranda?"

"Probably not. I'm married to my career. Besides, vampires don't marry often. They take companions." Somehow, she didn't think Remare was the marrying kind. Not after his experiences. And that was fine with her. As long as they were together, it really didn't matter.

"How is the dark and drool-worthy vampire doing?" Liz belted out a laugh any dirty old lady would be proud of. "I bet your vibrator is getting one helluva workout!"

Miranda picked a dandelion from a crack in the boulder and threw it at Lizandra. "None of your business, and I did *not* appreciate all the battery packets you guys got me for my birthday."

When the all-girl fan club broke out in hysterics, Miranda was sure her face heated.

"How many you got left?" Liz teased with a howl of amusement. "I bet not many!" That only elicited more laughter.

"Don't remind me." Miranda moaned. "He'll be back soon." She was planning to spend as much time indoors with her sexy vampire as they could steal to be together. Her skin was beginning to itch from wanting him so much. "I don't know how wives and girlfriends of soldiers do it. This has been hell."

"We did it," Tia said. "You love the guy, you stay faithful and you focus on the good memories."

"It's tough. But we get through it." Liz snickered. "That's why we have girlfriends. Movie nights and chocolate fests."

Max grinned. "And battery-powered dildos." Another bout of laughter erupted.

When Miranda noticed Tia looking down, she said, "I'm sorry, Tia, I didn't mean to be disrespectful." Tia's husband had been killed in the war in Afghanistan.

"It's okay." She smiled a little. "It's been a while."

Miranda checked out Liz. Her first husband had also been killed in the Mid-East war. They'd been so young when they married. After he died, Liz had wanted a father for her daughter, Casey, so she married a captain in the army. That marriage had only lasted six months. Hubby number two thought he could give orders to Liz like one of his subordinates. He soon found out that didn't fly with her. After the divorce, Liz said never again. And she'd meant it. She never remarried and probably never would.

"Hey, how's Casey doing?" Miranda quickly changed the subject. "Is she gonna be at the barbecue this weekend? What is she, eleven or twelve now?"

"Thirteen. And a major pain in my ass. Keeps wanting to come to Werehaven, even though I tell her she's gotta be at least eighteen. Moody as hell. Defiant. But she's my P.I.T.A., so I love her anyway."

"Thirteen?! Jesus, time flies. I seem to remember you telling me you were rebellious at that age."

"Me? Oh, really! Look at 'Miss I wanna dance on the stage at Webster Hall'."

"God." Miranda laughed. "Don't remind me. I still can't believe we did that."

"We did a lot of stupid things. Gran always said we'd get paid in full for the attitude we gave our parents."

"Karma," Miranda said. "It all comes back on us."

"Hey, can one of you throw down a water bottle?" Gavin stood at the bottom of the hill, his chest coated in a fine layer of sweat. Miranda still thought the Red Wolf was the handsomest and nicest of the males. He'd fallen in love with Liz, wanted to get married, and that had been the death shot to their relationship. Liz found another wolf, Cyrus, the White Wolf, to take his place. Miranda knew Gavin wasn't quite over it yet.

"Yeah, can I have one, too?" one of the blond twins from California called up.

Miranda still couldn't discern Drew from Daniel or how easily the other Weres could tell them apart.

"I will." Sasha grabbed a couple of bottles from the cooler and made her way down. "Hey, you guys need help down there?"

Max joined her friend. But Miranda thought it was more to ogle the handsome blond. Since Sasha and Max rented out Miranda's basement apartment, the twins were regular guests. Especially on movie nights. Miranda was grateful for the company. She'd been missing Remare something awful. Some nights were worse than others, but when the Weres came over, life felt good, right.

And wasn't that what friends were for, after all?

***

"Tell the little shit to gird his loins and learn some patience. My word is final or I'll take a whip to him when I reach New York," Magritte hissed to her agent in House Valadon.

"He has Mulciber's arrogance," Scorpio scoffed into his phone. "I'm not sure patience is his strong point."

"It had better become one, then. I want nothing interfering in our plans. If he wants to free his sister during the ceremony, that's fine. But he's to take no action against Valadon. Is that clear?!"

"I'll relay your message, but it's not easy reigning him in. Jeremy has certain aspirations, and he grows restless."

"Tell him I will meet with him once I arrive in New York. There'll come a time for his ambitions. But now is not the time!" She closed her phone and paced.

"Bad news, Magritte?"

"A thorn in my side, nothing more, Brandon." She examined his new hair color. "It's uncanny how much you resemble your brother." In truth, he was a pale imitation. But a necessary one.

"So I've been told. Enough to fool others?"

"We'll find out soon enough."

Chapter Six

"Come in, Aiden." Valadon tore his eyes away from his reports. All divisions of ValCorp were performing well. They should be; his directors were the best in their respective fields. He paid them generously to ensure their loyalty and was pleased with their performance.

Aiden shook his head in bewilderment. "How do you always know it's me before I even knock?"

"Your gait. You stride with determination. Gregori's footsteps are the loudest; makes sense since he's the heaviest. Tristan prances, makes sort of a tapping sound. And, you're the only one who hesitates before actually knocking." He leaned his head back on the chair. "The women have their own nuances. Now, what is it?"

Valadon could tell from Aiden's expression the news would not be good.

"Touraine informs us some of the European dignitaries want to come early for the wedding. A couple of days early. In particular, he mentions Calisar."

"I thought he might. His financial difficulties made my offer of remuneration more tenable." Valadon smiled. "Give him permission. I'll meet with him to see what he has to offer. Have any of our other agents in the High Court reported in?"

"Nothing of worth at the moment." Aiden's eyes were downcast. "I downloaded some photos of the cams in the city. We're still monitoring the major transportation areas to see if Brandon should make an appearance." He hesitated. "I found something unexpected. I sent the files to your email." His voice grew soft. "You will not like it."

Valadon immediately turned toward his computer and opened his email. "It's Miranda. At the New York Public

Library." The two stone lions near the stairs were clear enough in the background.

"Look closer at the man she's with. I enlarged his features on the next slide."

Valadon hit the tab and scrutinized the photo. It took only a moment before his breaths intensified as he seethed in rage. "Son of a bitch!" His hands fisted. "I'll kill her with my bare hands."

"That's Guy de Montglat, isn't it?"

Valadon knew the red rims around his irises were pulsing. He nodded once.

"I thought so. He's taken on the appearance of a college student. Maybe Miranda doesn't know who he is?"

Valadon slunk back in his chair. "She *knows*." He remembered his discussions about Montglat down in the archives with her. He tried to reign in his temper. He needed to think this through. Not react.

"Shall I have her brought in for questioning?"

Valadon swiveled in his chair as his breathing evened out. "No. Not just yet. Post agents on her. I want to know where she goes, who she sees. She works at the museum and then at New York University two nights a week. Find out where she goes when she's not there."

"Will do." Aiden rose to leave. "I'm so sorry—"

"Also, call Remare back." He exhaled slowly with deliberation. "I had wanted him to stay in Montreal for Nick's graduation, but my nephew tells me he'll be returning a couple of days after his finals, foregoing the ceremonies."

"This news will devastate them."

"Do *not* speak of this to anyone. If the agents question you, say it's routine or safeguarding. I will inform Remare myself when he returns."

"And Nick?"

"I'll notify when it becomes necessary. For now, this is on a need-to-know-only basis."

"Bree was with me when I downloaded the images. She knows something's wrong. What should I tell her?"

"I suspect your wife has been privy to many secrets. Does she know who Montglat is?"

"No. She wasn't in the courts when he was. To my knowledge, she's never met him."

"Good. Tell her it's an ongoing investigation, and he is simply a person of interest. No more."

"All right." He shook his head. "I can't believe Miranda would—"

"Neither can I. I'll get to the bottom of this. One way or another." Fury was riding him hard. How could he have been so stupid to trust her?! And, yet, some part of him wanted to believe there was a reasonable explanation. But he knew there couldn't be.

After Aiden left, Valadon wanted to throw something. Refusing to give free reign to his raw emotions, he paced instead. He'd been taught control. Had it branded into his very fiber. By a queen who demanded nothing less. A woman who was a master of deception, one who spun dreams and then turned them into nightmares.

Northern France, 1200

She was not the woman he'd thought her to be. Valadon panted from exertion. Magritte's latest lessons had been about control. She'd been a demanding lover and enjoyed taunting him.

"Do not come. Show that you have control." She whipped him, again, against his chest. The metal barbs at the end of the flogger tore into his flesh. Rivulets of blood dripped down

his skin. He healed almost immediately, but the pain was still excruciating.

His control was at its breaking point. He did not know of another vampire who could master his body's responses any better. "How much longer?" he gasped between clenched teeth, his fangs piercing his lower lip.

"Until I'm satisfied." She whipped him twice more for the disobedience. "You think you are the only talented lover in the court? You think there are no others who can do what you do? There are many, I assure you, who can do far more." She licked the fine line of blood across his chest. "Don't you understand I'm trying to make you better, more accomplished?"

No, he didn't understand. Sex was supposed to be an enjoyable act. Seduction an art form designed as a means to an end. But what Magritte demanded was something else entirely.

"Why do you continually fight me on this?"

"I don't like being manipulated." By the flash of anger in her eyes, he knew he'd said the wrong thing, but it was too late to take it back.

"Manipulated? My dear Valadon, you have no idea just how much I can manipulate you."

And, then, he felt it, the aching hunger that seared him and would not be denied. She had no need for the whip. Her mental abilities were the strongest he'd ever come across. And he'd just challenged her. To punish him or make him understand the full extent of her power, she unleashed her allure on him.

Vampires had varying degrees of capacities in arousing the emotions of another. The gifted excelled at making humans and vampires feel lust more intensely, more intoxicating than anything they could imagine. They would sacrifice anything to experience such sensations: Their wealth, their honor, even their children. With his talents as a lover, he never wanted to *use his allure against the weaker. He never wanted to master a talent so powerful it could bring a person to their knees. He had no need of lovers who succumbed because they were overwhelmed.*

Magritte had no such problem.

His body reacted. He tried to control it, but Magritte was too strong. He twisted against the restraints. His cock was harder than it had ever been. The buildup of pressure more painful than anything he'd ever experienced. He thought his testicles would explode at any moment. His body needed release, but she was restraining him as if she held his cock in her fist and squeezed the head to make coming impossible. The pain was unbearable. His voice vibrated with rage. "Why, Magritte?"

"Because you have a gift. You must learn to use it…or others will use it against you." She coated his body with lust so potent, he broke out in a sweat that soaked the sheets. His pants sounded like a bull rutting.

"Do you feel the lust riding you? The beautiful pain of desire. Do you know how many would kill to possess this gift? To feel what you feel? The old ones don't remember. They need the allure to remind them. Would you deny them?"

Right now, he would agree to anything, even spend another week in the tombs, if she would only grant him release. She called it a gift; he thought it a curse. He swore under his breath, no matter the needs of the court, he would never enslave another the way she had him. There were other ways to elicit pleasure, other ways of satisfying. Let the other lords in the court use their allure when the court demanded it. This was not him! This was not him, he kept repeating when she covered his naked body with her own, taking his cock deep inside her.

She rode him slowly, deliberately. He knew his eyes were glazed with passion and pain, and she desired him as such.

He'd come to realize, too late, she fed on his weakness. Fed on his vulnerability. Had been seducing him with promises of what he desired most. Success. She knew what he coveted, knew his ambitions.

And she held the key to his wants. She tightened her inner muscles around his cock, making him feel the tingling sensations even stronger. His balls were as hard as rocks now, and still, she rode him. He tried to blank his mind, but still, the dream was there: Escape this court, find his own territory. He desired freedom. Too late, she clamped down on him, and a howl of completion tore from his throat as he jetted stream after stream of cum inside her.

She leaned down to whisper in his ear. "Desire all you want. You belong to me. I own you."

*It was the only time he ever passed out from an orgasm. But not before a final thought—*But not forever. Not forever.

A few days later, he'd thought his punishment complete. How wrong he'd been. She'd sent him, one last time, to Durand's castle. If she thought him arrogant, she'd made sure he learned humility.

He didn't remember returning to Mont Helaire because he'd been unconscious at the time. As Valadon lay on his stomach on his bed, a young vampire of striking beauty attended his wounds. With his long dark hair and androgynous looks, he was a court favorite. Men and women desired him.

"Drink this," Kristoph requested. "It will help with the pain."

Valadon had no desire for any drugs that would dull his brain. He'd been tricked once. His body used for pleasure against his will. "Take it away," he groused.

"Let me bathe you with the healing oils. They'll help."

After what he'd been through, having another male touch his nude body didn't bother him so much. Especially by one who was trying to tend to his wounds. In truth, he ached in places he'd never imagine having such pain.

Kristoph rubbed the herbed lotion across his back. His dexterous fingers working in the soothing ointment.

"How do you tolerate it?"

Kristoph stopped his ministrations. "What do you mean?"

"The abuse by the elders. Durand's castle."

"Where I grew up, it was no different. My parents rented me out to visitors. They did not have the wealth you and the other nobles possess. My body is slender. I don't have the musculature you have. I couldn't fight them. We didn't have the money to send me to university. So, I use the only resource I have."

"Would you leave?" Valadon faced his healer. "If you had the money?"

"My parents sold me to Magritte. I know no other life."

"Someday, I'll have my own territory. I hope you come with me, Kristoph. There are better worlds than this one."

"I hope you get your own region, Valadon. You will need many friends and great wealth in order to purchase your freedom."

He planned to accumulate both. It would take time, but he would break free of Magritte's court. He would have his own lands and the power to rule over them. Finance wasn't the only thing he'd studied in the libraries. He'd read the histories of great rulers going back to the ancient Greeks and Romans. Many had engaged in licentious behavior in order to succeed. Even great Julius Caesar, as proud and determined as he'd been, had been made to assume the submissive position, that of a cinadeus, in order to accumulate the allies necessary for his advancement. Sex was just another commodity, a method of bargaining. Commerce.

"Be careful with your words, Valadon. Magritte has many spies in her court. You're one of her favorites. She will try to keep you on a short tether."

"She thinks she has me leashed." But he knew, in his heart, he would never be her lap dog, though on occasion, he would have to act the part.

"Choose your allies well, Valadon. Jealousy is rampant in the courts. Many will sell you out to curry favor with her."

And he had chosen his associates well. Until he'd suffered a bout of depression. During his malaise, he'd allowed himself to become vulnerable; he'd put his faith in one raven-haired beauty who'd betrayed him for her own selfish ambition.

For centuries, he'd never let another close to his heart. He'd had many women, some the most beautiful the world has ever seen, but none who'd claimed him as his beloved Lena.

Until one chestnut-haired authenticator came into his life. A human who had beguiled him with her cool detachment and analytical mind. One he'd put his trust in. Completely.

Valadon, you fool, won't you ever learn!

Chapter Seven

"Remare's chopper is inbound." Aiden was nearly vibrating with anticipation. "ETA twenty minutes."

Valadon smirked. One of his favorite lieutenants couldn't hide his relief. "Will you be so very glad to be rid of your duties as my second, Aiden?"

"Yes. This is *his* post. I was only keeping it warm for him. As much as I enjoyed working beside you, I'm much better suited for the communications room."

"Oh, I don't know about that. I think you did a marvelous job. Thank you for filling in while Remare was in Montreal. I'll make restitution when I can. I appreciate all the extra effort you put in. I know I asked much from you, but it was necessary."

"It was my pleasure. But I'm glad Remare is back. We missed him. All of us."

"No more than I." After Aiden nodded and left, Valadon thought how true his last statement was. He'd missed Remare greatly. Without his exuberant second by his side, he'd become ponderous and too much inside himself. Too much time on his hands for reflection. Too much living in the past.

Of all the vampires he met during his tenure at the High Court, Remare was the one he called friend. Of course, he'd made many acquaintances and some allies. And enemies. But he'd never truly bonded with anyone but the high-spirited Roman. He often wondered if that had been the reason Magritte kept sending Remare off to war or distant courts where abuse was rampant. She'd been jealous of their friendship and the bond they had and sought to keep him isolated. When she became frustrated at his lack of attention and unrequited affection for her, she'd devise ways of annoying them.

Like him, when Remare first came to Mont Helaire, he was so full of life and possessed great potential. Few others had his sardonic sense of humor and quick wit. However, after centuries in the courts, both of them were tainted by the games of the other lords. Each having experienced great loss, disillusionment and too many of life's disappointments.

Valadon had known then, if they didn't leave, they would wind up jaded, depleted of their dreams and desires. Fall into a life of debauchery and ennui like the other lords. He'd refused to let that happen to either of them. Much to the distress of the elders, he'd been able to win their freedom. A growl rose up in his throat. And, now, they were trying to trap him yet again.

A knock at the door. "Come in."

Remare swaggered in with a grin a mile wide. "The prodigal son returns!" Laying his briefcase over the couch, he turned sideways and raised one brow. "Miss me?"

"Of course." Valadon hugged him tightly, refusing to let go until Remare did. His brother in all things, except blood. More than Brandon ever was. Time and distance had taught Valadon that. "Much has happened since you've been gone. Some good and some not so." Valadon sat at his desk.

Remare went to the bar and retrieved his favorite bottle of Cabernet. "Aiden and Morel have kept me apprised of events and business." After pouring himself a glass, he sipped his wine. "Shall we start with the good or the bad?" He took the seat in front of Valadon.

"The good." Valadon didn't have the heart to tell Remare of his suspicions concerning Miranda. Not just yet. "How is my nephew? He did not return with you."

"Your heir decided to stay in Montreal a little longer. He assures me he will be back in time for your wedding. He insisted he wasn't a child and refused any guards."

"You assigned them, regardless?"

"Of course. He's not aware of their presence. I thought it best to keep it that way. I did, however, bring back another." Remare drank more of his wine. "Dione's granddaughter."

"Yes, Dione mentioned as much. As she saw fit to guarantee the safety of my kin, I have done the same for her. Selena is now your ward. You will see to her safety while she is in New York."

"I was afraid you would say that. Morel is getting her settled in. She's quite eager to meet you. And even more anxious to meet Cesare."

"And so she will. More good news. I've had meetings with Chase Lambert and our legal team, as well as with Victor. Even if we could not avert this wedding, we found an interesting way to protect ValCorp's assets."

"Do tell."

"I will. But I will need all the Elite Torians present when I do so. Soon. Your turn."

"Madame Lord Dione sends her regards. She is our ally, stronger and more supportive than ever. Many of her courtiers consider us friends and were very cooperative. I was able to ascertain more background history on some of the members of the High Court, as well as their followers."

"No mention of the whereabouts of my brother, Brandon?"

"There were a few leads I had Touraine track down, but sadly to no avail. Brandon knows we're searching for him. He doesn't surface often, and when he does, it's not for very long."

"As I thought. Thank you for the continual reports. They were thorough, as usual. I take it no progress on the discovery of my son?"

"Unfortunately, no. I made it a point to become friendly with several members of Dione's court. There were rumors but unsubstantiated. I did, however, discover Brandon does, in fact, have several offspring he has never acknowledged."

"Yes, I am aware of them, as well," Valadon sighed. "With all our people and all our resources, I was sure we would have unearthed my son's whereabouts."

"Magritte hasn't issued any more proofs of existence?"

"No. She's being cagey. She knows that's the one card she can hold over me." Valadon swiveled his chair. "Wherever he is, he is being well-protected. She wouldn't even tell me if he knows I'm his father."

"You injured her pride by leaving. Magritte is a vampire of long memory. She does not forget or forgive easily."

"I know." Valadon knew all too well of Magritte's tempestuous nature. He still bore the scars of her cruelty. "And the Vancouver deal?"

"You are now the owner of several properties in British Columbia. I inspected the real estate in Vancouver myself. You will be pleased with their proximity to the waterways. Construction on the main building is progressing according to schedule." Remare swirled his wine. "Lord Trenvier is an interesting person, a skilled negotiator. It appears you have his full support."

"I'm sure he found my offers more than reasonable."

Remare smirked. "Yes, he did."

"And, now, the bad." Valadon hesitated. "I want you to understand there is still the possibility a reasonable cause is at the heart of the matter."

"And which matter would that be?"

There was no easy way to tell him his suspicions concerning Miranda. He took out a folder and passed it along his desk to Remare. It took two seconds for him to realize who the person Miranda was arm in arm with. "I am sorry. There was no other way to prepare you."

"Have you," Remare cleared his throat, "have you brought her in for questioning?"

"Miranda's on her way here, now. She should be here momentarily."

"What do we know?"

"Not enough. Aiden found this image when he was checking police cameras on local tourist spots. He was searching for signs of our enemies. He found Miranda. As soon as he showed me the picture, I had our agents assigned to her. They've been following her, keeping track of her movements, reporting what she does and who she sees."

Remare ran a finger slowly down her image. "Does anyone else know?"

"Just Aiden. I was hoping she would lead us to Montglat's location. So far, nothing." His phone beeped. "She's here, now. I had her informed of your arrival. She knows nothing of our findings, as yet."

Remare closed his eyes as if in pain. "You want to confront her, now?"

"Yes. I thought, with your presence, it would be more difficult for her to offer a falsehood. Do you wish differently?"

Remare continued to stare at the photos. After a moment, he said, "No. Let's deal with this, now."

Miranda quickly brushed her hair in the elevator up to Valadon's penthouse office. When she'd gotten the text Remare was back in New York, earlier than expected, she dropped everything to rush here. Checking her makeup, she decided she didn't care what she looked like. Remare was back! Her heart was beating out a staccato. No matter how many deep breaths she took, she couldn't calm herself down. Her hands were shaking.

If she'd had time, she would have made plans for a sumptuous dinner and a wicked night of lovemaking. Well, that was still on the menu; she chuckled. She couldn't wait to feel his arms around her, inhale his woodsy scent and drive him wild with hungry kisses.

She felt her dress pocket for her keys. She had driven into ValCorp's garage so fast, she wasn't even sure she put the Jeep in park, let alone remembered the keys. She did. Calm down, she kept telling herself. But she was so giddy with laughter, she couldn't stop fidgeting.

When the doors to the elevator finally opened, she flew down the hall to Valadon's office. With a quick knock, she threw the door open and stared at Remare. Her heart was banging against her rib cage. He was still the handsome, drool-worthy vampire she remembered. His raven hair and goatee were neatly trimmed, and his penetrating brown eyes bore into hers.

She rushed to embrace him, breathing in his scent deep into her lungs. Tears almost threatened to break loose at finally being able to hold him again in her arms. She kissed him soundly, but he did not return her passion. Something was off. His body was stone hard. And he wasn't happy to see her.

Heart pounding, she searched his face for any hint of why he was so cold. "What's wrong?"

He turned from her.

"Miranda." Valadon pushed a folder across his desk toward her.

"What's happened?" She searched the High Lord's face. It betrayed nothing. She opened the folder and gasped. At a loss for words, she stayed silent. Not knowing what to say, she ran a finger down Montglat's image. "Oh!"

Chapter Eight

"Well, you should be proud of yourself. You've accomplished the impossible. You're going to marry a man who loathes you."

"Don't be so sarcastic, Magritte. This was as much your doing as it was mine." Vivienna smirked as she adjusted the neckline of her wedding dress so the tops of her breasts were clearly visible. "After all this time, Valadon will finally be ours, again."

"Yes, and all his glorious wealth. If you don't screw it up." Magritte came closer to inspect the dress. "Our people are already entering his territory. Some announced, others not so."

"He'll be angry when he discovers them."

"But, then, it will be too late. Our spies in ValCorp have supplied us with his latest financial earnings. Valadon is worth more than we originally thought. I was a fool to let him go. If the damned revolution hadn't been going on and we weren't in desperate need of finances, I never would have agreed to his leaving."

"Will you be summoning him back to Mont Helaire once the ceremony is complete?"

"Not just yet. I want you to make contact with our people there. You are to find out everything you can about his investments, his future prospects, any and all information pertaining to his holdings. It won't be easy. He'll be expecting a certain amount of snooping on your part." Magritte laughed. "He knows me too well."

"Does he have to die?"

"Regrets, Vivienna? That's not like you."

"Once we accrue the necessary funds, why bother with offing him? You know I enjoy playing with my prey."

"Because, my dear, dear Vivienna, once he learns of our duplicity, he'll be a force to be reckoned with. For all his human attributes, he can be murderous when it comes to protecting what he considers his. I will not have this coming back on us."

"I'm concerned about Vincent." Vivienna regretted confiding in Magritte about Vincent's true parentage. He'd been the one good thing in her life. And she loved him more than any other. "I don't know how he'll react to learning his father is Valadon."

"Your son is the least of my concerns. He will do as we have always done. He'll adapt. Too many in the European Commission have faulted. I can't have any more territories declaring bankruptcy." Magritte paced. "I thought we had seen the worst of financial calamities after the last world war, but the economic turndown has had far-reaching effects. We need to stabilize before solvency becomes out of reach."

"Don't you miss his touch, Magritte? His presence by your side?" Vivienna knew Magritte to be the most harshly pragmatic person she'd ever met. But she was still a woman. "He'd be a masterful addition to the High Court."

"Valadon would never agree." Magritte wound Vivienna's long tresses around her fist. "Love is a weakness, Vivienna. You seduced him and his second once before for the High Council. Never forget, you are on a mission."

"I'm well aware of my duty, Magritte. I will do all that is necessary."

Magritte released her. "See that you do."

Vivienna was glad when Magritte finally left. Her emotions were more aroused than she would have liked. For the last few months, memories she thought long-buried were surfacing. She had betrayed Valadon and Remare to further

her own ambitions. And they'd paid the price. But so had she. Long ago, she'd learned to keep her cards close to her chest, but one secret burned hotter than any other.

She hadn't planned on falling in love with Valadon, but she had. It had incensed her at the time. She'd been trained to toy with men's emotions, to manipulate and lure. Not to fall victim to her own emotions. She was one of the most beautiful women in the world and had learned to use her appeal wisely. She was wealthy, her chateau one of the finest, her fashion houses the most profitable in the world. Vivienna doffed the wedding dress and carefully placed it back in the wardrobe.

Magritte was right. Love was a fleeting thing, something transient, not lasting. Donning a robe, she paced. If only Vincent had been her natural born child and not Marlena de Avignon's. She exhaled slowly. Perhaps things would have been different.

She had to keep her wits; time spent on impossibilities was futile. She knew this, but still, some part of her yearned for what had been denied her— Valadon's love. If she'd only had more time, she could have convinced him to forget his beloved and learn to love her. But time was never on her side. She shook her head, clearing the last of her reveries. Better to focus on economic security she told herself. There was little volatility there. And monetary stability was worth more than the affections of a man.

Any man.

***

Miranda didn't dare look at Remare or Valadon as she studied the photo of Montglat and her. Nothing she could think of to say was going to appease them. She knew they were waiting for her to speak. Her stomach knotted. "I suppose if I said, it's not what it looks like, you wouldn't believe me?"

Remare's voice was icy. "You admit your involvement with Montglat?!"

Miranda felt the frigid air go through her. "He's a friend. Nothing more." She kept her chin up, though she felt her bones shaking.

"The High Council's number one spy is nothing more than a friend?" Outrage laced Remare's already harsh words. "Do you really expect us to believe that?!"

"It's the truth." Miranda's heart was thundering at the murderous look in Remare's eyes. It was as though he would strangle her with one hand and not blink as her life slipped silently away.

"Miranda, we need to know the truth," Valadon interrupted. "Our security depends on it. Sit down, both of you."

She sat on the couch, while Remare stood near the door with both arms crossed over his chest. He vibrated venom. If he had a sword in hand, she'd already be flayed alive.

"How long have you known Montglat?" Valadon asked.

She gave the High Lord credit for keeping his cool. Though, she sensed a similar rage simmering just beneath his skin. "Not long. I met him after I was shot. Protecting you." She hoped reminding him she'd took a bullet for him would earn her some sympathy.

"Where did you meet him?" There was no such consideration from Remare.

"At the public library." Miranda rubbed her hands. Not because she was nervous, but because the temperature in the room was dropping rapidly.

"Who approached who?" Valadon maintained his calm tone.

Miranda tried to remember. No way was she bringing Felicity into this discussion. Her friend didn't need to be interrogated the way she was. "He introduced himself. We started talking." She tried to reason with the High Lord. "He's not an enemy. He never once asked me about you."

"If that's true, how come he's never come forward to announce his presence in our territory?" Remare barely held back a sneer. "That's our protocol."

"He didn't want anyone to know he was here."

"And you didn't think that was a bit suspicious? Really, Mir-randa?!"

"I did. I asked Valadon if Montglat was a friend or foe." She rose to lean forward against Valadon's desk. "In the archives. I pointed out his picture and asked you about him. Do you remember what you told me? You said you didn't remember him ever being an adversary. If you had, I would have told you, then, he was here in your territory."

"Would you now?" Remare scoffed. "How convenient."

"Yes, I would have." Miranda approached Remare, bile rising in her stomach that her lover seethed with anger. This was not the homecoming she imagined. "I'm not an enemy, Remare. You know that. You *know* me."

"I thought I did. Now," he pointed to the photos, "I don't know who you are."

"Please!" She tried to hold onto his shoulders, but he shrugged her off. "You have to listen to me. Montglat is not your enemy." She shook her head. "He told me he was sick of European politics. He tired of it and 'went under'. He wanted no part of it."

"And you believed him." Remare raised a brow. "Not very astute of you."

Miranda felt her own temper heating from all the tension in the room. "Why shouldn't I? Aren't you the one who told me none of us are who we were centuries ago?" He'd told her that in Paris.

"Miranda, I think you need to tell us everything you know about him." Valadon kept his voice even, but she could feel the steel beneath it.

"Are you his lover?"

Her eyes narrowed at Remare's derogatory question. "No!" She glowered back at him. "And you should know better!"

Valadon interjected, "Why is he in my territory?"

"I told you. He was tired of the politics, the games the Europeans played. He wanted a reprieve," she waved her hand absently in the air, "an escape."

"Then, why didn't he seek permission to be here?"

"I don't know. I suppose he was afraid you would try to involve him in some scheme."

"Where does he live?"

Miranda's arms flew in the air. She chose her words carefully. "I have no idea. I've only ever met him at the library or at Bryant Park. I never asked where he lived. I never needed to know."

Remare cut in. "Why did you keep this from us?"

"Because he asked me to. I fail to see what the big deal is. He's here. So, what?"

Remare looked like he was going to have an aneurysm. "The High Court's leading spy is in our territory and you *dare* to ask that question?!"

"I don't believe he is a spy!" Frustration laced her words. "I believe he's here because he wanted to get as far away from the European Council as he could."

"You're his agent, aren't you?" Remare's tone was caustic. "He planted you here to spy on us. Who does he report to?"

Miranda rolled her eyes. "You've got him all wrong."

"I sense you're holding back, Mir-randa. What aren't you telling us?

She was getting exhausted from all their questions and doubts about her. Her heart hurt as if it were clenched in someone's fist. She faced Valadon. "I never lied to you. I would never endanger you in any way. Don't you know that?"

"If Montglat is in my territory, he's here for a reason. The fact he never announced his presence concerns me. Gravely."

"Who are Montglat's associates?" Remare asked. "Did he ever introduce you to any of his friends?"

"He never introduced me to anyone." She blew out a breath. "Why can't you just believe he's here to simply live, to visit the city?" Miranda realized how lame that sounded.

"Where is he, now?" Remare demanded. "I think it's time Monsieur Montglat and I met."

"I don't keep tabs on him. He's usually at the library."

"Where else?"

Miranda was losing her patience with Remare's snarky attitude. "I have no idea."

Valadon asked, "How can I get in touch with him?"

"Call him."

"I'd love to." Valadon removed his phone from his jacket. "What's his number?"

Miranda hesitated. If she gave them Montglat's number, could they triangulate his location? If so, would she be betraying Guy's trust? "I'm not sure. I can call him from my home and have him get back to you." She eased toward the door.

"You're not leaving."

Miranda heard the threatening tone in Remare's voice, and her gut felt eviscerated. What would they do to her to extract answers? Would they torture her? She wasn't sure she wanted to know. Returning to the couch, she rubbed the heels of her palms against her head and called out to Guy. She'd been practicing her mental abilities with him since he and Felicity returned from their cruise.

"Yes, Miranda? It's a beautiful evening; you must come to the park. Everything is in bloom."

"I'm in trouble, Blu. Valadon and Remare learned of your presence in Manhattan and think you're here to spy on them. They think I'm a confederate of yours."

Amusement laced his voice. *"How did they know I was in the city?"*

"They have photos of us leaving the library."

"I see."

"Will you please meet with Valadon to explain why you're here? I didn't dare bring up Felicity. Both Valadon and Remare are looking at me as if I'm some sort of traitor."

"I'm afraid not, Miranda. The minute I announce my presence, Valadon will set his guards on me. I do not wish to be apprehended."

"Call him, then. Blu, I need your help."

Silence ensued. *"I cannot call him without him tracing the number. I can, however, recommend an alternative."*

"What?"

"Will you lend me your voice? Our connection is strong enough that I can talk through you. This way my presence isn't compromised."

Miranda wasn't crazy about his idea. But the way Remare and Valadon were looking at her left little choice. *"Okay."*

Rising from the couch, she met Valadon's eyes. She could sense Guy in her mind. "Good evening, Lord Valadon. I hear felicitations and congratulations are in order for your upcoming wedding."

Miranda nearly gagged at the intrusion. It was her mouth the words were emitted from, but it was Montglat's inflections and slight British accent that reverberated in the room.

The startled expressions on Valadon's and Remare's faces were priceless.

Valadon rose. "Montglat?!"

"At your service."

"What have you done to Miranda?"

"She asked that I speak with you. I am honoring her request. No harm is being done. Though I must say, Vivienna?" Miranda felt the equivalent of a disapproving headshake.

"Instead of using Miranda this way, why don't you come to my office and we can speak man to man?"

"I would prefer not to. I know I illegally entered your territory, and for that, I offer my sincerest apologies. I simply didn't want others to know my whereabouts."

"Who are you working for?"

"No one. Like you, I left the High Court centuries ago. I found their petty politics tedious and no longer wished to serve. Surely, you understand my appreciation for discretion."

"Why are you in my territory?"

"For the enjoyment of your fair city. Nothing ominous, I assure you. But you are right to feel indignant at my lack of courtesy. To make up for my shortcomings, I shall send you a gift. One I think you will find most interesting."

"Montglat!"

"I would ask that you not disclose my presence here, but I fear I might be too late in that hope. If it assuages your vexed sense of propriety, know that I will be leaving New York shortly. Now, Miranda is feeling distressed, and I must leave. *Au revoir*, Lord Valadon."

"Montglat, don't you dare leave!"

Miranda gasped and bent over as Blu's presence left her. Nothing could have prepared her for the sense of violation, even though she had given her approval. Holding her stomach, she crawled toward Valadon's wastebasket and wretched. As she hadn't eaten much during the day, all that came up were the dry heaves.

Out of breath, her face heated and sweating from the exertion, she looked up at Valadon. "Don't *ever* ask me to do that, again."

"How long have you been able to speak to him that way?"

Miranda waved her arm in the air. "Not sure. Probably when you opened the channel." She dragged herself upright by clutching first the chair, then the desk. Inside her purse, she found her bottle of water and took long swallows.

Both of them continued to eye her with suspicion. "I was nearly burned at the stake because of you. Your brother kidnapped me and tormented me in a cell. I was stabbed, slashed and in a coma. I think I've proven my loyalty enough." She swallowed more water. "If you have issues with Montglat, you work them out with him. I'm leaving."

"Not just yet." Valadon strode towards her. "I need your pass key. I'm not sure what the hell is going on. But, in the meantime, I can't have an unknown having access to my building." He held out his hand waiting.

Miranda was aghast. "You still don't believe me?"

"Not completely."

Tears threatened to break lose. She fished in her bag for her security badge and handed it to him. "What about our work in the archives?" Miranda loved working there; she still had books she wanted to comb through for her own personal information.

"Suspended. For now."

She glanced one last time at Remare as Pink's song, "What About Us," played in her mind. The pull between them was still strong, and she wanted to touch him, simply cup his cheek. But he was a wall of ice. It was as if no emotion existed behind the dark deadness of his eyes. Miranda couldn't stand to see him this way. It hurt her heart too much.

She left before more tears rolled down her face.

Chapter Nine

"Do you believe her?"

Remare shook his head. "As much as I want to, no." He was still seething in quiet rage. He'd been manipulated by beautiful females in the past. His stomach felt as if it had been soaked in acid at the thought of Miranda being one of them. Of all the women he'd known, he'd least expected duplicity on her part. "If Montglat is in New York, he's here for only one reason. You."

"I agree. It's been centuries." Arms crossed, Valadon stared out the window. "Why would *Le Cameleon* choose now to surface? As far as I know, no one's heard or seen him in such a long time. And I pay well to be kept informed of such matters."

"I fear Miranda knows more than she is saying."

"You sensed that, too? I have my agents following her. If she reports to Montglat, we'll have our answer." Valadon glanced backward. "You'll be the one who questions her, again. Are you all right with that?"

"I would rather it was me than someone else."

"So be it. There is one other possibility to consider."

"Montglat has glamoured her." Remare's hand clenched as if missing his sword. "If I remember correctly, he was a vampire of many skills, admired and even feared in some of the courts. Known for his stealth. She wouldn't even know she was being used. Somehow, he targeted her. Knew from the pictures on social media, she was involved with you, had access where others did not."

"That is my greatest concern. And what he will do to her when she is no longer useful."

Remare didn't want to consider the possibilities. The thought of Miranda dying a horrible death made his body tighten. "I'll speak with her, again. I'll get the truth from her."

A knock sounded at the door, and a charming young woman with curly blonde hair entered. "Is now a good time?"

Remare smiled. "Lord Valadon, this is Selena of House Dione."

Valadon nodded at the unusually dressed woman. "It's a pleasure to meet you. Your grandmother and I have been friends for centuries. I understand you wish to intern with Cesare."

Her smile was ebullient. "Yes, it's been a dream of mine for some time now."

"I'm sure he'll be delighted to take you under his wing." Valadon seemed to be scrutinizing her. "I'll have Carla, one of his assistants, show you around."

"Thank you. I'm looking forward to meeting him. At school, Cesare is a legend."

Remare reached for the door. "If you will excuse me, I have some business to attend to. I will try to clear up that matter as expediently as possible."

Valadon nodded. "Keep me informed."

"Will do." He bowed. "Selena."

"Have you been to New York before? I don't remember meeting you, but yet..." Valadon sensed there was something charming about Madame Lord Dione's progeny. Her enchanting eyes held curiosity but also an intelligence and a perceptive nature usually seen in much older vampires. She seemed to be studying him as much as he was her.

"You wouldn't. I was a child the last time Dione brought me to New York." She laughed. "The only thing I remember is riding the carrousel in Central Park." Her smile was delightful in one so young. "Is it still there?"

"I believe so. And, now, you'll be attending F.I.T. What made you interested in fashion?"

"It's been a passion of mine for some time. I'm good at it. And Cesare's designs are awesome. I'm really looking forward to meeting him."

"As he is you. I hope you'll be happy here. Did Morel show you your room?"

"Yes."

"There you are." Tristan knocked and then huffed as if out of breath. "I was looking all over for you. Morel was called to the communications room and asked me to show Selena around. You shouldn't have disappeared like that."

"Sorry." Her voice said otherwise, and Valadon got the distinct feeling she was being on her best behavior. He smirked at her lack of genuine apology.

"If you're finished, I'll take her back to her rooms."

"It was a pleasure meeting you, Selena. I'm sure I'll see you at dinner. Tristan will escort you, now."

"I wanted to say thank you for this opportunity. It really does mean the world to me, and I'm grateful you and Dione were able to come to terms." After Tristan left, she hung back for a minute. "Oh, just one thing. No one calls me Selena, only my grandmother when we're at court. All my friends at university call me by my nickname."

"Which is?"

"Lena."

***

"Banzai!" Her voice louder than usual, Miranda shoved another shot glass with a fireball down the length of Werehaven's bar.

"Miranda, don't you think you've had enough?" Gavin asked.

She thought about it. "I don't know. Do you think I have? Lizandra said I should tie one on." She hiccupped. "I'm not sure I'm tied yet."

"I said to have a drink," the Were Queen huffed, "not to scorch my bar!"

"Oh, I was just having a little bit of fun. Banzai!" Another flaming glass went crashing down the bar, stopped only by Gavin's swift reflexes.

"Motherfucker! You're going to set the place on fire. How many have you had already?"

She considered the question. "Beats me! I stopped counting."

Behind the bar, Gavin dried off a glass. "She's wasted."

"*Ya think?!* Why'd you let her get so bombed?"

"Me? I cut her off two drinks ago. She summoned," he waved his hand for emphasis, "the bottle as soon as I turned away."

"I hate him!" Miranda's voice cracked. "He should have trusted me. Don't you think he should have trusted me?"

"Right now," the Were Queen crossed her arms, "I wouldn't trust you to walk a straight line, which I know you can't."

"Aww, you're just saying that 'cause you can't fling fireballs the way I can." Miranda tossed back the rest of her drink, the movement bringing on a bout of vertigo. "Whoa, who made the bar spin?" She clutched the rim for support.

"That's it. You're going to sleep this off." Lizandra grabbed her by the arm and pulled her down the hall.

"I can walk!"

"You're polluted!"

"Doesn't mean I can't walk." As soon as Liz let go of her, she slid into the wall. "Okay, maybe just a little."

When they reached her room, Liz opened the door. "Get your sorry ass in there."

Once Miranda lay down, the vertigo came back in full force. "Oh God, Liz, make the room stop spinning!"

"Mm-hmm." Liz stood with one hand on her hip. "You're going to have one helluva hangover. I've seen you drink. You can usually hold your liquor better than this. What the hell happened?"

"It hit me hard." She hiccupped, again. "I don't think I had much to eat today. I was so excited, so happy Remare was coming back today." A sob broke through her thoughts. "He hates me, now."

"He doesn't hate you."

"Oh, yes, he does! You didn't see him. He thinks I'm some sort of traitor."

Liz went to the bathroom and brought back a wet washcloth. She sat beside her and placed it across Miranda's forehead. "Now, why would he think that?"

"Thanks, that feels so much better. My face is so hot." Miranda tried to collect her thoughts through the thick haze of dizziness. "He thinks I'm a spy." She huffed. "He doesn't like the company I keep."

"What company?"

"I met a vampire. An ancient. He's a friend of mine. Nothing more."

"What's his name?"

"Boo. I mean Blu. A former agent for the vampire court. You know, you would think he would trust me." Miranda's eyes narrowed. "I bled for him. I even killed for him, protected him against a deformed creature. And, still, he has the balls to doubt me!"

"Wait a minute. Back up. Rewind. Who's this Blu?"

"I met him a year and a half ago after I got shot trying to protect Valadon. You would think they would show some appreciation, but noooo! Turn in your badge, Miranda." She lowered her voice to emulate Valadon's. "I can't have an unknown wandering around my building."

"You're hanging around a known spy?" Liz was confused and outraged. "Doesn't that sound a little strange to you?"

"*Former* spy. He gave that up centuries ago.'

"How do you know?"

"Because he told me."

Liz was giving her the hairy eyeball. "Mm-hmm. And you believed him?"

"No, no, no!" She waved her index finger in the air. "It's not like that." Miranda sat up and, keeping the cool cloth against her forehead, leaned against the headboard. "Blu's benevolent. Got tired of vampire court bullshit and walked away."

"And you know that for a fact?"

Miranda considered her words. "Yeah, pretty much. Look, he could have asked me about Valadon half a dozen times. He never did. He's here to get away from all the political intrigues." She exhaled. "At least, that's what he said. I believe him."

"And you and Remare argued about this?"

"Yeah, he thinks I'm an idiot or, worse, a spy. Where does he get off?"

"How'd he find out about you and this guy?"

"Someone took a picture of us leaving the library. Arm in arm."

"Jesus, Miranda. I can see why he'd be upset. I take it he just found out about this?"

Miranda nodded.

"And you've been seeing this other guy about a year and a half?"

"Not seeing, seeing." Miranda shook her head. "More like lunch every now and then. That's about it. Blu already has a girlfriend, companion."

Liz crossed her arms over her chest. "Now, let me get this right. Remare was sent away because he was boinking you. Valadon found out and exiled him. He comes back and finds out you've been hanging around with a spy."

"Former spy."

"He confronts you, and you tell him what?"

"The truth." Miranda shrugged. "He's not a spy, and we're just friends."

Liz sputtered. "You told him you've been seeing this guy, a spy, *former* spy, for over a year, and you don't think he should be upset?!"

"No, not really." Miranda thought about it. "Okay, I see your point. But there was no reason for him to turn his back on me." Anger and hatred she could deal with, but the way he spun away from her cut deeply.

"Really? I would have kicked your ass from here to New Jersey."

Miranda blinked. "But you know me."

"No difference. If I ever found out you were hanging out with a member of Red Claw and you didn't tell me for a year and a half, blood would be spilled."

Miranda gaped at her. "I would never hang out with the Red Claws."

Liz did the head tilt thing designed to infuriate.

"You trust me, don't you?"

"Not if you did something sneaky behind my back and lied about it."

"I didn't lie." She shrugged. "I just didn't tell him."

"A lie of omission is still a lie," they said in unison.

"I know, I know." Miranda held her head. "Jesus, no wonder he hates me."

"Girlfriend, you have got to talk to him. Explain every detail. Otherwise, he's going to have suspicions."

"Oh God, my head hurts." Miranda lay back down.

Liz rose and retrieved a cold bottle of water from the mini-fridge. "Here, drink this. It may help. We gotta get you sobered up. I'm gonna send Gavin in with some food and that green tea you like so much. You need sustenance."

After she left, Miranda curled into herself. God, she felt awful. The two vampires she cared most about suspected she was a plant. She hated them thinking that about her. When there was a knock at the door, she thought it was Gavin.

It wasn't. Remare closed the door behind him then stood staring at her.

Her heart banged against her ribs. When he didn't say anything, need overrode logic, and she sprang up to embrace him. She needed this. Needed him. Inhaling his scent infused her with emotional strength. "I'm so sorry, Remare. I should have told you from the very beginning. I'm sorry. Please forgive me."

"Why don't you start by telling me the truth?" The frost that had been in his eyes earlier seemed to have melted some. Even his tone was less harsh. "Tell me everything you know about Montglat."

Nodding, Miranda sat back down on the bed while Remare pulled the desk chair in front of her and sat. She told him what she could. She would not bring up Felicity but told him what she thought he needed to know.

After she was done, he continued to eye her. "And you're leaving nothing out?"

"Nothing pertinent." Doubt marred his handsome face. "Remare, I should have told you from the beginning. I just didn't think it was important."

"A high-ranking agent of the High Court is living in our territory, unannounced and uninvited, and you didn't think it was important enough to share with me?"

Miranda exhaled. "It never occurred to me, not once, that there was even the slightest, most remote possibility he could be here to spy on Valadon." She shook her head. "Not once, not ever, did he give me that impression."

"He's here for a reason, Mir-randa." No trace of hostility was evident in his voice. But, thankfully, warmth was seeping into his eyes.

"You think I got played?"

"It's possible. We will look into it. Our people are running background checks as we speak." Remare stood and replaced his chair at the desk. "Did he ever mention any friends or acquaintances he might be visiting while here in New York?"

"None. Like I said, I think he wanted to start a new life. Away from the courts. From what I saw of them in Paris, I didn't blame him."

He muttered, "What do you know of the courts?"

"I visited Vivienna's. Remember? I saw how those people operate. No, thanks."

"There's much you don't know." His eyes closed as if bitter memories were surfacing.

Miranda slinked up to him. "I missed you." She wound her arms around his waist. "Not the homecoming you expected, huh?!"

"Not quite." He brushed his lips against hers. "There wasn't a day went by I didn't think of you." He fisted her hair and pulled her closer for a much deeper, passionate kiss.

The butterflies in her stomach took flight, and her body melted into his. Relief enveloped her at the way he stroked her back, familiar touches in the night. Why did she always feel so much stronger when he was with her? What magic did he spin to make her feel all was right with the world, even when she knew it wasn't? A nick on her tongue, she tasted her blood. Her body heated, desire pulsing along her skin, strong and undeniable.

But through the thick haze of passion, something foreign was niggling at her. Something she knew but didn't recognize.

"Son of a bitch!" She pulled away from him. "You were entering my mind! Weren't you?"

He wiped the drop of blood away from his lower lip.

Wounded and outraged by the realization, her heart ached. "You would use the passion between us to...violate me?!"

"You're not telling me everything, Miranda. I'm not a fool. I can sense you're hiding something."

"And that gives you the right to rape my memories?!" Horror lanced through her.

"If you were honest with me, there would be no need to search your memories. It was hardly rape."

Her body vibrated with fury and pain as if he'd stabbed her in the heart. "To penetrate someone's mind without permission is rape. You took away my right to choose. Who *are* you? The Remare I knew would never have done something so cruel."

"Perhaps you didn't know me as well as you thought." Venom coated his words. "If I had suspected you were in league with Montglat or any of our enemies, I would have done much worse."

Tears of rage threatened. "Get out." She pointed to the door. "I don't know you, anymore."

"Fine." He reached for the door. "If you decide to be more forthcoming with the truth, you know where to find me."

The sound of the door closing had her falling back on the bed. She was shattered. There was no other word for it. Other women had used that word to describe how they felt after bad break ups, but Miranda had never understood the depth of the devastation. Her entire body felt bruised and battered. "This can't be happening!" Her insides hurt so bad, she curled into a ball and let the tears fall. The sobs wracked her body so badly she didn't hear the door opening.

"Miranda, what's wrong?" Gavin quickly put the tray on the desk and sat beside her. He pulled her into his arms, his warmth helping to slow her trembling. "Tell me what happened."

"I can't." She shook in his arms as more sobs escaped her mouth. "It was so awful." She hid her face in his chest, her tears dampening his shirt.

"I know, I know." He stroked her hair. "Take deep breaths. I'm sorry he upset you."

"He's a monster." She practically crawled in his lap. "I can't stand this. I feel like part of me is dead."

"We'll figure it out. As bad as it is, Miranda, you'll survive this. You survived worse. You have us. Liz and me. We won't let you do this alone."

Gavin's words resonated in her mind. Exhausted, she glanced up at him and palmed his cheek. "You were always there for me. Thank you."

"That's what friends do, Mira." He handed her a Kleenex. "Take a moment to breathe." He rose and brought the cup of tea to her. "Here, drink some of this. It will soothe your throat."

"Thanks." Miranda inhaled the calming aroma and sipped. It helped. "Gavin. Things are so screwed up. I don't know how to fix it."

"Tell me what's wrong."

She gave him the short version and he listened, asked a few questions and then offered support. "You need to make him understand the truth, Miranda. This is all one big misunderstanding."

"I don't think I could forgive him for violating my mind like that." The memory of it made her shudder. "The worst part of it was that he was using the attraction between us as a tool to get what he wanted." She put her hand over her heart. "Those feelings are precious to me, and he had no qualms whatsoever doing it." The thought made her want to vomit.

"I agree. He shouldn't have done that." Gavin exhaled. "He feels threatened by you. Sees you as some sort of danger. I don't think he'd have done it if he hadn't had a real good reason."

"That makes it all right?"

"That's not what I said. I've seen the way you two are when he's been here. It's obvious he has feelings for you."

She shook her head. "I wonder about that, now."

"I don't." Gavin stroked his jaw. "You didn't see him when he was leaving."

She glanced up. "How'd he look?"

"Shaken. Distraught, but he hides it well. He's a proud man."

"He should be upset. He hurt me."

"I know." Gavin brought the food closer. "I realize you're hurt, but Liz said you didn't eat anything. You need to keep your strength up. Can you get down a few bites? Lawe made these biscuits special for you. He said they're your favorites."

Miranda wasn't hungry, had no appetite, but she hadn't eaten much today and needed sustenance. Still warm, Lawe's biscuits melted in her mouth. She drank more of the tea. "How do I make this right?"

"If you're not ready to talk to Remare, how about Valadon? You said he wasn't belligerent with you. Would he understand?"

Miranda considered the idea. "Maybe." During their interrogation, if Remare was bad cop, Valadon had been good cop. "He wasn't as emotional as Remare." She rose. "What time is it?"

"Late, after midnight."

"I'm gonna go see him." She wobbled when she tried to walk.

"A little late, don't you think? Maybe you should wait until tomorrow. Let things settle."

She reached for her purse. "No. I might lose my nerve."

"Oh, no, I'm not letting you drive in the condition you're in. I'll take you. The twins can manage the bar tonight. I could use some fresh air."

"You don't have to, Gavin. I know you have responsibilities here. I'll drive slowly."

"As Liz would say, hell to the no."

When they were leaving, Gavin spoke to one of the twins, and Lawe came out and handed her a bag. "I made half a dozen, *cher*. You do right by them." He hugged her then went back to the kitchen.

"Was that Drew or Dan you were talking to?"

Gavin gave her a look. "Drew. You still can't tell them apart?"

Miranda looked at both of the twins. Identical hair styles, same height, weight. Even their clothes were the same. "Not really."

Gavin signaled to Liz up in the lounge, who was wrapped around Cyrus, that he was driving her home. No wonder Gavin wanted to get away for a while. Seeing an ex-lover with the new must have grated.

Chapter Ten

"You go on up. I'll wait here." In ValCorp's garage, Gavin adjusted the car seat so he was reclining.

Miranda said, "I don't know how long I'll be."

"It's all right." He leaned up and kissed her forehead. "I'll be here. Take as long as you need. Text me when you're finished."

"Will do."

She'd sobered up on the drive to see Valadon. They agreed to meet in his private quarters down in Valadon House. When the elevator doors opened, she was surprised no vampires were hanging around in the massive living area, either watching TV or in the kitchen having a late-night snack. It was eerie walking the empty halls.

After taking a deep breath, she knocked on his door and entered. He was at his desk, dressed in a black robe and silk pajamas. He looked up from his computer. "Miranda."

"Hello, Valadon." His huge poster bed with the black and gold duvet had already been turned down. There was a new, much smaller one off to the side.

"With all the foreign dignitaries coming in for the wedding, it was thought best to assign a guard to me at all times when they arrive."

Miranda remembered from the history books, monarchs often had sentries posted inside their bedroom to ward off any would-be assassins. She guessed the guards needed a place to rest, as well. "I'm glad you agreed to see me. Sorry for the late hour."

"It's quite all right. Would you like a drink?"

Miranda's eyebrows rose. *Hell to the no!* After fighting off the effects of the alcohol, she wasn't having another drink for a very long time. "I'm good, thanks." She sat in the chair in front of him. "I caused you concern today." She exhaled slowly. "I'm sorry. Remare came to speak with me at Werehaven." She wasn't going to tell him about the mental invasion; that wound was too raw. "I should have told you when I first met Montglat that he was in your territory."

"Yes, you should have." His eyes bore into hers.

"I've been trying to come up with a way to fix this." She laid her hand on his desk. "I know I made you doubt me. I get it, now. It's just...I never suspected anything malicious from Montglat. I still believe he's here for benevolent purposes."

"Do you know how difficult it is for me to believe that?"

"Remember when we were in the archives? You told me they used to call him *Le Cameleon*. I have no point of reference for that. I never knew him centuries ago. I don't know what he was like, then. I've been trying to see things from your perspective. I only know what he appears to be, now." She shook her head. "I screwed up."

Valadon seemed to be considering her perspective. "If you had known of his missions in the past, you would have been wary of him. You would have known not to trust him."

She leaned back in her chair. "Do you really believe people are the same as they were hundreds of years ago? Are you the same as you were back then?"

"I understand where you're coming from, but I believe people are essentially who they are. I can't believe Montglat has changed that much. Not after centuries of being an agent for our ruling lords."

"But you haven't seen him in such a long time."

"The fact that he came into my territory without announcing his presence, has been here for over a year—which we know of—indicates malice on his part."

"Maybe not. The only way we're going to resolve this is if you speak with him. Face to face."

"I invited him to ValCorp; he refused my offer."

"I'll talk with him. I'll get him to meet with you." She had no clue how she was going to manage that, but it was the only solution she could see.

Suspicion was back in his voice. "You hold that level of sway over Montglat?"

"I don't know." She shrugged. "But I'll try my best."

"He'll never agree to it; he's far too intelligent."

"Then, some place neutral to both parties." She yawned. The events of the day were finally catching up with her. "I won't stop trying until I convince him to meet with you."

"You're exhausted. Why don't you sleep here tonight? Today was arduous for all of us."

Another yawn escaped her throat, this one louder than the first. "I think you're right. Not going to fight you this time. But, if I stay, I'm claiming the guard's bed." As soon as she sat there, fatigue pulled at her. "I'm just going to close my eyes for a little while."

He chuckled. "I'm sure I have an extra pair of pajamas. You can change in the bathroom. This way you'll be more comfortable."

She took the silk threads Valadon retrieved from his dresser and closed the bathroom door behind her. A low whistle emitted from her lips. Even with just a night light on she could see the vampire king loved comfort. His black marble tub with streaks of gold had faucets resembling swan heads and was big enough for four people. The floor and wall tiles were the same colors of the tub, but what grabbed her attention was the painting on the side wall. It was a version of Monet's *Water Lilies,* and Miranda was sure it was an original. Wisely, it was encased in glass so the steam wouldn't ruin it.

She quickly changed and folded her clothes. His pajama top fell to mid-thigh. No way were the bottoms going to fit.

Valadon had turned the bedroom lights down low. "These are a little too long for me." She handed him his silk pants.

"I thought they might be. You do realize my bed is big enough for a small army."

"Not a soldier." *Flirt!* "The guard's bed is big enough for me." She returned his sexy smile. "Good night."

"Good night, Miranda." He removed his robe and pajama top. She exhaled slowly. He slid beneath the comforter and pulled the sheets over him. *Sexy beast! But not* my *sexy beast.* She covered herself with the blankets, and as soon as she lay her head on the pillow, sleep claimed her.

Valadon knew he was dreaming, but whenever he dreamed of Marlena, he fought to hold onto the precious memory. He was afraid one day it would slip away until she was but a figment of his imagination.

Marseilles, 1628—Nightfall

"I'll beat you to the cottage! You're getting old, Valadon, you can't keep up." Marlena laughed as she steered her horse *toward their secluded cottage.*

The sun was just beginning to set, but he could still see her long blonde hair flowing in the wind. He couldn't wait to feel the silken strands wrapped around his hand. He could easily outpace her; he'd been an accomplished equestrian for centuries, but he loved to watch her smile, and the speed of the race gave such a glow to her cheeks. "Be careful, one of these evenings you're going to go too fast, and your horse will throw you."

"You just say that so I'll go slowly. I have no intention of granting that request. Ha! I made it first."

"So you did. I suppose I owe you one wish, now. Whatever will my mistress desire of me, now?" He dismounted and tied

up their horses, then retrieved the parcel of food and wine. He was happy when her father and fiancé went on their business ventures. It was only then he could spend time with her. He'd bought the stone cottage from an old sea captain who decided to live out his years on the Spanish coast. This way his beloved Lena would have a place of peace and quiet to read and compose her poems. Had her father allowed it, he was sure she would have been a scholar.

"Ah, but my lover has already granted my wish. Come inside. I'll show you the latest drawings Marcel has been doing."

Marcel, the innkeeper's son, was talented in his depictions of the French seaside and the ships that came into port at Marseilles. Valadon would have to remember to bring the young artist paints and linens from his travels. "They're marvelous. Your young friend is quite talented. Should I be jealous?"

"He's barely fifteen years old, so I think you're safe in that regard. I prefer much older men, as you know." Lena knew he was a vampire. A select few human aristocrats possessed that knowledge, and as the daughter of one of their best allies, she too had become aware of his otherness. She kissed him and then led him to the fireplace where she was preparing the kindling.

He'd made arrangements with a local woodsman to make sure the cottage was supplied with enough wood to keep the fireplace going. He poured them each a glass of cabernet. "Try this wine; my friend Remare says the vineyards have been part of his family's Tuscany estate for centuries and they are the best in the world."

"But do they compare with the French wines?" She tasted it and moaned in pleasure. "I think your friend is right. This is very good." Her eyes danced with laughter. "Tastes almost as good as you."

"Scandalous woman." He took her glass, placed it on the table and kissed her passionately. "I've missed you."

"As I, you." Taking his hand, she led him to the bedroom.

He watched as she disrobed. In the near darkness, his fangs lengthened as she let the last of her clothes fall to the floor and climbed on to the bed. "Are you going to stand there all night, or offer your woman pleasure beyond her wildest imagination?"

Her laughter was music to his ears. He lifted her dress from the floor and set it on the chair then sat beside her on the bed. "Do you realize how truly beautiful you are?" He played with a strand of her hair. "I've traveled to many places in this world, none are as fair as you." He wondered if she would hold such deep affection for him if she'd known about his past, the acts of cruelty he'd been forced to witness. And the horrible things he'd done that he'd had to rectify his soul with so as not to go mad.

"I'm only as beautiful as you make me feel." She slid her hands up his arms to curl around his neck and untied the thong of leather holding his hair back. "And I have missed you terribly." She kissed him with far too much skill, talents he'd taught her. His body immediately tightened.

He broke from the kiss long enough to undo his clothes and then covered her body with his. "You are the light of my life, Lena. Never forget that. Even when I am gone for long periods of time. You are always in my thoughts." He nuzzled her neck, trailing butterfly kisses along her vein to her shoulder and then down to her breast. Her delicate nipple was already hard and waiting for his mouth to suckle.

She tasted like heaven, an angel sent to torment him with wants and desires he had no right feeling. He'd seen too many hells to realize life only offered precious moments; fleeting minutes of pleasure needed to be savored and enjoyed because of their rarity. And moments like this were becoming increasingly rare as his obligations and duties to the High Court intensified.

After tenderly biting down on one nipple and sucking it hard enough to have Lena moaning, he licked the sting, rolling his tongue around her areola, then administered to her other breast. Trailing kisses and tiny bites, he laved her navel, enjoying the way she writhed beneath his touch.

Pushing her legs wide to accommodate his shoulders, he settled between her thighs and used every technique he'd ever been taught to drive her insane with passion. He could hear her heart pounding as he licked, bit and stroked her intimate flesh. When her rapid breaths increased, he sucked her clit into his mouth and bit down. Her cries of completion aroused him more than he thought possible.

He quickly rose up on his elbows and entered her while her body still throbbed. Had he ever felt such warmth? Aware of his girth, he slowly inched deeper inside her. To cause her any discomfort when they were joined this way would be an insult to his very being. "You are so tight, my love. I'm afraid I'll hurt you."

She stroked his jaw. "You never have before. I like how you feel inside me. My body welcomes you, Valadon. There is no pain."

With every ounce of the reserve he learned at the High Court, he moved with a rhythm mutually pleasurable to them both. His own heart beat heavily in his chest. In his mind, he heard the sea battling against his ship as his thrusts became more pronounced. Sweat trickled down the side of his face as heat seared up his spine. He could feel her inner muscles contracting around his cock. Only when she screamed out his name did he plunge in deeper and allow himself to be sated. "I love you, Lena. I always will." He kissed her soundly.

"I love you, too, Valadon. Always and forever."

He rolled off her and barely caught his breath, when he heard a loud banging at the door. Her father, Lord Avignon, and her fiancé, Rocheforte, entered and stood horrified. Then, in a furious outburst, Avignon went for Valadon's throat with a sharp dagger as Rocheforte dragged Lena, naked and screaming, out of the cottage. Valadon shouted at the top of his lungs for them to let her go. His breaths a raging storm.

"Valadon, wake up." Someone was shaking his shoulders, but he couldn't break free of the horror. "It was a nightmare, only a bad dream. Wake up!"

The haze of sleep lifted, but his heart beat against his ribs in painful memory. "I'm all right; I'm all right," he breathed out. He lifted his body into a sitting position. Sweat poured down his chest. "Thank you, Miranda." He accepted the bottle of cold water she'd retrieved from the bar's refrigerator and swallowed a few gulps. "It was a nightmare I've had before. It didn't happen." He shook his head in part to clear his head and partly to remind himself. "It never happened. Not that way."

"Want to talk about it?" She settled alongside him on the bed and used a handkerchief to wipe away the perspiration from his face.

"No." He shook his head. Some memories were too personal to share.

"Well, this is a sight I hadn't expected to see." With arms crossed, Remare stood against the doorframe. "I knocked, but no one answered."

Miranda turned sideways. "Didn't hear you."

"Obviously not."

Chapter Eleven

Uncomfortable, Gavin twisted in his seat. Miranda had a nice Jeep, but it wasn't the ideal place to sleep for a man of his physique. With the underground garage dark and deserted, it had been easy to nod off. He checked his phone for the time when two men stepped off the elevator. At this hour, he didn't expect anyone to be around. With the window cracked open, he was able to hear their conversation. He sniffed the air to get a bead on their scents. One was unusual but not unfamiliar.

Something alerted him to the way the men moved. They whispered, but with his wolf hearing, he could hear their every word. Crouching down farther into his seat, he listened in.

"And you're certain the assassin will be in place in time for the wedding?"

"I told you, I would handle it. Everything is a go. But are you sure you want to proceed? Magritte was adamant in her last message Valadon was not to be harmed."

"Fuck her! I've waited long enough. I'm ready."

"You don't want to piss off Magritte. I've seen what she can do to other vampires. It ain't pretty. And someone of your looks, Jeremy, she'd take pleasure in torturing you."

"Not going to happen. My blood is one of the oldest lines, pure. I'm not afraid of her. Besides, if your man is as good as you say, they'll never be able to trace it back to me."

Gavin strained to hear more, but the two vampires had gotten into their cars and driven off. He checked the phone in his hand to make sure he'd recorded what he could. As soon as he'd heard the word 'assassin', he'd pressed record and tried to get as clear an image as possible, but with the darkness, the figures were hard to make out.

He immediately dialed Valadon's personal number.

***

"My right hand. Come, join us." Valadon welcomed Remare as Miranda slid off the bed and sat on her own. "There's nothing going on here that remotely smacks of infidelity. We were just talking."

Remare tossed off his robe and half-sat, half-reclined on Valadon's right. "Is that so?"

If he started smelling the sheets for any hint of sex, Miranda was going to throw the nearest object she could find at his head.

"Very much so," Valadon reassured him. "Miranda, why don't you join us? Come be my left hand."

Valadon and Remare were two of the most lethally sexy vampires she'd ever met. Each was exceptionally handsome and capable of using their allure. Together, they would be beyond temptation. Miranda didn't think her defenses would hold against them. "I don't think so."

Valadon laughed. "She doesn't trust me. I assure you I have no plans for seduction. I merely want to feel a sense of peace. Before all the madness begins when the European delegation starts arriving."

Miranda rose, but instead of going to Valadon's left, she moved to the foot of the bed and studied them. Something was niggling at the back of her mind, but she wasn't quite sure what it was. Together, they were every woman's wet dream. A fantasy of uninhibited erotic possibilities. Valadon was more muscular, stunning in his attraction, he could seduce the most ardent celibates. How the ancient sculptors would have gone mad creating his likeness. Remare's muscle tone was more striated, his veins prevalent across his biceps. His sensuality, cool and intoxicating, was a sharp blade capable of penetrating the toughest shields to pierce a woman's heart and have her yearning for more.

But strangely enough, Miranda wasn't aroused. Something was buffering her. Then, it hit hard, the ancient recognition that had been demanding attention in the recesses of her mind. How was it she'd never seen it before? Closing her eyes, she inhaled their scents deep into her lungs. It had always been there. But she'd been too blind to see it.

When she opened her eyes, Remare seemed to be studying her. "Mir-randa, what has you so rapt? It's not sensual awareness; I would know it if it was."

She blinked but, then, turned toward Valadon. "Since the first time I met you, I always thought you smelled like the ocean. At night. The brine thick in the air. I never knew why, but that was always the impression I had of you. Water."

Valadon was curious. "A hint of some cologne perhaps?"

"No. This is more instinctual. An essence I can just barely identify. But it's there." She turned toward Remare. "You were always my cave, my rock. You have always smelled like old growth forests, trees, evergreen, I think." She inhaled deeper. "Earth."

She looked at her hand. "As an *Elemental,* I have some control over the elements. But fire has always been my main element." She created an image of fire glowing in her hand then quickly quenched it. She faced Valadon. "You're missing one."

The High Lord nodded. "Air."

"I don't know what it means, but I have this very strong sense you pull power from us. In the book Gabriel found in the archives by Peralt, he believed the four elements worked in synchronicity with each other. Is it any wonder we're drawn toward you?"

"I'm not sure I'm following you."

She moved onto the bed and took Valadon's hand in her left and faced the palm up. Then, she hovered her right hand over it. "Don't you feel it? The hum, it's vibrating."

"Peralt was a maniac." Remare was not impressed. "He had many delusions about the effects of astronomy. I've read some of his books."

"Correct, but in some matters, he was right." Miranda reached over and took his hand. "Bear with me. I want to try something." She placed Remare's hand over Valadon's and let her right hand, the more powerful one, hover over theirs. "Feel the static energy." She closed her eyes, in tune with the pitch they were creating. When she glanced at them, each wore expressions of doubt. Until she clasped both hands between her own. A spark of power ignited between them. Knowing she was playing in uncharted waters, she quickly let it go.

Their countenances quickly changed to awe and wonder. "Not everything is in books." She explained, "Some things just exist. Imagine what we could do if we knew who the fourth was."

"Any clues who that might be?" Valadon asked.

Miranda had her suspicions. Only one person reminded her of the cool air, a voice drifting over currents of incredible power. Peralt had said only the chameleons could control all four elements. She wondered about the possibilities and the detriments of such power.

Valadon said, "Well, that is certainly something to think about for another time." He pulled her down beside him. "Rest. Just for one moment, let there be serenity between us." He lay back down, exhaled quietly and closed his eyes.

Miranda met Remare's dark stare. She was too tired, too emotionally drained to argue with him.

"When our guests come, I want a unified front. I don't want to give them any reason to think my House is weakened." Valadon's voice resonated. "Can you two work toward that end?"

"Of course." Remare nodded. "We are a strong House. They know this already. That is why they fear us."

"Miranda?"

"I won't be around much. You revoked my status, remember?"

"It's reinstated." Valadon turned to Remare. "Miranda has agreed to be my intermediary with Montglat. A meeting will be forthcoming between us."

"Really?" Remare's voice echoed with suspicion.

Miranda wanted to deny the fervent attraction between them, but as hurt and angry as she was, she could still feel the magnetic pull toward Remare. "Yes."

Valadon's phone started ringing. "Who the devil is calling at this late hour? It's nearly dawn." He rose to his desk and checked the number. "Gavin of Black Star clan requests an audience."

"Gavin!" Miranda smacked herself in the head. "I forgot all about him. He's in the garage waiting for me."

"Not anymore." Valadon smiled as he finished texting. "He's on his way to meet with me. You two stay here. Work out your differences. Can you manage that?"

Miranda tried to speak, but he silenced her with a hand. "I need my House in order. I cannot have any distractions. Things will be difficult enough with members of the High Court here." He drew his robe around him. The sleeveless one that made him look like a monarch from distant times. "Settle your differences." The vampire king had spoken.

And his word was final.

But Miranda wasn't going to stay in the same bed with Remare. Not after what he'd done. She got up and slid under the blankets of the guard's bed.

He turned on his side. "I don't think that's what Valadon meant when he said to settle our differences."

"Don't care. Not gonna argue with you. But this bed suits me fine." It was bad enough not trusting him, but Miranda wasn't sure she was strong enough to resist Remare's charms.

"You're not still angry with me?"

Miranda wanted to brain him, she really did. She slanted him a look. "You're lucky I don't throw a fireball at you."

A wickedly sexy half-smile. "I believe you already did that once before."

She was not going to melt just because Remare was the most amatory man she'd ever met. She remembered too well his sensuous touch. Wasn't going to fall for it. "You deserved it." Her voice was gravelly, even to her own ears.

He slid his hand slowly over the sheets. "This bed is far more comfortable than a guard's bed." His tone was seductive. "You should be here with me. You would sleep better."

She burrowed farther into the blankets. "I'm comfortable where I am, but thanks for your concern."

Frustrated, he groaned and lay his head on the pillow. "This is not the homecoming I had anticipated."

"Too cold for you? You should have thought about that when you iced me when you saw the pictures. You should have known me better."

"I admit I did react strongly. Those images were the worst I could imagine for you."

Miranda wasn't sure what she was angrier at, the way he had treated her in Valadon's office, as if she were a villain, a traitor he would like nothing more than to strangle with his own hands. As if their relationship, their intimacy, all they had shared had never existed. Or the fact he tried to violate her mind searching for answers. "You know what bothers me most, Remare? You weren't even sorry for what you had done. You felt you had every right to mind-rape me."

"That is not true." His tone sounded solemn. "And the fact you would liken me to rapists vexes me. Rapists take by force what is not theirs."

"Isn't that what you tried to do? Plunging into my memories without permission?"

"I didn't plunge, nor did I take. I merely searched."

Miranda's head hurt. "It's too late to have this conversation. You hurt me. I'm not ready to forgive you for that." She rose and headed for the door. "I can't sleep in the same room with you. I'm going to my guest room. We'll talk tomorrow."

"Mir-randa!"

"Let it go, Remare. I'm exhausted, and I don't want to fight with you." She closed the door behind her.

Making her way to the room she once slept in with Gabriel, she opened the door and was surprised to see Gavin under the blankets. "Gavin?"

"Miranda." His eyes were half-slitted. "Valadon said I could sleep here tonight. It's nearly dawn, and I need a couple of hours sleep."

"Me, too. Mind if I join you?" She did not want to sleep alone tonight. But, she in no way wanted to cuddle either. She grabbed a couple of extra pillows from the closet and built a wall on the bed between them.

"What are you doing?

"Remare might not understand the concept of puppy piles. And I don't want to argue with him, anymore." She slipped under the blankets. "How did your meeting go with Valadon?"

"Good. He offered me a job. Wants me to work security the night of his wedding."

Miranda hadn't even considered Valadon might need extra security, but with all the Europeans in attendance, it was probably a wise decision. Miranda turned on her side facing away from Gavin, who was turned on his side away from her. Not exactly what she'd imagined for Remare's first night back in New York, but then the fates enjoyed throwing her curve balls. "Tell me tomorrow." Yawning, she drifted off to sleep.

Remare growled in frustration. As luxurious as Valadon's bed was, without Miranda it was a cold, uninviting place. To hell with this, he thought. He'd go back to his own room. When he opened the door, he was surprised to find Valadon nearly asleep.

"I thought you'd be in the throes of passion by now. Seemed only right since you were in my bed, I should sleep in yours."

"Miranda wasn't interested in any romantic ventures." Remare sighed as he joined Valadon on the bed. "She is still angry with me. Tell me about this meeting she is arranging for you with Montglat."

"The details have yet to be worked out. When I know, so will you. I had an interesting meeting with Gavin. He was down in the garage when two of our own were caught plotting against me. He was able to record their little discussion. I sent the video to Aiden to clear up."

"Is it who I think it is?"

"Most likely. It seems they plan on some entertainment for my wedding. I hired Gavin to help with security. We'll go over the details tomorrow. I also have a meeting with Chase Lambert scheduled for the day after tomorrow in the main conference room. My legal team has done well in circumventing the worst of Magritte's plans to usurp my company. You'll be interested to see what they've come up with."

"I'll be there. Aiden has already updated me with most everything." Remare found it difficult to rest. His mind whirled with too many possibilities and his fingers beat out a tune on his chest.

"Has anyone ever told you that you make a poor bedmate?" Valadon slanted him a smile. "I can hear you turning over thoughts in your head. You never stay still for more than a minute."

"Miranda frustrates me; she should be here."

"Now, that would induce me to stay. Do you think she might...?"

"No!" The last thing Remare desired was any more complications.

Valadon laughed. "I didn't think so." He rose and put on his robe. "Rest well. I think I prefer my own bed. I might actually get some sleep there."

In the ensuing silence, Remare couldn't sleep. He missed his mate; she belonged with him, not in the guest room. He paced. He drank some wine. He paced some more. "To hell with this." Finally, he made the decision he would go to her.

Once outside her door, he briefly hesitated, thought of knocking, but entered quietly. A low growl emitted from his throat when he spotted Miranda in bed with Gavin. He inhaled but there was no hint of passion. When he spotted the wall of pillows between them, one corner of his mouth rose. Still, he did not like her in the same bed as Gavin.

He gathered her up in his arms and brought her to his room. After tucking her in, he climbed in, keeping a respectable distance.

Tossing and turning, it wasn't long before she woke. She cracked one eye open. "You really don't understand the meaning of choice, do you?"

"I did not think you would be averse to the idea. Besides, I didn't like you in bed with Gavin. Though, I do appreciate the pillow fort."

"Oh, brother!" Her voice was groggy with sleep. "You're incorrigible. Do not disturb me. I will not be responsible if any fire balls erupt."

He smiled sexily.

"Go to sleep, Remare." She tucked herself in and fell back to sleep.

Remare's heart warmed at her peaceful expression as she slept. Despite their differences, Miranda was his mate, even if she drooled a little on his pillows. Stubborn as a mule, he still loved her.

Content, he closed his eyes and let sleep take him.

Chapter Twelve

Miranda woke with a thirst she hadn't known in ages. When she spotted Remare asleep, she shook her head at his resolve. *Stubborn vampire!* They really did need to have a long conversation, but now was not the time. She knew without looking at the clock it must be sunrise; her powers always surged at dawn.

Borrowing Remare's robe, she made her way to ValCorp's kitchen and realized Escher must have gotten up early. There were bakery boxes on the breakfast nook full of pastries. After claiming a chocolate croissant and washing it down with a glass of orange juice, she felt a strange pull to visit the archives.

The vampires of House Valadon still asleep, the area was deserted and quiet. She wandered closer to the balustrade. Inhaling the scent only libraries possessed, she gazed out over the vast expanse of books and paintings of people long dead and wondered, not for the first time, why she always had such a strong sense of peace here. As if the place beckoned to her.

Here, she could think. Process her thoughts. But a feeling of uneasiness and dread pervaded her serenity. Remare didn't like secrets, even though he hadn't always been completely honest with her. Did she dare tell him she was related to Montglat? Would he accept her if she did? She knew he was angry with her because he could sense she was withholding information. She suspected it was the not knowing that irritated him the most. He'd been so enraged by the photos. How would he react if he learned her lineage?

Exhaling in uncertainty, she eyed the life-size painting of Bianca. Talk about beckoning, she snorted. Valadon's sister had always intrigued her. The more Miranda studied the painting, the line of her face, the impish smile, the more she felt as if Bianca was somehow trying to speak to her. Tell her something, but what?

Closing her eyes, Miranda stretched out her hand to see if she could sense anything. She knew there were those who believed in ghosts, spirits who lingered on the mortal plane, unwilling or unable to leave until some unfinished business was resolved. But Miranda wasn't one of them. Not a tingle. No drastic drop in temperature. Nothing. She lowered her arm.

Her family had died nearly twenty years ago, and no apparition had ever contacted her from beyond the grave. And she'd been close with her family. Why would Bianca, a vampire she'd never met, want to speak to her? She turned to leave when she felt a cold hand on her shoulder and gasped. Heart racing, she quickly turned. No one was there. Not a shadow, not a glimmer of anything supernatural. She shook her head and chuckled. "Geez, Miranda, maybe you should give up drinking."

She'd only taken two steps when she heard a woman's voice whisper, "Tell him."

That was no hallucination! Heart in her throat, Miranda quickly whirled around and saw what looked like an aura floating on the air. It hovered for one fleeting moment, then dissipated. Miranda stared up at the painting. Could Bianca have truly spoken to her? She scrutinized the portrait for any change, any hint of a spectral anomaly. "Who? Tell who, what?"

No answer. No response. Only silence permeated the cold, dark room.

Just then, the door opened. "I thought I might find you here." Remare joined her by the banister. "You're pale." He brushed a finger down her cheek. "You didn't sleep much last night. Perhaps you should get back to bed."

The attraction, always so strong between them, sprang to life, bringing an energy glow to the previously solemn room. "I won't sleep." Not after what she'd just seen. "Look, Remare," she pleaded, "Valadon is right. With all the foreign diplomats coming, he needs a unified front. I don't want to argue with you."

"I don't wish for any more hostility between us either. But you must understand why I reacted the way I did to the photos of you and Montglat. You can't continue to keep secrets from me." He rubbed her arms until he held her hands in his. "Especially when they have the potential to harm our House. Don't you trust me, Mir-randa?"

He'd said her name with the rolling *r*'s that always got to her. Did she trust him? She wasn't entirely sure. She knew she loved him, even though he'd bruised her heart.

"I want to." She let go of his hands. "But, sometimes, you make it difficult."

He moved a strand of her hair off her shoulder. "I'm not the only one." He stared into her eyes. "I nearly gave up my House for you."

She remembered that clearly enough. "I killed for you, bled for you. You should trust me."

"I do." Exhaling, he pulled her closer and kissed her forehead. "Despite my better judgment, I do trust you, when a wiser man would have his doubts." His arms circled her. "But I think Montglat is playing some game. One we don't have all the pieces to."

Miranda leaned her forehead against his chest and sighed. "I don't believe he is."

"I suppose we'll find out soon enough."

Miranda welcomed his embrace and held him tighter. How did she ever get to the point where she felt empty without him? That horrible, consuming void threatened to break her. She was stronger than that, but when she looked into his dark brown eyes, she saw so many truths, so much desire, it was as if her world was suddenly whole. She kissed him passionately. The familiar brush of his soft beard against her skin made her shiver in delight. But doubt gnawed at her. She broke from the kiss. At his questioning look, she said, "There's something I should tell you, but I'm not sure how."

"Why do I get the feeling I'm not going to like this very much?" His spine straightened as he released her. "Tell me."

"It's about Montglat."

He stood silently, waiting.

Miranda debated telling him. Her heart beat out a strong rhythm in her chest, and a fine layer of perspiration coated her cool skin. He'd said to trust him. Another deep breath. Their relationship was strong—forged in fires of misunderstanding and reconciliation. They'd survived hells in the past. And would, again. She was stalling. Considering taking the coward's way out. Miranda wasn't a coward. "He's my grandfather."

Nearly hissing, Remare stepped back from her. Suspicion glared on his face; the temperature in the room plummeted. *The Iceman* was back. Chilled to her very being, she reached for him, but he moved farther away. "Valadon needs to know."

"Remare," not knowing what to say, she uttered what was in her heart, "I love you."

His eyes remained dark. "I know." When he left, it was as if he took all that was alive and good from the room. She was alone. Again. In a dark and empty void. Her stomach cramped in agonizing pain. How could she feel such a complete utter sense of despair and still breathe?

That wonderful world where she was happy, half of a couple who loved and laughed together disappeared. She wanted to share her life with him, create more good memories.

And, now, he was gone.

Her heart beating erratically, she clung to the banister for support. That look he'd given her before he left spoke of dissolution. He'd lost faith in her. Her bear had cast her from his cave out into the storm to fend for herself. With one look, he'd made her feel insignificant. As if all that had been between them was suddenly and viciously ripped away. Of little consequence.

How could he do this to her?

What would happen when Valadon returned? Would he abjure her from his house? *So, this is what desolation feels like.*

Taking deep breaths, she sat at her worktable and placed her hands flat against the wood. She was done. She couldn't feel anything, anymore. Remare had hurt her for the last time. She couldn't take any more pain. The disappointment was too much to bear. Devastated by the sense of loss, she bent her head over her crossed arms on the table. There were no tears to shed.

The dead didn't cry.

Basking in her hollowness, she barely heard the door opening and lifted her head.

Valadon sat beside her at the table. "Is this true? Are you Montglat's granddaughter?"

Words would not form in her mouth, her throat too dry. She nodded.

Exhaling, Valadon inched away from her. "How long have you known?"

"Not very. I found out after we were searching the archives for information on Peralt. Before we raided the HOL's compound."

"Why didn't you tell me?"

"Because I knew the way you'd react." She exhaled. "And Montglat asked me not to." A weak smile surfaced. "If it matters, there's several generations that separate us." She shook her head. "He never told me how many."

"That's why we weren't able to discern her vampire blood," Remare interjected. "Her blood's mostly human."

Miranda nodded. After the way he'd annihilated her, she wasn't about to tell them Montglat was an *Elemental,* a "chameleon" who could control all four elements.

"Have you sworn a blood oath to Montglat?" Valadon's voice was deeper than his usual baritone.

Miranda was confused. "What's a blood oath?"

Remare answered, "It's when you pledge your loyalty to a vampire lord and his House."

"No. Of course not. He's never asked; why would he? I don't think he even has a House."

"I'm sure that he does," Valadon proclaimed. "You're just not acquainted with it."

Miranda shrugged and rubbed her forehead. She couldn't contain her anxiety, anymore. "Are you going to abjure me, now?"

"I should. Keeping a bloodline secret like that is grounds enough. But the fact that you offered the information to Remare without him asking, I'm inclined to offer you a pardon, if you acquiesce to one request."

Miranda's breathing sped up. "What request?"

Valadon smiled in a way that made her gut clench. "Swear a blood oath to me and my House."

Shocked, Miranda gasped. She suspected blood allegiances were for life. Sacred to vampires. She'd read up on kings of old. They had absolute power over their subjects. Could command them to do any number of immoral acts, not the least would be to order her to his bed. Not happening. "You'd have dominion over me."

"I'd have your loyalty."

Miranda started vibrating with a mix of rage and fear. "And what else?" She rose, tired of sitting, tired of feeling defeated. "What else does a blood oath entail?" She looked from one vampire to another, unsure if they would even tell her the truth.

"It's an essential bond between a vampire lord and his people. You need not fear me, Miranda. I wouldn't own you. You'd still be free to come and go on your own accord."

Instinct was screaming inside her head that there was far more dangerous ground here. She would discuss this with Felicity and Montglat. "Excuse me if I sound suspicious. But I don't know enough of your history or your customs to make an educated decision just yet."

Remare crossed his arms. "I told you she'd never agree."

"It's not an oath to take lightly. You should take time to consider it carefully. In the meantime, I would ask for another oath, more of a promise, really."

"And what is that?"

"Swear to me you would never willingly endanger me or any of my people."

That she could do. She'd never cause harm to him or his people. Except one. "And if one attacks me?"

"Then, you have my permission to kill her...or him." Valadon slanted Remare a look.

"I will give your request its due consideration." She leaned forward on the desk. Her ire heated to diamond hard. "But hear this. I killed for you. Those eleven HOL members at West Gate, I can still smell their burning flesh and hear their screams in my sleep. I took a bullet for you, was kidnapped, held against my will, mind-raped in a cell by your brother, Brandon. And *fucking* burned at the stake!" Her voice nearly rattled the ceiling. "I still bear those scars. I don't think you can question my loyalty. I've fucking earned it already!"

Furious, she gave Remare one last scathing look. "And you! You should know better." She shook her head in painful memory. "I lost people I cared about. Dearly. Dane died, horribly, because I asked him to investigate the HOL so I could help *you* in your investigation. I live with the guilt of his death every day of my life." Miranda's spine straightened. Pain turned to rage. "Don't ever question my loyalty, again."

She turned and left the vampires to ponder their own allegiances.

Chapter Thirteen

"If you stay together for any length of time, there will always be some disagreements."

"But, Felicity, you've been together with Guy for so long and you don't fight." Miranda thought it best to meet her former mentor at the coffee shop near NYU and make it look like a casual bumping into. She suspected Valadon was having her followed, and she wasn't about to get her friend in trouble.

Felicity laughed. "That's because you haven't seen us when we argue. I assure you we've had some beauts. One major one before we returned to New York."

"What about?"

Felicity sipped her tea. "Guy feels New York might become too dangerous when all the Europeans arrive for Valadon's wedding. Too many powerful people in one place at the same time. He wanted me to wait in Sardinia for him." She huffed, "Like that was going to happen."

"But you worked it out.

"Yes. We usually do. However, through the centuries, there were a couple of times I thought we'd end up going our separate ways," she sighed dreamily, "but we always managed to settle our differences. As I imagine you will with Remare."

"He's the most stubborn vampire in the world " Miranda blew out a breath. "I just don't know if we can make it work. His loyalty to Valadon is unfaltering."

"But you still love him?"

Reluctantly, Miranda said, "Yes. Though there are times I want to strangle him."

"Spoken by every woman, at least once, who has ever been in a long-term relationship. Now, tell me what else is on your mind. You've been hedging since you got here."

After recapping the incident with the photos of Montglat and the discord between her and Remare, Miranda exhaled. "Valadon wants to meet with Guy. There's no way around it. His resolve is unbending. Otherwise, he's convinced I'm a spy. Remare looks at me with suspicion in his eyes like I have traitor stamped on my forehead. It makes my skin crawl." She rubbed her arm. "I can't stand either of them doubting me. It cuts too deep. I was hoping you'd talk to Guy for me."

"I'm sorry things are so stressed between you and Remare and Valadon. The situation is further complicated by our past." Felicity leaned back in her chair. "My parents were strong opponents to Lord Valadon's grand unveiling. They refused to support him and the Progressive party in proclaiming our existence to the world. They left before the announcement was even made. I, too, have never revealed my vampirism. Guy and I both believed it would be safer that way." She exhaled. "Even though Valadon made good sense about technology and our growing inability to stay hidden."

"Did Valadon resent your family's beliefs?"

"I think he was disappointed. Understandably. He needed as much support as he could muster to deal with the fallout. There are still quite a few vampires who keep their identities secret."

"Mmm, secrets. Sounds like an interesting conversation you two are having." Guy kissed Felicity and pulled a chair to their table. "Felicity tells me you wanted to see me."

"Hello, Blu." As usual, he was dressed in a blue T-shirt, jeans, and sneakers. Miranda smiled. With his backpack on, he really did look like a grad student. "I need your help." She leaned forward and lowered her voice. "Valadon and Remare think I'm a spy for you. I hate having them think I betrayed them. They're a part of me. I know you said you wouldn't meet him at ValCorp, but this is very important to me."

"Valadon is a powerful vampire. I'm sure he has an army at his back. I, unfortunately, do not. If I agree to meet with him, he will no doubt try to apprehend me. I cannot allow that to happen."

"If I can work out some deal. If I get his promise not to seize you, would you consider meeting him face to face? I can't stand them not believing me. This is killing me." She shook her head. "The way they look at me eats at my heart. I can't deal with it."

Montglat sipped his coffee. "I see." He gazed around the area and remained quiet.

Miranda thought that was his way of saying no. Her shoulders sagging, she met Felicity's eyes and issued a silent plea.

"Guy, Miranda loves Remare." Felicity covered his hand. "Is there any way possible we can help her? She's absolutely miserable."

"For the last couple of months, I've heard little else. I should think, if he loves you half as much as you him, he would show some evidence of believing you."

"He thinks I'm mixed up in some sort of clandestine mission you've employed me in."

Guy smirked. "Always the wise and wary. Well, I suppose life has taught him to have a suspicious nature. I believe I would have my reservations if our roles were reversed." He closed his eyes as if considering the possibilities.

The silence grated on her nerves.

"It would have to be a public place, somewhere in the open air. I have it. Central Park, near Bethesda Fountain. Tell Valadon I will meet with him one hour before sunset. That should give us plenty of time to discuss whatever is on his mind. I would ask he come alone, but I know that will never happen. Tell him he has no reason to fear me. I'm not here for any nefarious reasons." He took Felicity's hand and kissed it.

Miranda's heart beat in earnest. "I wasn't sure you'd agree. Thank you. I would never have asked, but it's crucial to me."

"I realize that. Your happiness is vital to me, Miranda. I don't like seeing you so despondent. However, you will owe me. You are asking quite a bit from me. A risk I would not normally take."

"All right. I'm sure I'll owe you if you can convince Valadon you're not here to cause him harm." She hesitated. "There is something else you should know."

At their inquisitive looks, Miranda sighed. "Valadon asked me for a blood oath."

Their unified gasps had her shrinking back. "Yeah, I didn't like it much, myself."

Guy leaned forward. "What did you tell him?"

"That after taking a bullet for him, being tormented by his brother, and being burned at the stake, he shouldn't question my loyalty."

"Exactly what kind of vow did he want from you?"

"Some sort of pledge to him and his House. I told him I didn't know nearly enough to make that kind of commitment."

"Do be careful, Miranda. Oaths are taken very seriously in the courts and Houses. A blood oath is binding. Forever. It would be one thing to swear fealty to Valadon. Quite another to his House."

"What do you mean?"

Felicity fielded her question. "If anything should happen to Valadon, you would be bound to serve his House no matter who was in charge. The High Court could seize control and who knows who they'd put in charge. There are all kinds of dangerous variables."

Miranda rubbed her head. "I didn't even think of that."

"I would hold off on any oaths, Miranda. They may not be in your best interest. You told me Valadon is aware of your *Elemental* abilities. Any vampire lord would love to have you at their command. Show discretion."

"I have no intention of making any vows." She smirked. "Valadon thinks I've already pledged myself to House Montglat. I told him I didn't even think you had a House."

"That's yet to be determined." He smiled. "All right. It is settled. Tonight, then."

"Tonight?! So quickly?"

"Yes, if Valadon is so eager to meet with me, tonight. Let's get this over with. This way he won't have much time to conjure any disturbing plans."

Miranda was pretty sure Remare would be the one determining the strategies. She wasn't looking forward to this either, but if it would restore Valadon and Remare's trust in her, she'd see it through.

***

"All our people are in position."

Valadon didn't need Remare's assurance; he could sense their presence. He inhaled the fragrance of the blossoms in bloom along the trails in Central Park. The sun was beginning to set, but the warm spring evening only added to the park's beauty. Valadon looked over the area from Bethesda Terrace, wondering where Montglat's men were hidden. With Miranda on his arm, he made his way down the steps to the massive fountain.

Much to the disapproval of his irate second.

"I don't like this," Remare hissed. *"It's too wide open. Anyone can take a shot at you."*

"That is why you are here. I trust you will not allow that to happen." He laughed at Remare's growl of displeasure.

Glancing at the dark angel atop the fountain, Miranda led him to the north section where the row boats were on the lake. "It's safe. Montglat means you no harm."

"As I do him."

She exhaled. "I'm glad you two are finally meeting. I didn't like keeping his secret from you."

"I know." He smiled. "Thank you, again, for arranging this meeting."

Miranda glanced over his shoulder. "There he is, now."

Dressed in a blue shirt and casual slacks, he looked like any other tourist out for a late day stroll. Valadon remembered blending in was one of Montglat's greatest skills.

"It's good to see you, again, Miranda." Montglat tipped his Fedora toward her. "Lord Valadon, a pleasure, as well."

"I must admit I've been looking forward to seeing you." Valadon didn't like Montglat wearing sunglasses. He would have preferred to see his eyes.

"I'll leave you two to discuss whatever it is you need to confer." Miranda turned and walked in the direction of the boat house.

"Beautiful day out." Montglat gestured to the boaters. "I trust Remare has his men carefully secreted throughout."

"As I'm sure you do, as well."

Montglat smiled knowingly. "I offer my apologies for not announcing my presence in your territory. That was ill-mannered of me."

"Yes, it was. Would you mind telling me why you are in my lands? And why you saw fit *not* to ask permission first?"

"How do you know I wasn't here first?" Montglat grinned. "As I'm sure Miranda told you, I tired of the courts in Europe, their petty games. I wanted freedom." He glanced toward him. "Same as you, I suspect."

"Why New York? You could have gone anywhere; why choose my city?"

"I wanted to get away as far as I could. I considered Africa or South America. In the end, I chose America." He glanced upward as two eagles flew over. "The reason I didn't contact you was because I feared you would try to embroil me in your politics. I had no such desires for any type of involvement."

"How long have you been in my territory?"

Montglat faced him. "Not long, comparatively speaking."

Valadon continued to watch the boaters, ever watchful of the wooden areas where others might be hiding. "You want me to believe you're here on some sort of holiday? You know how unlikely that is?!"

"I served our High Court and their many intrigues for centuries. Some would say I was due for a lengthy vacation."

"And, yet, you survived, when many others did not."

"One does try his best to avoid such entanglements. Though it seems to me you've gotten yourself ensnared by Magritte, again. Was that due to carelessness on your part, or Magritte's cunning? In either case," he shook his head in disapproval, "Vivienna?! I could think of no other shrew less desirable to be married to."

"It was an arranged marriage. To halt the many inconveniences Magritte was causing in my overseas ventures."

"I didn't believe it was due to any lingering affection you had for Paris' reigning Madame Lord."

"Indeed." Valadon wasn't sure if Montglat's benevolent demeanor was an act or not. He knew of Montglat's missions too well to underestimate him. "I'm not convinced you randomly chose my city to hide in. If stealth was your goal, you could have chosen any number of places to take refuge in."

"True, but your city afforded wonders others do not."

Valadon followed his line of sight to the bench where Miranda was sitting. "Miranda Crescent."

"Yes, a fascinating woman. She's of my line. I'm sure she's told you that."

"She did."

"I like checking on my progeny from time to time. And Miranda has a habit of getting herself in trouble. You were supposed to keep her safe. She bears scars now she should not."

Valadon did not like Montglat's veiled implication. "I lost good people in my fight with Mulciber. Several were killed before I was able to defeat him." His anger spiked at how horribly Cyra had died and the emotional devastation Morel endured.

"Mulciber was a menace the High Court should have dealt with long ago."

"Yet, it was left for me to deal with." He faced Montglat. "I would like to see your eyes."

Montglat moved farther into the shade of one of the trees. He removed his glasses. "Satisfied?"

Not nearly! "I want your assurances you are not in my city to cause me or any members of my House any harm."

"That is not why I am here. I'm simply passing through, and the time will come, shortly, when I will leave."

Valadon could sense no duplicity, but still, the enigma that was Montglat remained. "You said you had a gift for me. What is it?"

"What do you wish for most?"

"A great many things. None, I'm sure, you can provide."

"Don't be too sure of that. Among my skillset, I've the ability to procure what others find impossible."

Valadon narrowed his eyes in contemplation. "If I hired you for a mission, would you accept?"

"That would depend on the task."

Valadon thought he had little to lose in revealing his conundrum. "I have a son I've never met. Magritte knows his whereabouts. I do not. She refuses to inform me of his location unless I marry Vivienna."

"Ah, she still enjoys playing *Mistress of Games*." Montglat seemed to consider the possibilities. "Children are to be revered. We have so few of them. Who is your son's mother?"

"A human who died centuries ago, Marlena de Avignon. She was promised to a wealthy merchant the High Court did business with, Rocheforte. Magritte refused my petition to turn her. Marlena gave birth to our child while I was away on court business. In fear of being disowned by her father and humiliated by her fiancé, who were away at sea, she entrusted the child to a midwife who, in turn, gave the boy to a noblewoman. That is all the information I have. I had my historians try to locate records of the birth, but to no avail."

"Magritte considered you one of her favorites. She would not have allowed you any happiness with your human."

"She did her utmost for that very reason." Valadon passed Montglat a memory stick. "This is the compilation my historians and agents have been able to solicit. I'm afraid it's not much."

Montglat played with the flashdrive. "GPS?"

Valadon smirked. "What do you think?!"

"If I accept this assignment, will you grant me access to your territory when I choose?"

"If you locate my son before the wedding, yes."

Montglat smiled beneficently as he pocketed the device. "Then, I shall find him."

Valadon watched as Montglat disappeared down the path into the shadows of the woods. Why did he have the sensation Montglat already knew the location of his son? Was that a possibility? A moment later, an eagle with a large wing span soared across the lake and rose high into the sky to join the other two eagles flying nearby.

Remare joined him. "The tracking device failed minutes after you gave it to him."

Valadon smiled slyly. "Did you think he wouldn't be able to detect it?"

"You gave him an assignment?"

"Yes. Strangely enough," he eyed the path Montglat had disappeared into, "I don't believe he means me any harm."

"Surely, you don't believe he's here on holiday?"

"Not at all. But, for whatever reason he is here, I think it's something personal. Something that hasn't quite come into the light."

Miranda joined them. "Did everything go all right?"

"Yes, for now. Your grandfather has a way about him of making someone feel secure. Whether or not he's sincere, time will tell."

She eyed Remare. "Satisfied?"

"Not completely, but for the time being, we have a truce."

"Can I give you a lift back to ValCorp, Miranda? My limo is parked over there." Valadon gestured toward Central Park West.

"No. Thank you. Since we're here, I'm going to visit Lizandra and Gavin at Werehaven. I'm glad you finally met him. In time, you'll see he's a good man."

Valadon kissed her knuckles. "In time." He watched as she took the same path Montglat had. "Were your men able to track him?"

"No." Remare walked alongside him to the limo. "Even Gavin said his scent disappeared as soon as he entered the woods."

"As mysterious as *Le Cameleon* is, I would rather have him as my ally, than an adversary."

"But can you trust him?"

"Until he gives me a reason not to." Valacon followed Remare's line of sight. "You keep looking toward Werehaven. Why don't you meet up with Miranda? There's nothing pending right now at ValCorp. I meant what I said about a unified front. Make peace with her."

"You've come to terms with my relationship with her? Completely?"

"Some would say it took me long enough." He remembered the palpable heat between them when Miranda chastised them for doubting her loyalty. Such fire in both their hearts was admirable to witness. And undeniable. "I want you both to be prominent members of my House. Even if the love you and her bear me is in friendship, alone. Go now, be with her. You have my blessing."

Chapter Fourteen

Miranda's excitement at seeing Lizandra sank as soon as she entered Werehaven. The jeering and howling of the wolves reverberated against the cave walls almost to a deafening pitch. The heightened energy made her skin itch. The Weres were known for their aggressive demeanor, especially when it was close to the full moon.

But it was usually the males who clashed.

As Miranda descended the spiral staircase leading down to the main dance floor, she watched in horror as Lizandra fought another female Were. Arms and legs thrashed as grunts were exchanged. The scent of blood and sweat saturated the air. Her heart hammering, she quickly scanned the crowd for Gavin but couldn't find him. Pushing her way toward the inner circle, she tried to get closer to her friend.

Fights between werewolves could turn deadly, especially when they battled for dominance, as was the case, now. She could make out Lizandra's opponent: Dori, the Red Claw spy Liz had been keeping an eye on. The tips of Miranda's fingers started tingling, and she knew instinctively she was readying a fireball.

"Careful, Mir-randa." Remare curled his fingers over hers and pulled her back against his chest. He whispered, "If you interfere, they will think Lizandra weak. You will cause more harm than good."

Grateful for his support, she leaned into him. Miranda didn't want to be overheard so she spoke mentally to Remare. *"I don't like this. Dori is a plant from Red Claw. She fights viciously."*

"As do all Weres when they are challenged. Lizandra is more than able to take her rival."

Miranda was aware of this, but still, her heart ached. *"I know she's a fighter, but I hate seeing this."*

Just then, Dori used her claws to slash Lizandra across her middle. The jeering increased to a thunderous crescendo. Miranda closed her eyes in pain, as if she'd been the one whose side was shredded. Something primal and dark was rising in Miranda; something she needed to keep contained. She wanted to kill Dori for what she'd done to her friend.

Snarling, each opponent circled the other, hatred evident across their faces.

"Breathe, Mir-randa. Lizandra will make her move, now."

Remare knew more about fighting than she ever would, and she trusted his instincts. Having him at her back helped her maintain composure.

In a move too sleek and fast to see, Lizandra slashed Dori's throat and swept her leg. The smaller Were went crashing to the floor. "Someone take that trash from here!" Liz bellowed. "Go back to your Red Claw Clan. Crawl if you have to!"

More howling and hooting echoed through the room. Most applauded wildly at their queen's victory. Miranda made note of those who didn't and those who helped the beaten Were. When she turned back, she sensed the pain the Were Queen tried to keep hidden as she held her side. She stood proud and victorious, her fist high in the air. "Black Star rules!"

More raucous cheering sounded throughout the room. Miranda wanted to hug her friend, but Cyrus beat her to it, kissing her in a manner that was brutal, but the way of the Were. She wanted reassurance Liz was okay but asked instead, "What happened?"

"Long story." She downed the drink Cyrus handed her and grinned. "I see you brought your favorite vamp." Liz nodded. "Remare."

"Lizandra," Remare greeted. "Always a thrill to see you."

"Ain't that the truth. Let's go back to my rooms."

Miranda followed them as the noise lessened and people resumed their drinking and socializing. Once inside her apartment, Lizandra pulled off her shredded top and lay across the couch. Her black bra also had a few minor tears.

"How bad are you injured?"

"A few scratches."

Cyrus retrieved some bandages and a bottle of alcohol from the bathroom. "You fought well. I'm surprised you let her slash you."

"Fucking bitch was faster than I anticipated."

Cyrus cleaned the wound and pulled out two broken fingernails. "Metal implants. That's how she was able to cut you so deeply."

Miranda inspected the broken nails. Each was tipped with steel shards. "This a usual thing?"

"No. Only a coward would enhance their claws." Liz winced as she turned sideways. "Miranda, I need you to leave so I can change and heal the wound."

"Right! I see you're in capable hands. I just stopped in to say hello."

"We'll talk another time."

"Yes." Miranda wanted to know more about what caused the fight but wasn't going to disturb her. Liz didn't like morphing into her wolf form in front of humans. Most Weres didn't. "I'll call you later."

"Ta."

Miranda made it halfway down the hall when she collapsed into the wall. Remare was by her side in a flash to steady her. "Are you all right?"

"I need a moment. My room's right here. Let's go there." As soon as they were inside, Miranda sat on the bed and held her stomach. Her body was trembling. Seeing her best friend in a bloody fight affected her more than she'd realized. "I can't stop shaking."

Remare sat beside her and put his arm around her. "Lizandra is Were Queen for a reason. She is the strongest of them all. That young Were never stood a chance."

"I can still hear them. The roaring's inside my head. She could have gotten killed."

"Not likely. She was measuring her opponent's ability. Sometimes, a combatant will allow a few hits to determine the other's skill and speed."

Miranda rubbed her head. "Could you get me a drink from the fridge?"

He retrieved a bottle of green tea and handed it to her.

She slugged down a couple of gulps. "Thanks. I can't believe it, but I'm actually hungry. I didn't have much today. I was nervous about the meet and greet. Want to go for a bite?"

"What would you like to eat?"

Miranda tried to suppress it, but a sexy smile escaped as she eyed Remare. "Something Italian."

He returned her grin. "I think I might be able to accommodate your request."

"You think she'll be okay?"

"Yes, I do. She has her alpha by her side. He'll take care of her."

"All right, let's get out of here. I could use some fresh air."

When they made their way top side, it was already dark, and the park nearly deserted. They walked along the path in the direction of his car. "So, what did Valadon think about the meeting?"

"He is amenable to the idea Montglat may not be an enemy."

She sensed his reluctance. "But you're not convinced?"

"I don't like unknowns. Too much potential for error."

Miranda inhaled the scent of the woods. Aside from the ugliness inside Werehaven, it was a lovely night for a stroll. The sky was a little murky, but the moon shone brightly. "I understand."

"Do you? I'd have thought you would try to persuade me otherwise."

Miranda shook her head. "No, I'm argued out. And I realize you have Valadon's best interest at heart."

"I had an interesting conversation with him before I came to find you. He accepts our relationship, strained as it is. He gave me his blessing."

Miranda scoffed. "At long last." She stopped to face Remare when they neared Bethesda Terrace. "We still have issues to work out." As angry and hurt as she'd been, her world was brighter with him in it.

He moved a strand of hair from her face and stroked her cheek with his thumb. "Yes, but I'm willing to work them out." His seductive voice was like a narcotic. "Are you?"

She searched his handsome face. No other man, vampire or Were, could ever affect her the way he did. The attraction between them was stronger than ever. For months, she'd craved his touch. Covering his hand with hers, she discovered the gift she had Morel send to him in Montreal. "You're wearing the bracelet I got you. I wasn't sure if you'd like it."

"I do. And I particularly like the inscription inside— Always and Forever."

She leaned into his caress. "I've missed you. More than you know."

"No more than I." He took her face in both hands and kissed her wildly.

Miranda felt her knees melting. The butterflies in her stomach were dancing. Or, she thought, it could be hunger pains.

He broke from the kiss and leaned his forehead against hers. "You're mine, Miranda. There's no escaping that for me."

She scoffed as she held him. "We're some pair, aren't we?!"

"But we are a pair." He moved to kiss her, again, when his phone rang. "Yes."

"Remare," Valadon said. "It appears your ward has slipped her guards. When I spoke with Selena earlier, she mentioned something about childhood memories. The carousel in Central Park was her favorite. Since you're there already..."

"I'll find her and bring her safely back to ValCorp." Remare ended his call and cursed in Italian. "My ward, Selena, has disappeared. Valadon feels she might be in the park in the vicinity of the carousel."

Miranda pointed south. "It's that way. When did you get a ward?"

"Montreal. I could go for the car, but I can run faster." He looked at her sandals. "Want to wait outside the park?"

"No." Miranda didn't like the idea of being abandoned. "I know this park like the back of my hand. I'll help you find her."

"Okay, then. Hold my cane." He scooped her up and threw her over his shoulder. Before Miranda could protest, he was off at a dead run, jumping over rocks and beds of flowers. Miranda wanted to scream "vertigo!" because of the preternatural speed at which he ran. She was being jostled every time his feet hit the ground. She was tempted to whack his butt with the cane when she started feeling nauseous. She'd have tossed her cookies, but luckily, her stomach was empty.

Finally, he slowed when they neared the carousel and lowered her to the ground. She held her sore ribs and took several calming breaths. "That was *not* pleasant."

He sniffed the air and then started searching the area. "She was here, but her scent is weak."

A noise in the distance. "The animals in the zoo." Miranda said. "Something's disturbing them." And they were off running toward the direction of the sound. A mist was settling over the area, but the trails were illuminated by the lamp posts.

"Her scent is stronger here. Selena," he yelled loud enough to rattle the monkeys in their habitat and the seals in their aquatic enclosure.

"Over here!" a female's voice cried out in the darkness.

A perky blonde, no more than twenty-one, appeared. Her curls draped a face Miranda could only describe as elfin. Her aquamarine eyes lit up her face. "Remare, I'm so glad to see you. I got lost and kept circling the area." She hugged him tightly.

"You're not allowed out without your guards. That was part of the agreement, was it not?"

She winced. "I know. But Tristan got tied up, and I thought I'd be back by now. I swear the subways were easier to navigate than the park."

Remare looked like he was going to pop a blood vessel. "You took the subway?"

"Yeah, sure." She shrugged. "It's no big deal."

His eyes narrowed. "Next time, you will have your guards with you, or I will see to it your privileges are revoked. Are we clear?"

She peered up at him. "I'm sorry."

Miranda glanced in the direction of the building housing the exotic plants. Still heated from their kiss and running, she said, *"I used to have fantasies about you and I having a* romantic rendezvous on top of the Rain Forest Pavilion." She wasn't sure why, but the thought of an outdoor sexcapade with Remare always excited her.

He checked their location and the skyscrapers to the east. *"High risk area. Too easy a target. Anyone with a telescope would see us. Choose another place."*

She shook her head at his pragmatic nature. *"The penguin preserve is pretty dark. Not too many tourists there. People would need infra-red eyeglasses to catch a glimpse."*

One corner of his mouth rose. *"Pick a date."* He gestured to the girl. "Miranda, this is my ward, Selena. She's the granddaughter of the Madame Lord of Montreal and my responsibility while she's studying here in New York."

Miranda was about to say pleased to meet you when sounds of growling started echoing in the dark woods around them. "Black Star runs patrols in the park." Her heart beating strongly in her chest, she listened intently, but could see no sign of the wolves. *"I don't think they're Black Stars. Liz told me sometimes Red Claws trespass on their territory."*

"Hand me my sword."

She unsheathed the sword and passed it to him. *"These wolves sound feral. Black Stars would have announced their presence by now."*

"Get behind me."

She stood back to back with Remare and Selena. *"I can create a firewall."*

"Not just yet!"

One by one, the wolves emerged from the darkness, their snarling lips pulled back from their canines. Her breathing intensified. *"Definitely not Black Star."*

"I count six. Now, seven. There are probably more watching, waiting. After I lunge, barricade yourself and Selena in the firewall."

"All right." Though if they attacked, she wasn't sure what she would do. She knew vampires were lethally fast, but so were werewolves. Each had supernatural strength and were predators, lethal in their pursuits. She didn't know which group was stronger and had no desire to find out.

Without warning, one of the wolves snarled and, fangs bared, charged them. The others followed suit. Remare cut them down, one by one, with swift strikes of his sword. The others started circling them. Miranda quickly erected a blue veil of flames around Selena, who exclaimed, "Whoa! That's so cool!" then cringed from the cold burn when she tried to touch it.

Miranda wouldn't leave Remare alone to fight the wolves. Instead, she used the sword cane as a conductor of her power and blasted them with energy balls, something she'd been practicing ever since fighting a certain blonde vampire.

Howls of pain erupted in the night. One particularly vicious wolf, the largest of the pack, drew closer, inching his way nearer to them, and Miranda's heart beat out a staccato. She wasn't sure who the wolf was going to attack, her or Remare, who stood ready with his sword.

"You were supposed to barricade yourself with Selena."

Miranda aimed the cane. *"Bite me!"*

One corner of his mouth lifted. *"With pleasure!"*

Suddenly, more howls rent the air, and other wolves joined in. Black Star's patrol pounced on the remaining wolves, and the fighting turned fierce. Blood splattered along the trail. When a red wolf bit down on the leg of the lead attacker, an anguished whimper slashed the air. The wolf twisted and half limped, ran in retreat, as did the remaining wolves.

Miranda made a fist and extinguished the flames. Remare took out a handkerchief and cleaned his sword as the new wolves took human form. "Good to see you again, Gavin."

Shirtless, each one was tall and muscular. Miranda caught Selena eying one of younger wolves who was seriously ripped.

"We heard you from the other side of the park. Damned Red Claws keep encroaching on our territory."

"Thank God you showed up." Breathing heavily, Miranda handed Remare his cane, still warm from her energy. "If I didn't know better, I'd say those wolves were on something. Their eyes were red, and they seemed too feral."

"Possible." Gavin shrugged. "What the devil are you doing this late out in the park? You're far from Werehaven."

She and Remare glanced sideways at Selena, who only shrugged and grinned.

"I had to retrieve a youth who was unaware of the park rules. She will not make that mistake, again, I assure you." Remare turned to his ward. "Isn't that right, Selena?"

"Sorry." Selena saluted him.

"Gavin, did you know Lizandra was in a fight with Dori earlier?" Miranda exhaled. "She kicked her ass, but she got cut, as well."

Gavin looked confused and then angry. "What?!"

"Yeah, some kind of disturbance. I went to see her, but the fight was already in progress. She didn't have time to tell me what started it."

"The white-haired wolf was tending to her." Remare added, "Apparently, Dori used metal implants in her nails. Some scratches ensued."

Gavin checked his phone and shook his head. "Still too proud to contact me." He shook his head in disgust. "Thank you for telling me. Do you need an escort out of the park?"

Miranda was going to say that would be nice but Remare answered. "We'll be fine."

Gavin pointed. "The exit is in that direction. One of my men will open the gate and lock it after you."

"Thank you."

After they were out of the park, Miranda studied the high stone wall. "Those fences are nearly ten feet tall, how do the Red Claws keep getting in?"

"For a werewolf, it's easy enough to jump. They use the trees as springboards. Or..."

"Someone's letting them in. She's got a traitor in her midst."

"Possible. Whatever the reason, it is a Were matter, one that I'm sure Lizandra and Gavin will work out. Are you still hungry?"

"I'm starving!" Selena chirped in. "Can we get something to eat, please?"

Miranda smiled at the girl's wide-eyed expression. "Despite all the ugliness, yeah, I'm hungry, too."

"All right, I believe I promised you something Italian. There's a fine restaurant on the West Side I think you would like." Frowning, he gazed at the way she and Selena were dressed.

"Italian?" Selena shrieked. "I love pizza! Can we get pizza?"

"I love pizza, too." Miranda grinned. "There's a great place on Forty-Fourth and Eighth, John's Pizzeria. It's a restaurant in a converted old church. They have other things on the menu and a pretty solid selection of wines. You'll like it."

Remare looked less than thrilled but nodded. "The car's this way."

When they reached the Theatre District with all the neon promos, excitely, Selena pointed to one of the electronic billboards. "Oh, look, it's a poster of Orion," She sighed in dreamy ecstasy. "His music is *so* cool, and check out how ripped he is!"

Smirking, Remare pulled into the parking garage. "Miranda was once engaged to him."

Selena leaned forward between them. *"No way!"*

"For a time. We broke it off a while back. He is cool." Miranda was amazed how fast his popularity had soared. She was happy for him and smiled back at Selena. "We're still friends." She wasn't about to tell her he was her roommate, even though he spent most of his time at ValCorp or on missions with his best pal, Bastien. "He's in Europe with his manager. They're checking out venues and doing security checks for next year's concert tour."

"Wow! Totally wow!"

After filling their bellies with food and drink, Remare drove them toward ValCorp.

Yawning, Miranda said, "Drop me off at my place. Please. I'm exhausted."

"I thought you were coming to ValCorp." He glanced back at Selena, who was pretending to be asleep, and lowered his voice. "I was hoping to speak with you."

"I'm not like you, Remare. I need more than two or three hours of sleep. The events of the last two days are finally catching up with me. I'm going to crash as soon as I hit the bed."

When he pulled up in front of her brownstone, he massaged the back of her neck and used his thumb to brush her cheek. "You're fatigued. I think I'm at fault for causing you stress."

"I wouldn't be so exhausted if I didn't care." She leaned in and kissed Remare, mindful Selena was sitting behind them.

"We'll talk soon."

Nodding, she smiled and made for her home. A quick shower and a warm bed was all she could think about. She already knew who she'd be dreaming about.

"She's pretty cool. I like her." Selena said. "You didn't tell me you were dating a witch."

"She's a lot more than that." Remare rubbed his jaw with his thumb. *And I like her, too!*

"You should have offered her chocolate. She probably would have come with us, then."

He shook his head as he drove down the street. "Miranda has more discerning tastes."

She sounded exasperated. "Did you at least send her flowers?"

"There was no time." He slanted her a look. "I had to retrieve one impertinent ward."

Selena snorted. "Wait a minute. Just one second!" She leaned forward. "You've been back two days and you haven't gotten any?" She fell back in the seat laughing hysterically. "Some sex god you are." More giggling sounded in the car.

"My social life is none of your concern."

Her teasing tone sounded sing-song. "Remare's in the dog house!"

He ground his molars. "Not another word from you. Unless you want to find yourself grounded at ValCorp."

"Okay." They hadn't driven more than a block when he heard her say, "Woof."

Chapter Fifteen

"I promise to be back before Valadon's wedding. I don't like the idea of you alone here in New York, when I'm gone."

"Oh, Guy, I think I can manage," Felicity teased. "You have your guards posted everywhere I go."

How did she know that? "You're too perceptive for your own good. Milan is beautiful this time of year, and Ryder is there. He just completed the purchase of that textile plant I wanted. He's becoming quite good at acquisitions. You can visit with our son and hear of his latest travels."

"I do that, anyway." She snuggled inside Guy s embrace. "I see no reason for me to leave. Unless, you know something I don't." She kissed him then tugged on his lower lip with her teeth. "Do you? Know something you're not telling me?"

"Of course not. It's just that I worry." He turned away to pace. "Some of the invited guests are not to my liking. They have long memories and will not be so forgiving if they should run into you. They haven't forgotten your family's refusal to abide by the Grand Revelation. One might be so bold as to try to teach you a lesson."

She laughed. "It's been twenty years, and no acts of recriminations have occurred. I'll be perfectly safe. It's you who should visit with Ryder. He misses his father."

"We met and had several conversations when he was out west in New Mexico petroglyph exploring. At least he stopped gambling at the casinos. I was afraid he would nearly bankrupt the Native Americans." He sighed. "I gave him the simple task of looking out for Miranda while she was on her museum exchange." He rubbed the shiny black stone he kept in his pocket. "I didn't expect he'd take her...flying." He exhaled. "His mark is on her."

"That was partly your fault. You should have told him what she was to him. Really, Guy, you keep too many secrets."

"I do what I must so the ones I care for most stay safe." He pulled her to him and playfully kissed her nose. "All right, then, I'm ready to leave. Promise me you will not try to deceive your guards. They're in place for a reason."

"I wouldn't think of it."

"I knew the High Court would make a play for Valadon. But I did not expect this of Magritte. Having him marry Vivienna is low even for her."

"Magritte is not used to having her wishes denied. She loved Valadon once."

"She put him through hell. I don't call that love."

"Some women don't deal well with having been spurned."

"I'm concerned for Valadon." Memories of centuries ago in the High Court started materializing in his mind. "Magritte has a taste for the unusually cruel. I fear she might be devising some other way of torturing him while she is here. Something I've yet to uncover."

"Valadon has his Torian army. They will keep him safe."

"It's his heart I worry about. You didn't see him after his beloved's death. He was completely devastated."

"He's had centuries to heal."

"There are some things time simply cannot heal. If anything were to happen to you, I doubt I could go on without you."

"You would." She laughed. "You'd be miserable without me, but you'd go on."

"Well, see to it that I don't have to." Guy played with the flashdrive Valadon had given him. He'd read all that was on it at NYU's tech department in the remote case there was a secondary tracking device implanted that could relay his location. There hadn't been. He'd thrown the original GPS in the lake before leaving the area. Whatever monitoring system ValCorp came up with, he smiled, Glatt Industries was always a step ahead in their Research and Development division.

And research was something he excelled in.

***

McGill University, Montreal

"Right then. We are done! All papers graded, and reports filed. I say we're out of here."

"I couldn't agree more." Nick Valadon relaxed into his chair. He'd enjoyed his first semester at McGill more than expected. Part of it was because of his friendship with Professor Vincent Deschanel, who'd given him a job as a teaching assistant. "I hope you reconsider my offer to come to New York. My uncle would put you up in one of our guest rooms, we have plenty of them and there's lots of great places to see."

"I'm sure there is. But hanging around with you or escaping the university to Quebec City with Professor Olivia Pembray for some R and R—hmm, tough choice there." Vincent laughed as he ran his fingers through his long hair. "Her beauty inspires my poetry."

"She is pretty."

Vincent playfully tossed one of his pens at him. "She's more than pretty; she's a goddess, but I wasn't referring to her features. I meant her soul. Olivia has a zest for life that takes my breath away."

As happy as Nick was for Vincent and Olivia, he was sad to be going back to New York. He'd grown used to being around Vincent. The two had hit it off almost as soon as they met. He'd never had an older brother, but if he'd had one, he'd want him to be like Vincent. He'd miss him when he was away. And Olivia. She was definitely sister material.

"Why so glum? It's the end of the semester; I would think you'd be glad to be going home. From what you told me, your uncle cares a great deal about you. Lord knows he's supplied you with enough guards."

"He has to; I'm his only heir. I wish I wasn't, though. I think I disappointed him before I left New York."

"You never did tell me what you did that got you transferred up here mid-term. Most students wait until the new school year begins."

"Let's just say it had to do with a girl. And some very bad choices on my part."

"Hmm, you're still so very young. You'll find another."

"Don't give me that *young* crap. You look like you're only a few years older than me."

"*Au contraire*, I have almost four centuries on you. That's a long time to make mistakes. And learn from them. What did this girl do, anyway?"

Nick gave him a look that said he wasn't going to talk about it.

"Fine. I'll ask no more."

"Thanks."

"Did you happen to tell your financier of an uncle you preferred to get your Master's degree in Fine Arts rather than business?"

Nick hadn't told Vincent much about his uncle or his business. Other than that he was a wealthy entrepreneur who worked in New York's Financial District.

"He'd kill me. I've already disillusioned him enough. Besides, I'm going to do both."

"You'll be stretching yourself a bit thin, my young apprentice."

"I can do it." Nick smiled. "I had a great professor in art history back at NYU. She was incredible. Introduced me to a world..."

"Is she the reason you're here?"

"No! Not at all. My uncle was interested in her for a while; she worked for him in his archives." He shrugged. "At least until she became involved with his best friend who happens to be his closest business advisor."

"Sounds like drama."

"It was. I'm glad I missed most of it."

"I don't get you. You have a great family from what you've told me. I would think you'd be excited to be going back."

"I am. Sort of."

"Every parent or guardian wants, or should desire, the best for their child. It goes with the territory. Be happy he's shown such interest in you." Vincent scoffed. "My father never did."

"Sure about that?" Nick gestured to the collection of postcards mounted above Vincent's desk. "You've either attended or were a professor at some of the world's best universities. I don't think you paid for it all by selling volumes of poetry."

"Hey, I don't just write poetry. I'll have you know, I've written several biographies and histories of some of the most well-to-do aristocrats in Europe. They paid handsomely. My mother does well for herself. She's in fashion in Paris. She wanted me to have the best education money could buy. I think she was making up for the lousy parents I had."

"But you love your mother. You've always said great things about her."

"She's my adoptive mother. My birth mother left me in her care and ran off with some wealthy merchant when I was an infant. My father never gave a damn about me or ever showed any concern. I met him once when I was around seven or eight. He came to my mother's house. When we were introduced, he took one look at me, a scowl on his face as if he had better things to do and sneered, *'Which one are you?'* I'll never forget it." Vincent snorted. "That was the extent of our conversation."

Vincent still remembered his father's cold green eyes. Vincent may have inherited that particular trait, but his hair had golden highlights he inherited from his mother. He was told she was a fair beauty but had no memory of her.

"Mother hired tutors in every subject. I think she felt that, if I was kept busy, I wouldn't dwell on it so much. Ask so many questions. I think that's why I loved poetry so much. All the grand eloquent elegies to love and desire. And the great adventure stories. That was my escape." He'd read so many books she'd even procured special tinted glasses to keep his sensitive eyes covered. He didn't need them to read, his eyesight was perfect, but she recommended wearing them so the light would not adversely affect him.

"Anyway, it was all a long time ago."

He still remembered how he, and the other children of the court, were sequestered whenever the adults decided to party late into the evening. One night, when he was barely eleven years old, he evaded the guards and hid behind one of the statues to watch how they played. It was a night forever etched in his memory. He could still hear the melodies of the musicians and smell the paint the artists used in their renditions of the revelry.

He'd heard whispers about sex, but that night, he learned much about carnal knowledge as the vampires drank their fill of their humans and enjoyed the pleasures of the flesh in every possible way with multiple partners.

The next day, when he questioned Vivienna about it, she promptly hired courtesans to teach him. That, too, was singed deep in his memory.

His mother still had many of the sensual paintings hanging along the corridors in her house. Over the centuries, she had collected several more erotic ones, some of which made his skin crawl.

Nick interrupted his reveries. "Your birth mother never returned to you?"

"No. When I was older, I asked about her. I was told she died at sea when their boat capsized somewhere in the Mediterranean."

"I'm sorry."

"Yeah, me, too." He'd long given up on having any relationship with his dad. If his father wanted nothing to do with him, then fine, he'd have nothing to do with him.

When he was nearly Nick's age, he accompanied his mother on one of her many travels to London. He'd become fascinated with the English Channel, appreciated its natural beauty, could still feel the fresh air on his face, taste its purity on his tongue. He'd loved the water, even wrote poems about it.

"Mother, can I take the last name of Channel? The water here is so peaceful. I find I rather like it."

He remembered she'd seemed pensive, at first, then narrowed her eyes, as if reflecting on it until she came to a resolution. *"Very well. If you must choose a last name, remember you are French, not English, my dear. Deschanel is a much better alternative."*

He'd liked the name from the moment his mother spoke it aloud and kept it through the centuries. And London was still one of his favorite cities to visit. Even though that was where he learned his mother was a spy for the High Court.

"Vincent, help me," Vivienna cried out.

After fighting with the last of the highwaymen who had assaulted and robbed them on the road to Dover, he'd rushed to his mother's side. She'd been grievously wounded, and blood was gushing from her side.

"Mother, feed." He'd ripped open his sleeve and pushed his wrist to her mouth. It was the first time she'd ever drawn blood from him. She'd always been generous in sharing her blood with him when he'd been hurt or injured in a fall from his horse.

"Find the satchel, Vincent. It's important. Gold and jewels can be replaced, but those letters are crucial! Do you understand?"

He did and searched valiantly for them. "I can't find them. The robbers must have stolen them."

Her look of utter despair urged him to continue searching. Finally, under the body of one of their guards, he was able to retrieve the leather pouch. "I found it."

Her look of relief and gratitude had stayed with him. He'd thought at the time she was only the lover of one of the members of the High Court. It wasn't until later he learned she was one of Caltrone's highest ranking agents. And Caltrone only answered to one other vampire: Magritte, Queen of all Vampires.

Vincent shook off his reveries. "Hey, what do you say we go over to Olde Tyme Pub and have a few before my departure. Better yet, why don't you come with Olivia and me to Quebec for a few days? You look like you could use some R and R, as well."

"Don't tempt me. It sounds great, but I have responsibilities at home."

Vincent reached for his jacket. "Okay, but let's hit the pub first. We deserve it after reading all those term papers."

"Now, that sounds like a plan."

Nick didn't like hiding his real identity from Vincent, but after he was nearly killed because he bore the last name Valadon, he had chosen Vischon as his new surname. He had considered taking his father's name, Korvo, but too many people still remembered him as a member of House Valadon. Only Madame Lord Dione and a few high-ranking members of her court knew his true lineage. He wasn't taking any more chances females would cozy up to him because his uncle was wealthy or that he'd make a great kidnapping victim.

Those days were over.

Now, he just had to figure out a way to get rid of his guards. Not that he minded palling around with Gregori and Irina. Gregori loved hockey as much as he did. He was a great guy, and it was obvious he was in love with his partner. Irina, Nick could probably do without, but they were a team, and he'd gotten used to her. Mostly.

But he was far too old to have babysitters. He was determined to prove not only could he handle himself in battle, but he could defeat any adversary. Vincent and he had decided to become sparring partners in several forms of martial arts. For a poet, his mentor was in surprisingly great shape and well-versed in fighting techniques. He taught Nick moves that increased his speed and skill. Even Remare would be impressed.

Gregori was a bit more reserved in his lessons. Something about not wanting to injure the *'heir apparent'*. *Fuck that!* He was a man, not a child, and didn't hold back in his matches with the powerful Torian. Once Gregori saw how much he'd improved, he finally quit holding back and gave Nick the workouts he wanted.

He longed for the day when his uncle would give him the respect he yearned for. Valadon had once sought autonomy. In time, so would Nick. But he wasn't a fool. Valadon was the most powerful vampire he knew, and he still had his guards. But he got to choose his enforcers.

The day would come when Nick, too, would decide for himself who his own protectors would be.

Chapter Sixteen

"Ah, Remare, join us. Arik was just informing me of some interesting tales of our European associates." Valadon welcomed him as the elevator doors behind him closed and he strode into the spacious living room.

Arik had replaced Brandon, as ambassador to the European Courts, when Valadon's brother had disappeared after trying to overthrow Valadon. The tall blond vampire had proven his loyalty many times to House Valadon over the centuries. After exchanging greetings, Remare sat beside Valadon. "And what tales might those be?"

Valadon explained, "Sending you away was a good idea, after all. Arik's been recapping those who've been salivating at the idea of my *'weakened'* House."

"Do tell."

"You never were one to mince words, Remare. It's good to see you, again."

"Likewise." Remare knew he was being curt, but the day's events were wearing on him, and he had much on his mind. Not the least was the woman who was probably asleep by now.

"When word of your discord reached the shores of the other side of the pond, naturally, there were those who sought me out for confirmation. The ones you suspected were the first to make contact. Of the three, I would say Merlinder appeared the most desperate."

"That doesn't surprise me. His financials have been precarious for some time now. Go on."

"I think he was hoping the High Court would name him as your replacement if you were to become incapacitated. And an end was made to your reign here in New York."

Remare snorted. "Vultures like circling when they think fresh meat is attainable."

"Especially when they, themselves, are most vulnerable," Arik continued. "I forwarded a copy of his debt portfolio to you. It is most substantial. And significantly more than the others who covet your holdings."

"Is he planning any moves against us?"

"Now that your reconciliation with Remare has been made known, I'd say no. If you were to ask me would he, given ample time and sufficient resources, I believe so."

Remare sensed Arik was holding back. "You look hesitant, Arik. Is there anything else you would like to share?"

"I've already sent my full reports to both of you. However, what I didn't include in the data is this undercurrent I sensed more than I could accurately report."

"What did you suspect?"

Arik sipped his wine. "What concerns me is this pervasive confidence in the members of the ruling court. I would expect anticipation, anxiety naturally. But there was little or none."

"Our High Court has always tried to keep the upper hand." Valadon scoffed. "Their arrogance is their greatest weakness. They think they are unassailable. They are wrong."

Arik nodded. "Magritte and her followers have more on their agenda than I could detect. And, believe me, I searched thoroughly for more information. Even our agents in the High Court said there were more than usual behind closed door meetings they were not privy to."

"They're not taking any chances with the upcoming wedding." Remare ran his thumb along the line of his beard in contemplation. "Any surprises they are planning for us they're keeping secret as possible."

"There was something else mentioned in the courts." Arik leaned forward. "Only a rumor. A whispering, really. Something about one of the old ones returning. I tried to find out who, but no one knew or was willing to talk about it."

"We have so few ancients left." Valadon asked, "Did you discover the source of this rumor?"

"No. But I made sure our agents are resourced quite well."

Remare's curiosity stirred. "Any mention of which region or locale of said old one?"

"Not as of yet, but I will keep on it. As soon as I learn anything else, as always, you'll receive word from me."

Valadon rose and shook Arik's hand. "Thank you for your continual support of my House."

Arik closed his fist over his heart and bowed. "Always and forever."

After Arik departed, Valadon asked, "What do you make of these rumors?"

"The European courts are in disarray. So many have suffered major financial losses. It makes them anxious. And a bit superstitious."

Valadon laughed. "I suppose so. We haven't had a resurrection in quite some time. The last ancient to rise was so disillusioned with the modern world, he went back to sleep. Can you imagine any of the old ones surviving in our technological realm? They would despise it."

"Perhaps." Remare gave it some thought. "But, with the right handlers, they could adapt over time."

"I received your text on Selena. I'm glad she is returned unharmed. I will speak with her tomorrow to make sure she is acquainted with our rules."

"No need. I already explained our expectations, thoroughly, and assigned Tristan as her advisor."

Valadon smirked. "How did he react when you told him?"

"Something about being 'over-qualified for babysitting detail', I believe."

"You look tired, Remare. I'm sure this wasn't the homecoming you expected. Have you made amends with Miranda?"

"For the most part." Something still was niggling at the back of his mind. The aching hollowness of his being beckoned to her. As if he was missing something vital.

"She is crucial to my House. Don't leave anything unsettled with her. Deal with whatever needs to be done."

Remare nodded. "I will."

Sensing the coming dawn, Miranda stirred awake. Yawning, she stretched and felt the tension in her body tighten and then relax. She'd fallen into a deep sleep almost as soon as her head hit the pillow.

A shadow moved near the window, his scent familiar and welcome. "How long have you been standing there?"

"Not long, Mir-randa. I enjoy watching you sleep. I feel compelled to stand guard over you." His voice was low, seductive, barely more than a whisper. "Somehow, you bring out the protective streak in me."

She patted the space next to her. "Join me."

He stretched out beside her. "The events of the last two days have been trying. I would not have wanted them for us."

Neither would she. He'd cut her deeper than she thought possible. "Is Valadon satisfied Montglat doesn't pose a threat?"

"For the time being. But, Mir-randa, I do not trust him." He lay back on the pillows. "I knew Montglat in the courts in Europe. He was very clever. There were times it was difficult to ascertain whose court he was serving." He faced her. "It's the not knowing that vexes me."

She rubbed his jaw. Whatever magic was between them stirred to life, and her body reacted. The attraction amazed her in its raw intensity. Would there ever come a time when he didn't affect her this way? "You hurt me. I didn't think I could feel as devastated as I did. I don't know how to prove to you that I would never betray you."

He took her hand and kissed her palm. "I never imagined you would know someone such as Montglat." Emotion blazed in his eyes. "I was wounded, severely, when I saw the photos. The spymaster is good at deception. I should have had more faith in your judgment, but knowing what I do, from centuries of experience, I had my doubts. Do you forgive me?"

Heat rose between them as it usually did whenever he was near. That magnetic pull, which always drew her to him, pulsed vigorously as if the air between condensed. Breathing became labored. Every time Remare walked into a room, it was as if the vibrations surrounding them magnified, heightening her sensitivity. "Yes, but I want you to promise no more mind invasions. You know me, Remare. You always have. You hold my heart in your hands. God, even a piece of my soul. You could destroy me, and I hate that you have that much influence over me."

"My love," he cupped her face, "there can be no more discord between us. When you hurt, so do I. You bleed, and it is my blood dripping to the floor. I will not harm what is between us, again. I swear to you."

His hand snaked behind her neck and pulled her to him. His kiss was so hot it seared her very being. How did this man, this vampire, have such power over her? She'd always been detached, intellectual, distant. How could he shatter her carefully constructed walls to leave her so exposed, so vulnerable? Tears threatened to break at the realization of the depth of her emotions.

Breaking from the kiss, he held her tighter to him. "You steal my breath, my sorceress."

As he massaged her nape, she rubbed her check against his shoulder. "You're wearing too many clothes."

Giving her a smoldering look, he rose and sexily began to unbutton his shirt, then tossed it casually over the chair. After he toed off his shoes and socks, his pants and boxers were next. As he stood naked before her, Miranda's breath became ragged. Remare was truly a work of art. Not an ounce of fat anywhere on him. His body was beyond toned, beyond ripped.

He was male perfection.

She breathed in his masculine, woodsy scent deep into her lungs. Aware of her arousal, Remare stroked his already hard cock. Teeth grinding, desire gnawing at her, she grew damp between her thighs. She wanted to go to him, take him deep into her mouth, rock his world, but her legs ignored the command to move. She groaned at her inability to reach him.

His sexy smile told her he must have realized her frustration, because he moved toward her and pulled the blankets off the bed. "Your turn."

Miranda yanked her tank top off and flung it on the floor. Her shorts were next. Not the sexiest outfit, she knew, but she hadn't been expecting company. Though, knowing Remare, she should have. She lay back on the bed with her arm behind her head and one knee bent, striking a sensuous pose. Her eyes heavy lidded, her voice seductive, she said, "Come here."

"As my lady commands." He covered her body with his, keeping his weight on his elbows, and gave her another soul-devouring kiss. Time didn't exist. Space no longer relevant.

She ran her hands over the smooth, cool flesh of his back. He was strong, powerful, masculine. She reveled in the way his heart beat against her own. Miranda wasn't sure she could hold on to her sanity much longer if he kept kissing her. Did she really want reality or was the mystical more enchanting? It was as if he pulled her to distant worlds she'd never known existed. The earth, as she knew it, didn't possess the magic he wove over her.

With him, she transcended the ordinary plane of existence and explored realms of passion that intrigued and beckoned. She basked in his love for her as it streamed through her, creating a wonderful floating sensation she only ever experienced with him.

He broke from the kiss and looked down at her and smiled. "Sorceress."

"Am not!"

"Are too. You threaten my control. Mir-randa, you make me feel things I did not believe possible." He slid his hand down between them to cup her. "You're wet. I've missed this. I used to dream about you this way late at night. It nearly drove me mad." He inserted one finger inside, and Miranda arched off the bed. "So tight. You must have suffered as I did."

"More. There were nights I couldn't breathe for wanting you."

Another finger joined the first as he pumped in and out of her. "And did you relieve yourself when the desire grew to be too much?"

"The best I could." Miranda laughed. "The Weres kept buying me fresh batteries."

Remare chuckled. "I had no such devices, but my hand got more exercise than usual. Come for me, Mir-randa. Let me watch as passion devours you."

Miranda's breaths turned into pants, her body tightening to the point of breaking as pleasure rode her high and rough. Remare sped up his ministrations until she screamed out his name and the world exploded around her. A bead of sweat dripped down the side of her face.

Opening her eyes, she saw Remare staring at her. "I think I know why they call it The Little Death; you look as if you're having a heart attack. I worry, sometimes, I may cause you distress."

"Not a chance, Remare." She grinned. "But you do take me to heaven from time to time."

"That is good to know. Now, perhaps you will take me with you." He nudged his cock at her core until he could glide into her swollen, tight flesh. Slowly, carefully, until he was fully sheathed in her warmth.

"I won't break, Remare. I promise you."

"I know. But some things you just don't rush."

Her body grew slick with perspiration as heat engulfed her. Whatever magic he wove invaded her body, desire so long denied intensified until she was no longer Miranda, but just a living, breathing entity. Instinct ruled, pure and possessive. It was as if her spirit mingled with Remare's and they became one. The thought terrified and tantalized. Her heart pumping wildly, her body tight nearly to the point of pain, she screamed out his name then heard his grunts as wave after wave of passion rode them.

Exhausted, he collapsed on her then quickly rolled them to their sides so as not to crush her. They lay side by side in perfect blessedness. Each completely spent by their exertions.

"I love you." Her breath sounded arduous. "Even if you weren't so damned good in bed, I'd still love you."

"It's good to know I come with benefits." He pulled her close. "I love you, too."

***

Gavin wove his way through the crowd at Werehaven and spotted Cyrus up near the lounge in Lizandra's chair. The white wolf with his long hair and chiseled body was hard to miss. Even Gavin had to admit, he'd never seen a Were larger than Cyrus. His fists tightened. No one was allowed on Liz's throne. *Did he think he became Were King because he was Liz's lover?* He could tell him that wasn't the way it worked. If Cyrus had any aspirations in that direction, he was going to be sorely disappointed.

Gavin climbed the few stairs to the dais. "Only the Were Queen sits there."

"She asked me to keep an eye on the club. I m following her commands."

"I heard Lizandra got cut tonight."

"She did. She's fine. It wasn't more than a scratch. She's with her girl tribe in her rooms." Cyrus looked him over. "I heard you had some fun on patrol. The Red Claws all dealt with?"

Gavin didn't answer to Cyrus, but not wanting to cause a scene, he said, "Yes, there were more, this time. Not far from the southern entrance. Brazen, don't you think?"

"True. Knowing you're on patrols, I'm surprised they even try. Persistent fuckers!"

Gavin didn't like the veiled insult about him doing patrols but would let it slide for now. He had other things on his mind. "I'm going to check on Lizandra." One day soon, he knew Cyrus and he were going to go at it. The Were reeked of ambition, it was in his eyes, something he kept carefully guarded, but was still there regardless. So was his air of superiority.

When he reached the Were Queen's rooms, he knocked then entered. As Cyrus said, Liz was surrounded by her female guards. "I heard you got injured tonight. Are you okay?"

The female Weres quickly rose. Tia, Liz's chief guard, said, "That bitch, Dori, cut her with metal shards imbedded in her nails."

"Is that so?"

"Yeah." Max added, "They dragged her sorry ass out of the place after Liz showed her who's queen."

"We'll see you tomorrow." Tia kissed Liz's cheek then made for the door with the others beside her.

"If you need anything, just call." Max winked at Gavin. "Liz really knows how to kick ass. You should have seen her tonight."

"That's enough, Max. You guys have a good night." Liz sat up and then winced when she tried to rise.

Gavin waited until they closed the door behind them. "You get hurt in a fight, and you don't think to call me?!"

"It was more a confrontation than an actual fight." Liz grinned up at him. God, he adored the way she smiled. "She got a few good hits in. But I bested her."

"Let me see the wound."

"No. There's nothing to see. After I changed, it healed. All's good."

"Is that why you wince when you shift position? Let me see."

Liz narrowed her eyes at his tone. Too bad. He may not be her lover, anymore, but damn it, he still cared about her. That didn't change. And he didn't think it ever would.

"Have a gander." She lifted her shirt.

Gavin examined her side. The bruises were almost all healed, but the discoloration still remained. "Who tended to you?"

"I'm not going to fight with you, Gavin. Not tonight."

"I'm not arguing; I'm merely asking."

Liz exhaled. "Cyrus dug out the bitch's nails. They're in the jar over there." She pointed with her chin.

Gavin quickly unscrewed the cap and examined the nails. "Jesus. They're like miniature blades." He raised a brow at her. "These are designed to maim."

"I know. That's why I had her thrown out. Permanently."

"You suspected Dori was a spy from the beginning, didn't you?"

Liz nodded.

"Then, why did you keep her around? Why'd you let her inside the club in the first place?"

"I wanted to see who she befriended. Who among us met with her. Don't worry. I only supplied her with information I knew would make it back to the Red Claws."

Gavin exhaled and shook his head. "Jesus. You used to tell me when you planned things like this. I guess you don't hold me in the regard you used to."

Liz met his eyes. Damn, the sea green color of hers held him captive. They were beautiful, like the rest of her. Whatever heat that was once between them rose. His instincts to mate rode him hard. Desire was a powerful emotion. More so when it was denied for too long.

"I hold you in the highest regard, Gavin. But I'm not going to explain each of my decisions. I *am* Queen."

"You never used to hide behind your crown."

"I never had to before." She tried to sit up, and he held her down. The electricity between them sparked. But she evaded his eyes.

Frustrated, he exhaled. "Don't. You need your rest. Even a queen needs down time."

"Gavin." She ran a hand down his arm. "I know you don't understand why we broke up. You just need to realize I do what I have to. I'm not perfect. I never said I was. I have reasons for everything I do. You're not a part of that, anymore."

"Cyrus is? You don't think I see through you? We were together for a long time. I know your moves. You expect a war is brewing with the Red Claws. You wanted someone like Cyrus at the vanguard. Protective much?"

"If a war does come, he'll be instrumental to Black Star. It's important he's here."

His ego just got slammed. "You didn't believe I could lead the clan into battle?"

"I wanted to be extra sure. Cyrus is huge; he instills fear in his opponents. You always inspired respect with the clan. That's not to say you weren't good enough. You're one of the strongest Weres in the pack, but you don't intimidate. You never have. So, of course, I have faith in your abilities."

"And in bed? Is he so much more than I was?"

The Were Queen did rise at his last comment. "That is no longer your concern."

She could cut him to pieces with her barbs. He knew that, yet he still wanted her. His heart beat out a staccato for her. And he could smell her arousal for him. "No? Your words cut, Liz, but your body tells another story." He turned and made for the door. "Tell Cyrus not to get too comfortable; his days are numbered."

Chapter Seventeen

"Your Olivia sounds wonderful. Perhaps, this summer, I'll take a trip to Montreal to meet her." Vivienna, Madame Lord of Paris, laughed with her son on the phone as he explained his travel plans. "I think taking in the sites in Quebec and the quaint towns along the St. Lawrence Seaway will be enchanting this time of the year. I'm sure you'll have a fantastic time. Be well, Vincent."

Ending her call, Vivienna turned to Magritte. "You heard? He's traveling north with his lover and has no plans to visit New York."

Magritte dug her nails into Vivienna's shoulders. "Splendid. We wouldn't want to announce his presence too early." The Queen of All Vampires studied her. "You've been reticent ever since we finalized our plans. You don't still have feelings for Valadon, after all this time? I thought I taught you better."

Vivienna could never forget Magritte's teachings. She'd been a willing, if not naïve, student. "Of course not. He was an experienced lover. One I took great pleasure in. Along with his second, Remare. Together, they were magnificent. Could pleasure a woman for days and nights on end." One eyebrow rose. "But you already knew that."

"Did you think I was blind? That I didn't see the way you looked at Valadon when he was at court? You were enamored of our Minister of Finance."

"Who wouldn't be?" Vivi shrugged. "He's incredibly handsome. Few vampires have his appeal...or his wealth."

"Yes. That is true. I knew, when he left the High Court, he would accomplish many great things." Magritte strolled around Vivienna's bedroom, examining her many erotic paintings. "But I never imagined he would accrue all that he has. He surpassed my greatest expectations. His affluence will help ensure the success of the European Commission. And you will see to it funds are diverted there. We count on your success."

"Never fear, Magritte. I know my responsibilities. We'll have control of his assets once the wedding is over. Our agents have provided us with the financial data we needed. He's ours for the taking."

"Yes. He is ours. Valadon is a great seducer. He did well in our courts. Be mindful he doesn't use his allure on you. He will own you if he does."

Vivienna scoffed. "Many before him have tried."

"And none have succeeded. I know. But none are Valadon. Keep your wits about you. As I've told you before, love is a luxury, an indulgence the bourgeois revel in. A transient thing. Fleeting. Like fireworks in the night sky, exploding in its magnificent radiance, it fades to dust before even hitting the ground." Magritte faced her. "But financial security. Now, that is enduring—something worthy of our kind. Remember, if you fail, we all fail."

"I will not." Vivienna was annoyed with Magritte's constant reminders. She knew well what it was to be insecure. Never again. "I remember his passions and his weaknesses. Trust in me. I will have him exactly where we want him."

"See that you do."

A knock at the door. Eric, her sometime lover and assistant, entered. "All the luggage has been transported. The pilot waits on your orders."

"We'll be down momentarily. Tell the chauffeurs to be ready."

Eric nodded then left. Vivienna was glad Eric was part of her entourage. Among his many skills, he was quite good at organizing her servants and keeping everyone on schedule.

"All right, then, I'll leave you to finish up. My own jet is waiting, and Brandon is already aboard." Magritte nodded to her. "*Au revoir, ma beaute.*"

Vivienna was glad when Magritte requested Brandon fly with her to New York. She knew Magritte and Brandon had been meeting secretly. What they were planning, she did not know. Probably some annoyance for one of the queen's less devout supporters. She shrugged. Brandon had been an adequate lover, but compared to his older brother, he came up lacking. Even his sexual games had grown tiresome. She knew, after decades of his penchant for the more exotic, Eric had requested, in fact, begged for no more. After seeing how long it took for his wounds to heal, she'd relented. Some of those scars had been so severe, they would never heal.

She glanced at one of the more sensual paintings she had commissioned of Valadon. While he slept, the artist had perfectly captured Valadon's nude form. But not his scent nor his intense animal magnetism. Opening a secret compartment in her cabinet, she retrieved another portrait of Valadon on a cliff gazing out at the setting sun. This one had always been her favorite. One she considered precious. He'd seemed conflicted, almost as if a part of his soul were missing and he could not figure out how to reclaim it.

Ah, but she'd been sent to make sure he shook off his malaise. The High Court had become concerned Valadon's continued depression would endure too long and requested she find a way to enchant the vampire back to his senses.

French Countryside, 1640's

"Monsieur Girard's madrigals have improved." Vivienna and Valadon ran from the coach to their country home. It was a fine stone structure set back from the main road. Caltrone had supplied her with the necessary funds to purchase it after she had completed a difficult mission for him.

"I think I prefer the tragedies of Shakespeare better." Valadon kept her sheltered from the rain.

Once inside, they removed their wet cloaks. *"Let's sit by the fire and warm up."* The servants, already gone to bed, had left a bottle of wine out with two glasses on the tray. *"You can tell me all about Shakespeare's plays. I favor his histories more so. But, when it comes to poetry, I still think Christopher Marlowe is more talented."*

Vivienna listened intently to Valadon's take on the gifted playwright and his use of iambic pentameter. She could listen for hours, enjoying his melodic tones. Vivienna sipped her wine. She never allowed herself to be captivated by a man. Caltrone and Magritte had taught her well how to seduce and be seduced, but Valadon was in a class by himself. They had solicited much information about him, but nothing had prepared her for his powerful charisma or striking features. She'd become fascinated with him and had to remind herself she was on a mission.

After they finished the first bottle of wine, they opened a second. Every now and then, Valadon's gaze drifted from her, as if he were reliving a memory. *"The next time we're in Paris, we must go see his latest play."*

"Yes, we must." She agreed as she casually loosened her bodice. *"He has such a depth of understanding when it comes to the weaknesses of mortals."*

"Of everyone." Valadon threw another log on the fire. *"You must be tired. We should turn in soon. This continual rain is sleep-inducing."*

Vivienna had done everything to make herself appealing. Her hair had been styled to perfection, her clothes revealing enough to entice. And she bathed in the latest perfumes from Arabia. She was not going to bed without him. "I think that's a wonderful idea."

Once in the bedroom, she removed her dress and stood wearing only her bustier and stockings. Glancing in the mirror, it was no wonder Magritte always called her 'Bell Fleur', her beautiful flower. She'd been born with impeccable features: violet eyes, fair complexion, fine bone structure and full lips. All of which she used for maximum appeal. Tonight, she donned a gossamer robe and remained in the doorway, watching Valadon.

He stood by the window, watching the rain fall, so silent, so still.

"Bed's turned down, and the room is warm. Won't you join me?" she asked in her most sultry voice.

When he turned to look at her, his jaw lowered. "I don't think I've ever seen you in that outfit."

"That's because I've never worn it before." She walked seductively toward him.

"Vivienna, you're one of the most enticing women I've ever met. But I don't think Remare would like this very much."

"Not so, Valadon. He's the one who encouraged me to keep you company." She opened her robe, revealing her feminine curves. "And keep you warm."

"He loves you, you know. It would be improper to play with his heart."

"Remare loves you, too. He said you spend far too much time by yourself. He wants us to be together, a threesome when he returns from war."

"He said this to you?"

"Yes. We both discussed it at length. He'd hoped you'd find another woman to raise your spirits. But, when that didn't

happen, he asked if I would consider taking you to our bed. He didn't have to ask twice. We both love you, Valadon. There's no deceit here. We simply want you to be happy."

Valadon brushed one of her curls behind her shoulder. "It doesn't seem right."

"I wouldn't worry about Remare too much. We agreed, when he is away at war for any length of time, he can satisfy his urges with whomever he chooses." She chuckled. "I'm sure he has already." She reached up and kissed him ever so slowly.

"Remare is too generous for his own good."

Vivienna laughed. "Neither one of us has ever had high regard for traditional relationships. We prefer to make our own rules. Perhaps that is why we get along so well. You've been alone too long, Valadon. Be with me." She caressed his pecs. "Let me show you what passion is, what it feels like to be alive. You've been depressed for too long. Isn't it time you returned to the living?" She brushed her lips softly against his. "To us?"

His eyes held that long ago look. Blank, yet with a yearning that had gone unheralded for too long. "And you're sure he approves of this? It's what he wants?"

"Of course." She stepped back, the robe falling away as she pulled the hair pin she'd woven her mane of raven hair around. Her curls cascaded down her back. His eyes were on her, hungry for a taste. She undid the strings to her corset, and soon, it joined the robe on the floor. "I'm lonely, too, Valadon…and chilled." She rubbed her arms, trembling either out of anticipation or fear he would reject her, she knew not, only that she wanted him.

He leaned toward her, hesitating, as if he were fighting a battle within himself. Finally, he pulled her close and inhaled her scent. She gradually released her allure, coating him in desire, the unrelenting need to embrace, to succumb to life's natural urges. He kissed her with the passion he must have had bottled up for nearly a decade.

Being in his arms was unlike anything she'd ever felt before, and she'd been with countless other men. His fangs brushed along hers, and their tongues dueled for ownership. In an instant, his shirt was off, and his bare chest was up against her naked breasts. Vivienna's breaths amped up as she was sucked into a vortex of passion that seared her very soul. Unwilling to wait for the bed, he sat with her in the chair by the fire.

Completely bare except for her stockings, she straddled his legs. He wrapped her hair around his fist and pulled her down for another devouring kiss. Vivienna's nails dug into his shoulders as she held on to him. Breaking from the kiss, she trailed her tongue down his jaw until she reached the pulsing vein in his neck. Her fangs bared, she bit him and swallowed his life's essence down her throat. She thought she knew passion, how powerful the allure could be, but nothing that came before prepared her for the waves of rapture that rolled through her as she consumed Valadon's blood.

He must have been starving for blood as well, because he nuzzled her neck then trailed kisses to her breast. He plumped the mound of flesh with his palm and then teased, nipped and finally sank his fangs into her. She felt his erection grow harder beneath her and rubbed her core against him. His growls of arousal sang in her ears as he finished feeding.

He quickly undid the fastening of his breeches and released his cock. He teased her by rimming her clit with it, circling but not using enough pressure to satisfy the swollen nub of nerves. He continued his circular motion, driving her wild with desire.

"Stop teasing me or I will punish you."

His laughter echoed in her mind. He plunged one finger in, stroking her to new heights of hunger. Then added another, his *hand coated with the evidence of her arousal, he plunged deeper and faster until she began panting. Satisfied he had her on edge, he pressed down on her clit with his thumb. Her screams of pleasure vibrated off the walls.*

Valadon positioned her over his cock, and she slid gracefully down, moaning at the pleasure of finally being joined. She rode him, teasing him with slow rotations of her hips until his eyes narrowed and his fingers dug into her waist as he encouraged her to speed up her movements.

But Vivienna wasn't easily swayed. She clamped down hard on him until he stilled. When he loosened his hands, she moved rhythmically, enjoying the ebb and flow of their union. A trickle of sweat rolled down the side of his face as he tried to maintain his control.

Gripping his shoulders with more force, she began to move in earnest, enjoying every growl and grunt he made as the fevered pitch of their lovemaking increased and intensified. Neither were content to come first and were holding back what they could so the other would climax. When it appeared he couldn't take anymore, he reached down between their bodies and pinched her clit.

Vivienna roared louder than she ever had during intercourse. His growl soon echoed hers. Exhausted, her head fell to his shoulder. It must have been their proximity to the fireplace with the burning logs that had her body glistening. She'd never felt such heat before, such depth of passion.

He removed his boots and breeches then carried her to the bedroom. After years of celibacy, the dam had finally broken. The red rims around his eyes pulsed with the life that had been missing for so long. He stared at her nude form as if he delighted in every inch of her. His body was sculpted to perfection. The glow of his skin with the sheen of perspiration added to his magnificent appeal.

Joining her on the bed, he continued their sexual escapades for hours, well into the next day and the day after that. Their sessions became contests of dominance, endurance and skill. Each testing the other, each desiring to prove their worthiness and superiority. His remarkable stamina shocked and exhilarated her. Their hunger, that insatiable thirst for more, grew stronger until they couldn't fuck anymore.

She summoned the servants to bring food, wine and blood. When they bathed, the sheets were changed, and fresh flowers were brought in to cleanse the air of the scent of their sex, only to have to be repeated for the next three days.

Breathing hard, Vivienna woke from her daydream with painful need between her thighs. Her skin was flushed and damp with perspiration. She placed her hand over her heart to slow her heartbeats. It had been centuries, but she could still remember every touch, the scent of their lovemaking, every detail of those nights in the cottage. They were some of her most wonderful memories.

When Valadon confided in her his desire to go to the New World and claim a territory for his own, she'd been faced with an impossible dilemma. By then, Valadon, Remare and she had been together for decades. How long before he grew restless and sought out another? What would she be left with? Her first allegiance had been to Magritte and Caltrone. It was her duty to report to them. Unlike her lovers' wealth, her family's fortune had been depleted; she needed Caltrone's support to maintain the lifestyle she'd grown accustomed to.

She'd never forgotten the look of inexorable disgust Valadon had given her when he realized she'd been the one to sabotage his plans to leave. It had taken nearly another century before he and Remare were able to buy their freedom from the High Court.

And, in the centuries since, no one had ever made her feel as alive as Valadon had. Not one lover had ever made her aware of what it was to truly love.

And, for that, she grieved.

Chapter Eighteen

"But why does he want to see us both? If it's a corporation meeting, shouldn't you be going alone?" Miranda asked Remare as she accompanied him down the corridor to Valadon's main conference room.

"Valadon specifically requested you attend. All the Elite Torians will be there, including Nick."

It had been months since she'd seen her favorite student and former assistant. She'd missed Nick terribly, but Morel had kept her apprised of his progress at McGill University, as well as Remare's well-being. The months apart had been rough, Valadon's idea of a punishment. She still thought he hadn't had the right to dictate their lives, but he was the king, after all.

As they neared the door, she wondered if the day would ever come when she and Remare could walk hand in hand down the hall without anyone raising an eyebrow.

He opened the door, and they entered. Valadon was at the head of the table, conferring with Chase Lambert, the young lawyer at the inquest into Cerise's dangerous games. Seated at the long rectangular table were the Elite Torians: Aiden, Morel, Gregori, Irina, Tristan and Katya.

"I see they got you, too." Gabriel rose and kissed her temple. "It's good to see you, again. He shook Remare's hand. "And you, too. Welcome home."

Before Remare could respond, the Torians stood and covered their fists over their hearts. In unison, they said, "Always and forever."

She knew, by the subtle tick in his jaw, Remare was touched and possibly humbled by the grand gesture of affection and respect.

He nodded to them. "Thank you. It's good to be home."

"Come take your seat." Valadon gestured to his right.

She sat alongside Remare as the Torians resumed sitting. Eyeing them, she wondered if they blamed her for Remare's absence, but she didn't pick up any negative vibes. And, as an empath, she was good at detecting emotions.

Valadon made eye-contact with her but addressed the group. "We're waiting on Nick, who is on his way here."

Aiden was sitting on Valadon's left, the seat Morel normally took as his third. She wondered if Morel had somehow been demoted for questioning Valadon's decision to exile Remare in front of the other Torians. She hoped not; Morel was a good man.

"Sorry I'm late. I had to take a phone call that was important to me." Nick bowed to his uncle and accepted the binder Aiden handed him. Dressed in a suit, he looked older than when she'd last seen him.

Valadon addressed them. "Let's get started. For the record, Bastien is in Europe with Orion, therefore, unable to make this conference. He will be apprised of all pertinent information at the conclusion of today's meeting. As always, everything discussed herein is confidential."

Miranda wondered why she was even there. She knew only what she'd read in the magazines about ValCorp's business operations.

"As you know, my upcoming wedding to Vivienna will be occurring soon." He sighed. "As much as we tried to circumvent Magritte's command, we were unable to do so. My thanks go out to Victor and our other historians for the research they did concerning covenants within the Vampire Nation and the mandates of the High Court. Special recognition goes to Morel for the many hours he put in working alongside Victor in the archives in addition to his other duties." Valadon faced his second. "And to Remare for his investigations in the Canadian courts."

Remare nodded to him. "All that could be done was done."

"And much appreciated. When word originally reached us of the High Court's intention of a merger between the European court and House Valadon, I had Lambert instigate measures to ensure ValCorp's solvency and protect that which is dear to me. Chase."

Lambert addressed the crowd. "Please open the dossiers in front of you to section one."

Miranda opened the black and gold binder to find a listing of ValCorp's finances. She inwardly gasped at the massive amount of Valadon's holdings. She knew he was a billionaire, but to see the spreadsheet with the actual numbers was staggering. His empire was comprised of real estate, hotels, transportation including cargo planes and ships, communication networks, various business holdings, and many investments. Miranda didn't bother to finish reading the list; it was too overwhelming.

Lambert said, "When the European delegation arrives, they will be under the same laws and covenants all American citizens are obligated to obey. However, given the history of the High Court and their financial difficulties over the last decade, we felt the necessity to ensure the survival of ValCorp's assets. Valadon and I came up with the following. Please turn to section two."

Collective sighs were heard throughout the room.

"I decided to partition ValCorp's resources. Each of you will receive a certain percentage of ValCorp for the duration of my marriage. Please be aware this is being done to insure Vivienna doesn't make a play for any of our holdings in case of divorce. Which I assure you will happen sometime after the wedding."

"But won't Vivienna's lawyers question the legality of these documents and try to fight their authenticity?" Tristan asked.

Valadon smiled. "That is why you will note the dates the documents were drawn on. We predated everything. Besides, I will offer Vivienna a one-time-only deal, quite substantial I might add." He glanced at Lambert, as if he and his lawyer had negotiated long and hard on the amount. "If she refuses, no further offers will be forthcoming. She'd be unwise to fight me on this. Vivienna is many things, but she's not a fool. Now, what I require from each of you is your signature on all the forms. Also on the non-disclosure agreement toward the back of the binder. Please look up at the board."

Miranda saw the financial breakdown. Everyone was allotted different divisions. Real estate went to Gregori and Irina, transportation to Katya and Tristan, communications to Aiden, Morel—financial investments, Gabriel—medical technologies. Bastien's share included ownership of Valadon Entertainment. Remare and Nick would receive the majority of the holdings in New York, especially the main headquarters of ValCorp. *Whew!* The amounts were staggering.

"In the case of my death—"

A roar of protest and shouts went up in the room.

Valadon chuckled. "I assure you, all precautions have been taken, but in the unfortunate case one of the delegates decides to take a shot at me, these holdings will suffice as my last will and testament. Hopefully, if all goes well, none of you will ever actually own any of this."

Chase said, "Please turn to section four. When Valadon's divorce is final, all holdings revert back to him. If anyone here decides to sell or transfer any funds... Well, you can imagine the consequences."

Miranda certainly could. It was a thinly veiled threat in case anyone got greedy, but she didn't think anyone present would be so foolish or disloyal. She was glad Valadon had taken steps to protect his assets. He'd worked hard for centuries to build ValCorp up into the financial empire that it was.

"There is one component yet not disclosed." Valadon clicked the remote, and an image of his beautiful archives appeared. "As Miranda has worked tirelessly with me in cataloging my works of art and helping me to locate disciples of Peralt, I wish her to have ownership of the archives."

Eyes wide, Miranda couldn't breathe. Valadon's art collection was worth a fortune! Some of his paintings were priceless. She just stared at him in disbelief, her heart hammering in her chest.

"Smile, people, stop looking so glum. I just made you all incredibly wealthy." Valadon smirked. "For the time being, anyway."

Lambert gestured to the documents. "Please remember this is a temporary transaction. In no way are you the true owners of the assets listed today. Something Magritte and all the European visitors need not know."

An applause rang out in the room for Valadon's strategy. Miranda blinked and shook her head. She examined the places Lambert had marked with X's where their signatures were required.

Nick was in heavy discussion with Lambert, asking questions and pointing to figures in the documents. He'd matured in his time away. His focus was intent, and sadly, gone was his ready smile that had so warmed her heart. She heard Nick whisper to Valadon, "I will do everything in my power to ensure your legacy continues." He placed his fist over his heart. Something she'd never seen him do before.

"I know." Valadon returned the gesture then addressed the group. "If everyone is finished signing, please return the binders to Lambert. He will keep them secure."

After everyone slid the binders back to the lawyer, Valadon stood. "Thank you everyone for your attendance today and your continuing loyalty." He closed a fist across his chest. "Always and forever." His vow of protection for his people reinforced. Each of the Torians returned the gesture.

"Miranda, Remare, please stay."

Nick apologized for being late. "I got a call from a professor of mine I've become good friends with. He was supposed to tour Quebec with his girlfriend, but an opportunity came up at McGill she couldn't refuse, and now, he has time on his hands. I want him to visit New York. May I invite him to your wedding?"

"Of course, if he's your friend, he is welcome in my House. Just give his name to Aiden, who will do the background check on him."

"Done."

"Nick," Valadon stood and spread his arms. "Welcome home. You were missed. Dearly."

Nick went into his embrace and hugged his uncle. "I know. I missed being here, as well."

He smiled at her and Remare then left with the others.

When they were alone, Valadon said, "Rosalyn has been busy decorating my catering hall. You will remember I once considered opening a restaurant here but decided against it at the time. I'm rethinking those plans, now. Would you like to see where the wedding will take place?"

"Sure." Miranda was curious what her friend would do with the place. Rosalyn had married Jason Morgan in a private affair in Finland with only family and a few close friends attending in order to avoid the craziness of the paparazzi. Miranda didn't blame her for her secrecy; she'd seen how crazy some of those reporters could be when she was engaged to Orion.

"Yes, I want to see the layout of the room. I'm sure Aiden advised on security measures?" Remare asked Valadon.

"Yes."

When they reached the selected floor, Valadon opened the doors to a magnificent ballroom with a high ceiling similar to the Rainbow Room at the Top of the Rock where she and Lizandra had once celebrated their birthdays. Huge arched windows decorated three of the walls, offering a breathtaking panoramic view of the city. At the far end was a raised dais, where she presumed the bride and groom and their attendants would be. Each of the windows and all the tables circling the dance floor were draped in black and gold, Valadon's colors. The center of the dance floor was glazed with ValCorp's insignia of a staff and flame.

Rosalyn approached. She hugged Miranda then faced Valadon. "Good to see you. So, what do you think of what I've done with the place?"

"Stunning. You've surpassed my expectations." Valadon kissed her cheek. "After the wedding, we'll use this room for socializing, dancing and music listening. My people spend too much time below; they need this. So do I. Thank you. I appreciate all your efforts."

Remare stood with his arms crossed by the window and gazed at the nearby buildings. "We'll have guards posted on the roofs. All security measures will be in place by the time of the wedding."

Miranda joined Remare. "You look disappointed."

"I am. I'd hoped we could locate Valadon's son in time to avoid this disaster of a marriage. I'm dismayed Valadon was forced into this arrangement and that I was unable to discover his son's whereabouts."

Miranda covered his hand with hers. "Valadon is certain he'll be able to finagle a way out after his son is made known to him."

"I'm uncomfortable with so many foreigners in our House." He stroked his thumb along her knuckles. "It is not a healthy situation. My gut tells me something may go wrong." His tone was pensive. "I don't like feeling this way."

Miranda had met some of the court members and wasn't crazy about their coming either. But Valadon didn't become a High Lord by being imprudent.

Vibrating with joy, Rosalyn joined them. "Will you be attending the transition ceremony? I would very much like you to be there."

Miranda was confused. "What do you mean?"

"There wasn't time to inform Miranda with all that's been going on." Remare said, "Rosalyn has received permission from Valadon to turn Jason vampire."

Miranda's spine straightened. She wasn't exactly sure what the ceremony entailed, but she was pretty certain it was a personal matter. Not one she especially wanted to witness. "Where will it take place?"

"Tonight. Down in the reception hall." Smiling, Roz radiated warmth and affection. "You missed our wedding. Jason and I would like you both to be there."

Miranda's butterflies started dancing in her stomach. She'd heard rumors about transitions. Gabriel had told her about the hell he'd gone through. But there'd been no preparation in his case.

"You'll tell me all that's involved, won't you?" She spoke mentally to Remare. *"So, I won't be surprised."*

"Of course, I will. I think you should see for yourself what's entailed."

"We'll be there." And, then, she'd know once and for all what exactly happened when a human became vampire.

The butterflies started dancing, again.

***

Jeremy held the phone in his hands and contemplated his decision. It was risky, certainly audacious. But he was the son of an ancient. Power flowed through his veins. Everything had to go according to plan. Timing was critical. The fallout from his actions would have far-reaching effects, but change was inevitable. The power structure in the old regime needed tweaking, and if it had to be him doing the modifying, so be it.

He'd studied the files Scorpio had compiled for him. Knowledge was power, but so was money, and he'd need more in order to buy the support he needed to achieve his goals. He'd already bought the support of one high-ranking member of the council. Others would follow.

But, first, he would free his sister from the hell she'd been damned to.

Chapter Nineteen

"I'm glad you're looking better. I never saw you fight like that. It got to me."

"That's why I don't allow you in Werehaven after midnight." Lizandra took another bite of the chocolate cake then pushed the plate away. "Weres are known to be aggressive. It's no big."

Miranda scoffed. People fought—Weres, humans, vampires. It didn't matter who, someone always got hurt. And she didn't like seeing her best friend injured. "If you say so." She finished her cake, then took their plates to Liz's sink and rinsed them off.

"So, how are you and Remare getting along; you guys all reconciled?"

"Yeah, for the most part. You know he can get pretty moody at times."

Liz laughed. "Don't we all."

Miranda smiled. "It wasn't quite the welcome home either one of us imagined." She was still shaken from the argument they had. "There's a lot about relationships I don't understand. I think I'm glad I stayed single for as long as I did."

"What don't you get?"

Miranda shook her head and tried to put into words what she was feeling. "Why some relationships last and others don't."

"That's because you spent so much of your life closed off. Studying. If you'd partied more, you'd have more experience."

Miranda raised a brow. "I partied quite enough, thank you very much."

"Relationships require a great deal of compromise. You're not used to making concessions; you're too used to having things your way."

Miranda thought about it. "I like things my way. Not crazy about the idea of having to make compromises."

Liz laughed. "No one does, but you have to, otherwise relationships suck."

Miranda thought Liz had the perfect relationship with Gavin. "Were you always happy with Gavin? You were together for so long."

"Most of the time." The Were Queen sighed. "But not all relationships are meant to last."

Miranda wasn't going to drill her about Gavin. The last time she'd brought it up, Liz nearly took her head off. "You think Remare and I have a shot at it?"

"God, I hope so. He practically drools on you, whenever you're here together. A person could get off on all the eye-fucking that goes on between you two."

Miranda snorted. "I meant between a vampire and a human, eh, *Elemental*. To tell the truth, there are times I almost forget he's a vampire. He's so damned civilized. And, then, there are other times I'm amazed I could ever forget. His *other* worldliness permeates every fiber of his being." She rubbed her hands. "I think I'm just scared."

"Jesus. You love him that much?"

"I try not to. Especially when he pisses me off. But, yeah, I do. We're attending a transition ceremony tonight. I think that's what's got my stomach in knots. Not sure I can watch a human turn vampire." She trembled at the thought.

"You said Remare wouldn't put any pressure on you; has that changed?"

"No. He's been good about that. But there's still so much about vampirism I don't know. I'm just not sure I can ever go through the transition."

"So, don't."

Miranda's jaw dropped. "Huh?"

"If it bothers you that much, you're obviously not ready. So, don't. He's not putting pressure on you, so why are you?"

"I guess I like to plan for the future." She shrugged. "He wants more time with me than a human lifetime. That's what worries me, living so long."

"Whoa, slow down. Why are you torturing yourself? Take one day at a time. See where it goes and let the future work itself out."

"I will. I am. The thought of remaining human, growing old, of having him watch me as my looks and health fade concerns me, too. Knowing, eventually, he'll find someone else when I'm dead and gone. Yeah, that kinda makes me want to kill someone."

"I think you're going to have to reconcile your fears. Decide which is more important to you."

"Yeah, I know. But, what if I do choose to become vampire, and Remare tires of me and leaves me for another? I'd still be vampire, but he wouldn't be with me."

"Girl, where are all these insecurities coming from?" Liz took her by the shoulders. "Remare loves you. He doesn't even look at another female when he's here."

"So, you think we have a chance?"

"Yes. If you're looking for some kind of assurance, you can just forget it. Life doesn't come with guarantees. You gotta make the best with what you have. Play with the cards you've been dealt and stop imagining all these what ifs. Even if things didn't work out, which I highly doubt will happen, are you ready to walk away from the best thing you've ever known because you're scared?"

"I don't know." Miranda broke away from Liz's hold. "I think my self-preservation instincts are working overtime.

God, I hate feeling vulnerable. I didn't feel this way with Gabriel or anyone else."

"You never loved anyone as deeply as Remare. Think of it this way. How do you think he feels? You don't think men have insecurities? I can tell you they do."

Miranda knew she'd become too self-absorbed, but Remare had really hurt her. He had so much potential to destroy her she hadn't even thought she could be affecting him the same way. "Remare calls me his sorceress. That I weave spells over him."

"Pussy-whipped, huh?!"

"Hardly. I don't know what's gotten into me." She shook her head. "Forget it. One day at a time, like you said. Hey, you want to walk with me upstairs, get some fresh air?"

"Sure."

Once they reached the surface, Miranda breathed deep. "It's almost summer. I can feel change in the air. And not just in the seasons." She rubbed her arms. "It's just this feeling I have." They both looked out over the swaying trees in Central Park. "Changes are coming."

"Yeah, I've been sensing that, too." Liz glanced back at the opening to Werehaven. "Let's hope they're good changes and not bad ones."

***

"Mir-randa, it's a rebirth, not a funeral."

"What's wrong with my dress?" Miranda glanced down.

Remare frowned. "Don't you have anything with color?"

"Not really, most of my gowns are black. It's sophisticated."

"As you are." He kissed her hand. "I'll have Cesare design you more dresses." At her raised eyebrow, he amended, "If you wish."

Miranda remembered what Liz said about compromises. "We'll see." She checked out Remare's dark suit. *Why is it okay for him to wear black and not me?*

When they reached the reception hall, Remare opened the door and ushered her in. She liked how he kept his hand on the small of her back. Possessive, yes, but somehow, it felt right. They said hello to the other Torians and moved forward. "Why is there a bed at the end of the room?"

"The transition may weaken Jason for a short period of time. He'll want to rest afterward."

Miranda felt the butterflies returning as soon as Rosalyn hugged her. She knew she was staring but couldn't tear her eyes from Jason. Remare had said this was more of a rebirthing ceremony, but to her, at least in part, it felt like a funeral. Like something vital was dying. She didn't know what to say to Jason, somehow "bon voyage" or "safe travels" didn't quite seem appropriate. She settled on, "Good luck, Jason."

Jason kissed her temple. "Thank you, Miranda. I'm glad you could make it. As for luck, I had all the luck I needed when I first met Rosalyn. She's my burning star."

Miranda glanced at Remare and wondered if he'd ever say something similar about her. She knew the others were talking, but this whole experience was so surreal to her, it was all white noise. When Roz and Jason left to greet others, she asked Remare, "Why is Gabriel here? Will they be needing a doctor?"

"Most transitions occur without incident, but there are rare instances when medical assistance is necessary?"

"What kind of instances?"

"Occasionally, some sort of complication arises. People have been known to change their minds at the most inopportune times."

She didn't think that was the case with Jason. "What other complications?"

"Jason's blood has been tested, and Rosalyn has been feeding him her blood for some time now. However, there are certain blood anomalies that remain undetected. Those people lined up to the side are there in case their blood is needed to complete the transition.

Miranda found the whole ceremony unnerving. She figured something as major as committing yourself so thoroughly to another should be done in private and not shared with such a large group.

Victor was up at the front, going on about life, love and loyalty. Transfixed on the medical equipment and the bed, she barely heard him. She wondered if Rosalyn and Jason would be engaging in any other personal practices. Her throat caught. A voyeur she was not.

Remare stood behind her and casually wrapped her in his arms. "Breathe, woman. I can hear your heart thundering in my ears."

His voice helped to calm her as her breaths evened. Valadon addressed the group, welcoming everyone to the event and Jason into his House. She hadn't known Jason would become a member of House Valadon, but she probably should have.

All was quiet in the room when music started playing from a side unit as Rosalyn and Jason sat on the bed. Was this really happening? Was she really going to watch this? Remare pulled her tighter against him. At this moment, she was grateful he had her back and wondered if he had his arms around her to stop her from fleeing or was merely lending support. Her hands gripped his wrists, and she smiled when she felt his bracelet.

Roz and Jason looked so blissful. They were smiling, and Jason laughed at something she'd said. Miranda was happy for them, still...

Jason removed his jacket, laying it over the bed and undid the first few buttons of his shirt. Then, he bent his head sideways so Rosalyn could sink her fangs into him. With one swipe of her tongue, she closed the wound. Then, she lowered the strap of her dress, and Jason repeated her action.

"The transition is done gradually. Always the vampire takes first, and then, the human follows the lead. Nothing is rushed. If there was going to be complications, we would have seen them by now."

Miranda heard Remare's whispered words, but they barely registered. She watched Jason carefully for any fitful movement. She worried he'd go into convulsions the way Gabriel had when he transitioned. She met her former lover's eyes. For a moment, they shared something. Humanity was not something easily relinquished. Especially in Gabriel's case, as he never wanted to become vampire.

The give-and-take process became more involved as Rosalyn began to take deeper gulps of Jason's blood. She could see his color changing, becoming paler, more translucent. Then, he took longer swallowing her blood, and his skin appeared healthier.

So, this was how it was done. Miranda exhaled. No hesitations, no reservations. Each of them giving and taking, dedicated to the transition. The love was so apparent between the two Miranda almost had tears in her eyes at the emotional impact of their shared joining. Rosalyn cared enough to want to share her life with him, for longer than a mortal's lifetime. And Jason had surrendered his humanity to be with her. If that wasn't love, Miranda didn't know what was. Jason had made the ultimate sacrifice for his beloved. And Rosalyn had given him the greatest gift a vampire could give.

"The process will go on for three days. Each giving and receiving until the vampirism is complete. Those days will be private between them."

She must have forgotten to breathe because she became dizzy. Someone had lowered the lights, signaling it was time for the onlookers to leave. The ceremony had gone off without a hitch. Miranda exhaled, relieved it was over.

"Let's get dinner, Mir-randa. You look a little pale."

Did she? Probably. No matter how much Remare had previously explained, nothing had prepared her for actually seeing it. "Can we go up to the roof first? I need fresh air."

Remare grinned at her nervousness. "If you want."

Once atop ValCorp, Miranda went to the edge to look out over the city. God, she loved how the skyscrapers lit up the night sky. The city was alive with its frenetic pace, people going about their business. The world hadn't stopped. Life continued as she knew it. Breathing in the cool evening air, she was better able to focus. "Thanks." She smiled up at him. "I think I got a little lightheaded in there."

Remare slid his knuckles down her cheek. "Are all your questions finally answered?"

"You have no idea what it's like. To be human and witness it. Nothing you said quite prepared me for the actual event."

"I suppose not." Remare's eyes glinted with laughter. "When you were a virgin, all that you'd heard about sex, did it prepare you for your first time?"

"Funny! She smacked his arm then laughed. "I see your point. I take it you've seen several transitions in your lifetime."

"More than a few." He moved a strand away from her face. "You're still a bit pale. Would you like to get something to eat or stay here a moment longer?"

She took one last loving look at her city and breathed deep. How she could be hungry after witnessing what she had, she wasn't sure. "I'm starving. Food is a good idea."

"Do you want to join the others in the formal dining room or would you rather dine in my rooms."

"Your rooms. We don't get enough alone time, and I'd rather not be around so many people just now."

"I'll have Escher bring us something."

Dinner consisted of sliced turkey with gravy and assorted vegetables. After they'd finishing eating, Remare bid Escher farewell in removing their empty plates. Why did she always feel better after a meal? Reclining on his couch, Miranda tucked one foot under her and had a moment to appreciate the Oriental décor of Remare's apartment. Every piece of art spoke of serenity, from the gold dragon with the ruby eyes to his Asian paintings, even his twin Samurai swords mounted on the wall presented an aura of tranquility.

"Would you like some wine?"

"Sure. When I was trying to figure out what to get you, Lizandra and I went shopping in Chinatown. We hit so many gift shops. I wanted to get you a dragon to match the gold one you have, but I couldn't find anything like it." She smiled. "At least not in my price range."

After handing Miranda her wine, he joined her on the couch. "That may have been difficult. The dragon was a gift from a Samurai master in Japan. It's quite old and one of a kind. Besides," he kissed her, "I'm quite fond of my bracelet." He wiggled his wrist.

"I'm glad." Alone time with Remare had been just what she needed. Their relationship had suffered some damage with their distrust of each other, but she was beginning to realize no relationship was perfect and all couples had their ups and downs. Though dating a vampire assassin had more complications than most. But, in the end, was it worth it? *Hell, yeah!*

Liz had said life didn't come with guarantees, and now, Miranda realized she didn't need one. She was lucky enough to have him in her life.

"So, what happens, now? I mean, after Madame Lord Vixen arrives with her entourage. For the life of me, I can't imagine what this place is going to be like for you or Valadon after she moves in."

"We go on with our lives as we have always done. Valadon will not allow Vivienna access to his personal rooms. She will have a suite set aside for her and her attendants. All the other dignitaries have been assigned rooms at the Plaza and La Pierre hotels overlooking the park. We considered having a few of the visitors as our special guests but realized others might be offended at not receiving the same accommodations. For security reasons, it is best not to have them all in one location."

"Does it scare you?"

"Having all of them here at one time? They've been here before…"

"No, I meant us." She pointed to him and her. "Does it scare you, sometimes, that whatever is between us is bigger than either one of us?"

He snorted but clasped their hands. "I used to worry a great deal about many things. Mostly at what Valadon would do. But, now that he's accepted us, no, I don't find myself considering such things." One knuckle glided across her cheek. "What's happened to make you ask?"

She held his hand against her cheek then kissed his palm. "I think seeing Lizandra getting injured weighs heavy on my mind. I was hurt badly before when you doubted me. I didn't realize just how deep my emotions about you were until I realized how torn apart I felt. So, yeah, it does scare me."

"No need, Miranda. I am in as deep as you. We're in this together. And I can't imagine what else we could possibly fight about." He kissed her forehead. "It's late. Are you staying the night?"

"No. I have to get up early for work tomorrow. And, with you around, I don't get much sleep."

One corner of his mouth lifted. "I can make sure you're relaxed. Perhaps a long soak in a warm bath."

"Mmm, sounds fantastic." She leaned in to kiss him. "Another time."

"I'm concerned you stretch yourself too thin. You don't have to work two jobs, Mir-randa. I can support you."

"And make me a kept woman?!" She feigned reproach. "No, thanks! I love my job at the museum. And I only work two nights a week at the university and never during the summers."

"The option is yours, if you ever change your mind. I just don't like the idea of you pushing yourself too hard. In any event, we're going to have several receptions for our visitors. Will you be here with me to greet them?"

Miranda sighed. She'd met some of the European visitors, wasn't especially eager to see them, again. *What did Liz say? Oh, yeah, compromise.* "If you want me to be."

Chapter Twenty

Miranda was making her way toward the elevator when Valadon surprised her. "Leaving so soon? I thought you'd be staying the night. Have you and Remare settled your differences?"

She nodded. "It's late. I do have a job to get to in the morning." She smiled sadly at him. In a few short days, he would be married to a monster of a vampire, one Miranda wouldn't wish on anyone.

"Before you go, I'd like to show you something. Do you have a minute?"

"Of course." She accompanied him to the archives.

He must have sensed she was tired, so he kept the lights low. He led her to the balcony overlooking his vast collection. For a moment, they stood in perfect tranquility, admiring the works of art. "You were surprised when I would put you in charge of my archives?"

"Yes. It speaks volumes of your trust in me. Are you sure I've earned it?"

He smiled. "If I wasn't, I would never have made you *Mistress of the Archives.*"

Miranda laughed at her moniker. "I'm honored. And I will never betray you."

"I know. Look across the open space. Tell me what you see."

"One of the grandest collections I've ever seen. Paintings from centuries past by some of the world's best artists. Unimaginable value. What do you see?"

"Memories. Priceless, as well." His voice, melodic and deep, was soothing to her ears. "Which is your favorite?"

"Not sure I have a favorite. They're all extraordinary in their own right."

"And if I said to choose one for your very own?"

Miranda's jaw dropped. He couldn't have just said what she thought he said. "Surely, you don't mean to say…"

"Theoretically speaking, then. Which one would you covet the most?"

In shock, Miranda turned and looked over the archives. "Honestly, I never considered it." Her eyes skimmed over the many works of arts. The only one that fascinated her was the life-size portrait of his sister, Bianca, and she would never want him to ever part with such a sentimental object. "To me, the paintings were to be admired from a distance. I never had an urge to possess."

"And yet, I did. Close your eyes."

She did.

"Which one immediately comes to mind?"

Bianca! Her breath caught. "I don't know. They're all so beautiful." Which one captivated her the most besides his sister's portrait? "Okay, I think I have one that stands out the most." She opened her eyes and stared at Valadon. "El Greco's *Opening of the Fifth Seal.* His mystical beliefs fascinated me."

"A good choice. Someday, I may gift you with it."

Miranda shook her head. "And why would you do that?"

"Because it will please me to no end." He took her hand. "But come, that is not the reason I asked you here."

"Where are we going?"

He surprised her by whisking her up in his arms and flying down the three flights of stairs. She felt like some phantom was transporting her into another dimension. She heard his laughter and smiled at his joy.

"Close your eyes and promise not to open them until I say so."

Miranda exhaled. "All right."

He carried her a few steps away from the staircase and put her down. She heard him flick a switch and then step back behind her. "Now."

She opened her eyes and gasped. She had to force air into her lungs in order to breathe. The painting was one she'd never seen before. In the background was the fireplace behind her in the reading area. But, instead of the sofa facing the fire, it was facing outward. Valadon stood behind it in a relaxed pose that spoke of his confidence and authority. Miranda was seated on the couch, dressed in a midnight blue gown, she too was smiling and projected an air of knowing, as if she had some special connection to things unseen. Her hand was clasped in another—one who wore a sapphire and gold ring.

Remare, also dressed in dark blue, stood sideways, leaning against the edge of the sofa, his hand reaching back to hold hers. His sexy grin hinted at his wicked sense of humor. Together, they provided an endearing cohesive presence, united in their happiness. The message Valadon was sending with this portrait wasn't lost on her. He'd accepted her relationship with Remare; they were a part of his world. Bound together in loyalty and friendship. And maybe something more. "Thank you."

Valadon leaned closer to her. "I thought you'd enjoy it."

"Asanti painted this."

"Yes, I commissioned it after Remare went to Canada. My way of an apology. If I hadn't reacted in haste, I never would have caused him or you the pain I did."

Miranda searched his green eyes. The High Lord hadn't always been completely truthful with her, but now, she sensed raw honesty. He truly was sorry for the damage he had caused.

"You never had reason to hurt us. We were always loyal to you."

"I understand that, now." He cupped her head and brought her into his embrace. "I should have long ago. You were special to me, and I lost sight of what was really important. I want you and Remare by my side. Always."

"We already are." As she said the words, she felt a bond strengthening between them, as if some secret pact had been reached between her and Valadon and Remare. She sensed the depth of his love and the joy he felt at having them with him. For the first time in a long time, she allowed his emotions to mesh with hers.

Discord had nearly torn them all apart. But, now, in his arms, she felt his vitality, the strength that bound them. He would protect them with all that he was. And all he asked for in return was their loyalty.

That she could give him. And more.

After Miranda left, Valadon perused some of his paintings, but the one that drew him was the portrait of Marlena de Avignon—his beloved, Lena. He stood studying her likeness. She'd been young, then, so full of life, spirit. He could still hear her laughter in the back of his mind, still see the way she smiled. He wondered what she would think of him today if she knew what he'd become. Would she forgive him his many sins? Understand his reasons for all he'd done?

"Rest in peace, Lena. I'm doing the best I can." As he walked away, he realized she would want him to be happy, to go on. Part of him never had. Perhaps it was time to let go of the past and move ahead with his life. He looked around the vastness one last time before shutting off the light. The darkness made him consider what was truly precious to him. His people were his reason for living, his family who he loved beyond measure.

When he neared the kitchen area, he heard sounds coming from within and wondered who would be in there so late at night. "Couldn't sleep?"

Selena swallowed a mouthful of ice cream then continued spooning more into her bowl. She made quite an impression with her hair up in a lopsided ponytail. Wearing a T-shirt, dark leggings and fuzzy slippers, she smiled up at him. "I like staying up late. When ideas come to me about drawing, I have to make the designs or I forget the next day what I'd been dreaming about."

"I see."

"Would you like some rocky road? I think it's the best, but Escher seems to have more chocolate chip mint than anything else.

"Sure." He joined her by the dining room table. "Did Tristan explain the safety measures we employ here in my House?"

She rolled her eyes. "Repeatedly." She started counting on her fingers. "So did Remare, Katya, Morel and Bree."

He didn't want to tell her she was eating Bree's favorite dessert. He'd have to remember to tell Escher to order more. "The rules are in place not only for your safety, but for that of all my Torians."

She grinned. "Rules are meant to be broken."

"Not in my House."

"Okay. I get it." Ice cream covered her upper lip. "You're responsible for my well-being. I understand and promise no more excursions without informing Master Tristan first."

Valadon winced at her words. "Please do not call him that to his face. I don't think he would appreciate it much."

"Fine. I wasn't planning on it." She swallowed another spoonful. "This ice cream is heavenly."

He found the young, irreverent vampire charming. "Are you sad to be away from your home?" He'd heard some students put on weight when they attended school in different regions.

"Nah. Besides, it's not the first time I've been away. Since I started college, I've spent summers interning at the major fashion houses in Milan, Paris and Rome. Dione said, if fashion was my thing, I should study with the best. Did you know, in ancient Greek mythology, Dione was Aphrodite's mother? The goddess of beauty."

"Yes. I did." He'd been collecting Greek artifacts for some time; maybe, one day, he'd show Selena his collection. "Of the fashion houses, which was your favorite?"

"No contest there. Milan, definitely."

"Really? I would have thought you'd say Paris."

"Hell no! Paris may be the largest epi-center for fashion, but I liked Milan. They weren't bound by so many rules and actually supported young designers. Not like that bitch, Vivienna." Her eyes widened when she realized what she'd said. "Oops! Sorry." Another eye roll. "I forgot."

"Not at all. Unlike some other lords, I like my people to be honest. I take it you and the Madame Lord didn't get along?"

"Stuck up...person. She never let me forget she was doing my grandmother a favor by allowing me in her fashion house. She used to peruse my designs and say something snotty like, 'You'll need another century before you can ever hope to join one of the major fashion houses.' She'd make some face like this." Selena squinted her eyes and wrinkled her nose as if she'd stepped in something putrid.

Valadon tried to hold back a laugh. "Yes, I'm told my intended can be judgmental, at times." He wouldn't share with the young vampire just how much he knew about Vivienna. And exactly how vindictive she could be. "She wasn't outwardly cruel with you, though, was she?"

Selena shrugged. "I'm the granddaughter of the Madame Lord of Montreal. But I bet if I wasn't, she would have been. The worst she ever did was invite me to one of her after dinner parties. I swear it was right out of an erotic historical text, like a Bacchanal festival. People going at it in groups. Major eww factor there."

Valadon was well aware of the indulgences of some of the European courts. Centuries ago, he'd participated in a few. "Rest assured, we don't hold celebrations like that here in America. At least not in New York."

"Good to know." She licked her spoon and placed the empty bowl aside. "I could have done without one of her boyfriends trying to cop a feel. I had to knee him in his balls one time for him to get the message. Brandon was such a pig." Her eyebrows rose, and her mouth widened at the realization.

"I take it you mean my brother." Quiet disgust burned in his stomach. "Brandon was never one to show much reserve. I apologize for his misbehavior."

"I told Vivienna he put the moves on me, and she just laughed, said I didn't know what I was missing."

Curious if Vivienna had the audacity to harbor his brother after Brandon had tried to usurp his throne he asked, "When was this?"

"About...two years ago."

He would file the information for a later date. Desiring to change the subject, he pulled her sketchbook closer. "Is this what you've been working on tonight?"

"Yes." Excitement rang out in her voice. "Want to see some of my designs?"

"Of course."

She opened the portfolio and pointed to several outfits he thought were appealing for people her age. Then, she turned a few more pages, and he thought the gowns exquisite, if not daring. "You have flare and courage. I respect that."

"Cesare says I need to harness my talent, not exploit it. I like him and the others I met at Valadon Creations. They seem like a fun group. Dedicated, but not hyper."

"Yes, they are very creative." He turned a page and saw a portrait of Nick reading a book. He met Selena's eyes, wondering if Selena harbored feelings toward his nephew.

She shrugged. "There's some of your other people in there. I doodle when I have time. It helps me think."

Valadon smiled when he found a picture of Remare leaning against a doorframe with his arms crossed and a stern look on his face. It was a pose he'd seen often enough. Selena had also done a drawing of Miranda in the park with blue flames shooting from her hand. Her defiant look intrigued him. His *Elemental* had a fearless streak that captivated and concerned him.

But it was the picture on the next page that had him catching his breath. "Who's this?"

"Oh, that's Professor Deschanel. He's mine and Nick's poetry teacher. All the kids love him. He always makes jokes about poets never receiving the recognition they deserved until after they were dead. But how their memories lived on long after they were gone."

Valadon traced the line of Deschanel's jaw and the curve of his lip. *So much like Lena's. Couldn't be.* He wanted to see the professor's eyes, but they were obscured with the reading glasses. "What color eyes does he have?"

"Not sure. Light, either blue or green. Maybe hazel."

He wished this sketch to be that of his son but knew his yearning and lack of sleep was clouding his judgment. "What's the professor's first name?"

"Vincent. We used to call him Professor V or Vincent until someone told us it was disrespectful. He's traveling in Quebec this summer, seeing the sights, doing the touristy thing."

"You're a wonderful artist. But it's late, now. Come, we should get some sleep." He knew he could use a couple hours of repose but feared the ghosts of the past would haunt him, still.

Chapter Twenty-One

Night had already fallen when Guy de Montglat stealthily entered Chateau Vivienna just outside Paris. How convenient the Madame Lord and her entourage were en route to New York. Only a few servants were still in the house, and those, he'd given the mental command to remain sleeping. Silently, he made his way up to her private boudoir. He scoffed at Vivienna's taste in art. She certainly enjoyed her erotica, but really, couldn't she find pleasure in something else? Perhaps a Monet landscape or a Georgia O'Keeffe.

No matter, he had business to conduct. He'd promised Valadon he would locate his son's whereabouts. He smirked. Most in the court thought Vincent Deschanel was one of Brandon's bastards, but the boy had never shared any of his uncle's more nefarious tendencies. Guy had already known where the vampire was when he'd made his vow to Valadon.

Besides his spies in the homes of the more prominent members of the Council, he'd had listening devices planted, as well. Ryder had installed most of the surveillance. He grinned with paternal pride. His son was getting too damned good at covert activities.

But, then again, he'd learned from the best.

While here, he would search Vivienna's private papers and journals for any birth records or proof of Vincent's lineage. But, in actuality, he was here for a far different reason. He'd long suspected it was Vivienna and Caltrone who had plotted Savinien's demise so that she could become the reigning Lord of Paris. They thought Savinien had died at the bottom of the Seine, but the ancient had survived with a bit of help and was getting ready to wake from nearly a century of sleep.

He wouldn't bother with her desk. Ryder had already gone through the secret compartments. And the safe behind her portrait. Vivienna thought herself clever with her agents in competing fashion houses. He wondered what they would do if they discovered she was guilty of corporate espionage. But that was not his concern.

With the secrets she kept, she would keep any correspondence hidden away where no one would think to look. But close enough to peruse when she felt the need. Somewhere only she would have access to. Or so she thought. He scrutinized her bookcases. He could feel a slight breeze on his hand. He used his device to locate the mechanism and pulled the latch. The bookcase opened. The scanner detected no other alarms in place.

He didn't have to go far. He noticed the slight deviation in the side wall where a few bricks were loose. He pulled them away to reveal a hidden compartment containing a metal chest resembling an old-fashioned jewelry box. "Whatever have you been hiding, Vivienna?" He was tempted to leave one of his salamander figurines behind as he occasionally did when he was known as *Le Cameleon*. But, then, she and the rest of the High Court would know of his resurrection. And that would simply not do.

At least, not yet. He quickly replaced the bricks as he found them and disappeared as silently as he'd arrived.

***

"Open the door."

"Give me a minute. Okay, got it. I'm glad Miranda's letting us use her cottage." Orion unlocked the door and flicked on the lights for Bastien, who was carrying their supplies. In his clumsiness, Orion nearly tripped on the rug. "God, it feels good to get away from the craziness of Paris." He folded the sheets that had kept the furniture from accumulating dust and put them in the closet.

"Well, I told you *not* to give the free concert in the city park." Bastien placed their box of groceries on the kitchen table. "You wouldn't have gotten mauled by your fans if you'd listened to me."

"Y'know, I just didn't realize how popular my music's become." He helped put some of the perishables away in the fridge. "I know you and Valadon have propelled my career, but it still surprises me, like I'm living in someone else's dream. It's so surreal. I'm afraid I'm going to wake up, someday, and discover it's all been an illusion." Orion shook his head. "I can't believe I'm actually famous. It's kind of a shock."

"It shouldn't be." Bas smiled up at him. "You're good. You should see yourself on stage. It's as if you really come alive there. You hold the audience spellbound."

"Thanks."

"No, really. I watched from the side. The way the lights hit you, it looked like you were glowing." Bas popped open a beer. "And your voice. Holy shit! I never thought anyone was that good live. I always thought producers enhanced the quality. But, damn, you hit notes I don't think mere mortals can hear. Rare, my man."

Orion thought of the one singer he opened for and, sometimes, sang duets with. "Except Tiseira."

"Yeah, except Tiseira." Bas handed him a beer. "But she's a vampire and has been a musician far longer than you."

Orion took a swig of his beer and relaxed. When his fans had rushed him at the park, bad memories of being attacked in New York had echoed in his mind. "Thanks for helping me escape. For a moment, I got worried there. Good thing we're fast on our feet."

"It's kind of my job to keep you safe." Bas put a hand on his shoulder. "I'd get scared, too, if the mad horde started rushing me."

Orion made his way back inside the living room. Even though it was late spring and fairly warm, he still wanted to build a fire. "Hey, do you know how to start a fire? We have a fireplace back in New York, but we're not allowed to burn anything. City ordinances. Too much pollution."

"Yeah, all our fireplaces in House Valadon are either gas or electric. I saw some logs piled up against the side of the house. Bring in a few."

After Orion dropped the wood near the hearth, Bas bent down and made sure the flue was open and then went to work with the kindling. In moments, they had the fire going.

"Thanks. I know it's not really cold out. I just like the idea of watching the flames."

"Yeah, me, too."

"It is so friggen nice here." Orion leaned back against the cushions of the couch. "I think I'm gonna ask Miranda if I can buy the place. She doesn't come here, anymore. Said it has too many sad memories, but she doesn't want to let it go, either."

"Yeah, she told me that, too, last time we were here." Bas sat beside him. "I told her my parents have people who could handle all the paperwork if she ever decides."

"I like the country." Orion felt a contentment he didn't usually feel. With Bas and him just sitting, having a couple of beers and enjoying the fire, life was good. "The air is so clean out here, and we have the woods out back to go exploring in. When the moon is full, it must be great to get a good run in."

"You'd like that wouldn't you, wolf?"

"Yeah. During the full moon, we change, and to be able to explore new terrain, to hunt, the instinct is very strong. It's exhilarating."

"Man, I'd love to watch you run. I first saw you in wolf form the last time we were in Paris. The way you tried to save me from my sister from hell after she tried impaling me with a hot poker."

"I went ballistic when I smelled your flesh burning." Orion barely kept his claws from manifesting. "I still can't believe your own sister did that to you."

"Yeah, I had a hard time, too. But she's made her choices. Isabelle was always out for herself. Even when we were young."

Orion couldn't imagine what Bas must have gone through, realizing what a monster his sister was. "I just wanted to thank you for helping me. It rattled me." Orion didn't talk much about when he'd first come to New York, but he felt compelled to confide in his best friend. "I never told you about the time I got jumped in Manhattan, did I?"

"You were attacked?

"Yeah. Stupid, I guess. I sat in at one of the local bars. Got to sing a few songs I'd written. Tips were really good that night. I didn't think anything of it. It was late, and I only lived a few blocks away, so I was walking home. Out of nowhere, I got jumped by three rogue werewolves. They must have seen the money I made that night and were waiting for me. At first, I thought they were only going to rob me, but they must have been feral. They tore into my flesh pretty bad, left me for dead. Not long after, Miranda found me. She lived up the block, so she got Lizandra to tend to me and brought me into her house to recuperate."

"Risky, with a wounded Were."

"Yeah, but she kept vigil over me until I healed. I owe her."

"I know." Bas rubbed his head. "Kinda hard to imagine her with Remare. Tristan texted me he's back, and all's well with Valadon."

"Seriously?"

"Yeah, supposedly he was on some covert mission up in Canada. Also, Valadon's idea of a punishment since they were sneaking around behind his back."

"Does Valadon still love her?"

"Don't know. But, from what I hear, all is forgiven. Anyway, he's getting married, and we gotta be back soon so as not to miss the ceremony."

"Still can't believe he's marrying that bitch."

"Yeah, it came as a shock to all of us. But Magritte has been after Valadon for some time. She never forgave him for leaving the European Council. That's why she picked the one woman Valadon can't stand."

"Pretty long to hold a grudge."

"Vampires have long memories. Rumor was Magritte had the hots for him something fierce. When he left, it was something like a slap in the face. She never got over it. I suspect she's been planning something like this for a good long while."

"Vindictive much?"

"Yeah, but my money's on Valadon. He'll figure something out. Or do as much damage control as possible. Anyhow, why don't you get a nap in? I'll cook dinner. You're in for a treat, wolf. I'm making medallions of beef ala Sebastien. You'll love it."

"If it's anything like the way Escher cooks, I'm sure I will."

Bastien hit him playfully with a pillow. "Hey, I'm a pretty good cook."

Orion laughed. "I didn't say you weren't."

"Go! I'll call you when dinner's ready."

***

"Our spy reports Valadon has reconciled with Remare." Gazing out the window of her jet, Vivienna was able to make out the lights of New York's skyline as she spoke to Magritte on her phone. "I told you their quarrel wouldn't last long. Especially over a woman, a human at that. They've been together far too long for any lingering discord. Your hopes of House Valadon becoming weakened due to division seem to be dashed."

"No worries. I know what he covets most and have never shied away from using his weaknesses against him. Our agents also report Valadon has been spending some alone time with the woman in question." Magritte's voice turned acerbic. "She's been spotted leaving Valadon's bedroom in the early hours of the morning."

Vivienna hated when Magritte took little jabs at her. All that would change once Caltrone became chancellor. As Queen of All Vampires, it was true Magritte held incredible influence, but the real power lay in the jurisdiction of the chancellor. Once Syrio stepped down and Caltrone took control, things were going to change. "Let him have his little indulgences. Once we're wed, he'll be honor bound. He loved me once; he'll love me, again. Miranda Crescent is of little consequence to me."

"I hear Vincent is traveling in Quebec. Dione has done an excellent job seeing to his well-being. He has a new lover and is quite happy living in Montreal. You were wise to send him to Canada. Ever since I informed him he has a son, Valadon's agents have been working overtime scouring the French countryside searching for any proof of his whereabouts."

"They will never find what they are looking for. I destroyed all records of his birth long ago." Vivienna never should have confided to Magritte she had adopted Valadon's son. But she never thought her confidant would turn against her. She should have known better. There was little Magritte wouldn't do to achieve her ends. And fewer people she wouldn't use to attain her goals. Vincent was Vivienna's son, the one good thing in her life. She would do anything to protect him, even if it meant circumventing their queen.

"We'll be landing in New York in a few minutes." Eric joined his mistress. "Arik informs me all preparations have been made for our arrival. There will be an informal dinner in your honor, and arrangements are being completed for the formal reception."

As one of Vivienna's assistants, he'd been privy to certain conversations containing information the High Lord would find invaluable. His tenure in her court was coming to an end. Never again would he allow himself to be taken in by a woman's charm. Her outward beauty masked a devious mind and a cold heart.

He knew what he was planning was dangerous. He didn't care. He'd spent the better part of a century being used as nothing more than a sex toy. Vivienna's lies and empty promises had been just that, nothing more than a means to an end. But he'd learned from her. Watched how power games were played and how people were used as pawns.

His days of being a pawn were almost over.

But the one he was concerned for most was Miranda Crescent. Magritte and Vivienna saw the woman as a possible threat to their plans, a subtle affront to their beauty by the High Lord, even if he hadn't had any such intention. Of the two, Magritte worried him the most. She was not mercurial like Vivienna; she bided her time and conspired. He listened in on her conversations, made himself nearly invisible, but her cunning was matched by her stealth.

However, he smirked, as difficult as it had been, he'd been able to procure one valuable piece of information he intended to use as his entrance into House Valadon. The trick, now, was getting access to the High Lord. With all the wedding preparations in progress, it would be a challenge. He would seek out Miranda and hope she remembered him enough to offer assistance. He'd liked her from the moment he met her. Unlike Magritte and Vivienna, Miranda did not delight in torturing or manipulating others.

Hell, he'd offered to pleasure her, but she would not take advantage of his low status in Vivienna's house. That was not so of the many other guests the Madame Lord entertained. He closed his eyes in memory and breathed deep. He hoped the High Lord was wise enough to subvert Magritte's games. Everything he'd heard about Valadon said he was intelligent. He'd have to be to deal with what was coming.

But much to their loathing, Valadon had once outfoxed them. The High Lord had had to sign an agreement forking over a substantial amount to the High Court, but he'd secured his freedom. Eric had already paid a terrible price with his blood and sweat. Pain and humiliation no one should ever know, but he, too, would secure what he valued most.

Chapter Twenty-Two

"Dinner was great, thanks." Orion finished drying off the last of the plates.

"Escher has us all watching some cooking show." Bas nodded. "I even caught Remare taking notes one time." He gestured with his steaming cup. "Does this bother you?"

"Why should it? I know you're a vampire. Besides, I've seen you drink blood before. The fridge in your apartment is loaded with the bagged and bottled stuff."

Bas shrugged. "It unnerves some people." He glanced outside the back door. "Hey, you wanna go for a walk. It's a clear night out."

"Sure. I could use stretching my legs some, especially after the meal you made."

"Ha, you Weres have the highest metabolism I've ever seen."

"True, we're big protein eaters. Let's go." When he stepped outside, he breathed in the cool, crisp mountain air. "There are so many different scents in the air. I can smell lavender, currant and...grapes."

"That's because the area is loaded with them. This is wine country. There are vineyards all over the place. Let's hike there." Bas pointed at the ridge. "I want to see what's up there."

They headed out. "Man, I miss this. I mean, I love living in New York, but the only place where we have any semblance of nature is Central Park. But here, it's just so great. Clean, unpolluted."

"Yeah, I like getting outdoors as much as I can." Bas exhaled. "Most of the work I do is indoors, so this feels pretty good."

They walked along in peaceful companionship, enjoying the sounds of nature. A few birds cawing, a rabbit hopping in the distance. As a Were, Orion's night vision was exceptional, so was his hearing. He imagined it was the same for Bastien.

Bas turned and smirked at him. "You up for a little exercise, wolf? I'll race you to the top of the ridge."

"You're on! Unless you need me to give you a head start."

"Fuck you! Vampires are faster than Weres."

"In your dreams, we can best you any day of the week; that's why we win all the hockey games."

"Oh, really? I thought it was because you cheated."

"I *never* cheat!" Orion feigned being insulted. "Don't have to. Can't say the same for some wolves, though."

"Okay, on the count of three. Ready?"

Orion nodded.

"Three." Bas took off flying through the woods as if he had radar, dodging trees, fallen logs and bushes. Orion was impressed with his speed. But vamps had nothing on the natural grace of the Weres. He took off after him. Soon, they were neck and neck, loping through the forest. The exhilaration of the run, of stretching his muscles, had him howling in joy. When they reached the clearing, both were out of breath and over-heated from the surge of adrenaline.

"Check out the stream. I bet the water is cold but refreshing." Bas walked to the creek and cupped some and brought it to his lips. "It's peaceful here. I like it."

Orion squatted down beside him. He used a handful of water to cool down his face. "How deep do you think the creek is?"

"Don't know. A couple of feet at least. Whoa!"

Orion didn't wait for him to finish. "C'mon! Let's get a swim in." Stripping off his jeans and T-shirt, he jumped in the stream, buck-ass naked. "It feels great." He felt like a kid, again, and started laughing as he splashed about.

A moment later, Bas joined him. "A little cool for my taste, but you're right, very refreshing."

They swam a couple of laps until they tired and then made their way back to the embankment. "Check out the precipice overlooking the water. We can sit there for a little while."

Naked, but dripping water, Bas used his shirt to dry off and then laid it on the protruding rock formation.

Orion followed suit. He rolled up his jeans and used them to form a pillow. "God, look at the stars. They're so bright. Can't see them in New York."

"Yeah, it's beautiful up here. Half-moon. I guess you won't be changing into your wolf form any time soon."

"I don't need the full moon to change. The instinct is strongest, then, but we can change any time we want."

"I've seen you twice in wolf form. You have one helluva pelt. Your black fur is thick, yet smooth. I bet it glistens in the moonlight."

"I guess it does." Orion raised one brow. "Is that your way of asking to see me turn?"

"I can't imagine you appreciating anyone asking. Vamps don't like showing their fangs either."

Orion considered his unsaid request. Anyone else he would have said no to, but not Bas. "If you want, I'll change. We usually don't let others watch, but I understand the curiosity." He rolled over on his side and breathed deep. The transformation didn't hurt, but he wasn't used to a non-Were watching him. His pelt was the first to slowly break through the skin on his back. He looked down at his hands and watched as the claws emitted. His feet contracted into the paws of a wolf. Extending his jaw, his snout emerged, and his wolf ears took shape. The process was gradual. Each section of his body steadily contorting to his animal shape.

In complete wolf form, he looked at Bastien who sat up staring at his new body. Orion tilted his head as if to say, "So, what do you think?"

"Amazing!" Smiling, Bas ran a hand across his back. "Fucking amazing. Handsome wolf. Do you have any idea just how remarkable you are?"

Orion nudged him with his nose. His way of saying knock it off. But, then again, he wondered how many vampires actually witnessed Weres turning. No wonder Bas was enthralled. He figured if Bas ever turned into a bat, he'd be equally transfixed. A howl broke from his throat, loud and long. Whimsically, he jumped on top of Bas and licked him. Playfully, he nipped at him and pushed him against the hard stone.

"Okay, okay!" Bas laughed as he wrestled with him. "I asked to see you change, not to get slobbered on."

Orion lay back down and slowly changed back to his human form. He shuddered then stayed silent for a minute. "Your impressions?"

"I think you're incredible. More than you'll ever know."

Orion felt the draw between them growing stronger. Despite his best attempt to ignore it, his cock hardened. He'd always been attracted to the vampire but had tried to keep his emotions hidden. They'd talked around their feelings, but Bas had made it clear his family had expectations for him. And family was very important to him. Still, he searched Bastien's eyes. "How incredible?"

Bas lay down on his back. "Enough to complicate my best laid plans."

Orion stretched beside him. "Sorry."

Bas linked his hands over his stomach. "Nothing to be sorry about."

They stared up at the mystical night sky.

"Simple never held much attraction for me."

Orion wasn't sure he was hearing Bas right. "Meaning?"

"I know you want more." He blew out a breath. "I said 'difficult', not impossible. Just the timing is off.'

"How?"

"I'm not ready for anything hot and heavy just yet."

"You're afraid of what people will think?"

Bas scoffed. "Please. Half the people at House Valadon already think we're sleeping together."

"And that doesn't bother you?"

"No. I'd hardly be the first, and I'm sure I won't be the last."

Orion hesitated in asking his next question. "Your family?"

"Aristocrats, vampire and human alike, have had gay lovers since long before I was born. Goes back to the ancient Greeks and Romans, before that even. Hell, half my father's friends have had male lovers at one time or another. It's no big deal."

"And yet?"

Bas faced him. "I'm not the only one who needs consideration. You're on the verge of becoming a phenomenal success with your music. I'm not going to do anything to fuck it up. And, right now, things are strained at ValCorp. People got twitchy with Remare being away for months; Valadon is set to marry the bitch from hell. It's just not a good time."

"Someday?" Orion grinned mischievously.

Bas reached behind Orion's hair and massaged his nape. "Maybe."

Whatever magic was between them intensified because Bas leaned in and kissed him. Torturously slow, erotic as hell. Orion's heart beat heavy against his chest.

Bas broke from the kiss and slid his lips over Orion's jaw. "Yeah, someday. Just not today. So, your compass can stop pointing north."

Orion frowned at his erection. "Unlike yours, my 'compass' has a mind of its own. This doesn't arouse you?" He pointed to himself and then Bas. "This, whatever it is, between us?"

"I'm aroused. I've just had centuries to learn reserve. Trust me, my mind is working overtime."

Orion smiled. "Good to know. I thought I was the only one."

Bas gave him a smoldering look. "You're not alone anymore."

"You want to hear something funny? When I first came to New York, I was clanless, a lone wolf. I tried to tell myself, it didn't matter. But it did. I couldn't go home. I never really felt I belonged there. So, I buried myself in my music. Even when I joined Black Star Clan, I had a home, friends. But something was always missing." Orion searched the sky. "I like living with Miranda. She's like my sister. Family. You're going to laugh, but honestly, I feel more at home in House Valadon than I've ever felt anywhere else."

Bas looked dumbfounded. "Seriously."

"I know it sounds strange, even to me. But it's the truth."

Bas seemed to be processing what he said. "I'm glad. As far as I'm concerned, you belong there as much as I do."

"Thanks." A sudden breeze picked, up and the trees swayed around them. "We should probably get back."

"Yeah, good idea."

After dressing, they walked back. When they reached the cottage, Orion felt more tired than he'd expected. The swim and the fresh air had been refreshing, but now, he just wanted to sleep. Not watching where he was going, he tripped on the same plank of wood he did when they first entered the house.

"You okay?"

"Yeah, hand me that hammer I saw in the drawer near the door."

Bas found it and brought it to him. "The wood is warped. Either from age or humidity. I don't think nailing it harder is going to do any good."

Orion wiggled the plank. "It sure is loose." Before he knew it, the plank buckled and revealed a hole underneath.

"These old homes go back centuries. I had the impression when we first got here, this part was the original house and the living area was added on. That's why the floor is uneven."

Orion sniffed the ground underneath and reached inside. "There's something here."

"What?"

Orion lifted a box wrapped in burlap. When he removed the covering, it appeared to be a small steel chest with roses engraved on the top and sides. He undid the lid and the scent of dried roses immediately assaulted him. There were old letters made of vellum and parchment. He took one out. "It's in French." He handed the bundle to Bas and inspected the rest of the contents, which consisted of jewelry, a hair comb, and other small objects.

"Love letters. Probably the lover of some married aristocrat. Centuries ago, monarchs often provided their mistresses with country homes, as well as apartments in the cities."

Orion found a ring buried on the bottom of the chest. He wiped away the grit. It was a black diamond with a torch etched on the side. "I might be wrong, but isn't that Valadon's emblem?"

Bas examined the ring. "Holy shit!" His breaths came faster. He went back to reading the letters. "Oh. My. God! Do you know what we found?"

"Not exactly."

"Valadon had a lover centuries ago. A human he loved very much. These are her letters. Look." Bas pointed to the signature.

"Lena."

"We gotta get these to Valadon. The roads here are dangerous at night. There's no lights, and some of the turns are tricky. At first light, we're out of here."

"Agreed."

They bundled up everything and replaced the warped plank. Orion did the best he could nailing the wood back into place.

Once upstairs, Bas put the small chest in his backpack. He retrieved a clean pair of boxers and after putting them on, he slid between the sheets.

"You want me to sleep in the other bedroom?"

"Yeah."

Orion turned to go.

"Come here, you fucker." Bas laughed. "Boxers stay on. Got it?!"

"Yeah, yeah. Where have I heard that before?" Searching his own backpack, he found and then slid on a clean pair. He pulled the blankets over his torso.

He lay on his back for a moment. After a while, he spooned Bastien from behind. "This okay?"

"Yeah, just don't keep poking me in the back all night long. It'll be dawn in few hours, and I want to sleep."

"Okay." For the first time in a long time, Orion was happy. He didn't have to have sex with Bas. He enjoyed just being near him. His friendship, their conversations meant the world to him. And, for now, that was enough. He yawned loud enough his jaw cracked.

"And no snoring."

"I don't snore, vamp."

"Do too, wolf. Loudly."

Orion laughed. He really did snore.

Not far from the cottage, in the shadow of a tall tree, Ryder lowered the binoculars. He'd wondered how long it would take the wolf and the vampire to discover the box. Hell, he'd even pried open the wood plank just enough so it didn't look obvious. "They found it, just as you knew they would."

"Thank you. All is going to plan. And now, we wait." Guy de Montglat nodded at his son. "There is one more mission I could use your assistance on. Interested?"

"Who's the target?" he asked, but as usual, his father's face betrayed nothing, but a knowing grin.

Chapter Twenty-Three

"Why are you here?" Rosalyn asked Miranda.

"Hey, I was invited." She glanced around the massive ballroom at the ambassadors and their spouses dressed in haute couture. Tonight's event was in honor of Valadon's greatest supporters and allies. His way of saying thanks to those who had remained loyal to him through the centuries.

"I meant, why are you here by the doors and not by that handsome vampire with the goatee?"

"He's playing diplomat, and I got tired of being arm candy and smiling at everyone. I swear I feel like my cheeks are about to split." Now, Miranda knew how it felt when she'd brought Gabriel to some of the museum's galas. He must have been dying inside but never said a word.

"I swear he gets more handsome with age."

Miranda slanted her friend a look. "Shouldn't you be with your hubby?"

"I was. He's resting comfortably. Gabriel's with him, now."

Miranda had worried about Jason. "No complications?"

"None, but we pretty much didn't expect any. He'd taken my vein many times before, so it was not a shock to his system."

Miranda breathed a sigh of relief. Watching the transition had rattled her.

"Besides, I needed a break and wanted to see how everyone liked the décor."

"Place looks wonderful, Rosalyn. You did a fantastic job. The Rainbow Room has nothing on you. Look at that view outside. I swear it's more awesome than the Top of the Rock.

"I think so, too. Oh, look, your man is signaling you."

Miranda turned to see Remare gesturing for her. "So he is."

"Go, I just stopped in to see how everything was going. I want to get back to Jason. Give Remare my regards."

"Sure. My same to Jason."

After Rosalyn blew her a kiss, Miranda made her way to Remare. She was amazed he affected her as much as he did. Whatever electrically charged atoms were in the air around them pulsed and became more potent the closer she got to him. She knew he was handsome, virile, but Remare had a presence no other did. He vibrated with life more than any other man in the room. It had always been so, right from the beginning.

She'd had her doubts about their relationship. His life was full of danger, covert operations and parties with ambassadors. She stayed safe inside her cubicle at the museum, researching artists and paintings. He went out on surveillance missions. She hung out at Werehaven with her friends. So many uncertainties had plagued her mind, but the one constant was the love they shared.

Maybe they wouldn't last the ages, but for now, she was happy. And intended to stay that way. "You called?"

Remare's dark eyes glinted with amusement; he took her hand and kissed her knuckles. "I missed you. I'm glad you came tonight. You look beautiful as ever."

"You do realize I own several formal dresses."

His grin widened. "I thought you could do with a few new ones."

"I do know how to shop for myself."

"And when was the last time you did?"

He had her there. She couldn't remember. "I hate shopping." There were so many other things she'd rather do: spend time with friends, watch old movies, do a bit of gardening on her roof. Anything but drag herself from boutique to boutique. She didn't know how other women had the patience to go through the whole process.

"I know. That's why I had your gown made for you."

"It's lovely. Thank you. But, next time, let me choose which one to wear."

"Hmm." His non-committal answer worried her.

"Everything going all right tonight?" She noticed several men and women wearing the little ear plugs with the spiral cords. "Do you have more security here or am I just noticing them more?"

"With these many foreign visitors, it was prudent to have more of our mid-level Torians in attendance." He slid his hand down her arm. "Will you stay with me tonight?"

Her body shivered at the minor contact. "Can't. As much as I would love to, I have to get up early for work."

"Could you not go in late?" His voice was seductive. "I would make it very worthwhile."

Miranda returned his smile. She had no doubt whatsoever he could do that and so much more. She liked it when Remare flirted with her. Big badass vampire could be charming when he wanted to be. Sometimes, all it took was just a look, a simple gesture or touch that sparked the connection between them. Those penetrating brown eyes of his bore into hers with a wealth of sensual promise. His scent conjured memories of nights between black silk sheets, of passion and pleasure. But the one thing that always turned her on was his voice.

Remare's tones could be threatening, at times—especially when he was angered, but he could also be sensuous, friendly and compassionate.

Sometimes, simply his companionship was enough for her to feel content. That there was hope in this crazy, messed up world. She stroked the line of his beard and eyed his lips. She was about to kiss him when suddenly the doors to the ballroom whooshed open, and a woman, more stunning and mesmerizing than any other, entered with such a flourish all heads turned in her direction. Her metallic gold and red dress hugged every curve, every dip of her body. Diamonds and rubies fit for a queen wove around her neck. Her raven hair was piled high with jewel-studded combs, and her flawless complexion gleamed in the light.

But it was her violet eyes that held the attention of everyone in the room. Vivienna.

Miranda's breath caught in her throat. "I thought vampires didn't wear red."

"Usually not. But I think Vivienna has a different intent."

It wasn't blood Vivienna wanted to convey; it was passion. And the Madame Lord made a bee line for one man only, Valadon.

"Wasn't this party for the ambassadors and their family?"

"It was. Vivienna always did like to make an entrance. I'd say she hasn't lost any of her skill."

"Jesus." Her dress shimmered with every step. "She looks like a goddess."

"We were informed of her arrival, but thought, after such a long plane ride, she'd remain in her hotel room until tomorrow. Come, we must offer our greetings."

Miranda hung back. "I think it better if you go. We didn't exactly hit it off the last time we met."

"Are you sure? Sooner or later, you will have to meet her."

"Let it be later." Miranda quickly kissed Remare. "I'm outta here."

He clasped her hand. "Get home safe."

"I will."

Once in the lobby, Miranda made her way down the hall when she ran into some of Vivienna's entourage. Valadon's guards seemed a little dazed, and Miranda had no doubt Vivienna had used her mental abilities on them. That would explain the lack of notification to Remare or any of the other Torians.

One redheaded man, sitting farther apart from the others in the shadows, turned in her direction. "Miranda."

She remembered the handsome vampire she'd met in Vivienna's home. The scars on his back from multiple whippings were unforgettable. She hadn't trusted the vampire when she'd first met him. He seemed different from the others, but deception was a way of life with some vampires. And they were good at it. "Eric. Long way from home."

"More than you know." He rose and hugged her. "I was hoping to see you." Careful not to be noticed, his voice was barely a whisper. "We have to talk."

She kept her voice equally low. "Not now. I'm on my way out."

"Please, sometime soon." Eric's hushed tone was urgent. "It's important. I need to speak with you. You have to get me an audience with the High Lord. I have information he needs."

"Why don't you tell him yourself? Why do you need me?"

"I can't approach him. He doesn't know me."

Miranda wasn't about to get sucked into whatever game Vivienna was playing. She'd earned Valadon's and Remare's suspicions once, she wasn't going to do it again. "Call him, then. If you can't get through, one of his people will relay the message."

"No!" he insisted. "This is private." Eric looked pained, and the pleading in his barely audible voice nearly undid her. "Please, Miranda. I helped you once. Remember?"

How could she forget? When Vivienna had been entertaining her guests at some sort of Bacchanalian festival, she tried to force Miranda's attendance. It was Eric who had pulled her away. She eyed the curious looks the others were giving them. "I'll think about it."

She was about to turn when the atmosphere around her suddenly turned frigid. Only one other time did she encounter such cold signifying an ancient. But Mulciber was dead, killed by the High Lord in a bloody battle for supremacy. This one was no less powerful, the pitch so intense the hairs on her arms rose in silent warning danger was close.

Straightening her spine, she slowly turned to face the vampire behind her.

Magritte, the Queen of All Vampires, stood smiling. But there was no warmth emanating from her, only razor-sharp calculation and an underlying current of animosity.

And that hatred was directed at Miranda.

***

Valadon watched as the crowd parted for the Madame Lord of Paris. Whispers of her beauty traveled quickly through the room. He had to admit she was stunning, but he knew beneath her exquisite façade beat the heart of a viper. "Welcome to New York, Vivienna. Had I known you were attending tonight's celebration, I would have sent proper escort."

His words were not lost on those around him. She was here without invitation, and he'd made certain his people knew that.

"I'm sure." She laughed. "But I thought you would enjoy my surprise."

"I take it your trip here was without incident."

"Of course. You'll have to do something about security. I wished to see the design floor, but your guards refused to allow me entrance. I was hoping to move my headquarters here."

Cesare, his chief designer, was standing only a few feet away and looked like he was going to have a heart attack. "I was under the impression you'd be working from your Manhattan office."

"For now." Her smile couldn't conceal the fangs she was proudly displaying. "But we can discuss business tomorrow. There's so much we need to talk about."

Not as far as Valadon was concerned. If she thought to take up office space in his building, she was sadly mistaken. Under no circumstances would he allow that to happen.

"So, the intended bride has arrived." Remare eyed Vivienna as one would a dangerous animal in the wild. "You're looking well, Vivienna."

"Remare. Handsome as ever. Did you enjoy your sojourn in Canada? A little chilly in the wintertime for my tastes, but you always did have a predilection for the cold."

Before the barbs escalated any further, Valadon decided to usher Vivienna to the side for a private conversation. "May I remind you, you are a guest in my House and subject to the same rules all my people follow."

The red rims around her irises pulsed. "I'm a queen or did you forget?"

"And still subject to my laws. What did you do to my guards?"

"A little haze to keep them from ruining my surprise."

Valadon reigned in his temper. "You will not use mental capabilities on any of my people. If you do, you will suffer the consequences. Am I making myself clear enough?"

"Valadon. You surprise me." She pouted. "I thought you'd be happy to see me. Magritte could have chosen far worse for you. I think she wishes she had named herself as your intended. Now, wouldn't that be a nightmare?"

"You're right. We do have much to discuss. But not here or now. This party is for the ambassadors, not you. If you make a scene, I'll have you escorted out."

She laughed. "And, still, you don't trust me. I'm going to be your wife. Don't you think a husband should have a certain amount of trust in his spouse?"

"I know you too well to think you could ever be trusted."

She laughed. "That was long ago. I'll tell you a secret." She leaned in close to whisper. "My entourage is downstairs. Magritte has just joined them, and they will be coming up shortly."

Valadon exhaled slowly and refused to allow the tic in his jaw to become visible. It was good he'd been taught discipline under the most severe of circumstances. By the Queen herself. The next two weeks were going to be a crucible of his patience and fortitude. "Then, we should greet them accordingly."

Chapter Twenty-Four

Miranda stood staring at the Queen. If Magritte was waiting for her to curtsy, she was going to have a long wait. Miranda didn't bow down to anyone. Not even Valadon. Though, she had to one time when Remare pulled her down beside him when Valadon had been elevated to High Lord. She smiled inwardly; at least Remare had provided a pillow before her knee went crashing to the floor.

Miranda eyed Magritte's bodyguards, and her heart rate sped up. She'd been weak once, but she'd trained with Lizandra and Gavin. And, now, with Montglat. After Guy returned from his cruise, Miranda had doubled her efforts at mastering her *Elemental* gifts. She'd become a lot stronger than either Guy or she had expected in such a short amount of time and was reasonably sure she could handle herself.

Magritte approached her. "Valadon's mistress, I presume."

"Archivist. And friend." Miranda shook her head. "Nothing more."

"Of course not. We're here to see the High Lord. Are you on your way up or out?"

Miranda didn't like the implied snark in Magritte's question nor the tension between her and Magritte's followers. "I'm leaving. But do enjoy the party. The banquet room has been properly decorated. I think even a queen would approve."

Magritte laughed. "So, you do know me. I wasn't sure if you did. Eric, make the appropriate introductions."

"Miranda Crescent, this is our Queen, Magritte, and ruling member of our High Council."

"A pleasure." Miranda nodded. "I saw one of your portraits at Madame Lord Vivienna's chateau. As impressive as it was, it doesn't compare with the reality." She heard the elevator ding as the doors opened.

Magritte sighed. "Imitations rarely have the fortitude to compete with the actual. Will you be attending Valadon's wedding?"

Miranda cordially smiled. "Presumably."

The Queen of All Vampires must have grown bored because she said, "Then, I'm sure we'll meet, again. Good evening. Eric."

Eric's eyes widened, and then, he bowed toward Miranda and joined Magritte's entourage near the elevator.

Before the doors closed, Miranda spied the steel in the older vampire's eyes. This was one vampire not to cross. The woman's façade was all proper etiquette and refinement, but underneath, Miranda sensed a monster—someone capable of great acts of cruelty if it suited her purpose. And she had no doubt it had, many times over.

Her favorite redheaded Were came beside her. "Staying out of trouble?"

She smirked. "Don't I always?"

"No. Not hardly." Gavin shook his head. "As a matter of fact, I can't think of anyone else I know who gets herself into as much mischief as you do."

"Oh, please. I've been on my best behavior for a long time now." She noted the spiral cord over his shoulder. "Remare tap you to do security?"

"The vampires thought having new faces at these receptions would be beneficial." He took her arm as they made for the exit. "Remare asked me to escort you home."

"I think I can manage on my own. He worries too much. But I would enjoy the company." She hooked her arm around his. "I'm parked on the street. Garage was packed. *Someone,*" she slanted him a look, "took my spot."

"*Someone* had to get here early to go over the schematics with Morel."

Miranda missed Gavin's friendly banter and was glad for the opportunity to hang with him. "Take West Side Highway to my place. I want to look out at the Hudson River."

"Okay. There's probably too much traffic on Church and Canal Streets, anyway."

After pulling onto the highway, Miranda opened the window and let some of the cool, fresh air off the river roll in. "I like it here." Laying back against the head rest, she breathed in deep. "Remare keeps a boat over there." She pointed to the docks they were passing.

"You and he are pretty close, now, aren't you?"

"Yeah. If you had told me, years ago, I would hook up with a vampire, I'd have said you were insane."

"You're happy with him, and he with you. The two of you practically start glowing when one mentions the other's name."

She laughed. "God, are we that obvious?"

"Not to an ordinary observer. But I've seen you with him several times, now. At Werehaven, mostly. You two seem to click. I'm happy for you."

Miranda wished she could say the same for him. Gavin just didn't have the 'glow' he used to when he was with Lizandra. She hoped, one day, he got it back. "Thanks. There are times when we want to brain each other. But, then…there are other times when…" She casually waved her hand in the air.

"Yeah, I get it." He pulled onto the exit leading to her home.

When he parked her Jeep in front of her brownstone, she said, "I'd invite you in, but I have work tomorrow."

"Don't worry, sweetness, I wasn't expecting an invite. I'll catch a cab up on Seventh." After locking the car, he handed her keys back.

"Gavin?"

"Yes?"

She knew she was sticking her nose where it didn't belong. "I wish you were back with Lizandra."

"Yeah, me, too." He kissed her forehead. "Unfortunately, my queen doesn't agree."

"Do you think, someday, she might change her mind?"

His crooked smile nearly undid her. "There's always hope, Miranda."

God, she hoped so. She leaned in and kissed his cheek then watched as he turned and disappeared up her street.

Once inside, she flicked on the lights and tossed her purse on the table. It was only then she realized she hadn't checked her text messages in a while. One was from Felicity: "Miranda, I have to be in the vicinity of your museum tomorrow. Would you like to have lunch at the cafeteria? Say, about noon?"

Sure. Felicity was one of her best friends. She knew her former mentor must be feeling a little lonesome with Guy out of town. She quickly texted her back then made for the bedroom.

***

"So, have you seen your fill of the city, yet?" Nick finished eating his sandwich and pushed away from the table at Angelique's, a café popular with NYU students.

"Not completely." Vincent leaned back in his chair. "I still think the Statue of Liberty was the most awesome of all the sites you showed me. You do know it was a gift from the French."

Nick rolled his eyes. "Yes, I was actually aware of that."

Smiling, Vincent teased, "Though, it doesn't compare with the Eiffel Tower and the boat rides on the Seine."

"We took the New York City cruise around the complete island of Manhattan; how could you possibly not be impressed?"

"I'm impressed! New York is a modern city; it just doesn't have the charm of the older ones."

"Really?" Nick was curious. "Which one was your favorite?"

Vincent seemed to reflect. "Not sure. Every metropolis has something to offer. There are some I loved teaching at: Edinburgh, Oslo, Zurich. Others where I met good people who became my friends: Madrid, Ferrara in Northern Italy, Athens. I liked the warmer climates and always found ways to enjoy myself."

"I'm surprised you didn't mention Notre Dame. Isn't that where you grew up?"

"Yes, and for a time, I considered Paris my home, but my mother thought I should travel and broaden my horizons. Before you were born, vampires could only stay in cities for a limited amount of time before arousing suspicion and being discovered. We had to age our appearance so as not to give away our true natures. It was tedious coming back as our own grandkids so we traveled a great deal."

"So, if Paris isn't your home, now, what is?"

"I have to tell you I've enjoyed Montreal a great deal. McGill has one of the best Humanities departments, a fine mix of old and new. I loved the short time we spent in Quebec City."

Nick smiled slyly. "Would Olivia have something to do with that?"

"She might." He laughed. "But it feels like home," he sighed, "more than Paris ever did."

"At least you got to travel. Aside from Canada, I've never really traveled, except when I was an infant. My uncle thought it safer until I got older. My parents died in France."

"I'm sorry. But at least you had your uncle to raise you. He sounds like a terrific guy. Are you sure he won't mind me coming to the wedding? I'm not usually known as a party crasher."

"As I am presently not in a relationship, you are my plus one."

"Thanks, again, for letting me stay at your apartment."

"It was a graduation gift. My uncle asked me what I wanted, and I told him my own place. I stayed there once before when I wanted time to myself or to entertain someone."

"The girl who got you in trouble."

"Yes. She who will not be named. It's history, but the apartment is mine, now, and you're welcome to stay for as long as you want. It has three bedrooms and plenty of living space."

"Thanks. I was unsure if I would make it down here. My mother cautioned me against New York, said it was high on the danger list. Like Prague in the eighteen hundreds wasn't."

"What happened in Prague?"

"Don't ask. Some memories are better left forgotten."

Nick couldn't agree more so he didn't push. "So, what else is on your 'must see' list?"

"Besides Central Park and the museums? You know what I'd like to see? Times Square. From the pictures it looks a bit like Piccadilly Circus in London."

"You know whenever you talk about your past travels you mention London quite a bit."

"I had good times there. Oxford was one of my best memories. I returned there often."

Sensing Vincent's melancholy, Nick said, "Well, all right, then, Times Square it is."

***

"Hello, Miranda." Felicity rose as Miranda joined her for lunch in the museum's restaurant. "I'm glad you could make it and not have to work through another meal."

"I don't always work through lunch." Miranda winced. It was true. She almost always wolfed down a sandwich at her cubicle while she completed reports. "So, what have you been doing since Blu's been out of town?"

"I have been scouring the local galleries in search of raw talent. You simply must come with me to SoHo to check out the new acquisitions. Alistair Calder throws wonderful gatherings at his gallery I think you might enjoy."

"Sounds good. I will make time for it." Miranda started grinning. "So, are you up for some gossip?"

"I thought you'd never ask. Rumors throughout the vampire community spread fast. We heard Vivienna made a grand entrance last night."

"Oh, Felicity, I wish you'd been there. Rosalyn has done a wonderful job with the banquet hall. It mirrors any of the high-end reception halls New York has to offer. Black and gold linen and drapes and Swarovski crystals all over."

"I bet. Somehow, I didn't think Valadon would spare any expense. I sure would have liked to have been a fly on that wall."

Miranda felt bad Felicity's family had been Conservatives who opposed the Progressives Valadon spearheaded during the Great Reveal. It had been twenty years, but sour feelings die hard. "You should have seen the red and gold dress Vivienna was almost wearing. She left very little to the imagination. Her boobs clearly on display."

"I've never known her to be anything else but flamboyant. She does so enjoy the attention."

"I beat a quick retreat when I saw her. You will never guess who I bumped into in ValCorp's lobby."

"Who?"

"Magritte."

"*No way!* She showed up? I didn't think she left her stronghold in France very often. Besides, I thought last night's ball was for Valadon's ambassadors."

"It was, but neither woman seemed to care. I kind of feel bad for Valadon. I don't know how he's going to handle being married to Madame Lord Vixen."

Felicity's head fell back in laughter. "Oh, that is just so apropos." She clapped her hands in delight. "I wouldn't worry too much about Valadon. If there's anyone who can handle either one of them, it's the High Lord. He spent centuries doing business for the High Court and their associates. I'm sure he'll deal with them with aplomb."

Miranda sure hoped so. She was still shaken by the bad vibe she'd gotten from Magritte. "It's frustrating that he even has to." She sighed. "I know marriages are arranged for political reasons, to ease tensions, whatever. It just seems so…wrong."

"Don't you mean archaic? I couldn't agree more with you. But Valadon's no fool. I bet he's already taken steps to safeguard his considerable fortune."

"I guess." Miranda shrugged.

"So. How are you and Remare getting along since Guy agreed to perform a certain task for Valadon? No more suspicions?"

"We're working it out. It really hurt to think he doubted my loyalty. It shook me."

"Stay in a relationship long enough you learn to weather the storms. Life with Remare won't be easy. But I have faith in you. From what I remember Remare was a good man. His loyalty to Valadon commendable. A man of honor. I liked that about him. That and his incredibly good looks."

"He is a man of honor. I've always respected him for that. As far as his handsomeness goes, Felicity, you have no idea. Unless, of course, you've seen him naked before?"

"*Miranda!*" she huffed. "When would that have been possible? And my imagination is just fine, thank you very much."

Miranda laughed. It felt good to share a moment of enjoyment with her friend. "Hey, you want to see a movie tomorrow? I hear there's a new release on Georgia O' Keeffe. It's supposed to be very good."

"Hmm. Now, that sounds interesting. She's always been one of my favorite artists."

"Let me check times, and I'll get back to you." Miranda glanced at her watch. "I've got to get back soon. Have you heard from Guy lately?"

"Yes. He's working on some business matters but promises to be back before Valadon's wedding."

"Good. I'll text you when I know where and when the movie is playing."

"All right. Be well, Miranda."

"You, too!"

Chapter Twenty-Five

"Be reasonable." Valadon's voice sounded deeper, even to his own ears. After giving his intended bride a tour of ValCorp's major divisions, they were taking refreshment in his formal dining room. "I've considered your requests, but there is simply no space at ValCorp for your design department."

"There would be if you'd make room." Vivienna huffed. "Your building is certainly large enough to accommodate my staff."

"Unfortunately, you and your people would be a major distraction to those I already employ. Your beauty far too compelling for them to concentrate. So, my final answer is no."

"You mix pleasantries with resolve. Very well, I'll continue to run my company from the Mid-town headquarters." She smiled seductively at him. "I do believe that is the first compliment you've given me in quite some time."

"You don't require approval, Vivienna. From what I remember, you always did exactly as you pleased with little regard for the viewpoints of others."

"Not true. There are a few whose opinions matter." Her fangs peeked out of her mouth.

"You and I both know this marriage isn't based on any affection between us, but rather on coercion, so you can stop with the flirtations. They are neither necessary nor desired."

"There was a time when you welcomed such affections. I'm sad to see you've become so distant. Or is your mistress the only one who warms your cold heart?"

"The only mistress I have is ValCorp."

She laughed. "I noticed she wasn't at the ambassadors' reception. Are you keeping her hidden, afraid her appeal will be diminished by those of your own kind?"

"I believe he keeps her sequestered in the archives." Magritte joined them after meeting with his accountants and going over their financial books.

"If you're referring to Professor Miranda Crescent, she works part time in the evenings in my archives. She's of no interest to you. She is merely an associate and a good friend."

"The archives. Perhaps you should keep an eye on your art collection to make sure none of your paintings go missing," Vivienna snarked. "People of her station yearn for what others have."

Valadon resented her innuendo. "Unlike others, Professor Crescent isn't motivated by greed, but rather a deep appreciation for art."

"Enough." Magritte raised her hand to halt the discussion. "The pre-wedding reception will be starting in a few hours, and I wish to return to my hotel suite to get ready. Lord Valadon, your financials are in accordance with the tithes you've sent us. We look forward to seeing you tonight."

He nodded to the women as they left.

***

Waiting outside the movie theater, Miranda glanced at her watch, again. Felicity was late, and that was so unlike her. If anyone was fanatic about promptness it was her former mentor. Miranda began pacing and then decided to send her another text. Finally, her phone rang, and she noted Felicity's number. "Thank God, I was worried about you."

"Hello, Miranda." Her blood chilled. "It's been a while. Remember me? I certainly remember you." He made a depraved slurping sound. "And the way you tasted."

"Brandon!" Heart in her throat, Miranda staggered and braced herself against the side of the building. Valadon's brother who had kidnapped and tortured her. "Where's Felicity?"

"Oh, I'm sorry. Your little friend won't be able to make the movie tonight. She's a bit tied up." An image appeared on her phone of Felicity, bound and bleeding on the ground.

Her voice was ragged. "You monster, he'll slaughter you for this!"

"He'd have to find me first, but if he did that, then I'd have to kill your friend. She was your advisor at NYU, wasn't she? Meet me at Grant's Tomb. If I see anyone with you, her spine gets severed. You have one hour. Tick. Tock."

The phone call ended. Miranda's breaths came hard and fast. She tried to contact Guy, but there was no response. Brandon wanted her for a reason. He knew she'd call Valadon, pull him into some sort of a trap. Miranda wasn't going to do that. Neither was she going to meet the fiend alone. She considered calling Remare, but with all the foreigners at ValCorp, she'd be creating a dangerous situation there. Her mind was racing. This could be a ruse. She held the side of her head. Everyone knew she was involved with Remare by now, didn't they?

Did Brandon think both vampires would come for her? Was that what he intended so some nefarious plan of the High Council could take place when Remare and Valadon weren't there to stop it? Did he want Remare coming to her rescue so that Valadon would be left without his number one Torian? That was definitely a possibility. One she was not going to let happen.

She wasn't the weakling she'd once been when he'd held her captive. She was human, but with some awesome *Elemental* gifts she'd been refining under the tutelage of a very powerful vampire.

She looked up at the street sign. She was on West Seventy-Sixth; she could drive north on Riverside Highway or... Since she was this close to Werehaven, she'd call the Weres for back-up.

"Gavin, what are you doing there?" Nearly out of breath, she gasped. "I thought you'd be at Valadon's reception tonight."

"Night off. I'm working the wedding. What's wrong, Miranda? You sound stressed."

"I am!" *Very!* "I need help. Can you and Lawe and a few of your buddies meet me Uptown? I have to see someone I'd rather not. I can't explain, right now." She glanced at her watch, again. "I'll be at a Hundred and Twentieth near Riverside. There's an old church there. Okay?" She figured two blocks away from the monument would be enough distance not to be detected.

Damn it! This was her fault. She'd been the one to suggest the movie. Brandon, or one of his flunkies, must have been spying on her. And, now, he had Felicity. Miranda shook her head to get the image of Felicity and the blood-soaked ground out of her mind. She wanted to mentally contact Felicity, but they'd never shared blood. She knew her friend didn't have the power or the talents Guy possessed.

As a Blueblood, Brandon could do some serious damage to her. And the bastard would get off on it.

***

"Tomorrow's the day. Are you sure you're up for this?" Remare smirked at Valadon as they greeted more well-wishers at the reception.

In truth, Valadon was tiring of the parties and just wanted it all over with. "I've dealt with worse." Valadon scoffed. "You should have seen the tantrum Vivienna," he gestured with his flute of champagne in her direction across the ballroom, "threw when I informed her that her rooms were separate from mine."

"I take it that didn't go over well with Madame Lord Vixen?"

Valadon raised a brow at his choice of words.

"Miranda's moniker for Vivienna. They didn't hit it off when they first met in Paris. Speaking of which, here comes Bastien and Orion. I think it would be wise to keep our young wolf away from Vivienna." She'd slashed Orion's throat when he took exception to the way she had treated Miranda.

"Sorry, we're late. We had engine trouble with the jet in Paris, and it took longer than we expected."

"That's all right." Valadon put a hand on Bastien's shoulder. "You texted you found something you wanted me to see?"

"Yes. I stored it in my room, but I think it's something you should carefully examine."

"I will." Valadon faced Orion. "My intended wife is here. Do you think you can control your enmity so no disturbances occur?"

Orion gave him a wolf grin. "I'll try my best."

"Make sure there are no conflicts," he instructed Bastien as he and Remare continued mingling. "Where's Miranda? I haven't seen her tonight."

"She dislikes these parties and wanted to spend some time with a friend whose husband is away on business."

"Anyone I know?"

"She didn't say, and I didn't ask. Apparently, we're working on our 'trust' issues."

"Call her. I think she should be here. Her friend can come, as well."

Remare tried to reach her on his phone. "Odd, no answer." He tried, again, with the same result.

"Let me extend the invite. This is supposedly my party." Valadon eyed Vivienna, who acted every part the queen she believed she was with her sycophants hanging on her every word. Shutting all else out, he tried to contact Miranda. Picturing her in his mind, he sent the mental message, *"Miranda?"*

She slammed her natural shields down harder than she'd ever used with him before. Something was wrong! Normally, she would just tell him it wasn't a good time. He tried, again, this time with more force. *"Miranda? Are you all right?"*

"I'm sorry, Valadon. I'm meeting with Brandon. He's taken a friend of mine hostage."

A growl tore through his voice. *"Where are you?"*

"On the West Side. Please, Valadon, stay away. He wants to lure you here. That's why I didn't contact you. Don't worry, I've got this covered."

"Who's with you?" he demanded.

"A few Weres." She locked her shields, effectively shutting him out. But not before he glimpsed an image of Grant's Tomb.

"I have to leave for a while." He looked around the ballroom for his Torians and mentally contacted Tristan and Katya. "Brandon's back in New York."

"Let me go after him. This is your reception." Remare's voice was steel. "I will deal with him."

"Brandon is my brother; if anyone deals with him, it will be me. Stay here. Protect my territory. I need you vigilant in case anyone decides to make a move against ValCorp."

"Allow me to come with you."

"No. I need you here. I'll be in contact, I assure you." He turned and left before his second could offer any more arguments. There was no telling what Remare would do if he knew Miranda was with Brandon. He had Tristan contact several of the mid-level Torians to meet him in the garage.

***

Miranda made her way furtively toward the Tomb with the Doric columns and the Neo-classical architecture. The Weres were already hiding in various spots not far from the domed monument. Tucked in her boots were the two long daggers she'd often carried when out alone at night. But her real power lay in the energy balls she'd been learning to throw. Heart beating firmly in her chest, she reached the top of the stairs and looked around. Heat was already gathering in her fingers. The rotunda was in shadows, but she spotted Felicity's crumpled body in the corner. It looked as if she'd been flung against the wall and slid down to puddle on the floor.

Miranda rushed to her friend and nearly slipped on the pools of blood. Brandon had torn out one side of her throat. She was alive, but barely. The Dark Angel within Miranda woke and demanded vengeance. She spoke softly. "Blu?"

Felicity's voice was barely a whisper. "Airport."

Damn it! There's no way he's going to get here in time! She held her hand over Felicity's neck to help with the healing.

"How touching! I tried to keep her alive, but I was in the mood for a snack." Brandon's snarky voice sounded behind her.

She turned to see he had lightened his hair to look more like Valadon. His face was thinner, narrower. A perverted shadow of his brother. Handsome, yet evil. At that moment, all she wanted was him dead. Sensing her eyes turning blood red, she raised her hand in his direction and unleashed an energy blast.

Startled, he rattled back on his haunches. "Vivienna was right!" He laughed and clapped his hands in delight. "You do have some talents of the *Elementals*." He snarled, "Shall we find out just how many?"

A voice she didn't always recognize as her own answered, "Why not?" She blasted him, again, this time with more force.

He took refuge behind a column and fired a searing strike her way.

Miranda quickly took cover behind another column. The last time she witnessed vampires fighting was when Valadon and Mulciber had exchanged volleys. She wished she had one of Remare's swords in hand but knew she wasn't anywhere near proficient enough to go against Brandon. But what she had, she'd use to her advantage.

She called the winds off the Hudson River to her defense. Just enough to keep him disconcerted so she could increase the size and intensity of her energy balls. Her power was exhilarating and imbued her with a sense of confidence. The noise of their battle grew loud enough to wake poor old Ulysses and Julia in their sarcophagi.

Brandon applauded her efforts. "This makes me wonder why you didn't use your powers when I had you in the cell. You must have wanted my touch more than I thought."

Bile rose up in her throat. She'd been chained to a wall when the bastard had played with her. "Only a viper would ever want your touch. What's the matter, Brandon? Still can't deal with Valadon being better than you?"

Another volley of energy blasts hit the column and the wall behind her, quicker this time. She must have hit a nerve. "You can try to look like him all you want. You'll never be him."

"I don't need to be him. He sits high on his throne, safe at ValCorp. Fool doesn't know his days are numbered. Did he really think he could lure me into the open by sending his watchdog away? He insults me with his obvious ploys."

"You can't defeat him. You saw what he did to Mulciber."

More volleys were shot her way. One nearly singeing her hair. She searched the walls for something to deflect her energy balls the way Lizandra did bank shots playing pool.

"I don't have to defeat him." Another blast. "With my contacts in the High Court, he'll soon be history. And you along with him."

She'd already expended most of her stores of energy and didn't know how much she had left. Never having been depleted before, she didn't anticipate exhaustion overwhelming her so fast. Breathing hard, she looked around for something to spear him with, but there weren't any objects to use.

Until she spied the metal handrail near the stairs.

***

"Where is Valadon?" Vivienna slithered up to Remare. "He's missing his own party."

How could he have once fancied himself in love with this woman? Had he been so blinded by her beauty he couldn't see her reptilian nature? "He's taking an important call; he'll be back shortly."

Vivienna seemed to be scrutinizing him. "In all these long years, you never sought out a territory for your own. Were you afraid you wouldn't be able to hold it?"

"Charming as always, Vivienna." He wondered how long before she spewed her poison. "You and I both know if I had desired a dominion of my own, I'd have pursued one. That has not been the case. Loyalty is what keeps me here. Something you know very little about."

"There are many types of loyalty." Her violet eyes seemed to be glowing. "I've always been loyal to my goals. Had you been more ambitious we might have ruled together."

Not in a million years! "It's your ambition that will be your undoing, Vivienna. Enjoy your success while you still have it." Remare nodded to her and made his way into the crowd. Any more of her presence and he'd become ill. He checked his phone one more time to see if Valadon had texted him. Still no word. It was the not knowing that was testing his patience.

He would circulate and greet their guests with the poise he was anything but feeling.

So far, the night was proceeding without incident. Each of his Torians were strategically placed in sections of the ballroom should any trouble result. It was too damned quiet, and his skin was itchy. He felt as if something vile was in the air, but he just couldn't figure out what.

***

Lizandra was so going to kick her ass. Gavin and the other Weres had rushed in when they saw Brandon winning the fight. The question of who was stronger: Weres or vampires had been answered.

Brandon was a Blueblood, stronger than the average vampire, and nearly eight hundred years old. She'd underestimated him. He was more powerful than she'd thought. He dislocated Lawe's arm after the powerful Were grabbed him from behind. When Gavin attacked, she was sure he would be victorious until Brandon pulled a move she hadn't seen coming and flung him against the wall. The sound of bone crunching had her stomach roiling.

Outraged, Maxine jumped on Brandon's back using her short, but powerful legs to headlock him while she beat on his head. "You go, girl!" Miranda whispered as Brandon tried to peel her legs away from his neck. The twins tried rushing him, but he kicked them, their bodies flying through the air.

"*Never engage an enemy who is stronger. But, if you must, use speed as a deterrent. And, if that doesn't work, use every dirty trick in the book!*" Lizandra's words echoed in her head. Miranda was quickly running out of ideas. She had one last fireball burning in her hand, waiting for when Brandon pounced.

Turned out she didn't have to wait long. Without warning, he reached around the column and pulled her up from the floor. In a blur of motion, he slammed her against the marble before she could throw the fireball and punched her across her jaw. Blood spurted, and her teeth rattled. Her lip was swollen, yet he pulled her closer. "Foreplay's over. Now, let's see…"

"Brandon!" Valadon's voice bellowed through the halls of the Tomb. The High Lord walked toward them. Miranda used her arm to wipe the blood from her mouth.

"Well, brother dear, it's good to see you, again."

"Why are you attacking my people?" Never taking his eyes off his brother, Valadon pulled her to her feet. "Come to ValCorp. Whatever differences we have, we can settle them there."

"And face High Lord Valadon's justice. I think not." Brandon made a mocking noise as he sarcastically shook his head. "Marriage to Vivienna? You must be losing your mind; the Valadon I know would never allow that to happen."

"What do you know of it?"

"More than you," he taunted. "They'll strip you bare, and whatever's left they'll leave for the vultures."

Seeing them together, Miranda thought she was seeing double, but Brandon radiated evil far darker than his brother.

When Valadon tried to take his brother's arm, Brandon flung him across the hall. Valadon spiraled in mid-air and was on his brother a second later. The two combatants fought furiously and so fast Miranda couldn't see their punches or power blasts. She quickly went to check on Felicity. Her still form scared her, but she saw the slight rise and fall of Felicity's chest as she breathed.

When she spotted Maxine, the Were gave her the thumbs up and smiled, albeit her body was twisted in a bent position. Gavin crawled to where Lawe was and manipulated the arm to pop back in its socket. The twins were inching nearer to Max. She figured they were all right, too. If not bloodied and bruised.

Valadon had wrestled his brother to the ground and was pinning him down. His baritone vibrated off the walls. *"Why?"*

"Because I couldn't stand the sight of you!" Brandon spat at his brother. "You could have had a stronghold in France, but you just *had* to come to America. You abandoned our home, let our lands fall to foreign invaders."

"I gave you everything you ever wanted. *Everything!* And, still, that wasn't enough for you."

Brandon was slowly reaching down inside his boot as Valadon raged. Miranda flung herself in their direction and wrestled the dagger away from him. "He was going to kill you with this." She handed the knife to Valadon.

"She's right, you know." Brandon's cruel smile was a manifestation of his malice. "You will never be safe as long as I'm alive. I'll come for you, again. When you least expect it." He wanted to torment Valadon to the very end. Knowing his brother still harbored affection for him, he used those emotions against him. The sadist enjoyed causing pain, seeing Valadon hurt gave him pleasure.

"Tell me what you know of Magritte's plans," Valadon demanded.

"Go to hell!"

Miranda watched as Valadon narrowed his eyes and pierced Brandon's brain with his mental power. She'd seen him do the same thing to Peralt from the communications room at ValCorp. Brandon tried to mentally fight him, but he was no match for the High Lord. He made a grab for the dagger, but Valadon held it firm in his hand.

"Valadon," she whispered, "you have to kill him. The next time he comes for you, you may not survive."

Valadon gazed down at his brother. So many emotions crossed his face she could only imagine what hell he was going through. He placed the dagger's point over Brandon's heart. She covered his hands with hers. "This way you won't have to live with it." Miranda's heart beat against her ribs as she waited for him to strike the killing blow.

Everything froze, time stilled in that moment as everyone in the Tomb watched and waited.

Rage and sorrow warred in Valadon's face. Reality versus sentiment. After a moment, he shook his head. "I can't. I can't kill my own brother."

"I have no such compunctions." Out of nowhere, Guy de Montglat appeared and tossed a silver web over Brandon and hauled him over his shoulder. The ancient far, far stronger than anyone in the building. "There's a special place in hell for those like him." When Brandon fought to break free, Guy flicked his hand, and Brandon fell into a deep sleep.

Several of Montglat's companions helped the Weres to their feet.

"What will you do to him?" Valadon asked.

"Imprison him in a cold, dark place like he once did to a friend of mine. I assure you, he will never escape to cause you further harm."

Miranda glanced back to where Felicity's body had been. "Felicity?"

"She sleeps. It will take time, but her body will repair itself."

Guy smiled at Valadon "Now, you owe me one."

Before she or Valadon could say anything, Guy and the rest of his men disappeared. Miranda knew vampires couldn't dematerialize, but they moved so impossibly fast humans thought they did.

The Weres joined them. "Thank you for your assistance." Valadon nodded to Gavin. "My men are on their way here. As annoyed with me as they are, I told them to hang back. I wanted to talk to my brother first. They should be arriving shortly."

"We'll wait outside until they do." Gavin walked alongside Lawe as the twins limped beside them. Max winked at Miranda as she left with them.

Miranda joined Valadon on the stone bench adjacent to the wall. "Going to yell at me for not contacting you first?"

"No." He rubbed both palms against his forehead. "I would never do that." He pulled her closer to him and held her against his side. "I searched his mind before Montglat arrived. You were right; he would have kept coming after me until he finally succeeded in killing me."

Miranda felt the undeniable grief and disgust emanating from the High Lord. She circled her arm around him. As an empath, she sensed the depth of his loss.

"Brandon and I were once good friends, true brothers. We learned business from our father, rode through the woods near our home together, went on many adventures. We laughed and celebrated many events through the centuries. And, now, that will never happen, again."

Somewhere along the way, jealousy had reared its ugly head. And, instead of love and respect for his older brother, loathing and envy had taken root. She had no doubt Magritte and Vivienna had manipulated those aspects of Brandon's personality to suit their own ends.

"I'm sorry." What else could she say? No one could ever go back and change time or the decisions they made.

"Me, too." His voice was raw. "Why didn't you ever tell me what Brandon did when he kidnapped you?"

Miranda froze. The color quickly draining from her face as she pulled her arm away from him. "You saw what he did when you searched his memories?"

"I did. I am so sorry. Remare and I suspected as much. We had Dr. Amira examine you. There were no signs of rape. That's what she told us."

"No. There wouldn't be." Miranda rose and stood against one of the columns. She remembered every minute of the hell Brandon had put her through. "Fiend that he was, cut his fingers and inserted his blood inside me to heal the wounds." Her voice sounded acerbic. "Said he didn't want me looking messy when he presented me to you."

Miranda crossed her arms over her chest, partly in anger and partly to stop the shaking. "He considered me your plaything. A toy he wanted to use and discard so you could never have it, again. He wanted to break me to hurt you. Brandon searched my mind for memories of you. He wanted to replicate having sex with me the way you did. Fuck with my head. He was so angry when I tried to fight him in my mind. And, then, he became even more hostile when he couldn't find what he wanted. He made me think it was you when he was inside me. Total bastard."

"Miranda, I—"

"Don't!" Enraged, she turned to him. "Don't look at me with pity in your eyes. I didn't want it, then; I certainly don't want it, now. Pity doesn't do anything for anyone. I'm not a fucking victim. I'm a survivor. So, don't lay any sorrowful looks on me. I'll hate you for it."

He nodded. "Does Remare know?"

"No. And I would appreciate you not telling him. I don't need to relive it. Talking about it doesn't help; it only makes it more real. I'm over it. Let's move on."

Valadon's heart was breaking. Miranda had survived such cruelty at his brother's hands. Because of him. Because he'd let it be known he had feelings for her. Was it any wonder she'd shied away from his touch? He closed his eyes in memory of the times she flinched when he'd barely touched her. Now, he had images seared into his brain of his brother's vindictiveness. How could he have been so blind? Others, through the years, had tried to tell him of his brother's malevolence. He'd thought the stories greatly exaggerated. Now, he knew better.

"How can I make this up to you?" he whispered aloud as he joined her by the column.

Her eyes seared into him. "By never repeating it. You only give him satisfaction by letting it cut into you. You once asked me for a vow of loyalty. I'm asking you, now, for your promise not to relay any of it."

"If that is what you want, you have my word." He gently touched her elbow. "Did Gabriel know?" His son had been her lover and her doctor; surely, she would have told him. No wonder she'd fled from him to the one vampire who was more human than any other. Every time she saw his face, she'd have seen Brandon's. It pained him to realize he'd never had a chance with Miranda. His brother had seen to it.

"If he suspected, he never asked. And I never told him."

"I'll keep this between us. He placed his palm over the side of her face, his fingers barely brushing her wounds. "Take my blood, Miranda. I don't offer it often. You're in pain. It will help heal your injuries."

"Not a blood vow?"

"No." He shook his head. "You've tried to protect me more than once, now. Let me help you." He lifted his wrist and bit into it.

Miranda didn't like the idea of tasting Valadon's blood. It somehow felt like a betrayal to Remare, but her body was sore all over; if it wasn't for the column, she wasn't sure she'd be standing. She knew once the adrenaline wore off, her body would crash. She took his offered wrist and drank. As soon as the liquid hit her stomach, she could feel a warming sensation pulse through her body. She shivered then licked the wound closed, even knowing vampires healed themselves. "Powerful stuff." She smiled up at him.

"That it is." He gestured to the street. "Our people have arrived. Let's go home."

Chapter Twenty-Six

After turning down Valadon's offer to take her back to ValCorp, Miranda drove to Werehaven with her friends. She knew she owed Lizandra an explanation and would rather talk face to face with her best friend. And she admitted it, she wasn't quite ready to see Remare. It was a toss-up who would hit the ceiling harder and rip her a new one. One confrontation at a time.

A mild headache was forming behind her eyes. So, she was grateful when someone dimmed the lights in the room with the Jacuzzis where she soaked soothingly in the warm water. Only the twinkling lights lit up the murals of the Caribbean islands and clear turquoise sea on the cave walls. Leaning forward, her head rested on her forearms which were hugging the edge. Even though Valadon's blood went far in healing her, she was still tender in spots and wouldn't lean her sore back against the rim.

Depeche Mode was playing on the sound system with one of her favorite songs, "Waiting for the Night". Somehow, that song always relaxed her.

Lizandra slipped into the tub in front of her. Being in a room full of naked Weres used to offset Miranda. Not anymore. She waited for Liz to say something, but the Were Queen only smiled at her. Miranda knew she was patiently waiting for an explanation.

Gavin joined Miranda in her tub. Using one of the large sponges, he began to gently stroke her shoulders, letting the heat from the water soak deeper into her skin. "Now, you do know Lizandra is at her most cunning when she is silent?" he whispered in her ear.

Miranda looked up sideways at him. He winked at her and continued sponging her back. She took a deep breath then faced Liz. "There's a reasonable explanation—"

"*Reasonable?!*"

Miranda knew she was in trouble by Liz's tone.

"Really, do continue. I'm so eager to hear why my best friend thought she could take on a Blueblood vampire in the middle of the night without contacting me first."

"In all fairness, Miranda called me first for back-up." Gavin went silent when Liz glared at him. Miranda thought she saw sparks emitting from her eyes.

"I did not think I could 'take on' Brandon. I merely went there to scout out the area. Hijinks ensued. A little blood was spilled. Bad vampire was captured, and all ends well."

A wave of water splashed over her. The Were Queen was not amused. Miranda used the towel Gavin handed her to wipe the water from her eyes. "Okay, okay. I should have contacted you first. I didn't. I'm sorry. But there just wasn't time—"

"*Wrong!*" Liz pointed one of her lethally long nails in her direction. "You *make* time!"

Miranda smiled sullenly and nodded. "I will." She recapped the night's events in enough detail to satisfy the queen, with Gavin and the others supplying more particulars she'd forgotten.

"I see. The only thing saving your hide is that you at least tried to contact me first." She slanted a look at Gavin, and Miranda knew they'd be having words soon. The grin on Gavin's face was his way of saying, *'How does it feel to be left out of the loop?'* Apparently, he was still pissed off Liz hadn't contacted him when she'd been hurt fighting.

"Are we good, now? I've gotta get down to ValCorp. I'm sure Remare is gonna want to hear my version of the night's events, as well."

"We're good. As long as you promise not to do anything as stupid as you did tonight."

Miranda didn't think she acted foolishly. She'd been trying to protect both Valadon and Remare. Okay, maybe testing her evolving powers on a Blueblood wasn't the best idea, but she'd walked—eh, limped—away still standing. "Okay."

Lawe entered the cave and immediately went to the music system. She heard him mutter, "What crap is this?" He promptly changed the music to Bob Marley. He smiled at her with his gold teeth and started dancing. All the Weres applauded and started swaying to the beats.

Miranda looked around the cave with her friends by her side. This was her tribe. They'd adopted her into their own. Each one of them had fought and bled for her tonight and not one of them complained or hesitated when called. And they'd gladly do it, again. God, she loved them.

But there was one irritable vampire waiting for her down at ValCorp. Explaining why she hadn't called him earlier was probably not going to go over well.

At all.

***

"Come in." Valadon called out when there was a knock at his door. Bastien and Orion entered.

"What the hell happened?" he bellowed when he saw Orion's face.

Bas answered. "Orion was overcome with the need to address Vivienna for the time when she slashed his throat. He made a derogatory comment—"

"She called me a mongrel!" Orion interjected.

"And one of her guards took a swing at Orion."

Valadon exhaled. Normally, he'd be angry one of his people acted inappropriately when they had visitors in his

House, but there was something about the young Were that made him hide a smile. "And what did you call her?"

Orion winced. Hesitating, he thinned his lips.

Bas said, "I believe the words 'prima donna' were used. Among others."

"Will you kindly refrain from using pejorative terms in the presence of my guests? I have quite enough to deal with without having to worry about my own people."

"Yes, sir." Orion seemed to relax.

Noticing the box under Bastien's arm, he asked, "What do you have there?"

"This is for you." Bastien laid the box down on his desk. "We found it buried beneath the floor in Miranda's cottage in France. There are some letters in there pertaining to you. I believe it's centuries old."

Valadon began examining the contents. "Anything else?"

"Not at this time."

He watched as his Torians turned toward the door. "Orion. A word if you please."

***

When Miranda exited the elevator, she made for the kitchen, instead of going straight to Remare's rooms. She knew she was stalling but needed sustenance. As soon as she spotted Orion making a sandwich her jaw dropped.

"What the hell happened?" they said in unison.

"Fight."

"Same." Miranda knew her eye was still a little swollen, though she applied plenty of concealer. At least the gash on her hairline had disappeared. Mostly. "Who with?"

"One of Vivienna's dickhead guards. Valadon said I'm banned from the wedding to avoid any further 'incidents'. You want a sandwich? There's plenty of turkey."

Miranda frowned. She didn't think she could keep any solid food down. "Is there any turkey soup in there? Escher makes great soups."

"I don't see any." Orion searched the fridge. "Want anything else?"

"Nah, I'll just have some tea."

He filled a cup with water and was about to nuke it.

"You don't need to heat it. Just bring me a spoon with the cup."

He set it down in front of her then sat across from her at the breakfast nook. She found one of her green teabags and raw sugar packets on the bottom of her purse. Using her ability, she heated the water and dipped the teabag in.

Orion shook his head. "I know you have powers, but it still amazes me when I see you use them."

She sipped her tea, enjoying the aroma and the warm liquid. "No cookies in the fridge?"

"I didn't see any. Now, you mind telling me what happened to your face?"

"Altercation with a bad guy. Valadon kicked his ass. All's good."

"So, that's where he disappeared to tonight. Remare know?"

"Probably." She sighed. "If not, he's going to."

Orion smiled. "No wonder you wanted cookies. Courage lacking?"

"Nah, just tired." Miranda grinned. "It's been a long night."

After a while, when she'd finished her tea, he said, "Time to face the music."

"I'm stalling, aren't I?"

"Pretty much. Want me to walk you down to his rooms?"

"I got this." She slid off the stool. "See you tomorrow."

As she walked down the corridor, she was trying to figure out what she was going to say to Remare when Vivienna appeared in front of her. And she didn't look happy.

The feeling was mutual as the air vibrated with heated tension. "Vivienna."

The Madame Lord's lips twisted cruelly. "I take it you're the reason Valadon had to leave our reception tonight."

"Possibly. But I'm sure he had other matters more important to attend to."

Her violet eyes glared with hatred. "Slut! Do you really think he'll have time for you when he's married to me?"

"I think Valadon will do whatever he chooses. He is king around here."

"And, when I'm queen, you'll be history. No one will even remember your name."

After her fight tonight, she was in no mood to trade insults with the vixen. "You won't be hearing from Brandon anytime soon." She tilted her head. "Or ever again for that matter."

Vivienna's expression turned to horror.

Miranda thought she sensed loss but doubted the viper had feelings for anyone but herself. She couldn't resist a slight grin. She knew it was petty, but it felt good.

For a moment.

Vivienna's eyes narrowed as she stared at her. Miranda must have been more tired than she thought because she suddenly found herself flying through the air and crashing into the wall. She slid down to the floor unceremoniously, taking a moment to catch her breath. Her ribs felt bruised, if not broken. She heard feet pounding in her direction.

When she looked up, Remare had one hand around Vivienna's throat, pinning her against the wall a foot off the ground. Both had bared their fangs. Miranda knew he was strong but was still amazed at his strength.

Valadon lifted her to her feet. "What happened?"

Miranda held her stomach, glad she hadn't eaten anything. "She blasted me."

Vivienna huffed as Remare let go. "She insulted me."

"You may want to ask her why she was so upset at finding out about Brandon's dear departure."

The Madame Lord's fists tightened, and Miranda thought another blast was forming.

"Vivienna! My office, right now!" Valadon's patience seemed to be tested to its limit. "Everyone else, back to your rooms. Remare, take care of Miranda."

"Of course."

Once inside Remare's apartment, Miranda sighed in relief.

Until she saw her lover's agitated face. "Something you forgot to tell me about earlier?"

She hated when he got all snarky with her. She'd dealt with his sarcastic self before. Probably would many times to come in the future. She smiled. "Short version or long?"

Remare crossed his arms over his chest and cocked his head. "Why don't we start at the beginning?"

***

"I was willing to let your insolence slide at the party when one of your guards attacked Orion. From what I understand, he may have inadvertently started it. But this, I do not condone."

Vivienna sat facing him, her bosom clearly on display. "Valadon. With our wedding tomorrow, some of my guards are a bit stressed. Surely, you can understand their excitement."

"My people are to be respected! If you attack any one of them, it is an attack on me! Such offenses will be met with severe consequences. Do you understand me?"

"As you wish, but maybe you should remind them, after the wedding is complete, I will be their queen and should be accorded all due reverence."

"Wrong!" Valadon was going to settle this, once and for all. "When we are married, you become my wife, not queen. You will *not* assume any of the responsibilities or privileges Madame Lords have in their own territory."

She was taken aback. "Surely, you jest?!"

"I do not. This is *my* territory with my laws." He leaned forward. "And my rules will be obeyed by *all* my people."

She slinked closer to him. "Perhaps your edicts need amending."

"Perhaps not." He would brook no further discussion. "Now, what is this about you and Brandon? You harbored a known criminal, a traitor who tried to usurp my throne and would've killed me for it."

"Reports didn't reach our shores until after his failed *coup d'état*. Maybe, if you had shared information more willingly, we could have avoided such dangerous liaisons."

Valadon knew she was lying through her pearly white teeth. He'd received certain letters in her hand and in his brother's to know she'd conspired along with him. Proof of her guilt and insurrection. A crime commensurate with dire penalties. "Just how many spies did you and Magritte plant in my building?"

"Valadon, how could you accuse me of such prosaic exploits? Don't I have enough to worry about with my own territory?"

"A domain you should keep to. While here in my lands, I expect you to reign in your ambitions." He deepened his tone. "You may not like what comes back on you. Now, I trust your accommodations in my House are suitable to you and your staff. I suggest you return to them. I have work to finish up."

She gazed around his rooms. "When will my things be transported here?"

"They will not. Your rooms will remain where they are, now."

She looked astounded. "We'll be married. Is it not customary for the wife to bed down with her husband?"

"I have no such desires." His eyes bore into hers. "These are my private quarters and will remain so."

"Then, the marriage will not be consummated, and Magritte will not be obligated to hold up her end of the agreement."

"History records many marriages not consummated until one or two years after the ceremony and are considered legal." He slowly revealed his fangs. "I'm in no rush."

Her temper spiked. "I take it you intend to enjoy the pleasures of your mistress?"

"I have no mistress," he exhaled, "but if I did, I would prefer her company to yours."

"Have you've forgotten the pleasure we once shared?" She smiled seductively. "Do you really think another can offer the passion I did?"

A block of ice could give more affection than her. "I plan to investigate your involvement with Brandon. Thoroughly. If I find out you conspired with him, you will regret your actions. Immensely." As good an actress as Vivienna was, she couldn't conceal the rapid beat of her heart. "I bid you goodnight, Vivienna. Sleep well."

He smirked as she stormed off, slamming the door behind her.

A few moments later, there was a soft knocking on the door. He couldn't wait to hear what platitudes she would now offer after his threat sank in. "Enter."

Selena appeared and gazed down the hall before closing the door. "Please tell me you're not really going to marry that witch." She feigned vomiting.

"Selena, it's very late. What are you still doing up?" Her semi-transparent nightgown wasn't lost on him. The outlines of her delicate breasts peeked through the opening of her robe.

She took the seat vacated by Vivienna. "I couldn't sleep." She took a deep breath and met his gaze. "I wanted to ask you for a favor. But I wasn't sure you'd be keen on it."

After dealing with Vivienna, he was charmed by Selena's youthful innocence, though he expected she was quite capable of feminine manipulation. Her winsome smile enchanted him. Surprised, he felt something cold cracking inside him. He dared not think it was the wall he'd built around his heart. "Ask me what you want. You need not be shy about it."

"You know how you assigned Tristan and Katya as my bodyguards? And how they've had to pull double duty with all the preparations going on in this place?"

"Go on."

"I watched Tristan training some of the new Torians, and I...wondered if...I might be considered a candidate?"

He blinked in surprise. "Absolutely not. You are the granddaughter of a Madame Lord. I doubt she'd appreciate you engaging in potentially harmful activities."

"Please. Hear me out. I know the city is dangerous. I'm not frail. Dione made sure I trained with her people. Her second, Tristan's father, Sanduval often gave me lessons. I want to get better. I want permission to train with Katya. And, hopefully, learn how to use armaments with Tristan. What danger is there if I'm taught by the best? Surely, you have confidence in your own people. You say protection is your main goal. What better way to protect me than to let me train?"

Valadon rubbed his jaw. He admired her spunk and willingness to learn. "Your grandmother would not approve."

Her smile was back. "And if she does?"

"Then, we will continue this discussion after my wedding." He considered her request and the possibilities. "If, and this is a major if, I consent to your training, it would be focused on the basics. No weapons, yet. Your progress would be carefully monitored."

"That's all I want. A chance." Her eyes lit with enthusiasm.

"Go, then. I'll speak with Dione and see if there is some resolution we can agree on."

"Thank you." She rose and reached his door.

"By the way, Selena. You need not use seduction as a means of getting what you want. I much prefer honesty."

She laughed but let the sleeve of her robe fall revealing her bare shoulder. "So do I." And, then, left him alone.

He grinned at her provocation. "Little minx."

Chapter Twenty-Seven

"And that's all of it." Miranda sighed as she finished relaying the night's events to Remare.

He studied her for a long while before speaking. "You do realize I'm Valadon's chief strategist. That I've fought in countless wars and battles and was victorious."

Miranda winced. "Yes."

"And, yet, you thought Brandon could out-maneuver me? That he knew more about strategies and tactics than I?"

"I only knew he was laying some sort of trap. I sensed he wanted to lure Valadon away from the party for some malicious purpose. If I contacted you and you left the party, Valadon might have been more vulnerable without his number one enforcer. I was only trying to safeguard you both."

He rubbed his neck. "You have little confidence in my abilities."

"No." She took his hands in hers. "You protect everyone. Who protects you when you need it the most?"

"Valadon. We've had each other's backs for centuries."

"Granted, I was running on adrenaline. I thought it through the best I could. I wanted to save my friend and hopefully, somehow, capture Brandon for you and Valadon. I knew the party was important to you and him. I thought you deserved some relaxation and enjoyment after all you've been through."

He cupped her cheek. "Little is more important to me than your well-being. Promise me you will not keep something so serious from me, again. Trust me to come up with a solution amenable to all parties."

She gingerly leaned back against the cushions. "You're such a badass, Remare. Is it so difficult to accept I'm getting stronger?"

"Difficult? No. But you don't have the years, no, centuries of dealing with complicated situations I have. Nor the strength. You should have told me."

"Then, teach me. Show me how to move like you do. Faster. I got some good hits in on Brandon. It was his speed that outdid me."

"I don't want you to have to fight. I have soldiers for that."

"But you don't want me to get hurt. Neither did Lizandra. She and Gavin taught me self-defense and some other moves." She wasn't going to add how much Blu had been helping her with her energy bolts. "But I need to be quicker. Will you help me?"

"I suppose you're only going to get yourself in more trouble if I don't." He seemed to consider her words. "But, if I do, I want your promise you will call me first if or, more than likely in your case, when you find yourself in a dangerous situation."

"Okay. I see your point." She'd been afraid he would tear into her for not contacting him first. He didn't. "Can I crash here tonight? I'm exhausted."

He nodded. "Take off your shirt and lay down on the bed. You keep wincing every time you turn sideways. I want to examine your ribs."

"All right." She climbed the two steps to his bedroom and tossing her shirt over his chair lay down on his duvet.

He sighed. "Your side is bruised." His fingers gently traveled along her ribs.

She glanced up at him. "Sensitive there."

"Any sharp pains?"

"No. It's kind of dulled." She thought Valadon's blood and soaking in the hot tubs had alleviated the worst of it, but then, Vivienna blasting her into the wall had only aggravated it.

"Roll over."

"Woof."

He thinned his lips. "Not funny."

She turned, knowing her back was probably worse than her front.

"More bruises, mostly near your shoulder" His hand traveled over her ribs. "I don't feel any cracks."

"I don't think there are any, but yeah, a little tender. Vivienna got me good. I had little warning of what she was going to do. Otherwise, I would have deflected her blow."

"Lower your jeans, I want to see if there are any more bruises."

She did.

He promptly whacked her ass. Hard!

"Oww! What's with the butt smacking?!" She massaged her sore cheek.

"That's for not having faith in my abilities. Maybe, next time, you'll remember to call me. Now, finish undressing and get under the sheets. I'm going to take a shower. I'll join you in a moment." He lowered the lights until only shadows ensconced the room.

"Remare? I'm sorry."

He nodded then closed the bathroom door.

After shedding the rest of her clothes and slipping under the blankets, she buried her nose in his pillows and inhaled his scent deep into her lungs. She loved sleeping in his bed. Being with him always made her feel...good. She had friends whose company she enjoyed. Made her laugh. But, with Remare, she was alive.

And happy.

When he opened the door, he was naked, and his hair was slicked back. She admired his body. God, Rodin and the ancient sculptors would have had a field day sculpting his likeness. Not an ounce of fat anywhere on his chiseled body. His arms and thighs were defined as were his pecs and six pack. His cock made her mouth water. No fig leaf would ever be big enough to cover it.

He smirked as if he knew what she craved. "No sex for you tonight until your body heals." He joined her under the sheets.

"I'm not in *that* much pain."

"No. But it's late, and you're exhausted. I want you to take some of my blood. It will help heal you."

Miranda was leery. She'd already taken Valadon's. Would taking Remare's be too much? "All right."

He sat up against the headboard and cut a small opening over his heart. She bent her head and drank his life's essence. The copper taste no longer offended. The fact this was becoming familiar should have concerned her. It didn't. After she swallowed a small amount, she licked the wound closed, marveling at how quickly he healed.

She hugged him. "Remare." Her eyes met his. "I love you."

He smiled. Not his usual sexy smirk, but a gentle smile that conveyed his emotions, his deep affection for her. "I love you, too. Though, there are times I want to take you over my knee."

"What's wrong with just taking me?" She kissed up the side of his neck and jaw. "I'd like that very much."

He raised a brow. "No nookie for the naughty."

"I thought you liked me when I was naughty?"

"Not tonight. You need to regain your strength."

Miranda sighed and burrowed deeper into his chest. It felt so right being in his arms, his bed. Just lying beside him. Relaxed, the events of the day came back to her in crystal clarity. She'd endangered her friends by going to Grant's Tomb. They'd fought and bled for her. Images of them laughing and smiling in the hot tub room surfaced. Memories of the heat so apparent between Lizandra and Gavin, yet denied, haunted her.

So did images of Valadon's pain and sorrow. Not just for the loss of his brother, but for what she had suffered at the hands of Brandon. A sob escaped her throat. Then another. And another. Until her tears were drenching Remare's chest.

"Mir-randa." He held her tenderly as he searched her eyes. "What is it? Why are you crying?"

His gentle tones undid her. She tried to speak but couldn't; she was so overcome with grief. Her stomach began to spasm. She knew she was crashing. The effects of the emotional stress of the night hitting hard. Her throat hurt from her sobs. She clung to his arms and bent her forehead against his chest.

He lifted her chin to him. His eyes were a softer shade of brown than she'd ever seen before. "What's wrong?"

So many things she wanted to tell him but couldn't find the words. She gasped for air. What came out of her mouth surprised her. "There wasn't any turkey soup left." She half laughed, half-whimpered. "Escher makes great soup, and I really wanted some, but there was none." Another sob escaped her. "My Aunt Meg used to make me turkey soup when I wasn't feeling good."

He held her close. "I could make you some." He sounded uncertain. "I'm not sure where I would find a turkey at five in the morning, but I'm sure I could locate one."

Miranda started laughing at the thought of Remare searching the grocery stores for a turkey. The sobs returned until they quieted. "It's not just that. Valadon was so crestfallen tonight. He vacillated between killing and sparing Brandon. He was so torn; it hurt to see what he was going through."

She shook her head. "The Weres got injured. They fought bravely, but Brandon was vicious. He flung them against the walls." She sniffled. "I can still hear bones crunching."

"Later, in the hot tubs, I saw how Gavin loves Lizandra. He still wants her, but they're not together, anymore. I hated seeing them apart. They belong with each other. Why can't they just be happy?"

He kissed her forehead. "Mir-randa. You're taking on too much. Valadon has been conflicted about his brother for some time. They were once close. We tried to warn him in the past, but he focused only on the good. Now, he knows better. He will deal with it." Remare held her close. "Weres heal much quicker than humans. They are most likely recuperated by now." He sighed. "As for Liz and Gavin, I have no idea what their relationship is. I only know what mine is. And how fortunate I am to have you beside me."

His thumb stroked the side of her face, and she leaned into him, taking his palm in hers and kissing it. "Make love to me. I need you tonight."

He grinned. "As my lady wishes."

Covering her body with his, he nuzzled her neck and butterfly-kissed her jaw until he found her mouth. Miranda warmed at the tenderness in his touch and returned his caresses. Their tongues tangoed in a sultry dance that had her toes curling. She slid her hands up his back enjoying the sensation of cool skin over strong muscles. Somehow, when they were connected this way, she felt as if she were absorbing his strength. She broke from his kiss. "Nothing feels this good. When I'm with you it's as if the world doesn't matter, anymore. She held her palm up. "Can you feel it?"

His eyes narrowed. "Feel what?"

"The earth's vibration. I can't explain it," she shook her head, "but I know the sun is rising. There's this hum. I can sense it."

"My sorceress. You enchant me, still." He kissed her palm, then his lips met hers with more passion than before.

She wondered if the breaking dawn was affecting him the way it was her. Her nails dug into his shoulder as her other hand massaged his neck. Need, more powerful than ever, was driving her. Pushing her to claim this vampire as her own. Instinct evolved to new heights as she succumbed to the intoxicating euphoria of his magic.

His lips slid across to her neck where he nipped and licked his way down to her breast. He laved her areola then sucked her nipple into his mouth. Miranda arched off the mattress as the pleasure coursed through her. "Remare," she whispered in a voice more sultry than usual.

He looked up at her and smiled. "Too much?"

She chuckled. "Not enough."

"Patience." He resumed his ministrations, kissing his way to her other breast and nipped his way past her navel to raise his head between her thighs.

"Are you sure you're up for this?" he teased. "I can stop if you need me to."

"I'll kill you if you do." Laughing, she pushed his head back down.

The thing with Remare was that he liked to tease. Slow rhythmic circles with his tongue had her practically begging for more. Her eyes were glazing over as he dipped and sucked on her intimate flesh, except where she needed him most.

"Tease."

His eyes were heavy-lidded. "Naughty girl." His tongue swirled and caressed, driving her insane with ripples of pleasure. Her fingers dug into the sheets. If he didn't let her come soon, she would wind up tearing the material. When she thought she could take no more, fly no higher, he bit down gently on her clit, and she screamed as pleasure tore through her. He continued sucking on her until she roared out his name.

When he thought her worthy of mercy, he gave one last long lick then leaned forward and kissed her quickly. "I like it when you pant for me."

"I'm panting! I'm panting!" She chortled, her body coated in a fine layer of perspiration as her heart beat sturdily against her ribs. "You do me in every time."

"I know." He rose over her and settled between her legs. Positioning his cock at her core, he nudged at her opening until he was barely in an inch. Watching her with blistering intent, he moved in deeper then withdrew and repeated the action until she was arching her hips high to meet his thrusts. Together, they danced in magical rhythm, each unwilling to break their stare, their hold on one another, until Miranda felt her body tightening and the blood pounding in her head so strong she came, again.

Remare drove himself in deeper until he, too, shouted his pleasure. Nearly collapsing on her, he rolled them over on their sides. They lay together in blissful silence. After a while, he said, "I've missed you. More than I should. You steal my concentration. I should be focused on Valadon's wedding, yet my mind travels back to you all the time."

"Yeah, me too. Hardly a day goes by when something doesn't remind me of you. And I find myself wondering what you're doing and where you are."

He pulled her into his embrace. "I'm glad." He kissed her temple. "We should sleep. Tomorrow, ah, later today is going to be very busy."

"Don't remind me." Her voice sounded warbled as she drifted off to sleep. Safe in Remare's embrace, she knew the nightmares that haunted her would stay at bay.

Chapter Twenty-Eight

Closing his eyes, Valadon lay back in his chair after perusing several of the letters he'd discovered in the box Bastien had given him. Age had weathered the vellum some, but the handwriting was still legible enough for him to read.

Lena had written often to her confidant, the midwife, Celia. Lena had loved their baby greatly and regretted giving him up. She had cried for months after being informed of his supposed death. Her words tugged at his heart, and shades of his familiar melancholy returned.

But the journal entries written by Celia intrigued him even more. She had hated lying to Lena but was instructed to do so by the noblewoman whose name she had carefully omitted. For a few years, Celia had stayed in a small chalet on the woman's estate, helping to raise the boy.

Celia believed the Madame loved the boy as if he were her own, but the child had cried incessantly, as if he missed his natural mother. And the noblewoman had little patience. When the boy was old enough he was brought to the main house where many attendants and tutors saw to his well-being.

After her dismissal, Celia returned to her stone cottage, afraid her life was in danger. She'd known who the child's real parents were and feared she posed a threat to the Madame, even though she'd sworn never to reveal the child's true identity. She noted in her diary the times she visited the estate and saw the boy was happy and well-adjusted. She, too, felt remorse for not keeping the boy with her at her small cottage, but, then, he'd never have known all the luxuries the noblewoman provided.

Had he known Lena was pregnant, Valadon would have seen to her safety and provided well for the child. He wondered about the man his son had grown up to be. Was he as arrogant as some of the other lords he'd known in Paris? Was he benevolent? Valadon hoped so. Did he resemble his mother in any way? Or his father? The questions persisted in the back of his mind.

Images of who he thought his son might be fluttered before him. A youth dressed in silk outfits riding a horse. Another of his son enjoying a party. A young man at his studies. One thing Valadon was almost certain of—his son would have been well-educated. Affluent men during the seventeenth and eighteenth centuries usually were.

Valadon examined the ring he'd once given Lena. He remembered the night he gave it to her. It was a beautifully engraved piece with his emblem beside the black diamond. Rummaging deeper into the box, he found what looked like a small piece of metal. At first, he thought it a coin, but on further inspection it appeared to be a totem of some sort. On one side were the words, *'Justice Pour Tous,'*—Justice For All. He turned the coin over and smirked.

A lizard was engraved on this side, or more accurately, a chameleon. Montglat had kept his word to send him a gift, after all.

***

"So, how does this look?"

"Pretty good." Nick glanced at the suit Vincent was holding. "I'm glad you went with the black on black. It suits you."

"I'm kind of excited for tonight. And, here, I thought I would be spending the summer touring Quebec's wilderness." Vincent pushed his long locks from his face. "Do you think we'll have time to get a haircut?"

"Of course." Nick wasn't nearly as excited. Valadon had explained it was a marriage of state, a business deal carefully negotiated. Nothing romantic. Hell, when, or if, Nick ever decided to marry, he was damned sure he was going to be in love with the woman and she with him. Still, it bothered him he'd been lying to someone he considered a friend. "We have hours before the ceremony. It's a midnight affair. Do you want to go out for breakfast?"

"It's way too early to be up and about." Vincent smiled. "Surely, some restaurant around here delivers?"

When Valadon approved his choice of apartments, Nick had been too intent on moving his stuff in rather than stocking the fridge. Except for his required bags of blood, there wasn't much to munch on. And, as sustaining as blood was, vampires required more nourishment to maintain their muscular form. "I'm sure there is. What are you in the mood for?"

Vincent arched his back. "Large coffee, croissants, eggs Benedict. And some orange juice."

Nick got to work ordering from the deli around the corner. "Food will be here in half an hour."

"Good, because I'm starved." Vincent gazed out the large plate window. "Clear sky. Hardly any clouds. Something tells me it's going to be a memorable day."

"I suppose so. Listen, Vincent, can we talk for a few minutes?"

"Of course. But, hey, don't feel obligated to play tour director. I know it's a big day for your uncle, and you probably have things to do. We've already seen the Statue of Liberty, Central Park, the New York Public Library—which was amazing, by the way—the Empire State Building and countless museums. I think we can take some time off to just kick back and relax."

"Yeah, that works for me. However, there's a few things you need to know. About tonight. I think you might want to sit down for this."

"All right." Vincent sat across from him on the sofa, concern marring his handsome face. "What is it?"

"Remember when I told you the reason I transferred up to McGill University was, in part, because of a girl?"

"Yeah, you told me not to ask. I figured it must have been painful, so I backed off from asking any questions."

"She tried to kill me." Nick shook his head, part of him still had a hard time believing he'd gotten himself in such a situation. "Seriously kill me. To curry favor with Edgar Renworth. You see my uncle is a business tycoon. He has a lot of enemies. Renworth was a competitor who lost an important contract because we were quicker on the uptake."

"Jesus. I heard the corporate world was competitive. But, really, do people kill each other over business deals gone bad?"

"Some do." Nick rubbed his jaw. "There's more. You see, my name isn't Vischon. I changed it because people were always warming up to me, thinking they could use me to get some financial deal going with my uncle."

Vincent's eyes narrowed. "What you said about your parents? That was the truth, wasn't it?"

"Oh, yes. That's not something I would ever lie about. But my last name..."

Vincent was eying him with curiosity. "Which is...?"

Nick closed his eyes, hoping his friend wouldn't hate him for keeping something so significant from him. Or, worse, see him as an opportunity. "Valadon. My last name is Valadon."

"Oh God!" Vincent stood. "Don't tell me you're related to the High Lord of New York?! *The* Valadon I've read so much about. The same vampire who spearheaded the Great Reveal and made adversaries of half the Vampire Nation? *That* Valadon?"

Nick rubbed his neck. "Yeah, but from what I hear, almost all the Conservatives who opposed his reformation later agreed with his decision. He was right, it's impossible to stay hidden with all the new technology."

"I agreed with his decision. But I also know an awful lot of vampires who strenuously disagreed. They chose to remain veiled." Vincent held his jaw. "Not sure how much longer they'll endure that way with all the satellites." He looked at him and grinned. "Got any more surprises you want to share?"

"Isn't that enough?"

"I'd say so." Keeping his hands behind him, Vincent paced. "I can see why you would want to hide your identity. It makes sense."

"I was hoping you would keep my secret. When I go back to McGill. I don't want people fawning over me because of my last name." Nick shrugged. "Or worse."

"I won't tell anyone. Though keeping this from Olivia... Yeah, that's going to sting."

"It's probably better she doesn't know. I would hate it if she started treating me differently."

"She wouldn't. But you have my word I won't tell another soul."

"Thank you. It means a lot to me. I didn't want to tell you either, but I didn't want it to come to you as a shock when I introduce you tonight."

"I'm finally going to meet this uncle of yours you talked so much about. I should've known something was up when you avoided saying his name."

The buzzer sounded. "Food's here."

"Great. Next time, wait until I have my caffeine to spring news on me of that caliber."

"Deal."

***

Valadon looked up when he heard someone knocking. "Enter."

"I have the report you requested." Carla walked toward him. "You said not to send it in an email, so I brought it when I saw the light beneath your door."

"It's very late. Shouldn't you be asleep?" His melancholy seemed to drift to his burgeoning spy. Her understated demeanor deceived those who did not see her as a threat. But her keen intelligence and stealth were to be admired. Unfortunately, her brother, Corbin, had gone missing when the HOL had been abducting vampires. He was now feared dead.

"I don't sleep much."

Neither did he. He glanced at the data. "As I thought. Thank you for bringing me this. Can I offer you a drink?"

She shook her head. "Thank you, but no."

He poured himself one, anyway. "Your instructors have all positive things to say about you. As always, you have my deepest gratitude for all your efforts."

"Thank you for recommending me for the covert operations program. I find my life has more purpose than just the designs I do for Cesare."

"Does your family still have hope your brother may be still be alive?"

"My mother does." Her gray eyes met his. "My father doesn't think so."

He only realized, now, Corbin had been her twin and detested telling her the next. "We may never find him. You realize this, and you still want to be one of my agents?"

"Of course. I know my brother may never be found. I've accepted it."

In sympathy, Valadon rose and took the young woman in his arms. "I'm sorry." He inhaled the citrus scent of her hair. "I wish I had better news to share with you."

"It's all right." Her eyes held such sadness. "I know you did your best."

When she turned and reached for the door, he surprised himself by saying. "Would you be interested in staying the night? I've decreed having a guard with me at all times. It seems I don't always follow my own rules." Instead, he'd made the two rooms closest to his the guards' quarters. In truth, he didn't want to disturb his Elite Torians. Remare had Miranda, Katya was with Tristan, Aiden with Bree, Bastien and Orion were sharing a room, and Gregori was with Irina. He was happy each had found solace with another. Only one basked in solitude: Morel, who he hoped one day would find happiness, as well.

Her eyes widened when she glanced his bed.

He smirked as he pointed. "The guard's bed is over there."

Letting go of the doorknob, Carla slowly stepped toward him. Unzipping her dress, she let it fall to the floor and pushed it away with her toes. Resolved, she stood before him, wearing only a lacy black thong. Her breasts were full, and her nipples erect. Her feminine scent permeated the air to the point where his fangs slowly elongated. He'd thought he wanted companionship tonight, but his body yearned for far more. "You realize I'm to be married later today."

"If you'd rather not." She bent to retrieve her dress.

He stopped her. "I didn't say that. I just want you to be aware, if you stay, the invitation is for tonight only."

"Understood." Rising, she met his eyes as her hands traveled up his chest to his nape. Her lips were soft as she kissed his jaw and then his mouth.

It had been so long since he'd been with a woman, one who enchanted him as Carla did. She didn't want him because she sought to curry favor for advancement, or for bragging rights that she banged the king, or any of the usual reasons women came on to him. Like him, she wanted companionship to alleviate the biting ache of loneliness and to forget, for at least a little while, the harrowing pain of loss. He kissed her, thoroughly enjoying her taste of apricots, and laid her on his bed.

Quickly removing his shirt, he covered her body with his, enjoying the sensation of her embrace. He kissed the line of her throat and nipped just deep enough to draw a thin line of blood, which he quickly lapped up. Surprised, he stared down at her. She'd been keeping a valuable secret from him. "You're a Blueblood."

She lifted one shoulder. "My family lost much of their fortune during the World Wars before they fled to America. We no longer have the status we once did. Like them, I wanted to make my own way." A half smile. "I didn't want to be treated differently because of my ancestry."

She tasted like heaven. It had been so long since he'd fed from another Blueblood. "I'll keep your secret. But you deserve more." He sighed. "I don't know how yet, but I'll find a way to restore some of what you've lost."

She massaged his nape. "I'm not asking for any favors."

Her pride intrigued him. "No, you're not. But I will consider it an honor to make restitution." He rose and quickly removed the rest of his clothes, carelessly tossing them to the floor. When she began pushing her thong down, he removed the scrap of black lace and pitched it aside. He smiled as he bent over her. Then, he took her in his arms and kissed her as passionately as she was him. He needed this. Needed to feel alive, again, needed to share.

Crazed with lust, he took her pert nipple into his mouth and sucked. Her sighs of pleasure aroused him even more. After laving the other one, he quickly turned her over on her stomach and kissed down the length of her spine. When she trembled beneath him, he caressed her from the shoulders to her hands which he held affectionately. Rising up, he slid his fingers to her wetness, plunging one inside her core. She was tight but aroused. A growl tore from his throat.

Her breaths ragged, she lifted her hips and spread her legs wide in welcome, and he would have taken her that way, but he wanted to watch her face as he penetrated her. See how she reacted to him. He gently rolled her until her eyes met his, then bent his head and licked her core slowly and thoroughly until she was arching off the bed and gasping for breath as the orgasm rocked through her. Kneeling between her thighs, he lifted her hips to his and positioned his cock at her opening. He would not thrust too hard or too quickly. This was not a woman who had gratuitous sex often. He would take her slowly, patiently.

His eyes boring into hers, he thrust into her one slow inch at a time, enjoying the moans escaping her lips until he was fully seated inside. They began to move in earnest, now. Her rising to meet his strokes and him rotating her hips to welcome him and retreat. Sweat coated both their bodies as he continued to pleasure them.

Smiling, she surprised him when she used her inner muscles to clamp him tighter. He lifted one of her legs and pulled it over his shoulder, the excitement building in her face. She was close, but he would not let her come too quickly.

If this was his last night as a bachelor, he was going to enjoy the night for as long as he could. The corner of his lips tugged upward. And make damned sure she did, as well.

Chapter Twenty-Nine

Miranda couldn't stop staring as Remare finished dressing. Naked, he was a handsome devil. Suited up in formal wear—she sighed—he was beyond drool-worthy. The golden epaulettes and braided ropes on his navy jacket reminded her of the uniforms officers wore in nineteenth century France. The short jacket barely reached his hips, but the curve of his backside was still visible. Of all the men she'd known, Remare had the nicest butt. Definitely bitable; she smirked. And she had. Plenty of times during the night.

After spending the better part of the day in bed, lounging, loving and talking, she was ready for some fresh air. She just wasn't sure about tonight's main event. "Are you sure you want me at the wedding? Vivienna is *not* going to welcome my presence."

"Of course, I want you there." He slipped on a pinky ring matching the larger gold and sapphire one he always wore. "You are my beloved." He grasped her arms and kissed her forehead. "Also, you have an uncanny ability to observe things others do not. Indeed, your perception is admirable...and needed tonight." He frowned. "I'm still not comfortable with the prospect of so many foreign diplomats in one room at the same time."

"You think someone is going to take a shot at Valadon?"

He exhaled. "I fear that may be just one possibility. With the room crowded, it will be difficult to keep aware of everyone's movements. More security is in place than we've ever had before. Metal detectors at every entry point. Hopefully, there will be no surprises."

"All right. Help me with the dress. I still don't know when you had Cesare design it."

His face lit up. "I've been waiting patiently to see you in it."

"Had to do the make-up first." After slipping into it, she turned so Remare could do the zipper. The gown clung perfectly to her curves. The material cool to her touch. The silken layers of midnight blue looked good on her, and with the two small crescent-shaped moons on the bodice, the dress was stunning. She studied herself in the full-length mirror. "Not too shabby."

"You look beautiful." He nuzzled her neck. "As always. Except you are missing two things. He retrieved a necklace of exquisite sapphires and diamonds and secured it around her neck. Then, he fastened a bracelet of the same gems around her wrist.

"Jesus, Remare. They're magnificent."

"As are you. Ready?

"I think so. Gotta say, butterflies are doing calisthenics in my stomach. I have a bad feeling about this wedding."

"All security measures needed have been implemented. Valadon even hired Gavin and some of the other Weres; they'll be posted on the roof and those of the nearby buildings. We'll be fine."

But, even as he said it, a nagging feeling of dread persisted.

***

The assassin made his way into the banquet hall. Knowing where the cameras were, he still kept his face averted. Even with the wig and latex mask that made his nose appear broader and cheekbones flatter, he took no chances. He'd attended other functions where he casually mingled with guests and acted as if he were one of the invitees. Blending in was one of his specialties. He felt the device secure in his pocket and eyed the location he would make the hit from.

Looking up at the dais, he smirked. Where better to see a monarch fall, than in front of an audience.

All logistics complete, he made his way to the bar. Masking his accent, he ordered a Stoli on the rocks. Surveying the crowd, he spotted a stunning blonde, and his heart beat faster. He allowed himself a slight smile. She'd once been his lover, in another life, another country. Her escort with the steely eyes was massively built; he would need to be to keep her protected. They thought him dead, *a ghost*. He wondered what her reaction would be when she saw him, again. But, tonight, he wasn't here for her and casually made his way toward the back.

A safe distance away, he raised his glass and saluted her. "*Nostrovia*, Irina."

***

Miranda enjoyed walking down the corridor with Remare, arm in arm. There was a time when she'd feared they'd be found out and hated sneaking around. Now that their relationship was common knowledge, it felt good not having to hide, anymore. When they approached the golden doors to the ballroom, she chuckled. "I'm glad Valadon didn't choose to name it after himself." *Welcome to Rosalyn's* was clearly etched over the entranceway.

"He thought, after all the hard work and long hours Rosalyn put into the banquet, she deserved the credit."

The doors opened, and Miranda was struck speechless. During the day, the room was stunning, but at night, it was simply spectacular. Strings of Swarovski crystals shone brightly from the ceiling. The largest near the center with gradually smaller ones fanning out. Huge exotic flower arrangements decorated the walls between the massive windows. Whoever had designed the ultra-modern lighting with the chrome fixtures had outdone himself. The place sparkled like a wonderland. Up at the dais, two large ice sculptures of swans faced each other. To the side of them were marble statues of the ancient Greek gods.

People were drinking, socializing and seeming to have a good time. Music was playing. Evidently, vampires had the reception before the actual wedding. They made their way around the circuit, greeting and socializing with Remare's old friends. After a while, her face hurt from all the smiling. She spotted Gabriel approaching them.

"Good evening, Miranda. Remare."

"Nice to see you again, Gabriel." Miranda hugged him. "I wasn't sure you'd be here."

He lifted his champagne glass. "Of course, I'd be here. Big night for Valadon, even though the circumstances are somewhat circumspect."

"To say the least." Remare shook his hand. "I'm glad you're here tonight. Valadon would have been disappointed if you'd declined his invitation. Excuse me for a moment; Aiden is signaling to me."

"You look fantastic." Miranda slid her hand down Gabriel's arm. "Snazzy."

"Nice dress. Couldn't miss the matching color with you and Remare. Most of Valadon's Torians are in black and gold."

"Not you. The dark gray looks great on you."

"Thanks." He sipped his champagne. "So, are things good between you and Remare?"

"Yeah. We have a few differences, but we're working them out."

"I watched you walk in with him. I hate to say it, but you look good together. Happy."

"Thanks. We are." She hoped, someday, Gabriel found someone he'd be equally happy with. "How's the research coming? You still at the foundation?"

"Yes. I'm working with a committee on genetics. It's fascinating to hear how others are progressing in the field."

"I'm sure it is."

After they chatted a while, Gabriel excused himself. "I'd better go pay my respects to Dad before he thinks I'm avoiding him."

The High Lord was decked out in a stunning black suit. No one could doubt he was a king, especially with the floor-length purple sash draped across his chest and over his left shoulder. Miranda wanted to speak to Valadon, but she wasn't sure what to say. Congratulations was out. Sorry you have to marry the bitch from hell, was probably not an appropriate thing to say at a wedding. She sighed. Maybe it was better she remained silent.

When a server passed by with a tray of champagne, she took one of the crystal flutes and raised it in his direction. *I'd wish you luck, Valadon, but I think you're going to need a heck of a lot more.*

Valadon's laughter echoed in her mind. *"I agree. Thank God, I already have 'a heck of a lot more'."*

Damn! She'd forgotten how easy he could slip in her mind. *"Sorry."*

"It's quite all right. Remare shares your sentiment and said something similar earlier. Enjoy the party."

Miranda spied Remare laughing with friends and decided not to disturb him. The Torians were decked out in high formal wear. Irina looked stunning in a black clingy dress which emphasized her svelte figure; Gregori was equally striking in his suit. Together, they made a handsome couple.

She rubbed her head, feeling a headache coming on. Glancing out one of the arched windows, she saw lightning flash in the distance. A storm was coming in off the ocean. She wondered if she had time to run back to Remare's room and get her migraine medicine. Letting Remare mentally know she'd be back in a moment, she made her way down the corridor and bumped into Eric, who was dressed in a deep lavender and maroon suit. Vivienna's colors.

"I'm so glad I found you." He exhaled as if he'd been running. "I was coming to talk to you. Did you get a chance to speak to Valadon?"

"I'm sorry, Eric. He's been very busy. Why are you breathing so hard?"

"I need to leave Vivienna, but I can't do that unless he grants me sanctuary. Miranda, this is very important." He glanced down. "I have information he needs to know."

"Tell me; I'll get the message to him."

"No. He's not going to accept me into his House unless I have something substantial to offer. And, trust me, what I found out is significant."

Probably something to do with vampire politics. "I'll try to get word to him. He's a bit occupied, right now, but I'll make every effort, okay?"

Nearly collapsing in relief, Eric kissed her cheek. "Thanks. That's all I ask."

"Where's Vivienna?"

"She asked me to see if the party was in full swing. Madame Lord likes to make an entrance."

Miranda didn't doubt it for a moment. "Everyone's in there that I can see."

"Okay, I better run back. And thanks, again."

She wasn't sure what to make of Eric. She'd learned to be skeptical. Especially of those in Vivienna's court, but in her gut, she felt he was genuine.

Once in Remare's room, she found her handbag and retrieved her medicine. Grabbing a bottle of cranberry juice from his fridge, she took a mouthful and swallowed the pills. Gazing at the bed, she wondered if she could just take a nap, but Remare would probably kill her if she missed the wedding. Hurrying, she locked the door and made her way back to the party.

"Oh my God, Miranda. You look great!" Nick greeted her as the elevator doors opened.

"Nick! It's good to see you, again." She hugged him. "We haven't had a chance to talk since you've been back. I've missed you."

"Thanks. I read your emails. Especially the ones on your museum's new acquisitions."

She eyed his friend.

"This is Vincent, my professor and friend from McGill."

"We've met," Vincent informed him. "I took your advice and looked west. You were right. The sunsets are more magnificent." He kissed her cheek.

Miranda felt a spark of electricity run up her arms similar to when Valadon touched her. She almost didn't recognize Vincent with his shorter hair. Her face heated. "It's good to see you, again." The last time they'd met he'd been wearing dark sunglasses; now, he wore tinted ones. She wondered what his eyes looked like; there was something familiar about him. "McGill is a fine university. You must be happy teaching there."

"I am. Very. You must come up and visit, sometime."

When they heard a noise down the hall, Nick said, "We'd better get inside. I've yet to make my congratulations to Valadon."

They made their way into the banquet hall. Once inside, Vincent's phone began ringing. "It's Olivia, my girlfriend."

"Take your call." Nick nodded as he made his way toward Valadon. "I'll introduce you to my uncle later."

While Vincent moved to the back corner of the room where the restrooms were located, Miranda searched out Remare.

"There you are." He kissed her temple. "I see Nick has finally arrived."

"Yes, he came with one of his professors from McGill…" Before she could say anything else the DJ announced the arrival of the bride.

***

"Go, now," Jeremy instructed Scorpio. "While the wedding is in full force with Vivienna's arrival, no one will see you slip away. Release Persephone from her prison cell."

Scorpio nodded, then turned to make his way down to the lowest region of Valadon House. With everybody in a celebratory mood, it would be easy to disappear into the dark region and free Mulciber's daughter.

***

Everyone turned in the direction of the doors as Vivienna's entourage entered, wearing her colors. When the Madame Lord appeared, there was a communal gasp. The woman radiated splendor. Her raven hair was piled high with sparkling diamonds and ringlets of curls draped down her back. More diamonds adorned her ears and neck, stunning in their brilliance. Her flawless pale complexion seemed to glow whenever she moved into the light. Miranda didn't like the vampire, but even she was awestruck by the woman's beauty.

Gazing at Remare, she spoke mentally. *"Have to say, she's outdone herself."*

"An exquisite study in dichotomy: as beautiful as she is on the outside, her façade masks the heart of a viper."

Miranda couldn't agree more. Exhaling, she brooded over Valadon's fate. Shaking her head, she was disgusted. Valadon had been forced into a marriage he never wanted. Marriage should be about love, commitment between two people with common goals. Vivienna only cared about herself. Valadon deserved so much better. All this so he could ascertain his son's whereabouts. She hoped the European contingent hadn't played him, and they would give him the information he needed.

"Let's join them." Taking her arm, Remare moved them toward the dais where Victor, their sage, stood on the top step, waiting to preside over the ceremony.

Was it wrong to wish for a speedy divorce before the wedding even took place? Apparently, others agreed with her; Miranda heard people making bets on how long it would last.

Valadon and Vivienna were on the third step of the dais. Remare and Miranda stayed to the side. Her stomach contorted with the awful wrongness of the situation. All Valadon wanted was to find his son, a child he'd had with his beloved Lena. Magritte knew this was his weakness and used the information to blackmail him. The only thing keeping Miranda from being sick was knowing Valadon would outfox them, somehow. She snorted, at least he'd taken steps to protect his venerable fortune.

She must have missed Victor's words because someone handed him the ribbons he would place around their wrists. First Valadon's and then Vivienna's colors. When they exchanged blood kisses, Miranda looked away. Applause rang out in the crowd. She refused to clap, not for this calamity.

Vivienna turned and smiled down at her. "You see, he only weds one worthy of him. Not those who are lacking."

Miranda didn't bother to filter her words. "You don't deserve him."

Before she realized she'd spoken aloud, Vivienna gasped and then glared at her. Miranda felt like a thousand daggers were stabbing her skull. She clutched Remare's arms as she faltered.

"What's wrong?" Distracted by the wedding, he hadn't noticed what the Madame Lord had done.

She clutched her head. "Vivienna is cutting into me."

He maneuvered between her and Vivienna and somehow stopped the mental torture. "You *dare* attack a member of our House?"

"She insulted me. As queen, I will punish anyone who offends me."

"You are *not* queen. Get over your jealousy, Vivienna. Miranda is mine and poses no threat to your marriage."

"Yours?" She tilted her head as if in contemplation. "Is that so?" She eyed Victor and smirked. "If she is truly yours, why don't you marry her?" She casually waved her arm. "We have the sage; our people are all gathered. Or is this simply a ploy to protect Valadon's human?"

Miranda felt her cheeks to see if her eyes had bled. The pain had been so brutal, she was sure blood stained her face. She was relieved when her fingers came away wet only with tears.

A low growl escaped Remare's mouth. "Mir-randa. How would you feel about marrying me?"

Her head snapped up. "Are you insane? She's only trying to cause trouble."

"This, I know." One corner of his mouth lifted. *"In trying to cause harm, she may have given us a boon. Let's not waste it."*

"This is her wedding! And Val's! I'm not going to ruin their day." Outside the window, lightning illuminated the sky.

"Listen to me." He held her arms. *"Vivienna sees you as a threat. I cannot keep my eyes on you twenty-four-seven. The minute my back is turned, she will try to harm you, again. Let me protect you. If we're married, she won't have cause to see you as a rival. Vivienna has a way of eliminating all competitors and making it look like accidents. Please, Mir-randa. Let's do this so neither one of us has to fear her retaliation."*

Miranda searched Remare's soulful eyes. More emotion than she'd ever seen before. As the girlfriend of a vampire assassin, she could deal. But being Remare's wife? She had no clue what that entailed or how dangerous it could be. As far as she was concerned, she was already married. To her career. *"We live different lives."*

"Yes, we do." He brushed back her tear-stained strands of hair.

"This won't work." She stroked the line of his beard. *"It can't."*

"We make it work." He winked at her. *"And, if it doesn't, you can divorce me. But, for now, let me sleep in the security of knowing Vivienna will not try to hurt you, again."* He slid his hand over the side of her head. *"I love that fantastic mind of yours. I don't want to see you wounded, again."*

Did she dare consider going through it? She looked around at the crowd. Not one person was there from her friends. No Weres, no people from her job. No one. But Remare. "Lizandra will kill me for this." Liz was supposed to be her person of honor.

He laughed. "She might try to kill us both. We'll have to come up with some way of appeasing her." He lifted her chin. "Please, Mir-randa. Will you marry me?"

She never expected to hear those words from Remare. How could she do this? She gazed up at Vivienna. Would the Vixen Queen really try to kill her? Would she succeed? Miranda tasted her power; it was stronger than she'd imagined. Could she continue coming to ValCorp and not be afraid the vampire would endanger her? Would the vixen make her death look like an accident? She could. Remare was waiting for her answer. *"If we do this, it's not a contract between us. Just a bond. We end it as soon as we realize it's not working, okay?"*

"Your faith in me is beguiling." He smirked then brought her up on the third step and addressed the crowd. "Ladies and gentlemen, your attention, please. I have an announcement."

Miranda glanced at Valadon. *"He's trying to protect me. Vivienna made a threat against me. She suspects we're involved."*

Valadon grabbed Vivienna, who looked like the picture of innocence, by the arm. Remare must have spoken silently to him, because the High Lord eyed him and then Miranda and nodded his consent.

"A happy surprise." He grinned. "Miranda has agreed to become...my wife."

The applause echoed loudly throughout the room as she leaned into Remare's embrace. The shock of hearing it aloud made her heart beat out a staccato. When the crowd quieted, they faced the sage.

Miranda's breaths quickened as Remare took her hands in his. His eyes were more intense than she'd ever seen, the red rims pulsing. She knew Victor was speaking but he sounded so far away even though he was only a few feet from them. Remare slipped off his pinky ring and slid it on her finger. Miranda felt her knees go weak. As no one had ribbons in the colors Remare favored, he gave his midnight blue handkerchief to Victor, who folded it around their wrists.

"I take only a taste of your blood." He bit her neck, and Miranda nearly collapsed. *"Your turn, my love."*

Oh, no-no-no! Miranda couldn't bite him with so many watching. Her heart was hammering in her chest. She couldn't do it. *"I can't."*

"Miranda, if you don't, you will humiliate me in front of everyone."

She needed to do this. Remare bent his head, and she leaned closer, his scent of pine infusing her with strength.

Her mouth on his neck; somehow, she found the courage and bit. His blood filled her mouth, and she quickly swallowed. Her stomach nearly lurched.

The ceremony complete, people shouted and applauded wildly. It was only then that she realized she'd given Remare a blood oath. Unable to comprehend the significance, she saw Irina gasp and hold on to Gregori's arm. Clutching her stomach, Miranda understood her sense of shock; she was feeling pretty much the same.

She thought she would faint, there was a buzzing in her head, and so much was going on around her. People congratulating them, shaking hands, offering well-wishes, but her eyes locked on Vincent who was steadily making his way through the crowd. He'd taken off his glasses, and Miranda saw his eyes were the same as Valadon's.

Vincent approached the High Lord with tears threatening to break loose. He glanced first at Vivienna. "Mother." Then, at Valadon with curious anticipation. "Father?"

Valadon looked as if he'd seen a ghost. He stood rapt as so many emotions crossed his face: shock, confusion, wonder. Then, finally, adoration. Blu had once told Miranda blood recognizes blood. Apparently, he was right because Valadon pulled Vincent into a tight hug. The father-son reunion was so heartwarming Miranda thought tears of her own would break lose.

Vivienna stood motionless. She, too, was in shock. As was Magritte who stood with anger coloring her visage.

Suddenly, the buzzing sound contracted, and a popping sound was heard. Someone had fired a shot at Valadon, but instead of it hitting the High Lord, it hit Vincent! In the back of his neck, a vampire's only vulnerability. His body crumpled to the floor.

Miranda pushed people away to get to them. Vampires were hard to kill, but they weren't impervious. Sever the spinal cord, and they died. Just as the assassin intended.

She thought the windows would shatter when Valadon bellowed in rage as he held Vincent's limp body in his arms.

Miranda joined them. So did Vivienna. When the Madame Lord spotted the bullet-shaped dart embedded in his neck, she went to pull it out.

"No! Don't." Miranda grabbed her arm. Aghast, Vivienna attempted to slap her, but Valadon stopped her.

"What is it, Miranda?"

"He's in shock." She sniffed the wound. "It's not a bullet." Her hand hovered over Vincent's neck. "It's not severed. Not yet."

"How do you know?" Vivienna demanded.

"He still breathes." Miranda could feel the bio-electrical current still running through his body. She wondered if the electrical storm raging outside was somehow enhancing her own abilities. "It's a coil. Copper."

Remare knelt down beside her. "We've kept an eye on the weapons our enemies have been manufacturing. If it's the device I think it is, it's in the shape of a spider, but instead of several legs, there are three tentacles that wind around an object." He glanced at Vivienna. "If you had pulled it out, you would have killed him."

"Valadon. Keep everyone away. I can loosen it."

Valadon instructed his Torians to escort everyone from the banquet hall. The room soon emptied.

Gabriel stayed. "Do you need help, Miranda?"

She shook her head. "There's a vibration here. I think the device has some sort of microchip embedded."

"It does. Be careful, Mir-randa." Remare warned, "Some of those devices are known to self-destruct, along with whoever tampers with it."

"Good to know." Miranda closed her eyes and focused her power on the area of Vincent's neck surrounding the device. "The tentacles imbedded themselves around his spinal cord. They have barbs on them. Devious makers of the device." She breathed deep. "I've undone one." She was glad the components were copper. If it had been made of plastic or synthetic fibers, she wouldn't be able to feel the metal's frequency. "The second one's fighting me, as if it's been programmed to stay coiled."

Miranda concentrated harder than she'd ever done before. Blood began dripping down Vincent's neck. She met Valadon's stare and saw his red rims were pulsing. In that moment, she wondered how anyone could mistake the High Lord for a human. His Other worldliness vibrated all around him, as if music from another dimension were playing. "An energy boost would help, right now."

Valadon leaned toward her as his penetrating gaze seared her. An epiphany about why he'd once frightened her ignited. Valadon had depths of knowledge, ideas and emotions from the various centuries he'd lived through. Answers to unimaginable questions. Keys to doors she wasn't ready to open. The vastness of it all was unfathomable. It woke something primal in her, something dark. It wasn't Valadon who'd scared her, but the beast within, yearning to break free, that she kept carefully caged. She promptly locked down those thoughts.

His voice cut into her reveries. "How?"

She smiled calmly at him. "A touch." She moved closer to him, the pull between them too strong to deny. His attraction seemed to be a living, breathing entity as if his water element was reaching—striving for the warmth of her fire, the natural magnetic pull of opposites.

His energy rubbed against hers, coating her with more power. Just when she thought their lips would meet, he stroked her arm. And that was the source she needed. "Second one's undone."

Valadon and the rest seemed to breathe easier.

The third coil was the toughest. Each of the barbs had imbedded themselves in the spinal column. She carefully summoned them to unwind, one barb at a time. The scent of copper was making her nauseous. What world she absorbed power from she didn't know, but it felt as if she was drifting. Energy flowing through her fingers as natural as the air. Breathing deep, she removed the last barb. After pulling it from Vincent's neck, she handed it to Remare. "You may want to have your men look at that."

Valadon cut his wrist and dripped blood into Vincent's wound. His body quickly absorbed it. Miranda was amazed at how fast vampire blood healed injuries. And, as a Blueblood, Valadon's blood was very powerful.

Gabriel moved in closer. "Even though the wound is closed, I think we should take him to the infirmary. His tendons might have been injured. I'd like to take a sonogram. Just to be sure."

"I called for a stretcher." Valadon nodded. "Amory is on his way."

When Miranda tried to stand, she swayed. Remare caught her. "Are you all right?"

"A bit woozy. I could use some water."

Someone handed her a bottle, and she greedily swallowed several mouthfuls. "I think I need to lie down for a while."

The last thing she remembered was Remare swooping her up in his arms.

Chapter Thirty

Staying in the shadows, Orion moved silently through the darkened levels beneath Valadon House toward the dungeons. Trailing Scorpio had been fairly easy. Wearing the electronic ear plug, Aiden had alerted him when the spy had left the reception. Orion hated missing the wedding but understood the importance of Valadon's request. Weres could move very furtively in the darkness. Having trained with Bastien, he knew how to keep a safe distance without being detected. But, just in case anything went wrong, he had a gun strapped to his side. And back up was close by, Gavin already in position.

The Torians had provided him with a salve that masked his scent as a Were so the dhampire wouldn't detect his presence.

When Scorpio neared Persephone's cell, he called out to her but must have realized she'd be in the deep sleep of vampires and set upon unlocking her door.

Once Scorpio entered the room, he cautiously moved toward the sleeping form, but before he realized it was a mannequin wearing Persephone's clothes, Orion quickly shut the heavy metal door and Gavin secured the lock, trapping him inside. The two Weres knuckle-tapped. "One less rat to worry about."

Orion contacted Bastien. "Mission accomplished." There was some discussion about locking Scorpio in with Persephone, who'd earlier been moved to a different cell, but it was felt the two would kill each other, and Valadon wanted Scorpio alive. For the time being, anyway.

"Let me out!" the dhampire roared. "I've done nothing wrong. I was merely checking on her."

"You can tell that to the vampire king when he comes to visit. He'll be having a few questions for you. If you're smart, you won't waste his time." Gavin chided, "Maybe he'll show you the same consideration you showed him."

Scorpio banged his fists against the door until Orion shut the small metal opening that allowed for conversation between jailor and prisoner. "Let's get back upstairs."

***

As Miranda awoke, her mind was still groggy but she knew she was in the infirmary by the smell of antiseptics. Glancing up at Remare, she said, "I had the strangest dream you and I got married."

Remare chuckled. "Check your left hand."

The sapphire sparkled at her. Miranda shook her head to clear the cobwebs. "No way!" But, then, all the events of the night came rushing back. "And you're good with this?"

"Of course. I did ask you, didn't I?" He glanced sideways. "Though, I don't think Valadon's marriage will last very long."

Miranda glanced to the side where a small crowd was gathered around Vincent. "Is he all right?"

"Resting. Gabriel says he's doing fine. He just wants to keep him here overnight for observation."

"You knew!" Valadon's words seared as he tried to contain his rage in barely controlled whispers. "You knew, all this time, but you chose to keep my son from me. Why?"

Vivienna sighed. "He's my son, too. I adopted him when he was an infant. I had no idea he was your son until after. I thought he was one of Brandon's bastards."

"Don't lie to me! You knew Marlena de Avignon was my lover and that she bore me a son. You knew, and you kept this from me!"

"I didn't know! Not until years later. You had no interest in me. You told me to go to hell, remember?! You wanted to leave the safety of the High Court to come to America. What kind of life could you have shown Vincent? It was all wilderness! Spartan. I gave him every comfort. He never wanted for anything."

"Keep your voices down!" Gabriel hissed.

Valadon looked like he wanted to strangle Vivienna.

"Father," Vincent whispered. "Don't harangue my mother. She told me when I was a youth I was adopted."

Valadon hovered over Vincent. "How are you feeling, my son?"

"I'm fine. A little tingling in my fingers and toes."

Gabriel was there in an instant, examining Vincent's eyes with a pen light. He squeezed Vincent's hand. "Any numbness?"

"None."

Gabriel used one of the wooden tongue depressors to brush against Vincent's foot. "How about here?"

"No. I can feel that."

Everyone let out a collective sigh.

Vincent looked up at Nick and smiled. "I guess this means we're cousins. Now, I know why I warmed up to you so quickly."

"I had absolutely no idea." Nick gave the others a dark look. "You know you were shot, right? You should be thanking the person responsible for your being alive." He glanced at her.

Miranda waved. "Glad to see you're awake."

Vincent looked confused. "How?"

"Long story. It can wait. I'm just glad you're looking better." She threw her feet over the side of the bed and tried to stand. Remare was there to assist as she swayed.

"Vincent," Valadon explained, "this is Miranda Crescent and her...husband, Remare, my second in command."

"It's good to finally meet you. Your father and I have been searching for you for a long time." Remare glared at Vivienna.

"As soon as we were made aware of your birth, we began our investigation."

"I thought Brandon was my father." Vincent looked up at Vivienna. "Why didn't you tell me?"

Vivienna appeared to be composing herself. "By the time I realized you couldn't be Brandon's, Valadon had already left me. Your demeanor was far more reserved than your uncle's." The Madame Lord glanced at Valadon. "I was afraid he'd take you from me."

"This is all very touching, but I still haven't finished my examination. Do you think this little family reunion could be held later?" Gabriel asked, "Somewhere other than my infirmary?"

Vivienna looked aghast. "You employ the most acerbic people."

Valadon smirked at Gabriel. "At times, I do. But, in this case, the doctor is right. I suggest we move this discussion to one of my conference rooms where we'll all be more comfortable."

"I want to come." Vincent tried to stand but became wobbly.

"No, you don't." Gabriel helped him back to bed. "I can probably fill you in on a few details. Valadon may be High Lord of this House, but in the infirmary, I'm lord, and my word is final."

Valadon grinned. "Take good care of your patient, Doctor. I trust you'll keep your barbs to a minimum."

Feigning hurt, Gabriel covered his heart with his hand. "You wound me. Would I do such a thing?"

"See that you don't." Valadon ushered everyone to the exit then turned to Gabriel. "Guards will be posted in and around this location. If there are any deviations, contact me immediately."

The last one to leave, Miranda glanced back at Vincent and Gabriel, who pulled a chair closer to Vincent's bed.

"Now, bro, do I have a story for you."

Once in the corridor, Morel approached Remare. "There's something requiring your attention."

"Can it wait?"

"It can, but I think you may want to see it, now."

Surrounded by his Elite Torians, Valadon said, "Go. Meet me in the conference room later."

Miranda stayed with Remare. "Do you want me to accompany you or would you rather I wait in your rooms?"

Remare raised an eyebrow to Morel, as if waiting for a reply.

Morel shrugged. "Your call."

"As my wife, I think you should come." He linked their fingers and brought her hand to his lips.

"I thought I was imagining your nuptials. I suppose congratulations are in order." Morel winked at Miranda. "Do I get to kiss the bride?"

"No!" Miranda and Remare replied.

Once in the communications room, Aiden rose from his seat and addressed Remare. "We scrutinized the surveillance tape of the wedding. There's something you should see."

Aiden's wife, Bree, joined them. "Is it true?"

Miranda held up her left hand.

They watched in silence as Aiden rewound the video. "Everything seemed to be progressing well with the ceremony. When the assassination attempt happened, we replayed the tape in slow motion. This is what we found."

Miranda watched the images of Valadon and Vivienna near the dais. Several Torians were nearby, as were some of Vivienna's people.

"Watch the trajectory of the shot fired," Morel said.

"There's a clear path to Valadon. Except for one person."

Miranda thought Aiden meant Vincent, who'd been hit by mistake. She gasped when she saw who the intended target was. "That bullet wasn't meant for Valadon, was it?"

Remare growled. "Play it back. This time, slow it down to two point five."

Aiden adjusted the controls, as directed. Everyone was congratulating Valadon as one person stood in front of him. It was only at the last second that Vincent blocked the shot and took the hit.

"The intended target wasn't Valadon." Remare turned to Morel and Aiden. "Magritte was."

The leader of the Vampire Nation, Queen of All Vampires, Magritte was one of the most powerful vampires in the world. And someone had wanted her dead.

Remare was stone cold. "Who else has seen these videos?"

"No one," replied Morel. "Everyone else was at the wedding. Aiden and Bree were the only others in the room with me. We thought you should know as soon as possible."

Remare sternly nodded. "Valadon must be informed immediately." He rose. "Do not discuss your findings with anyone. Is that clear?"

Both Torians and Bree nodded.

As they walked down the hall, Miranda asked, "Who do you think hired the assassin?"

"Undetermined." He rubbed his jaw. "She has many enemies. Any one of them could have decided to take her out. My guess is someone who covets her power and position. Someone who stands to benefit from her demise."

"Remare, that device was meant to torture before it eventually killed."

"Yes, I know. Someone wanted her to suffer. And I'd bet they wanted to watch, as well." He turned toward her. "I think it best you wait in my rooms."

Miranda nodded. She didn't want to become embedded in any more vampire politics. And Remare, her husband—geez, was she ever going to get used to that word?—needed to focus on the business at hand. "Let me know what's going on. When you can."

"I will." He kissed her forehead then turned and left.

Miranda was halfway to her room when she ran into Eric in the hall. "Is everything all right? I can't believe someone tried to take out the High Lord at his wedding."

She didn't bother to correct him. "Listen, Eric. I can't get to Valadon, right now. You need to be patient."

"I can't." He seemed to be jumping out of his skin. "There's already talk we'll be leaving. I have to see Valadon before we go. I'll never get the chance, again."

"Eric?"

Miranda turned to see Rosalyn approaching.

"My God, is it really you?" Her hand was shaking as she reached out to touch him. Tears glistened in her eyes.

"Rosalyn, dear sister. Oh, God!" Eric threw his arms around her and held her tightly as if he let go she'd disappear. "I thought about you so often."

"Why didn't you come home?"

He loosened his hold on her. "How could I? Mom and Dad forbid it. They disowned me for joining Vivienna's court."

"No, they didn't! They were heartbroken when Vivienna told them you no longer wished to return because you enjoyed the excitement of the Parisian court."

"I *never* said that! I hated her court. I wanted to return to Finland, I swear it. Vivienna told me our parents forbid it."

Miranda's heart warmed at the brother and sister reunion but didn't think this a safe place for revelations. "I think you better continue your conversation inside your rooms."

"Come with me." Rosalyn grabbed his hand and led him in the direction of her room. "We have much to discuss."

"What a night for family reunions," Miranda muttered as she watched them depart.

Once inside Remare's room, she locked the door and plopped down on the bed. The events of the evening were catching up with her and exhaustion was setting in. Just when she thought she'd fall asleep there was a loud knocking on the door. "Who is it?"

"Orion. Open up."

As soon as she unlocked the door, Orion brushed past her. "You got married?!"

Miranda winced. "Ye-ah."

"Didn't you think you should tell someone first?! I just found out from Bastien."

"It happened really fast. I swear. Vivienna tried playing her mind games with me. She hurt me. Badly. When Remare saw what she was doing, he asked me to marry him so she wouldn't dare do it, again. To protect me. It seemed like a real good idea at the time."

His eyes widened. "You mean no other Weres know?!"

"Noooo!"

"Oh man, you are so fucked! When Lizandra finds out, she's going to rip you a new one."

Miranda rubbed her head in frustration. "None of this happened the way it was supposed to. We were supposed to stand up for each other. No one was there from my side, no Weres, no humans from work, ha, no family members."

"So," he grinned, "do I congratulate you or get you drunk?"

No more drinks, she thought. The one glass of champagne she had at the wedding had made her dizzy. Sighing, her smile was lopsided. "I guess you congratulate me."

Orion grabbed her in a bear hug. "I never thought I'd see the day. My God, I always wanted the best for you. You're married to the second most powerful vampire in all of New York. You sure you know what you're doing?"

"Not a clue." She laughed. "But we're going to try to make it work. No more sneaking around. We're going to take it one day at a time. See where it takes us."

Orion started laughing. "Well, it won't be boring. I can tell you that much."

She propped herself up on the bed, and Orion sat near the edge. She didn't think she'd mind boring all that much, but with Remare, she couldn't imagine things ever getting dull. "Did you know Valadon found his long-lost son?"

"Bastien told me some deets." Orion rubbed his neck. "It's hard to imagine Vivienna being a mother to anyone, but Nick said he's a standup guy."

"I met him once in Paris. Briefly. At Vivienna's house. He's a poet." She wondered if Orion heard any of the other news. "You heard about the assassination attempt."

"Yeah, the Torians are all looking into it. Bastien's packing to go on some sort of secret mission."

"How're things going between you two?"

"Pretty good. We stayed at your cottage in the French countryside. It's beautiful there. We found a box underneath one of your floor boards. It had letters and stuff from Valadon's former girlfriend. Bas and I flew home as soon as we could to give it to Valadon."

"In my cottage?"

"Yeah, buried deep. I only found it because I tripped on one of the planks. Bas says the box was centuries old. It contained one of Valadon's rings he must have given the girl."

Miranda was shaking her head in disbelief. But, then, she'd heard stories of long lost works of art buried in basements. "Didn't find any old paintings, did you?"

"Nah, no such luck."

"What's going on, now, with Valadon?"

"Oh man, you should have been there. Valadon was so furious at Vivienna I thought he'd kill her for keeping Vincent from him."

Just then, another knock at the door.

"Who is it?" Miranda asked.

"The one who is going to kick your ass from here to hell!"

The Were Queen had arrived. And she was not happy.

Chapter Thirty-One

"You knew!" Valadon was furious with Vivienna as he paced in his conference room. "You knew all this time and chose to keep my son's identity a secret. I knew you had a taste for cruelty, but why?"

"I told you." She circled away from him. "I didn't realize he was your son until he began to show patterns so unlike Brandon."

"You committed fraud against me. This marriage will be annulled as soon as I can get my lawyers to draw up the papers."

"You dare to do such a thing?" Outrage laced her voice. "How have I committed fraud?"

"You deceived me by keeping valuable information from me. I will make you a generous offering. Once. Take it and leave my territory."

"I will not! Not as long as Vincent is here."

Valadon scribbled a number down on a piece of paper and shoved it toward her.

She laughed. "As if."

"Consider your actions carefully, Vivienna." He waited a moment to deliver his *coup de grace*. "I have Brandon in custody. You harbored a known traitor in your territory, among other illicit acts." His voice was menacing. "I can cause you far more damage than you can ever do to me."

Vivienna's eyes widened as she gasped. "Brandon is a known prevaricator. Don't believe a word he says."

"I don't have to. I read his mind when I apprehended him."

The Madame Lord of Paris had the grace to look horrified.

"You gave him sanctuary in your home after he tried to usurp my throne. You, he and Magritte conspired against me to get control of ValCorp. Shall I list all the crimes you're guilty of?"

"Brandon was always jealous of you. You knew that. Where is he, now?"

"In a safe place. One he'll never escape from. A very dark, cold place." His eyes bore into hers. "One I wouldn't mind seeing you in. Now, do we have an accord?"

Her eyes seemed to be racing as if she were searching for some sort of viable alternative, when none surfaced, she capitulated. "I'll accept your offer. On one condition."

***

"That's her." Gabriel wheeled Vincent down the aisle in the archives to where Marlena de Avignon's portrait hung. "She's my great, great, multiple times, grandmother. Your mother. Valadon told me stories about her."

Vincent tried to rise, but Gabriel put a hand on his shoulder. "It's best to stay sitting." When Vincent had expressed his desire to see her portrait, the only way Gabriel would allow it was if he stayed in the wheelchair. He wasn't taking any chances with his half-brother. "She's beautiful, isn't she?"

Vincent nodded slowly. "I have no memory of her."

"You wouldn't. You were only an infant." Gabriel gazed up at the portrait. "Back then, pregnant, unmarried women didn't fare well. Valadon was away on business, and she had no one to turn to but the midwife. You're lucky you wound up in an aristocratic household."

"I know. I had many advantages others did not," Vincent said as his eyes stayed glued to the portrait. "Vivienna made sure I never wanted for anything. She loves me."

"A bit temperamental, if you ask me."

"Among other things, but she's still the only mother I ever knew." Vincent shook his head. "I can't tell you how overwhelming all this is to me. I can't believe I have a father. And that he's Valadon."

"Well, in that regard, I can sympathize." Gabriel exhaled. "He's my father, as well." When Vincent glanced at him, he added, "He turned me. When I lay dying, over a hundred years ago. We'd been friends. My family was ambushed by Rogues. I barely survived. When I woke, it was during the terrible transition."

"You didn't know what was happening?"

"I wasn't given a choice. Valadon made it for me." Gabriel exhaled. "I resented him for a long time. It's only recently I've come to terms with it."

"How did Valadon know you were one of Marlena's descendants?"

"He told me he kept track of all of her children through the centuries. I was the last living one. He couldn't let me die. I've accepted it."

"So, we really are brothers."

"Afraid so." Gabriel smirked. "Welcome to the family!" He pointed to the life-sized portrait that hung high near the ceiling. "That's your Aunt Bianca. Nick's mom. She died not long after he was born."

"Nick looks just like her."

"That he does." Gabriel rubbed his jaw. "He's not much like Valadon, though."

"I wish I had known them. It's like I have this whole new family I know little about."

Gabriel reached up to retrieve Marlena's diary. "Don't try to figure it all out at once." He handed the tome to Vincent. "This is her journal. I've already read it. You might get some insights."

"Thank you." He thumbed through the pages. "I'm getting tired; would you take me back to my room?"

"Sure. You need your rest. In the next few days, if you have any questions, I'll be happy to answer them."

***

"*What? The? Fuck?!*"

Miranda grimaced as Lizandra stood waiting for an answer. "Yeah, that's pretty much how I felt."

"You get married, and you don't even invite me? *Me!? Your best friend!*"

"As I tried to explain to Orion..." She was going to kill her friend, who'd taken off as soon as Lizandra had shown up. "It happened very quickly. Vivienna used her mental abilities to make it feel like she was stabbing my brain. Remare saw the pain I was in and offered to marry me to keep me protected." She exhaled. "He made a really good argument."

"I don't believe you! Couldn't you wait one lousy day?!"

"Nooo! Not really. All the people were there; the sage was there. We were all dressed up." Miranda collapsed onto the sofa. "I have no blasted clue what I'm doing. I'm flying blind on this one."

Lizandra softened her tone. "Are you happy?"

Miranda shrugged. "I'm not unhappy. Confused. Worried. In shock, pretty much sums it up."

"Holy crap! You really are married. When Gavin called, I thought he was pulling my leg. You really did it! You married Remare!"

"Yeah. I sure did. We have a lot to work out."

Lizandra sat near her. "You will. You and he love each other. You'll find the answers."

"Think so?"

"Yeah. Know so. I'm just so surprised. I can't believe you're married. *Holy, holy shit!* How's Remare dealing with it?"

"He's laughing his ass off at the irony. Vivienna was trying to hurt us. She wound up uniting us."

Liz narrowed her eyes. "Vivienna?"

"Valadon's new wife. She sees me as some sort of competition; that's why she hurt me. And why Remare married me. He said she couldn't be trusted. But, as his wife, any attempt on me would be seen as a declaration of war." She shrugged.

Just then, they heard a commotion out in the hall, when they opened the door Rosalyn was furiously shouting at Vivienna, who seemed nonplussed. Suddenly, slaps were given, and a fight broke out.

Lizandra asked, "Which one are we rooting for?"

"The redhead, she's a friend of mine." Rosalyn landed a punch to Vivienna's jaw. "The dark-haired woman's Vivienna, who just slammed Roz into the wall."

"Should we join in?"

"Probably not." But, as soon as she said it, Vivienna raked her nails down Rosalyn's arm. "She's the one who slashed Orion's throat."

A vicious growl tore from Lizandra's mouth as she joined the fracas. Miranda tried to keep Rosalyn away from the fighting as the other two went at it like banshees. Arms and legs moving in all directions, too fast for her to follow. Blood and hanks of hair fell to the ground as they slashed at one other. Sounds of material being ripped and torn echoed in the hall. But, when Vivienna aimed a well-placed kick in their direction, Miranda used her powers to deflect the blow.

Screams and growls rent the air as the combatants fought for supremacy. People came running from both ends of the corridor until one deep, male voice roared, "*What the hell is going on?!*"

Valadon and Remare stood with their arms crossed. Miranda saluted her new hubby. Gavin was trying to hide his smirk. The Torians helped the women stand. Lizandra licked the blood from her fingers and smiled at Valadon. "I hear congratulations are in order. You, too, Remare."

"If this is your way of felicitations, I think you need to work on your social skills," Remare quipped as he lifted Miranda's arm so she could stand.

Liz grinned. "Just a little misunderstanding between friends."

"I request an audience with you. As soon as possible," Rosalyn addressed Valadon then glared at Vivienna as if she wanted another go.

"I have no wish to stay here a minute longer if this is the way you run your House, Valadon." Vivienna huffed, "That woman should be whipped for her insolence."

"The way you whipped and tortured my brother?" Rosalyn was seething. "I'll see you in hell before I allow him to return to your court."

"Eric joined my court because your own was too tame," she looked derogatorily at Rosalyn, "too dull."

"You kept him prisoner. He never would have chosen the life you gave him."

"Enough!" Valadon bellowed. "Everyone, go back to your rooms. I will sort this out later today. The last thing I need is any more upheaval in my House. Understood?!"

Apparently, they did, because everyone left. Except for Lizandra. "I offer my apologies. I usually don't start disturbances in other people's homes, but it looked like Vivienna was going to slaughter the redhead."

Gavin quipped, "I suppose it didn't dawn on you to call for help."

Lizandra smiled charmingly. "Not at the time."

Miranda's heart warmed at the heat between her two Were friends. Maybe there was hope for them, after all.

When Remare peered at her, as if waiting for an explanation, Miranda shrugged. "Hey, I was just trying to hold Rosalyn back."

They eyed the blast mark on the wall.

Not feeling the least bit guilty, but trying not to grin, she shrugged. "Oops!"

Chapter Thirty-Two

"Do you believe her?"

"Of course not!" Valadon slanted his second a look. "We both know Vivienna would say anything to protect her own hide. She's guilty as sin."

"But she took your offer?"

"Yes, but she did request one concession."

"Which was?"

"She made an interesting case for the stability of the ruling court. If two main Houses were at odds, it may not bode well for the entire Vampire Nation. She asked I wait a certain amount of time before going public with our annulment."

"How long?"

"I'm considering that, now."

Remare shook his head. "And the matter of the assassin?"

"He boarded a commercial airliner bound for Zurich hours after the attempt. Our agents are tracking him. It was good we had our people positioned on the roofs of the nearby buildings. The Weres reported our uninvited guest rappelled down the north side of our building into a waiting car. We tracked him to the airport. I'm betting his employer will not be happy with his failure."

"You didn't want him apprehended here?"

"No." Valadon swiveled his chair. "Let's see who he reports to."

"Who did you assign to track him?"

Valadon's eyes lit. "One I'm delighting in. An agent of remarkable talents."

"Female?"

"Quite."

Remare groaned. "Not one of the mid-level Torians? This mission is too risky."

"I'm aware of that, but I have every confidence in her abilities."

"And the other?"

Valadon smirked. "Someone with uncanny skills of subterfuge."

"All right, then. Stay behind your veil of secrets." Remare exhaled. "I'll find out, anyway, in time."

"I'm sure you will. Since I plan to have her presence here more often in the future."

"I'm sending Bastien and Tristan to track down the makers of the device. We suspect it's being manufactured in Austria. Our old friends at Ehrlich Industries. Tristan believes it is a prototype they've been rumored to be working on."

"Good. Keep me apprised of their findings."

Remare nodded. "There are so many in the courts who've wanted Magritte dead for centuries. But I'm surprised they chose now to strike."

"I'm not. They waited until she was far from her own territory, without her myriad of guards." He swiveled in his chair. "Many lords have suffered severe monetary losses they have yet to recover from. Some have borrowed luxuriously from Magritte and are heavily in debt to her. Now, who among our esteemed guests stood to gain the most from Magritte's death? Who seeks to curry favor with her possible replacement?"

"Several. I find it interesting the only high-ranking council member who was noticeably absent was Caltrone. But he's made it known he wants to be chancellor when Syrio steps down."

"And who's been in bed with Caltrone for some time, now?"

"Many. Who do you suspect?"

"One with ambition, audacious enough to plot this out in my territory. Can you imagine the fallout if the Queen had fallen in my House, under my protection? It would have cost me a great deal of discomfort and inconvenience with the other lords. Blame would have fallen in our laps."

"I'm having Aiden check the financials on the top ten on our watch list. Someone must have paid a substantial amount to the hitter. Do you suspect Vivienna had a hand in this?"

"I suspect her of a great many things. Of this, I'm not sure. Let's see what our agents uncover in Zurich."

"Magritte will not be pleased she failed to procure controlling interest in ValCorp. She will try, again; you know that."

"I do. But she'll wait to strike, again." He exhaled. "There's nothing left to do tonight." He rose and clasped Remare on the shoulder. "Go home to your wife. I'm sure she misses you."

"You're not going to disavow my marriage, now that the foreign dignitaries are leaving?"

He shook his head. "I think I'll let you and Miranda work that one out. You allowed Vivienna to manipulate you."

"I let her think she was manipulating me."

"And now?"

"I have a wife." He grinned. "One who I love very much and plan to spend whatever time I can with."

"Give her my best."

"I will."

***

"I don't see why I can't come." Orion flopped down on Bastien's bed and watched his friend pack. "We've worked well together on missions."

Bas slanted Orion a look. "Not this time. I need Tristan with me. He knows more about weapons than anyone. And he's a great tracker."

"Hey, what am I, chopped liver?!" He pointed to his nose. "Who's better than Weres at tracking?"

"You're great at it. But Tristan has years of knowledge and experience you don't. He's studied weapons and manufacturers of armaments for decades. He's already doing the research on the device that nearly killed Valadon's son. Besides, it was Remare who assigned us."

"Remare. I still can't believe he and Miranda are married." Orion rolled to his back. "And that I missed it."

Bastien laughed. "It was unexpected. But, you know, he looks happy. I'm glad he's back. The place wasn't the same without him." He zipped up his backpack. "I'll be gone a few days, a week at most."

Orion peered up at him. "Stay safe." He rose to get the door for Bastien. "I still think it should be me going."

"Stay here tonight. It's almost morning, anyway."

The heat between them intensified as the room grew smaller. Orion tried to pull his eyes away from Bastien's lips, but his hunger was too demanding. God, he loved the way Bastien smiled. Not quite a smirk, it was sexy as hell with his slightly raised eyebrow that always made Orion's stomach flip.

Before he knew what was happening, Bas let his backpack fall to the floor and pinned him against the door and kissed him. He. Fucking. Kissed. Him. Full on the mouth. Orion's arms locked around him, and for one blessed moment, he knew what heaven felt like.

Bas broke from the kiss. "I'll be back before you know it. That was something for you to remember me by." He winked then closed the door behind him.

Orion leaned against the wall. It took a minute for his breaths to subside. He broke out in a wide grin and howled loud enough for the whole House to hear.

***

Valadon slowly opened the door to Vincent's room. Even with the lights on low, he could perfectly see his son's sleeping form. And Gabriel, who had fallen asleep in the chair next to him. Not to be left out was Nick, who was sprawled out on the sofa. *His boys!* Though none of them were boys, anymore, they were still his children, and he was overcome with pride for each one.

In the coming days, he would spend as much time with Vincent as possible. He wanted to learn all about his upbringing and travels. Aiden had downloaded and reported as much as he could about Professor Deschanel's professional history: The universities where he'd taught, the cities he'd lived in. But very little was known about his personal life. Valadon would make it his business to find out.

He'd been robbed of nearly four hundred years of memories. He wanted to strangle Vivienna. There was nothing he could do about the past, but he would make sure as hell his son knew who his father was and that he was loved. Regret tugged at him; Vincent would never know his biological mother, Lena. She'd be so proud of their son and the man he'd grown up to be.

And Gabriel. His other son slept with his mouth open, snoring lightly. Lena would have been pleased to know so many of her descendants had lived happy lives. Valadon had seen to it that they did. Though he'd been unable to spare Gabriel the pain and horror of losing his family, he'd been well-provided for. Valadon wondered how having his brother around would affect him. Would it make Gabriel more grateful for what he had, instead of angry for the things he didn't?

Both sons had Lena's smile and the curve of her jaw. Her legacy wasn't lost. He hoped she rested in peace in whatever great beyond existed. *Sleep well, my love; you are not forgotten.* And he'd make sure both sons knew what a wonderful woman she'd been. And maybe, in time, he could finally let go of the ghosts who haunted him.

He glanced at his beloved nephew. Nick had grown up without really knowing his mother, as well. Bianca had been more precious to Valadon than any other relative. He'd made sure he and the Torians filled Nick with stories about her and his father, Korvo. Their love was a story to last the centuries. Favorites in every court they visited. An enchanting couple, their lives cut down too early by an unfortunate plane crash.

One he still hadn't been completely satisfied with the technical reports. He sighed, but there was nothing he could do to bring any of them back. The past was gone. What he wouldn't give to have just one more day with each of them. Vampires lived long lives. They had more time to appreciate the ones they loved. But they also lived with the pain of loss for far longer.

He made a silent vow each would know how precious they were to him.

***

Before he began his wedding night with Miranda, Remare had one last errand to complete. He knocked on Vivienna's door and entered.

"You!" She continued packing. "Are you here to gloat?"

"Why would I?" He leaned against one of the posts of her bed.

"We would have been happy. I would have made him forget the past. He would have learned to love me, again."

"You live in a fairy tale, Vivienna. Let it go. Let go of the past. Valadon has moved on. So should you."

"As you have?" She narrowed her eyes. "There were rumors circulating in the courts you'd had an affair with Valadon's mistress. Did you fall in love with the human, too?"

"Miranda is my wife, now. I intend to keep her as such."

"A human!" Vivienna laughed. "You surprise me. You never had a taste for humans before. Is this what living in America does to vampires?"

Remare had learned long ago never to allow vampires like Vivienna to know his true feelings. The old vampires played with emotions the way children played with toys. And, like infants, they often broke them. "Living in America has little to do with it. We simply choose not to live in the past but look forward to the future."

"We had a good relationship." She slinked up to him, her hands traversing his chest. "Remember the fire between us?"

He'd once thought her beautiful, certainly one of the most stunning women in the world. But Vivienna was ruled by her passions, primarily her desire for power "I remember many things." He brushed her arms away. Only one woman had the right to touch him so familiarly. "Not the least of which was your ambition."

"Did you never wonder, if I hadn't fallen under Caltrone's spell, just how happy we could have been? You, me and Valadon. We traveled to so many of the courts. I remember many great evenings we shared." She sneered. "Do you really believe you can find such passion in the arms of a human?"

He already had. "There's more to life than passion, Vivienna."

"Of course there is." She backed off when she realized her charms were wasted on him. He'd seen beneath her façade to the viper underneath. "But you didn't come here to reminisce, so why are you here?"

"Too true." He straightened and stepped away. "Valadon wants you informed he's granted sanctuary to Rosalyn's brother, Eric." Had he known the young vampire had information concerning Brandon, he would have arranged an audience sooner. He clicked his teeth together. "That was a rather nasty trick you played on him. Even for you."

She scoffed. "People are either pawns or players. He wanted in on my court. I gave him access." Her violet eyes glittered with lust. "He experienced pleasures others have only ever dreamed about."

Remare wasn't going to remind her the youth had suffered miserably because of his curiosity and ignorance. He'd seen the scars on Eric's back for himself, the evidence of Vivienna's passion. "I wish you well, Madame Lord." He turned away. "May your travels be safe ones."

She couldn't refuse one last shot at seduction. It was her nature. "Will you be visiting my court any time soon?"

Unlike her, he'd shut the door on the past a long time ago. "Oh, I doubt it. I really doubt it."

Chapter Thirty-Three

"What are you doing?"

"Getting ready for work." After changing into a pair of slacks and shirt, Miranda was putting the last of her cosmetics away. She glanced at Remare, who was leaning against the wall.

"You do realize it's our wedding night?"

"It was. Unfortunately, you had to work. It's morning, now, and I have a job to get to."

"You can't be serious! You'd rather work at the museum than see to your husband's needs?"

"My *husband* had to work late and missed his own wedding night. Just as well. We had a lot of visitors." She counted on her fingers. "Orion wishes us well, as does Selena, Rosalyn, Gavin and Lizandra."

"So does Valadon and the rest of the Torians. Don't go to work, Mir-randa." His voice was seductive. "Stay here...with me."

"Sorry. Your job is important to you, as mine is to me."

"My *job* is seeing to the welfare of those employed at ValCorp. There is no such urgency at the museum."

"Are you implying your work is more important than mine?"

He moved closer to her. "People can die if I ignore my responsibilities."

Remare had many good qualities; his arrogance wasn't one of them. "You don't think highly of what I do, do you?"

"I didn't say that. But you must admit more rides on my obligations than the validation of whether a portrait was painted by a grand master or an apprentice."

Miranda wanted to brain him. She really did. But he was just oh so charming with his half smile and hooded eyes. And she'd married him. Faults and all. "After work, I'm going to go to my home and try to get a few hours' sleep. I'll pack an overnight bag and meet you back here. It would be nice if you had dinner waiting. I'm sure I'll be hungry."

A low growl sounded as he snaked his arms around her. "I'm hungry, now."

She kissed him lightly. "Be that as it may, I have a career that means as much to me as yours to you. Get some sleep. You didn't get much last night. I'll be back later tonight."

Frustrated, he ran his fingers through his hair. "This is not the wedding night I had anticipated."

"Likewise." She exhaled. "You realize our marriage won't resemble anything normal. We both work long hours, and sometimes, travel is necessary."

"Normal is overrated. I don't expect anything typical. Actually, I prefer it otherwise."

"We never discussed marriage."

"I told you I wanted to spend decades, if not centuries, with you."

"True. But I think the first thing we have to work out is where we're going to live."

"I hoped," he waved his arm around the apartment, "you would move in here with me."

"That's a huge request. I've thought about it. I love my house. I've decorated it with knickknacks I've collected from my travels. And it has memories of my family."

"I have several homes, Miranda. If we're to be husband and wife, we will need to live together."

"Agreed. In time. For now, I want to stay one or two days at my house, a couple here with you and, if you want, a couple at your town house. I can't just leave my home. I'm not ready yet. But I'm willing to work at it."

"I realize the suddenness of all this." He exhaled. "For a time, I will agree with you. But, eventually, I want you to move in with me."

"Would you consider living in my home?"

He shook his head. "Your place is too small Whether the apartment or the town house, safety is more prevalent in mine than in yours."

She stroked the line of his beard. "Even with all the security measures you've installed?"

"Yes."

He was right. She knew it. But she didn't have it in her to let go of her home. She was too attached. "Truthfully, Remare, do we have a chance at this?"

"We do. Both of us will have to make compromises. But, if we're honest with each other, I'd say we have a very good chance."

"I hope so." She kissed him, and his passion made her knees weak.

He slid his hands down to cup her ass and then lifted her to the bed.

She laughed. "We don't have time for this."

He kissed her soundly. "We make time."

Miranda could hardly breathe, being consumed by Remare's desire. "You make me happy. But you also make me late for work." She rolled to the side of the bed. "I'll be back later tonight." She knew if she stayed any longer, she'd be calling off work, and she wouldn't let that happen. Not with a desk loaded with responsibilities.

"Mir-randa."

She looked back, knowing her face was already heated with passion.

His yearning was a palpable thing. "I love you."

She'd said the same words to him when they'd argued in the archives. She returned his words. "I know." Smiling, she closed the door after departing.

***

Valadon thought it proper to pay his final farewell to Magritte, who was soon to leave to go back to Paris. "I trust you will have a safe trip back to Mont Helaire."

"Yes. Wouldn't it be fitting if you decided to come with us?"

"Hardly. I have my own territory to rule over. And you have yours."

"In all these long centuries, have you never given thought to how your homeland is fairing?"

"I know very well how the courts of Europe are doing. The media covers them quite thoroughly."

"And, yet, no fondness for the people you once called friends?"

"My friends and family are with me, now."

"Several of the European courts have faltered. Fallen into financial ruin." Her voice was caustic. "This may not have happened if you were still our Minister of Finance."

"Speculating of should haves, could haves, would haves, Magritte? That's not like you. From what I remember, you always leaned toward the pragmatic."

"I do what is necessary to ensure the survival of the Vampire Nation. You may not approve of my methods, but I see to it we endure."

"As do I. Of my House."

"I never thought isolationism would manifest so deeply with you. It is a fault I do not admire."

Valadon didn't miss the veiled threat, but he too had taken steps to safeguard his House. He debated telling her of Aiden's findings regarding the bullet's trajectory. But, if Magritte was eliminated, who was to say her replacement would be any less Machiavellian in their pursuits? "You left the reception immediately after the attempt on my life. Were you worried the assassin's bullet may have been meant for you?"

Her face blanched. "There will always be those whose ambition rides them too much. We do what we must to protect ourselves."

"We do, indeed."

"How is your son? I've heard he is recovering nicely."

"He is. His security will be paramount to me in all his future endeavors."

"And the assassin? Has he been apprehended?"

"Unfortunately, during the commotion, he was able to vanish. I think it best we all watch our backs even more than usual."

"I agree." She walked toward the door. "My offer of hospitality remains open should you change your mind about visiting Mont Helaire."

He shook his head.

She seemed to hesitate then faced him. "Did you ever love me?"

"Never." The word left his mouth before he thought better of it. "You taught me many things; love wasn't one of them."

Her eyes cooled, and she smiled knowingly. "Good." Then closed the door behind her.

After the last of the foreign dignitaries had left, Valadon walked toward his penthouse office. He wanted to see the sunrise, feel the warmth on his face. It was a good thing the windows were tinted. As a Blueblood, he was stronger than most vampires. But the downside was he still couldn't tolerate the sun, not completely, even with the ointments his company manufactured. He held his hand to the window and looked out over his city.

The dawn always possessed the hope of a better day—a promise the world would begin anew. Unsatisfied with being indoors, he retrieved his special sun shades from his desk drawer and ascended the stairs up to the roof. He couldn't face the sun directly without consequences, but he could stay in the shadows.

He reflected on the last few days. In his heart, he had hope for the people he loved—for those he considered family. And he would do whatever was necessary to keep them safe. Once outside, he looked down at his emblem of the eternal torch above his corporation, the symbol of his power. He pressed his fist to his heart and made a vow to keep them protected. "Always and forever."

With his sun shades on, he watched as the sun cleared the horizon. Felt the vibrations in the air as the clean, cool breezes of the morning swept over him. There was something magical in the earth's energy he could almost grasp in his hand. A power so profound it exhilarated and made him happy to be alive.

Turning his head to the heavens, Valadon raised his arms high into the sky and roared to the morning angels, his defiance of the dark forces that worked against him, his belief in those he loved and his faith in his own abilities. An affirmation of what it was that made him a king. When the first few rays of sunlight kissed his face, he felt the promise of a new day beginning.

And smiled.

***

Miranda took the afternoon off from work. She had to appease Jordan by taking on another assignment, but since she welcomed the new task, she was good with it. Anything to have gotten some much needed sleep. But now, after a few hours repose, she was revved to see her new husband. She'd called earlier to let him know she was on her way.

Opening the door to his apartment, she called out, "Remare?"

"Up here, Mir-randa."

She climbed the two steps to the bedroom to see a naked Remare sprawled on their bed. Just beyond him was a table set for a romantic dinner for two.

She leaned against the wall and smiled. "I suppose you're the appetizer."

He glanced down at his cock and then smirked. "Some would say I'm the entrée."

She laughed and jumped on the bed with him. "I missed you. Greatly." She thoroughly kissed him. "If I wasn't starving, I'd say food is way overrated."

"After you demanded I keep you fed?! I'll not have you saying I've deprived you of bodily," his eyes narrowed with lust, "needs."

"I couldn't stop thinking of you today. Everyone wanted to know why I was smiling. Until I showed them the ring."

"Were they disappointed they were not invited to the wedding?"

"Not after I explained it caught me by surprise, as well. Did I tell you Lizandra wants to throw us a party to celebrate our nuptials?"

"As does Valadon and the rest of the Torians. It's good the people we care most about want to share in our happiness."

"I'm glad, too. But it will have to wait until I come back from London."

He abruptly sat up. "When are you going to London?"

"Jordan conned me into it. In exchange for taking the afternoon off and the next two days. I told him I was in desperate need of a honeymoon. He wants me in London this weekend to validate and procure a painting that's on loan to the London Museum."

"On loan, hmm." He rubbed his jaw. "Wouldn't their museum want first dibs on it?"

"Not in this case. They've already used up their fiduciary funds."

"The vampire lord of London is a friend of mine. I can come with you."

"This is not a vacation. I am going there to work. One day to travel, one day to validate, and one more to fly home. I'll be home in three days."

"You'll take two guards with you and my jet."

"I don't need guards. I'm working for my museum, not hanging with your old cronies. And a commercial airliner is fine."

He lifted a brow. "Orion, then?"

Miranda exhaled. Actually, she could use the companionship. "Okay."

"And my jet?"

She remembered the nightmare of his plane going down. "You had problems with it recently, didn't you, coming back from Europe?"

"The plane is fine. I've flown to Vancouver and back several times on business. I assure you it is safe. Do you think I would allow my wife to fly on an unsafe plane?"

Miranda thought about it. "Is it as nice as Valadon's jet?"

"Nicer." He snaked his arms around her. "The only difference is the color scheme and a few minor conveniences." His lips captured hers. "A proper honeymoon should be three or four weeks. Not merely a couple of days."

She ran her finger along the side of his jaw. "We'll just have to make up for lost time, then." She kissed him, again, as he pulled her under him. "You make the world disappear."

"I'm going to make a lot more disappear." He had her undressed in mere seconds.

She giggled. "Not sure how, but I think this is going to work between us."

"It will. We'll have our disagreements, but we'll work it out. I like the idea of you being my partner. Either in work or in life. I want you by my side."

"I think you like me under you, as well." She grinned. "But, yeah, I like being with you, too. My lover, my partner, my husband."

"Let's work up an appetite. There's plenty of food. To start, I believe you requested turkey soup. We also have pasta with medallions of veal in a fine marinara sauce."

"My appetite's up." She rubbed against him. "Yours is, too."

Remare grabbed her and kissed her senseless. She'd never seen him happier. "Let's make some magic, my sorceress."

Epilogue

"You look angry, Magritte." Vivienna sipped her wine in Mont Helaire's main reception room.

"Of course I'm livid. We lost one of our best spies in Valadon's court. He was invaluable in providing crucial information. If you hadn't screwed up the wedding with your son's inopportune arrival, we would've had Valadon where we wanted him."

Vivienna was glad her son was now protected. She had despised the way Magritte callously wanted to use him to manipulate Valadon. "I told you, I had no idea Vincent would travel to New York. The last he told me he was on his way to Quebec's preserve."

Magritte was seething. "It's no matter, now. Another opportunity has presented itself."

"Concerning?"

Magritte's wolfish grin promised pain. "Lord Acton."

Fabian approached. "Madame, your guest is waiting for you in the parlor.

"Good." Magritte's eyes darkened in anticipation. When she opened the doors, her temper hadn't abated. "So, you thought to challenge me?"

"I can explain."

"I'm sure you can." Magritte smiled. "You think, because you have Mulciber's blood running through your veins, you have the power of an ancient. You're as arrogant as he was. Where is he, now? Her voice reverberated off the walls. "Answer me!"

"He's dead."

"As you should be. The only thing keeping you alive is because I've found a purpose for you."

Defiance laced his words. "What purpose?"

Magritte enjoyed playing with her prey and stroked his face. "You're quite handsome and talented from what I hear."

He had the audacity to look smug as if his beauty intrigued. "You must admit our goals are the same, and with me running ValCorp, we'll benefit immensely."

He thought he could seduce her. He was about to learn just how painful seduction could be. "You're not half the man Valadon is. An ambitious fool who lacks discipline. Let me show you what a true ancient can do to those who lack restraint."

Unable to fight her power, Jeremy fell to his knees before her. "It wasn't me!" She reduced him to crawling. "I canceled the contract." He fought for breath. "It was someone else!"

"Who?" demanded the *Mistress of Games.*

***

Ryder continued playing with the beads of his bracelet as he sat in the hotel lobby. On another assignment he'd worn the beads in his hair. He smirked; that had been one of his better missions. But, now, Miranda was married. Happily, from what he'd heard. He was glad for her. She deserved whatever joy her new husband could provide. He sipped his coffee and checked his phone, again, for the text he was waiting on.

Sighing, he was eager to get back to Milan. The summers there were incredible. Zurich was attractive enough, but it wasn't home. It was nearly summer, now, and still, the cool breezes chilled him. He'd been shadowing the lovely agent Valadon had assigned to track *The Ghost*, the assassin known for leaving no trail.

He had to admit, she was good. She'd changed her appearance three times since their plane touched down, but it was her scent he recognized. Citrus. He'd promised his father he would stay with her until she completed her mission. And, if the person going up to the assassin's hotel room was who Ryder thought it was, their mission would soon be coming to a close.

***

Miranda was dreaming. She'd had this same dream several times before. A cave, dark, the scent of old earth. Women chanting. The familiar scent of incense burning. Lavender and other herbs. She drifted until she came upon the grotto where the women were singing in a tongue that was foreign, yet hauntingly familiar.

The woman who danced in the fire laughed and sang with the others. The crystals surrounding them pulsed with life, but this time, when the woman turned and met Miranda's curious stare, her eyes turned dark with horrendous fear. Something was terribly wrong. Poison. Someone had poisoned the crystals. She started shrieking as the flames turned black and began consuming her flesh. Her screams rent the air as the crystals darkened, and the fire quickly spread to the other women turning them all to ash.

Screaming in horror, Miranda woke to the sound of Remare urging her to wake. She could taste the horrible scent of smoke in her mouth. "It's only a dream, Mir-randa. It's only a dream. You're safe here with me." He held her in his arms, soothing her with words of comfort.

"Water, please."

Reaching back to the end table, he handed her a small bottle of Pellegrino.

She drank heavily, the cool liquid soothing her dry throat, then gave him the bottle back.

Valadon burst in the room, and a moment later, so did Orion. Her screams must have been louder than she'd thought.

Still breathing heavy, she looked up at them with regret for having woken them.

"Jesus! I had a nightmare, Miranda, you were surrounded by flames. It scared the hell out of me," panted Orion.

"Interesting. I had the same dream." Valadon sat on the bed and touched her arm. "Are you all right?"

She was about to tell him she just needed a moment to catch her breath, when Orion grasped her hand. With all four of them touching, a bolt of current seared through her, increasing her natural energy levels to a new astounding height.

Dropping Orion's hand, she leaned away from Valadon, backing into Remare's chest. She kept his arms around her. When she saw their faces, she knew they had felt it, as well. "You found your fourth, Valadon. I'm fire." Her hand slid over her husband's. "Remare's earth. You're water. And Orion is the fourth element, air." She smiled up at him. "With the way you sing, your notes float on the air."

Slowly raising her eyes to the High Lord, she instinctively knew with whatever primal gifts she possessed. The undeniable sense of knowing that perplexed, yet reassured her. "You're the most powerful of us all. We belong to you. You never needed a blood oath. We've always been yours."

She glanced down and then back up at Valadon. "You're the chameleon."

Author's Note:

If you enjoyed this book, please leave a review at the vendor of your choice

Coming Soon

Veil of Destiny, Seven Deadly Veils, Book Five

While vacationing in London, Miranda and Remare learn of an old book that may contain clues to the destiny of Others, *The Book of Origins*. Encountering allies as well as adversaries, their search will take them from ancient libraries to London's darker and more sinister sections. And to an old castle whose eccentric inhabitants may know more than they are willing to impart.

Haunted by dreams of a mysterious woman, Miranda has long yearned to discover her *Elemental* heritage and uncover truths concerning her abilities. However, some secrets are never meant to be unveiled and may destroy what she holds sacred. Remare agrees to help Miranda, but fears their search may arouse the interest of an old enemy bent on revenge.

They will try to keep each other protected from the forces trying to drive them apart. But the fates may have different plans: A destiny neither one of them never imagined...nor desired.

Diana Marik is the author of the Seven Deadly Veils Vampire Series. She grew up in New York City and has her MA in English Literature from Hofstra University. Before becoming an author, Diana worked as an educator, mental health therapist, yoga instructor and camp counselor.

Among Diana's passions, traveling is her favorite. One of her favorite places to visit is the American Southwest and her home away from home, New Orleans. When not writing, Diana loves discovering museums. In her leisure time, she enjoys going to the movies and hanging out with her friends.

Diana is currently at work on her latest novel in the Veilverse and would love to hear from her fans. She can be contacted at www.dianamark.com

Silent Violence

By

Michael Morton

A Fallen Empire Novel

Chapter 1

Draconis Sigma System (Post Conquest Year 499)

Captain Fremont McMannus of the 76th Microgravity Strike Team, or MIST, had done a lot of things throughout his Marine career; leading a boarding action against an Imperial cruiser in the middle of space battle struck him as one of the dumber ones. Still, a prize was a prize and the battered forces of the Terran Union could use all the ships it could capture.

The assault force he led, two platoons and his command team, were strapped down inside the five Type-31 Boarding/Assault Boats, affectionately called "Babes" by the Marines. With a stealth coating and active emission controls, it gave the Marines the best chance to make it to the target and back to their ship when the job was done.

"Five minutes out, Cap." The pilot's voice was calm and even, as if flying through a raging space battle was an everyday jaunt for him. The engagement in the Draconis Sigma system was massive, with ships of the Terran Union Eighth Fleet battling one of the last New Empire punitive expeditions dispatched to 'quash the rebellion.'

This is the biggest action in the last few years and it's on the small side compared to the engagements of the two last decades. Desperate fighting on every side to break away from the Empire, preserve it, or settle old grievances. Now everything and everyone in these so-called Succession Wars is tired and broke. Especially him.

On cue, a small wall panel broke loose as the Babe sharply adjusted course. It hit the deck soundlessly in the depressurized hull and sat there for a moment. When the jets cut off and microgravity returned, it floated upwards and began to drift lazily through the cabin.

McMannus turned back to his display screen. The two platoon commanders accompanying him on this action, Second Lieutenants Ishido Kan and Harry Webb, were split-screened across the top of the display. Their target took up the bottom half of the screen and the picture was good enough to see jagged holes, melted armor and a massive hole in the aft section.

"Okay, Ishido, Harry, you clear on your targets?"

Kan nodded, his young face eager. *"Yes sir! We'll take the main boat bay and press towards the engine room."*

His other platoon leader was a few years older, having spent some time in the ranks before going to Officer Candidate School. *"Aye aye sir. We've got the spinal mount access panels and then the bridge."* He paused and grinned wryly. *"I take great pleasure in that hole in the engineering section. All nice and blacked out. Wouldn't want them firing that baby while we're slipping through the maintenance hatches."*

"Well, you two cause a ruckus so we can dock and blow the main airlock. Then we'll split the ship in half between you. Just be sure it's a big ruckus so we don't have a greeting party. VIS, gentlemen."

His screen flashed at him a priority signal from the flagship, so he put his junior officers on hold while he answered it. The screen showed the flag tactical officer from the *TUS Missouri*, one of the last surviving Union battleships.

"McMannus, go."

"Captain, updated orders from Admiral Besson. You have a new target; the flagship of the enemy fleet, the battleship Emperor's Grace and Glory. *Her main drive was just shot out and she's drifting. The Admiral wants her and the commander as prizes."*

"He wants us to... board a Grausian battleship?"

The lack of expression on the other man's face showed he knew what he was ordering them into. *"She can't maneuver, so she can't effectively use her spinal mount. We're targeting* her small batteries now. *The destroyers Hoel and Johnston are maneuvering to take them under continuous fire and they'll be available for naval gunfire support once you're aboard. Two strike fighter squadrons are also being vectored in on her to eliminate their radars and point defenses. She'll be blind and toothless for your approach."*

"Great. We'll get there and be shredded by their troops once onboard. Two platoons can't do the job!"

The screen split in half, now showing a display of the tactical map around the enemy battleship. *"We're cross-attaching three platoons from other assaults. You'll have overall mission command, given that each platoon comes from a different MIST."*

His stomach clenched up over the thought of trying to coordinate actions between platoons of four different MISTs. Standard practice for taking a ship was to capture either the bridge or the main engine room. The first would secure important prisoners and control over the weapon systems but control of the latter would prevent a self-destruct and give them complete control over the ship's systems. Calling up the layout of a Grausian battleship was easy since both sides were fighting with the same equipment and databases and he made a quick evaluation. "Copy, flag. Send orders to my Third Platoon to stand ready to support the assault. Requesting at least one other platoon standing by, too."

"Negative, Captain. The Admiral has missions for the rest of the boarding parties. However, he has not specifically tasked your Third Platoon, so I'm sending those orders now." He looked to the side and typed in a command. *"And all four MISTs are now under your command. Good luck."*

McMannus cursed under his breath. His body automatically shifted with the acceleration and course change as their pilot steered them towards the battleship. *This is going to be tricky. I have to go after both the bridge and engine room at the same time. Then there's armory. If we don't move fast, the Grausian marines on board will get to the heavy weapons and then life gets really interesting.* He analyzed the trajectories of all the approaching forces and made a decision.

The single screen was replaced with three new ones when the other platoons connected to his communications relay. Three new helmets appeared, with a tagline under each one. First Lieutenant Yoshiaga of the 50th. Second Lieutenant Lindvig of the 30th. Staff Sergeant Hladík of the 45th. "Marines, this is Captain McMannus. I'm transmitting your objectives now. Based on existing trajectories and avoiding the main gun fire cone, the 76th will hit the boat bay and proceed to the engine room. Lieutenant Yoshiaga, you will assault through the spinal mount accesses with the objective of the armory. Lieutenant Lindvig and Staff Sergeant Hladiks, your objective is the bridge. Coordinate your assaults through the main airlock and cargo locks."

They acknowledged their orders with the air of men who'd been given unenviable tasks. They all realized the odds against them. With nearly forty Marines in each platoon plus his command team, he had just over two hundred Marines to take on a ship with a complement that numbered over two thousand.

Once he was finished passing out orders to the other platoons, McMannus clicked over to his command channel and briefed Harry and Ishido on the new plan and their roles. Then he called out, "Gunny, private channel."

Gunnery Sergeant Yembe Mulongo had served with McMannus for the better part of three years and he recognized the emotion behind the taut command. "*Just another day in the black, sir. We'll handle it. I know Hladik; he's solid. The rest, well, they're Marines.*" His voice was measured and calm and it helped McMannus center himself.

"This just went from a routine boarding to a real cluster in a heartbeat."

"*Things usually do, sir. Remember Tannenberg Gate? We're probably going to need the Third Herd before this is all through. I'll get with Bates and start things moving. Double normal loadout for everyone.*"

The third platoon of the 76th, along with his executive officer First Lieutenant Robin Haskins, was still back on the *Missouri*. When he commed, her screen showed the backdrop of the launch bay. "Reading my mind, Robin?"

"Just being prepared, Boss. Word came through from the flag bridge and Lieutenant Beauchamp and I are stacking everyone for loading."

"Coordinate with the Gunny on loadouts. Things are likely to get out of control fast over there. Make sure everyone is loaded and ready to deploy on my word."

"Good copy, Boss. Good hunting."

*****

In 1st Platoon, Lance Corporal Jordan DeMarco looked around the cabin as they blazed towards their target. The word had just come down from the CO about their new objective. He couldn't move very much in his shock frame but his right leg began to fidget. *This isn't like a station assault or dropping on an asteroid base. A battleship is serious business!*

The armored Microgravity Assault Combat Exosuit (MACE) amplified his every movement. The fidgets translated into his heel thumping up and down on the deck. His squad leader, Sergeant Aaron Baines reached out with his left leg and gently kicked Jordan's vibrating leg. *"Lock it down, DeMarco."*

"Sorry Sarge. Just… thinking."

"That's your problem, DeMarco. You think too much. Let the Old Man and the Lieutenant do the thinking. Your job is to follow orders."

"But what if…"

He didn't get very far with that as Baines sighed loud enough to drown the channel. *"I said, knock it off, DeMarco. You got a job to do, you do it and don't get your head spinning like a bad thruster."*

Chastised, Jordan kept his mouth shut. The other six Marines in his squad were sitting like him, although with their visor tint on, he couldn't tell what they were doing. Ricks was likely playing a game on his screen. Van Hook was sleeping; the tilt of the helmet made that obvious. *I wish I could sleep.*

*****

McMannus' viewscreen now showed the massive bulk of the *Emperor's Grace and Glory* while they made their final approach to the boat bay. The trajectories of the other platoons were on track to meet their objective entry points as well. All seemed quiet and the intermittent laser and particle beam fire from earlier was missing, thanks to the two Union destroyers having systematically targeted and destroyed any secondary battery that got off a shot. The two ships were behind and above the assault force now, still in position to provide cover fire should it be necessary.

This proved to be the case when a previously-silent particle beam battery lashed out, catching a Babe from the 30th dead on. The small craft vaporized, caught in the energies of a beam meant to punch a hole in a larger ship. Lindvig's icon disappeared off his HUD a moment later. As his own ship began to juke around, Fremont contacted the 30th's platoon NCO. "Staff Sergeant Hudson, proceed to the target and get out of their line of fire but do not dock. You don't have enough to force the main airlock. Stand by to reinforce one of the other assaults."

Heavy laser fire from the supporting destroyers lanced into the battery emplacement, destroying it in a spray of plasma and debris, Hudson acknowledged the change in command and orders with a curt, *"Aye aye, sir."* His own Babe continued dodging back and forth, attempting to make itself less of a target while they closed the final distance to the battleship. The massive airlock doors that served the boat bay loomed in his display.

A red light over the forward airlock came on, signaling contact with the enemy hull was imminent. Moments later, everyone shifted in their shock frames when the Babe made contact, the floor vibrating under their feet with the impact. The light over the airlock switched from red to yellow and Marines unlocked their frames to stack up in position at the bow.

Each of the five Babes was now lined up horizontally along the boat bay door seam, with only a few meters separation between them. Mounted on the jowls of the assault boat's snub-nosed bow was a massive pair of hydraulic spreaders, similar to what emergency personnel used to free trapped people from the mangled wreckage of a vehicle crash. Ten pairs of hydraulic pistons worked in unison to pry the boat bay door apart. They didn't need to create much room.

The forward hatch on each Babe slammed open as soon as the airlock light went green, providing enough room for the four waiting Marines to shoot through the gap. They went through feet first and abreast of each other, propelled by their maneuvering packs and hearty shoves from their teammates. Their laser rifles lay flat on their bodies until they cleared the gap and then they came up, searching for targets. The inductive pad on the palm of each Marine's MACE relayed the data from the rifle's electronic targeting scope to the Heads Up Display on their helmet, allowing the Marines to shoot wherever the rifle was pointing.

*****

Jordan moved with his team into the boat bay. It was both cavernous and confining. The walls were distant and yet the whole thing was crowded with small craft, docking collars, airtight personnel transfer tubes, gantries, hoses and sundry equipment. The team moved as one, taking a sharp turn to avoid the noses of the docked small craft barely three meters from the bay door.

"Shit, this looks just like the bay on the Missouri!"

"Shut up and do your job, Ricks." Baines led the team to the gantry that held numerous sealed tubes leading to the small craft. The other teams in the first wave split the three gantries between them. Baines gave hand signals to provide overwatch on the airlocks leading in. *"Watch your sectors and call out if the Impies make a push. Mind the friendlies setting up for the breach."*

Jordan scanned his section of the inner hull, with two airlocks in sight. Ricks was two meters to his left and Baines two to his right. His palms were damp inside his gloves and his breathing came ragged in his ears. The suit beeped a warning at him that his pulse and respiration were above nominal and he took a deep breath to steady himself.

He kept his weapon trained on the hatch itself as Marines from the second wave took up positions on either side of the maintenance airlocks. When they were set, Baines took them off overwatch. *"Right. They got it. Over to Objective Bravo. Overwatch and cover fire."*

They scanned the distant main transfer tube, watching the other Marines landing and taking up positions around the central axis. They could see Grausian sailors running through the airlock back towards the battleship interior. The assaulting Marines swiftly set small explosive charges on the frame and backed away quickly.

"Stand by for breach. Ready heavy weapons."

The charges went off, silent flashes in the vacuum of the boat bay and the tube fractured into several pieces. A heavy gunner stepped up and fired several rounds from his M901 Barrett plasma rifle into the airlock doors, spot welding them in place. That, combined with the vacuum beyond the door, ensured that no counterattack would be coming from that avenue.

Jordan was already turning back to the airlocks when Baines ordered them to prepare for breach. *"Follow through and reconsolidate beyond the locks. The LT is tagging the rally point, so mind your HUD and don't get fucking lost. That means you, Ricks."*

They held their positions while the third wave assault teams stacked up at the five maintenance airlocks and set breaching charges. The fourth wave was already on the way, aligning themselves in a single file to assault the airlocks. The element leader in charge of each stack reported back to McMannus once they were ready.

*****

McMannus was still inside his Babe, letting the sergeants organize the assault and overseeing the attacks of the other platoons. *Gotta hit them all at once; overwhelm their ability to respond.* Seconds ticked away while he waited for the green lights. Finally, Yoshiaga and Hladik signaled they were in position. Over the general channel, he broadcast, "All assault elements, go go go!"

*****

Five nearly simultaneous flashes lit the entire boat bay. Each was strong enough to fracture the entire airlock door in its frame. Decompression did the rest, shooting the fragments into the open bay. The assault teams from 2nd Platoon streamed through the openings, weapons firing at anything which moved. Here and there, a Marine staggered or fell, depending on what he or she was hit with. Medics pulled these aside, slapping emergency patches on the holes and, if necessary, triggering the automed medical functions built into the MACEs.

Baines led them through the breach. *"Watch your sectors, people. Don't trip over the bodies."*

Two Grausian sailors lay on the floor, vacc suits filled full of holes. Blood trickled from the wounds and streamed in globules towards the blown airlock. Jordan stepped sideways to avoid as he followed his squad leader.

The rally point was in a passageway wide enough for three MISTers abreast. He could see a squad pounding down the hall towards the main transverse passage, which would take them directly to the main engine room. As the other team from their own squad joined them, Baines started moving. They took off at jog, weapons at port arms as they moved towards their main objective.

*****

McMannus followed his headquarters team through the jagged frame of the airlock into a narrow corridor. Bullet holes and scorch marks were scattered here and there but there was little evidence of a pitched battle. Both Harry and Ishido reported minor resistance at all the hatches, easily overcome.

"Whisper Six, Whisper One. We've reached the main transverse passage. Ongoing minor resistance. Proceeding to objective."

That was Ishido, heading for the main access to the engine room. His effort would face the most resistance but would also draw the most attention from the defenders.

"Whisper Six, Whisper Two. We've reached the lift access. Negative resistance. Proceeding according to plan."

Harry's job would be to approach the engine room from a different vector, either above or below the main deck and force an entrance that way. With any luck, Ishido and 1st Platoon would keep drawing the defenders to themselves and make it easier for Harry's 2nd Platoon.

Meanwhile, he had a battle to coordinate. He tagged on his HUD an intersection ahead as his temporary command post and waited for his security squad to set up a perimeter. His C3 operator halted next to him and McMannus motioned to him. "Sparks, show me the overall picture."

The tech manipulated the controls on the battlecomp, extending its telescoping arm. This projected a 3D holographic display of the ship's floor plan. The areas controlled by each unit were represented by different shadings on the map, along with known enemy positions and strengths.

The Grausians' response was becoming more organized than he was comfortable with. Yoshiaga's assault through the spinal mount had been clean and unopposed but he was now hitting stiff resistance. They weren't even halfway to the armory. The 45th was making decent progress towards the bridge but they were under strength for their objective. The bridge might even be more heavily defended than the engine room. His only ready reserve waited in space for his orders. He had to put the enemy off balance. *Reinforce success. Carry the battle swiftly into the enemy's rear.* With that thought in mind, he ordered Hudson and his two squads to reinforce the 45th and the bridge assault.

The deck shuddered under his feet, a sharp vibration that was accompanied by a brief stomach lurch that meant a fluctuation in the artificial gravity field. Since they were all magged to the deck it shouldn't affect his people but this was a new development. "All MIST units report. Who hit the argrav generators?"

He got negative responses across the board except for Harry. "*Think it was the naval gunfire, Whisper Six. We're closest to the hull and felt impacts before the explosion.*"

McMannis considered this new development. If the destroyers could take out more of the argrav, his people would have a better shot at this thing. Nobody operated in microgravity like a MISTer. He motioned to Sparks. "Contact the *Hoel* and *Johnston.* Find out who took those shots."

He studied the changing situation on the map, which showed Hudson taking his people in support of the 45th. Meanwhile, Yoshiaga's situation was becoming more and more bogged down. The enemy held the armory and the approaches, making it a difficult prospect to assault. Even attempting to envelop the armory from above or below wouldn't help. It was designed to be isolated from access from the other decks. The only good part is that the 50th was in a perfect blocking position to prevent reinforcements from making it to the armory.

Sparks signaled to him. "*Sir, I have the Hoel's combat information center on the horn. Call sign Locomotive. Johnston is standing by, call sign Tampico.*"

"Locomotive, this is Whisper Six. Request fire mission."

"*Roger, Whisper Six. Send it.*"

He filtered the map to display the ship's systems, selected the argrav generators closest to the exterior hull, double checked his own people's positions and transmitted the data to Locomotive. Taking those down would get them close to microgravity in most of the ship. "Locomotive, Whisper Six, fire mission. Target data transmitted. Cleared hot, over."

"*Whisper Six, Locomotive. Target Number One through Five, in sequence. Shot, over.*"

A new voice came over the radio. "*Whisper Six, Tampico. Shot, over.*"

McMannus switched over to the general channel. "All MISTs, stand by for microgravity. Naval gunfire impacts at the attached coordinates. Be ready to execute Spiderwalk. Hit 'em hard and fast when things go into freefall. This is our element, people."

"*Whisper Six, Locomotive. Splash, over.*"

"*Whisper Six, Tampico. Splash, over.*"

"Roger, splash, out." Seconds later, the hull vibrated again, a double jolt that caused the whole deck to quiver. Briefly, the walls swirled in his vision until his inner ear adjusted. "Locomotive, Tampico, Whisper Six. Target, repeat, over."

The destroyers were adjusting their positions for the next round of targets when a call of "*Contact!*" came over the HQ channel. His security team opened up, pouring fire into the attackers from the covering positions they had established. Gunny Mulongo gave him a hand signal that he was handling it and crab walked over to the corridor while McMannus turned his attention back to the battlecomp. He didn't have enough people to hold a perimeter. They had to take and hold their objectives fast before the Grausians started hitting back with a vengeance. Committing all your reserves before the other guy did was a huge risk but from the information he had on hand, it sure seemed like the ship's crew was already all in.

"Sparks, message to the XO. I need the rest of the 76th over here ASAP."

Minutes later, Gunny Mulongo reported the attack was broken up and Locomotive and Tampico were calling in another salvo. The deck shook again and they were in microgravity for several seconds. When gravity returned, however, it was less than the standard gee.

"*Whisper Six, Whisper Two. I have micro.*"

"Roger, Whisper Two. Execute Spiderwalk." Minutes after he said that, the gravity in their area changed rapidly, going from stronger than a gee to about a half gee in the space of a few seconds. Then the familiar double impact shook the ship again, stronger this time as the remaining argrav generators struggled to compensate. There was the familiar stomach drop of zero gee and then gravity was history.

*****

Jordan kicked in his mag boots as his stomach lurched. Then the Old Man came over the general channel. *"All Whisper elements, execute Spiderwalk."*

With practiced motions, his squad began breaking apart into pairs. Jordan and Ricks demagged and hit their suit jets for a second, propelling them to the ceiling. They flipped before they reached it and magged their boots to the new surface. The Marines began scaling the walls and ceiling like massive bugs.

When inside a ship in microgravity, most crewmembers stuck to the established layout and magged themselves to the nominal deck. Besides making it easier to navigate the oftentimes complicated interior of a starship, not everyone could handle the three-dimensional thinking required to ignore a 'down' vector. The MIST did things differently. Their suits also had electromagnets on the hands, knees, toes of their boots, the chestplate and the backplate of their MACE. Then there were magnetic grapples they could attach from waist, calf and shoulders, allowing them to bound from point to point with speed. With practice and they got a lot of practice, a MISTer could scuttle up walls and across the ceiling like some grotesque, four-legged spider using hands, feet, chest and grapples.

"Down is the vector," Baines called. He was still on the old 'floor' but Jordan's mind reoriented itself. Corridors became holes in the floor and they began to walk down the hole, staggered to provide supporting fire and not flag each other with their weapons.

The Grausian sailors defending the next intersection were more organized. Their weapons were the Grausian version of the MIST's PW-93V and the 4mm needles would tear apart a typical suit and could even damage a MACE given enough hits. Jordan knelt, his knee magnets securing him to the deck and opened fire. Ricks was next to him and they alternated firing at the defenders in short, aimed bursts, the exoskeleton taking up most of the recoil. Baines led the rest of the squad forward at a lumbering run. Then they unmagged and jetted forward, weapons snapping back on retractable slings as they drew their vibrodirks.

Landing among the defenders, the six Marines slashed vacc suits to ribbons in seconds with practiced efficiency. It wasn't necessary to go for the kill but simply to spill their air. The spacers went into panicked motions, trying to seal the long tears with emergency patches and more often than not fell back limp as their efforts were in vain. Jordan and Ricks joined them as the struggles of the last Grausian ceased. Rick hollered and slapped his squadmates on the shoulders. *"Bad ass! That was certifiably bad ass!"*

"Shut it, Ricks. We ain't seen any Impy Marines yet. Take them down and then you can celebrate." Baines pointed at the intersection corners. *"Overwatch, people. The rest of the platoon will come pounding through here soon."*

*****

"Whisper Six, Whisper Five. Enroute, ETA five minutes."

"Roger Whisper Five. Standby for mission orders." He watched the changing situation on the display. Just as he was about to order her to reinforce the bridge attack, a panicked call came in from Lieutenant Yoshiaga.

"Whisper Six, Shujin Three! Enemy reinforcements are here. They have Gvit!"

The big, rhinoceros-like aliens were usually not found aboard ship. Their large size caused problems maneuvering in the corridors, they ate massive amounts of food and were generally unpleasant to be around. A new feed opened up in his display, mirroring what Yoshiaga was seeing. Two massive, armored creatures were pounding up the corridor, ignoring laser and plasma fire to reach the 50th positions. They had a golden colored 'I' on their breastplates. Behind them, armored Grausians with a similar logo followed, weapons at the ready.

"Shit. First Legion. What the hell are those sonsabitches doing here?" The only thing he could think of was that this admiral was a lot more important than most if he had the Empress' Own on his ship.

Yoshiaga's people concentrated their fire but there were only so many weapons that could be brought to bear. The first Gvit collapsed a few meters from the 50th position, arms struggling to pull itself forward while blood poured from its wounds, a richer red than human. It shuddered to a stop after a few seconds but the second one hit the Marines like a battering ram.

It swung a massive vibroaxe like it weighed nothing. Two Marines were sliced in half, their MACE suits insignificant against the creature's strength and its weapon. Another Marine let loose a Barrett blast at close range, causing the signal to blur into static for a few seconds. When it stabilized, a massive fist filled the screen. The picture dropped out completely.

"Dammit!" The plan shot to hell, he switched channels. "Whisper Five, your objective is to secure the armory. High probability there may be one or more Gvit there from the First Legion and other Legion personnel. Take charge of any 50th survivors."

He had to give it to Robin. She responded levelly, "*Roger that, Whisper Six. Secure the armory, rescue the 50th and be ready for First Legion and Gvit.*"

Muttering a curse under his breath, he called Gunny Mulongo. "Whisper Seven, move us out. I don't want to be caught by any roving ship's crew or Impy Marines. Follow Mr. Kan's path; it should be clear for now."

"*Copy, Whisper Six. Ready to go when you are.*"

He motioned to Sparks to pack it up. Things were getting far more interesting than he would like. They had to pick it up or be crushed by a foe that outnumbered them at least ten to one.

His command group caught up to the rear section of Ishido's 1st Platoon. They were deployed across the primary access corridor to Main Engineering, drawing the defender's attention while Harry's 2nd Platoon maneuvered against the secondary access to the powerplant.

Sparks updated the map with the new positions of all the units involved. The XO and 3rd Platoon were reconsolidating after boarding the ship and shaking out into an assault formation. 50th was a shaded circle around the armory, with sporadic reports from various Marines but no consolidated position. The 45th and 30th platoons were making good gains towards the bridge but were still far from their objective.

"Whisper Two, Whisper Six. Status?"

"*Whisper Six, Whisper Two. Buttoned down tight. Prepping demo now. Give us five mikes to get through.*"

It was five minutes he didn't think they had but it was necessary. "Whisper Six copies. Whisper One, standby for a mad minute in five mikes. Whisper Two, report when ready."

Both platoon leaders acknowledged. When Harry's people were ready to force the entries, Ishido's platoon would open up with everything they had at full rate of fire to draw attention to themselves and away from the flank attack to force an entry.

A few minutes later, his exec broadcast, *"Whisper Six, Whisper Five. Am assaulting the armory now. Be advised, an unknown force of 1st Legion personnel have already exited this location and are believed to be headed your way."*

"Great. Just what we need." He didn't need to look around to see that his command team was completely inadequate to stopping that counterattack. Should he turn Ishido one eighty to meet the attack? Impossible, they were locked into a firefight with the engine room defenders. Pull 2nd Platoon from its assault? It was the only force he had. The 1st would continue with their assault but it would be a lot more expensive.

"Whisper Two, Whisper Six. New orders. Redeploy from current positions to meet a counterattack from the armory. Be advised the OPFOR may include First Legion personnel with heavy weapons."

There was a pause and then Harry's chipper voice came through. *"Whisper Six, Whisper Two copies redeployment. About time First Legion came to a party we're throwing."*

Dammit. "Whisper One, Whisper Six. Cancel mad minute and flanking attack. Commence direct assault on objective."

"Roger, Whisper Six. Pushing now."

"Whisper Seven, Whisper Six. Keep us up close against 1st during their advance. No gaps."

*****

Jordan poked his PW-93V around the corner, watching the display of the corridor on his HUD. The small weapon was designed for the close quarters fighting aboard a ship or station and the integrated sight was connected to his HUD via cable. It displayed the barricade and a brief image of a weapon poking through a gap. He fired a burst and withdrew the weapon before it was hit by return fire.

Next to him, Ricks waited a few seconds and then thrust his weapon around the corner, firing at the defender who had fired at Jordan's weapon. All around the intersection the cat and mouse game continued. Two understrength squads of MISTers alternated fire, trying to pick off exposed defenders so they could assault through the blocking position. But the exchange wasn't all one direction. The scorch mark and half-melted MACE suit across the way from a detonating M901 battery pack showed the futility of trying to use the bulky weapons in the same fashion as the PW-93Vs.

Baines crawled up next to Jordan. *"Whaddya got?"*

"At least a dozen back there that we've counted returning fire. And that's after we took out five of them. How's Ibiza?"

"Doc's got her sedated for evac. The grenades cracked the suit and she's got internal damage. Van Hook didn't make it back to the aid station. You're second team lead, now."

Jordan gave him a thumbs up. "What's the plan, then? We're stalled out here."

Through the tinted visor, Jordan saw the smile. *"What else? Get ready to descend into the madness. We're the main effort now so we have to push hard and fast through these motherfuckers before we get swarmed. Screw this plinking shit. The LT's massing the grenade launchers. Stand by to assault."*

As the twelve Marines readied themselves to go over the corner, three grenadiers pushed their PAW-95s over the edge and emptied their six round magazines. The 20mm grenades burst across the barricade in a flurry, filling the corridor with debris and dust. Baines led the charge over the edge, calling *"Follow me!"*

The MISTers made no attempt at a coordinated assault, instead activating the suit jets for speed. Weapons blazing into the smoke and dust, they hit the remnants of the barricade with a vengeance.

Magging to the deck beyond the barricade, Jordan found himself face to face with a Grausian Marine struggling up off the deck. Not waiting for the alien to get his bearings, he put his weapon inches from the other creature and fired three bursts. The needles chewed their way through the armor in a split second and the Grausian was tumbling backwards from the momentum imparted, having never fully magged to the deck.

Around him the others were engaged in their own struggles, weapons blazing and vibrodirks slashing. The smoke and dust were still swirling in the micro-g and targets slid in and out of sight. Letting go of his weapon, which retracted on the sling to mag itself to his pack, he drew his vibrodirk and waded into the chaos.

*****

McMannus coordinated with Harry to deploy his unit across the most likely avenues of attack from the armory. With any luck, they'd be facing probes on all of them instead of one massive push. They could handle small probes but if the Grausians punched a full assault on one position they would be through.

The assault continued on the Main Engineering accesses. A steady trickle of casualties came back but they were gaining ground. The defenders were stubborn but disorganized. Ishido just needed more time.

*****

Jordan stood up from Ricks' prone form and turned off the med alarm on his suit. Sergeant Baines was propped up against the wall with the corpsman working on him. Looking around, he saw three other members of the squad, all junior to him. "Right, people. Form up on me."

He kneeled next to Baines and touched helmets with him. The older man's voice was tinny through the connection and he spoke haltingly. *"You got this, DeMarco. VIS."*

"Roger that, Sarge. VIS."

Standing, he motioned to the ad hoc fire team. "Follow me." They headed down the corridor, muzzle flashes visible in the gathering haze.

*****

A few minutes later, Harry reported the First Legion personnel were pushing forward piecemeal, trying to force multiple penetrations to relieve the attack on the engine room. *"Bloody uncoordinated, Whisper Six. I doubt there's an officer among them. They're just throwing themselves at us."*

"Good copy, Whisper Two. Keep them off our backs a little while longer. Break break. Whisper Seven, detach the command squad and feed them into the assault. Maximum effort."

While his command squad moved up, McMannus watched several firefights in progress at the 1st's position. The legionnaires did have some heavy weapons but they displayed a distinct lack of cohesion. It kept them from following up and forcing a breakthrough. All Harry's people had to do was hold in place and let the Grausians break themselves against their positions.

Clicking over, he saw that Robin and 3rd Platoon were in a heavy firefight. They had to fight against both arriving crewmembers and legionnaires still in the armory itself. Bad luck gave them the timing to coordinate their attacks, with the legionnaires opening up with heavy weaponry and the crew charging the 3rd's positions.

He and Mulongo saw Robin's screen go blank from the impact of a plasma thrower on her position. Seconds later, her icon disappeared from Sparks' projection.

"Dammit! Sparks, show me Whisper Three…," His voice trailed to a stop as Lieutenant Beauchamp's icon also vanished from the screen. "Shit shit shit. Whisper Three Seven, Whisper Six. Report!"

He heard nothing for several seconds and then Staff Sergeant Holcomb came up on the net. *"Sir, it's going to hell down here! We're getting hit from both sides. XO and the eltee are down. I don't know how much longer we can–"*

Later, McMannus wasn't sure if he or Holcomb went off the net first. There was a flash and something slammed into him from behind. His magboots held but the blow doubled him over, slamming his chest plate into his knees. Trying to demag his boots, drop to the deck and draw his weapon as white spikes of pain radiated across his chest called for more dexterity than he thought he had but he managed it. Sparks was firing over his prone position while the Gunny was firing from a braced position at a corner.

Coming at them from behind were several Grausian sailors, their off-white vacc suits easy to identify. Their charge was nothing more than suicide, with Mulongo and Sparks taking them down one by one with precise fire from their PW-93Vs. The one with the grenade launcher was last, suit shredding from the repeated impacts before he could load another round.

Gasping, he hit the transmit button. "Whisper Two, watch for leakers! Consolidate as needed."

While Sparks kept watch on the corridor, his senior NCO checked him for damage. *"Suit's good, sir. Some dings and scratches but nothing vital hit from the outside. How's your internals read?"*

His personal internals were still stinging but the suit's readouts showed good pressure, temperature and O2. "Good to go, Gunny. Guess I called it wrong sending the command squad forward."

"*No sir. We need to force that objective. My bad for not watching our six.*"

"We'll call it even. Help me up."

Gunny went to get some of the less-badly wounded for rear area security while McMannus and Sparks set about reestablishing the battle picture. 2nd reported sealing the breach that leaked their attackers and that there were no more legionnaires left in the assault, just sailors.

"Roger, Whisper Two. Advance on the armory and aid Whisper Fi–." He paused, collecting his thoughts. "Aid 3rd in holding that position. Keep them off our backs. Break break. Whisper One, status on the objective."

"*We're almost at the main doors, Whisper Six.*"

"Roger. Coming to you."

Reaching the last intersection, they arrived to see a plasma bolt impact on the outside corner of the corridor wall. It sent a spray of molten metal across the corridors. In the microgravity and vacuum the droplets tumbled unevenly. With well-honed instincts, the headquarters team turned their helmets away from the scattering of white-hot particles. "Whisper One, you need to do something about that."

The response back was a laconic, "*Working on it, sir. I'd really like to know how someone got a plasma thrower from the armory before we got here.*" The wall shuddered slightly from incoming rounds, stitching the intersection where the vastly reduced 1st Platoon and the headquarters team were gathered.

"Not important at the moment, Mr. Kan. It's here and Gunny now has a mess of slagged bits on his armor. I suggest you hurry before he gets upset." *And before anything else hits us from behind.*

The intersection was briefly illuminated from their end of the corridor when three Barretts opened up in rapid succession. From the engine room entrance came an even brighter flash and the deck vibrated a second later.

"Got him, Captain!" Lieutenant Kan followed up on the detonation and ordered his platoon into the assault. Several Marines threw themselves flat in the corridor, laying down suppressive fire while their mates unmagged from the deck behind them, Jordan and his ad hoc fire team amongst them.

With practiced skill, they bounced up to the ceiling in the microgravity environment and oriented themselves in a wedge. They'd had time to plan this assault. Using the electromagnets in the gloves and their internal suit jets, the Terrans zipped down the length of the corridor, their commander in their van. As before, within seconds the assault element was in and behind the defending Grausian sailors and the few Imperial Marines that had made it back to the engine room. The support element ceased firing when their mates entered the fray.

The assault force jackknifed into a feet-first approach and used their momentum to barrel into the defenders. Sailors scattered across the deck and then the MISTers layed about with their vibrodirks, slashing unarmored suits with practiced ease.

*****

Jordan was one of the first to reach the sealed hatch to the main engine room. Checking the panel, he grabbed the first Marine he saw with an electronic 'can opener' and pulled him over to the door. "Get this thing open!"

Moments later, Staff Sergeant Salazar showed up with another Marine tech and put him to work at the hatch. Jordan was already organizing an assault stack at the door. *"Good work, DeMarco. You got it here. I'll keep feeding you Marines to shove in there. Make it count."* Then he disappeared back into the haze.

*****

McMannus turned to Gunny Mulongo, who'd taken over monitoring the rest of the battle while he focused on the engine room assault. "Status, Gunny?"

The slender NCO looked up from the battlecomp display where he'd been updating the status of the company. "*Sir, Whisper Two reports no further probes. Either they're done or they've refocused on the bridge assault element. He's linked up with Sergeant Jeffries and the survivors of 3rd Platoon and they have a solid position. He's also found what's left of the 50th.*"

Looking over the display, McMannus winced. 3rd had taken better than forty percent casualties, including the platoon leader, platoon sergeant and his XO. The 50th was even worse off; he doubted there was anyone left alive higher than a corporal. But Harry had held off the counterattack, secured the armory and gathered the survivors into a blocking position to prevent the Imperials from interfering with the seizure of the main engine room.

"What about the bridge assault?" Not that it mattered; once they controlled the main engine room, the ship was theirs. The 30th and 45th had run into stiffer resistance finally and hadn't reported success. Whatever Gunny Mulongo had been about to say was cut off at Kan's excited whoop over the radio.

"*We are in! Sweep and secure, people. You know the drill.*"

The captain turned to look at the all-too few remaining Marines of 1st filing in through the now-open hatch, weapons at the ready. Of the one hundred twenty Marines in the 76th who'd boarded the Grausian battleship, he had less than ninety effectives left between the three platoons and his headquarters section. He didn't even know the casualty figures of the attached platoons but they had to be at least as high, if not higher. All because Fleet Admiral Besson had to have a prize in the last days of the war. Still, they'd taken a battleship, the flagship of the last Imperial fleet to challenge the nascent Terran Union and that was a unique prize. He sighed and prepped the message for the Admiral on their success.

Chapter 2

Hadfield Station, Terran Union, one week later.

An alarm was ringing but since it wasn't General Quarters, he ignored it. After a few seconds, since it hadn't silenced on its own, Free rolled over onto his stomach and blindly fished about on the side table for the room controls. The incessant ring had woken him from a mercifully dreamless sleep that he wasn't willing to abandon quite yet.

After a moment of blind fumbling trying to locate the damned panel, he tried to open his eyes. They were sticky and felt as dry as sand. The alarm was coming from his commpad. It was a non-emergency call, which is why he hadn't clued in on it at first. He could feel his head starting to pound in time with the pulses as the ringing continued.

As much to save himself as to answer the call, he tapped it for audio-only. His voice was harsh and scratchy as he answered, "McMannus. Who is this?"

"Free, it's Taggert. Sorry to wake you this early when you just went on leave but the Old Man wants to see you."

He lifted his head from the pillow and looked at the commpad with bleary eyes. *Oh eight hundred.* His attention switched to the mess in his room. Several liquor bottles stood on the coffee table across the room and clothes were scattered around the room. *Shouldn't there be...* and that was when he became aware of a warm body next to his. Rubbing his face with his hand, he said, "Right Tag, I can do that. Pulse me the details, because I'm going to need... a bit to get ready."

The answering chuckle was warm and friendly. "Roger that, Free. Old Man said you needed some downtime after the Draconis action. It's non-duty related, so he'd like to meet for lunch. Message on the way."

The commpad beeped as the connection was cut and the body next to his moved. A sleepy female voice asked, "Honey? Who was that?"

His head dropped to the pillow as he relaxed again. It was Aileen in bed with him. One thing made sense at least. "Duty literally just called, love."

She sighed and rolled over, one arm draped over his back and her head pillowed next to his. Her legs twined with his and her lilting voice was soft in his ear. "I put your uniforms in the closet when they got back from the cleaners. And the hotel has unlimited hot water and room service. You don't have to leave for hours yet."

"What about your store? Fleet's in, so there's bound to be sailors with money to burn."

"Desirae's opening today. She'll be okay for a few hours without me." Her tongue tickled his ear. "And check out isn't until eleven."

He rolled over to face her, placing his hand on her cheek. "You think of everything. I knew there was a reason I kept you around."

He felt almost human when he and Aileen checked out. She kissed him goodbye and headed for her store on the outer rim of the station. Even though his head pounded slightly with each heel strike, he kept up a brisk pace. When he caught a lift at the elevators near the hub, the security scanner recognized his bio-signature as military and unlocked the military levels for him. As the lift sped through the station, his commpad buzzed at him and the flat tones of the computer voice came through his earpiece.

Meeting with Colonel Garza in one hour at Smedley Butler Dining Facility.

Unlike some others, he didn't use a custom voice of a celebrity or other public figure. It seemed undignified in the middle of a combat situation to have some damned celebrity calling out targets.

The lone Marine sentry saluted as he approached and Fremont automatically returned the salute. His bio-signature unlocked the access hatch and he stepped into the entrapment area. It took only a few seconds for the sniffers to clear him and the opposite door opened. Now that the treaty was being signed and the Grausian threat ended, Union security was relaxed dramatically. It was not much more than a few months ago when the sentry would have been in full battle rattle with the rest of his fire team backing him up and access to the hatch would have been through a winding maze of collapsible, steel plated emergency barriers that rose from under the decking of the corridor.

On his way to his office, he passed a room filled with thirty plus Marines in a transition class. Another Union policy measure, meant to boost the economy and recover from the endless series of battles with the other races. Fewer people were needed in uniform and more in the workforce. Also, with all the available planets in the newly created Demilitarized Zone (DMZ), the corporations were looking for people with the skills necessary to survive in a not-so-friendly environment. Word was they were paying three times what the military paid. Considering a lot of the military's growth was from draftees during the last part of the independence wars, he supposed it was a good way to re-acclimate battle-hardened Marines to life off the battlefield.

Stepping into the 76th MIST company area, he heard the unmistakable sound of a sonic cleaner in the hall. Up ahead, crouched over the machine as he cleaned the bulkhead was Private Lafayette Dempsey, his head bobbing in time to whatever beat was on his headphones. Free paused, considering the sight. The serious casualties suffered at the battle of Draconis Sigma, when they led the capture of the Grausian flagship meant that there were a lot of faces missing in the barracks on the trip back. Soon there would be a lot of new faces as the replacements arrived. But Lafe cleaning a bulkhead for his various and sundry offenses to Gunnery Mulongo's sense of order was a solid reminder that some things never change.

The young private looked up as his company commander passed him, his usual grin in place. He started to rise but the captain waved him back down. He did pop his earphones out, though. Lafe may have been a skater extraordinaire (his own words) but he was the soul of courtesy. He claimed it was due to the lessons his pappy back in the Bayou beat into him. "Cap'n, what are you doin' hea-yah? Gunny find a bulkhead for you too?"

McMannus chuckled. "No doubt he could, Lafe. No, duty calls. In this case, as I was sleeping one off. And I'm not going to ask what you did to deserve this, because no doubt you do deserve it." He paused. "Gunny made sure it's not going to interfere with your separation appointments?"

The private shook his head, a woeful grin on his face. "Aw naw, suh. Ain't transitioning out no more."

"And why would that be? Find out you have warrants still out for you in the Real World?"

"Suh, I got this life figgered out. Be starting all over again as a civvie and… well, there ain't much for me back home. Only joined up cause the judge was a friend of my pappy. Sides, me and Gunny had a talk. Bout my future in the Corps. He thinks I might have one, if'n only t'clean the bulkheads."

McMannus stared at the younger man, as memories of the backwood colony world he used to call home flickered through his mind. "You and me both, Lafe. You and me both. Carry on, then."

He continued on to the front office and was surprised to find his Second Platoon commander, Harry Webb, typing with dogged determination on a terminal. Harry popped up from his chair but took his seat as his commander waved at him to sit down.

"Mr. Webb, shouldn't you be depriving a bar of its gin somewhere?"

"The good stuff is all gone, sir and I shan't waste my time on the rest. Besides, I need to get these after-action write-ups done."

"Harry, you hate paperwork. You hate thinking about paperwork. You even hate it when someone nearby is doing paperwork."

The young man hung his head. "Guilty as charged. Although that should be a standard of behavior, not something to be ashamed of."

"What's on your mind, Harry? Something had to drag you in here besides a dogged determination to abuse yourself."

His lieutenant sighed and motioned at the screen. "Uni application. One of the benefits they're offering as part of separation is tuition assistance. Everyone in my family has a Master's degree or better in something. I thought I might take a swing at an advanced degree myself."

"My, my. Harry Webb voluntarily subjecting himself to lectures, report writing and exams. What is the universe coming to?"

"I will draw the captain's attention to the fact that a university has both male and female attendees. Some lovely, impressionable young thing might take a fancy to a lad who's been a space marine."

McMannus laughed. "Ladies do love the uniform. Very well, Mr. Webb. Carry on with your paperwork and dreams of impressionable young coeds."

Once in his office, McMannus opened up the company reports and reviewed the latest status. Colonel Garza tended to ask off-the-wall questions about unit readiness and he wanted to be prepared for that possibility. He worked on that for almost thirty minutes, until a message from the Regiment Personnel office informed him his replacements were delayed en route, with an arrival date 'to be determined.'

Great. With all the separations and discharges going on, I bet we're going to get less than half the number we need. He started going through the organization charts, trying to develop alternative schemes in case they did get a much smaller number of personnel than they were expecting. At ten to eleven, he rose and left the office. Harry was still hard at work on his application, frowning at the screen and mumbling under his breath as he typed and backspaced.

*****

The chow hall was central to the regimental spaces in the station, meant to serve several hundred personnel at once. Those of lieutenant colonel and higher rank had a private Officer's Mess but Colonel Garza usually liked to eat in the Enlisted Mess with the rest of his Marines. So it was a bit of a surprise when the assistant adjutant, Captain Blaine Taggert, met him at the entrance and told him to head to the private room.

Colonel Garza was alone in a room set for over a dozen. Free walked over and took the offered seat across from him. "Colonel. Are we going to be joined by anyone else, or…"

"No, Free, just us. I have a little something… actually, a couple of somethings I need to talk about with you." Tag walked in with two trays and set them down on the table and then left all without saying a word. A small grin played over his face as he left.

"Boy better not get transferred to Intel. He can't keep a secret to save his life." The colonel reached into the breast pocket on his uniform but kept covered what he pulled out. "Free, I hope you know you did a damned fine job in Draconis Sigma. We've never captured an Impy battlewagon before and likely the way things are, no one will ever again."

McMannus shrugged, looking away. "We paid a high price for it, sir."

"Not as high a price as many thought. And some thought it was too high a price to pay for a certain unnamed Admiral to have bragging rights, but that's Fleet politics for you. Word is, he's parlaying that into a political ticket. He gets his and you'll get yours because everyone still agrees it was masterfully done. And that makes this a real pleasure." He slid a small case across the table.

Free took it curiously and opened it. Inside were a set of gold oak leaves. He looked up at the older man, who grinned and said, "Not official yet but the general himself is signing off on it. Orders'll be cut within a month or so and we'll probably lose you not too long after that. I'm pushing for battalion XO, or at the very least, an S-3 somewhere."

He sat, stunned. As a mustang, a prior enlisted man, making Major was something he didn't expect until towards the end of his career. He had four years prior enlisted time, with another nine as an officer. His majority shouldn't have been for another couple of years and anything beyond that was as ephemeral as... well, as a dream.

The other man cleared his throat, drawing Free's attention again. "Now that the happy news is delivered, I have some less than appetizing news. Son, how many of your people have put in for separation? Or already in transition?"

He knew the answer right away, courtesy of his pre-lunch review. "Only one in transition already, sir. Twelve more have filed their paperwork and I have at least that many who've expressed interest. Since we went on leave almost as soon as we got in, I don't think many of them have had a chance to really consider the opportunity."

"That's what I thought." His boss leaned back, sighing. Shaking his head, he said, "Free, in about forty-eight to seventy-two hours, Union High Command is going to freeze all individual separations and instead move to a mass demobilization. The politicians passed the new defense bill and military end strength took a big hit. To meet those goals and they're under pressure to do so rapidly, the brass have decided to demobilize whole units and even decommission entire squadrons of ships. Older classes, or those too damaged to be repaired within the reduced budget."

"Whole units... I assume since you're talking to me, the 76th is on the block?"

"The 76th, her sister units, the whole damned regiment. Word is this post will be a battalion at most come next year. And these sweeping cuts aren't going to be kind. There is no money being set aside for any transition niceties, like retraining or education. We're going to see a force reduction on a massive scale and done quickly to meet their budget goals."

The realization hit him like a shock of cold water. "That means you're…"

"I was advised that my retirement paperwork would be looked upon favorably and expedited. Probably six or seven months from now." Garza toyed with a fork. "There's going to be an officer's call the day it hits the news officially but I'm telling you this now. You're headed out of here and you'll land in a good spot, Free. A rising star and even though they're downsizing, they'll be looking for a core cadre to keep things going. You could go far in the new Corps. I don't doubt there's a command in your future. It may mean some staff work for a while but that's the way the game is played."

McMannus sat back, his mind whirling. His company, gone. The regiment, almost certain to be deactivated and colors cased. The whole world was turning upside down. He looked at the man across from him, who suddenly looked old and tired. "What will you do, sir?"

"Oh, I don't know yet. Grandkids are still young and my son is talking about the opportunities on the frontier. He's a botanist, you know. Lot of good work for people like that. Maybe I'll join them and try my hand as a colonist. I'm not that old, by God!"

The rest of the lunch was strange to Free; half work on how to draw down the regiment to a battalion and half musing about the future of the worlds in the Demilitarized Zone. They were both certain that it wasn't going to be easy for them. Too many left over elements from the war (from all sides), pirates pouncing on unguarded shipping lanes and individual worlds fighting over valuable resources. The elation of his pending promotion faded into the background; set aside to be enjoyed later, when he had time.

Later on, he messaged Gunny Mulongo that he wanted an all-hands call with everyone he could get a hold of by tomorrow. Most of the company was on leave but they needed to know what was going to happen. He owed them that and this was probably why the Old Man told him. A quick call to the other company commanders and an oblique reference to upcoming news confirmed that. The word would be getting out to everyone they could reach.

He was back at his quarters by 1500. He debated a quick workout but decided instead he had to talk with Aileen. This affected her, them, as well. A quick call to the shop to confirm she was in and he was off to the lower level mall. As he walked, he paid closer attention to the news. Normally he was only worried about events that could develop into something they would be sent to take care of. Now he listened for word about the changes in the Terran Union and beyond.

The markets were up, of course, since the treaty was all but signed. But the talking heads spoke of 'peace dividends', 'a return to normalcy' and 'focusing on the needs of the people instead of aggression'. Corporate CEOs were animated about the possibilities in the DMZ and commercials everyone advertised the amazing opportunities that could be had for those with the spirit of adventure.

He waited in the front of the store while Aileen was working with her current set of customers. She had built her own alterations and custom tailoring business through the years by hard work and long hours and the sweat and love she poured into it meant it had become a very successful small business. She didn't need him to support her.

Will she go along with this? We haven't talked about marriage seriously, because neither believe we need a piece of paper to define our relationship. Still, we've been together almost three years despite the war and the deployments. Is that enough for her to uproot herself and start over in a new place? Is it even right to ask her to do this? There's plenty of other officers who are married and move their families with them everywhere they go but is this right for us? I guess the real question is, do we need each other for mutual support? Sure, we can each do it alone but aren't we better together?

Aileen motioned him into the office when the customers had left and greeted him with a kiss. "It's not like you to be done this early. To what, or who, do I owe a favor?"

"Still on leave, babe. Lunch with the Colonel was... interesting."

"Interesting, he says, and leaves me hanging. Come on, then, out with it."

"I... It was..." At a loss for words, instead he pulled out the case with the oak leaves and handed it to her. She opened it with a small frown, which lit up into a smile as she realized what it meant.

"This is what he wanted to tell you? When? Oh, this is grand!" She squealed, throwing her arms around his neck and kissing him soundly.

He smiled into her beaming face. "It'll be a few months yet. He said the General himself was signing off on it."

She bounced up and down, rolling her eyes. "We can't wait months to celebrate! Let's go to that nice little Italian place we always like! I'll close early and we'll spend the night with some great food and a nice chianti."

Free's smile faltered. "Allie, there's more. With the promotion comes a new assignment. Off station."

She stared into his eyes, stunned. "Oh..."

He held her close, hands on the small of her back. "It's sure to be another station assignment. Probably a staff position, which means no deployments. And...,"

She put her hands on his chest and pushed him away gently, her face blank and gaze unfocused. Stepping away from him, she walked over to the door of the office, arms folded across her chest. He stood, frozen and at a loss for words, waiting for her to speak. After several long moments, she turned back to him. Sniffing once, she swiped at her eyes with both hands. "When?"

Free shrugged. "A few months. Probably no more than six. Allie, I…"

She walked back to him and planted a small kiss on his mouth. "Well, we have time to talk, then." But she wouldn't meet his eyes. "Now come on, we've got some celebrating to do! You call and make reservations while I tell my crew we're closing early."

*****

The next morning was the last day of his leave and it dawned much like the previous days'. They had celebrated late into the night, finishing off a bottle of champagne after the wine in the restaurant and then made wild, almost frantic love. They had neither discussed his impending promotion and move nor had they talked about any future plans. It was a mutual avoidance and it seemed to carry into the morning. Aileen was still asleep when he got out of the shower and he dressed quickly and quietly. As the door hissed closed, he saw that she lay unmoving, her back to him but it looked like her shoulders shook in small motions.

He headed to his office, intent on burying himself in paperwork. Pausing at the entrance to the 76th canton, he reached up and touched the wooden plaque that hung over the hatch with the unit motto, "Violentium in Silentio."

Violence in Silence. That we were. And now I'm supposed to accept that everything we've done throughout this war, the people we've lost, will fade into the history books in a few weeks. Shit. I need something to do to keep my mind off that and everything that went unsaid last night. Given that most of the unit was on leave or in the sickbay, it was a pretty light load. The replacements were now canceled, a sure sign that Colonel Garza was right about the pending demobilization.

Leaning back in the chair, he stared across the 76th office spaces. The cubicles didn't make a difference; it was the people who sat in them and in the barracks. He'd been with the company for over five years now, first as a platoon leader, then executive officer and now commanding it. It was a bit unusual to be here that long but when the fleet is constantly deployed, the transfer of personnel to new billets was limited. Plus, his former company commander had been a genius at manipulating the assignment system.

As much as anywhere, the 76th is home and these are my people. I know them better than I know anyone else. New recruit or old salt, we've fought side-by-side in action after action over the years. And now I'm not just leaving for another assignment where we might meet up in another unit down the road. They're getting pushed out and we'll never meet up again in uniform.

Realizing that train of thought was going nowhere, he pushed it and went back to work. At lunchtime he grabbed a quick bite at one of the local vendor stalls before heading to the gym. He had no messages from Allie all day and had sent none. There seemed to be nothing to say, or at least nothing to say that wouldn't cause a fight. He wondered what this evening would bring.

Gunny had set the formation in one of the micro-g courts, where freefall versions of hockey, ulama and other sports were played. The Marines were well at home here, as they used the micro-g courts for both sports and training. McMannus entered to find most of the company there and they were clustered around one end of the court. Gunny Mulongo called the area to attention as he drifted towards the 'ceiling, then grabbed a handhold absently and swung to face them.

"At ease. Thanks for coming in while on leave. I know Gunny wasn't supposed to twist any arms and I trust he didn't have to twist hard. I wouldn't have had this formation except there are some things happening here in the very near future that affect everyone and the Colonel and I wanted you to hear it from us first."

Looking around at his people, he paused. There were missing faces aplenty from the Draconis Sigma action and it showed. The tight buddy knots and small groups were there but they seemed smaller and tighter. Like the loss of a member had pulled them closer together. He remembered being like this, post-Massacre, as a young private. Lieutenant (and now Colonel) Meagher had pulled their asses out of that bloodbath but they'd lost a lot of people. The survivors, well, they felt like members of an exclusive club now.

"Sometime in the next few days, you're going to see this break in the news. A massive drawdown of the armed forces is coming, now that the treaty is signed. It's going to mean demobilizing a significant portion of the military. All the services are going to be affected." He scanned their faces. All were attentive but there were quite a few whose focus had grown sharper. Perhaps they had sensed something was up from the newscasts. "I have it on very good word that instead of processing individual separation requests, they're going to begin mass separations, whole units and ships. Anyone who hasn't already been approved for separation is going to fall under this new process. And it's not likely to be a kind process as we're shown the door."

There was the expected buzz of conversation, punctuated with phrases like, "No fuckin' way!" and "Those assholes!" Aside from the angry faces, there were plenty who were realizing just what this meant for their future. In particular, he noted Lafe Dempsey and Harry Webb, each realizing the abrupt termination of their dreams.

He waited for several moments until the outbursts had died down and Gunny had put them at ease again. Looking across the sea of familiar faces, he said quietly, "We've been through a lot. We've sacrificed a lot and lost friends. And after all of that, this is what we get in the end. It's a giant shit sandwich and we've all got to take a bite. The only consolation is that it isn't personal. Thousands, tens of thousands of others will be going through the same thing. That's a small comfort, I know. Especially when you're trying to start new jobs and careers. Despite the push to explore and colonize in the DMZ, it's going to be a tough new start for everyone."

He pushed off from the wall with a gentle motion and drifted towards them. As he got to within a few feet of the front ranks, he grabbed a handhold and arrested his motion. "Just remember who you are and what you did. You broke the Grausian deathgrip on the human race that's held us for five hundred years. You kicked out the scavengers who wanted our worlds in that aftermath. And you did what no one else has ever done; you took a battleship away from the enemy. If you can do all that then you can handle what's coming next. You can handle it and beat it. Then you'll keep doing impressive shit wherever you end up. I'm proud of each and every one of you and no matter what happens, that will never change."

*****

Aileen entered the apartment quietly, closing the door with a faint click. Free still heard it but didn't move from the recliner. A highball glass and a bottle of cheap bourbon sat on the coffee table in front of him, half-empty. Whatever she'd been ready to say when she got home was set aside as she took in the scene.

She walked over to stand next to his chair. "Free, what's wrong?"

He rubbed his eyes with the fingers of his left hand. "I'm a fucking hypocrite, that's what."

"I see," she said cautiously. "And what exactly are you a hypocrite for?"

Instead of answering, he leaned forward, picked up the bottle and splashed a few inches in the glass. The bottom of the bottle hit the table at an angle as he tried to set it down and Aileen reached down to help steady it as Free righted it. With the caution of someone who realizes they are drunker than they thought, he gently placed the bottle on the table. He spent several moments looking at the glass before wrapping his hand around it but did not lift it to his lips.

"Free…. Honey... " She knelt down next to the table and gently unwrapped his fingers from the glass. Holding his hand in hers, she tried to look into his eyes but he wouldn't meet hers. Behind the alcohol blur, she saw his brown eyes were fiery hot.

"I had to tell them today. The Union is demobilizing on a massive scale and they're getting kicked out without so much as a thank you. They're getting shafted and I'm getting a promotion and a future!" He waved a hand at the ceiling. "I stood there and told them 'we' were getting the shit end of the deal but I'm not getting crapped on, am I?"

He abruptly yanked his hand from hers and stood up, a bit unsteady but he didn't appear to notice. "Told the whole company, or what's left of them. They broke their asses out there! Kicked the door in on a goddamned Grausian battleship and wiped the deck with them but do they get any thanks? Fought every fucking engagement for the last fifteen years to throw off those Scalies and push the Chimps back and what do they get? Don't let the door hit you in the ass on the way out!"

He was breathing heavily now, swaying in place as his head spun from the alcohol and adrenaline. Aileen moved slightly and he looked down. Her eyes were wide but he saw no fear, no concern, only… surprise? She took a slow breath and looked down. When she spoke, her voice was low. "I didn't know you felt this bad about it."

"Bad? Bad? Allie, I feel… ripped in half. Broken. They're my Marines. Mine. I've been part of this unit for five years now. It's more than just people who work together. It's like, like family."

Aileen stood then, her face finally showing an emotion, grief. "Now you know how I felt, Free, when you told me. I thought we could have something together. Here! The war's over! You don't have to go out there and risk your life! You could get out, too. There's bound to be plenty of opportunities for you!"

"Allie, you're saying exactly what I had to tell the company. Yes, there's going to be lots of opportunities but there's going to be thousands of ex-military looking for jobs."

"I know people here on the station. I'm on the small business council. A few words in the right ears and I'm sure I could get you something!" Tears were trickling down her cheeks and her voice broke at the end.

"So I should just take any job that comes along? Would you? Would you be dependent on my charity if the situation were reversed?"

She grabbed his hand and held it to her chest. "What does it matter if it's charity? We'd get to stay together! And... plan for the future. Maybe get married. Have a family and a life."

He reached out and cupped her cheek with one hand, the other still held by hers. Softly, he said, "Allie, we can do those things wherever we are. Why is it so important to stay here?"

She closed her eyes. "It's not the place, Free. You're right." And when she opened her eyes, they bored directly into his, fierce and unrelenting. "It's your job. You go away and I never know if you're coming home again. You risk your life time and time again and maybe that was okay during the war but now it's done! You don't have to do that anymore!"

Leaning forward, he kissed her forehead. "I don't have to but I can't just up and leave my Marines. I have to do something. I don't know what but I can't just leave them like this."

She let go of his hand and stepped back towards the door. Swiping at the tears on her cheeks, she said, angrily. "What about me? Will you do something for me or just leave me like this?"

"I want you to come with me. Be with me. Wherever we do, whatever we do. For always, Allie."

Her shoulders slumped. "Just wait at home, not knowing if you're ever coming back. That's what you'll do for me?" She turned and opened the door. "I don't know if I can do that for you. For us. You'll always be a Marine and the Corps will always come first, I guess. There's no changing that."

And then she was gone.

*****

He sat alone in the apartment for the rest of the night. The bottle sat, forgotten on the table. Thoughts and ideas chased themselves round and round in his head; the company, the drawdown, the promotion and Allie. No matter how he tried, he couldn't make them fit. Like trying to fit together magnets at the same pole, they always repelled each other.

Starting awake, Free looked around groggily until he realized he was still sitting in the living room chair. His back ached, his eyes were sandy and the fog in his head blurred his thoughts. Only the drive of duty pulled him into the shower, got him dressed and out the door. He remembered nothing of his trip to the Marine base and he shut the door to his office upon arriving. By rote he logged in to his account, noted the messages awaiting his review and then sat for a very long time, lost in thought.

A distinctive triple rap shook him out of his reverie. "Yes, Gunny?"

The door opened and in strode the Gunny, uniform creased to perfection and back ramrod straight. He held a tablet up and said, "Sir, training schedule for your review. Now that our people are coming back off leave, we've got to get those hangovers run out of them."

McMannus stared at him in disbelief. "Training schedule, Gunny? Now? After what I told you yesterday?"

Laying the tablet on his commander's desk, he said, "Now more than ever, sir. You reminded them what they did as Marines. Now we remind them they are still Marines. That they will always be Marines, no matter where they go or what they do."

McMannus ignored the tablet for the time being. He leaned back in his chair, considering the older man. Gunnery Sergeant Yembe Mulongo had been a Marine for eighteen years, only a few more years than himself. Yet the man seemed ageless and timeless, with a stoic quality that befitted a man in his position. "Gunny, can I ask you a personal question?"

Mulongo assumed a parade rest position. "As the Captain wishes."

"Oh, take a seat. This isn't an inquisition." He waited until the man had sat down and then continued. "What will you do? After separation, that is?"

Several moments passed before the other man answered. "I haven't given it much thought, sir." His eyes looked up and away. "Guess I'll figure it out when the time comes. Got to be somewhere I can put my skills to use. The worlds in the DMZ are bound to be full of opportunities. You know the old saying; chaos and confusion means money on the table."

"Money on the table? Like hiring yourself out as a bodyguard or something?"

"Or something." He relaxed a bit in his chair and looked at his boss. "I have relatives out there. They've talked about how things are now. It's wild at times and hardly much TU presence. They've talked about setting up their own militias and such but none of them have military training. That could lead to something."

McMannus shook his head. "You could be a sergeant major in the militia, then. Got a nice ring to it, huh?"

Mulongo gave a short smile. "Big fish in a little pond. Not much room to swim. And it'd be ground-based. Maybe not for me, then. Micro is where I belong."

"You and me both, Gunny. You and me both."

His senior NCO gave him an odd look. "Sir, I heard some things. The Lance Corporal network, you see. About you and... well, your status."

"I see." McMannus sighed heavily. "Yes, the Colonel gave me some heads-up on what's coming down the pipe, for me and all of us. I guess I'm the only one with good news, though."

"It's well-deserved, sir. Not everyone could have done what you did. And kept as many of us alive as you did." He leaned forward, eyes intent. "Don't feel guilty about being rewarded. The Lord knows we don't get enough recognition for what we do. Take it and do good things for other Marines, sir."

"Thanks, Gunny. I appreciate your confidence and candor. It just feels like I'm running out on the company. Not everyone is going to land on their feet after this."

"No but it's not like they're without skills. Micro training and being able to handle a suit for hours on end? Plenty of zero-g construction firms will be jumping at the chance to get their hands on our people. And that's not something the dirtdogs can compete with, either. Shipping companies, too. Understanding that micro-g doesn't mean 'no mass' and working with heavy objects in vacuum is worth something too. These kids will find something in micro if they want."

The captain rubbed his face with his hands. "Alright, Gunny, you've convinced me. It still feels a bit like I'm running out but I'll be damned if I'm going to whine about it anymore.

Mulongo rose and nodded. "Can't have the CO slacking off. Looks bad to the ranks. I'll await your signature on the training schedule. If you approve, we can start after chow tomorrow with basic drills in the micro-g courts."

"Right. Thanks again, Gunny."

After the door closed, Free leaned back in his chair, drumming his fingers on the armrests. Mulongo painted a decent picture, post-separation. At least he hoped it would be like the man said. Someone who was trained in micro-g and able to withstand being in a suit for hours at a time was not very common. People who lived and worked in space had to have a basic understanding of micro-g and vacuum and be able to don a suit in an emergency but that wasn't the same as moving and maneuvering yourself and other objects.

Returning his attention to his terminal, he began working through the waiting messages. Near the top was a surprise, something that had come in just this morning from his old commanding officer, Colonel Tom Meagher. Back when he was a private, then Lieutenant Meagher had been Free's platoon commander, assigned to the security detachment of the U.S.S. *Caledonia*. Their escape from the trap the Impy forces had laid in Glarius, which had resulted in a near-complete assassination of Terran military leadership, was nothing short of miraculous. Four years later, Captain Meagher had recommended Corporal McMannus for a commission and continued to be a mentor throughout his career.

Intrigued at the timing of the message, Free opened it with some anticipation.

Free;

Congratulations on your promotion, no one deserves it more. The 5th Marines will always be in your debt for what your guys did at the Tannenberg Gate. If the Impy's had managed to get even one more ship through, we would never have gotten off planet ... but I digress.

I heard through my own sources about the 76th being disbanded and everyone getting tossed. I know you still have a job but the war is over and you and I are men of action. In debt to you, I'd like to offer you a staff job with my new company, Hibernia Arms LLC. We'll be doing private military contracting, mostly out in the DMZ. I know you're not a ground pounder, so I can't offer you a command position, but I expect you could easily handle operations planning.

Having said that, I know you won't take it. I'm sure that your skin crawls with the thought of sending others into battle while you reap the profits from a safe desk, as does mine. Here's a thought, though. I have a line into the

*Demobilization and Reutilization Management Office. I'm
pretty sure I can get someone to declare, say, a company's
worth of MACE suits unsuitable for further use and surplus.
And it just so happens I'm looking at the log report of the
76th right now. Did you know that your entire outfit's
equipment is being sent to the DRMO as excess? Matter of
fact, it seems Hibernia Arms just purchased the lot for a
song. I wonder who we could unload them off to? A ground
infantry unt can't use MIST gear. I'll have to give my S-4 a
severe reprimand and dump these somewhere.*

Call me, all ansible charges reversed to Hibernia.

Tom

P.S. Sergeant Major Huy said you owe him.

He sat back, stunned. Meagher was obviously leaving the
service. Perhaps he was offered a generous retirement, like
Garza? And becoming a 'private military contractor'? In
simpler terms, a mercenary.

Free searched his memory on mercenaries. There hadn't
been any for hundreds of years, or at least, none of any note.
The legions were the iron fist of the Empire and they were
merciless, even with each other during the Rebellion. The
military history courses at OCS covered Terran military
operations on old Earth, however. The balkanized nature of
the planet prior to meeting the Empire had led to 'private
military contractors' operating in both open security and
covert direct action roles. They could be used in situations
where governments either could not or did not want to act
openly or to prevent the widening of a conflict to war
between nation-states.

So humans had done it before. Selling your skills for
money instead of serving your nation. Put that way, it
sounded… dirty. But then, he thought, someone who worked
for a corporation sold their skills for a paycheck. Being a

mercenary, a private military contractor, was just another form of business.

He leaned back in his chair, mind working on the issue. Hiring out as mercenaries was certainly something for his people to do. Given what Meagher had said, he wasn't likely to hire them, though. However, as micro-g specialists, the MIST had a very specific skill set. That was exactly his line of thinking before Meagher's message. So was there a place for them to get hired in their specialty?

Or... Should they form their own company? The Colonel's comment about the suits; was that what he was suggesting? He reread the message. It certainly seemed like that. So say they did form a mercenary company specializing in micro-g operations. There were Legions aplenty that did ground combat but working in vacuum and low gravity situations was almost uniquely a Marine and more specifically, a MIST mission set. All Marines trained to operate in vacuum and micro-g but the Microgravity Strike Teams excelled in it. They were the point teams on assaulting enemy ships, orbital facilities and stations on planetoids and moons. They also were the first line of defense against such assaults.

Mulongo's comments about the colony worlds setting up their own militias came back to him. Things were probably a bit hairy out there and he'd also said that chaos and confusion led to money on the table. His Marines could take advantage of that. And wasn't that just what he'd been thinking through on the things they could do?

But who would lead them? As that thought came to him, he realized he was thinking of himself. After all, if they were going into combat, he wasn't going to let anyone else but himself take them into harm's way. Harry Webb and Ishido Kan, his two surviving platoon leaders, were coming along nicely but neither was quite ready for this kind of independent operation. He would need an executive officer and probably a small staff as well, since they'd be operating on their own. They'd need intel assets, a logistics officer, their own armorer and suit technicians… His mind flipped through the staff billets, automatically noting what was needed and coming up with his preferred candidates. There were going to be a lot of military folks out of work in the coming months. He should get a jump on hiring.

And as he thought that through, he realized he was starting where Aileen started. She began her own business with very little idea of where it would go but she did it. She poured her time and energy into it and her employees respected the hell out of her. She had made it into something and that made her feel good. He hoped that he could do as well as she had and feel as good as she did. After all, he was doing something for his Marines instead of abandoning them. Promotion be damned! This company was his life. He couldn't just leave them hung out to dry. And this was something they were good at. They could do this.

Of course, that assumed the company wanted to follow this path. Maybe some had other ideas about getting out now that the war was pretty much done. He wouldn't keep anyone who didn't want to stay. But with the prospect of being dumped out into the streets so abruptly, the thought of staying with your unit might appeal. He laughed to himself as he sent the Gunny a message to set up another formation tomorrow and then come see him. One thing was certain; he would need Yembe as the core of any unit he was going to form.

*****

The company was once again the micro-g courts. They were doing small unit exercises, practicing using walls and various objects to adjust their trajectory as they maneuvered towards their objective. It was probably one of the most difficult aspects of being a MISTer, because once you launched, you couldn't adjust your course without using a maneuver pack and you didn't always have them. Plus, they were a nuisance if you were trying to get somewhere without being detected. Coordinating a four man fire team or eight man squad so there weren't any collisions and everyone got to where they needed to be required a lot of training and practice.

Today, Gunny had them maneuvering in squads by platoon, with the lead squad in each platoon then competing with each other. The din as he entered, unnoticed, was deafening as the uninvolved Marines cheered for their side or shouted insults at their opponents. There was a frantic knot of bodies where the lines of advance crossed towards objectives and Free watched as Corporal Pimental got her people untangled swiftly and efficiently. Mulongo nodded in approval and said in a voice loud enough to be heard over the din, "She's coming along nicely and the squad respects her. She'll make a good sergeant and squad leader."

McMannus clapped him on the shoulder. "Here's hoping she wants to use those stripes."

They waited until the current exercise had finished and Gunny Mulongo called the room to attention as the captain floated down to the gathering. The company slowly accreted around him and he stopped approximately in the middle of them.

Magging his boots into place on the deck, he said, "Good afternoon, Marines!"

The response was crisp and he smiled broadly. Pivoting in place, he pointed to his face. "You may be wondering why I'm so happy, especially given the news I delivered yesterday. Wonder no more! We are Marines; we improvise, adapt and overcome. And that's what I'm planning to do here in the very near future. Now the usual expectation is when an officer is smiling, shit is going to roll all over you. The shit rolled downhill yesterday. Today, we're pulling ourselves out of the pile and cleaning up."

McMannus pointed to Corporal Pimentel. "Christiane, that was an outstanding job you did just now. Gunny is also impressed with your work and he tells me it's time to make you a permanent squad leader instead of acting. Who am I to argue with him? Congratulations!"

As the Marines next to her expressed their approval, he continued, "You may be thinking you'll only get to be a sergeant for a short time but there might be something else on the horizon. Are you interested in continuing to use those stripes?"

She nodded with emphasis. "You bet, Captain!"

He then pointed at Lafe. "Private Dempsey, would you say you're good at being a Marine and especially a MIST Marine?"

Lafe rubbed the back of his head with a sheepish expression on his face. "Waal Cap'n, there's some that would say I'm not but yeah, I say I'm pretty good at it."

He called on several other Marines in turn, asking each one the same question. All were those who had thought they were going to continue on in the Corps instead of separating. All answered in the affirmative. Then he held up his hands and asked all of them, "What if there were a way you could keep doing what you're doing? It wouldn't be as a Terran Union Marine but you'd still be a Marine and you'd still be doing micro-g work."

Their confusion at his question was plain on their faces but he put his palms out in a 'hold up' gesture. "We'll get to the answer to that in a minute. Mr. Webb, are you still thinking of going back to school once you get out?"

The lanky Brit shook his head. "Uni's bloody expensive, sir. I'd need a job first and save up. And getting a job is going to be a dog's breakfast with several million of us hitting the streets."

"Do any of you disagree with him? No? He's got it right. The job market is going to be flooded with tons of you apes, all with very similar skill sets. It's going to come down to who you know, not what you know. Anybody know anyone?"

Most shook their heads in the negative, although a few volunteered that they might go back to the family business.

"And if that's what you want to do, then do it! I know a lot of you joined up to get the Impies out of our space and we've done that. You've done your part and nobody would begrudge you wrapping things up here."

He pivoted in a slow circle, making sure he had everyone's attention. "But for those of you who are worried at the prospect of being dumped out into the street with nothing but the clothes on your back, listen closely. I'm going to propose something quite unusual, something that we Terrans haven't done in centuries."

*****

Free was feeling pretty good as he sat down at the ansible terminal and punched in the code for Hibernia Arms. Meagher's promise of supplying them with MACE suits was real as Staff Sergeant Dunbar, a 76th member who'd been on light duty with Supply due to an injury, had discovered at the depot. A bit of paperwork, a few bottles of good booze and the suits were theirs while being marked 'unsuitable; disposal required'. Dunbar was now working on a full company's worth of weapons to get 'lost' in the shuffle of demobilization and settling his own affairs so he could join them. Free figured that was at least worth a bump in rank to Gunnery Sergeant.

In the end, he had almost ninety percent of them volunteer to become private military contractors. He planned to talk to the other companies, hoping to recruit more Marines and fill out the ranks. They'd accepted himself as commander, with Harry and Ishido as platoon commanders and Gunny Mulongo as senior NCO. Almost all the platoons would remain intact and any other personnel he was able to convince would fill out the ranks or even become a third platoon.

The call connected and the face of his old commander appeared on the screen. His face creased in a grin when he saw his former subordinate. *"Hey, Free! Long time no see.*

Sorry to hear about the demob but I'm guessing you're handling it in stride?"

"That's about right, sir. Took your advice and we're forming our own company. Haven't decided on a name but the kids want to keep the unit designation at least. All thanks to some helpful advice."

"*Well, that's what I'm here for. Get your suits from DRMO yet?*"

"Doing that now. Thanks again for that. Now we just have to find our first contract. I'm hoping you have some advice on that. That's not something they taught in Expeditionary Warfare School."

"*Well now. Lemme see.*" Meagher turned to another screen and scrolled through it for several seconds. "*I thought so. Have a look at the Pavo Real system in the Denovo Sector. We got word that they were having some problems with a developing insurgency. People that work the belt want to split off and form their own government. It's starting to interrupt their trade. Thought we might be interested but turns out it's all in the high orbitals and beyond.*"

"Well, well, well. That does sound right in our lane."

Meagher smiled and hit a button. "*Transmitting the file now. Go out there and make a name for yourself, Free. The field is ripe for a new player, especially one with your particular set of skills.*"

His inbox chimed as a new message arrived. "Roger that, Colonel. Stay safe and keep your powder dry."

"*Same to you, Free. Good hunting and see you out there in the DMZ.*"

*****

He worked steadily throughout the rest of the week on both sides of the job. On one hand, he had to fill out the endless paperwork the TUMC required, no matter that everyone knew they weren't going to be around much longer. On the side, he sketched out what an independent company would need. No longer would they have the support of the government and its established supply chain. They would have to find, buy, or maybe steal what they needed to operate.

A message from Sparks popped up on his terminal near the end of the day, announcing he had a civilian visitor. The person who came to his door, however, was not a civilian despite his business attire. There was something familiar about him, too.

Free stood and offered his hand. "Fremont McMannus. What can I do for you, sir?"

The man shook his hand with a firm but not overstrong grip. He looked to be in his late forties, with gray at the temples. "Ezekiel Vestry, Captain. Thanks for taking time to see me."

"Vestry. Weren't you on Admiral Bhatra's staff back during the Charee campaign in '93?"

His visitor smiled. "Nice to be remembered. Yes, I was the assistant G-2 for the good admiral. And you were a newly minted captain, if I recall. Never forget your first company command, do you?"

Smiling, McMannus motioned to a chair. "So what brings you to the 76th, Mr. Vestry? I'm assuming it is 'mister', correct?"

His visitor put a finger to his lips and pulled out a small electronic device. Placing it on Free's desk midway between the two of them, he pressed the power button. A low hissing noise emanated from the device.

"A little precaution, Captain. We don't know who else might be listening."

Free regarded the white noise generator with unease. "And why are we worried about who might be listening?"

"In my line of work… that is, my previous line of work, you always assumed someone might be listening. In this case, I know for a fact someone has been listening to you. For example, the fact that you've convinced a large number of Marines to join you in a private venture has come to the attention of some highly placed people. As well as some people who think it's not a bad idea."

Free's stomach clenched up but the cold wash of anger overrode the fear. "You're spying on me?"

"Not me, Captain. I'm no longer working for our mutual employer. As a matter of fact, I was forced out a few weeks ago as the treaty was getting ready to be signed." He paused, looking at the device with a sour expression on his face. "Don't take it personally. Intelligence collects on a large number of conversations, verbal and electronic, on the TU military bases. We had a number of leaks early on in the war against the Grausians, so it was necessary at the time to find and stop those leaks. Unfortunately, the practice continued long after it was needed."

"So why are you telling me this? And why are you here?"

Ezekiel said in a low voice, "I… we want to join you."

"That's not what I expected to hear. We? Another spook like you? Why aren't they here?"

"No, the other person is my daughter. We want to get out of the TU, for our own reasons."

Free sat back and regarded his visitor with narrowed eyes. "And just what are you running from?"

"My past." He smiled sheepishly. "Yes, I know it's cliche. But when I was 'invited' to retire, it was also made clear that remaining in the TU was not in my best interest. Normally, people at my level are sought out by the major defense contractors, not necessarily for what we know but who we know. Relationships open doors, which leads to lucrative contracts."

"I sense a 'but' coming."

"The flag and general officers I know are also being forced out, part of the 'peace dividend'. The men and women who designed, fought and won our independence from alien rule are now being retired, one by one, to make room for the new crop that are playing to the peace movement. Which means I wasn't of much value to the corporations. The DMZ is a different matter, though. Plenty of opportunities there."

"Sure sounds like you're bringing some baggage with you. That's not comforting. What happens to you in the DMZ?"

"I become just another private citizen. And I'm not bringing danger down upon you. As long as I'm out of the TU and not in a position to influence the new politics, they'll leave me alone. They have other things they'd rather spend their resources on."

"Okay, let's say you're not bringing more problems down on us. Why should I hire you?"

"I can help, Captain. A career in Naval Intelligence gave me access to a great deal of information and my focus area included many of the systems that are now in the DMZ. I know the economics, the politics, the alien races and the people in these systems where you need to be hired. Insider information, as it were."

"Well, I can't say that won't be helpful. But why drag your daughter into a situation like this? Doesn't she have other family members she can stay with? We don't know what we're going to run into out there and a combat unit isn't the best place for a family."

"You'll have to consider that situation eventually, Captain. Your people aren't going to be by themselves for long. You have your own dependent, after all. Aren't you worried about dragging her into this?"

Free paused his retort, thinking about Aileen. And what about others in the unit who had spouses or family? "I... hadn't thought that far ahead. Guess that's another thing that's going to be different being a private contractor. Planning for dependents."

"And protection of such. After all, why fight you when your opponent can go after your families?"

"And you want to bring your daughter into this?"

He smiled. "Alanna just graduated from The Basic School a few weeks ago and was commissioned in the TUMC as a second lieutenant. Then just a week ago, before she reported for duty, she received a notice that she was being placed in the inactive reserve, to be called to active duty if needed. Or she could accept termination of her commission without prejudice and a small sum for 'career realignment'."

"Lots of that kind of thing going around."

Ezekiel nodded, sighing. "She's always wanted to be a Marine. Didn't take her old man's advice to go into the Navy where there's some class. Now, though… Captain, she has a degree in accounting. She's a trained Marine officer. And she's had the benefit of a father who has passed along the lessons he learned in twenty-five years as an intelligence officer."

"Pretty damn impressive. You must be proud of her."

"I am. And it was her suggestion that we join the 76th together, not mine. Her thought was that the accounting degree would be very useful as an assistant supply officer. But she's also willing to go through micro-g training as well and truly become a MIST Marine, if you'll have her."

"Yeah, I realized earlier I'm going to need staff and logistical support, since I can't count on a higher chain of command. So what about you? Thinking S-2?"

"That's right. If you'll have me as well." Ezekiel sat back in his seat and watched Free with his calm, gray eyes. There was no expression at all on his face but a slight tension in the set of shoulders made Free think he was betting everything on this decision.

On a hunch, he opened the file Meagher had sent and spun the screen around. "What do you know about the Denovo Sector and specifically the Pavo Real system?"

The former intelligence officer scanned the information, nodding in a few places. "System has an extensive asteroid belt. Better than three times the size of old Sol's. Lots of raw materials for the war effort came from there. And that didn't make many friends among the miners when they didn't see the profits the system government was realizing from the sales. Started organizing work stoppages and riots."

"So we'd be facing disgruntled miners? Breaking up strikes and protests? That doesn't sound like what they need a MIST unit for."

"Let me think… The strikes and riots lead the government to stop using most of the low orbital processing and terrestrial sites. Too easy for the miners to use them to get down to the planet and stage more public protests. Instead, most of the stations were moved to the belt. They claimed that it made processing easier and quicker. What it really did was tighten the yoke. Air, water and food was all shipped up the gravity well or brought in from cometary bodies. All had to be paid for with ore. That's the last I remember. Things must have really gotten worse if they're ready to hire a mercenary unit."

That's more than I knew an hour ago. So he knows his stuff. At least about this contract. Will he be useful on other contracts, or on campaign? And do I really have a choice? A man who knows the worlds of the DMZ and a fellow officer. Sooner or later I'll need a staff to help find the right contracts, pick fights we know we can win.

Free stood and offered his hand. "Okay, then Ezekiel. Let me be the first to welcome you and your daughter to the new 76th MIST. Or at least, provisionally welcome. Once we all get kicked out and can actually stand up the new company, then it'll be official."

His new intelligence staff officer stood, the tension draining from his shoulders and took the proffered hand. "Thanks, Captain. I appreciate your trust in me."

Free pinged Gunny Mulongo to come to his office. "I'll introduce you to Gunnery Sergeant Mulongo, my senior NCO. If we're going to be working together, we'll need to know each other. Speaking of which and not that it makes a difference but what rank did you retire at?"

Ezekiel smiled briefly. "Captain. Naval captain, that is. But as I said, I'm retired now. So it's just Ezekiel."

"Sure thing, Zeke."

A pained expression crossed the older man's face. "Please, never call me that."

*****

Finally, there was only one thing left to do. He had given her a few days to process and now it was time to see if she was still talking to him.

He waited until just before closing before he went to Allie's store. She was helping a customer when he walked in. He saw her look up at him and then she turned back to her customer. Once she was done, he walked over. She looked tired and there were dark shadows under her eyes.

Running her fingers through her hair, she gave him a small smile. "Free. Is there something I can help you with?"

He smiled back and shook his head. "Just came by to tell you a few things. First off, you're right. I am a Marine and will always be one. No surprises there."

She started to say something but he held up a hand. "Please. Just a few more things. You're right that I don't need to risk my life for a government or something grandiose like patriotism. And I never really did. I always did what I did for the Marines on either side of me. They're the ones I fight for. So that's what I've come to tell you. I wanted you to know that I won't be taking that promotion and heading off to another assignment. And I am getting out. But I'm also staying a Marine."

Her face clouded over in puzzlement. "You're getting out but staying a Marine?"

He took her hands in his. "You're not the only one who can start a business. I'm going to be a Marine where I can; out in the DMZ. I... we, really, most of the company is coming with me; we're going to do something that hasn't been done in a long time but now is the time for it. We're going to form our own company and try our hand as private military contractors. No more fighting and dying for some faceless politician. We get to pick our fights and we get paid what we're worth. And most importantly, we're doing it for each other."

Hope and confusion swam across her face. "Free, that's such a huge unknown. What if it doesn't work?"

"Allie, my dear, we'll make it work. You haven't seen what a couple hundred determined Marines can do!" He leaned forward and touched his forehead to hers. "I'm hoping you can meet me halfway on this. But don't answer now. Give me six months out there in the DMZ to set up a place; a base of operations. Then I'll let you know where to come, if you want. I've heard there's going to be lots of opportunities out there for a smart person. We can make our own start, together, out there. What do you say?"

She sniffled once and swallowed heavily. For long moments, she was silent. Then she said, "Six months, you say? That'll give me time to design a new uniform for your company."

*****

Alpha Centauri, Terran Union

Thomas Flatley and Oliver Beck waited for their boss in the small break room outside the executive conference room at Galactocity. Flatley was thin and prematurely balding but presented an aura of quiet competence as he worked steadily on his tablet. Beck was almost the opposite, tall, broad-shouldered and dressed in a simple jumpsuit, with a head shaved bald and a neatly trimmed blond goatee. He stood at the back of the room, with a clear line of sight to the door, cup of coffee in his hand.

When the meeting ended, Winfield Cross left near the end, still talking with the CEO. They parted at the elevators, with the CEO smiling and nodding. After the doors closed, Cross motioned for them to join him.

"They just signed the treaty. It was broadcast live via Ansible, with much fanfare. The politicians are giddy at what they've accomplished. As if they had an original thought in their heads. Very well, gentlemen, we have our instructions. In a few weeks or so, the Union will announce a new initiative aimed at boosting the postwar economy. This new DMZ will be open for business and Galactocity intends to capture those markets in our area."

Lean and athletic, Cross had worked hard to become the Vice President of Market Development for Galactocity, keeping it on the stock exchange as a top performing company. He had a proven track record for finding weaknesses and exploiting them ruthlessly, all for the company's benefit. Those who did a good job for him found their careers immensely improved and the converse was true for the underperformers. They walked to his office as he talked and inside, he closed the door and turned on the white noise generator in his desk.

"We've been allocated the markets in the Denovo Sector. Thomas, you'll lead the market analysis team. At the same time, I'll want you to do a thorough but private investigation into the local shipping concerns. We have to be ready for not just competition from the Terran companies but those local as well. They'll have the markets sewn up and personal relationships in place with the markets. I want those identified for Oliver so we can plan to sever them."

Turning to the large man, he tapped the desk. "Oliver, put together the personnel you think you'll need to investigate our options for disrupting the local companies. I'd prefer to use unsavory elements already in place. See what they'll need. The company will have any number of small arms that can be conveniently 'lost' and made available. It should go without saying that there should be no trail back to Galactocity, of course. I'll also want a thorough analysis of the military and police forces in the region."

*****

Tau Ceti, Terran Union

Cassandra Vickers walked down the hall to Oscar's office suite, heels soft on the plush carpet. StellarMart may have supplied almost every system in the TU but their office motif was currently in an old Earth phase. Soft earth tones, plush carpeting and muted artwork were meant to soothe employees and make for a more productive environment. She didn't care what they chose for the decor but it was better than the last round, which had consisted of whites and blacks with minimal furniture. At least this didn't hurt her eyes.

She waited as several people filed out of his office, all in deep discussion and taking notes on their tablets. None of them noticed her standing there, a skill she had perfected.

Oscar was leaning over his administrative assistant's shoulder as the young man typed. Her boss looked up as she entered and gave her a brief smile as she walked over to stand next to him. He preferred to be involved in the details, 'down in the trenches' as he liked to say. Sometimes it was annoying but you never had to slow down for your boss to catch up that way.

Oscar stood and stretched as they concluded their edits, clapping his assistant on the shoulder as he saved the file. "Good job, Eric. Pass that around to the team and then take off for the day. And now for you, Cass. You're back and just in time. How was your trip?"

She followed him as he led her into his personal office. Waiting until he had closed the door, she let her disappointment show. "We didn't find him, Oscar. I definitely think Everett's gone into the DMZ."

He shook his head. "I'm sorry, Cass. What happened to him during the war was a travesty. I had hoped you would find where your brother disappeared to."

She crossed her arms over her chest. "Well, I did what I thought I should. If he was a competitor or new market, I'd have a lot more resources at my disposal. But I won't cross those lines for my own personal business."

Oscar sat in his chair, a small smile on his face. "What if we could blur those lines?"

Cassandra looked sharply at him, her normally soft brown eyes sharp. "What do you mean?"

Waving his hand at the outer office, he said, "We're looking at the DMZ markets. The TU pull out means it's a free-for-all on the economic side. Every single major interstellar corporation and a few of the smaller ones are putting together a market analysis on those systems closest to the TU. That's Denovo, Clements and Tien sectors, by the way. Over forty settled systems and whoever can get there first and lock in exclusive contracts stands to make a lot of money."

She smiled now. "And you'll let me be in on it?"

He rubbed his hands together. "Well, as part of StellarMart's Public Relations team, isn't that part of your job? Establishing corporate trust, promoting brand loyalty, developing consumer and purchaser relationships?"

"Yes but I have a feeling you want me there for my other specialty. Things like finding corrupt bureaucrats, digging up blackmail material, hacking computers for inside information and applying leverage to the terminally recalcitrant."

"Well, yes, that's a given. But Cass, this is a major opportunity. It's going to get crowded, what with everyone poking around the same markets, talking to the same government bureaucrats, lining up the same buyers. I'm sure the pressure will be on and that may lead to some… funny business."

She leaned against the door, arms still crossed but eyes alight. "Funny business. I like that. Better than corporate espionage."

"Well, let's try to keep it at that level. The StellarMart Board is not ready and it seems none of the rest of our competitors are ready to take it further right now. But without any TU oversight in the region, some enterprising souls may decide on their own to ramp things up. I'd like you there primarily to protect our people against such adventurous souls while doing your own surveillance on their activities."

"And perhaps, in the course of my surveillance, I might find something about my brother?"

He spread his hands. "Personal stakes make for powerful motivations, don't you think? I think you'll be very inspired to closely watch everything developing in the DMZ. So keep your bags handy, Cass. You'll be headed out to the Denovo region in a few months, once the market analysis teams gather and sort their data. Pick your team, although I'm pretty sure I know who you'll take. The Board has authorized a Jump Ship solely for this purpose and you'll have your own dropship besides the one for the main team. Salani Kusari will be leading the main market analysis team.

Cass nodded. "She's the best outmaneuvering people and getting what's she's going after."

"I'll have a quiet talk with her about your team's abilities. I think you'll get along well with her and she's not the type to micromanage. Just keep feeding her information so she can make the kill and you'll get along just fine."

Smiling, she turned and opened the door. "Thanks, Oscar. This means a lot."

"Well, you just happened to be in the right place at the right time. Besides, you are the right person for the job. I trained you myself. I pity anyone who gets in your way."

Chapter 3

Pavo Real System, two months later

Fremont and Ezekiel sat in the outer office of the Minister of Trade and waited for their appointment time. They wore TUMC undress uniforms without insignia, except for a 76th patch on the sleeve and rank on Free's collar. Aileen's uniform design was still months away, so this would have to do for now.

"You'd think he would see us right away when the three largest freight lines in this region have filed complaints about stolen ships and cargo." Free got up to go look out the window, unable to sit any longer.

Ezekiel continued to sit, legs crossed. He didn't look up from his tablet. "He's letting us know he's in control of this situation, Free."

"But he's not in control."

"Which is why he wants to show he's in control." The older man closed the cover on the tablet and smiled up at him. "The more people lose control, the more they want to show they haven't."

Free shook his head. "Mind games. I'll never get my head around this stuff."

"You will. Just takes some practice."

The assistant at the desk looked up from her screen. "The minister will see you now, gentlebeings." A buzzer sounded and the double doors to his right opened.

They walked to the door, Ezekiel a step behind and to the left of his boss. The minister's office was neither as large nor as sumptuous as Free was expecting. The red-skinned Illryian behind the desk was not much of a surprise. The race as a whole took to trade matters like a duck to water. It made sense to have one managing your commerce. Most governments in the DMZ were composed of a multitude of species. Free didn't have a lot of experience with this particular race, but the minister seemed to be young for his position. *Probably why he's trying to show he's in control; he has very little experience with not being in control.*

The alien came around his desk with a broad smile, his six-fingered hand wrapping around theirs in a human-style handshake. "So nice of you to come by and present yourselves, gentlebeings. I do hope we can do business with each other. Pavo Real has a lot to offer."

They sat at his invitation on a small sofa while he pulled an armchair over to sit across from them. He watched expectantly as Ezekiel opened his tablet and projected his screen on the tabletop in front of them.

"Here are the costs for hiring the 76th, by month. You'll be getting two platoons and associated support personnel for this price to provide security against the insurgents on your stations. Also included are the costs expected for combat action, to resupply after said action and a requirement to treat injured troops at the government's expense."

"Yes, yes. My deputy minister reported back to me on what she believed were successful negotiations. Are you gentlemen here to change the terms?"

"No. The terms are satisfactory. We just want to hear from you about what was expected. Your deputy left some areas a bit vague."

"I see. And what areas would that be?"

Free leaned in. "The Terran Union Navy patrols required by treaty, for one. Why haven't they done anything? Secondly, what are we to do with any insurgents we catch, sir? Your legal system covers crimes like this but this contract doesn't give us law enforcement powers."

The minister looked uncomfortable. "Well, those are both difficult situations. The Terran patrols haven't started yet and we've been told that our internal politics aren't their concern anyway. As for the other, the government has de facto jurisdiction over the entire system but in practice any place beyond our low orbitals often has their own system of rules. Lack of resources to station personnel out there in numbers to enforce our laws is the primary reason. The insurgents have taken advantage of that situation."

"That's not my question, sir. I can't legally arrest those who we catch or surrender to us. Just what are we to do with them?"

"Well… I thought… that is to say… I mean, they're the enemy. Certainly you wouldn't want them taking up arms against you again?"

"Minister, my people are combat troops, not executioners. We will not kill prisoners for you. Either you send law enforcement personnel with us under my command, to arrest any prisoners we take, or your government grants the 76th authority to legally detain our prisoners. With associated bounties to be paid on their safe return."

"Bounties! That's absurd. We don't want them here!"

Ezekiel cleared his throat. "I think you're missing an important aspect of this, sir. By allowing us to detain prisoners for prosecution by your legal system, it shows them that fighting against us is not a lost cause. Jail is certainly a better option than death. It also tells them that they're going to get prison time, not death. That's a reason to surrender rather than fight to the death, which would be hard on us and politically costly for you. Finally, your government will appear as the legal authority in this system, with the power to punish criminal acts. We all win in this case."

The bureaucrat at back, eyes distant as he considered the implications. "You make some very good arguments. Yes, I do appreciate how you can spin this situation. Very well. Let me discuss with the Minister of Justice and see if he can spare personnel to send with you, or issue a legal ruling that you can lawfully detain your prisoners. Was there anything else?"

When they walked out of the ministry building an hour later, Free sighed heavily. "That was one of the weirdest negotiations I've ever been in. I knew being a mercenary was going to be different but this is a whole new level."

Ezekiel shook head. "Contractor, Free. We're contractors specializing in armed combat or security services for financial gain. That sounds better than 'mercenary'."

"It means the same thing!"

"Yes but mine sounds better in polite conversation. Which you will be doing more of in future contract negotiations. You have a lot to learn, grasshopper, before I'm ready to let you negotiate without me."

"Grasshopper?"

"Old Earth term. Never mind." His commpad chimed and he glanced at it. "Ah, Alanna's reporting from our new digs at their main station. Apparently, they need some work. Something about not letting a dog sleep there."

Free sighed again. "Let's go see. We just got here and already the government is screwing us over. At least that's a situation I'm familiar with."

Chapter 4

Plancius Station, Pavo Real System, One Week Later

McMannus, Gunny Mulongo, and Harry Webb were going over the equipment reports when the door to their ad-hoc command section opened to admit a very haggard-looking pair. Ezekiel had been working long hours to analyze all the data both the Justice Ministry and their Customs Administration had provided on the insurgent activity. There were only so many hours in the day and he was the only trained intelligence analyst. McMannus intended to fix that at some point in the future and all he could do right now was assign Ishido to help him out. His platoon sergeant could handle things without him for now.

The younger man hooked a chair out and offered it to Ezekiel, who sat in it heavily. The younger man sat with a bit more grace but not much. Both men had bloodshot eyes and the older man's hair was mussed but they were both smiling.

"I take it from those shit-eating grins that you've found something." McMannus leaned back in his chair, starting to smile himself.

"That we have, sir. That we have. These so-called insurgents are children compared to a Naval Academy-trained mind."

Harry looked up at that. "I thought a Naval Academy graduate had to take off his clothes to count to twenty-one."

"Listen here, you young pup… Never mind. Wasted effort. You can't learn a Marine nothing unless you bury his face in the mud first."

They all laughed. "Okay, Ezekiel. What have you got?"

Ishido moved to the room's computer and activated the briefing screen at the far end. Manipulating the controls, he brought up a map of the system while the intelligence officer picked up a laser pointer. "So far, our enemy has made pretty good use of the high orbitals and asteroid belt bases.

Everyone out there is pretty separated from anything that happens planetside, as they only get one month of leave out of twelve. Most of those roughnecks spend it drinking and whoring anyway."

Mulongo tapped the table. "Pretty good recruiting out there too. Some of those rockhoppers get to thinking it's easier to hit a freighter than mine ore. And mining lasers make pretty good anti-ship weapons, up close."

Ezekiel nodded and pointed to several locations in the belt. "These are what the government thought might be the key focus areas. Lots of traffic in and out of these stations, more than is necessary to deliver ore for processing and to pick up air, water and supplies. Lots of political unrest there, too. There's not really room to stage a protest or riot on these stations, not like before. Graffiti and work slowdowns become the medium of protest. The problem is the government police sweeps didn't find anything. The leading theory was a mole in their department somewhere that was warning the insurgency leaders to go to ground on the stations. They stopped doing them a few months ago. Too costly for too little return."

"But you thought differently?"

"Exactly. The government analysts were so focused on the activity on the stations they didn't follow up on the trajectories of the ships that were excess to the traffic profile. That's what we've been doing mostly, following these ships as they were tracked on and off through the system. Want to know what we found?"

"We're dying to hear it."

The viewpoint on the screen zoomed out of the belt and scrolled outsystem, tracking towards the nearer gas giant. Before it got there, the view zoomed back in on a ghostly image of a large station. The laser pointed danced across the image. "This is, or would have been Fleet Base AP-01. The Navy was going to install a non-nominal Jump gate here to supplement the zenith jump point. This was early in the Succession Wars, when we were on the defensive and needed to open another front. Construction started but was never finished because the strategic situation changed, making it unnecessary. It was abandoned and left unfinished."

His fingers steepled, McMannus sighed. "I assume this build up is for some reason."

"Gentlemen, I give you the enemy base. All those trajectories end up here."

He stood and walked over to the screen. "How sure are you of this?"

"I rate this as high confidence." He frowned. "What I don't know is when to find them there. The data we have is fairly limited on a time plot. Our data set only covers the last few months. I'd need more data to establish patterns of movement beyond this."

"So, we need them to run to their base." Turning, McMannus pointed to Harry. "Mr. Webb, when you need your enemy to move in a particular direction, what do you do?"

Harry shot to his feet and braced to attention. "Sir! A commander has two options, sir! He can mount an overwhelming attack to force the enemy from his present position, sir! Or he can maneuver in a way to make the enemy's present position untenable, forcing the opposing force to leave their current position. Sir!"

Laughing, he motioned Harry to sit. "Thank you for that energetic display of military discipline, Mr. Webb. It will be duly noted in your performance report that you are a kiss-ass of the highest degree. And Harry is correct, gentlemen. We need the insurgency leadership to leave their positions of their own volition and congregate at that station so we can sweep in and grab them all in one fell swoop."

Mulongo leaned back in his chair. "Stampede."

"What?"

"Stampede. Cause a ruckus in one location that gets them all panicked and moving in the direction we want."

McMannus took his chair again. "What do you suggest we do to cause this stampede?" He looked around the table. "The floor is open, gentlemen."

Ishido, quiet up to this point, cleared his throat. "Sir, they usually bug out when the cops come calling. Maybe another sweep? A very loud and obvious one, focused on the insurgency leadership that involves a detailed inspection of those stations."

Ezekiel slapped the table. "I like it! They've shown in the past they can get prior warning of these sweeps. And something like this fits the previous operational patterns the government has established. They wouldn't suspect an ulterior motive to this. It's just another opportunity for them to show that the government forces are incompetent and have no way to enforce their authority."

Their commander looked around the table at his de facto staff. They nodded in agreement. "Very well, people. We have the beginnings of a plan. Ezekiel and Ishido, get some rest. We'll need fresh minds when we start pulling together all the elements, to include bringing in the locals. Harry, let's you and me start working up a maneuver scheme to get us to this old Fleet base as unnoticed as we can. Gunny, get with the NCOs and prep our people for action, quietly. This will be our first action since striking out on our own. We will have no Fleet support and no one else to call on for reinforcements beyond some questionable local forces. We have to be locked tight on this. No mistakes."

Chapter 5

The next day was a quiet buzz of activity within the 76th spaces. Security was tighter than usual, although the locals were still unused to their presence and didn't comment on it. Gunny Mulongo had the whole unit on workup, from checking MACE suits, to cleaning weapons, to preparing ammunition loadouts.

Newly pinned Corporal Jordan DeMarco checked the hold of the shuttle one last time and gave a thumbs up to his squad leader. "All clear, Sarge. That's the last of it."

"Right. Okay people, take a breather until the next shuttle docks. Get some water or a piss. No fucking off, though. That means you, Santis."

Lance Corporal Brian Santis gave him a pained look. "Aw Sarge, why you gotta pick on me like that?"

Sergeant Baines jabbed a thumb at the stripes on his sleeve. "Cause I've been in long enough to see skaters with more style than you. I don't know what you got away with at your previous unit, Santis but I own your ass now."

Jordan chugged down some water as Santis continued to bitch under his breath. Capping the bottle, he passed it over to the lance. "Brian, drink. We've been working our asses off and don't need you down as a heat casualty."

Private Avery Bennings laughed from where she sat against the wall, water bottle in hand. "How could you tell? Fucker's half out of his mind half the time anyway."

Santis threw her the middle finger and grinned maniacally. "Wrong. I'm out of my mind all the time. The Green Weenie wiped it all away and replaced it with moto bullshit! You'll never be the Marine I am!"

She made a face. "Eww. Why would I want to be you?"

Jordan ignored their banter as he took a look around the dock. At least half the company was here, working to unload their gear and ammunition from the ships that brought them here. They'd been on station just a few days but the Captain had them working overtime to unload. Like he needed them soon.

Baines leaned on the wall next to DeMarco. "You got that look, Jordan. You're thinking too hard."

"It's just… this is too fast. No 'hurry up and wait' bullshit here. The Old Man's got a bug up his ass about something."

His sergeant snorted. "DeMarco, it's either 'hurry up and wait' or 'get this shit done now'. Always been that way in the Corps."

"No. There's something different about this. You remember the guys taking away the ammo? They were starting to divide it into basic loads as they went."

"So? Maybe Gunny wants to be efficient when it comes to issuing it."

Jordan stared at him until he looked away. "Right. Gunny never does anything without a reason. So you think we're going into action soon?"

"I don't know. But I wouldn't plan on libo anytime soon. Something's up."

*****

In the command section, Harry and Ishido were working at terminals on their tasks. Harry was drawing up assault plans and checking available imagery for pictures of the Fleet base to get an idea of what kind of position the insurgents held. Ishido was reviewing the previous police sweeps of the asteroid stations and cross-referencing that against ship movement patterns. And Ezekiel and McMannus were in his office hashing out what and how much to tell the Pavo Real government.

"You have to feed them something that gets them motivated, sir. Otherwise word will get to the insurgents that this isn't a determined sweep. Tell our employers we identified movement patterns that suggest the insurgents are preparing to launch a counteroffensive. They're stockpiling weapons and ammunition at these stations. That ought to get them fired up to do a very serious search."

"That could work. I'd have to bring in a few of their key people on the actual operation, though. Since we demanded their guys deploy with us or give actual authority to detain, we need their cooperation."

"The chance of a secret getting blown is equal to the square of the number of people who know about it. Keep it to just a few and preferably no one involved in actual operations."

McMannus rubbed his eyes and leaned back in his chair, staring at the terminal. It displayed a zoomed-out system view, with their target at the center. "We have to tell someone in a position of command what we're planning. We're going to need their help to get to the target."

Ezekiel reached over and opened up a datafile, importing the contents into the display. Multiple lines began appearing on the screen, tracing lines to and from the asteroid belt. "I thought about a way. These are all the ship trajectories I was working with before. Now watch when I remove the regular haulers."

Most of the tracks disappeared, all of them from the belt to the main planet. Only about a dozen remained, most of them heading into the outer system. Tapping the screen, the older man said, "There's our opportunity. Ships still fly outsystem, mostly government survey ships but some mining vessels headed for the gas giants. There's a market for rare volatiles that can only be found in quantities in a gas giant's atmosphere. These ships make runs every so often when the prices are high enough to justify the fuel cost."

His boss stared at the screen. "So we charter… shit, that's a strange concept. We charter one of these mining ships to get us close to the target and then crash their party."

Vestry traced the route on the screen. "We have to get to the target and back as well. Someone has to pay for the roundtrip fuel costs."

"I bet you're going to tell me that's a lot of money. Of course, if we bag the insurgent HVTs, then it's money well spent. If not us, then who's going to pay for it?"

Ezekiel leaned back in his chair, smiling. "My vote is our employers. Plus, that's in the contract. They have to provide transport to any station in the Pavo Real system. This just happens to be a non-standard station."

"I knew there was a reason I kept you around. All right, so can we sell this plan to them?"

"Boss, I just know that's their hidey hole. Know it in my gut. We just need to encourage them to use it when we want them to. After that, it's time to clean house and wrap up the problem. Or at least, wrap up the problem we were hired to solve."

McMannus swung out of his chair. "Okay. Let's grab a shuttle to the surface and tell our employers how to spend their money and move their people."

*****

They hadn't made it to the docking ports for the station-to-surface transports when Free's commpad pinged with a message from Sparks. "Sir, just got a message that some VIP from the Ministry of Justice is on his way to see you. ETA twenty minutes. What should I tell them?"

His boss sighed. "Tell him I'll be there. Show us on our way back."

"Roger that, sir."

As they headed back to the 76th area, Ezekiel grinned. "Well, it saved us a trip."

"Assuming this guy can make the right arrangements. And is willing to listen. And agrees with our plan."

"You know what your problem is? You're far too optimistic."

Their VIP was Chief Marshal Thisk, the chief law enforcement officer of their Pavo Real Policia Nacional. He had the bearing of someone who'd worked his way from the ranks. He was also a Clu'Lachan, the six-limbed snakelike aliens who had fought both for the Grausians and then against them when they realized the other subject races actually had a chance of winning.

Thisk was accompanied by two others of his kind, although neither spoke nor offered their names. Instead, they took up positions near the door, sidearms and other police accouterments on their belts and harness. The males tended to operate in fraternal groups of threes, unless death or injury prevented that. The females did whatever they wanted.

The Chief Marshal gave the two of them the salute of equals in his culture, two fists clenched on his chest. "Captain McMannus of the 76th Microgravity Strike Team, I greet you in the name of the Ministry of Justice. May your hunt be fruitful. My thanks for taking time to meet with me."

McMannus and Vestry returned the salute, and motioned the other to a chair as they sat. "Chief Marshal. The sun shines bright upon you and your clan. I assume you're here to learn how we can put an end to your insurgent problem?"

Thisk narrowed his eyes. "You have been here, what, ten days total? Most of that spent unloading and settling in. Yet you have found the answer we have struggled with for months?"

"Chief Marshal, you're a lawman. You hunt criminals. I assume that they have certain patterns, certain methods which you recognize. We hunt soldiers, which is what these people consider themselves. They act like soldiers, not criminals. So we know what to look for, to find them."

"I see. So what do you propose? How do you find them and stop them?"

Motioning to Ezekiel with one hand, Free turned his terminal around so the Marshal could see the screen. "Over to you. Run him through your analysis and our plan."

Fifteen minutes later, the Marshal was grinning. "Oh, this I like! Very much so. We make a great show of cleaning house and send those scum scurrying for their holes. I only wish I could be there to see their faces when you kick in their door!"

"Then we have a plan, Marshal? And the government can get us a mining ship for transport?"

The Marshal's face closed down and he spread his hands. "Alas, I am here at the orders of the Justice Minister, who gets his orders from the Prime Minister. These orders send your people to the belt stations for security and garrisoning. He wants to put the fear of your weapons in these people. This is included in your contract."

McMannus sat back, stunned. "All of my Marines?"

"Well, maybe not so much. The Ministers, they are not warriors. They do not know how these things are done. If we have just a few of your people at each station, with your weapons and your armor, it shows the rabble we mean business. This is what the Prime Minister wants and now so does my boss. They have to show the public that they are making progress on this issue." It was hard to tell, but the Marshal looked a bit embarrassed as he said this.

His fury mounting, Free leaned forward, eyes intent on his visitor. "Let me understand here. He wants me to distribute my Marines piecemeal among, what, four or five stations? They'll be sitting ducks by themselves! I can't even reinforce them quickly if things go south. What about your officers? Will they be there to back them up?"

Thisk spread his hands. "Regrettably, no. I am even more constrained than you are. But I can put together these sweeps your plans call for."

Ezekiel leaned forward, cutting his boss off. "Hold on, sir. This can work to our advantage?"

McMannus turned to him, eyes blazing. "Really, Mr. Vestry? How can putting a squad at each station, eight Marines, work to our advantage?"

"We time their deployment to start just before the sweeps. Then we make them part of the sweep with the police. If the insurgent leaders know we're also looking for them, they'll definitely bug out."

"Not if they ambush us first."

"That's not their operational pattern. They're using classic Maoist tactics, which makes them predictable. You know, 'The enemy advances, we retreat.'"

He stared at his intelligence officer levelly. "How sure are you of that? We're taking a big risk with this. And if I deploy a platoon for this operation that only leaves us one for the assault."

"High confidence, sir. And it adds to the impetus for the enemy to bug out for home. We need them to run if we have any chance of ending this in one strike."

Free turned to Thisk. "And you can get us a ship to take us to the target? What about some of your officers to come with, to take them into custody?"

"Hah! I would pilot it myself if I could, if only to see those cabróns' faces when you take them down! Yes, you will have your ship if I have to stand on the Minister's desk to get the money. And I have just the agent to send with you, one who knows their way around vacc suits. Been in and out of one since they were walking."

"They'd better, Marshal. Cause that station isn't likely to have much air when we're done with it."

Chapter 6

McMannus stood next to the loading dock as 2nd Platoon boarded the system shuttles. Harry Webb stood with his platoon sergeant, going over last-minute details. They were all in their MACE suits, with a full combat load. Not knowing what kind of reception that was waiting for them, he intended to give his people every advantage he could.

Gunny Mulongo stood next to him, dark eyes watching the scene with that quiet patience he was known for. Only the lines around the corners betrayed his feelings.

"I don't like this, Gunny. I really don't fucking like this one bit."

The senior NCO chuckled. "Don't have to like any of it, sir. Just gotta do it. Since when has liking it been part of our job in the Corps?"

"You know, technically, we're not part of the Corps anymore."

Eyes wide, Mulongo looked over at his officer in shock. "Not part of the Corps? That's a fucked-up way of thinking, sir."

His boss smiled back at him. "Well, they say no matter where you deploy, you carry the Corps with you. I guess we're just stretching the definition of a deployment."

"Better, sir. Don't scare me like that. My heart can't take it."

Harry walked over them, tucking away his tablet. "Lads and lasses all tucked away in their beds, sir. Right sorry they're going to miss the action and all at the end, too." His own expression was hopeful.

"Sorry, Harry. I flipped a coin and you lost out on this one." He stepped in close. "Remember what I told you, son. We convinced the police to let you use this shuttle to check on the stations, so use it! Keep moving so you aren't a sitting duck. Make sure everyone is on their toes for an odd reaction. We think they're going to bug out, so let them.

Don't corner them and don't let the cops put you in a situation that you can't shoot your way out of. Remember to use the screen door if you need to."

In MIST parlance, leaving via the 'screen door' was exiting a ship or station via the nearest air lock, or making one yourself. If an enemy wanted to follow a MISTer outside the hull that was just fine.

"Roger that, sir. Don't worry about us. Just don't let Ish get lost in that mess of a construction site. Lad can't navigate worth a damn. Got us lost right and proper at TBS."

Clapping him on the shoulder, McMannus laughed. "I'll watch out for him. Now, off with you. VIS, Harry."

"VIS, sir. Gunny." Harry saluted and headed off to his ship.

"Fuck me, Gunny," McMannus whispered. "This is worse than my first time as a butterbar. I sure hope we got this nailed down."

"Mr. Vestry seems like a pretty smart guy, sir. We'll get these fuckers."

*****

The rest of the day and most of the next was taken up by training and assault rehearsals on the station exterior. While most of the 1st Platoon had come over together, there were enough new faces to warrant some extra training. Free and the Gunny took turns overseeing the exercises and Free once again vowed to find himself a new executive officer.

Harry reported a successful deployment of 2nd Platoon, with nothing more than dirty looks so far. The cops had yet to arrive, so for now Harry had them doing simple sweeps in open areas, so they wouldn't get caught somewhere isolated.

Good as his word, the Chief Marshal sent over one of his officers. Curious, Free met her himself at the front gate to their area. It was another Clu'Lachan, but female. Shorter and stockier than the males, Agent Drusk looked like she would fit right in the Marines of the 76th. She had also brought her own vacc suit with her and he walked her back to the suit room, called the 'Morgue', so she could stow it away with their MACEs.

"The government ones are shit. Plus, I have my own special modifications."

Free looked up from the suit she was laying out. "Really? You're rated in suit tech and repair?"

"No. Not officially. But you learn enough if you survive long enough. And I do know electronics. If you give me your freqs I can patch in easy enough."

"It'll take more than that." He tapped his commpad. "Sparks, meet me down in the morgue. Bring whatever you need to add a civilian comm unit to our network."

"Aye aye, sir. On the way."

"Morgue?"

"Marine thing. You'll get used to it. You work with Sparks and he'll get you set up. Your boss tell you what's up?"

Her tongue flickered in and out rapidly, the Lachan equivalent of laughter. "You're going to kick in the door and I get to stuff the survivors in a cell. What could be better than that?"

"Apt enough. Ever been in a firefight in micro? Or in vacc?"

"Not a firefight, no. Had a crazy Grausian put a hole in my suit when I found her stash on the hull of her ship. Let me tell you, that O2 alarm is scary enough when it's low. It's really terrifying when there's a breach alarm with it."

"You've seen that part of the elephant, then. Good. Not that I expect you to be in the front of the fight. But there's no telling what'll happen after we take the station. I'm going to offer them a chance to surrender once we have control but if one of them has a blade stashed…"

"Oh sure. I'm there to show them an easier way out. A prison cell is a lot more comfortable than being spaced."

"Good enough." Sparks came into the room with his comm gear. "Sparks, hook Agent Drusk into our network. Command and general channels, with a private one to me."

As Free walked back into the command section, both Gunny and Alanna Vestry met him. There was a bit of confusion as Alanna attempted to defer to the NCO but Mulongo simply stepped back. "After you, Lieutenant."

She shook her head. "I was taught not to get between a Gunny and his objective."

"That's only on the battlefield or in the bar. Please, ma'am."

She nodded and presented her tablet to Free. "Sir, I finished the loading sequence for a standard mining ship. You said you wanted to see that."

He stared at her, eyebrows raised. "Did you crosscheck with Lieutenant Kan or Gunny Mulongo?"

Her face fell. "Um, no sir."

He stepped past her towards his office, motioning to his senior NCO to follow. "Do that first, Ms. Vestry."

Once inside the office, he sat heavily in his chair and rubbed his face with his hands. "God save me from overeager butterbars, Gunny."

"Oh, they gotta learn sometime, sir. As things go, this wasn't too bad. Remember the newbie that loaded without even checking with his CO?"

"Hey, I at least knew something. I was enlisted and had done that shit before."

"The command section staff heard that chewing out through two closed doors."

"He was only pissed because I did it right. Okay, what's up?"

"Report from the last exercise. I think we're there. New guys are fitting in like they've been there all along and they cut seven seconds from the breaching standard time."

"Good. All right, give 'em some downtime but no liberty. I need us ready to deploy on a few hours notice and we don't need any leaks on what we're planning."

"Aye aye, sir. Any news about a ship?"

McMannus checked his computer. "Nothing in the last few hours. While I believe the Chief Marshal can make miracles happen in his own organization, I'm skeptical about this."

"And we can't do our own checking without giving away some of our intentions. This mercenary stuff is harder than it seems."

"Private military contractor, Gunny. We're contractors, not mercenaries. Sounds better, I'm told."

Mulongo snorted. "Can't pretty up what we do, sir."

Chapter 7

First thing the next morning, Agent Drusk was at Free's door. "I have something for you. The Ministry finally got a ship for you to use. Want to see it?"

"Hell yes." He pinged Gunny, Ezekiel, and his lieutenants to meet him at the dock slip Drusk provided. "What about the sweeps?"

"Eh, that's not so good. The paperwork alone takes days just to get everything moving. Must be nice to move with so little."

They headed out towards the docks. "I can move faster but I don't have the resources you guys have. It's a trade-off."

The ship at the listed slip was a standard gas mining ship. The hull was a simple framework with three pods, for controls, crew and engineering. Stacked on top were several massive cylinders to transport the volatiles. It looked sturdy and well-kept and the name *Sirena* was painted in yellow on the control pod, along with the image of mermaids frolicking.

The ship's master was a different matter, however. A Charee, he stared up at them sullenly and only grunted when Drusk greeted him.

She turned to Free. "Don't mind his attitude. Salva Anagrii knows how to fly a ship, don't you, Sal?"

"Whatever you say." He mumbled something else under his breath, shifting his four-foot frame back and forth.

She flicked her tongue in and out. "Sal, like many in this system, hauls regular cargo when he's not making the volatiles run. Seems that while he's a good ship captain, he's not so good at smuggling. We caught him many months back with some items that weren't on his manifest. Nothing dangerous, so we've been holding back on the paperwork in case we needed something. And now we do."

"Bastards. Just let me pay your fine and we'll be done."

"Oh no, Sal. We need you and most especially, your ship."

Free examined the ship's master as the rest of his people arrived. The alien was unhappy and nervous. Exactly what a Marine didn't need for the master of his delivery vessel. He tried to calm the waters. "Captain Anagrii, this isn't likely to be dangerous for you. Just get us to where we need to go and then back again. You probably face more danger when you skim those gas giants."

"So you say. What do you know about taking care of a ship?" The fur around his face fluffed up and his eyes blazed. "This is my family ship, five generations back!"

Free stepped forward and looked him in the eye. "Trust me, Captain. We know very well how important it is to keep our ride home safe. None of us have any desire to go dutchman out there in the black."

The ship's master licked his lips nervously, eyes sliding from Free to Drusk and back. "*Daskha*! What choice do I have?"

As Alanna and Ish talked about loading with the captain, Drusk pulled Free and Mulongo aside. "Sal isn't violent. But I wouldn't put all my trust in him. Like a child sometimes. He needs a minder, you know, to watch him when we leave the ship."

Gunny looked over at the man in question and then back at Free. "One fire team ought to do it, sir. Just enough to watch over the control spaces."

"One less fire team on the assault."

"Well, since you're taking your command squad in, they're actually up one team."

Free cocked his head and looked at his senior NCO. "You know, it's very aggravating when you read my mind and tell everyone my plans."

"It's in the job description, sir."

He turned back to Drusk. "Okay, we have a ship. We have Marines who want to kick in doors. We have a police officer. Now all we need are some rabbits."

Gunny smiled. "Steers, sir. Steers stampede, not rabbits."

Chapter 8

A few days later, McMannus and Alanna were going over the supply report when Ezekiel poked his head. "It's going down. They're bolting for their hole."

Alanna immediately activated the room's screen and loaded up their feed from the government sensor while her commander called Gunny, Ishido and his platoon sergeant to the room.

They all watched the screen expectantly as one by one, ships left the belt stations. As their courses were computed, several highlighted in red and a projection popped up on the screen, showing them heading for the abandoned fleet base.

"And there we go, sir. The word is out and the rush is on to get out. Hell, the cops haven't even made it halfway there." Vestry was grinning and tapping his fingers on the table.

McMannus moved to stand next to the screen, grinning. "They're nervous. I like it. It'll make them sloppy. They've done this drill enough they know how it goes. Time for us to flip things around them. Alanna, what's the arrival projection for the last ship?"

She tapped a few keys and the projections changed shape. Most were narrow lines but one was thicker. "This one will arrive last, assuming no one changes their burn rate. Estimated arrival in fifty-four hours."

"Okay. We want them settled in and playing the waiting game for the cops to leave. Make them think they've outsmarted their enemies once again and they'll be fat, dumb and happy. Let's give them say, twenty-four hours on site before we hit it. What's our departure time on that assumption?"

"With a thirty hour trip for us, that means leaving in forty-eight hours."

He stood. "Alright, people. That's it then. Ish, get your looking over the station plans we have. Start drawing up your assault plan and bring me something in the next few hours. Alanna, sit in with Ish and his NCOs so you can do some on the job training. Ammo issue will be six hours prior to launch. Gunny, get a fire team and go with Agent Drusk to Captain Sal's slip and lock him down, quiet like. All crew to be recalled from shore leave within twenty-four hours. Mr. Vestry, keep monitoring the situation and let us know what changes."

Chapter 9

Beyond the Pavo Real asteroid belt, Pavo Real System

Jordan and the rest of his squad stepped out into the dark, leaving the safety of the freighter behind. In the distance, visible only as a highlighted square on the HUD was their objective. The Marines of 1st Platoon, now calling themselves Kan's Killer Klowns, activated their suit jets for the specified duration, giving them a vector towards the station.

The platoon was spread out in an arrowhead formation, two squads to either side of the command team. Even with his suit's magnification, he could barely make out his mates. There was no way the people on the station could see them.

It was going to be over an hour's journey to the target. Jordan called up some music on his player and settled into the slow drift towards their target.

*****

The white knuckles on the four prehensile 'hands' of the *Sirena's* Master stood out against the black plastic of the armrests. He licked his lips nervously as they watched the display showing the supposedly abandoned mining station together. "Your men, they do not show on the display. How do you know they are where they are supposed to be?"

Free answered absently, eyes on the countdown timer on the screen. "Training, Mr. Anagrii. Training and rehearsal." A single blip appeared briefly on the screen and flashed three times before disappearing. Smiling, he clapped him on the shoulder. "Relax, Captain. We've done this kind of thing before against much tougher targets. Now, I'm headed out to join my people. Corporal Deboeck and his team are staying here to guard you. Just keep on course and be on the lookout for our signal for pickup."

He sealed his helmet as he left the bridge and checked his weapon. Despite Dunbar's best efforts, they hadn't been able to get PW-93Vs for everyone yet. Still, they weren't expecting fully armored Grausian Marines anymore. Just regular people armed with whatever they could steal or buy on the black market. For the Marines who didn't have a PW-93V, the Remberg 765 shotgun should be enough for this collection of targets.

And there was also the matter of limiting collateral damage on the stolen goods. His employer (and damn, wasn't that a strange word) was emphatic about recovering the material the insurgents were holding. That word had come a mere twelve hours before they launched. Ezekiel had immediately argued that it wasn't part of the contract, which had resulted in a contract modification. Now that they got five percent of the recovered value of the goods, it was in their interest to limit damage as well. Only the best shots in each squad had PW-93Vs; everyone else (including himself) had Rembergs with both buckshot and non-lethal rounds.

Corporal Deboeck nodded at him on the way out, his pose casual as he leaned against the bulkhead near the ship's bridge, with Agent Drusk next to him. Captain Anagrii was in debt to the Pavo Real government to transport the 76th to the pirate base but he was also the only guaranteed ride home. The fire team on the bridge would ensure the *Sirena* was still there when the action was completed.

It was unlikely this rundown station had sensors able to detect a man-sized object in a MACE, with its external camouflage array. The three-flash signal told McMannus that Kan was in position on the station's hull at the specified breach points. Since they hadn't seen a reaction from the station, 1st Platoon ought to be able to force entry into the station with complete surprise.

Free, his headquarters team, and a security squad were now going to make a very visible exit from the *Sirena*, focusing the insurgent's attention solely on them. This would allow Kan's people to breach and enter the station with surprise. At least that was the plan.

Entering the cargo bay, he saw Sergeant Cantore had everyone suited up and ready to exit the bay. Taking his position in the front of his Marines, McMannus signaled the bridge.

"MIST to bridge. Ready for insertion. Open the cargo bay."

The star field spun in their vision as the *Sirena* skewed sideways to bring the station into view. It was a mass of spars and lattices, looking like a spider's web which had been through a storm. Only one section looked complete, a bulbous structure composed of several habitat units strapped together on the central spine. Five ships were docked at the central tube, a hash of small freighters, shuttles and other unidentifiable hulks. The exterior was unlit and what few portholes showed no interior lights.

They activated their suit jets, HUDs displaying their trajectory as they aimed for the structure. At this distance, McMannus couldn't make out any personnel airlocks, so he centered his reticle on the docking tube. His breathing was regular and even as he watched the rest of his 'assault team' spread out in a mass with him. They were far enough apart that an attacker could only target one of them and they stayed out of each other's own fire arc.

"Uh, Captain, this is Sirena. These bastards are telling me they're going to fire on my ship!"

"Negative, Sirena. We're not tracking any exterior weaponry and their ships are powered down. Just keep calm and maintain your position."

They were still several minutes out. Enough time for the insurgents to deploy some of their own outside, if they were willing. That would tell him where their airlocks were, although Ishido should be covering the obvious ones. But the station remained dark and there was no movement outside.

When they got within one hundred meters they began their braking maneuver. He felt his heart rate quicken. This was the most dangerous point of the approach, as they were easy targets and couldn't maneuver without throwing off their chance to land. Seconds ticked away as the station grew larger and larger. The tube had airlocks for a dozen ships, so he picked the one furthest from the docked ships as his entry point.

They hit the hull around the docking collar, grabbing cover from the protruding hull elements and his radio crackled. Garbled words came with static as Sparks fed him the traffic he was picking up. No one would be able to hear their own conversations due to their encrypted comms but he could hear others. It sounded like they were trying to communicate using low-power sets.

"Sparks, see if you can break through their encryption. Let's find out what they're planning."

"*Aye aye, sir. Shouldn't be too hard. Looks like civilian-grade stuff. Just be a minute.*"

McMannus waited as Gunny arranged the security squad to cover the airlock and stationed a man with the electronic 'can opener' at the hatch controls. True to his word, Sparks had the enemy comms decrypted in short order.

"*I'm fuckin' tellin ya, they's Marines. We practiced that kinda open order suit assault in the war.*"

"*Marines or not, there's only about a dozen. We have three times their number. Shut up and be ready.*"

McMannus clicked over to the general channel. "Whisper Six to all Whispers. At least one Marine in this bunch. Be ready and I would really like it if we could take that one alive. Whisper One, standby to execute."

Three clicks answered him. He switched back to the enemy channel and turned off his encryption. "Enemy commander, this is Captain Fremont McMannus of the 76th MIST. By order of the Pavo Real government and the Ministry of Justice, I order you to surrender."

A laugh was the first thing he heard back. "*Surrender? To those fucks? Hell no! Come and get us, screwhead!*"

"Well, I tried." He clicked back over to the general channel. Whisper Seven, go. Whisper Two, go."

The airlock cycled open, controls overridden. Pieces of small debris streamed out past the Marines of his security squad as they jetted inside. The two lead Marines raised their weapons, flashes silent in the vacuum.

"Clear. Two tangos down."

*****

The telltales on the airlock went green and the hatch cycled open. It was a maintenance hatch, barely big enough for a MACE. Santis took up position at the entrance as Bennings went to work on the inner door. Safety protocols would normally prevent the inner door from opening while the outer door was open but the MIST knew there were ways around that.

The rest of the team stacked up behind Santis. It was only the four of them, given the small size of the entrance. Jordan was number two in, with Sergeant Baines behind him. His breathing sped up as he waited for the door, a slight fog forming around the nose piece in his helmet.

The door cycled and pieces of trash and other unidentifiable debris streamed past them. Santis went in fast, jetting to the nominal ceiling. However much he complained, he knew his micro-g. Jordan was right behind him, taking a low position in the short corridor. An empty suit rack lined the left-hand side of the room and there was a sealed door at the far end. Judging by the way it was bulging, it wasn't airtight.

Baines landed a few steps ahead of Jordan and Bennings came in after him, triggering the lock closing sequence. The inner station door returned to normal as the station's life support struggled to replace the lost air. Red lights were flashing over the inner door.

Baines motioned to the door. "DeMarco, Santis. Breach and clear."

Jordan unmagged from the deck and triggered a burst from his jets. They spun him around until he was feet first at the door. Santis gave him a three count and then opened the door. Jordan was already moving after 'two' and jetted through the door at head height, clearing the top with inches to spare.

He hit the opposite wall with both feet, knees bent to absorb the shock and magged on. The corridor beyond the door curved left and right and he scanned both directions. A figure in a motley vacc suit came around the bend in the slow walk of magnetic boots, weapon in both hands held across the chest. Jordan raised his Remberg and shot him twice, heavy slugs punching through the unarmored suit with ease. The figure stopped in mid-stride, one leg magged to the deck and the other floating free. Blood pulsed from the holes in globules.

"One tango down. Hall is clear."

*****

As his security squad streamed down the docking tube to the airlock at the other end, McMannus took in the reports. Ishido's people had breached the station at six different points and killed seven insurgents. They were now going room to room, clearing the area. In many cases, the insurgents had been caught without their helmets on and in the rapidly decompressing station it was a simple matter to detain them as they gasped for air.

Reaching the airlock at the entrance to the station, Sergeant Cantore took charge once again on entry. He arranged one fire team for entry and motioned to the controls. *"Sernak. Crack the door."*

The three of them stayed out of their way as this hatch yielded as easily as the outer one had. It was a large airlock, able to hold at least a half-dozen bodies. The entry team knew their jobs, arraying themselves at the inner door while Lance Corporal Sernak worked at the controls.

The inner door opened to a long passageway. That was all they had time to notice as bullets began impacting around them. McMannus didn't even need to give orders to scatter. Sergeant Cantore dispersed his squad in four directions, using microgravity to their advantage.

Free and the other two used the doorway as cover, now that there was plenty of room in the lock. "Gunny, Sparks, keep their heads down while I check with Whisper One."

The two began alternating fire down the passage as he ducked back. "Whisper One, Whisper Six. Front door is open. Meeting stiff resistance."

"*Whisper Six, Whisper One. We have eleven tangoes in custody. Seven additional dead. I can send a squad to clear your way.*"

"Copy Whisper One. Coordinate with Cantore on the movement. Make sure you keep those prisoners secure." He clicked over to the enemy channel. "Enemy commander, it's all over. Surrender now and let us take you into custody."

He waited for several seconds but there wasn't any answer. "Last chance, pal. We're in and already rounding your people up. Make it easier on yourselves."

There was a series of clicks on the channel and then the voice he had tagged as a possible veteran came on. *"Fuck it, man. I told them you was trouble. Alright, alright. You win."*

*****

A short time later, the *Sirena* was docking at the station while the prisoners were assembled in the docking tube. There were seventeen total, all with the motley suits of miners. They were back in their own helmets, which were covered with opaque polymer bags. Their hands zip tied in front of them. Behind them, sixteen bodies were laid out.

Ishido clumped over, fingers working on his sleeve tablet. "We've cleared all the rooms on the station and opened up all the docked ships. As far as we can tell, there's no one else here, sir."

Free looked over the ragged collection of prisoners and gave his subordinate a thumbs up, since they were all still suited. "Casualties?"

"Five minor suit breaches, no serious injuries. Suit patches took care of the breaches and Doc checked them out. Boss, these guys weren't carrying any serious firepower. Shotguns, pistols, that sort of thing. No energy weapons or explosives."

"Well, sure. They weren't expecting trouble here. Just brought their personal stuff. Okay, get 'em ready for loading."

Drusk met them at the ship's airlock. "That was amazing, Captain! You got them all?"

Free walked her down the line of prisoners. "All that were here. We've searched every corner of the station and haven't found everyone else. The count matches the capacity of the ships that are docked, too."

Her rapidly-flickering tongue was easily visible through the faceplate. "Justice will send people to recover the ships. Let's get them loaded aboard and back to Pavo Real. And then these egg-suckers get to learn what it's like dirtside, for many years to come."

Chapter 10

Aboard the Sirena, Pavo Real System

McMannus, Ishido and Mulongo were compiling their after-action notes and expenditures for their report in the freighter's dingy crew lounge when Drusk entered. They'd been underway for several hours and she'd spent quite a bit of that time compiling her report and then communicating with Justice. It was hard to tell, but her face seemed grim in contrast to her earlier jubilance. She wore her uniform harness and her badge was prominently displayed.

"What's going on, Drusk?"

She walked over to their table and nodded brusquely. "Captain. I request that you and your men bring the prisoners to the cargo bay. The Justice Minister has a message for all of them and that's the only space large enough. I'm having Captain Sal pressurize it now."

Standing slowly, he nodded at his platoon commander. "Ish, turn out a couple of squads for this. Drusk, we're gonna want to move them in small groups. Less chance of them getting ideas."

"Of course, Captain. I'll be in the bay, setting up the comm equipment." She turned without another word and strode out.

Ishido was already on his commpad to his platoon sergeant. McMannus turned to Mulongo. "I don't like this, Gunny. What can't wait until we're back on Plancius Station?"

His face was grim. "I suspect we're all not going to like this. Feels like the Green Weenie is about to strike again."

*****

Fifteen minutes later, the seventeen prisoners were assembled in the cargo bay. Drusk had set up a projector to display the image against one wall. Currently, it showed the image of the Justice Ministry seal. She stood next to the airlock door and motioned for Free, Ishido and Mulongo to stand with her. A line of Marines in MACE suits, weapons at port arms stood between them and the prisoners.

She leaned over and whispered to Free, "Would you have your people seal their helmets? More intimidating that way. The Minister wants to really hammer home that they're going to get what they deserve."

Free nodded and gave the command himself. Twelve visors slid into place, turning the bulky armored suits into faceless hulks. The prisoners muttered to themselves until the screen came to life, displaying the head and shoulders of the Justice Minister.

"You have been detained by the lawful authority of Pavo Real. Your actions to date warrant serious charges. We will not let you get away with running amok just because you believe you are owed something by this government. To that end, you are charged with assault on officers of the law, resisting arrest, armed robbery, piracy and most importantly, insurrection against the lawful authority of the duly elected government."

His words were interrupted by jeers and catcalls but this was a recording. They were too far out for a live broadcast. They quieted down once they realized he couldn't hear them.

"--my pleasure to announce that, having been tried in absentia for your crimes, you are found guilty on all charges. The court sentences you to death. Agent Drusk, carry out the sentence of the court."

Free turned to look at her as the prisoners began to shout. She was backing through the airlock and motioned for them to follow. He did, intending to get an explanation and his two subordinates came with him. The line of Marines stood firm, magged to the deck. Their weapons were still at port arms. Once the four of them were through the lock, she closed it. They could still see the bay through the plexiglass window next to the hatch and watched the prisoners continue to rant.

"Dammit Drusk, what's going on in there?"

She looked at him, face gray. "I am doing my job, Captain. As ordered by the Minister." Reaching over, she pressed the button to open the cargo bay doors with deliberate intent.

"Shit!" Free turned on his commpad. "All Whispers in the cargo bay. Commence res–"

His voice died as Mulongo slapped his hand over his CO's microphone. "Sir, we can't."

"Gunny, they're murdering those men and women!"

"No sir. The lawful authority of this system is exercising their form of government. We can't interfere without being charged with a crime ourselves."

"But...," Free's voice trailed off as Mulongo raised his own commpad. Through the viewport, he could see the struggles of the prisoners slow down. Mouths gaped open, reaching for the air that wasn't there. Already more than half were motionless and drifting out the open doors.

"This is Whisper Seven. All Whispers, stand down and take no action. I repeat, take no action. The first Marine I see move from their spot will answer to me."

Free looked around. Drusk was standing stiffly, her gaze fixed on the viewport. The muscles of her jaw were taut and her expressionless eyes didn't move from the scene. He looked over at Ishido. The lieutenant wasn't as controlled as the police officer. His face was pale and he swallowed heavily. His eyes were a bit wild as he looked over at his commanding officer.

With an internal sigh, Free raised his commpad. "This is Whisper Six to all Whispers. The representative of the Pavo Real government is carrying out a legal order from their Justice Minister. We did the job we were hired to do, Marines. That is all."

Ishido raised a hand to point at the viewport. "Sir. There are cameras in there too."

Free looked to where he was pointing. Sure enough, there were cameras mounted to the walls. They were positioned to catch the bodies as they drifted out the open bay doors. As the last body left, Drusk closed the doors and began to repressurize the bay. He turned to her.

"What the hell are those cameras for? Some sort of gruesome example?"

She wouldn't face him. "Exactly, Captain. The footage is already being broadcast back to the home planet. Soon, it will be edited and rebroadcast out to the entire planet and system, along with the criminal records of those people. Everyone will know what happens to those who rebel against the government. The people of Pavo Real will feel reassured that the government is in control. Those who are still at large will be afraid."

*****

Jordan numbly walked into their berthing area with the rest of his squad, having stowed his MACE in the rack with the others. The rest of the platoon gathered around as they entered, questions flying fast and furious.

"What the fuck happened? They just spaced those guys without warning!"

"What'd the Old Man do? We heard the general broadcast but what happened in there?"

Baines looked over at another squad leader. "You saw?"

"A couple people were watching a feed from the suit cameras. They told people, those people told people and then everyone was watching. What the hell, man?"

His sergeant shrugged. "Beats me. The Captain says it was all legal. Says they were tried in court and that was it. Game over, adios and suck vacuum."

Jordan sat on the edge of his rack, staring off into space. Jessica paced back and forth for several steps and then dropped to the deck to crank out push-ups. Santis flopped into his rack, put his headphones on and closed his eyes.

Baines walked over. "You got that thinking look again, DeMarco."

"Just wondering if this is what it's going to be like from now on, Sarge. I thought we were headed out here to, I dunno, make things better."

"You popped that guy in the station without a second thought. That was your job and you were doing the mission. If you had known what was going to happen in the bay, would you still have moved those guys in there?"

"Sure but-"

"But nothing. It's still like it was back in the Corps. Officers do the thinking and we execute the mission. Besides, you trust the Captain, right?"

"Well, yeah…"

"And he ain't never steered us wrong, neither. Always tried to look out for us. You know he turned down a promotion and staying in, right? Decided he was coming with us out here."

"Shit. No, I hadn't heard that. But yeah, you're right. He'll look out for us, I know. I just don't like being used like this."

Baines laughed. "How's this different from back in the Corps? They used us all the time, put us in shit situations and we got the raw end of the deal a lot."

Jordan laid back, hands behind his head. "Yeah but this time we've got a choice. They only hired us. They don't own us. Unless…"

"There's that thinking look again."

"Unless they're trying to own us. Make us look so bad we can't find another contract. Then they come to us with a crap offer but it's the only offer we got. Then what?"

His squad leader looked disgusted and slightly scared. "Shit, DeMarco. You keep thinking like that and you're gonna keep me up all night." He turned and walked away.

Chapter 11

Plancius Station, Pavo Real System

Their arrival at Plancius Station was low key. No one met them at the dock and Drusk nodded a dispassionate farewell as she departed. The men and women of 1st Platoon filed off the ship, relief at being back on station competing for a concern that went beyond being alive.

Free had Ishido stop them in the docking bay. "Alright, take a knee."

They lowered themselves down, clustering in a semicircle around their commanding officer. "First off, let me apologize for putting you in that situation. My intent was to reduce the amount of resistance you would face by offering the insurgents an alternative. It worked, at first. Clearly, the government here is more ruthless than I expected."

He paused, turning in place to look at all of them. "You all did nothing wrong. I know you feel dirty right now. We fought the Imperials, the Charee, the Clu'lachan, and the Ilryians for almost twenty years and we never did anything like this. But remember this. We were in and done with no casualties. We got our high value targets and now we're back home. You did me proud back there. So well done, Marines."

Ishido stepped forward. "Let me add my kudos. You were on the bounce and did the mission. Once we get everything cleaned and stowed, I'm authorizing rotating seventy-two passes all around. Dismissed."

There was a brief cheer and the 1st Platoon rose to their feet. As they filed out of the bay, Ezekiel and his daughter entered. He waited until the Marines had cleared out before approaching.

"Captain, this is my fault. I'm the one who had the bright idea to push for criminal charges. I just never thought they'd go this far."

McMannus shook his head. "We both pushed for that and we both failed to see how far they would take it. Forget it, Ezekiel. Lesson learned for next time. It's over and done with."

Alanna produced a tablet and turned the screen towards them. "That's it, sir. It's not over."

The video playing was that of the spacing of the prisoners. But the camera angles showed the backs of the Marines in the foreground as the prisoners gasped their last. The video lasted for over a minute with a ticker that read, "Insurgency leaders captured by the Terran mercenaries. Federal court convicts and sentences to death, with execution overseen by the mercenaries."

McMannus looked up at Vestry, horror on his face.

The older man nodded. "That's been playing nonstop since a few hours ago. Worse, Harry's out of touch. I'm hearing from some people in the Justice offices that the law enforcement sweep is… becoming excessive."

"You can't get ahold of him? Nothing at all?"

"I'm limited to using the station comm system and the mining stations are under communications restrictions. Nothing in or out except official government traffic."

"Right. Let me get out of this suit and changed. Then we'll go hit up the Chief Marshal for some answers."

*****

The Chief Marshal wasn't on the station. He was back groundside, 'coordinating law enforcement efforts' and 'briefing the Justice Minister.' Or, at least, that's what his staff told them.

"What about communications with my Marines out there? Why can't I talk to them?"

They were in a briefing room with a senior agent, a human named Controveros. He smiled thinly. "We're trying to limit the spread of information so we can catch anyone who didn't run. I'm sure you know how that kind of thing works, yes? Rest assured, our people are working alongside yours. Once we have everyone we need in custody, then we will reopen the channels."

Free slapped the table. "Dammit, that's not good enough! If my people are in trouble, I need to know!" He half rose as spoke, voice rising.

The agent's smile changed to a frown. "You think we are putting your people in trouble? You're mercenaries You live off of trouble!"

"Not unnecessary trouble. Look, you need to let me talk to my officer. I have to-"

He was cut off by a wave of the hand. "And I'm telling you no. You will be allowed to communicate when the time is right. Instead, you should be looking at your redeployment plans for when we are finished catching the rest of the ringleaders."

"Redeployment plans?"

"Yes. Per your contract, you must provide security for the specified stations."

Free threw up his hands. "But we caught all the insurgency leadership!"

Controveros shook his head and the frown deepened. "The ones we know of. And who's to say someone will not step into the empty places? No. You are contracted to us for six months for security work. Unless you want to break your contract?"

Ezekiel laid a hand on Free's arm, who shook it off. Vestry then grabbed his boss by the elbow and squeezed. The agent's face was getting red and he needed to defuse this before things got out of hand. "Captain, I'm sure the federal police will be done soon with their sweeps and then we'll be able to contact Lieutenant Webb. And we will honor the terms of the contract. We're all on the same side. Right, Agent Controveros?"

The other man stared at Ezekiel, lips pinched. "As you say. All in due time. Now, I have duties to attend to. We will be in touch regarding moving your mercenaries out to the stations." He stood, motioning at the door.

Minutes later, McMannus and Ezekiel were outside in the corridor. They walked in silence for several more minutes, Free leading the way. His subordinate let him, knowing his boss needed to get his temper under control. Finally, they stopped at a small bar that was mostly empty.

Before Free could order anything, Ezekiel paid for a whole bottle of the local tequila. He motioned his boss to a small table in the back as he collected two glasses with the bottle.

The foil seal on the top came off easily and he poured a small amount for both of them. Then, giving a small salute with the glass, the older man tossed his back with a single easy motion. The cough a few seconds later brought tears to his eyes. "Okay, that was damned foolish. I shoulda known what kind of crap this was when I saw the foil."

Free sipped his more cautiously and made a face. "Honestly, it might be better to get it over with quickly." He tossed the remainder back and set the glass down, indicating another round.

This time, when Ezekiel raised his glass, he matched the gesture and nodded in the general direction of the 76th area. "To a job well done and no casualties."

They both tossed back the drink, coughed and this time Free poured another round. Ezekiel led the toast this time. "To fucking bureaucrats and their inability to see the big picture."

This time they didn't cough. Free looked at the bottle. "Fuck me, I think my throat is numb."

Vestry poured another and toasted his boss. "To your unintelligent intelligence officer, who negotiated us into a corner."

Free put his hand on the other man's wrist. "No. We were both there. Instead, here's to a couple of fucking new guys in the contractor business, who are learning it the hard way."

"Fine. I'll drink to that."

"Okay, now what? We're stuck in this system for at least six months. The government is using us as boogeymen and implying that we are their executioners. What can we do?"

Ezekiel shook his head. "Right now, not a goddamned thing. They have us cornered. Best we can do is stick it out and try not to get set up for any other atrocities. I'll see what I can come up with to try and counter the negative publicity. Then we get another job in a different system and leave Pavo Real in the proverbial dust."

"Now that's something worth drinking to."

*****

When McMannus and Ezekiel got back they had an officer's call with the platoon sergeants to relay what they had learned. Once they were done, Gunny Mulongo cleared his throat.

"Sir, something else for you to chew on. Sergeant Baines came to see me while we were still in transit. Relayed something one of his squaddies had come up with on this situation." He passed Jordan's concern to the group.

Vestry shook his head. "Company store." Alanna looked puzzled, then nodded with a grim expression.

Their boss leaned back on the edge of his desk. "Explain, Mr. Vestry."

"It's an old technique, used to be practiced on Earth. People working for a company were paid in company scrip. Then they had to buy all their goods and equipment from the Company store, at prices that were just high enough that they had to borrow against their next paycheck. Always kept them in debt to the company and they could never leave."

Ishido looked disgusted. "And that's what they want to do to us? Why?"

"Doesn't matter. We're not going to let it happen." McMannus pointed at Ezekiel and his daughter. "You two are lead on this. Figure out what we can do to avoid going into debt, make sure our name isn't associated with illegal acts by the government and find us our next contract."

He began to pace the small office, rubbing one hand on his chin. "Gunny, we have *got* to get in touch with Harry and warn him. Get Sparks and ping the Lance Corporal Network. Figure out how we can get word to him without breaking the Pavo Real laws."

Done with his pacing, he nodded at Ishido. "You and I are going to work up operational patterns. You'll have to take your platoon out next, or possibly even at the same time as Harry. Let's start working on courses of action to cover our bases. I'd like to keep a good chunk of our people mobile, even if it means living in a system boat."

"Alright people. We have a new mission and lots of work to do. We had a victory on the field but the war's not over. We just changed opponents."

Chapter 12

Two days later, Gunny Mulongo had worked his magic and established an 'unofficial' communication link with Harry. It was audio and text only and there was a lag of a few hours but it was something. The Justice Ministry was running public service announcements and dominating the news broadcasts with the success of the new 'peacekeeping' efforts on the troubled stations. Since the raid, there were no official reports of violence or unrest on the stations. Harry's backchannel reports of the situation weren't the same as what was on the air but he had no incidents and they hadn't had to use their weapons yet.

McMannus and Ishido were still working on deployment schedules. They hadn't been told to send out the 1st Platoon yet. He wondered if indications of unrest here on the main station would change that. Then his forces could be split between the high orbitals around the main planet and the mining stations in the belt. He said as much to the others.

"Thing is, we're really the only mobile force they have in the system. Their police force in the high orbitals and beyond is barely bigger than we are, they're scattered on all the stations and they have to stay there for the most part."

The four officers were sitting around a folding table littered with takeout food containers. Ezekiel pointed his fork back in the general direction of the Justice Ministry offices. "I've learned that when they did their sweeps, they either shut down some offices or stripped them down to the absolute minimum in manning. That's one reason they hired us, to augment their people."

"Let's face it. Our employers want us to guard their property. We've got four major stations and seven minor ones. I would rather not have less than a squad at each one but with only nine squads I don't see how we can manage it."

Ezekiel pointed at the deck. "Five major stations. And yeah, that's a problem."

Alanna cleared her throat. "Ish and I have been looking over the contract. It doesn't specify how many people are to be at each station. One thing I know is that if you're first in line, you get what you want. We should be presenting our own plan for how to secure those stations rather than letting them do it for us."

Ishido nodded. "With that in mind, we've developed a new operational concept. Their stations are mostly symmetrical across their belt. What if Harry and I split the belt between us? That's two major stations and three to four minor ones each. We put a squad at each major station and then have the other two squads on a roving patrol between all the stations. We rotate the squads every few weeks to keep people from getting bored or too well-known. You keep the command group here to meet the letter of the contract."

McMannus frowned. "Where will we get the ships for the rovers?"

Alanna opened up her tablet to show the contract. She scrolled to one paragraph and tapped the screen. "That's on the government to provide. Says right here in the contract that they're on the hook for transportation between stations. If they want to do things by the contract, then it works both ways."

He looked at the two younger officers. "Ish, that means your people don't get a lot of down time. And it means we're nailed to the floor here on this station, which is several days travel from the belt at a full gee acceleration at best. If things go sideways, you can't count on us reinforcing you."

Lieutenant Kan spread his hands. "Sir, would you rather they spread us out by fire team and we have no ships available? At least this way we'll always have two squads mobile and ready to respond to incidents."

McMannus sighed and shook his head. He looked at Vestry. "You've been quiet this whole time. You put them up to this?"

"Nope. The kids thought it through on their own, it appears. And it's a sound plan, if a bit rough around the edges. Fact is, this is about the best way to do things and keeps us from being spread super thin."

"Alright. You two write this up tonight and I'll take it to the Ministry first thing in the morning. We'll show them we can do our jobs and still meet the letter of the contract."

Chapter 13

McMannus returned the next afternoon with a triumphant grin. "They bought off on it. I actually got to talk to the Chief Marshal via vidlink and briefed him directly. I think he's a bit embarrassed at the way his government used us and he agreed with just about every aspect of the plan. The only hitch will be getting enough ships for four squads. Ish, we might have to make do with only three roving patrols, with the fourth one here. That means we might be able to send it as reinforcement if it comes to it. They can grab a ship like they did the *Sirena* to use if necessary.

Ishido nodded and called up their plan to make the change. "We can make do, sir. It'll spread out the revisit times but the squad here can reach any station quicker than one of the rovers."

"Here's the other shoes they dropped on me. One, the government is in talks with some of the other systems directly connected to the Colon High Station jump portal. They're very close to signing up together in a loose confederation. Lowered tariffs on trade, security cooperation, that sort of thing. Which ties into the other thing. In a few months' time, Pavo Real will be hosting a trade convention for some of the major Union corporations. Seems the corps can smell money out here in the DMZ and are anxious to lock in these markets."

Vestry snorted. "Of course they are. Which means Pavo Real and its partners will want to show off their very safe neighborhoods where nothing will happen to the fat merchant ships coming through the jump gate."

"Exactly. My guess is they're going to want us to ensure there aren't any incidents on the stations. Which means they need us to be everywhere at once keeping the peace. Thing is, I can't tell if that means tighter or looser rules of engagement. If anyone pops up causing trouble, are they going to want us to squash it right away with extreme prejudice, or are they going to want a gentler approach so it's not a major news event?"

The intelligence officer smiled. "Either way, it's a win-win for us."

His boss gave him a puzzled look. "Mr. Vestry, in my considerable time working for the Terran Union, I don't believe I've ever encountered that situation."

"Wouldn't be surprised. Governments aren't made to have win-win situations. That's why we will enjoy this one. Look, if they want us to go hard core on any tangoes that pop up, that's not a problem. Our guys can do it with their eyes closed and we get the reputation of being tough and difficult to beat. If they want us to go soft, we don't look like faceless monsters in armored suits. We know they don't have any weapons that can seriously damage our suits, so we can use less-lethal measures without risking casualties. I think it's time to use that media coverage to our advantage."

"I hope you're right. It'd be nice to not get screwed over in the bargain for once. Okay, Ish. Make ready everyone but one squad, your choice, for deployment the day after tomorrow. I've been informed there'll be media coverage for this, so put on a good show. It's not just a dog and pony show, it actually helps us out."

"Roger that, sir. Everyone and everything will shine bright under their lights."

"And be careful out there. Just because we beat them handily once doesn't mean it'll go that way the next time."

Chapter 14

Alpha Centauri System, five months later

"In summary, the Denovo Sector represents a market worth one point seven billion. The central node of Pavo Real is the key to the shipping lanes, having no fewer than seven jump points that connect it to other systems. Color High Station provides the jump gate in the system and provides warehousing, transshipment docks and hundreds of thousands of cubic feet of station under air is central to dominating these markets."

"Thank you, Thomas, for that thorough market analysis. Are there any further questions?" Winfield Cross looked around the table. There were headshakes from those around the glass table as they made notes in their tablets and examined the figures in the holographic display at the center of the table.

Smiling slightly, Thomas Flatley nodded his thanks at his boss as he closed the presentation and leaned back in his chair as Cross continued.

"Now, we have a great deal of preparations to make for our entry into that market, people. The board wants to be first to develop this region and our division is leading the charge for Galactocity. The upcoming trade conference in Pavo Real will involve all of the major corporations on this side of the Union. Brand new markets mean they'll all be sending their best people to negotiate with the locals. We have to be prepared to go toe to toe with them and more importantly, to win those exclusive rights!" He slapped the table lightly. "I expect preliminary reports from each division in say, two weeks? No less than that. We do this right and there will be accolades and more importantly, stock options all around. Now that the war is over, the DMZ is ripe for development and Galactocity intends capture the finest of those markets."

As the group began to disperse, Winfield looked at Thomas. "Don't leave. I have a few details I want to go over with you."

"Of course, sir." Thomas leaned back in his seat, smiling.

As the rest filed out, Oliver Beck entered the conference room, looking out of place among the business suits leaving it. His presence caused those exiting to shy away from him as he stood next to the door. Once they were gone, he keyed in a code at the door panel which caused it to slide shut as a red light came on over the door.

"Room is secure and the anti-monitoring system is active, Mr. Cross."

Winfield nodded and waved a hand at the man. "Join us at the table, Oliver. I don't want to keep craning my neck to look at you."

The large man quietly took a seat at the table as Cross turned back to Thomas. "And now; the special analysis?"

Thomas turned off his tablet. This information was sensitive enough that he had it memorized and it was the reason he was here in person, instead of briefing by ansible. "The region has seventeen shipping concerns; this being defined as operating three or more ships. The largest operates seven ships. None are jump capable so all depend on the jump gate at Colon. Three lines are wholly owned by their respective governments. All have extensive contacts in the twenty major markets in the region, in many cases personal or familial. Their financials and personnel information are on a secure drive."

"Debts? Outstanding contracts? Personnel problems?"

"All there, sir. Each concern has more than one vulnerable point, most of which are financial. When they start losing shipments and ships, it's going to hurt. Some are borderline right now. They won't be able to fulfill their contracts or even keep their ships running. We can move in at that point and offer competitive rates, with safety and guaranteed delivery backed by Galactocity's name."

"Very good, Thomas. I'm not about to let this conference dictate our entry into the market. We're going to put our competitors off balance before it even starts. When they get there and find out the local companies are getting hit with our 'pirates', they'll reevaluate the security situation and hesitate to commit to signing their contracts. That's the opening we need." He turned to the other man. "What about the political situation? Oliver, how are the various governing bodies prepared to respond to pirates insystem?"

The big man shrugged. "None have significant military forces. Most are strictly for customs and immigration. The armed craft in most systems are primarily concerned with either law enforcement activities or the security of the stations at the jump point and the immediate operating area around key facilities. There are no 'navies' to speak of."

Cross smiled and nodded his head. "This is sounding better and better. Have you both identified key elements within the governments who are amenable to our proposals?"

Thomas tapped his tablet. "I have several contacts on five worlds, including Pavo Real. Bureaucrats are the same everywhere; overworked, underpaid and underappreciated. All have proven susceptible to the funds we advanced and are ready to do us favors in return."

Beck took up the thread. "Like its old Earth namesake, this system handles a significant percentage of the traffic in the region through the jump gate at the Colon High Station. Pavo Real recently concluded a treaty with their nearest trade partners to form a semi-political body called the 'League of Denovo'. While primarily concerned with internal trade, they do have some loose agreements on enforcement of immigration and customs laws and extradition of criminals."

His boss leaned back in his chair, eyes on the ceiling. "Now that could be trouble in the making. But it's new, you say?"

"Yes, sir. Only within the last three months."

"Well, something that young can be easily fractured. Or taken advantage of, since none of the partners have full trust in the other yet. I want both of you to take a look at how we could make that happen. Or how we could use it to our advantage. No sense in destroying something we can use. What about mutual defense pacts?"

"None, sir. As a matter of fact, none of the entities have the right to pursue criminals into each other's systems."

"Well, that's good to know. Especially for you, Oliver. What do you have for me in your primary area?"

Oliver, like Thomas, had memorized his brief. "I have three teams ready to deploy with me to the Denovo operating area. Any more than that will create an unacceptable signature, both in the region and on the company books. The primary team will operate on Colon and be our interface with our contractors. The mobile team will have their own ship and conduct our caching operations and be available to transport the other teams. And the influence team will in fact break apart once it transits into the other systems. They will conduct information gathering and be our contacts with the people we previously discussed, in case we need them to act. I will act as the liaison between all the team, with Pavo Real being central to those operations."

"And our ability to disrupt existing trade functions in those systems?"

"We have contracted with an organization that meets our criteria; a willingness to operate outside the law, the ability to move questionable cargo quietly and enough resources to take on the targets we have in mind. Given our assurance of providing the cargo manifests ahead of time, they're ready to begin operations against the shipping lines we designate. I'm convinced they're primarily interested in making money, not trouble. Casualties should be minimal or nonexistent, as long as the crews don't put up a fight. This is about the cargoes, not the ships or the people. However, in the event we need to escalate, I have secure cutouts to contact two other groups who have no qualms about that sort of thing. They will also make suitable sacrificial lambs when the time comes. Once you give the word, operations can begin in about three weeks."

The VP nodded. "And the weapons? Both for them and us?"

Beck gave a small smile. "Team two will travel via their own ship and begin to emplace the caches in the region. These will be small arms and ammunition only, with the serial numbers logged as lost in action or disposed of due to unsatisfactory testing during manufacture. The coordinates can be made available to whomever we choose, whenever we choose. For the other, our TU Navy contact assures me that when we ask, light ship-mounted weaponry will be made available to protect ourselves from pirate activity."

"Fine, fine. I have a separate team ready to make those modifications. We'll seem like a dream come true against pirates and none of their ships will have military-grade hardware like ours. I also have the assurances of Admiral Besson that the limited TU patrols in that area will be 'unavailable' for anti-piracy operations. Their instructions will be to watch for treaty violations, not internal issues. What else?"

The ex-military man frowned. "The mercenary units in the area. While most of them are ground based and of limited utility against pirates, there are a few who can operate in deep space. The reconstituted 76th MIST, for example."

"Mist? What's that?"

"It's an acronym. Stands for Microgravity Strike Team. Former TU Marines. Experts in microgravity and vacuum work. Word is, they stayed together after the drawdown and are now for hire. Anti-piracy, station defense, boarding actions, that kind of thing. They're also providing training to the security forces. They've already had a successful contract in the area and could become a serious crease in our operations."

"Fine, fine. Make a file on them and anyone else you think might be an obstacle." He pointed his finger at Beck. "If they get in the way, make arrangements to have them removed. Your disposable groups, for instance. There's too much money at stake here to let some military has-beens get in my way."

He paused, smiling at the larger man. "Oh and no offense meant at the 'has-been' thing."

"No sir. Of course not."

"Alright. Get to it. Thomas, make him a copy of your file so he knows where to put pressure. And be ready to head back out in a few weeks. I want you in position to report on timing. This upcoming conference Once the local lines are ready to break, we need to be ready to snap up that market share."

*****

Cassie smiled at the message from Oscar and left her desk. Her destination was on a different floor, one behind multiple security doors and protected by anti-eavesdropping devices of all kinds. Inside were the small group of specialists StellarMart employed to both protect their corporate intellectual property and acquire other companies.

Her usual team sat in a four-person cubicle, although there were only three of them. Selena's monitors and VR equipment took up most of the fourth desk along with a number of cases of specialized equipment. When she walked in, they were engaged in a spirited debate about the latest movie to hit the web.

Vera was the first to notice Cassie and held up her hand to shut down conversation. "What's up, Cassie?" The accountant was in her mid-30s and looked exactly like what she was, complete with hair in a bun to wearing old-style glasses.

"Pavo Real is hosting a trade conference in a few weeks. StellarMart will be participating and we're a go for our side."

Janik smiled and cracked his knuckles. "Another challenge. Fun." The big blond was a man of few words, except when he was practicing his social engineering skills on an unsuspecting target.

Their raven-haired hacker whooped in delight. "Yes! A new audience to witness mah skills and respect mah authoritay! You watch, Cass. I'll own their networks in just a few days."

"Let's not go overboard just yet, Selena. We're still on a tight leash for now, so keep things above board. We're just gathering information for now."

"And for later?"

"Later will come. Now, let's start putting together our list of equipment. Plan for being there anywhere from a couple of weeks to a few months. And yes, plan ahead for things to get down and dirty with the other corps. Oscar says this market is going to be heavily contested."

Chapter 15

Colon High Station, Pavo Real System

"This is bullshit, DeMarco. Why the fuck are fixing someone else's broke-ass shit instead of busting someone's ass?"

Jordan replied absently, attention on the laser welder just barely visible through the polarized face shield of his MACE. "Whatsa matter, Santis, you have a problem working civilized hours and getting libo almost every night?"

The lance corporal adjusted his grip on the panel that DeMarco was welding to the merchant ship's hull, careful to stay out of the beam's path. "Well, no. But we all signed on to this merc thing to kick in doors and blow shit up. Not fucking scrape hulls and do a field day on someone else's shit. Fuckin' merchie. You think this guy ever did any maintenance at all?"

"If he did, I can't see any sign. But good for us that he didn't and has the money to pay." DeMarco toggled off the polarization on his helmet screen and checked the weld. Satisfied, he straightened and looked around at what was going on. The Colon High Station maintenance yard was filled with ships of all sizes, both jump capable and insystem. Fireflies winked from the hulls and small craft darted through the congestion, outlining the scope of work underway in this massive deep space shipyard. And 1st Platoon (Kan's Killer Klowns) of the 76th MIST were temporarily part of that work force.

Above, the massive jump gate of Colon Tower was visible, even from over a hundred thousand kilometers away. Every few minutes, you could see the inky blackness of a jump portal appear, although the ships transiting through were invisible at this distance. Santis clumped across the deck to stand next to him. "Man, all the action is out there! And we're fucking stuck here."

"Give it a rest, Santis. The Old Man has to pay the bills somehow. We haven't had a contract offer since we finished up with the govvies. It's like peace broke out all over the region. Ain't nobody sticking their heads up for us to shoot at right now." He hefted the welder and turned to their next repair site. "So come on, we got five more panels to finish or Staff will have our ass."

The all-hands alert sounded in their earpieces, followed by Lieutenant Kan's voice. "Exercise Exercise Exercise. All hands take cover. Rounds inbound. I say again, rounds inbound. All hands take cover. Exercise Exercise Exercise."

As two Marines scrambled awkwardly around the massive shape of the engine bell, Santis continued grumping. "And we got the fuckin' el-tee throwing exercises every shift! What kind of hard on does he have for these things?"

Their head-up displays switched to exercise mode, displaying several yellow trajectories coming from empty space, simulating the kinetic rounds inbound. The lines terminated at the ship they were working on. Several impact icons appeared on the hull further forward but none near them.

Kan's voice sounded again over the radio. "Exercise Exercise Exercise. Two casualties mid-ship from first squad. DeMarco, make the recovery. Baines, covering fire from your team. Second squad, engage simulated targets and provide covering fire for the assault element. Third squad, prepare for assault. On the bounce, Klowns!"

None of the platoon were armed, of course. But their onboard computers could simulate outgoing fire just as well as incoming. Santis grumbled about that too, until DeMarco thumped him on the helmet.

"Shut up, moron. Soon as we get over the curve of the hull, what do you want to bet Staff will be there, monitoring the exercise and listening in on our comms?"

"Oh. Yeah."

"So stay the fuck shut up and do it right. I swear to God if you screw this up for us, I will beat the ever-living shit out of you."

"Okay, man. I got it. By the book, you'll see."

The two Marines came over the hull into the simulated fire zone in a low crawl, darting from protrusion to indent to make the best use of cover. Sure enough, Staff Sergeant Salazar was standing about twenty meters from the two 'casualties', watching the recovery effort unfold.

DeMarco reached them first and touched helmets with the closest one, allowing them to speak without getting on the radio. "Hassan, where you hit?"

The swarthy face grinned up at him. "My balls, man, my balls! Put some pressure on them with your hands before I bleed out!"

"Fuck you, Snackbar. Your system says you took a round in the chest and right on through life support. You're dead, man."

"Nooo, don't leave me! Don't let me die in the cold depths of spaa-ace!"

Salazar broke in on their conversation. "Private Takbar, can it. You're a casualty. DeMarco, what's the drill here?"

"Tag 'em for retrieval later and move to the next casualty, Staff!"

"So get your ass in gear and help Santis. Takbar, shut up or I'm freezing your suit."

"Aye aye, Staff," they chorused. Hassan lay still as DeMarco moved to help Santis. "What do we got?

Santis slapped PFC Benning's leg. "Round through and through. Suit sealed it and I double sealed it against air loss. Bouncer cracked the faceplate and spilled some air but I put a patch on it. Good thing, too, so we don't have to look at her ugly mug."

Bennings gave him double middle fingers. "Works both ways, asshole."

Salazar cut in. "Nice work, Santis. That was on the bounce and well executed. I guess you do actually have a mind you can put to work."

"Oh, gee, thanks, Staff. Does this mean you like me?"

"It's not my job to like you, Santis. Only to make you the best Marine you can be." There was a pause and then he continued, "Or kill you trying. Maybe both. Now back to work, Marines. Exercise is over."

*****

A few hours later, as they filed out of the airlock at the end of the shift, Salazar tapped DeMarco on the shoulder and motioned him off to the side.

"Yeah, Staff?"

"You're doing good work with Santis. He was really on the ball getting to those casualties."

DeMarco sighed. "Had to threaten to beat his ass to get him to shut up and work."

"Bitching comes with the uniform. He may need a reminder now and then but that's why he's still a PFC." He paused, considering. "Keep it up and you'll be ready for sergeant soon. The eltee's got his eye on you, DeMarco. Don't fuck this up."

The other man stepped back to watch the rest of the platoon as they turned in their tools and cleaned off their suits. DeMarco followed them in, lost in thought. *Fuck me. Sergeant? Back in the Corps, I thought that would be years away. Now I could be leading a squad in a few months.* The thought was both exciting and frightening. The action on the Grausian battleship led to his promotion to corporal and team lead but what it had taken to get him there wasn't necessarily something he wanted to repeat.

*****

Harry and Ish leaned over Alanna's desk as she hammered on the keyboard, eyes half-closed in a frown. She'd always been able to concentrate on the task at hand despite the environment and had learned over these last few months how to ignore the other two when she needed to. It was a vital skill, given that the three of them shared an office meant for one person.

"See, Ish? Poor lass is working her fingers to the bone. Hasn't had any fun for ages. Going to be a shadow of herself soon."

Ishido nodded sagely. "I concur, doctor. What do you prescribe?"

Alanna rolled her eyes as she continued to type. "What are you two up to now? And don't try to rope me into one of your schemes."

Harry put his hand on his chest, eyes wide. "My dear Alanna, we're merely thinking of your wellbeing! It's our duty as fellow Marines to ensure the health and welfare of our fellows at all times. And I daresay you're not well at all."

She finished entering the numbers into the supply list and looked at him. "Of course I'm not well. I'm doing the work of three people to make sure the company has what it needs."

Ishido stepped around the low wall of her cubicle and put his hand over her mouse. Before she could react, he clicked on the 'save' button. "Exactly our point. You've been working yourself to the bone and need some relaxation."

She clicked on the save button again, just in case Ishido had missed it. "I know how to relax. I've got a good book I'm—"

Harry cut her off. "Book! Naw, mate. What you need is some real Marine relaxation!"

"I know how to drink. I did go to college."

Harry waved a hand. "Lightweights. Besides, you're a Marine officer now. You have a reputation to uphold."

"So you want me to go get drunk. Now?"

"Why not? You're not a mean drunk, are you? Break things, insult people, puke on the floor?"

"No!"

"Then you're coming with us. Besides, Captain's orders."

"What?"

They both nodded. "Yep. The Old Man said to get your head out of the computer and blow off some steam. Those are our orders, so you have to comply. Don't want to upset the Captain."

"But…" Her objections fell on deaf ears as they gently lifted her out of her seat. "I've still got a mountain of entries…"

"And they'll still be there tomorrow. And the dependent transport is coming tomorrow, which means a ton of work for everyone that's a higher priority. So tonight, you're coming with us."

*****

The three lieutenants staggered out of the elevator into the foyer of the 76th garrison area. The two Marines on duty smiled to themselves. "I.D.s, please."

Harry produced his first, as the other two fumbled through their pockets. "Come on, people. Don't leave the poor man hanging. Private Danniker, I apologize for the state of my comrades. Just not as skilled as I am in their relaxation."

Danniker gave her platoon leader a tight grin as she scanned his ID. "You're the expert, sir."

"And don't you forget it, Danniker. Let your mates know your boss can drink anyone under the table."

Ishido and Alanna finally produced their IDs and had them scanned into the system. The other sentry, Lance Corporal Rimer opened the access hatch and braced to attention. "Lieutenant Webb and a party of two, arriving!"

Alanna staggered through the door, followed by Ishido. Harry waved a finger in front of the guard. "Flattery will get you everywhere, Rimer. Don't you forget that."

As the hatch closed, Danniker burst out laughing. "Holy shit, they can really tie one on!"

Rimer shook his head. "You think this is something? Wait till the Lieutenant really starts drinking."

Inside, Harry and Ishido made sure Alanan got to her quarters. As her door closed, they turned to see Ezekiel standing a few meters down the hall, half-hidden in shadows. He nodded as they approached.

"Nice job, gentlemen. And I assume you were gentlemen the whole time?"

Ishido nodded vigorously but Harry drew himself up. "Now shee… see her, sir. Your daughter is a fellow Marine officer. Cap'n said to get her to relax and we did so. Ain't nothing more to it."

The older man nodded again. "Apologies, Mr. Webb. Just a father's reaction coming out."

As Harry and Ishido made their way past him, Ish mumbled, "Besides, she knows some very obscene drinking songs."

Chapter 16

The next day was a flurry of activity and excitement. The ship carrying the company's dependents was arriving from the TU. The married personnel were excused from yard maintenance work to greet their loved ones and get them settled. After work, the captain had authorized release of company funds to pay for a welcome party.

Jordan waited with the others at the waiting area. He and Lucy weren't exactly married but she'd been willing to travel hundreds of light years to be with him. If that wasn't commitment then nothing was. And she said she was bringing him a surprise. The captain was there too, a bunch of flowers in his hand. *Funny, the Old Man didn't strike me as the romantic type.*

Free tried not to fidget as the speakers announced the docking of the shuttle. He was pretty sure Aileen hadn't changed her mind. No, he was sure she hadn't. He was just afraid she might have. *Argh. Knock it off. She'll be on the ship.*

The corridor from the security station had a dogleg so they couldn't see anyone approaching. The appearance of the first person around the corner was a surprise but the shouted greeting was quickly joined by others as more arrivals appeared. Free took a moment to watch his people finally rejoin with their loved ones they had left behind. They didn't exactly have the ideal situation here, without a contract in place but at least this gave them time to settle in. It felt right, too, having everyone here now. The Company was complete.

The stream of arrivals had slowed and Aileen still hadn't appeared. McMannus kept smiling at the arrivals, welcoming the ones he was familiar with and congratulating them on coming out here. Finally, she came around the corner, walking with a very pregnant young woman. Free heard the corporal waiting nearby gasp and then shout, "Lucy! That's your surprise?"

Aileen stepped aside as the young man ran up and wrapped the woman in a very protective hug. Smiling, she turned to Free. "Well, don't I get a hug?"

He enveloped her in his arms, burying his face in her hair. "God, it's good to finally see you again. I know I said wait six months but now I'm kicking myself for making it that long."

She laughed softly in his ear. "It was worth the wait."

He released her with some reluctance, although he kept hold of her hand. When she looked down at that, he laughed. "Not in the Corps anymore, my dear. And I'm the Old Man. No one is going to give me the stinkeye if we hold hands."

"I'm liking this mercenary gig more and more."

"The dependent quarters are all set up. A bit smaller than the stations in the Union but they're all ours. For now. The contract with the station will run a few more months but we get room and board with our pay. Bonuses too, which the troops are eager to earn."

"Are we staying here, then?"

"Here on Colon, for a while. Given that it's central to multiple systems, it's a good place for us to stage out of into the other places. We're trying to work a longer-term contract with them and we're just about there, I think. Gives us some stability and a place to call home." He nudged her. "And I think I found a good location for your shop. It's off the main market area but…"

She poked him in the ribs. "Business later. I have other plans for you today."

*****

Oliver Beck walked off his ship onto Colon High Station with casual disinterest, as if an interstellar journey was commonplace to him. Pretending to be a corporate drone on business was an easy cover and provided him and his other team members with reasons to visit many parts of the station. Dozens arrived and left every day, so a few more wouldn't be noticed. His forged identity and travel documents easily withstood the attentions of the Customs and Immigration officer and he continued on to the baggage pickup. While waiting for his bags, he saw the others of his team arrive one by one.

Exiting the arrivals section, they all headed separately for the hotel area of the station. Colon High Station was a massive structure, built to manage the traffic that supported over a dozen systems that connected to and through the Pavo Real system. The Grausians constructed the original station but the flow of commerce funded several expansion efforts over the years until it was as big as some of the major terminals in the TU.

They all took rooms in the same hotel, one known for specializing in business travelers. Over the next several days, they would take rooms under different names in other hotels, mostly lower class but a few high class as well. Then the rest of the team set out to conduct their own in-person reconnaissance of the station.

Once unpacked, Oliver set up his secure communications set, a briefcase-sized terminal that contained devices to provide encryption, voice modulation and filtering and signal monitoring. It was a simple matter to install a pirate tap on the commercial line, so he could place calls without giving a number and location. He made calls to four different businesses, leaving messages stating he was on station and wished to meet to discuss contract fulfillment. The criminals he was dealing with owned all four of those businesses and this would ensure they got his message that their prearranged deal was now active and they would collect the manifests of the target ships in the next few days. Once this was done, he dressed for a casual dinner and headed out to meet with the rest of his team.

They arrived individually at the restaurant, a noisy place that made monitoring their conversation very difficult, if not impossible. They discussed the small changes that were necessary now that they had first-hand knowledge of the station and its patterns. Over the next few days, key station personnel would be contacted and supplied with funds to ensure their participation in the plan, which mostly consisted of looking the other way and letting the team know if someone started looking too closely at what was going on. Once the manifests were acquired and sorted according to their target list, they would plan their attacks and begin execution of the plan. The first phase of the operation was to cause general unrest, so the targets would be necessarily broad to cause the maximum impact. In later phases, they would target specific lines to put them out of business or up for sale, depending on Galactocity's needs.

Oliver liked the opening stages of an operation. So many pieces in play and so many things to coordinate meant that he was constantly on the move and always considering options. It was when he felt the most alive and now nobody was shooting at him while he tried to do it. All he had to do now was monitor the results and make any changes necessary to ensure the continued success of the plan. The official Galactocity business development team would be arriving in a week for the conference and he intended to set the stage to maximize their bargaining efforts.

Chapter 17

En route to Colon High Station, Pavo Real system

Captain Patil stepped onto the bridge of the *Calcutta*, tea in one hand and a pastry in the other. Unable to fall asleep, he'd filched a pastry from the breakfast tray (privileges of rank) and headed for the bridge. If nothing else, the monotony of the blackness of space would help him relax. He'd been in space since he was fourteen and it felt like home.

"Evening, cap. Everything all right?" Pilot Second Class Murphy started to drop his feet off the console but Patil waved him back.

"Just fine, Joe. Couldn't sleep. Got some Company paperwork to review and I'm hoping that and the view outside will put me to sleep." He sat down heavily in his chair and put the tea and pastry on a side tray.

"Picked a good time for it. 'Bout halfway to the jump point nearabouts. Ain't nothing on the close-in radar."

The chime from his console startled both of them. The screen flashed the message 'Emergency Communication' in bright red letters.

Joe dropped his feet to the deck and punched a command into the console. "Well I'll be damned. Cap'n, we got an SOS from a ship nearby. It's the *Beowulf*. Lost her drive to a power plant failure and they're drifting."

Patil pulled his own repeater screen from where it was stowed on the side of the chair. "See if you can locate her. She's not within ten thousand klicks or the beacon would already show on the radar. I'll check the database on her."

Minutes passed while both men worked on their tasks. Patil was the first to announce, "Found her. New Discovery lines intersystem ship running a route from New Lisbon to here. She's a fast intersystem ship, runs luxury goods and passengers. That ought to be good for a nice chunk of change when we rescue her. Anything yet on radar?"

"I think so. At least, it's the only non-asteroid registering. Got something about twenty-eight degrees to port and below the ecliptic. Her vector is updating but it looks like she's got a low velocity. Want me to plot an intercept?"

"Yes. The system logged the emergency signal anyway, so we'd have to answer some hard questions at Colén High Station if we didn't at least try to answer it."

*****

Five hours later, with the bridge fully manned and his engineering crew ready in the airlock to transfer over, they watched the helpless freighter grow larger in the viewscreen.

"Damn. Look at that carbon scoring. Is that debris in her shadow?" The navigator fiddled with the resolution, trying to get a better look.

"She's lucky she didn't blow completely. What's the radiation readings? Does the EVA crew need shielding?"

Joe shook his head. "Not getting anything beyond the background."

The communication tech reported, "No response to hails, sir. The emergency signal keeps repeating but nothing else."

Patil sighed and leaned back in his chair. "I hope we're not too late. Okay Joe, get us in position to deploy the EVA team. But keep an eye on those energy readings. Be ready to roll us if needed."

Joe was about to respond when the radar began beeping furiously. Their attention was captured by what they saw on the viewscreen, as two small craft came into view from behind the crippled freighter. One looked like a standard surface to orbit transport, complete with winged control surfaces and aerodynamic streamlining. The other was bulbous and squat, looking more at home in the airless depths of space. Both ignited their engines and began moving toward the *Calcutta* together.

"Captain, I have an incoming transmission from one of those craft. They're demanding to speak to you."

Patil motioned to the screen. "Put them on."

"Attention Captain of the Calcutta. Cut your drives and prepare to be boarded. Any resistance will be met with severe consequences. Cooperate and no one will be hurt. We just want your cargo."

*****

Free looked up as the sentry escorted Agent Drusk into his office. He waved her to a chair and leaned back in his. She sat stiff-backed, as if expecting the worst.

"Relax, Agent Drusk. I don't bite. Unless you're a recalcitrant private who seems to think the world is one big happy place to explore without consequences."

Her tongue flicked in and out, once. "I was not sure, after…"

"We all get orders we don't like at times. Some more than others. You were just doing what you were directed to do by a legal authority. I'm not going to hold that against you. Your bosses, on the other hand, are on my shit list."

Her hands twisted in her lap. "It wasn't the first time I've killed anyone. I've used my weapon in the line of duty. But they were all self-defense. I've never been an… an executioner." She looked up at him, eyes questioning.

He sighed. "Neither have I. When you go to war, there are rules, believe or not. The Terran Union has specific laws that are in effect during military operations, one of which is you don't execute prisoners. That's what was driving my reaction at the time. Even though those prisoners were lawfully sentenced by your court, I'm not an executioner. I made that clear before to your government. It seems they didn't take me seriously."

"Sala Thisk didn't want it done that way but he was overruled."

"Sala? The Chief Marshal is your uncle? Is that why you were assigned to us?"

"No! Well, mostly not. I am the most qualified in a vacc suit and I have fought in microgravity, true. But did he have other motives in assigning me? Probably. And that is very much the reason behind why I am here now."

"Here in an official capacity? Again, Agent Drusk, I'm not inclined to look favorably on any sort of job offer from the government. Whatever you have had better be worth our time. I might even charge extra to cover legal fees."

She pulled a data card out of her harness pocket and laid it on his desk. "This data is courtesy of the Chief Marshal, in a somewhat unofficial request. Three merchant ships were attacked in this system the last two days. The cargoes were quickly and efficiently removed. There were no deaths and only a few minor injuries when some of the crew didn't comply quickly enough. We suspect some of the organized crime gangs but given what we just went through, my uncle would like your assessment of the data. Is this just criminal activity or are we looking at a new set of rebels?"

Chapter 18

Jump Point, Tau Ceti System

"Ladies and gentlemen, this is your pilot. We're about to dock with the Jump Ship. Please buckle up and prepare for weightlessness. It'll only be a few minutes and then we'll be in their grav field."

The announcement paused the music in Cassie's earpiece, interrupting her thoughts as the star field slowly slipped by. She'd started out thinking her way through their strategy and ended up wondering where Everett had slipped off to in the DMZ. As a former Marine, he had been to a number of systems during the war. He'd always had the gift to find common ground with strangers so she had no doubt he could find a place to land. *He'd have been better in this job than as a Marine.*

Her team moved back to their seats with practiced ease, although Selena was already in hers. She tightened her seatbelt with one hand as she manipulated the data in the VR world with the other. She obediently opened her mouth as Vera came by with the anti-nausea meltaway strip.

"Thank you, mother," said Selena.

Vera snorted. "You'd puke your guts out or smack that oversized noggin of yours on the ceiling without me to look after you. Damn right you should be thanking me."

Selena blew her a kiss and then flipped her off with one gloved hand. Janik chuckled and also took the proffered medication. "Remember her first time in zero-g? You think holding her hair off her face so she could puke in the bag would teach her some manners."

She flipped him off with the other hand. "You can both kiss my hairy ass. Just know this; records of your private moments can find their way to interstellar social media. I have that power in these magic fingers." Her gloved fingers wiggled, as if casting a spell.

Cassie snorted, tightening her own seatbelt. "Alright, settle down. Selena, does everyone have their alternate IDs loaded?"

"Done and done, boss lady. Janik is now Queen Trinity, a down on his luck drag queen looking to revive his singing career. Vera is Matilda Quackenbush, a recent divorcee looking to live it up and hook a hot hunk to put out the fire between her legs that her ex could never satisfy. And you, my dear annual evaluation writer, are a lost princess of the Empire, seeking the hidden treasure which will proclaim your lineage and allow you to overthrow the current incompetent lardass on the throne."

Vera rolled her eyes while the big Swede looked thoughtful. "I have never explored that side of my sexuality before. And I do have a lovely singing voice."

Cassie chuckled. "Okay, maybe not quite what we need out here. Save those for the next mission. What do you really have?"

Selena pointed at Janik. "All weights, all classes Master Cargo Handling license. Should be able to get him a job in any dock we want. And if they peel back the surface layer, he's fleeing a TU murder charge from a bar fight. That should make him a target for any corruptible elements."

Janik cracked his knuckles. "I didn't mean to kill him. But his face screamed for a rearrangement."

She pointed to Vera. "CPA certified, with average marks from a backwater university. Lots of experience in handling the books for shipping lines. And loads of cash in several well-hidden bank accounts, of course. Break out the jewels, dearie. You have a taste for expensive things, although you don't go for flashy."

Vera called up their inventory. "Hmm. A nice watch, maybe a string of pearls. Something understated but pricey."

Selena popped her VR goggles on top of her head and bowed from the waist, limited by the seat belt. "I, as befits my mastery of subterfuge and obfuscation will remain hidden in the shadows, manipulating data streams like a spider in her web. Of course, a serious probe will expose my investigations, namely that I'm gathering information on the various corporations vying for market shares in the DMZ. Which I will make available for the right price. Finally, our dear leader will remain her beautiful and talented self, as a public relations shill for StellarMart where she can move about in the open and trick unsuspecting bureaucrats into giving away government secrets with just a crook of her finger."

Their ship shuddered slightly as it docked with the massive Jump Ship. The computer wizard pumped her fist in the air. "Yes! How's that for dramatic timing, people? Bow down to the master."

Cassie shook her head as everyone clapped. "Alright, settle down. Save your energy for when we actually get there.

Selena, excellent work, as always. Remind me to ask corporate about paying you what you're worth."

The hacker snorted and slid her goggles back on. "I won't hold my breath."

The intercom came to life and the pilot announced, "That's it, folks. We're docked and sealed to the JumpShip. Countdown to jump is just over an hour, so if you have any transmissions you need to make before we leave the system, now's the time. As a reminder, it's two jumps to Pavo Real, with a recharge time of two days in between jumps."

Cassie waved for everyone's attention. "You know the drill, experienced interstellar travelers that you are. Keep checking the company buffers to see if there are any last-minute instructions. And one last thing. Corporate is still playing this one above board for now, so if you run into another team, watch and listen but keep your distance. We'll be told when things are supposed to go hot. That means no pirate taps right now, Selena. I don't want to be made an example of if someone over there gets lucky."

"Understood, chief. I promise, no sticky fingers."

The next hour was spent waiting for the other company ships to dock and for the Jump Ship navigator to plot their course to the Pavo Real system. They did a final review of the various corporations in the Denovo region, the key government officials and the reported shipping tonnages that crossed the region.

Vera looked up from her screen. "By the way, just from a quickie analysis, these numbers aren't adding up to me."

Janik didn't even bother to look at her. "That's what you get for buying your degree online."

She ignored him. "I'm serious, Cassie. I can't put my finger on it but there's something hinky about these profit & loss numbers we got from the Colon High Station. It's managed as a private concern, so we may not have all the numbers. But it's been bugging me ever since we got the data dump and I started massaging it for route planning."

Cassie mirrored Vera's screen on her own. "What are you seeing?"

The accountant highlighted several boxes. "Just my gut feeling right now but these tonnage numbers seem low for the tariffs collected over the last few years. Conversely, the port fees are low for the amount of tonnage in the system. I need to do more calculations and narrow down some of my estimates for data we don't have. But I think someone over there is playing a shell game with these numbers to hide something."

Janik popped his head over his screen. "Most likely smuggling. Very common in the frontier areas, especially when the Grausians were here. It's almost like they expected it to happen and as long as you gave them their cut, things were good."

Selena snorted. "An empire as old as the Grausian one, graft has become part of their way of life."

"Okay, then." Cassie waved for silence. "Vera, keep on it as long as you think it will affect our estimates for tonnage and traffic throughput. A few percentage points at this stage of negotiations aren't a serious concern. See if you can find any government kickbacks or payouts tied to it. Graft would be normal and something we can use. But if it starts looking like some frontier corporations are playing shell games with each other, set it aside. They're not our targets right now."

As they settled back into their research, Cassie reviewed the key people she'd picked out for further work. Werner Herzberg, senior executive in the Ministry of Foreign Affairs. His name was associated with the efforts to form the League of Denovo and received the lion's share of the news coverage, to include being at the President's side when he signed the treaty. He would know the most about the politics of the region. The trick would be finding the right carrot to get him to share what he knew with her.

Félix Varela was next on her list. As the Deputy Chief of Operations at Colon High Station at the jump point, he would be in a position to know the most about the actual traffic through the region. His boss was a political appointee but Felix came up the hard way, starting at the docks. There probably wasn't any part of the station he didn't know. *Including the best ways to smuggle goods in and out. Vera definitely needs to check his finances. And see what he knows or doesn't know about the books not balancing.*

Her last subject was Chief Marshal Thisk, the top law enforcement officer. She needed to be aware of what he knew, because if his office suspected her or her team of any activities they didn't like, she wanted all the advance warning she could get. But she was also curious to see just how closely he was tied to the politics of the League, now that it was official. The new influx of trade would put serious demands on his people to enforce their customs and immigration policies, which were part of the Justice Ministry. *And I wonder what he knows about hinky numbers at Colon? They have their own security but there are still government officials checking the ships, crew and passengers. More unanswered questions.*

Chapter 19

Colon High Station, Pavo Real

Free stepped into their unofficial command center carrying a bag of takeout. His whole command staff plus Sparks were there, working on their terminals with furious intensity. He set the bag down and started setting out the containers of empanadas and assorted sides. Sparks jumped up to help but his boss waved him back to his terminal. "Finish what you're doing. I can handle food service for now."

Several minutes later, Vestry stood up and put his hands on the small of his back. "Damn, that smells good. And trust me, we've earned it."

McMannus gestured at the layout. "Load up and tell me what we've got."

As they got their food, Alanna displayed the familiar system map on the big screen. There were three X's in red on the map, all outside the asteroid belt they'd become familiar with over the last six months. Ezekiel used an empanada as a pointer.

"Alright. The Justice data has been thoroughly massaged and vetted. What you're seeing here are the official records of the three attacks on merchant vessels. They were all outbound to the jump gate when they were hit. They were all skillful takedowns, professional jobs that were executed quickly and quietly. I'd bet money we're looking at organized crime, not a resurgence of the rebels. Those miners only had one approach and it wasn't very subtle."

Harry nodded. "I can vouch for that. Those buggers had a very direct way of thinking and didn't worry too much about doing things cleanly."

"Very well. We believe that organized crime, not a resurgence of the rebels is causing problems in the system. Is this something we can leverage? I don't want to be a policeman but if they need us to take down pirates operating from hidden bases in the belt, that is something very much in our job jar."

Vestry considered the empanada. "I think the better question is, is it something we want to leverage? After all, we didn't exactly leave on the best of terms."

His daughter nodded in agreement. "They tried to screw us over, got caught and our final payment was made with ill-grace. I'm still going over the last supply delivery to see if they shorted us or gave us crap."

"Getting screwed over by the government was something we had to take in the Corps. Out here we don't have to take it. But what are our options, people?" McMannus leaned back in his chair, chewing slowly. "Besides, the boys and girls are getting antsy."

Ishido groaned. "That's putting it mildly. I've written up five people, including a corporal. And not even for serious charges but silly stuff like starting fights in the barracks, putting graffiti on the walls and running a gambling ring."

Mulongo looked up at that. "That's not serious?"

"They weren't gambling for money, Top," Ishido said. "Salazar would have been all over that. No, they were betting on astrilid races. You know, those things that look like a cross between a hamster and a lizard? The Grausians created them as pets for space travel because they adapt well to micro. Anyway, the troops were racing them and the winner got a place of honor in the barracks and bragging rights. People were spending money on costumes, trophies and other stuff like that and those because the things they were betting with. They even built a damned medal podium."

Alanna stifled a laugh while the Gunny just stared. "Just when I thought I'd seen everything," he mumbled.

Ezekiel tossed the remains of his meal back in the bag. "So we need some action for the kids before they go completely bugfuck. But is going back to the very people who tried to screw us a good idea?"

Everyone was quiet for a moment until Alanna cleared her throat. When her boss looked at her, she looked around at everyone before speaking. "I realize I'm the youngest and most inexperienced here, so maybe I'm speaking out of turn. But from a business perspective, we have something they want. We should be able to charge market price, as the saying goes. Maybe we should let them come to us first with a proposal? What they offer will tell us just how much they need us."

Harry grinned. "Oh, I like that. Newbie's got the right idea, Skipper. Let them dance to our tune for a change."

Vestry leaned over to tousle her hair. "And here I was wondering if you actually learned something in school."

She responded by slapping his hand away. "Knock it off, Dad. I'm not a kid anymore."

McMannus stood up abruptly. "No, you're not, Ms. Vestry. You are definitely thinking like a mercenary. Something the rest of us need to catch up to you on. Right. Harry, Ish, come up with something to burn off that excess energy. Maybe a wargame? Winner gets extra liberty and bragging rights, the loser gets latrine duty for a week."

Harry's eyes gleamed. "Suggestion, sir. Let's record it and offer copies to some high-ranking bigwigs. Let them see what we can do. Bit of advertising couldn't hurt. Especially when First gets its ass kicked."

Ishido rolled his eyes. "Dream on, pal. I've been running my guys through drills every day. We'll wipe the deck with you."

"I like it, Mr. Webb. Add that to your planning. Meanwhile, we have three other tasks. One, I'd like to draw up some terms we need to include in our contracts as standard boilerplate from now on. Lessons learned from our first contract. Ezekiel, you and Ms. Vestry draft those up and then we'll review. Two, we need to start planning for the upcoming trade conference. Harry's advertising can be one piece of that but we also need to be ready for any of these corporate types who come calling. Put together a standard dog and pony show for them. Mr. Webb, the video marketing was your idea so you get this one. And three, we need to continue to update our intelligence on the shipping losses in-system so we can evaluate any offer that comes to us with an actual threat assessment in hand. Ish, you've done that before so this one's yours."

He leaned forward, hands on the table and looked at each one. "We got lucky on our first contract. No casualties, we got paid and learned some valuable lessons that didn't cost us too much. But I don't want to rely on luck. Ms. Vestry can think outside the box easier than us right now because she's new to being a Marine. The rest of us need to unlearn some of those lessons that were pounded into us and start thinking like mercenaries, not government military types. That's the only thing that's going to keep us going and winning."

*****

Their maintenance shift completed, Jordan, Santis and Bennings stepped out of the lift onto the Colon Mercado Balboa. Hassan was on extra duty, having caught Salazar's attention one too many times. Taking up nearly an entire ring, the main commercial center of Colon High Station was active day and night. Since the port never shut down, neither did the merchants looking to take the spacer's money.

They immediately headed for the Loco Burro, the bar the Klowns had adopted as theirs. The locals had learned after a few weeks to check who was there before entering, although the passing ship's crews often didn't care. And for the most part, the Klowns left them alone. Unless, of course, some unkind things were said about Marines or mercenaries, in which the Klowns felt obliged to invite the offender outside for a spirited discussion on said topics.

The bar was mostly empty, except for a few spacers. It was still early for most shift workers, so the team settled down to enjoy their drinks. Or try to. Santis was still complaining about the maintenance work they had to do instead of going out and killing things.

Bennings sighed. "He ain't wrong. If I'm stepping out into the Black, I want it to mean something, not fucking scrub work."

Jordan nodded and took a sip of beer. "Yeah. If we wanted a civilian job with regular hours, we wouldn't have signed on here. Did you hear about the fight between Curtis and Sloane?"

"Yeah, Sloane's an ass and nobody likes the way he hums out of tune but Curtis didn't have to break his jaw."

Jordan took another swallow. "Things are only going to get worse unless we get another contract. The Old Man has to be planning something, I know. We've all heard the rumors of pirates in-system. Sooner or later, we're going to be tasked against them. I think that's why the lieutenant has us running all those drills. And did you take a close look at the supplies we off-loaded the other day?"

She looked at him over the top of her glass. "Didn't Baines tell you to stop thinking so much? You may get worried, but you end up bugging the shit out of the rest of us."

"I can't help it. One thought leads to another and then they start having little baby thoughts with each other."

"Speaking of little baby thoughts, how's Lucy doing?"

He leaned back, a goofy smile on his face and launched into a long description of feeling the baby move. Avery silently congratulated herself on getting his mind off his professional worries.

Chapter 20

Cassie stepped into the large conference room, bringing up the rear of the StellarMart team. The public relations effort really began after the deals were signed, so she was a background figure until that happened. That was just fine with her. She took a seat against the wall, in the middle where she had a good view of the whole room. Representatives from the other corporations filed in, human and alien alike, taking their seats at the table while their assistants took seats by the wall. At the front of the room, two members of the government team conferred in low voices over a laptop.

"*Audio visual check,*" whispered Selena in her ear. Cassie turned her head in small motion, the small camera in her glasses capturing the whole room on video feed and piping the data back to their suite.

"*Okay, that's good, Cassie. Running facial recognition now. I'll be able to let you know about anyone flagged as high interest as they pop up.*"

She sipped her tea and watched the room settle down as the heavy hitters filled up the table. These were the top sales and marketing people, heavy on the Illyrians, sent to impress and inform the locals on the benefits of partnering with their company. She could safely ignore the sales pitches and focus on the ones here who, like her, were not pitching a product but instead bringing other services.

There was a brief stir at the entrance and then a man and woman entered in military dress uniforms. They looked somewhat like the TUMC dress uniform but instead of a bright blue with gold braid, it was a more subdued navy blue with gray trim. Given they were the only military uniforms present, she suspected they were part of the 76th. The man was the older of the two by at least a decade; she barely looked out of college. He took a seat at the table and she sat behind him, along the wall.

"Fremont McMannus, Cassie. Popped up right away. Head of the mercenary company known as the 76th MIST. That's em eye ess tee, short for Microgravity Strike Team. Consists of former TU Marines, demobilized in 499 after the treaty was signed. Almost all of them chose to stay together and form their own company with Captain McMannus in command. They were previously in the employ of the Colon government for counter-insurgency operations in the asteroid belt. No active contract on record now."

She noticed that he paid little attention to the room, instead scanning through a document on a tablet held by his female counterpart and asking a question now and then. *Scoping out the next players in the arena? Looking for a new contract?*

The conference began with a welcome from their hosts and a speech from the trade minister. As the representatives of the corporations introduced themselves, Cassie used the opportunity to get a good look at each member of their teams. Selena would save their images to file and they could do a workup on them later.

"Okay Cassie. Here's the download on the mercs. They had a six-month contract with Pavo Real to deal with a minor rebellion in their orbital stations that was affecting commercial traffic. It just wrapped up a little over a month ago. Initial scan of the news reports say it was successful, with the mercs taking out most of the rebel leadership in one surgical strike. No new contract since then. The system has been quiet with no further incidents reported and no outstanding shipping insurance claims."

Cassie tapped out a message on her commpad. *###Mercs here for reason. Gov't reps don't mind. Find out why no new contract. Add to security topics and prep package for my mtg w/Justice###*

Across the room, Thomas Flatley watched the proceedings from the wall seats. As a market analyst, he didn't rate a chair at the table. That was fine, since he knew who was really running the show for Galactocity. More importantly, he had a direct line to Mr. Cross. It was his analysis which enabled their covert effort and that would put these frontier hicks on the defensive. They'd be ripe for the plucking by the marketing team, who would get the kudos publicly but he knew Mr. Cross would reward him personally.

So far, there was nothing new here for him. He didn't care what the other corporations were doing, as long as it didn't interfere with their own efforts. Flatley supposed some of them, maybe even all of them were running their own covert efforts but none were as ambitious or decisive as theirs. No, the only real fly in the ointment was that mercenary unit, the MIST. They could be a serious impediment to their operations if they weren't handled right. Beck said he had it handled but Thomas didn't get to where he was by relying on other people's analysis. He opened his tablet and began running searches on everything related to the TU Marine Corps, MIST units and one Fremont McMannus.

*****

The morning briefings ended at midday for lunch, which was a buffet-style affair with numerous standing tables where the diners could mix and mingle. Cassie walked casually among them, plate of finger food in hand, catching snippets of conversation here and there. Already, the corporate players were setting their hooks in the locals; promises of franchises, sole source contracts for materials and predictions of job growth. She'd heard it all before and ignored it. This wasn't what she was here for.

It wasn't until she passed a table of gloomy-looking people that she slowed her pace and perked her ears.

"I'm telling you, it's not just some lone wolf. I was there when Captain Patil recounted their capture to our adjusters. Those pirates knew what they were doing and were not screwing around." The human was wearing a regular business suit without any logos on it.

The Charee nodded. "I've got a cousin who works for the port authority. They should be on the watch for our lost cargoes but no official notices were issued. And he says that the unsavory elements on the station are throwing their weight around to keep things quiet. He's scared and he fought in the war. I think those crooks have decided that it's open season on us now."

The third, a Grausian, looked around. "Isn't that why they spent our taxes on those mercenaries? Shouldn't they be hiring them to do something about this?"

The human snorted. "Not likely. As far as I can tell, they don't have any ships of their own. And the government doesn't have anything to send either. No, I heard they hired a merchie like us to take them out to a suspected pirate base. Held a gun to the captain's head, too, so he would leave them stranded."

Cassie continued her stroll, this new bit of information running through her thoughts. It was only hearsay but it was another data point. This could affect consumer confidence and the government had to be seen doing something. *Are the MIST a professional outfit or were they a bunch of thugs in uniform? And what was this about piracy in this system? That wasn't in the dossier supplied.*

Stopping at an unoccupied table, she pulled out her commpad and sent a message to her team. *###Heard rumors about piracy in-system. Check gossip on the docks re: cargoes targeted. Crosscheck against insurance claims. Injuries? Which lines? How often? Top priority.###*

Selena replied almost instantly. *###On it. Lots in public pages on mercs. Still digging in govie databases. Sending public file now.###*

Cassie scanned the pages, looking for anything that stood out. Decorated TU unit, forced out after the treaty, stayed together and formed a private military organization. *Hmm.*

Interesting choice of careers. I wonder why? Didn't they get their fill of fighting in the Succession Wars?

Reading further brought her to Pavo Real, which was their first and only contract. She read the public releases with her PR lens. Past the effusive praise and standard news boilerplate, she saw there weren't reports of much actual combat. The station assault that resulted in the capture of most of the insurgency leadership had the most detail but was still maddeningly vague. All the news reports after that mentioned security work on the mining stations. The official news reports concluded that the key security provided by the mercenaries contributed to the end of the nascent insurgency effort. There was effusive praise for the Justice and Trade Ministries for having the foresight to bring in experts to deal with the terroristic threat posed by the insurgents. *Which continues to beg the question; if they were so successful, why are these combat-hardened Marines running around in the DMZ without a contract? Or did they become a bunch of thugs no better than those they fought?*

She searched the room, looking for Captain McMannus. He was the key to this. A man who could convince a hundred-odd Marines like Everett to drop everything and head out to the DMZ could be a force to be reckoned with. His actions would determine just how stable these markets would be for the foreseeable future. She spotted him near the front, engaged in conversations with several of the Colon station officials. Their discussions didn't seem to be too deep, so it was time to find out what she could.

As she crossed the room, her gait became daintier, and her face took on a vapid smile. She nodded and waved at people as she passed the tables, her course a straight shot at McMannus.

Timing her arrival at a natural pause in the conversation, she beamed her brightest smile at him. "Captain McMannus, could I steal just a teensy bit of your time?"

He smiled at her and nodded at the others, who drifted off. She held out her hand. "Cassandra Vickers, StellarMart Public Relations. But everyone calls me Cassie."

He turned to her and took the proffered hand with a gentle shake. She realized he was only about as tall as her own five foot eight. "A pleasure, Ms. Vickers. What can I do for StellarMart? By the way, my compliments to your communications division. We use their parts for our suit radios and the failure rate is extremely low. Very durable stuff you guys make."

She forced a blush and put her hand to her chest. "Please, just Cassie. And thank you, Captain! I'll make sure to pass on your feedback. I'm sure they'll be so glad to hear it! They were such a big part of the war effort. I remember reading in our last internal company newsletter that they're retooling for commercial communications equipment. But I'm sure we can still provide for your needs, Captain. After all, the military is still a valuable customer. My job as a public relations agent is to ensure our customers remain happy with our products. Perhaps I could set up a separate meeting to discuss your company's needs?"

"That would be most welcome, Ms. Vickers. Being on the far end of the supply chain can be a bit disconcerting."

"And we intend to change that, Captain! New trade routes and a steady flow of products to our new customers out here. Everyone can be part of the StellarMart family and enjoy the end of the war. It'll be so nice to step away from a full wartime footing, don't you think?"

He gave a small smile, making no attempt to hide his feelings about her statement. "The war with the Grausian Empire may be over for now but there are plenty of fights to be found here in the DMZ."

Putting on her shocked face, she laid a hand gently on his arm. "Oh, yes! I heard people talking about pirates in the system! Can you believe that? But I'm sure you can handle them, right?"

Fremont nodded and his smile warmed slightly. "Of course, Ms. Vickers. That's what we're here for."

Moving closer to him, she gushed, "I'm sure pirates are no match for an experienced unit such as yours! They're probably too scared to come after you. The government should be glad once again that you're here. After the way you helped end that nasty insurgency – which led to all of us being able to come here, by the way – you should be able to command your own price to deal with those nasty pirates."

His smile froze. "One would think, Ms. Vickers. One would think." The arrival of the young officer who accompanied him prevented further conversation as she announced it was time for his meeting.

Captain McMannus shook her hand briskly. "Nice to meet you, Ms. Vickers. I'm sure we'll see each other around."

As they left the room, Cassie messaged her team. *###Something happened w/76th contract with govt. Find out!!!###*

Her eyes narrowed as she considered his expression when she mentioned the insurgency. There was something else going on that both the government and the mercs weren't saying. Maybe it was nothing but if the 76th was going to be the linchpin to safe and secure trade in this system, she needed to know what had happened.

Free and Alanna entered an empty conference room about halfway down the corridor. Before closing the door, she glanced back the way they'd come. "You looked like you needed rescuing, sir."

"Not quite rescuing but your interruption was very welcome. That young lady was a little too much to take in at once. And now that I'm thinking about it, she was pressing pretty hard for some information."

Alanna stayed by the door. "Likely that glib-talking airhead routine is an act. These corporations aren't going to send the 'B' team to negotiate multimillion credit contracts. Better watch out for her."

"Crap. I was being polite and told her to come by and talk about our supply needs." He gave her an evil grin. "Guess that'll be up to you, Lieutenant."

She frowned and looked down. "Sir, if I may…"

Free tamped down his first reaction and nodded. "Go ahead, Ms. Vestry."

"I think my father should meet with her first. If she really has more designs than just selling products, he'll be able to ferret that out. He's taught me a lot but I just don't have the experience he does."

He thought about that and nodded slowly. "Very well. After our last negotiating experience, he and I talked about going into future ones with our eyes wide open. If Ms. Vickers is not what or who she says she is, your father is the best one to find that out. But I want you listening in, if not in the room. As my supply officer, you'll be doing your own negotiating, too."

"Copy that, sir. I trust myself against some local merchants where only a few thousand credits are on the line. When we start talking about millions, that's where I get nervous."

Chapter 21

Oliver walked through the casino doors and headed for the slots. He selected a machine at random and accessed the credit line he'd set up the day before. It took nearly ten minutes of mindless playing before his contact sat down beside him. Either the man hadn't spotted the other member of his team or didn't care. *Probably didn't spot him. These people may know how to steal but they don't know shit about tradecraft.*

As they both played their machines, the man spoke. His accent, a derivative of old Earth German, made him a bit difficult to understand. "Our arrangement is off to good start. All ships on list visited and we get the cargoes. Good money for them. First time doing big jobs across several systems. Challenging but boss is happy with arrangement. When can we expect next targets?"

"Tell your boss I'm happy they're happy. My people will deliver the next target list shortly."

"Justice is getting involved. Watching ships, watching people. They know us, know our people. Could be hard getting manifests. Will be problem soon, maybe even slow down the jobs. How you want to handle?"

"What I want is results for the job I hired you for. I made it clear I wasn't going to be paying them off and I wasn't going to tolerate any interference, from Justice or anyone else. I picked your group because I thought you had a way to handle the heat. Was I incorrect in my assessment?"

"No. We can handle it. We just think you would be concerned about how."

Oliver stood up and turned to go. "The only thing that concerns me is a slowdown in operations. We can handle getting the cargo data to lower your profile. Meanwhile, do what you've been paid to do and handle Justice in your own way. As long as you continue to deliver results, that's all that matters to me."

*****

Oliver left the seedy casino and headed for the nicer section of the station. It was now time to work the other side of the plan. Entering an upscale restaurant, he sat down at the bar next to Flatley and ordered a soda water with lime. The analyst frowned. "No drinking on duty?"

"Something like that. My work doesn't mix well with lowered inhibitions."

"Ah, yes. Okay. Sorry."

The larger man waved off the apology. "Our contractors are concerned that Justice is starting to interfere. I told them to handle the situation in their own way. I expect the results will be messy and public and probably start either tomorrow or the day after."

Thomas nodded. "It will cause an uproar and people will become worried about security. The news about the pirate attacks is already making the rounds among the participants. When it becomes clear that law enforcement is powerless, it'll increase the uncertainty among the other corporations. I'll pass the word to our team that things will be unsettled soon so we're ready to exploit any gaps."

The bartender arrived with the soda water and they paused their conversation until he had moved away. Beck sipped at his drink and stared at the mirror behind the bar, watching the crowd for several seconds. "I have to travel to the other systems and talk with our people out there, see what progress they've made. Unfortunately, operational security prevents any significant exchange of data via ansible. Before I go, how did the first day of the conference go? Are there any problems with the other attendees?"

"None so far. It's early yet. They're still feeling their way around the situation, I think. Any sign that others were here ahead of us?"

"Nope. The station people we have on the payroll haven't reported anything, at least."

"That mercenary unit you mentioned was at the conference yesterday. And they're going to be presenting towards the end."

"Oh? What were they doing?"

Thomas frowned. "Nothing, as far as I could tell. Just listened to the presentations and talked with some of the presenters. There didn't appear to be any serious conversations or the start of negotiations. There's no report of them being back on contract with the government, or with anyone for that matter. The fact that they're presenting could mean they're in the market for a new contract. Curious situation."

Beck tossed back the last of his drink and stood. "Hell, I don't care if they sit around with their thumbs up their asses for the next hundred years. As long as they stay out of our way."

*****

Cassie entered their suite and kicked off her shoes with a sigh. Vera looked up briefly from the couch and nodded a greeting before turning back to her screen. She had set up a double-headed display and was working between different spreadsheets on each one. Selena was no doubt working in her own room and Cassie let her be, choosing instead to get a sparkling water from the refrigerator. She leaned back against the kitchen counter and took a swallow, eyes shut.

"Rough day at school?" Vera's fingers kept clicking away as she spoke and her eyes didn't leave the screens.

"First day is the most fun; meeting all the players involved and seeing where their starting positions are. It's the second day that's always tiring. Now that you know who is who, you have to plan who to talk to, who needs to see you talking to them and watch who they're talking to. There's a lot of maneuvering for positions even though you're not sure which position is best and lots of doublespeak. My brain is fried."

"And just think, you get to do it again for the rest of the conference."

"Lucky me. Hopefully armed with the information I've asked my minions to get for me."

Vera smiled. "I'm pretty sure the webmistress was successful in her searches. I could hear lots of cackling and promises of doom through the door. As for myself, I haven't been quite as successful. I've run some additional analysis on the packet we got from corporate, trying to figure out who and what the other corps will go after. That's already in your inbox. Now I'm back to the profit/loss for this station. I still think there's something off here and I have a hunch it's going to be important. Otherwise, why go through so many cutouts to conceal it?"

Cassie shrugged and capped the bottle. "I trust you'll figure it out. Janik down at the docks?"

"Yep. He said don't wait up for him. I'm guessing he'll be working the bars tonight. He's after the info you wanted on the losses to the pirates. Maybe he'll learn something that can help me."

"Baby steps, Vera. This conference is two weeks long. No need to rush things. Okay, time to visit the webmistress and find out what she knows."

"Oh, she knows everything. She's very fond of pointing that out. Good luck."

The door opened to Cassie's knock and a gloved hand beckoned her to enter the dimly lit room. "Gimme a few seconds to back out of this search. I went down quite a few rabbit trails and I just want to wrap up those loose ends."

Cassie found a chair and sat with a sigh. When Selena was deep in her information web, she ran on her own time. Patience was required to extricate her. This time it was a welcome break and she leaned back, trying to turn her brain off.

After several minutes, Selena pushed her googles back on her head. "Okay, boss lady. I take it you want that info you pinged me on?"

"Yes, if you have it."

"If I have it? Boy, do I have it! Where do I have it? Hang on." She slipped her goggles back on. Seconds later, a display came to life and files began to open. Cassie moved to stand next to the screen as text and images popped to life.

"Okay. Item the first, where the 76th is on their contract. They don't have one. Or rather, they don't have a contract that leverages their military skill set. Right now, they're working in the Colon maintenance yard, performing ship repairs and refits. A scan of multiple sources shows a distinct lack of need in the surrounding systems for a professional military company specializing in microgravity operations."

"And why didn't they hire back with Pavo Real? I got the distinct impression from their boss there was something between the government and them but are things bad enough to sour business?"

"Hard to say. They completed their contract successfully and ended the insurgency. Like I told you before, no complaints by either side in court or in the press. There is some negative press from some liberal elements in other systems that the mercs used excessive violence, especially in the execution of their prisoners."

"They executed prisoners? I'd think there'd be more than negative press."

"Well, they didn't exactly execute them. The government held trials in absentia while the mercs were still in transit back with the prisoners. The courts convicted the prisoners and sentenced them to death within a matter of hours. A law enforcement officer with the mercs carried out the sentence and the mercs were used to prevent the prisoners from escaping their fate." Selena called up the video from the freighter and played it.

Cassie nodded as she watched. "Oh, I can see how that could be interpreted. Very good use of framing and positioning. It looks like the mercs are somehow responsible for the execution. And the voice track is well done. Says the proper and legal things, taking credit for enforcing the laws while making it seem like their hands are clean."

"Eggsactly. All done proper and legal by the government, even if it seems unethical. Which probably explains why the mercs are keeping their distance from Pavo Real and hiding up here. They probably don't have the money to leave the system. And where would they go?"

"Their boss is going to present on the next to last day of the conference. A promotional pitch, maybe? They don't seem to be desperate for work just yet."

"Should I take a look at their finances? Maybe a few inquiries on their expenditures?"

Cassie shook her head. "Let's not run the risk of irritating the people with the big guns. And speaking of big guns, that takes me to my second research task. What's this about pirate activity? Why wasn't it in our read ahead packets?"

"New information, boss lady. Only a couple of weeks old. Publicly, there are reports about three different ships from different lines hit. All local, meaning not Terran corporate. However, by digging through some of the financials and I'm waiting for Janik to confirm a few things, I think there's been at least seven vessels hit. And not just in this system but the other members of this new Denovo League."

"Not everyone's reporting being hit, hmm? Lack of insurance? Lack of confidence in the government doing anything?"

"Maybe a bit of both. Here's another curious point. Almost no injuries and no deaths. Whoever is behind these attacks is definitely more interested in cargo than in mayhem."

Cassie sat back down. "That could be an implied threat. Don't report us and we won't hurt you later."

"That too. If so, it seems to be working."

"Okay, this gives me an angle to work on the government side. As profit-hungry corporate types, we would be interested in anything that would threaten our bottom-line.

An unstable security situation definitely falls into that bucket."

"And in the course of your maneuvering, find out why they haven't hired the 76th? Sneaky."

"It's the obvious question, isn't it? We need to make these pieces of the puzzle fit together. The competition is going to find out about the pirate activity sooner or later. That'll get them jumpy. Depending on what I learn about the local plans to deal with the threat, I might even leak the info myself. Then we know when they know and start the ball rolling on our terms. Either way, we get to be ahead of the pack depending on what we learn."

The hacker cackled from her chair. "I love watching you in action! Okay, what else do you need to be magnificent out there?"

Reenergized, Cassie pulled out her tablet and began going over her notes. Her meetings tomorrow just got more interesting and had new strings to pull on. With any luck, one of those strings would trigger a reaction she could use.

Chapter 22

The next morning, Cassie walked out of the station manager's office, her face locked down on a corporate smile. Only when the elevator doors closed did she allow herself a small smile of triumph. Mr. Variela and his boss were well versed in the doublespeak that pervaded bureaucracies everywhere but she had learned from the best in the Union on how to read between the lines. The station manager was clearly out of his depth in matters of interstellar economies and station operations. He was a politician, more used to boardroom discussions about abstractions. Felix let slip a few things and his body language on her questions pointed towards more involvement in the day-to-day workings of a major economic hub.

Which confirms some of Vera's suspicions. A station with this many jump points would have more than its fair share of smuggling and that always sticks to greedy fingers. Felix either cooks the books to hide the fact or provides bureaucratic cover to the various operations on station. I'd guess the latter. He doesn't seem smart enough to be on Vera's level.

The elevator took her down, past the Mercado Balboa and hotel levels to the docks. Janik had sent her a message and she needed to meet with him. He was working these docks so he couldn't just break away. She stopped at a ladies' room to remove most of the makeup needed for corporate-level drone interactions, leaving just enough to show she had made an effort in the morning. Her jacket was reversible and she switched it around to the plainer side. The heels came off the shoes with a twist and went into the jacket pockets.

She left the restroom looking like a minor office worker, complete with datapad and perpetually worried expression. A few minutes search brought her to Janik's dock and some choice invectives shouted across the bay over misfiled paperwork got him away from the crowd.

She pretended to show him the datapad, adding in a few emphatic gestures. "What did you find out about the pirates?"

His expression was one of exasperation but his words were more chilling. "That they're not pirates in the usual sense. Just like the rest of civilization, this station has its own crooks. Most do smuggling or data brokering and have been since the Grausian rule. It's a part of business here and well organized. I was told within hours of starting work who I would pay for protection and what the standard rate was."

He supplied his own theatrics to hers while continuing. "Just over a week ago, someone new came on the scene. They set up an exclusive arrangement with one gang, the Hoffmans, to hit specific ships. All of us on the docks were told not to look too closely at anyone checking manifests."

She gave him a final wave of her hands. "Great. We'll talk more tonight. See what else you can find out about this mysterious new player. See you back at the rooms." Stalking off, she projected the very image of a pissed-off, overworked clerk but her mind was adding what she'd just learned to the other facts. This trade conference was becoming a lot more intriguing by the day and the addition of unexpected players was making her life more complicated.

*****

Around Colon, groups of station security personnel accompanied by Justice agents made polite and not so polite inquiries on the usual suspects. Doors were sometimes forced and there were a few chases through the corridors and passages. Ships were impounded and searched and while some contraband was found, it wasn't what the Justice agents were looking for.

Through it all, the Hoffman leadership watched and measured. It was obvious the old arrangements with their contacts in the Ministry of Justice were either no longer in effect or the people on their payroll were not effective in controlling the investigation. That was bad but survivable.

The losses incurred by the investigation were minor compared to what they were being paid to attack the merchants, not to mention the monies received for the fencing of the stolen cargoes. But acts like this could not be allowed to continue and those whom they paid to ensure it wouldn't happen needed to be punished. To do otherwise would be bad for business and as noted, had the potential to interfere with future profits.

Plans were discussed and a way ahead decided upon. There had been arrangements with Justice agents and leadership before and arrangements could be made again. Once, of course, the Hoffmans were back in an acknowledged position of power. Meanwhile, the Ministry of Justice would be taught a lesson in the use of power.

*****

Back in their rooms later that evening over dinner, Janik laid out in more detail what he had learned. "There are three main gangs here on Colon. The smallest group are the Ghost Dragons, who focus on running the gambling action Next are the Black Suns, who control the prostitution and drug trafficking. But first and foremost are the Hoffmans. They control all the other types of action. Nothing happens on this station without their fingers in it. The other two pay them for the privilege of operating here. It sounds like they've been in the business since the Grausians established the station. Oh and Selena, the Hoffmans have significant cyber capability. They do the majority of the information brokering for several systems."

Selena nodded. "Fits with what I've seen so far. There's a well-organized information gathering effort on the networks, which means someone here eventually learns anything that's on the network. And that information then goes up for sale."

"I suspect the Hoffmans have quite a few station people in their pockets, then. We all know how private information can be used to align people to your will." Cassie picked up the glass of wine and stared into it. "So we have an active criminal element influencing the security of the region. Not entirely unexpected, although perhaps the level of insecurity is more than what we'd like."

Standing, Vera began to clear the table. "It's just another factor in the calculations. Payoffs and accommodations with criminals are part of doing business. Some people just hide their criminal activities better than most. Whoever ends up with contracts out here will figure out how to make it more profitable to not attack ships. They always do."

Nodding, Cassie leaned back in her chair. "And if that's us? How do we make it more profitable to leave our ships alone?"

Vera placed the dishes in the sink. "One thing at a time, Cassie. We have to win the contracts first."

"Yes, we do. And lowballing our costs without taking into account the losses to criminal activity will not be looked upon kindly by senior management. If the customer isn't going to tell us how bad things are here, how do we find out?"

Selena poked chopsticks at her. "You have an idea, boss lady. I can hear the gears turning."

Cassie smiled and sipped at her wine again. "Maybe I do. Thanks to my ever-so-helpful minions, we know about an organization that has had experience with instability in the Pavo Real system and dealt with it. I think tomorrow I should take the good Captain McMannus up on his offer to come by and visit. And maybe make them an offer that looks irresistible to someone who is currently unemployed."

*****

Free did his best to assist Aileen in prepping dinner but they got in each other's way enough she finally shooed him out. "I appreciate the help but I got this. You set the table and open the wine."

"Aye aye, ma'am."

"Are you going to attend the rest of the conference?"

"No real need until our presentation at the end. I met with the people Ezekiel said might have some work but nothing panned out. The rest of the conference is supposed to be their pitches to the government and station bosses and then contract negotiations. Nothing really that interesting for us."

She handed him a platter and turned to get the rest. "Well, it would be nice to know who's leading the pack. For future planning purposes."

He laughed. "Why Aileen O'Connell. Are you asking me to collect insider information for you?"

She walked over to the small table and set her dish down with a casual motion. "Of course not, Captain McMannus. I would never dream of involving an upstanding Marine such as yourself in any impropriety."

He put his dish down and gathered her in his arms. "Well, as it happens, I'm not in the Terran Union Marine Corps any longer. I'm a mercenary and we are well known for our improprieties."

"Is that so? Well, maybe I can convince you later to do some insider investigations."

"There would have to be a very good incentive. We mercenaries care a lot about the bottom line."

Their kiss was interrupted by an incoming call on the circuit Free had Sparks put in for 76th business. He sighed and unfolded himself from Aileen's arms. "McMannus here."

"Sergeant Kodala, sir. We got that Agent Drusk on the line. Says it's real important she talk to you, in person. Told her you were off duty for the night but she's insistent. Real nervous in the service, like."

Aileen nodded and started to leave but Free motioned her to stay. "You're part of the unit now. You can hear this stuff."

She sat and he nodded to Sergeant Kodala. "Put her through."

Drusk looked terrible. Her skin was gray and her eyes were haunted. She spoke like she was keeping control with an iron will. "Captain McMannus, thank you for taking my call. I assure you it's important."

"Of course, Agent Drusk. What can I do for you?"

"The Chief Marshal is coming to Colon and would like to meet you tomorrow morning, first thing. Justice would like to discuss a contract with the 76th."

Alanna was right. "Not a problem. I'd like to bring my intelligence and supply officers with me, if that's okay. And so we can come prepared with the right kinds of paperwork, just what kind of contract would this be? Security again? Training?"

"We need you for direct action, Captain. About three hours ago, someone struck multiple Justice offices and at least two small craft. We have seventeen injured civilians and three dead agents." She shook her head and took a deep breath. "We know who it is, Captain. We just don't have the firepower or the training to go after them."

Free nodded in sympathy. "Very well, Agent Drusk. Direct action won't be cheap, though. And it tends to be very messy."

"Understood, Captain. But either we respond to these *pendejos* in kind or we're done as a valid law enforcement agency. The Justice Minister himself approved this contract and says you can have what you need to see it done right."

"Very well. We'll see you in the morning."

After the call disconnected, he turned to Aileen. "Well, that was probably a bit more than I wanted to expose you to right off the bat."

She nodded grimly. "Brings back some memories of the early days of the Collapse. You never knew when a Grausian fleet was going to pop into the system. But I guess these guys aren't in that league. I mean, who goes after cops except criminals?"

McMannus nodded. "That's who we think has been acting up lately. Pirate actions have increased in the last couple of weeks and they're good. We were wondering if the government was going to bring us in to handle them. Looks like they waited too late."

Aileen started to eat and nodded at Free to do the same. "Think if the 76th gets involved that we'll be targets next?"

His fork froze halfway to his mouth. "Shit."

She smiled. "You have a way with words, honey. Eat your dinner, it's getting cold. We'll solve that issue tomorrow."

Chapter 23

As soon as Free, Ezekiel and Alanna returned to the 76th area from their meeting with Marshal Thisk, he ordered the duty guards into their MACE armor. To Harry, Ishido and Mulongo, he said, "We are now at increased force protection levels, gentlemen. All access to our areas will be through this main entrance. Secure and seal all other entrances and place cameras on them. No one is to leave our spaces alone; minimum two personnel together, preferably more. We'll also need to put a standing guard on the dependent living quarters."

Ishido made the necessary notations to the duty log and Mulongo called up the additional guards for the quarters and the front. Harry gave a low whistle. "That bad, sir?"

Ezekiel downloaded his notes to their file system. "That bad, Mr. Webb. You've seen the reports on what happened to the Justice people and offices. As of today, we are on contract with Justice, only they're not going to advertise that right away. That'll give us an element of surprise, we hope. We should be getting a massive data download soon from their intelligence people on the known criminal organizations on Pavo Real and Colon; people, locations, capabilities. They also have footage of some of the suspects and they're currently matching them against known gang associations."

"At some point, once our employers come up with a target list, we're going to hit them. Justice wanted us out there tomorrow but we managed to talk some sense into them. Mostly because I promised when we did hit them, we'd come down like a ton of battle steel." He paused, looking around. "These aren't soldiers we're going up against. These scum used firebombs on offices, kidnapped and spaced agents and threatened families. Those insurgents were playing games and got spanked for their efforts. This time, we're going to show these people what it means to truly go to war."

*****

Cassie stepped out of the lift into a short hallway that led to an airtight door. Two armored Marines stood guard outside the door and their blank visors and bulky exoskeletons were imposing as hell. They were both armed with a short-barreled automatic weapon but thankfully neither were pointed at her. One of them stepped forward and held out a hand, palm out. A metallic voice issued forth from the suit speakers androgynous in its computer-modulated tones. "I'm sorry, ma'am but entry to this level is restricted. No unauthorized personnel."

She stopped and slowly raised her personal commpad. The screen flashed with her business card. "Good morning. I'm Cassandra Vickers, StellarMart Public Relations. I'd like to speak to your commander, please. I have some business to discuss with him."

"Wait there, ma'am. I'll call for someone."

Both guards went still for several seconds and then the one who spoke to her said, "Very well, ma'am. An escort will arrive for you shortly. Please leave your personal weapons with us."

Cassandra smiled gaily. "Oh, I'm not armed."

The head cocked slightly, as much as the armored helmet would allow. "Ma'am, you have a four-inch blade in the cuff of your left boot. And a steel wire wrapped in your belt. Would you please remove them?"

Her smile faded, to be replaced with an ironic grin. "That's a fair exchange of information, I guess?" She slowly bent down and even more slowly removed the holdout blade from her boot. Then she undid her belt, again with exaggerated slowness. Holding both out, she waited for the Marine to take them.

"Exchange?"

"She means we both learned something about each other, Private Hendrickson." The man who came through the door was older, in his fifties with graying hair. He was dressed in casual business attire and appeared to be unarmed. "Ezekiel Vestry, Ms. Vickers. I'm here to escort you."

"Mr. Vestry. Very nice to meet you." She silently cursed herself for her smugness. Of course someone would be monitoring the entry! Now he knew two things about her and she knew nothing about him. With a silent sigh, she followed him through the open door and into a small room with a computer terminal. He keyed a code in and indicated for her to place her commpad next to the terminal.

"I manage the contracts for the company and thus have the best understanding of the corporate mind. This will register your pad and establish you as an authorized visitor while you're in our area, Ms. Vickers. Please stay with a 76th escort at all times and don't try to enter any doorway which doesn't open for you."

She smiled brightly as she took her commpad back and followed him into the hallway. "Why Mr. Vestry, you act like you think I'm going to spy on you! I'm just here for a business meeting with the premier mercenary unit in the DMZ and to make sure we have a good working relationship."

He smiled back at her, with just a hint of irony in it to tell her he saw through her act. "Of course, Ms. Vickers. Just our standard security protocols. I'm sure you understand. Now, Captain McMannus will be tied up for a while longer, so I'm here in his stead."

They entered a small conference room and he waved her to a chair. "And it should go without saying that any information about our current status and readiness is only available to prospective employers. Are you here in that capacity, Ms. Vickers?"

She decided to keep to the corporate drone facade with Vestry. There was something entirely too sharp about him. "Cassie, please, Mr. Vestry. And not right now. StellarMart has no policy set for the employment of private military contractors for this market, so I'm afraid we won't be looking to hire you in that particular capacity just yet."

"Ezekiel, then. What can we do for you, if you're not looking for some door-kickers?"

She cocked her head and gave him a confused smile. "Door-kickers?"

"A military idiom. It means soldiers, marines in our case, especially ones who are trained in forcible entry operations."

"I see. Well, Ezekiel, I'm part of an advance party from StellarMart working with the local system government to open the markets here in the DMZ. Now that the war is over and industry is making the shift away from military production, we'd like to expand our customer base and the worlds out here are ideal candidates." She gave him her best public relations smile, full of promise and enthusiasm. "However, our board felt that an assessment of the local government's ability to provide security and the status of the current private security firms was also in order, given the unstable nature of this region. Union military patrols are still getting started and they're mostly focused on watching the other races. And that nasty business that just made the news has us concerned, as well."

He nodded. "Perfectly understandable. And you came to us because we concluded the anti-insurgency operations and you want our assessment on the security of the Pavo Real system."

Damn, he's good. "Why yes, Ezekiel. My, it's so nice working with a professional. As the face of StellarMart in this region, my Public Relations department would so love to reassure the public of an uninterrupted flow of StellarMart goods and services and stable prices. Would you be able to help us understand the current security situation and what could be done to help stabilize it?"

"Cassie, don't you think that's the job of the government? Public safety and security are their responsibility."

She leaned forward in her chair and put on an earnest face. *Time to bait the hook and see if he bites.* "Ezekiel, I've done my homework. The system government wouldn't have hired you if they could reassure the public of their safety of this system on their own. No, what I'm looking for is the facts behind the scenes. As the door-kickers, as you put it, you're the ones in the best position to assess a threat and the response needed for it."

"And if the government disagrees with our assessment?"

"Not your problem. We would be your customer. You're not currently working for the government, are you?"

"I'm afraid I can't provide any information on our current contract or future negotiations."

Very smooth. "In any case, we would be looking for information from both of you. The government has one take on the situation, informed by their politics and desire to grow their own system. Your take on the situation is less biased towards the existing elements here but also focused on a specific solution. Two sides of the equation, as it were. Just think of it this way; StellarMart is willing to pay for a professional analysis from experts in the field."

"I see. So you're not hiring military contractors but you are willing to pay them for their opinions?"

Come on, little fishy. Take the nice bait. "If you like. It's not like you'd have to do work you aren't already doing. What is the likelihood of an attack on a particular ship or company, what goods are being targeted, what countermeasures would be needed to handle the threat. That sort of thing."

He stood and paced to the front of the room. "We don't come cheap. A thorough security analysis is going to cost you. And can you funnel that kind of funds to a mercenary company without questions being asked that might be challenging to answer?"

"Perhaps payment in kind instead. A little quid pro quo, if you will. Shall we start with a discounted rate on munitions and supplies in exchange for the information we're seeking?"

He gave her a broad smile. "Now we're talking business. What kind of discounts are you thinking of?"

Twenty minutes later, she and Vestry had hammered out the basic terms of their exchange. She sent it off to Vera to prepare the contract and waited for it to come back. Vestry sat behind the terminal and began to gather the information they bargained for.

As he worked, Cassie took a deep breath and let the corporate persona slip a bit. "Ezekiel, would you mind if I asked you about something else? Something not related to this contract or in fact, not related to StellarMart at all?"

He looked up from the terminal. There was no expression on his face but his eyes bored into hers. "That's a rather unusual request, Cassie. But you can ask."

"It's about my brother. He was a Marine in the war. He survived but we don't know where he is."

"I see. And you think because we're a former Marine outfit we would know him?"

She blushed. "Not exactly. Everett, that's my brother, he always said that the Marines were different from the other services. Marines tend to stick together, he said. I was wondering if maybe you had heard about him since you arrived out here. The last we knew he was heading into the DMZ."

Ezekiel nodded but frowned. "The name doesn't ring a bell with me but I'm former Navy. However, I will ask Captain McMannus if he knows anything about your brother."

"Thank you. He used to be a staff sergeant. Everett Vickers is his name. If anyone in the 76th knows anything about him, I'd appreciate the opportunity to talk to them. As I said, this is personal. Nothing to do with StellarMart."

"We'll see what we can do, Cassie."

She left the 76th without meeting Captain McMannus but she had in her possession a data chip with the latest intelligence they had on potential criminal organizations and other 'unstable elements', as Vestry had put it. She also had a healthy respect for Ezekiel Vestry's bargaining skills. Of course, she hadn't come quite prepared to negotiate a contract but opportunity was knocking here. Now she had something more to go on for leverage. And maybe she would learn something about Ev.

*****

"Well, Ezekiel, how is StellarMart these days?"

Vestry didn't look up from the terminal he and Alanna were working on. They were adjusting the budget based on the projected prices from the StellarMart contract. "StellarMart is the same as any corporation, sir. Always concerned about the bottom line. Ms. Vickers is another case entirely, however."

McMannus leaned against the doorjamb. "I take it she's not just another pretty face in a business suit?"

"Oh no. Not in the slightest." He turned to look at the younger man, a broad smile on his face. "She reminds me of me, in some ways. If that young lady isn't an operative of some kind, I'll eat this terminal."

"Should we be worried about her being in our area, then?"

"I had the rooms swept after she left. Nothing. No, I don't think we have to worry too much about her right now. She has larger fish to fry; namely, the bureaucrats and policy makers on the worlds they're going after. I suspect the intel she gathers on us will become part of a larger portfolio, as they look to get the exclusive rights to the markets in this system and others."

"That confirms what I was seeing in the briefings the other day. It looks like a major marketing push is about to start in this region. What does that mean for us?"

"This puts a new light on the piracy actions. These corporate types are always watching the bottom line. Unexpected losses and unstable markets tend to make them nervous. I wish we'd had this information before we renegotiated with Justice but we got the best deal we could with the information we had. I'll slip a few words in the right ears here on Colon that a station security contract might not be a bad idea to help reassure people. A place like this will be central to everyone's business. The amount of tonnage transshipped and stored, as well as the business on station will be a significant factor in everyone's bottom line."

"It's about time we started getting more options out here. I'd rather have to turn down contracts than beg for them." He gave the older man a wink. "I would say keep on this but I think you would anyway. Ms. Vickers really lit a fire under you, didn't she?"

"Professionally, yes. Like I said, I see some of me in her. It'll be a good challenge for me to keep up with her. See if I still got it."

Alanna muttered under her breath, "If you're talking about a swelled head, then yes, you've still got it."

He blew her a raspberry. "You just watch your old man run circles around that young pup. She won't know what hit her."

She stood up from the terminal and pulled her tablet from the dock. "The only thing that hits her will be the smell of your nasty old man cologne. Captain, I have the StellarMart order ready for your signature. I was able to increase our munitions purchases by twenty-five percent and secure spare parts suitable for the MACE suits."

He held out his hand for the tablet. "The good news just keeps on coming. This is very timely, as Drusk just messaged me with our first mission. They want to set traps for the pirates and identified four freighters outbound from the gate in the next few days that would be likely targets. They've examined the manifests and picked the ones with the most expensive cargoes. They wanted to send out everyone on these ships but with our new contract language in place I refused within the terms of the contract. Instead, I'm sending out two squads from each platoon."

The intelligence officer frowned. "What happens if they get into more trouble than they can handle?"

"That's the second part. Both Harry and Ish will rotate quick reaction force duties on a Justice patrol ship, stationed here. First sign of trouble, they burn for that location. And that lets me keep two squads plus the command element for local security." He looked at Alanna. "And you get to further your education. Since you didn't get to go to Infantry School or Basic Microgravity, you will accompany one of the QRF squads as a supernumerary to whoever's in command. A little on-the-job training in commanding a unit and practice operating in micro."

Alanna nodded once, her face expressionless except for her eyes, which danced in excitement. "Aye aye, sir."

He then pointed a finger at Vestry. "You, mister intelligence professional, get to work on figuring out where these pirates are getting their intel. Justice has a minimal presence here on Colon. Drusk is here temporarily, so you can probably liaise with her. But…"

The older man nodded. "The insider threat is the biggest unknown in any situation. The fewer people we let know, the easier it is to control."

Turning to go, Ezekiel paused. "There was something else, at the end. Ms. Vickers asked if we knew anything about her brother. Seems he was a Marine who disappeared into the DMZ either during or after the war. I said I would ask around to see if anyone knew him."

"That's an odd request. I assume you didn't promise anything."

"Just that I would ask. If anyone does know him, she'd like to talk to them."

"What's his name?"

"Everett. Everett Vickers."

McMannus paused, his face fixed. "Well, now. That's a new twist."

"You know this guy?"

"I know the story behind it. So does the Gunny. Staff Sergeant Vickers was caught in a very interesting situation and got court-martialed because of it. So he escaped detention, huh?" There was a bit of admiration in his voice.

"Sir, please don't keep information from your intelligence officer."

"When we're done with this situation, Mr. Vestry. I'll talk with the Gunny and platoon leaders about this. I don't know where Staff Sergeant Vickers is currently but if she is his sister, the Corps owes the family. See if you can verify her identity and relationship, please."

*****

Ezekiel tapped on the notification bell on Alanra's quarters. She opened the door and raised her eyebrows.

"Coming to see if I'm going to bed at a reasonable time?"

"No. I'm past that. Trying to keep you from reading in bed was a losing bet. And there were worse things you could be doing, especially once you got older." He paused. "Can I come in?"

"Oh! Yeah, come on in. I'm just double checking my kit for deployment."

He stopped inside the doorway, taking in the scene in front of him. His daughter had laid out everything on the table and couch in an orderly fashion. He wasn't familiar with Marine gear but knowing her, it was likely by the book. And then some.

She stood in the middle of the room, frowning at the neat little piles. "I know I got everything from the manual. Ish will quiz me on that but Harry is likely to ask me off-the-wall questions to see if I'm thinking outside the box. Especially since the Captain keeps pointing out that I'm the best at it. But I think–"

"Alanna." He said it with enough volume to get her attention. "Sit, please."

She smiled as she sat, nerves finally coming to the front. "It's the Captain, right? He's decided he needs me here more, right? I'm not going?"

Her father sat across from her. "You're going. That hasn't changed. The Captain knows you need more experience and this is a good, low-threat opportunity. But low threat doesn't mean no threat. A scared opponent can still get a lucky shot and those MACEs aren't impervious."

Pausing, Ezekiel gathered his own thoughts. "I guess what I came here to say is, don't take chances. Please be as careful as you can."

She looked around at the gear scattered throughout the room. "It doesn't seem real, does it? When they pulled my commission, I thought I'd never serve in uniform again. Let alone deploy as a Marine. And now…"

"Now you're scared but don't want to admit it?"

She drew in a shaky breath. "It shows that much, does it?"

He shook his head. "Honey, we're all scared on that first mission. My first combat assignment came after I'd been in for several years already and I was still scared shitless. There we were, going into action against the Grausians to get free of their rule. I was on the flagship, one of the heaviest ships we had and I had a hard time getting enough spit to swallow when the action started."

She stared down at her hands. "I remember Mom watching the news feeds all the time, trying to see what was happening."

"At least I'm here and can see you off." He reached out and took her hands. "I have no worries about you doing your job. I just want you back safe. Listen to Ish and Harry, pay attention to what's around you and don't take unnecessary chances."

Smiling, she squeezed his hands. "I promise, Poppa."

Chapter 24

Cassie sat at the cafe, sipping on an espresso and watching the crowd. The Mercado Balboa was central to the business section and open twenty-four hours a day. The crowds ebbed and flowed but a place like Colon was never quiet. Her tablet told her it was the equivalent of a late night but you would never know it from the hustle and bustle of the place.

So many people passing through here. So many lives on display. Was Ev here now? Or had he passed through here before? Without staring at them, she noted the cameras that watched busy corridors and storefronts. All that data, recorded by the station. She reached a decision and picked up her tablet and earpiece.

Selena answered on the fourth ring. "Sorry boss lady. I was busy with some sniffers on my trail and didn't see your call. Whassup?"

She spoke with care. "Selena, in addition to your other searches, I'm adding a specific person to your list. Sending a picture now."

"Sure, what's one more… Cassie. Umm, is he involved?"

"No. But Oscar said it was okay to use you guys for this. As long as it doesn't interfere with your primary data gathering activities."

"Nope. I can set up some automated searches, since all I'm looking for is a rough match. It will at least tell us if he's been here."

"Good. Thank you. And I promise, this has been cleared with the right people."

"Cassie. I trust you. You don't have to say any more. Besides, I should have thought of this myself."

She clicked off and sighed.

*****

The Hoffman hacker tapped his foot in time with the music coming through his earbuds. The others in his section might go for technopop nonsense but he preferred the classics. Everything old Earth had to offer from the masters, he made sure he found it. Sometimes, he imagined himself as their contemporary, his fingers on his keyboard like theirs on the piano. They created wonderful music while he created.... Well, he didn't really create the data. He just found what he was told to find and put together the file on the targets he was given by his seniors in Hoffman.

A notification pinged on his screen. His primary responsibility was searching the station video records for whomever was sought. That included finding someone before anyone else. This meant he needed to know when someone else was looking for people he was looking for.

A few commands and he was in the station archives. Everything seemed normal at first glance but his tripwire program had detected a search for a person on his list of people whose movements they were interested in. He needed to find out who was searching and what exactly they were looking for. His bosses would be very interested to see who else was trying to deal in the information business on the station.

Chapter 25

Shipping Lanes, Pavo Real System

Jordan and Brian lay prone on the hull of the freighter, hidden by the shadow of the communications array. The ship approaching theirs grew larger in their HUDs as they waited for the command from Sergeant Baines.

"What the fuck is Staff waiting for, DeMarco? I can hit him from here."

The corporal ignored the complaint, watching the closing distance tick down to the predetermined range. Anyone coming within two hundred meters of the freighter, after being repeatedly warned away, would be considered hostile, not incompetent. That range was well under the safe operating distances for non-docking ships and only a pirate or a cripple would get that close to another ship. *Sometimes Brian forgets little mission details like that.*

The range dropped below the limit and still the other ships didn't maneuver away. "Okay, Santis. You've got your shot. Take out his drive. I'm ready on the reload."

The lance corporal stood and raised the AT-8 launcher. It only took him a few seconds to acquire his aim point and launch. The rocket exited the tube in a spray of inert gas and traveled ten meters before the motor ignited. As it sped to the target, Jordan moved up behind the other Marine to reload the tube.

The AT-8 CGAH (Cold Gas Anti-Hull) was the standard for breaching operations against small craft. The high explosive squash head round created a hole in most hulls sufficient to allow a suited man access. It was also effective at putting holes in vital equipment and this first round was sent directly at one the two main drive pods, mounted on booms aft. It impacted as they finished reloading and they were able to see the jet of flame erupt from the side of the pod. The suspected pirate began to spin at a weird angle from the impact and Brian struggled to get a proper lead on the second pod. The other engine came alive as the pirate struggled to get control of his ship.

"Shit, this thing's all over the place. Switch to laser?"

"Stand by. Let me get the damned thing on." Jordan aimed the linked laser designator at the second engine pod. The other ship was much closer now and he suddenly wondered if it was going to hit. Before he could decide whether or not to fire, Baines came over the net.

"Stand by on the hull. Ship's maneuvering to avoid the pirate."

Their engines ignited as both Marines knelt to lower their center of gravity. The maneuver pushed their ship out of the path of the tumbling pirate and they watched as it slid past, jets still firing to stop the roll.

They were positioning to fire again when the first engine, which had been trailing debris and was now lit from within by an orange glow, suddenly exploded in a bright white light. Both men took cover behind the comm array again, as debris sped past. Pieces bounced off the freighter's hull and the dish antenna they were beneath for several seconds.

"DeMarco, you good up there?"

"Roger, Sarge. We found cover. No holes and no worries."

"Good. Come on inside, then."

"What about the pirate?"

"He's lost all power. Either the explosion or the debris killed his plant. We're calling for his surrender now and then we'll take a walk in the Black to round them up. Good work, Marines."

Santis whooped over the comm. *"Fuck yeah! I killed me a pirate ship! Hey Jordan, can I paint a kill marker on my armor?"*

*****

The intelligence officer popped his head around the door into the captain's office. "Preliminary report from our first op. They stopped the attack and captured four. A Justice cutter will pick them up. No casualties on our side."

McMannus smiled and leaned back in his chair. "That goes well with what I learned. Agent Drusk sent our next mission. Seems one of their snitches gave them some info on a very interesting ship that left Colon yesterday."

Vestry motioned with both hands. "Give, give. What do we know? People, vectors, armament?"

"All that and more. They believe this ship belongs to the organization that hit Justice. Some criminal family called the Hoffmans. It's a fast freighter that has allegedly been involved in smuggling before, so it's been on a watch list. The source said it left with twenty people above and beyond the normal crew, carrying 'a lot of guns.' And the source said their boss told them what ships to hit and what cargo to look for. Drusk says the Minister himself gave the go ahead to deploy us to take the ship down. They're tracking it with their own deep space scopes and have a pretty good vector for it."

"A fast freighter makes for a pretty good interceptor and a smuggler might already be armed. Smart; get them out between the shipping lanes and hit targets on the fly. The question is, where do they get their intel on who to hit? You can only tell so much from the external scans on a ship and they have to make sure the cargo is worth it. Who's giving the orders on who to hit, when to hit them and what to take?"

"One question at a time. Justice is sending a ship to stop and board the freighter for a 'customs and safety' inspection. I'm sending two squads along under the 2nd platoon NCO, Staff Sergeant Brown. Harry will just have to miss out, because we're still working our way through the larger problem."

Chapter 26

Deep space, Pavo Real system

"There's our target, Staff Sergeant. Good thing we knew where to look, cause I've got fuck all on passive sensors. They're running on minimal power plant output. Enough for life support and passive sensors, I'd say."

Staff Sergeant Jessica Brown watched the display the pilot indicated for a few minutes as they closed. "Do you think he'll run once we hail him?"

"Oh, there's a chance. How's he going to explain what he's doing out here, nearly shut down? He could claim comms failure or computer issues but once we get aboard it'll be easy to discover the truth of that story. I give him a fifty-fifty shot of running. If everything on their ship is legal though, he may try to stick it out. No law against wasting your time just hanging around in space."

"When you're sure he's not going to run, we'll deploy outside. Then we stick close to the hull and be ready to bounce across once you've docked. We might have to blow a hole to get access, so make sure your people are in suits when they come over."

The pilot whistled and shook his head. "Man, that's some crazy shit. I've done EVA for repairs but only when we've been coasting. Under accel, that's something else."

"Just another day in the Corps for us. You haven't lived until you've ridden outside a juking Babe in a combat zone."

"I prefer riding my babes elsewhere but I get your meaning." He punched some numbers into the nav computer and a timer started. "Twenty minutes until we're too close for him to outrun us."

"Good enough." She turned and went back to the passenger section. The seats had been removed to make enough room for seventeen Marines in MACE suits and two Justice agents in their own EVA suits. They sat on the deck for the whole trip, with only a few breaks to stretch their legs, one at a time. Most slept; a MACE wasn't a bed but MISTer learned to make do inside their suit. At least they didn't have to have their helmets on. The agents learned a whole new definition of uncomfortable but they hadn't complained either.

"Up and at'em, Marines!" Jessica barked. "Jump off in twenty minutes. Shake it out, take a piss if you need to. Time to earn your pay and step out into the Black."

The usual grumbles greeted her announcement as they struggled to their feet. They were all itching for this fight after being stuck in the ship for this long. She walked over to the two squad leaders to go over the deployment plans. The airlock could fit only two Marines at a time, so instead they would simply seal off the cockpit and depressurize the whole compartment. Then they could open both airlock doors and deploy in a few minutes. Afterwards, the agents could repressurize their interior for docking.

The two Justice agents, Baylor and Quinonez stood off to the side. Their EVA suits prominently displayed the Justice logo and "Policia" in bright yellow letters. Quinonez was senior and he had a grim expression. "These guys are supposed to be part of Hoffman's organization and they are some scary people. We ID'd some of the guys on board as their heavy hitters. Including the crew, there's over thirty people over there. That's about twice your count."

"True. On the other hand, we have micro-g on our side. And that makes a huge difference. Just watch and see. We'll herd the survivors to the airlock and you can take it from there."

They looked at each other and then back at her. "You're going to leave some of them alive?"

She snorted. "We don't just go in and destroy everything. Well, we can and we have but only when the occasion calls for it. The Corps has found that an overwhelming display of firepower is usually sufficient for people to reconsider their life choices."

*****

Twenty-two minutes later, they were magged to the exterior hull. The alleged pirate ship was highlighted in their HUDs and Jessica had assigned landing points. First squad would assault with both teams while the second squad would send in one team. The last team was her reserve, remaining with her on the Justice ship until needed.

Their pilot signaled. *"Staff Sergeant, they finally answered our hail. Just like I thought, they're claiming electrical issues. Broken comms and trouble restarting their reactor. I told them to be ready for us to dock to render assistance. That's pretty standard for us."*

"Roger. Don't open your hatches until I give the signal. We'll jet over before you dock and be ready on the other locks."

"Oh, trust me, we're more than happy to let you take the lead on this. Kicking in the front door is as scary as it gets."

"Not as scary as we are. And we won't be using the front door."

*****

When there was only a few hundred meters separating them, Jessica gave the order for the assault team to go. Her HUD displayed the twelve figures leaving the hull in groups of four, angling for their assigned landing spots. One to assault the airlock on the opposite side and capture the bridge, one for the cargo hatch to secure the center of the ship and one for the engine maintenance hatch near the drives to secure the engine room. The last was the riskiest, because if the pirates decided to light off their engines while the team was still forcing the hatch, they could be crisped in an instant. That meant they would be the first to go when the Justice ship docked.

The two ships came closer and closer and there was no sign of activity from the pirates. *Of course not. They're expecting police officers and only a few of them.*

The docking tube extended from the Justice ship and made contact with the target airlock. From her position, she could see the telltales turn green, indicating a solid lock. "Execute."

The engine room team disappeared from view around the drive protrusions, moving with the quick bounding motions only a MACE suit and MIST training could provide. It should only take them a few…

"Whisper Two Seven, Whisper Two One. We're inside the engine room. No air, looks like they've already depressurized."

"All Whispers, go for breach." She clicked over to the Justice frequency. "They're already depressurized over there. Probably waiting to hit you as soon as you open their airlock. Stay put, we'll handle this."

The cargo lock team was inside in seconds but the other personnel airlock team reported a jammed hatch. "Blow it," she told them, then clicked over to the Justice frequency. "We're blowing an airlock on the starboard side. Standby to adjust your position."

"Whisper Two Seven, Whisper Two One. Two tangos KIA in the cargo bay. I have one WIA via suit breach. Be advised they have what appear to be LR-8s."

"Whisper Two Seven copies. All Whispers, watch for laser weapons. Advance with caution."

"Fire in the hole!"

From the far side of the ship a jet of sparkling particles erupted into space. The pirate ship shifted visibly, starting a slow roll to port. The docking tube flexed with the roll, showing a bow in the middle of the tube. She felt the vibration of their maneuvering thrusters almost immediately and the docking tube straightened.

"Whisper Two Seven, Whisper Two One. Engine room is secure and drives offline. Two tangos KIA, three prisoners."

"Whisper Two Seven copies. Defensive positions against assault. We're going to start pushing them hard from the other entry points."

"Whisper Two Seven, Whisper Two One Bravo. Advance from the cargo bay stalled at the entry to the main passageway. They're barricaded in that central corridor pretty good. Minor suit breach, patched."

"Roger. Whisper Two Two, status?"

"Whisper Two Seven, at the bridge now. Hatch is sealed tight and we're taking automatic weapons fire from the main passageway. Minor suit damage. Three tangos KIA at the airlock on your side."

She called up the interior plan of the ship Justice had provided. The main passageway directly connected the engine room and the bridge, with only one major juncture to the cargo bay. The majority of the 'passengers' had to be in that area. They were probably in their rooms in their quarters when the attack started and were now stuck like a rat in a pipe. She needed to keep them bottled up or they would overwhelm her people.

"Right. We're going to keep the pressure on them from both sides. Whisper Two Seven assaulting the other airlock." She clicked over to Justice. "Retract the docking tube. We're going in through that hatch."

They kicked off the hull and jetted over to the pirate ship as the docking tube folded back onto itself. Standing on the pirate hull, with the airlock at their feet, Jessica stood back as the fire team leader arranged her people. This hatch opened without issue, since the pirates had wanted the Justice agents to come inside. Three bodies in motley EVA suits floated in the vestibule inside the airlock and blood globules floated around them. The other airlock was directly across from theirs, with the other assault team taking turns returning fire at the defenders in the main passageway.

Her team cleared the area by clipping the bodies to the exterior hull. The pirates were continuing to send a hail of fire down the passage. She watched as pieces of the wall and ceiling seemed to disappear as if by magic as bullets tore through them. Burn marks appeared on the bridge bulkhead. Not enough to breach that thick wall, unfortunately. Her people were careful not to expose themselves past the corner of the intersection as they set up to send fire down the main passage. Once they were set, Jessica selected the frequency their pilot had used to communicate with the pirates earlier.

"Attention, enemy commander. Your ship is boarded and we control your engine room. I request and require your surrender to the lawful authority of the Pavo Real government. You have one minute to comply."

There was silence for several seconds. A harsh voice then asked, "*You're arresting us? For what? You've killed several of my crew without provocation. You should be the ones under arrest.*"

She sighed audibly into the comm. "I'm not fucking around here. Surrender or we will kick the door in and nobody survives."

"*Try it, bitch. We've got some surprises for you.*"

And so do we. She gave hand signals to the two teams with her to lay suppressive fire down the passage and then follow with grenades. Then she told Two One what they were doing and to hold fast.

Two MISTers on each side of the passage poked their PW-93Vs around the corner, using the feed from their built-in sights to aim down the corridor without exposing themselves. They fired several bursts of suppressing fire and then ducked back as the other four tossed grenades down the hallway. Hours of practice in micro allowed them to bounce the explosives into the open doorways along the corridor. Designed to shred Grausian battle armor, the grenades pierced the thin interior walls with ease. The four explosions made the deck and walls vibrate briefly and thin streamers of smoke drifted into the passageway.

The first four MISTers pulled themselves around the corner. For them, it was a crawl down into a rectangular hole in the ship, with the engine room at the bottom of the tunnel.

One Marine on each wall, the floor and the ceiling provided complete coverage and spread them out so they weren't getting into each other's field of fire. The magnets on their MACEs kept them attached and flush to the surface.

When the first team had gone several meters, the second four stepped over the corner and down. They were walking down the floor and ceiling in pairs, providing overwatch for the assault team. Any pirate who stuck his head out of a door received a burst of fire and usually did not stick their head out again.

The first set of rooms had received the brunt of the grenade blasts. The walls were shredded metal and plastic and the Marines on the walls stuck their weapons around the doorways to scan the room with the attached sights. Once they confirmed it was clear (either by visual inspection or by firing at anything moving), they kicked off and 'hopped' over the open space.

The second set of rooms provided enough resistance that each earned a grenade. Bits and pieces of metal, plastic and ship's equipment streamed out into the hall after the explosion. A quick inspection and they were moving again.

Jessica watched from their original position at the airlock intersection. The team leaders were doing their jobs and she didn't want to bump their elbows. Things seemed to be well in hand until she saw one of the walking MISTers go to their knees as a puff of vapor exploded out the back of the suit.

Turning her head, she saw the bridge door was open and the end of a laser rifle barrel poking out the open doorway. Pivoting, she jammed the end of her weapon around the corner and squeezed the trigger on the first thing she saw in the doorway. The bullets tore through the standard EVA suit the pirate wore and impacted on the front view screen.

She continued past her pivot to step into the open hatch, kicking the body into the bridge as she advanced. It wasn't a very big room, barely large enough for the pilot, navigator and ship's captain. The other two pirates were still in their seats, working feverishly on their panels. They didn't even look up as she entered, calling to them on the pirate frequency.

"Right, hands the fuck up right now! Let me see them!"

The figure in the captain's seat reached for a pistol clamped to the console and she put a burst into his helmet. The body sagged in the chair as blood streamed into the cabin. The final pirate raised both hands in a slow, easy motion, wiggling its fingers to show it had nothing in them.

"Whisper Two Two, Whisper Two Seven. Bridge secure. Status?"

"*Whisper Two Seven, Whisper Two Two Echo. Two Two is down. One other KIA, life support damage. Objective secure. Unknown enemy KIA, seven prisoners.*"

She sighed and called Quinonez. Time for them to come on over and make the arrests while she got her people back under air so they could treat the wounded. And mourn the dead.

Chapter 27

Colon High Station, Pavo Real System

"Captain, report from Staff Sergeant Brown. Objective captured and enemy forces neutralized."

McMannus let out the breath he'd been holding. "Casualties?"

Harry was trying for a professional look but the pain came through in the creasing around his eyes. "Two KIA, sir. Sergeant Kwan and Lance Corporal Napolitano. Seems the buggers had some LR-8s. Last generation but unexpected. Bit of a shock at that, Staff says."

Rubbing his face with both hands, McMannus nodded. "Good times had to end someday. All right, what's their ETA back to the station?"

"Seventeen hours, sir. They have nearly a dozen detainees, sir. Justice agents confirm no orders to space."

"Tell Staff to watch them carefully, Harry. I'm authorizing some tactical interrogations but nothing else. Let's find out who else they may have out there."

"Copy that, sir."

McMannus tapped the comm button for Vestry's office. "Mr. Vestry, have you got any specifics you need from the pirates?"

The man stepped into the room a few seconds later. "Indeed I do, Captain. Mostly confirmation of some things we suspect. Is this from the most recent op?"

"Yep. Send your questions to Staff Sergeant Brown. Maybe some tips on how to get that info. We're not used to doing this kind of stuff."

"Of course, sir. Things like this are best left in the skilled hands of a professional."

He gave his intelligence officer a sideways glance. "Bold words from a man surrounded by the very bruisers he denigrates."

"Denigrate. That's a big word, Captain. And speaking of skilled hands, Drusk would like my help."

"Doing what, pray tell?"

"She thinks they might have a surveillance target that's linked to the pirates. The problem is, they're not sure. He's not doing anything criminal but he seems suspicious. They thought I might have another angle."

"Alright. Anything to help, I guess. Is this covered under our contract?"

Vestry waggled his hands. "Gray area. Another item to add to lessons learned, I guess."

"Let us know what you learn, then."

*****

 Oliver sat down at the desk in his hotel room and opened up his electronics case. This was one of his primary rooms, an upscale executive suite where a man with expensive-looking luggage wouldn't seem out of place. Moreover, it had good network connections, vital for the work they were doing here.

He set about checking the various electronics and making sure they were connected to the network. In the first few days on station, they had planted a number of cameras and microphones at key locations. This room was their command post and someone was here at least once a day to check the recordings to see if the computer had flagged anything.

Today, however he was checking on the newest cameras they had installed. The 76th was rapidly becoming a problem for his operation, as he thought they might be. The Hoffmans were quite upset at losing one of their ships and he needed to see if the mercs were going to continue down this road. Even though there wasn't anything in the news, he was quite sure the government (or possibly station management but that was less likely) had hired the 76th to do something about the piracy actions. The question was how they had picked up on the Hoffman ship.

The team had a hell of a time getting cameras to monitor the mercs. The only elevator to their garrison was heavily guarded and he noticed right off the bat that it was swept for monitoring devices on a regular basis. He needed another way to listen in and watch what they were doing.

Following the mercs would take up too much of their time. However, the Hoffmans had people to put on that task. Every bar, every nightclub, every restaurant they went to would have at least one listener to see what juicy tidbits they dropped.

The bureaucrats on the payroll were also on the task. They would be able to get him details of the contract, which would provide valuable information on what the 76th was and wasn't being paid to do and for how long. Maybe they could wait them out, risking a slower performance on the piracy front for less interference from the mercs. *Mr. Cross might not like that plan, however. By the time this conference ends, we need to have the other corps off-balance and slow to let contracts.*

There was one last area he could do some intelligence gathering. He'd done a lot of despicable things for the Union during the war and this was about the lowest he'd gone. The only difference now was that he was getting paid a hell of a lot more to do it.

The newest cameras were watching and listening at the entrance to the 76th dependent quarters. He'd had a hell of a time getting them installed and it had cost more than he'd expected bribing the station maintenance personnel to put them in. Not to mention the risk if they were discovered, which given the inexpert nature of their installation, was very likely. However, the computer was tagging and cataloging everyone as they appeared on camera and crosslinking them against the members of the 76th. Within a few days, he'd have a complete database on the 76th, both active members and dependents. Then he could apply some appropriate leverage.

*****

Ezekiel watched the security video feed closely. Three Colón Station security officers, two humans and Grausian, watched with him but he doubted they saw everything he did. They were looking for criminal activity, not an intelligence operation and had likely dismissed the man sitting in the bar across from the docks as just another pedestrian. But to Ezekiel, the man screamed 'operative' as surely as if he'd been wearing a sign. He sat watching the docks, which most people usually ignored. Once you've seen one cargo loading operation, you've seen them all. He sipped his drink like any other patron but his eyes never left the docks. Most people at least looked into their cup from time to time.

"How long are we going to watch this guy? He's doing nothing except doodling on his tablet." The Grausian sitting at the desk, Vallas, yawned to emphasize his point. The other two nodded, clearly bored as well.

Ezekiel sighed. "He's not doodling. He's taking notes on what cargo is being loaded."

All three looked at him, two wearing identical confused expressions but Vallas had a wary look. "What? How can you tell that?"

"When you doodle, you either make short, deliberate strokes or long flowing, continuous ones. Writing involves a series of specific motions."

One of the other officers leaned forward to get a better look at the monitor. "But how does he know what's being loaded?"

The intelligence officer pointed at the screen showing the dock. "A container smaller than a standard unit indicates either a special order or something that requires specific handling. That likely means it's valuable. Containers that require a heavy-duty hoist to get them on and off the transports mean it's either something heavy or it has special packaging that requires careful handling. They could be valuable so it gets noted. Finally, containers that have life support units attached mean it's something that can't be exposed to vacuum, so it's delicate and also likely valuable. Once he knows which ships are carrying the potential targets, they know which manifests to get a look at."

"But that's only the ships here at the dock. What about the big freighters?" That was Lieutenant Comey, nominally in charge of this shift. He was about thirty pounds overweight but had been doing security on the station for nearly twenty years. Still, he was looking for the small con, the local crime that worried the merchants on station and interfered with the small tourist trade. The things that would get the government involved.

"They don't care about the grain or the ore. Too heavy and not worth enough to resell. See, he's watching that loading operation very carefully. Notice how his hand motions are regular and even. He likely has his own shorthand on type, size, number and ship name. Even if you picked him up and looked at his notes, you wouldn't know what he's got on there."

"But we are going to pick him up, right?" Comey's hand hovered over the comm unit.

Ezekiel leaned back and sipped his coffee, noting that Vallas was slowly reaching a hand towards his personal commpad. "Nope. We continue to monitor him, both physically and electronically. Then we find out who he reports to. Then we watch that person and on up the chain. We build target folders on each of those bastards; habits, movements, contacts and so forth. When it does come time to roll them up, we'll know everything we can about their whole network."

Comey barked a laugh as Vallas relaxed. "Here I thought this spy stuff was going to be flashy and high-speed. It's nothing more than a stake out on a grander scale."

"Just about like that, Lieutenant. The only difference is when the MIST takes someone down, we don't worry about niceties like arrests and warrants. We'll track them back to their base and squash them at the source."

"Heh. Like to be in on that."

"Only if you don't mind spending hours at a time in a suit and out in the Black, Lieutenant. That's the only way we do things."

Comey shuddered. "No thanks. I hate just going out on the hull for security inspections. I don't know how you guys handle all that empty space."

Ezekiel smiled. "It does take a special kind of person. Thanks for your cooperation in this investigation. I'll make sure you get a copy of what we send to the Ministry of Justice and that your names are mentioned. It's been a pleasure working with you."

*****

Ezekiel knocked on his commander's open door. "The target folders are ready for review. Got time for it?"

McMannus nodded and rose. "How many?"

"Three for now. One guy on the docks taking notes, the person he's passing those to and a guy in the security office."

"Shit. A mole in the security office?"

"We knew there had to be at least one guy on the inside, sir. I'm guessing that Vallas, my suspect, isn't the only one. There's probably at least one person in the shipping office, too. This kind of thing takes multiple people on the inside to be as successful as it has been."

He leaned back in his chair and looked up at the ceiling. "And what do we do about them?"

"Right now? Nothing. When the time comes, after we take down the pirates, we can hand them and the evidence over to the local authorities. Maybe I can swing a bonus on that, too. After all, we're only contracted to eliminate the pirates, not their inside people. But I suspect that the Chief Marshal would be very happy if we handed that information over to them for action. Then he would have successes, too. If we're going to be sticking around here, it might be good for some folks in positions of authority to owe us a few favors."

"See, this is why I keep you around. I'm just a simple military guy. I can't think like that."

Ezekiel laughed. "Sure, Free. You're about as simple as a fusion drive."

Chapter 28

Cassie settled down on the recliner with a glass of wine and waited for Selena. It had been a long day already and tomorrow was going to be even longer. Her feet ached from the fancy dress shoes and she longed for a hot bath.

With even less patience than Cassie felt, Vera called out, "How much longer, Selena? We've all got things we need to do!"

The hacker came out of her room, tapping away on her tablet. "Hold on a few more secs. Just enabling the white noise generator…" Soft static began to play through the room's speakers.

Cassie raised her eyebrows and sat up. "Do you actually think someone is listening in on us?"

Selena put a finger to her lips and then went back to her tablet. After a few more taps, she smiled. "There. If anyone can get through that, I'll dance naked down the main concourse."

Janik gagged and Vera rolled her eyes. "Eww. This had better be worth the mental image you just gave me."

The other woman merely smiled as she turned on the main entertainment unit and mirrored her tablet display. "Serves you right for having a dirty mind. Okay, you're wondering why the secrecy. Well, if you were listening to Janik the other day, you'll remember the Hoffmans control the information market around here. And by control, I mean own one hundred percent."

Still images began flashing up on the scene. Each one was of a member of the various Terran corporate teams in different locations, to include the shower, in bed and other less pleasant scenes. "You think I have my fingers in a lot? These people are serious voyeurs and they own the station networks. I have been working my butt off to get data and cover my tracks while I'm doing it."

Cassie nodded. "So that goes into the portfolio on this station. Why do I get the feeling this isn't the particular reason why you called us here."

"Got it in one, boss lady. Have to make sure they don't know what we know about what they know." A new set of windows opened on the screen, displaying various docks and warehouses. All seemed to be from security cameras and one began to play, showing men and women hurriedly unloading a ship at dock. Everything removed from the ship went straight onto cargo trucks, without scanning or inspection. "This cargo was one of the recent piracy incidents. Officially reported as lost and insurance claim filed. It happened in the next system over but the shipment originated here. I know this because I scanned the labels on the containers and ran them through the customs database."

That earned the hacker a look from her boss. "What did I tell you about pirate taps?"

"And this wasn't one. I had a valid login, spoofed from a legal account."

Cassie opened her mouth and then closed it. "Fine. Continue. Why do we care about this?"

The video feed changed. The time stamp was from a few days before the first recording. This time, cargo was being loaded onto a ship by the porters at the dock. Janik sat up and pointed a finger. "I helped load that ship!"

"Yeppers." Selena manipulated the recording to zoom in on one of the porters, bringing Janik's face into focus. "Did you see anything unusual that day?"

He looked at her, confusion plain on his face. "Unusual how?"

She switched video feeds again. This time it was from a camera further down the dock, looking down the corridor instead of into a slip. The activities of the porters were barely visible. The image electronically zoomed in on a food stall across the way. A man sat there, bowl in front of him. They watched him take a bite from time to time but his attention was focused on the ship being loaded. He made notations on his tablet from time to time.

"There. That's the unusual piece. Someone was watching you load and making notes on what was being loaded. And I will bet a real steak dinner he's linked to whomever is behind the piracy."

Cassie walked over to the screen. "What makes you think he's not Hoffman?"

"Hoffman would hack the port servers and go for the manifests digitally. However, Justice has put increased security on those files, which means an increased risk of setting off an alert. So whoever is running this operation will have to use more old-fashioned methods, like this." Selena paused the video and brought up a screen with multiple graphs.

"I've run the data we originally got from Colon through various filters and pivot tables. Losses to theft run about five percent. That's about standard for an outsystem like this. Inside the TU losses rarely get above one and half to two percent but those are under more strict regulations. Not going to find those here. Still, I would bet that Vera's hinky spreadsheets are due to station management involvement in these nefarious activities."

The accountant nodded. "Cassie, I'm not ready to point any fingers but I'm fairly certain that some highly placed people on Colon are involved in covering up illegal activities. To what degree is the piece I'm working on nailing down."

"Well, we knew that was a likely input into our negotiations. Very well, Selena, you look like you've got more to show us."

"Losses to piracy during that time period were barely half a percent. Hoffman is surely responsible for most of that, although those rebels had a hand in it too. But in the last few weeks, piracy losses have jumped to over nineteen percent. Losses to theft remained about the same."

Vera nodded. "I can confirm that. But what does it mean?"

Cassie tapped the screen. "Selena's right. If Hoffman could effect almost a three hundred percent increase in the loss rate, why weren't they doing it before? Why now?" Turning back to her team, she nodded. "Because someone is paying them. Someone who is new to the scene."

Janik slapped his thigh. "It's one of the corporates!"

"The question is, which one? Who started playing dirty before the conference began?" Cassie began to pace the small living room. "Okay. New priorities. We need to find out who's poisoning the negotiations here. We thought we could use this to our advantage but it turns out someone is already manipulating the system. I really don't like getting beaten to the punch."

Chapter 29

It was the middle of the day so this section of the station for the various nightclubs and bars was mostly deserted. Their destination, the Kater Blau nightclub, was unlit and no doorman stood outside. Still, the door opened automatically at their approach and Oliver and his team stepped inside the entrance, pausing to let their eyes adjust. The lighting inside was low, except for one table near the back. Three people sat there, with two rough-looking men flanking the table.

Oliver continued forward to the table while his men fanned out to cover the rest of the room. There was no sense in giving these animals an edge. He wanted the thought to remain in the forefront of their tiny minds that he was calling the shots and wasn't afraid of them.

There were two men and a woman sitting at the table in the back of the room. At least one of them represented Schattenmannschaft, or SMS. One of the two groups he'd mentioned to Mr. Cross, the SMS was the violent arm of the Hoffmans. They provided muscle for hire to whomever paid the most and was concerned the least about bloodshed.

One of the men was dressed like he'd just come in off a ship, jumpsuits and mag boots. A pistol rode in a shoulder holster. He was seated between the woman and the other man, who was visibly uncomfortable. His clothes looked out of place on him; stylish and yet ill-fitting. The woman was in what appeared to be casual business attire, collared shirt, jacket and slacks. Once Oliver was next to the table, it became apparent her clothing was tough synthleather and ballistic cloth, cut to resemble more respectable clothing. The pommel of a knife protruded ever so slightly from her cuff as she waved him to a chair opposite theirs. Oliver sat down in it like he owned it.

The woman, whom he only knew as 'Ana', indicated the bottle of whiskey and four shot glasses sitting in the center of the table and he shook his head. Some of these groups just wouldn't do business with a person who didn't drink with them but he would be damned if he would dance to their tune. She poured three glasses, which she and the man next to her tossed without taking their eyes off him. The other man sipped at his but made a face at the taste.

Think cause you can rough up some spacers or knife some gangbanger in an alley you're tough? He just smiled in return. "Things are going well. Losses among our targets are up over three hundred percent. The Terran Union corporations are starting to get antsy about the security out here, which is exactly what I'm paying you for. But I'm guessing there are new problems or we wouldn't be meeting. What exactly is wrong?"

Ana frowned. "Hoffman trades much in information, ja? And on this station we own these systems. We know when people are snooping where they shouldn't. So we want you to know there is someone else here now, also very good." Her accent was crisp and cultured and she sounded amused.

"So? Why should I care?"

"They are skilled enough to learn much of our operations. Pieces by themselves don't tell much but when you put them together, like a puzzle, the picture becomes much clearer. We believe this someone is building a very good picture of what's happening between you and us. Inquiries into manifests and orders. Downloads of ship schedules and who was working the docks for those ships. Accessing the station security video archives. And not just what we are working on but many aspects of our organization's operations."

"Okay, we have a spy in our midst. Find them and get rid of them."

"As I said, they're skilled. Hard to catch in the act, good at leaving false trails and covering their tracks. Skilled enough that if they were an independent actor, we might offer them a job instead of killing them. But very soon they will know exactly what we are doing, or Justice will get their hands on the information and then what?"

"I don't care if you offer them a job or send them out the airlock. I pay for results on the targets we give you." Beck tapped the table for emphasis.

She watched his fingers and smiled. It wasn't a pretty smile, more at home on a predator sighting their prey. "Hoffman has pirate taps on the station network at all levels. Complete coverage, ja? This person was traced to a hotel hosting the conference delegations. So is a Terran Union person."

He took a breath. This was the game she was playing. What he said next had to be done carefully or the entire operation would be at risk. "Again, I pay for results on what we contracted on. Security is your business. What about using station security? Arrest them on some jumped up charges and hold them until after the conference is over?"

She looked at the third man. He swallowed heavily. "Um... there is too much at stake here. We don't know how much they know. Better to get rid of the problem, uh, permanently."

Fucking drone. Can't even say it out loud. "While I can't condone or even pay for an operation against a Terran corporation and in fact officially advise against it, I also can't tell you how to conduct your own security operations. Do what you need to do, then. Just let me know before it's about to go down so I can do damage control at my level."

"Oh, you're very good. Classic doublespeak." She smiled and stood and the other two men stood with her. Her accent roughened. "All asses covered, ja? Is good. We take care of it. No more worries."

*****

Oliver secured the door to his room and activated the extra security measures he'd put in place. Mr. Cross needed to be aware of this kink in the plans and the possible blowback on them. *I don't think he'll disagree with the adjustment but he's going to be pissed.*

Activating his own equipment, he composed a message for ansible transmission. Galactocity had their own encryption protocols but Terran Union Intelligence could break those if they choose. For that matter, anyone in the company with a high-enough clearance could decrypt the message. This had to be said carefully.

Attention: Winfield Cross
*   Vice President for Market Development*
From: Denovo Market Development Team
Subject: Security

Sir,
It has come to our attention that competitive interests at the Denovo Trade Conference are developing in a new direction. We have instituted information security protocols as per your guidance during the planning session. Losses to date are minimal but we deem these proactive measures necessary to secure our essential information. Once more complete data is available on the efforts and personnel involved, we will provide another update.
Very Respectfully,
Thomas Flatley, Market Developments

He signed it with Flatley's corporate certificates and sent it. The other man was unaware Oliver had his certificates but Cross had made it clear in a private conversation before they left that Beck had to have plausible deniability at all levels. Flatley was a market analyst and part of the official team but an ex-Special Forces officer would be out of place. This was fine with him; he preferred operating behind the scenes.

Things would come together fine as long as Ana gave him a few hours warning before they hit their targets. He sent a coded message to the rest of his team to be ready to activate their contingency plans. If there was some blowback they wouldn't be caught unawares.

Chapter 30

"If I hear one more freighter captain whine about the protection we're providing, I'm gonna lose my shit."

Ezekiel looked up from his terminal at his boss. They were processing the latest after-action reports in the conference room and McMannus was glaring at his own terminal.

"Can't blame them for being worried, sir. They're civilians, not used to this kind of violence. Fights in bars, customs agents looking for kickbacks, yes."

"If we had a ship of our own, I wouldn't have to worry about them. I'm not asking for much. Big enough to carry a platoon, with a pilot I can trust not to bug out once we've dropped." He paused. "I'm whining, aren't I?"

His intel officer put both hands up in the air. "You don't need me to tell you that. But yes, you are. As long as it's just me in here, I'll listen. I might also tell you to put on your big boy captain pants and suck it up, too."

McMannus stood up, smiling. "Point taken, Mr. Vestry. Whining duly noted and completed. Now, I'm going to exercise a little commander's privilege and take off early for lunch. Aileen has been wanting to try that latin fusion place down on the mercado, so I think I'll surprise her today."

"You do that. Maybe you'll come back in a better mood."

The captain flipped him off as he left the room. Ezekiel smiled again, tapping a note on his to-do list. *Find a ship.*

*****

Oliver hadn't expected Mr. Cross to respond this quick but there was the message in his inbox.

To: Thomas Flatley
From: Winfield Cross
Vice President for Market Development

Subject: Security Upgrade

Mr. Flatley,
Please ensure all proper security measures are in place to prevent data losses and maximize our ability to compete in the market. Take proactive approaches as needed to secure our essential information and corporate intellectual property.

He smiled as he read. The key phrase, 'proactive approaches' was the go-ahead to implement the security contingencies they had, both for the mercenaries and to protect against a double-cross by the Hoffmans.

*****

Free and Aileen sat in a small booth near the front window of the restaurant, the remains of their lunch on the table in front of them.

"This was nice, Free. I assume you'll be able to do this more often?"

"I should. Now that I'm not writing reports for colonels and generals, you'd think I would have more free time. But somehow, it's not working out that way."

She laughed. "Finding out that running your own business isn't as easy as you thought?"

"Hell, I hadn't really thought about it at all. I knew it would be different but it's not what I thought. Payroll. Buying supplies instead of heading to the depot. Dependent issues, although I have my eye on a smart person to help me with that."

"Welcome to my world. Just wait until it's time to do taxes."

"Wait, what? Oh, shit. How do you even do taxes as a mercenary company?"

Aileen was laughing harder now, tears leaking from her eyes. He glared in mock anger at her. "Sure, laugh at my lack of knowledge. I suppose I look like a brand-new butterbar to you, trying to navigate the wilderness of small businesses."

"Oh Free. You should have seen the look on your face."

"You will continue to see it, my dear, until you help me replace it with something better. After all, you're stuck with it and me now."

She paused at his tone of voice. "Free…"

He reached out to take her hand. "Now that you're here and living the life of a mercenary dependent, is this something you'd like to continue?"

Her fingers intertwined with his and her smile changed, from mirth to shy joy. "Free, I would… there they are again." Her gaze shifted to the window.

Outside, a man and a woman sat at a cafe table across the corridor. They were both looking in their direction, in a none-to-friendly manner. Free's right hand slid across the table and down to his sidearm. "Who are they, Ally? Where have you seen them before?"

"I know I saw them the other day, when I was closing up shop. And a couple of the other spouses have mentioned to me they thought they were being followed. I don't know who they are, though. Do you?"

"I have a hunch. Ally, pass the word to the rest of the spouses to report anything suspicious to the duty sergeant. We have to watch out for ourselves now. I'll see about increased security at our Back Gate, where you guys come and go. And speaking of which, we should go. Now."

Chapter 31

Oliver hung up the phone and took a deep breath. SMS was doing the hit tonight. They had identified the target as personnel from StellarMart. That team was going to be eliminated and with them, the risk to the plan. *So why am I worried? Because SMS might screw it up and someone could get away? No, they're too used to cleaning up messes. It's the questions that are going to be asked afterward and the attention brought to bear on the situation. That's what Cross wants to avoid. People will ask, 'Why StellarMart and none of the other corporates?'*

Because they got caught with their hands in the till. Yes, that's something the others will accept. And StellarMart will too, if there's someone to tell them that's why it happened.

He picked up his tablet and opened it to the contact sheet from the conference, with a listing of the key members and where they were staying on Colon. He checked the hotel and room identified as the target location and, with a nod, picked up the phone.

Cassie was changing into casual clothes when Vera knocked on her door. "Call for you, boss. Someone from the conference, he says."

McMannus? Vestry? She picked up the extension in her room. "Cassandra Vickers speaking. How can I help you?"

"Ms. Vickers. We haven't met yet but I'm here at the conference as well. I've come across some information that will benefit both our organizations. Do you think you could meet me and discuss it?"

The voice was male and the tone was direct. This was a person used to getting what he wanted. *The question is, what does he want? Does he know about the actor behind the pirates?*

"That's a very interesting proposal. What kind of information?"

"The kind you don't share over an open line. It's vital information and we should really talk, Cassandra."

We've gone from Ms. Vickers to Cassandra. From direct to friendly. "Okay. You've piqued my interest. Where and when?"

"As soon as you can get there." He gave her the name of an eatery in the Mercado. "You won't regret this."

Cassie dressed in a business casual outfit, one that could hide her needler, knife and stun stick. "I'm going out for a meeting, Vera. Looks like someone else might be onto something and they want to share information."

Vera waved with her coffee cup. "We'll be here, slaves to our corporate masters."

*****

The eatery was mostly empty but the man in the back booth waved to her as she entered. Approaching the table, she took his measure. Tall, head shaved bald, neat goatee. Fit and sitting with his back to the wall. Probably ex-military.

She sat across from him. "Well, I'm here. Suppose we start with your name and who you work for. That way we'll both be on an even footing."

He smiled. "I'm sorry, Cassandra, it doesn't work that way. You can call me Mr. Smith, if you like. But since I have information you need, I call the shots."

"How do you know I need the information you have?"

With one hand he gestured at the bustling market beyond the window. "The outcome of this trade conference will make or break careers. Multimillion credit contracts will be signed here in the coming days and we both know those will shift the power balance in the region. We also both know what our respective masters are willing to do to get these contracts. Unfortunately for you, StellarMart won't get to share in the wealth."

"And how would you know that?" Her tone was cold and her eyes were like ice.

"Because I know what you've been doing, Cassandra. You and your team. An admirable effort but now that you've been discovered StellarMart will have to cut its losses or be embarrassed in front of their peers."

She shifted in her seat, leaning back with one arm draped over the back of the seat. The other arm was in her lap, hand conveniently close to the needler. "Embarrassed how? And what do you think I've been doing?"

Smith leaned back as well, only both his hands remained in view. "Well, since you arrived on station, you've had a hacker gathering information on the other corporate teams and on the local government representatives. Much more information than is necessary for standard negotiations. Perhaps for blackmail purposes? That's likely what the others will think."

Cassandra forced a scornful laugh. "An amusing story. But not one people are likely to buy."

He tossed a data chip on the table. "A record of your searches and the data gathered."

She didn't reach out for it. "That could be easily faked."

"Yes, it could. But the others will know their own data on there is authentic, so the implications would be hard to ignore. StellarMart would have to do a lot of explaining and tap dancing and likely this will mean withdrawing from the negotiations."

"So why tell me this? What do you gain from it?"

"Full disclosure here. My company is also working in the shadows. The only difference between us and you is that we didn't get caught. But we can help StellarMart avoid losing more than just a hacker team. You're our leverage on that front. I'm telling you this so that your company will owe us a favor."

"What do you mean, 'losing a hacker team?'"

"You know by now that there is a criminal element controlling the buying and selling of information. They're very unhappy with you. You've gathered information on them and their businesses, information they don't want to get out. The fact that you've also been talking to the mercs is another negative in their books."

She laughed, hiding the sinking feeling in her stomach. "Their criminal activities aren't even part of our research."

"They would beg to differ with you on that. In fact, you've learned far too much about their activities and who they're dealing with." He checked his watch. "And in about three minutes, one of their strike teams is going to hit your rooms and eliminate the team you've got there."

She slid out of the booth but before she could stand, he had grabbed her arm. "You won't get there in time, Cassandra. And you wouldn't be able to affect the outcome. You'd just die with the rest of them."

"Get your hand off me or lose it."

"Consider this some corporate goodwill. We could have had all of you eliminated. I chose to save you, so you could carry the story back. Everyone here will soon know that StellarMart crossed a line and suffered the consequences. You get to live and the price is to be both the messenger and the scapegoat. After all, it was your investigations that brought this on you."

She struggled but he had her at an awkward angle. His grip was absolute on her arm and she had to sit as the pain on her elbow increased. "What do you want?"

"Nothing. I've already achieved my goals; saving you and eliminating your team. Now, I'd advise you stop here and consider yourself lucky that you're alive. Leave off your piracy investigations and you'll continue to be alive. You may congratulate yourself on some very fine investigative work. So good that you were too close to finding us out." He slid out of the booth now, releasing her arm as he stood and smiled down at her.

"Bastard."

"Not quite but I understand the sentiment. This is your only warning. And remember how easy it was for them to find you the first time." With that, he left the eatery.

Cassie pulled her tablet to call but it had already pinged with a message from Selena. The subject line read, 'GTH Plan'. A video file was attached.

*****

The night clerk at the hotel looked up as the exterior door slid open, her standard welcoming smile on her face. That smile faltered as she watched the group of people that came in. All were dressed in dark clothing and carried duffel bags. The lead man flashed her a smile and a nod. She nodded back, nerves causing the smile to falter. They entered the elevator without saying a word. With a shaking hand, she picked up the phone to tell the security guard, on his rounds, to come back to the lobby as quick as he could.

Vera yawned and looked at the clock on her computer. After midnight. She got up and headed to the kitchen for some more coffee. Janik was snoring softly on the couch, his jumpsuit unzipped to the waist. A quiet muttering came from behind Selena's door, punctuated with occasional audible curses.

The door buzzed, the sound of an incorrect code entered. She paused, halfway out of the kitchen, coffee mug in hand. Janik mumbled something and sat up halfway, eyes blinking sleep away. The door buzzed again and Selena shouted through her door, "Bad guys!"

Vera dropped to one knee and pulled the holdout needler from her ankle holster. She heard Janik hit the floor with a thud. The door buzzed a second time and a muffled curse came from the other side. She scooted back to hide next to the bar that divided the kitchen from the living room, keeping the couch between her and the door. Janik was low crawling around the couch towards her, his own needler in hand when the door panel exploded in a shower of sparks. They both heard the door being wrenched open and through the smoke she saw a figure stalk through the open door.

Raising the needler and aiming was surreal. They trained for just such an emergency but Vera had never fired at a real person before. Her finger was already squeezing the trigger before she thought about it. Janik squeezed off two shots in rapid succession. The person staggered and dropped to the floor on the other side of the couch, out of sight. She squeezed off another shot into the open door, certain there were more attackers beyond.

Her teammate was almost to her when an arm appeared in the doorway. It tossed a small object into the room, where it bounced off the wall next to her and landed inches from him. They both stared as it exploded in light and sound, deafening and blinding them.

The blast knocked her flat on her back. Her head was spinning and she felt nauseous. Scooting backwards with an awkward motion, she tried to get around the bar and take cover behind it. The carpet gave way to the smooth surface of the kitchen floor and Vera huddled up close to the bar, behind its dubious protection and blinking at the spots in her eyes. A blurry image of Janik's hand came into view from the direction she'd come, grasping at the smooth floor. She heard a dull sound and the hand spasmed and went still.

Breathing rapidly, on the edge of panic Vera held the needler out, pointing this way and that as she desperately tried to clear her vision. She fired once, twice, three times at what she thought were people. Another faint boom and a sudden pain in her chest took her breath away. She fell over, gasping. There was an enormous pressure on her chest and the spots were giving way to gray as her vision narrowed to a small tunnel.

And then everything went black.

*****

With one hand, Selena hit the key to send the emergency alert to Cassie and the StellarMart lead while the other was activating her own room defenses. She'd upgraded the door lock on their suite and her room but there wasn't much she could do about the door's integrity itself. They would break it down eventually.

The progress bar on the data wipe was filling in quickly and she'd just finished backing up her data to the drive on their ship only a few hours ago. Cassie would know where to look. There was only one thing left to do. She dove behind the bed as the lights went out and the fans went into overdrive on the wall vents in her room. Designed to keep air circulating, they could also be reversed to evacuate the air in the event of a fire. Safety protocols prevented this from happening unless directed by the station's fire management system but Selena had taken control of their rooms on the first day.

She pulled the emergency respirator out from its stash and clamped it over her face. Already she could feel her skin tighten as the air pressure dropped. The pressure imbalance would make it extremely hard to open the door, assuming they could get past her lock security upgrades.

Dull thumps came from the other room. Selena fought to control her breathing, the mask tight over her nose and mouth. She heard the ding from her system as the data wipe completed. Good. Next the power supply would overheat and start a meltdown. Nobody was getting anything from her systems!

The door panel buzzed as they attempted to override the controls, then shorted out in a shower of sparks. She thought she heard someone yell from the other side and smiled. Whoever was trying to get past her security just got a huge shock when the panel shorted. *That ought to give them second thoughts! And with the motor now shorted out, that door won't move in its tracks short of breaking it down.*

The room shook as the door exploded inwards, sending shrapnel scything into the bed and walls. Air rushed into the room and she felt heavy steps reverberating on the floor. A black clad figure came around the bed, rifle pointed at her.

Selena sighed and let go of the mask so she could give her assassin double middle fingers when he pulled the trigger.

*****

Cassie was breathing heavily as she watched the video of her team being killed. Selena's hidden cameras caught more than she wanted to see. The attackers wore non-descript black clothing and used their weapons with deadly efficiency. She was glad to see that her team got at least two of their assassins but it was cold comfort.

Now what? Go back to the main StellarMart team? And do what? If I start my own investigations, they'll be all over me. And they just might go after everyone else this time. Her stomach churned as she ran through various options *Go to ground for now. I can't get completely off the grid which means those Hoffman goons will find me sooner or later. So maybe I give them something to find.*

It took a bit of searching to find the cheaper part of the station. It hadn't been part of their research or info packets. She rented a room on her personal card and used her real name. No point in giving too much away too early. Then she went out and found a liquor store, where she purchased several bottles of cheap alcohol. A few personal items and her quick disguise was as good as she could make it.

She settled down in the room, eating bad takeout and sipping at the even worse booze. One bottle had already been emptied down the bathroom drain when she had pretended to take a long bath, after making sure as she could there weren't any cameras in the bathroom. Her tablet held all but the most recent files her team had compiled, so she reviewed those where she could cover the screen. She would figure out what was really going on here and how she could get revenge for her people.

Chapter 32

"Captain, I think I've found just what we need for a ship of our own."

McMannus looked up from the report on the latest pirate takedown. Ishido and his people had gotten lucky, bagging two would-be pirates in as many days. It was a welcome change from worrying about the security measures and the people who were watching them. "And what would that be, Mr. Vestry? A surplus Union frigate? Maybe a Babe?"

"Almost as good. There's a former Union Navy pilot here on the station with his own ship. Not jump-capable of course but big enough to transport a platoon or more with ease."

"And why would said pilot want to give up the life of ease as a civilian and join up with us?"

Vestry leaned against the door jamb and smiled. "Because he was prior Navy and also because he was almost court-martialed."

He put the tablet down and leaned back in his chair. "I knew intel officers had weird ideas now and then but you're going to have to explain this one to me in a bit greater detail."

Ezekiel tapped on his own tablet and an image appeared on the other man's computer screen. It was a head and shoulder picture of a man in Terran Union undress uniform, golden wings prominent on his chest. "Meet former Lieutenant Commander Neil Eisen. Fourteen years' service, executive officer of a combat search and rescue squadron. Recipient of a Silver Star and two Distinguished Flying Crosses."

"Okay, he's a certified badass. What's this about a court-martial?"

"Five years ago, during the assault on the Kingston system, his squadron was in support of the ground assault. Things didn't quite go as planned and the assault force had to consolidate their positions. His flight was on their way to pick up a cut off unit but were instead ordered to return to base. The ground commander was going to use orbital strikes on the enemy concentrations and was willing to sacrifice a few people to get as much of the enemy as he could.''

Vestry grimaced. "Knew a few generals like that myself. Anyways, Eisen pretended to have communication issues due to enemy jamming and made the pickup anyway. His commander backed him but the general charged him with disobeying orders, in combat. Whole thing was on its way to a general court."

"So he got cashiered?"

"Funny thing about doing the right thing. The case was dropped and Eisen was 'invited' to separate. Honorable discharge and all. Apparently, someone in JAG realized if the case went to court that everything would come out into the open, including the order to abandon that cut off unit. Bad press for the general and everyone involved."

"Generals do hate bad press, especially when they have more stars in mind. So now Mr. Eisen is in the DMZ making a living as what? Freighter captain?"

"Pretty close. From what I've learned, he's been on the straight and level since getting out. No law enforcement run-ins, no bank problems on his ship."

"Back to my first question. Why would he give all that up to join us?"

"Put yourself in his shoes. He does the right thing, making the pick-up and instead of a medal he gets the boot. He got screwed by a general who cares more about orders than people. Sir, you are the exact opposite of that general. Let's go meet him and then you put on your most charming face and ask him to hire on."

*****

Captain McMannus followed his intelligence officer through the beat-up hatch. The inside was dim, lit only by a few flickering lights that had seen better days. Low volume music reached his ears, a twangy yet peppy tune that mixed a country & western with bollywood.

The interior was a long, narrow affair. None of the drinkers at the bar took any notice of them as they passed, instead hunching over their drinks and lost in their own minds. One didn't come to this kind of bar for good booze or quality companionship.

The far end of the room was lit by several table lamps, shining down on the poker table but leaving the player's faces in the dark. Hands moved in the light, moving chips and cards back and forth as the game progressed.

Ezekiel halted them several feet away. Leaning in, he whispered, "Our guy is the one with the very large silver ring on his thumb."

McMannus nodded and watched the game progress. There was no telling how long it had been going on but the man they were here to meet was either very lucky or very good, judging by the stack of chips by him.

After a few hands, Eisen tapped the table. "Deal me out for a few. Got some business to take care of."

Standing, it became obvious the man was short, maybe five foot four. He walked past them and they turned to follow. He led them to a table and motioned for them to sit. "So, I understand you're looking to hire a ship."

McMannus held up a hand. "Not a ship. We're looking to hire you, Mr. Eisen."

"Semantics. Me, the ship and my crew go together, so you hire one, you hire all."

"And hire isn't quite the correct word. We want you to join us."

"I left that military crap behind me a long time ago. Now I just fly cargo." He leaned back in his chair, a pleasant smile on his face. "I'm not your guy. But out of curiosity, why me?"

Ezekiel smiled. "Because of why you left the service."

The pilot snorted. "You want me because I was nearly court-martialed? That's a fucked-up reason."

"Not because you were on the way to a general court. The reason you were charged is why we want you. Anyone who disobeys orders to make the pickup can't be all that bad."

Eisen's smile changed, showing teeth. "Oh, I can be bad. And thanks for opening an old wound."

McMannus leaned forward. "Cut the crap, Mr. Eisen. You got screwed over, you took your lumps. Quit crying about it. The 76th needs someone like you and yes, we need your ship and crew. I'm offering shares as an officer for you and NCO ranks for your crew. You know what a MIST unit is. You've flown a Babe in combat and flown combat insertions on just about every type of platform. And you care about those you deliver."

The other man eyed him. "You make a pretty speech. I didn't think Marines knew more than a few grunts. Anyway, I'm done with that combat shit. It's not like we have a destroyer or frigate backing us up with their firepower anymore."

"It's not like you're going to have to fly into the teeth of a Grausian battleship either. We need a pilot we can trust to deliver us to the target and take us home again. I'm tired of relying on merchies and their fickle dispositions. With them, every time I have to leave a fire team or God forbid, a squad behind to secure our ride home. With you, I can deploy the whole platoon and count on pickup and a ride home, no matter what. Once the troops know who and what you are, they won't worry about their ride and focus on the job at hand."

Eisen nodded. He toyed with the ring for a few moments. "Who pays if the ship gets damaged?"

"Comes out our operating budget. Same for supplies and if we can get them, armament. Plus we can command a higher price if we have our own transport."

Eisen toyed with his glass for almost a minute, eyes staring off into the darkened room. "Okay. Let me talk to my crew first, though. My chief is former Navy but the loadmaster came up through the merchies. Good man with cargo and knows his way around the docks. Knows how to drive a hard bargain. I have to be sure they're on board."

The 76th commander held out his hand. "From what I've seen, your crew will follow where you lead. Welcome aboard, Lieutenant Eisen. Come on by our spaces tomorrow or the next day and we'll get you properly on the books. And then we're heading out in four days on an op."

The pilot shook his hand. "What, right away? No hurry up and wait?"

The other two got up to leave. "You're not in government service anymore. For mercenaries, time is money."

"You know, I left as a lieutenant commander."

"You also had to deal with generals. I'm much easier to work with."

As they headed back to the office, Vestry flipped out his tablet and made a notation. "I'll check into that loadmaster's background. If he's suitable, I'd like to sound him out for some field work for me. We could use some eyes and ears on the docks. Nice charm, by the way."

"You want nice words, go work for a general. If the loadmaster is interested, clear it with Eisen first. I don't think he'd like you poaching his crew's time."

"Unlike you, I'm the soul of courtesy. For example, I would never think of enlisting another man's subordinate into my service without letting him know first."

Chapter 33

"Mr. Smith here."

"Mr. Smith, this is Ana. We spoke earlier this week, ja? Let us speak again and soon."

"I have a scrambler for this line. Do you have one and the codes I gave you?"

The woman at the other end sounded amused. "Are you afraid to be seen with us?"

"The more we meet where other people can see, the more opportunities people have to put us together. Now, do you have a scrambler or are we done here?"

"Fine. Engaging now."

There were several buzzes on the line while Oliver watched the signal on his terminal. It steadied down into a regular pattern as the two systems established a handshake and shared codes. "Alright, we're secure. What is so urgent?"

Her voice held a buzz to it, courtesy of the digital filtering. "It is those mercenaries. We have lost too many ships, too many people. Now they are hiring a ship of their own, which means they are not tied to the locals. You must do something."

"I must? I'm paying you for results. If you're having operational security issues or just have incompetent people, that's your problem to fix. If they're hiring locals, then why can't you convince those people they don't want to be hired?"

"Your money means little if we are dead. And too many of ours are dead or captured. Those in custody of Justice can be freed but to go against the guns of those armored beasts, no. No amount of money is worth that."

Beck sighed to himself. *I knew this was coming. They're not insurgents or paramilitary types.* "Fine. I have other assets who are willing to do these things. But their pay comes out of your cut."

"Our cut is nothing if we are not operating. Twenty-five percent."

"Your cut is nothing and your risk is greater without the intelligence we provide. Fifty percent."

"Very well. But until these mercenaries are dealt with, we are being more careful with target selection. And we will tell you which ships after we hit them."

Paranoid as hell. Not bad. "Fine. As long as they meet the target criteria, your security measures are acceptable."

Ana hung up without another word. Oliver immediately flashed a message to his team and Flatley.

H getting antsy. Increase personal security measures. BPT activate secondary contractors.

He went to the closet and pulled out a case he hadn't opened yet. Inside was a disassembled FN modular weapon system and plenty of ammunition. With quick, expert motions he reassembled it and inserted a magazine. This version, with a collapsible stock, short barrel and shoulder sling was ideal for carrying concealed. It complemented the concealed pistol he always carried. Things were about to get very exciting on station and he wasn't going to get caught by surprise. Then he phoned Flatley and told him to come over right away.

*****

Oliver held his pistol at the ready as he checked the camera he'd mounted outside the door. Flatley stood there, looking tired and nervous but appeared to be alone. Stepping back and opening the door, he motioned the other man inside. "Anyone following you?"

"Two of those Hoffman goons. They're not very subtle."

The ex-military man locked the door and replaced the anti-kick plate. "They don't have to be. They control a significant portion of the illegal activity on this station and more importantly, have a number of highly placed station and government people on their payroll."

Flatley sat at the small table and sighed. "I don't see why you couldn't come out–"

Beck cut him off. "Because of those Hoffman people. They know about this place but not my others. They also know about you and that we work together. We've given them nothing else to watch, just confirming what they already know."

"Fine. Why am I here?"

"They're getting antsy about the mercs. Apparently, they've suffered too many losses."

"Are they going to be able to handle the 76th? Because those guys are going to really upset our plans if they keep going the way they are."

"I'm not going to use the Hoffman organization. I have another option, instead. One of those more violent groups I mentioned to Cross."

The analyst rubbed his hands over his face. The bags under his eyes were showing. "I've been talking nearly nonstop with the marketing team. They went from being on top of the world on the initial piracy news to almost ready to pull out. The team chief has them in hand but even he's getting worried."

"I got this. But I need you to ping our people in the government bureaucracy. I have to have a nice juicy tidbit to slip to this group. Something they'll really bite on. Once they do, I'll give them a location of one of the weapons caches so they can really hurt the mercs when they go after them."

"And that will end the problem?"

The former military man shrugged. "Nothing is sure in combat. And the 76th is good, I'll give them that. But this works in our favor either way. If the mercs get hurt badly and that is a possibility with the weapons we're supplying, they cease being a serious threat to our plans. If our contractors get beat, then we cease operations altogether. Makes it look like the threat has been neutralized."

"Yes. Yes, we could make that thread pay out. If the security situation stabilizes, the locals are going to be desperate to hook any corporation still around to negotiate. Terms and rates can be adjusted to entice even the most reticent. That's assuming you can give us advanced knowledge?"

Oliver nodded. "I have comms with my contractors and a contact that will let me know what the 76th reports back to their Justice handlers. Win or lose, we'll know before anyone else here."

******

McMannus finished introducing the newly minted Lieutenant Eisen to the rest of the command staff. "Tell the boys and girls they don't have to worry about their ride anymore. We now have someone who is both part of the unit and understands very well what it means to deliver troops to the target."

"Also tell them if they puke on my deck or otherwise make a mess, they're cleaning it up." Eisen wore the undress grays with ease, already seeming like he'd been with them the whole time.

Harry raised an eyebrow at the pilot. "You've flown a MIST insertion before, then? Cause we don't puke unless some hotshot vacc jockey thinks he has something to prove."

"Not a boarding action, no. But I did combat search and rescue for most of my career."

"Say no more then. Welcome aboard."

Sparks popped his head in the room. "Cap'n, priority message from Justice for you."

McMannus hurried out of the room as the rest looked at each other. Harry rubbed his hands together with a big grin. "Just in time, mate. This is where we earn our big money!"

Eisen rolled his eyes. "Great. I'm so thrilled. I'll make sure to stock up on crayons for in-flight snacks."

Chapter 34

"Mr. Vestry, Mr. Kan, proceed with the mission brief."

Ezekiel stood and walked to the front of the room. The screen flickered and changed to display a scaled view of the whole system. It zoomed in to the second planet in the system and to the sole moon orbiting it.

"This is Metztli, which previously supported a heavy metals mine. The Grausians abandoned it some thirty years ago after it became too costly to operate. Justice had it on a watch list of potential bases supporting smuggling operations, given its easy path to the jump point. Turns out they were correct."

The display on the screen shifted, now showing fuzzy optical images that quickly resolved into a series of three domes and other assorted structures. A bulbous ship squatted on a landing pad near the domes. He manipulated the images to show several perspectives of the surface. "These images are less than a day old. The ship you see is the *Gacela*, a government fast courier. It arrived at the jump gate three days ago and went missing shortly after that. An organization known as the Red Ghosts has claimed responsibility and is demanding ransom for the crew and passengers."

The image changed to show a human male; head shaved bald, a ferocious black mustache and a much-broken nose. A list of charges appeared next to him. "This is one of our high value targets for this op. Piotr Mierzejewski, head of the Red Ghosts. As you can see, Justice has quite the file on him. He's got warrants from Pavo Real and the neighboring systems. We get a bonus if he comes in alive."

Lieutenant Kan took over at this point. "Our mission is twofold; rescue the crew and passengers of the *Gacela* and eliminate or capture the Red Ghosts. Given that this is their primary base, we're expecting serious opposition on this mission. We estimate their strength at thirty to thirty-five personnel, given the available life support capability of the habs. With that in mind, we are committing 2nd Platoon, half of 1st Platoon and the company command section. This mission has top priority, so we're temporarily suspending the anti-piracy ops."

"We'll travel to the target on the *Calypso*. Travel time is about fifteen and a half hours. Lieutenant Eisen will be in communication with Mr. Vestry and receive the latest intel before we drop." The screen changed back to the moon's surface. Four green ovals appeared around the perimeter of the base. "Once there, the assault will proceed in two phases. 2nd Platoon will lead the initial assault, dropping on these zones and rolling up their sentries to capture Objective Alpha, the landing field. They will then secure Objective Bravo, the *Gacela* and any other ship that happens to be there and set up a defensive perimeter to prevent a counterattack from the hab domes. At that point, the Captain will drop with the command section and the section from 1st to begin the assault on the hab domes. These are Objectives Charlie One through Three, starting with the northern one. 2nd will support the hab assault as needed but its primary job will be to provide security for the flanks and maintain the evac route."

The perspective zoomed in to show a view of the surrounding terrain from the ground level. The mine was in a crater at the base of a mountain range. "Key terrain includes the crater rim and this ridge." He highlighted the ridge closest to the crater. "We'll want to sweep these to remove any snipers and ensure we maintain the dominant terrain."

Captain McMannus stood and took over the controls from Ishido. A picture appeared on the screen of a human male, older and distinguished-looking. "Thank you, Mr. Kan. One last thing, people. Just to make the pucker factor higher, this isn't just any courier. It was carrying the Pavo Real Deputy Foreign Minister, on his way back from visiting the other members of the League. The government received a very large ransom demand within an hour of the ship landing there. This was no coincidence. Someone leaked that itinerary and set up the kidnap attempt. Rescue of the minister is top priority. We need him alive and unharmed. After the mission is complete, we will focus on locating and securing any intel on who set up the kidnap attempt. The Red Ghosts don't normally do this kind of thing, so someone in the government has to be feeding them inside information."

The screen cleared and he looked around the room. "Doing this right will build our reputation and get us better contracts. I know we didn't use to think like that but this is how things are changing. Now, that's not to say I want glory hunters out there. We go in, do our job, rescue the hostages, capture the bad guy and go home. Simple as that. We've all done asteroid assaults. Mind the gravity, watch your air and guard each other's backs. VIS."

They stood and echoed his last comment together. The captain turned and clapped Ish on the shoulder. "Sorry, Mr. Kan. Since you got the last assault it's Harry's turn on this one. But you won't be idle. I'm leaving you in charge of the dependents and our base. If the Red Ghosts get a message out or our OPSEC fails, things here could get interesting. When the assault starts, you're to lock down the base and all dependents. Full security measures and full load out until we return. Take no chances."

He turned to the rest of the group. "Let's mount up, people. Platoon and squad briefs on the *Calypso* enroute."

*****

Beck watched the *Calypso* leave the dock on a feed pirated from station control. Once he was sure they weren't changing course, he went to his rented room and set up his anti-tap gear on the room's commlink and called his contact on station for the Red Ghosts.

"Yeah? Whatchoo want?" The voice was rough and slightly slurred, no doubt from the bottle he had in his desk drawer.

"This is Mr. White. You should let your boss know that the mercenary unit known as the 76th MIST just left the station to attack your base."

"What? That's bullshit! How do you know?"

"That's what I do. The real question is, what do you want to do about it?"

"We'll handle them. Bunch a washed-up mercs? Pfft! Piece a' cake."

Beck rolled his eyes. "You have no idea what you're dealing with. Do you know what a MIST is? No, of course you don't. Let me enlighten you. These Marines are experts in microgravity and vacuum work. Their job in wartime was to assault heavily armed warships and defeat the crew onboard. Your puny small arms aren't going to do much to them and your lack of tactical ability will be on full display as they take you apart in a bloody froth."

There was a long pause. "So why do you care?"

"My employer views the MIST as an obstacle to his plans. As such, they need to be taken care of. Your organization can be the tool that handles this obstacle, if you're willing."

"And what'll cost us?"

"Right now, nothing. We'll even give you the weapons necessary. But later on, when I ask for a favor, you'd better drop everything to do it."

"Weapons? Like, the good shit?"

"Yes, the good shit. Even some plasma weapons, which should toast those armored suits the MIST uses."

"Then hell yes! We'll burn those fuckers up and take their shit, too."

"Of course you will. The weapons are located on planet near your base. Here are the coordinates."

Now that I'm done with that scumbag, time to let the boss know. Using his own terminal, he placed a secure ansible call to the cutout number. "There was some vapor building up in the system but I found a mechanic to take care of it. I'll let you know when things are cleared up."

If the MIST happened to eliminate the Red Ghosts and their base, it was one less loose end for him to take care of once this operation was completed. He still had the SMS around to take care of them here on the station, if it came to that.

Chapter 35

Enroue to Metzli. Pavo Real System

The *Calypso* was under acceleration, making the trip seem like a luxury to the Marines, who were used to spending hours in micro. Even with the boost, it was still hours of travel to their target, which allowed plenty of time to brief the units on their targets. The MACE suits were able to display a simulation of the terrain at the base, which allowed them to plan at least the initial phase of the assault as best they could.

While Lieutenant Webb worked with Staff Sergeant Brown and his squad leaders on their deployment, McMannus, Gunny Mulongo and Staff Sergeant Salazar went over the standard floor plans for the habitats. Given that they were several decades old and had been inhabited by the Red Ghosts for an unknown amount of time, there were likely to be modifications. Entry points were noted, as well as life support controls. They were pretty sure the hostages would be in the hab, since the *Gacela* was too small and cramped to accommodate an adequate guard.

"I'm concerned about the courier ship, sir." Gunny Mulongo highlighted it in their displays. "She could be a staging location for the enemy. If they had to displace people from the hab so they put their hostages in there, then we could be looking at a squad or more in the ship."

"So what do you suggest, Gunny?"

"Well, in our previous life I'd say station an anti-armor team there and pop the lock if it opens. But I'm guessing our employers would like their ship back in one piece."

"Good guess. We're going to have to keep random destruction to a minimum in this line of work. Don't want damages to come out of our profits."

"In that case, I recommend a sniper team with LR-9s on overwatch. Anyone pops their head out the hatch that doesn't look like a hostage, we take them down." Three red circles appeared on the display. "These all have good lines of sight to the hatch."

Staff Sergeant Salazar frowned. "We have one LR-9 in 1st. But I'd hate to leave someone out of the assault."

McMannus shook his head. "Me too. Trade with Staff Sergeant Brown. Overwatch on the ship or ships is their mission. The LR-9 would be too dangerous in the hab, anyway. Too easy to breach the walls."

"Speaking of breaching, sir. Are we going in the easy way or the hard way?" The Gunny tapped the image of the bureaucrat. "Once we drop on their perimeter, they'll be ready for us."

"With three habs and three squads, we can't afford to go slow. I want to crack two of them first, using 1st Platoon with the command squad in reserve. Maybe we'll get lucky and find our targets on the first try. If not, then we can use all three squads to use on the last hab. Mierzejewski will feel the noose tightening around him."

"And will he do something stupid then?"

McMannus tapped the image of the criminal boss. "The Red Ghosts have a reputation for violence and a lack of empathy for their targets. They've also survived quite a while in this system. I'd say Mierzejewski is going to want to use his hostages for negotiating an escape, especially once we cut off all his escape routes. If he won't surrender, we'll go in fast and hard. We don't have to worry about damage to the habs."

*****

Eisen brought the ship into a low flight path, barely five hundred feet above the surface, which was easy enough with the lack of atmosphere. They had approached from the far side of Metzli to avoid warning their opponents. The pilot looked back at his new boss. "Okay, we're set on the planned ground trace. The release point is in seven minutes, after which I'll put her into a figure eight pattern over the base."

"Copy that. You'll get the first look at the target so sing out if something looks off from the last visual image." McMannus made his way back to the cargo bay, where the platoon was assembling. Lieutenant Webb and Staff Sergeant Brown were at the back of the formation, probably going over some last-minute details.

"Ready for a walk in the black, Mr. Webb?"

"Piece of piss, skipper. Be done in a jiff and have a spot of tea ready for you when you come on down."

"Sounds good to me. Let's pay our respects to old Piotr and retrieve that wayward bureaucrat. Six minutes to drop."

Harry saluted with a jaunty smile and secured his helmet. As he headed for the front of the columns, his voice rang out on the general channel, "Second Platoon, who are we?"

"Weasels!" Came the shouted reply.

"And what do we do?"

"First in, last out!"

The overhead lights went out and a hastily rigged red light by the cargo doors at the rear came on. It began to open slowly upwards, the blackness beyond a yawning void. Gunny Mulongo called out over the comm. *"Stand to!"*

The Marines stepped into two four columns, facing the rear doors. *"Check suits!"* came the next call.

Each Marine checked the suit in front of him, while the Captain and Mulongo checked the rear person in each column and then each other. As each check was completed, the Marine toggled on a green LED on their suit helmet. Soon, the bay was filled with green lights.

Eisen's crew chief was standing by the rear hatch, alternately watching the red light and checking out the door. The star field was now fully visible but nothing could be seen of the ground. They were approaching from the shadowed side of the planet and wouldn't be in full sun until they were less than two minutes from dropping.

"Captain, I'm picking up radar signals. Nothing approaching detection range but they're radiating. They might know we're coming." Eisen's voice was calm and cool and McMannus thanked Ezekiel silently that he didn't have to deal with a panicky civilian.

"Copy, Mr. Eisen. Continue on course."

He looked over at the Gunny, who gave him a thumbs-up. Jumping against a ready enemy wasn't anything they hadn't dealt with before and at least this time they weren't dealing with defenses that could obliterate them with one shot.

As the ground features suddenly became visible through the hatch, the crew chief said over the open channel, *"Two minutes!"*

Mulongo repeated, *"Two minutes! Stand in the door!"* Lieutenant Webb and Staff Sergeant Brown stepped forward, the columns moving with them.

The red light flashed twice and the crew chief pointed at the deck. *"Braking! Mag on!"* A civilian ship like the *Calypso* didn't have pod-mounted thrusters to fire in both directions, so they were approaching rear-end first. Everyone was already magged anyway but the doublecheck didn't hurt.

Mulongo repeated the call and they felt their bodies sway backwards with the forces exerted by the engines. Then the engines cut and the green light came on.

The crew chief and Mulongo were shouting, "Go!" over the radio but neither Harry nor his platoon sergeant needed the command. Both unmagged and stepped through the hatch into nothingness beyond, with the rest of their platoon in rapid succession.

As McMannus watched his people disappear over the ramp, Eisen reported continuous radar hits. *"Tracking stuff only, though. No fire control. But I'd definitely say they were ready for us."*

"Whisper One, Whisper Six. Condition Red Two. I say again, Condition Red Two." This was the call for a hot drop zone, where the enemy was prepared but no ground to air defenses were firing.

"Copy Whisper Six. They're boiling out of their habs like ants. I think-" His voice cut off in a crackle of static. Both men stepped forward to look out the hatch as the section from 1st Platoon and his own command squad began lining up for their drop.

Eisen had halted short of the landing field, letting the Marines use the jets on their MACE suits to carry them to their objectives. The Captain's HUD showed him each Marine's position as they dropped to the surface. The neat columns were beginning to scatter across the visible sky as each Marine maneuvered violently.

The reason for their evasive actions became apparent when a ball of white plasma shot forth from the landing pad, near their target ship. It streaked past a juking MISTer, the range giving the target enough time to adjust course. Two other pirates fired their own plasma weapons from other positions near the landing pad, with one of them scoring a hit in a shower of sparks and slagged metal. The unlucky victim, Private Davies, began to tumble in mid-flight, suit flashing red in the command display. Without waiting for the platoon leader, McMannus triggered the suit's emergency response protocols. It would automatically land so the Marine could at least have a chance at being recovered. The health monitor was offline, so he wasn't sure if Davies was dead or not.

Harry's voice came back online. *"Sorry Whisper Six. Had to juke about. One of those bolts nearly took me head off. Where'd they get Barrett's?"*

"Whisper One, worry about that later. Priority targeting on those positions."

"Copy. Grounding now."

They watched as Webb's platoon hit their assigned landing zones, squads mostly intact. The plasma fire had only scored a single direct hit and it became apparent from the scattered positions that the pirates weren't really prepared for a mass drop. They were concentrated on the landing pad, probably figuring the 76th would land their ship and disembark from there.

Each squad moved in a coordinated fashion, identifying and concentrating on the pirate positions. These were set up in piles of equipment or in small craters next to the field and the pirates at least had some familiarity with controlling their movements in low gravity environments. They were able to use their cover well, firing and dropping back without bouncing too high.

However, from up above, McMannus had a god-like view of the battlefield that gave him the ability to locate each position, which he tagged on the BMC3 terminal and transmitted to his people. The MISTers then proceeded to show the pirates just how to maximize the use of the low gravity to make pop-up attacks on their opponents. While his teammates put out covering fire, a MISTer would make a suit-assisted leap straight up, firing as soon as they saw their targets. A kill shot wasn't necessary, as the pirates' suits were unarmored. A single 4mm flechette could make a huge tear in their suits, forcing the pirate out of the fight to scramble to patch the hole. He had stripped out 1st Platoon to arm most of 2nd with all the PW-93s they had to maximize his firepower on the assault.

It took less than ten minutes from the start of the drop to Lieutenant Webb's call of *"Objective Alpha secured. Two KIA and four WIA. Two of those will need evac; the bloody plasma fried their computer controls and life support's gone a bit wonky."*

"Copy Whisper One. Clear a site and we'll land. Status on Objective Bravo?"

"Whisper Six, doubt there's anyone in it. Ship looks solid but the hatches are open and power's off. I'll send a team to check it out."

*****

They landed a few minutes later and hustled the casualties aboard. McMannus led his assault force in bounding hops across the landing field towards the habs.

They were spread out in a skirmish formation, preventing a single hit from taking out multiple targets. The habs were set back about a hundred meters from the field, in a roughly triangular setup. The center hab was closest to the field but he wasn't going to put them in a situation where they could be hit from both sides.

He was about to give the order to the Gunny to deploy for their assault on the left-most hab when Sparks pinged him.

"Sir, I've got a transmission in the open from the hab. Could be the enemy commander."

"Right. Patch him through to me."

Seconds later, a harsh voice came online. *"...you scodney gits! I'll make yer sorry fer touching down on me bach! Come on, then!"*

"Enemy commander, this is Captain Fremont McMannus, 76th MIST, representing the legal authority in this system. You have two minutes to lay down your arms and surrender your hostages."

"Oi, asshole! Why don't you fuckers bugger right off? Try and come in here and those fuck-tirds won't be long. Be funny to watch them suck vacuum."

McMnannus switched channels back to his command circuit. "Sparks, can you localize his transmission?"

"Negative, sir. He's using the main antenna to broadcast."

Turning to Mulongo, McMannus gave hand signals for him to deploy for an assault on Charlie One, the hab to the left. Then he switched back to the open channel. "Your hostages die, then you die with them. I'll have no reason to keep you around."

"Ha! You think those Justice types will stick us in the clink? We saw what you lot did to the last batch."

Shit. I knew that video would come back to haunt us. "There are no Justice agents here. Only us. I give you my word that any who surrender will live to stand trial back on Pavo Real."

"Yer jest chatting me up so you can bust on in. I can see you doongi moving around out there. Tell you whot; I'll give you one for free. Ain't no one in that hab. Now you got fifty-fifty on where I be. Them's good odds in my book."

He's stalling. Telling us the left hab is empty is begging for us to check it out and make sure. It buys him time for… what?

Mulongo signaled they were ready to hit the hab. This would just be the squads from 1st Platoon, so he still had his command squad in reserve. Plus all of Webb's platoon back at the landing field. So why did he feel like they were about to step into something nasty?

Fuck it. "Execute."

The two squads simultaneously breached the two airlocks of the hab, forcing the doors to stay open as they streamed in. He waited, sitting on his anxiety as he waited for a report.

"Whisper Six, Whisper Two Seven. No opposition on entry. Hab is on minimal power and dark. We-" His voice cut off in mid-transmission as the hab exploded. It wasn't a large explosion, more of the building expanding visibly and then flames jetting out of the weak points in the structure. The walls and roof began to break apart and then collapse slowly in the moon's low gravity.

"Gunny, take the command squad and see who's alive in there! Whisper One, get me a squad for assault actions. Whisper Eight, prep for casualties." McMannus was bounding towards the structure himself as he gave orders. "Sparks, get me a better signal. My HUD is showing all kinds of interference on their signals."

They reached the debris pile and started moving the pieces aside. The lack of an atmosphere prevented any fires from continuing and the low gravity allowed them to maneuver even the largest pieces aside. The first two MISTers were pulled from the remains of the hatch almost immediately. Their armor was scorched and blackened but the integrity was intact.

The Captain sat both of them down on a nearby rock. "Can either of you tell me what happened?"

Private Ramek sucked on his water nipple and swallowed. *"Dunno, sir. Staff Sergeant put me on door guard and took the rest inside. Then, boom."*

"Cap'n, same with me. After the airlock it was a straight corridor to an interior hatch. Couldn't see much more being at the rear of the column. But I think the hatch was rigged cause I thought I saw it open just because it went to shit."

They all turned as Gunny announced another one and then over the comm they heard Staff Sergeant Brown. Her voice was weak but thready. *"Whisper Six, Whisper Two Seven. What happened?"*

"Whisper One Seven, I think you tripped an IED. Status report?"

Her voice remained weak and she seemed to have trouble breathing. *"I'm… okay, I think. No suit alarms but I'm pinned. Can't move anything."*

"Copy that, Whisper One Seven. Standby. We're digging you out. Do you have signals on anyone else?"

Her reply disappeared in a burst of static, followed by an ear-piercing squeal. He gritted his teeth and watched the two privates also making faces at the noise. Several seconds later, the squeal disappeared but was replaced with multiple overlapping transmissions.

McMannus toggled the command override, cutting everyone but his platoon leaders and sergeants out. "Whisper Two, sitrep!"

Harry was breathing heavily. *"Whisper Six, I've been a right wally. They did a runner on us and come out of the old mining shafts. Stand still, you wanker. Right, still trying to get an accurate count but we're all mixed up. It's dirk time and no bones about it."*

"Whisper Two, copy. VIS and finish it fast. Whisper Seven, sitrep."

"Whisper Six, we've pulled four more out but we're taking intermittent fire from Charlie Two. Sparks has neutralized the jammer the OPFOR deployed."

"Right. Whisper Seven. I'm taking these two here with me and Sparks and lay down suppressing fire. Continue rescue operations." He signaled the two privates to follow him. "Tag any suspected sniper locations."

"Whisper Six, already marked. Two, possibly three. Looks like they may be using SV-17s."

More mil standard weapons. First plasma rifles and now sniper weapons. Where the hell are smugglers getting these? "Copy Whisper Seven. Commencing suppression now."

He assigned targets to each of the three MISTers with him and observed the hab for any new spots. The sniper positions seemed to be cut directly into the hab wall itself rather than a hatch or other normal opening. *That means the hab is probably already depressurized, which means the hostages aren't in there. That leaves only one place left.*

Alternately watching the hab and typing on his sleeve keypad, he sent a message to Webb.

*When current OPFOR contained or eliminated, send two squads to last hab. Likely
hostage location so breach with speed and be prepared with rescue bubbles. Will
draw attention here. Signal when ready.*

With a spray of molten metal, Private Ramek's helmet exploded. There had been no warning, no flash of a firing weapon to give away the shooter. It could only have been a laser. They ducked behind the debris and McMannus called out to Mulongo. "Whisper Seven, watch out for laser fire. Have you dug up anyone with a Cigar yet?"

"Affirmative, Whisper Six. Where do you want it?"

"Take out Charlie Two. The hostages aren't in it so no reason to keep it. Watch it, they have at least one laser."

"Good copy, Whisper Six."

McMannus looked left and right. There was enough debris for them to spread out some. He slapped the legs of Sparks and the other private and gave them hand signals to displace and commence pop-up firing. Maybe they could get lucky and it might distract the enemy from noticing the rocket team. Since the AT-8 warhead could breach ship hulls, this flimsy hab should be no problem.

"Whisper Six, heavy weapons team in position."

"Copy, Whisper Seven. Standby." He got his own PW-93V ready and signaled to the other two. They all popped up at the same time, spraying the hab. "Whisper Seven, go!"

The AT-8 used nitrogen to expel the projectile several meters and then it ignited its rocket motor. The rocket streaked in from his left and impacted on the hab right at door level. The high explosive squash warhead did its job, expanding into a pancake of explosive before detonating. A blast wave over a meter across slammed through the thin walls and interior structure of the hab. It expanded as it went, tearing through the load-bearing walls. Almost immediately, the hab began to sag towards the impact point as the weight of the upper section pulled it down. It was a slow-motion fall in the one quarter gravity but there was enough to do the job.

Two suited figures spilled out of the upper part of the structure as it fell and they riddled each with flechettes. One was wearing an especially bulky backpack, likely the laser sniper. "Nice work, Whisper Seven. Can you free a team to check for any remaining hostiles?"

"Roger, Whisper Six. We're just pulling the last survivor out. Everyone made it, although there are two with life support damage. They're on their way back to the ship now."

"I copy. Whisper Two, status?"

"Whisper Six, it was a bit dodgy there for a bit. But Alpha is resecured and I have a present for ya."

The video feed from Webb's suit showed a man in a vacc suit that was painted blood-red, with a white ghost face on the chestplate. He was in a vehicle of some sort, which started at his waist and flared out into treads. It mounted a set of jets on the rear, allowing it to move in vacuum as well. Right now he was on side, one tread shredded. His suit integrity was still good, because he was giving the lieutenant a double middle finger.

"Whisper Six, meet ya counterpart. Old Piotr himself. Led the counterattack in this collection of odds and sods. Got him and five other EPWs. Our side has three WIA, one KIA. Skipper, they had PW-89s. Couldn't use them for shit but a lucky burst caught Corporal Mackey just right. Where'd they get these things?"

"Good question, Whisper Two. Okay, police everything up. I'm on my way over to talk with our friend there."

The Red Ghost leader was still as uncooperative as he'd been before. "Look, Piotr. I already promised you that you'd live to stand trial. But if you let those hostages die, you're signing your death warrant yourself. But if you cooperate, when I turn you over, I can attest to the fact you weren't party to cold-blooded murder."

The glare from the shaven-headed man was palpable but the effect was spoiled by their position. *"You wanna piece of me, ass-wipe? Why don't you come closer, so that I can whip your arse."*

Piotr was still on his side in the dirt and the position had to be uncomfortable. McMannus stood over him, PW-93V cradled in his arms. The other smugglers were secured in the hold of the *Calypso* and there was a squad ready to breach Charlie Three. If they could get the pirate's cooperation, then maybe they could wrap this up quickly.

Sighing, the mercenary captain kneeled a safe distance away from the pirate. "Look, that video had some shock value but now they're regretting it, within Justice at least. It's done us no good either. I don't want a repeat of it and will not let that happen to you. But if I have to report that the hostages died because of your actions…"

The rugged face relaxed and a sigh briefly clouded the helmet with moisture. *"Bloody wanker. Fine. Both doors are rigged with delay timers. But that's the only thing None of me men are inside. All the hostages are in the central room, with helmets on but radios disabled. Couldn't risk them calling out, ya know?"* He gave instructions on how to disable the triggers which McMannus relayed to Webb.

"And now you. What the hell is this contraption and will it explode if we set you upright?"

"It's me own bloody design. Never had use of me legs, so I's had to improvise in gravity. Jes flip me over and I can do the rest."

"Fine. But no dodgy stuff or I'll have Mr. Webb here pop the other track."

Chapter 36

Colon High Station, Pavo Real System

Cassie wrinkled her nose at the smell of her room. She'd been holed up here now for three days and the inactivity and smell were getting to her. There had been some trips out to check on a few things and she always made sure to come back with more cheap booze. *I have a plan, I think. The only question is, will they play along? I have information they need but I have to convince them to listen or else it's worthless.* Her tablet pinged at that moment, notifying her of another blocked attempt to remotely access her ship's database. That was the tenth attempt and she wasn't sure how much longer the security lockout would hold.

She checked her appearance in the mirror. Cosmetics and an artful use of hair gel made her look exactly like how she should; someone coming off a multi-day bender. Her jumpsuit was shabby and patched but hid the business suit underneath. It was the best she could find on the budget she had, what with all her clothes lost in the raid. *I just hope the guards don't think I'm some sort of hack salesperson.*

On leaving her room, she followed her usual routine until she reached the liquor shop. Instead, she passed by it and into the clothes shop two doors down. The displays in the front hid the view of the dressing rooms near the back, something she'd plotted out the day before. Inside the cramped closet, she skimmed off the jumpsuit and stuffed it into a corner. Rough voices filtered through the closed door, demanding to know where she was. The shopkeeper, paid off in advance, denied seeing anyone come in as Cassie slipped out of the dressing room, down the corridor and out the back door. She followed the maze of narrow corridors and hatches until she reached a bathroom. A few minutes work in the mirror and her appearance was changed, with hair and makeup now approaching a more business-like level.

Twenty minutes later, Cassie exited the elevator at the 76th entrance and stopped short. The normally open hall that led to their entrance was a maze of metal walls. A bright light flicked on and shone right at her face, blinding her.

"Halt! State your business!" The voice was computer-modulated and impersonal, booming through the small space.

Hand in front of her eyes, she blinked away tears. "Cassandra Vickers, here to see Captain McMannus!"

"Use the terminal to your left to enter your information." The light moved away a little so it was no longer blinding her, although she still couldn't see anything of the entrance due to the glare. There was a small data terminal and she punched in her information with shaking hands. She put down both the Captain and Mr. Vestry as people she wished to see. Maybe one of them would be available.

"Stay there and don't move. Your information is being processed."

After several long minutes, the light clicked off. "Proceed through the entrapment zone to the entry control point."

She walked forward cautiously. Now that she wasn't blinded by the glare, she could see that the barriers were shoulder-high and very sturdy-looking. They formed a dog leg she had to navigate and she heard movement outside the barrier as she went through. As she passed a very obvious metal detector, it went off.

"Remove your weapons and place them in the bin next to you."

With slow, careful movements she put the needler, knife and stun stick in the bin. This time the detector didn't go off as she walked through and after another dog leg she was at the main hatch. It was reinforced steel and gastight but it opened for her soundlessly. On the other were two armored Marines waiting for her.

"Follow us, ma'am."

They took her to the same conference room as before. Inside were Ezekiel Vestry, dressed in a simple jumpsuit and two young officers, a man and the woman from the conference and they were both armed.

"Well, Ms. Vickers, what brings you to our neck of the woods again? Come to negotiate for more information?"

She swallowed. "Mr. Vestry, I'm afraid I've come with my hat in hand. I need help and have nowhere else to turn."

He frowned. "What about your company? Can't they help you?"

"That's… no. I can't go to them without putting them in the same trouble, or worse."

"Ms. Vickers, if you're in trouble you should go to the police."

Her knees threatened to buckle as she stepped forward, hands in an iron grip on the back of the chair. "Mr. Vestry, I can't be sure of the police. Of anyone here on the station besides you."

Vestry looked at her once more, eyes lingering on her white-knuckled grip and relented. He motioned to the chair. "Please, sit. Tell me more. I'm very interested in your characterization of the station personnel, especially law enforcement."

Minutes later, after she had relayed her story and showed them the video of the attack, Vestry turned to the male officer. "Ms. Vickers, this is Lieutenant Ishido Kan. The Captain is not currently on station and Lieutenant Kan is in charge."

The young officer spread his hands. "I'm sorry for the loss of your team, Ms. Vickers. But to repeat, what can the 76th do for StellarMart?"

"It's not StellarMart. It's me. And you." She sighed. "Look, I'm done at StellarMart. I screwed up and got my team killed and then on top of that StellarMart will have to withdraw from the conference. If I'm not fired I'll be working some menial job that will bore the shit out of me. I can't fix that. But I can get revenge for my people and help you in the process."

"Help us? Why?"

"Because the same people who got me are out to get you. They're the ones behind the pirate attacks and they're doing the same thing we were trying to do; manipulate the negotiations. Only you're screwing up their plans by finding and stopping the pirates." She cut off the flow of words and swiped a finger across the tears threatening to fall. "And because I couldn't help my brother but I can help you."

Vestry leaned forward now. "That's a strong accusation. Do you have proof?"

"Yes. It's on my ship's database. For now it's under lockdown but the Hoffmans are very good at getting access to secure systems. I can't be sure how much longer it'll be safe. I need… would like you to escort me to my ship so we can get that information. Then you can have a copy to use as you see fit."

"I… see. So you're contracting for our services, then?" Kan leaned back in his chair, tapping his fingers on the table.

She looked down at her hands. "No. I doubt I could afford you. I'm asking for a favor, Lieutenant, to accomplish something that will help the both of us."

Ezekiel shook his head. "We only have your word on that. If you're in trouble with the wrong people, we don't want to get in the middle of that."

"The Hoffmans already don't like you. It's not like you're on their Christmas card list."

The lieutenant looked over at Vestry, who nodded. He turned back to her and gave her a grim smile. "We would very much like to have that information. You have your escort, Ms. Vickers. The only price is a copy of your data. Consider it a family rate. The Captain told us about your brother. He's one of us and we'll help you."

*****

Cassandra walked in the middle of the diamond formation set by the four Marines. People saw the heavily armored figures coming down the corridor and scattered from their path. Fortunately, their path to the docking slips wasn't heavily populated.

At their slip, she keyed in her access codes and thumbprint to gain access. The corporal left two Marines on guard outside and then followed her in. "In case someone got here before you, ma'am."

She didn't think it was likely. The ship's access logs showed that no one had come aboard since they'd docked but if these Hoffman people were as good as Selena, they could have doctored the log. A wrenching pain stabbed her guts as she remembered her webmistress. Never again would she make her jokes about their cover identities or proclaim her mastery over the networks. *I'll get them for you, Selena. You, Vera and Janus will all get your revenge.*

She sat at a terminal, the one she'd used several days before on their trip out here. The compartment echoed with the laughter and jokes from that time and she screwed up her eyes to stop the tears. Blinking watery eyes, she accessed the secure database Selena had set up. Sure enough, the most recent time stamps on the access logs were during the attack. Hitting the backup button, she turned to the corporal. "I'm downloading the files to a data stick now. It'll be a few minutes."

Corporal Jordan DeMarco nodded. "Ma'am, my orders are for you to make two copies. You carry one and I'll carry one. Mr. Vestry also said to tell you they're going to crosscheck both copies against each other."

She sighed and nodded at the main panel. "Very well. They'll come out over there when the downloads are complete."

They both waited in silence for several seconds as the computer hummed away. Jordan took advantage of the wait to look around at the corporate ship. He hadn't been anything that wasn't either military or freighter and neither spared money on comforts. The workstations looked new and unworn and the seats were self-adjusting memory gel. It looked like the back of the room had a complete kitchen setup, with multiple drink dispensers for hot and cold beverages. He turned back to his VIP, feeling her gaze on his.

"Admiring the setup, corporal?"

"Yes ma'am. We don't have anything like this."

She sighed. "Yeah. I took my brother for a tour when he was home on leave and he said I had the sweetest gig in the universe. Now I'd trade it all for…" She stopped, not knowing exactly what she would trade it for.

Jordan waited but she didn't continue. He was about to ask if her brother was the guy scuttlebutt was going on about but the team at the main entrance commed just then.

"Corp, we got some guys down the end of the slip giving some bad looks. Bout seven or so. No weapons I can make out at this distance but they're giving us unfriendly looks."

"Roger. Be ready. A few more minutes here and we're done." He said to her, "Ma'am, that was my team outside. There are some people out there who might be ready to cause trouble. Soon as you're done, we'll go. Can you move fast?"

She kicked off the cheap shoes she was wearing and walked over to a locker. "I'll put on some mag boots. Less comfortable but it gives us more options. And yes, I do know how to use them."

As she was sealing the boots, several things happened. The computer buzzed, with a panel opening and revealing two identical data sticks. And the team at the main airlock reported taking fire.

"A couple shots, corp. Hit the docking hatch and ricocheted into the hall. Seems like standard slugs."

"Take cover and return fire on a valid target, Jess. We're on our way."

Santis poked his head in the compartment. "We going to kick some butt, DeMarco?"

Cassandra stood and picked up the data sticks. Handing one to Jordan, she looked at him expectantly. He stored it in a secure pouch on his belt. "No, Brian. Our mission is escort and return. No time to play. Head out front and give me a wedge in the hall. Push forward to the end of the slip and secure the position. Remember, engage valid targets only. Watch for non-combatants."

The other Marine left as Jordan switched to the company channel. "Whisper One, this is Whisper One Three Bravo. Taking hostile fire. Slug rounds, no damage or injuries. Prepping for exfil."

He motioned for Cassandra to stay behind him as they went to the main airlock. His scanner showed that the other three were about halfway down the corridor. "Bennings, any signs of hostile activity?"

"That's a negative. Soon as we started heading down the corridor they scattered."

He thought about that. Why fire a couple of rounds and then run when approached? *To get us to bunch up.* "Hit the deck!"

Five people popped around the corner at the end of the dock, LR-8s in hand. The laser fire was invisible to the naked eye but Jordan's HUD showed the pencil-thin beams streaking past. All three Marines on his fire team were well-trained and hyped in anticipation of combat. They dropped to the deck, although Takbar wasn't quite as fast or lucky as the other two. One of those beams intersected the right shoulder of his MACE, vaporizing ceramic and metal with a flash.

The emergency air loss alarm sounded in the dock and red lights began flashing. The other four beams had penetrated the far end of the docking arm with ease. Jordan stuck his Remberg around the corner left-handed and fired three times rapid fire. "Pull back to the airlock. I'll cover you!"

Bennings grabbed the struggling lance corporal and helped him to his feet. Santis fired short bursts from a prone position, being the only one with a PW-93 in the team. There was a body on the ground at the enemy position but the rest had taken cover behind the corners. Fortunately, the LR-8s were bulky and a man without an exo would have a hard time firing one-handed around a corner. *They'll have to expose themselves to fire.*

The other two made it inside the airlock. Their VIP had enough sense to clear the narrow accessway and stood well back inside the ship. "Santis, displace!"

Brian pulled his feet up underneath him and pushed to his feet, backing towards the airlock. Jordan fired at each corner, not seeing a target but trying to keep them from peeking around the corner. As his teammate made it into the airlock, Jordan hit the 'Close' button.

"Whisper One Three Bravo, Whisper One. Do not engage hostiles. Remain in the ship and await extraction."

No shit, lieutenant. Aloud. "Roger Whisper One. Be advised hostiles are armed with Lima Romeo Eights. One suit damaged, one hostile down. Target is secure on the ship."

"Whisper One copies. Hold tight, DeMarco. We'll get you out of there."

He looked at Bennings. "How's Snackbar?"

The Marine in question gave him a thumbs-up. "Minor suit breach. Patch is holding. I think some of it got me. Or maybe something melted from the suit. My shoulder is on fire."

Jessica didn't look up from where she was working. "Shoulder joint's fused, Jordan. Lower arm's fine but he'll have shit all for leverage."

Jordan nodded and began rapping out orders. "Right. We're going to be here for a while. Snackbar, pop your upper chest plate and let's get a look at the damage to your shoulder. Santis, guard the lock. Ma'am, is there a medical facility on the ship?"

Cassie hesitated, then shook her head. "Fuck it. I'm already screwed as it is. This way."

She led them down the main hall and past the computer room to a locked door. It opened at her key card swipe, revealing a sterile-looking room with a single exam table in the middle of the room. The room lit up as they entered and the exam table came to life, lights flickering and the monitor above it showed 'Ready for patient'.

"Shit, this is better than most medical bays I've seen!" Jessica helped the wounded Marine onto the table.

Jordan looked over at his Cassandra, eyebrows raised. She looked sheepish. "We do… did a lot of work that wasn't exactly on the level. And we tended to operate outside normal corporate channels. Having your own autodoc was considered a valid expense. Having used it myself, I agree."

He filed that bit of information away for later. "Then I'm guessing those folks outside will have a hard time getting in?"

"If they try conventional means, yeah. But this ship isn't military. It doesn't have a hardened hull or any kind of defenses. They could force the lock and given what I know about their tech skills, it should be easy for them."

"Shit." He keyed his comm. "Whisper One, Whisper One Three Bravo. Hostiles have their own can opener ability. Unknown how long we'll be secure here. One WIA with suit damage."

"Copy. We're working on solutions here. We ccn't go starting a firefight on the station with an unknown force. But we'll figure something out."

He relayed the information to the group. "Guess we'll have to sit tight until they figure something out."

Cassie motioned for Jordan to follow. She led him back out to the airlock, where Santis was on guard. At the suit locker, she pulled out a sleek personalized vacc suit. It had her name and the StellarMart logo on it. "I'm qualified in this thing and I have no issues walking outside in it. What say we take off and stiff these creeps with the bill?"

Chapter 37

They watched the completion bar march to one hundred percent in silence. It wasn't necessary but they all seemed to feel better knowing it was done. Alanna ejected the data stick and walked over to put it in the safe. Ezekiel leaned back against the desk and smiled at Cassie. She was still in her vacc suit, helmet sitting on the table.

"Well done, Ms. Vickers. Alanna and I will review your findings and hopefully it's enough to get Justice to put their full weight against the Hoffman organization. And perhaps we'll find out who's behind the whole scheme as well."

She looked at the terminal, whose desktop was far different than the ones she was used to. Selena's chaotic mess of shortcuts, Vera's neat rows and columns and Janik's nearly empty screen except for two folders, labeled 'Family' and 'Beer'. "That would be nice, Mr. Vestry. I don't expect you to go after them. In fact, if it really is another corporation, then you would quickly be outclassed. And they wouldn't fight in a way you're used to."

"True. And enough of this 'Ms.' and 'Mr.' business. You've fought alongside us. Just Ezekiel and Cassandra, yes?"

"Cassie, please. And thank you. Now what?"

"For one thing, let's get you some clothes to replace that vacc suit. Very nice work, keeping up with the Marines, by the way." He led her out of the conference room and down a corridor.

"I think they held back for me, if you really want to know. But it's nice to see my training wasn't wasted."

They went into a storeroom and he let her sift through the available uniforms for her size. "It's a very… eclectic set of training you have there. I know there's more to you than you let on but I suspect there's a lot more than we would even guess."

"I'm… was very good at my job. Corporate espionage is an ugly phrase but that's what we did. We would gather all kinds of information that our bosses could use to influence our competitors, sway our customers and end up with the most profitable deal they could make. Pirate taps, fake accounts, breaking and entering, you name it, my team and I could do it. It's amazing what you can plant on someone's outer hull to give you access to their databases." She began to strip off the vacc suit. Ezekiel turned his back as she did so. "You don't have to do that. I've got a bodysuit underneath."

"My mother would have my hide if I peeked on a lady undressing that wasn't my wife. Call me old-fashioned. But I do, in fact, know what it takes to gather that kind of information. I'm not just a pretty face around here."

She laughed. "Oh, I never thought you were just that. Our little fencing match on that first day told me you were way more than you appeared. And you can turn around now."

He showed her where to rack her suit and then led her back to the conference room, where Alanna was glued to her terminal. "Dad, you have got to see this stuff!"

"Like father, like daughter," he said, with a whisper and a smile. Motioning for her to take a seat at the conference table, he sat at his own terminal. "There's coffee and tea at the bar in the back. I'm afraid I can't let you wander around but I suspect we'll need you here anyway to answer the innumerable questions we're going to have.

*****

"The Red Ghosts have failed. We need to take matters into our hands now."

Oliver checked his call log and saw nothing recent from his contact on Colon. "How do you know they failed?"

"The mercenaries sent a message to Justice a few hours ago, confirming the capture of Mierzejewski and the rescue of the hostages. They are getting ready to return to the station. We have conferred. It is time to end their threat once and for all." The voice on the other end was scrambled but he was pretty sure it was Ana. He was also pretty sure she wasn't happy.

"Taking on the 76th is a tall order. If they can take down the Ghosts when they're ready for them, how well will you fare?"

"How well can they fight when we hold their people?"

His blood turned to ice. "You're going after the dependents? That's… risky. It may not turn out the way you think."

Her voice roughened. "That corporate swine you let go? She recovered her database with their help. And she's with them now. How long before Justice gets that information, hmm? All your nice plans go up in smoke then, nein? No big contracts, no money for anyone then. Do you think about that?"

Shit. Cassandra, you just had to stay in the game. "Fine. What do you need from me?"

"Weapons. Like what you gave the Ghosts. Even the odds."

"I don't have much on station but you can have them."

"And your team to help us fight off the mercs when they come to rescue."

"What! No. That's not part of the deal we made. We supply weapons and information only."

The lights in his room went out in an instant and the emergency ones stayed off. The only light from his console. It stayed dark for several seconds and then his vid unit activated. The screen showed a camera feed of their meeting in the casino. Only his face was visible; the man at the next machine was out of the frame. The speakers came to life and replayed their conversation.

"Would you like to see other ones? We have all meetings recorded. Very embarrassing for your company if these surfaced on public networks. Galactocity bosses be very unhappy, ja? Worse still if Justice gets them. You have been to prison, Mr. Smith?"

He sat for a few seconds, fuming. *All this time I thought I was being careful. But using SMS to take out the 76th was still within the scope of the plan. I just didn't expect to be caught up in my own web. And these are criminals. Not used to the chaos of war. I think the Hoffmans and SMS have outlived their usefulness and a lot can happen in the swirl of battle.* "Fine. But there's only two of us."

"There are four in your team here on station, Mr. Smith. Or should I say, 'Mr. Oliver Beck?' Please do not try to hide from us anymore. It will not go well for you. Now, you are trained in microgravity, yes?"

"We are. Not as well as the MIST but we know how to fight out there."

"Good. Let us plan to give them a very warm welcome when they arrive."

*****

The two sentries on duty at the front entrance to the 76th compound were relieved every two hours, the video feeds showed. Oliver tapped the door on the screen. "Best time to hit them is about fifteen to twenty minutes after shift change. Enough time for the guards that just went off-duty to relax, maybe get a drink or snack. The two who just came on duty will have settled into their routine and everyone will be just a little off-balance."

The SMS hit team waited outside the lift entrance. They were deep in the bowels of the station, in an area completely under Hoffman control. People moved about, checking weapons and readying their gear. The criminal organizations had better than two hundred goons to go after the mercs. He'd only been able to supply a dozen battle rifles, three Barretts and a handful of PW-93Cs, which the leadership immediately took for their own use. Still, they had an amazing array of firepower themselves. Shotguns and handguns made up the majority of their armaments, with a few battle rifles and submachine guns from earlier decades.

However, their most dangerous weapons would stay in a secure room, physically away from the fighting.

Hoffman's ability to control the battlefield was frightening. They only gave him a small display but they could remotely control lighting, doors, communications and even the environment itself to a degree. The 76th had removed all station cameras inside their compound, which limited initial planning. But the assault teams would plant wireless cameras and repeaters as they went, so the fog of war would gradually dissipate under their view. He was feeling a bit better about their chances.

Already they had shut off outside access to the compound, although the inhabitants didn't know it yet. Lifts were being rerouted, deliveries delayed and communication lines to the outside were ready to be cut. Assault teams were quietly being deployed to the levels above and below the compound, out of sight of any prying eyes.

"And their families?" Ana had her operators switch the screen, which now showed a much more open passageway. Two sentries stood guard behind a makeshift barrier. A winding path led through the obstacles, with turnstiles in two different places.

"That's easier and harder. Defenses aren't as tight here but unless you move fast and hard, they'll get that blast door on the other side closed. All your hacking skills won't count for anything if they disconnect it from the network. And trust me, you may be able to get in and out of systems with ease but the MIST are experts in breaking systems."

Ana studied the screen and compared it to a floor plan on another screen. "Twenty meters and we're inside their defenses. There will only be four of them. How hard can it be?"

"I'll leave it to you, then. Let's talk about the outside battle. How many of your people can you put on the station hull?"

She shook her head from side to side. "Twenty, maybe thirty. Is that enough?"

"Not even close. The best we'll be able to do is slow them down." At her stubborn look he sighed. "These guys are used to dropping on Grausian-held positions in the face of heavy fire. Last I checked, you don't have any heavy weapons beyond what I gave you. Most of the people you put outside are probably not coming back."

"You're going outside."

"Because you're forcing me to. And I intend to come back. All your specialty hacking skills will be useless out there. The Black is unforgiving and doesn't care how good you are with a computer. No air is no air and one misstep turns you into a dutchman." He shook his head. "Unfortunately, we need to slow them down. The longer we can keep them from interfering with the inside battle, the better our chances are of capturing their dependents. So that's what we focus on doing."

"Fine. Tell my people how to fight them. Slow them down or it will be bad for all of us." She motioned to one of her people already in a vacc suit. "Klaus! This is Mr. Beck. He will show you how to beat these Marines."

Klaus grinned, a snaggle-toothed thing. "Ja, ja, is gut to fight outside! Wind in your hair, sunshine on your face! We going to haf lots of fun!" Giggling, the criminal flashed another smile and clumped off, calling for his team.

Oliver turned to look at Ana, who shrugged. "Those who are good at working outside are quirky. Just get him pointed the right way and Klaus will be the merc's problem."

"Fine. We'll cover the closest airlocks and be ready to deploy before the 76th gets here." She turned to go but he grabbed her shoulder. As she frowned back at him, he motioned at the monitor. "This had better work, or they will take your organization apart. There won't be any place in this system where you can hide."

Chapter 38

Metztli orbit, Pavo Real System

McMannus walked back to the cargo bay where the MISTers had set up their temporary racks. Nothing more than a floor-mounted rack for the MACEs, it served well enough to allow a Marine to slip in and out of his suit with minimal movement. Already they were sitting in clusters on the deck, cleaning weapons and gear. Meanwhile, the minister and his crew had reboarded their ship and were already traveling back home.

He walked over to the corner where the wounded were bedded down. With multiple people dead and wounded, this was one of their more costly battles. *I need to hire some doctors. Or at least proper corpsmen. Another thing I didn't think of when I hatched this wild idea.*

Still, the mood was good. Everyone was in high spirits, despite the casualties. They'd had a major battle against a serious opponent. Something more than just pirates, who usually gave up or cut and run just as things were getting interesting. As he wandered about the groups, he heard war stories, fun poked at each other and reenactment of kill shots. It was almost like being back on a warship after a battle.

Gunny looked up from reassembling his PW-93V. "Sit down, sir and take a load off."

His boss sat, looking around the bay yet again. "Feels like old times, doesn't it?"

"That it does. Kids are feeling good, casualties were light and we're gonna get paid extra for this. So do us all a favor and take the worried look off your face."

"Shit. Was I being that obvious?"

The NCO smiled. "Celebrate with them. They want the Old Man to feel good too. Worked hard to get you that 'W'. Ought to enjoy it with them."

The loudspeaker sounded with Eisen's voice. *"All hands, ready to boost for home. Stand by for one gee."* A cheer sounded throughout the bay.

*****

Colon High Station

The lift signaled an incoming car to the entrance of the 76th compound. The alert was out about possible reprisals on their visitor, so the sentries were already locked and loaded. One was behind the main barricade at the door, while the other was to the side of the lift doors, about three meters back. This allowed them to fire without hitting each other.

When the doors opened, the interior of the car was dark. Neither Marine lowered their weapons. Corporal Xiang called out in a booming voice, "State your business!"

Nothing moved in the darkness of the car. Xiang triggered the spotlight, hoping to catch a glimpse of something. The light revealed six oxygen cylinders, mounted in two rows of three, horizontally on a rack. The photosensitive sensor on the rack captured the incoming light and a circuit closed, triggering an electrical charge to the blasting caps on the cylinder heads. In an instant, the pressurized gas escaped, turning the tanks into makeshift rockets. They slammed into the barriers, trailing fire as the escaping oxygen ignited.

Xiang was slammed against the far bulkhead as two cylinders caught his barrier squarely, ripping it from the mount and throwing it back against him. The impact stunned him, his MACE flashing multiple failure indications on his HUD. Private Horrocks, off to the side, witnessed the tanks destroying the barrier material and ricocheting around the room. Caught by surprise, he froze for several seconds, trying to process what had just happened.

This was enough time for the elevator car to ascend, revealing the SMS assault team hanging on below the car.

They leaped to the deck, spraying shotgun rounds into every corner of the now-darkened room. This was enough to shock Horrocks into action. He returned fire, his Remberg shotgun cutting down one attacker with the first shot.

"Whisper One, Front Gate! We're under attack! They're–" Whatever else he was saying was drowned out in the screech of electronic noise as the second wave of SMS terrorists deployed a battery-powered jammer. The survivors of the first wave were trading fire with the lone defender. It was an uneven exchange, as his MACE shrugged off most of the pellets while their makeshift armor often proved unequal to stopping slugs from his Remberg. However, enough rounds were flying at the Marine that after taking down the first three attackers, his suit was breached in several places and his left arm wasn't working very well.

Xiang shook his head, trying to clear his blurry vision. He was having trouble moving his legs and there was something blocking the lower half of his visor. A terrible screech sounded in his earphones. He struggled to move, to get to his feet and do something. Something tapped his visor and he could barely make out the muzzle before the flash blinded him. A second shot completely pierced the helmet armor and ended his life.

Horrocks was on one knee now, ducking behind the mangled debris of the barriers and trading shots with the unknown attackers. He still couldn't get through on the radio and there was no sign of the corporal. He'd been on the battleship assault and this felt worse. Things were going to hell and he didn't know what was going on or if help was coming. Motion in the corner of his eye forced him to leave cover to turn and a slug slammed into his shoulder. The Remberg clicked on empty as he fired at the shape across the room and he fumbled for reloads. Something slammed into him from behind, knocking him off balance and spilling the rounds on the floor. He jabbed backwards with the butt, feeling its impact on something that gave. Two more shots hit him in the chest in rapid succession, toppling him onto his back.

He struggled to rise but someone was stepping on his arms. Then there was another person on top of him, shotgun raised. Three shots in rapid succession ended his efforts to rise.

At the entrance to the dependent area, the attackers were several seconds behind the first attack. They had to wait for confirmation that the attack had gone off before triggering their own. Thus the sentries here were warned as soon as the explosions at the Front Gate triggered the lockdown procedures. Unfortunately, the timing of the attack happened as several of the 76th family members were returning home.

A half dozen SMS attackers burst from around the corner at the far end of the corridor, firing their shotguns and pistols with wild abandon. They weren't necessarily trying to hit anyone but trying to cause panic among the civilians caught crossing the barriers. The two sentries had just begun to hurry them along when the attack happened, so neither was ready for the attack.

Their first reaction cost them a chance to open fire on the exposed attackers, as both Marines moved to place their armored bodies between the civilians and the attackers. Bullets and shot impacted and bounced off them and the barricades, sending a whirlwind of deadly lead into the corridor.

Lance Corporal Cavallari and PFC Hames turned to return fire, their Rembergs deadly against the exposed attackers. There was another wave just behind the first and this one was shielded from the return fire. The last of the first wave went down before they reached the barriers but their comrades were only meters behind them. Two of them went to one knee, firing their battle rifles. The heavy slugs slammed into the MACE armor, staggering the two Marines.

Inside the 76th compound, Lieutenant Kan had reached the armory and was armoring up while taking status reports.

"Simultaneous attacks at the Front and Back Gates. Unknown attackers, mostly shotguns and pistols. Front Gate sentries are down and not responding. Back Gate is holding but we have three civilians caught in the crossfire." Sergeant Valenti was in the Orderly Room, trying to coordinate the response. The security camera screens were filled with static. He had no information on how many attackers there were and what had happened to the two sentries. Horrocks and Xiang were in his squad and Ish heard the anguish in his voice.

It was no less for him. This was his platoon. "Go to lockdown on the Front Gate, Valenti. Reinforce the Back Gate until the civs are clear and then lock it down, too. I'm almost done, be there in two mikes."

Valenti hit the two large red buttons on the security panel labeled 'Front Gate Lockdown'. The first button deactivated the lift door access, preventing the door from opening unless it was manually cranked open. The second button cut the main door power, again preventing anyone from opening it unless they access the manual controls. Since the access panel for those controls was on their side of the door, these attackers weren't getting through without explosives or a heavy-duty cutting torch.

The Hoffman hackers couldn't prevent the main door power cut off, since that was a local switch. But they could prevent the lift override from happening and another assault team made their way onto the deck. They joined the survivors of the first wave at the main door and demands went back for a cutting torch.

Back at their control center, Ana snarled at the delay. "Verdammt! Fine, they want to play games with the power? Berg, cut their power completely. Let's see how these *scheiesse* like playing in the dark."

Behind her, Oliver rolled his eyes.

At the Back Gate, Cavallari and Hames were making better use of the barricades. The second wave had gotten to the entrance without serious losses but the security measures worked as planned. The winding path funneled the attackers into a killing zone and the Marines took turns popping from behind cover to punish the terrorists. The lights went out but the low-light gear on his MACE gave him a clear view on his HUD.

Cavallari sank back down behind the wall. His left shoulder servos weren't working anymore, courtesy of the damned riflemen. "Reloading," he called out, fumbling through the magazine change with the stiffened limb.

"Hank, my Remberg took one for me. I'm down to my pistol."

"Right, Pete. Stay down and wait for them to get close, then." He clicked over to the platoon net. "Whisper One, Back Gate. I don't know how much longer we can hold."

"Cavalry's on the way. Civs are clear now."

"Stay low coming out. They got snipers with battle rifles."

To emphasize his point, a heavy-caliber bullet hit the barrier above his head, causing the whole panel to ring. Resisting the urge to return fire, he crab-walked a few paces and waited for the attackers to get closer.

The other two members of the off-duty fire team were waiting at the access hatch from the main compound to the Back Gate. Ish briefed them. "Reinforce Cavallari and defend the barricades. Keep your eyes peeled; they used some kind of explosives at the front to take down the barrier. Hold as long as you can and pull back when necessary behind the blast door. I don't have to remind you who you're defending out there."

The hatch opened and the lead Marine started to go out in a crouch but rounds began hitting the wall around the door. Ish put a hand on the other Marine's arm. "Cavallari, can you provide some suppressing fire?"

Rounds were hitting the barrier along its length over his head in near constant rattle. "No can do, sir. I'm pinned down."

Kan shouldered his PW-93V, one of the few they had and nodded at the first man. "Be ready. I'm going to give you some covering fire."

He went low through the door, hugging the near wall and stepping forward several steps. Waiting a three count, he popped up and began firing short bursts at any targets he could see. As he did so, the rest of the fire team poured out into the corridor and made their way to the barriers.

As soon as they were under cover at the barriers, Ish rolled back around the hatch, breathing heavily. His armor sported several dents now and he took a second to marvel at his escape. There had to be at least ten tangoes out there, pushing hard for the entrance. And he had only eight more Marines inside to defend the whole compound.

One of the off-duty privates came running up to him, arms laden with magazines and more importantly, a case of a dozen grenades. They only had tanglers, not fragmentation but it was better than nothing. A tangler grenade threw out a spray of quick-hardening adhesive that needed a special solvent to dissolve. It was used by security on ships and stations because it didn't risk puncturing the hull or damaging key equipment. Since frag grenades were in short supply out here, the last shipment of munitions from Justice had included three cases of tanglers.

He motioned to the private. "Get low and when I fire, shove that case out into the corridor. Cavallari, I'm sending out a case of tanglers and magazines."

The two new Marines were able to provide enough covering fire with him that Hames was able to dive over the barricade and reach the supplies. As he belly-crawled to each of his fire team, Ish closed the hatch. He motioned to the door controls. "Stand by here until relieved. If I give the signal, drop the blast door."

"Sir, won't that cut off the team at the gate?"

Ish nodded as he turned to go. "Let's hope it doesn't come to that."

The rest of the off-duty members of 1st Platoon were nearly finished gearing up as Ish made it back to the orderly room. Valenti was working on the computer terminals with an increasingly frustrated face. "It's no good, sir. I can't get anything. No network access, no comms, nothing. Lights and basic power are out all across the compound and housing. Backups for us kicked in but it's only good for ten minutes. We're isolated here."

Kan looked over his shoulder as the security panel. "What about air? Environment still good?"

"So far. The override on the elevator didn't work. Camera's going to die here in another few minutes and then we'll know dick all about what they're planning."

His boss slapped his shoulder and forced a grin "Their plan is to come in and kill us, Valenti. Only two ways in here, so it's not a hard problem to solve. So how about we prep a warm welcome for them?"

*****

Ana looked over at Beck, now in his armored vacc suit. She had just sent their only three LR-8s up the lift to support the attack on the dependents. A heavy-duty plasma torch was being loaded on the other lift, to breach the front gate. "Those had better do the trick. You said nothing about tanglers. We have solvent but now we waste time going back for it."

He shrugged. "This was your plan, Ana. If you had given me some advance warning, we might have gotten more information for you. Welcome to the joys of mission command."

Her eyes flashed but she held her comments back. "What do you suggest now?"

"You mean, how to conduct a frontal attack on a fortified position? Be prepared for heavy casualties. And really that's your only option now that they're alerted. Get those LR-8s into a supporting position, have them open up and then send everyone in a fast charge. You'll lose some getting there but then you'll be amongst their positions. Even then, don't stop. Push forward and take that blast door. Feed 'em some meth or other shit to get them over their fears."

"My people aren't soldiers. They don't have the discipline to–"

He stepped forward and cut her off, his voice a savage whisper. "Then you and your other leaders get up there behind them and," he poked at the PW-93C she held, "encourage them to charge. Make them more afraid of you than of the enemy."

*****

Cassie stood at the door to the orderly room and watched Lieutenant Kan talking with the other lieutenant and Ezekiel. The young man was downloading the floor plans to the compound and housing area to his tablet before the main power died. His brows were furrowed slightly and his fingers trembled slightly as he tapped in the commands.

He looked up to see her standing in the door. With a wan smile, he shrugged. "Not much of a rescue after all, I'm afraid."

The former operative stepped into the room, mag boots clunking on the floor as she put a heavy pack on the table. "I think I have a way around the communications problem."

"I don't think you can fix the circuits with a tool kit. Even one that's," he peered at the label on the pack, "Vacuum-rated."

"Remember what I said about my previous job? Tapping into commlines to gather information also means I can send messages. I can tap into the station array and get a message to your boss." She frowned. "The only problem is, I need to get outside to do this. Kinda hard to do right now."

Ezekiel nodded in satisfaction. "I like her idea. And the Hoffman's won't expect us to send someone outside."

Kan frowned. "You've done this before? Well, getting people outside the hull is our specialty." He opened a channel. "Sergeant Baines, get me a team to open a screen door. Ms. Vickers is going to go outside and get a message to the Captain."

Minutes later, Cassie was suited up and standing with the two Marines from her trip to the ship. They were in a dead-end of a maintenance corridor far from the front entrance. One Marine was setting up a temporary airlock in the corridor about ten feet away while the other was carefully placing explosives on the floor.

Jordan talked as he carefully set the charges. "Ma'am, once this blows, this whole area will decompress rapidly. Even with your mag boots it could be dicey. If you look in the bag by my feet, you'll find some hand magnets. You can slip those over your suit gloves to give you extra support."

Cassie fitted the slip-magnets and glanced nervously at the charges. "Won't I have to worry about the blast?"

"Only if you're standing next to them. Directional cutting charges, so it will mostly go through the floor. The temporary airlock will be far enough back to get you out of the danger area. Now, we're right next to the outer hull here. The plans we got from the station people said this area should have had a hatch but I guess the contractor screwed that up. No problem. We're used to making our own doors."

"I haven't exited this way before. I mean, I've practiced what happens during explosive decompression but the assumption was you were trying to stay inside the ship."

The young man turned to smile at her. "Nothing to it, ma'am. You stay inside the station until the area decompresses. Then you exit through the hole. Two simple operations. Just take them in that order."

Santis called out. "Ready here, Jordan. Just waiting for you."

Jordan placed a small remote in her hand. "Press the clacker when you're ready. We'll leave you a second temp airlock kit here so you can come back in when you're done. Unless…"

"Unless they're out there and see me?"

"Um, yeah. The LT said to remind you of that. Don't want to let them in through a back door, you know."

"Got it. If they see me, I'll lead them on a merry chase back to one of the normal air locks."

"Good luck then, ma'am. Hope you can get us through to the Captain."

Cassie watched them finish sealing up the airlock and test it. Once she had a thumbs up from the corporal, she turned to look at the far end of the corridor. Sealing her helmet, she then lowered herself to a squatting position and activated the boot and hand magnets. Once she felt secure, she triggered the remote.

Flame spread briefly along the floor from the charges and smoke filled the corridor. Then a patch of the floor over a meter square disappeared, taking the smoke with it. She felt the air press against her as it followed the smoke outside but her magnets held her. In just under a minute, her suit told her there was zero atmosphere around her.

Unmagging, she made her way to the hole and looked down. The view was dizzying, staring down into the vast deepness of space. The view slowly changed as the station rotated and Cassie took a second to orient herself. Then she kneeled and with the communications kit strapped to her back, she pulled herself through the hole and onto the station hull.

Chapter 39

"Cap, you want to come up to the bridge for a bit?" Eisen's voice was just a bit too casual.

"What's up, Mr. Eisen?" He made sure the door to the bridge was closed.

"Put on the headset and then you tell me."

Pulling on the spare headset, he heard a familiar female voice repeating the same message over and over.

"Whisper Six, this is the corporate airhead. Please respond. I have a message for you."

He looked at the pilot. "I know that voice. The question is, why is she calling and in the open?"

"Can't be good."

McMannus thought for a moment, then keyed the microphone. "Corporate airhead, what's your message for Whisper Six?"

"It's from Whisper One: Fort Alamo. Need cavalry soonest."

"Fuck. Mr. Eisen, call the Gunny and Mr. Webb up here, please. Then calculate your best time to Colon, max burn."

"Max burn on this tub is only three gees, Cap'n. This ain't no military ship. I'm guessing that particular code phrase means the shit has hit the fan?"

"Best possible speed, Mr. Eisen. Our base is under attack and we have to get there ASAP." He keyed the microphone back on. "Corporate, stand by for new arrival time. Are you with Whisper One?"

"Nope. I'm outside, tapping into the station communication array. They're cut off from comms and power. Hoffman made their move on you, Captain. They're going after your families."

"Those people. Anyone else? Is station security getting involved?"

"As far as we could tell, it's just the Hoffmans. I think station security is sitting this one out. Too many of their people are either on the Hoffman payroll or too scared of them."

He thought for a moment. "See if you can get a hold of the local Justice office. There should be an Agent Drusk on station. She might be willing to help."

Neil looked up from his navcomp. "With the velocity we've already built up, I can cut about five hours off the trip. Maybe five and half if you don't mind some extra velocity when we get there. Instead of a zero-zero docking approach, I can do a flyby and you drop on the station like you did on Metzli."

"Then set it up." Webb and Mulongo arrived at that point and McMannus explained briefly to them the situation. "Get everyone suited up and on the deck for a sustained high gee burn. That includes the wounded. Mr. Eisen, I'll signal you when we're ready."

To Cassie, he said, "We'll be there in about five hours. Tell Mr. Kan that I said he is to hold out that long, using all resources at his direction."

"Gotcha, Captain. We'll be waiting for you."

*****

Hull of Colon High Station

Cassie manipulated the settings on the comm tap. It was easy enough to get a broadcast to Kan, as she had their frequency and channel and the two Marines were just inside for a relay. But getting a message to Justice was harder, especially if she didn't want to call attention to her efforts.

After several abortive attempts, that burned up far too many minutes, she grimaced. "Screw it." She had the comm codes for the Justice office but trying to leave an encoded untraceable message was blocked by too many security measures. So instead she called them direct.

"Justice Ministry, Colon Station. How may I direct your call?"

"Agent Drusk, please. This is Cassandra Vickers and I'm calling from the 76th MIST." The line clicked and a pleasant hold music started playing. The incongruity lasted only for a minute before a female voice answered. "This is Agent Drusk. I am required to inform you this call is being recorded. So, just who are you, really? There is no Cassandra Vickers registered with the 76th."

"Sorry about that. I'm not part of the unit but I am working with them. Or they were working for me. Whatever. This is important, Agent Drusk. Captain McMannus asked me to pass you a message. The Hoffmans have launched an attack on the 76th compound while most of the unit is off on a mission for you. They're after their families, probably to get the 76th to leave the station. I assume you've heard nothing of this?"

"No. Nothing on the station security channels and no broadcasts." There was the sound of keys clicking. "Hmm. There's a hazmat spill reported near the 76th compound. They're warning people not to travel near there."

"That's it. Can you get security camera footage?"

"That's… odd. I'm getting a 'technical failure' message when I try to access the servers." She paused and it lasted for almost a minute before Cassie spoke up.

"Agent Drusk? Are you still there?"

"Yes. Yes, I'm here." Her tone was distracted. "What is it that Captain McMannus would like from the Ministry of Justice?"

Cassie opened her mouth to respond but the shock of the question kept her from speaking. *They got to her, too? We are so screwed.* Gathering herself, Cassie swallowed. "Please help us out. I know you don't have many officers on Colon but maybe you can rally station security. Distract the Hoffmans. The Captain is on his way back at a high burn but it'll still be five hours until he gets here. Please! Think of their families!"

The line was quiet for several seconds. "Officially, there's no evidence of a crime for us to respond to. So I'm sorry, Ms. Vickers but I have no reason to deploy a tactical team or involve station security. If Captain McMannus has any further requests, he can relay them to me when he transfers his prisoners upon his arrival."

As Drusk was talking, a text message played out in Cassie's HUD. It read

> *Radio monitored. H is watching our*
> *offices. Need time to deploy a team.*
> *Hold on a little longer.*

Cassie felt her stomach unclench. "Please send help as soon as you can, Agent Drusk. We'll be waiting."

*****

Lieutenant Kan stared grimly at the downloaded plans. He had to hold out for five more hours. The Front Gate wasn't his problem; that entrance was reinforced and doubled as a gastight hatch. They would need to burn or blow through it and he had a pair of sentries stationed far enough back they wouldn't get caught in any blast. The hall beyond doubled as a defensible position, with interconnected offices and lockable doors. They had placed tanglers on trip wires and scattered stuff all over the floor to trip up anyone coming through. Anyone coming through there would get hit from all sides.

"We need the dependents in a more defensible position if the enemy gets past the blocking position." He zoomed in on that section of the plans, with Ezekiel and Alanna at his side.

She pointed. "The only place large enough for everyone is the series of compartments set aside for school and community get-togethers."

"Lots of room for a defense in depth, if we can get them moved back quick enough." Her father pointed at the corridors running through the place. "A good team could use these to do hit and run attacks, slow any attackers down."

"It will have to do. Alanna, you get the job of organizing the evacuation. Talk with the Captain's lady. She knows a lot of the dependents and can help out. Mr. Vestry, I'm sorry but you're going with them. I don't need you here and you're not trained in a MACE. One more weapon in the last-ditch defense might make a difference, though."

Ezekiel sighed. "Kinda expected that. We'll do what we can."

Kan looked up and motioned Jordan to come over. "Corporal DeMarco. Lieutenant Vestry is going to organize an evacuation of the dependents to a defendable location. Take your team and establish defensive positions along the entry corridors. Hold at all costs. Understood?"

Jordan nodded crisply. "Oo-rah, sir. Fuckers won't get past us."

"We'll hold here as long as we can and kill as many as we can. Captain will be here in five hours, so we just have to hold that long. Off you go. Sergeant Baines, see to covering fire so they can get through."

That left six plus him inside the compound, with a five-hour clock running. Against who knew how many people who were intent on taking their families hostage. *Grausian battleship my ass. I don't know how we're going to pull this one off. I don't know what I'm more scared about.*

******

Lieutenant Vestry and her father walked with Aileen down the corridors, knocking on doors and telling people to get moving. No personal belongings, just food and water if it was easily carried. Diapers and formula for the babies. It wasn't difficult to get them moving. They'd heard the alarms and gunfire and the power had been out for quite a while now. But it still took time. Flashlights and headlamps flicked up and down the corridors as people hurried away.

Jordan stopped his team further back. "Right. Brian, Hassan. Break off here and start scouting out strongpoints. I don't want them to get a straight shot back this way, so figure out what we can do to divert them from the main corridor. The more they have to wind their way through rooms and offices, the easier it'll be for us to slow them down."

"Got it, Jordan. Me and Snackbar will figure it out, no problem. Be like laying false trails for the shore patrol after some midnight requisitions."

"Bennings, make sure all the light switches are off. I don't want them to come on in the middle of a firefight and throw us off. Then start pulling heavy shit into the corridor. I want barricades in several places; something decent enough for a few shots before we displace." As the three of them went off, he walked over to report to the lieutenant.

Alanna nodded, Remberg slung across her MACE. Her father also had one, although he was only wearing a ballistic plate vest. Both had tangler grenades and Ezekiel had a set of nightvision goggles. "I have every faith in you, Corporal. We're going to make the best barricade we can at the entrance to the safe room. There's a couple more people who know how to use a weapon, so we won't be totally defenseless."

"We'll do our best to make sure you don't need to use them, ma'am."

Aileen was looking at him with a worried expression. "Just the six of you to defend us?"

"Lieutenant Kan is holding the main entrance with the rest of the platoon that's here, ma'am. If anything gets past them, they won't be in great shape. They'll be scattered, leaderless and confused. That makes them great targets."

"Free will be here to save us."

He nodded solemnly. "Of that I have no doubt, ma'am. The Old Man won't let us down."

******

Lance Corporal Cavallari paused, listening. The enemy's fire had shifted. There were more pauses in the firing and rounds were coming more and more from the same side of the corridor.

"They're getting ready to try something. Check your mags and be ready to pop up. Whisper One, you copy my last?"

"Roger. Let us know what happens as soon as it does. I've got another fire team ready at the door to back you up."

He didn't have to wait long. The fire trickled away and then there was a flare of light from the barricade. The smell of burning metal came to him about the same time as a scream from one of the Marines. Low crawling, he shifted to their position to find a slagged hole in the metal of the barricade that corresponded to a melted patch on the back of the unmoving MACE of Private Riviera.

"Get low, get low. They've got lasers! Whisper One, OPFOR has high-power lasers. They're burning holes in the barricade and I've got one KIA already!"

"Understood, Cav. They're targeting the door too. Be ready for them to follow up with an assault force."

Automatic weapons fire sounded from the enemy positions, followed by yelling and some screams. A few more bursts, interspersed with more white-hot holes in the barricade and then he heard dozens of throats cry out with furor. The deck vibrated with their footsteps as they charged his position.

"Let 'em have it!" He popped up and fired three rounds and then ducked back down. As he shifted to a new firing position, he heard the other two firing. Popping up again, he was surprised to see how close the enemy was, less than ten meters away. He emptied his magazine into the charging mass and dropped down to reload. A sharp pain in his left arm made him gasp and his suit breach alarms started going off.

It hurt to move his left arm and he had no feeling left in his hand. Fumbling with a magazine, he got it in place just as one of Hoffman goons leaped over to his side of the barricade. The man tumbled to the ground and Cavallari flipped his weapon over and slammed the bolt home one-handed. He raised the weapon carefully and fired one shot, taking his target in the throat as he rose.

"Whisper One, they're in our position. My left arm ain't working so good."

"Stand by, Cav. We're gonna pop a smoke grenade and deploy. Be ready for pickup."

He listened to a single Remberg bang out five shots in rapid succession. There was no pistol fire from Hames. "No good, sir. We're done for. It's time to close the blast door."

"Just hold on, Cav. We'll get you out."

"No sir. Close that door. We'll keep them busy as long as we can."

Lieutenant Kan looked down at the red button for the emergency door closure. It triggered a mechanical release on the springs holding the door back, so the lack of power wasn't an issue. Closing his eyes, he mashed the button with the heel of his hand. The hollow 'boom' of the door slamming shut resounded through the deck.

"Alright Marines, you all know what comes next. Let's get ready to give them hell. No one gets through that door unless their dead body is falling through it."

Chapter 40

Ana paced back and forth in their small ad-hoc operations center as the reports came in on the closure of the blast door. Oliver had to admire her self-control. She didn't swear or rant and rave about how things or people had failed her. Her face had that fixed look he'd seen on other commanders, whose battle plan had gone to shit and was now trying to figure out how to recover.

Fuck it. I may not like her but I still need them. "It's a minor setback. Get some plasma torches, like they use at the maintenance yard. Cut through the hatch and we're in business."

She glared daggers at him. "That will take time. Already, station security is on me, whining about not being able to keep this quiet for much longer."

"Fuck 'em. I assume you have something on them, something that keeps them working for you? Remind them that you own them. As a matter of fact, make them get those torches and haul the things up here. Put 'em in their place and let's get this operation moving. We've got less than eight hours to get this thing done before the rest of the 76th gets back here."

"Don't you think I know that?" She broke off, swearing now under her breath in German. "We've lost over twenty people already. If this keeps going the same way, we won't have the people we need to run our operations. The Black Suns and Ghost Dragons are watching us all the time and they'll jump us if they think we're weak."

Well, now. "Okay. That problem I understand. My company would be willing to work a deal with you on that. Provide some personnel, off the books, to shore up your operations. In return, we would continue the partnership that we have now. We could use your connections and leverage within the government, for example."

The crime boss regarded him with suspicion. "That helps you later. What helps us now if our competitors decide to take over our businesses?"

"I can have a dozen armed and trained operatives here in a week. Another two dozen in a month. If they take something away from you, we'll help you get it back. With interest."

"And if we stop the attack now? Cut our losses?"

Oliver laughed. "Then we're gone and you get to face the wrath of the 76th alone. You think they'll just forgive and forget?"

Her composure cracked the tiniest bit and she licked her lips with a nervous gesture. "Very well. We continue and see this through. But if your men don't arrive within a week…"

"Once we're through here, I'll send the message. I think we'll both enjoy the fruits of this new relationship, Ana." *Right. Win or lose, you'll bleed yourselves dry in this fight and your competitors will wipe you out. Then there's nothing to link Galactocity to you.*

*****

The Metzli assault force lay on the deck of the *Calypso*, with three times their own body weight pressing against them. The MACEs helped somewhat with that, with air bladders filling and deflating in rhythmic motions to keep the blood from pooling. Their training included being subjected to high-gee accelerations and prolonged burns but never for this long. He and Eisen agreed to a ten-minute break at the halfway point but that was all the time they could afford.

There had been no official communications from Colon since their report on departing orbit. Repeated calls to the Justice office went unacknowledged.

He held his temper in check and kept breathing. There was nothing more he could do for now.

*****

Cassie finished her trek across the station hull to the main passenger ship slips. She hadn't seen another soul on the way but now there were tour groups and sightseers clustered here and there near the airlock. *Perfect for my needs. Blend in with the tourists and get back into the station. Find Drusk and help however I can.*

The main corridors of the station, at least in this public area, seemed to be business as usual. The monitors weren't showing any alerts or warnings and the crowds milled about in their expected patterns. No panic, no tension. She'd stashed her suit at a public locker and went immediately to a gift shop. Now she was dressed in a 'Colon: Living the High Life' jumpsuit with multiple corporate logos on it. She had a backpack with an image of the Jump Station embossed in bright neon colors. Her mag boots had been replaced by 'genuine Pavonian cultural footwear,' whatever that meant. But now she blended with the crowds on this part of the station. It wasn't very far to the public offices and she put on a worried face as she walked through the security checkpoint. Lots of tourists came here, for visas, lost passports, notary services and the like.

The public offices corridor was more subdued and quieter but the palpable zone around the two Grausian thugs was even more pronounced. Oh, they were dressed like everyone else but you could almost feel the menace they radiated. And they had stationed themselves with a direct line of sight to the Justice front hatch.

None of the station security officers paid them any attention. In fact, they seemed to be going out of their way to not notice them. *Well, I can do something about that. It'll cost me my favorite knife but it'll be worth it.*

She continued her slow approach down the corridor, eyes seemingly fixed on her tablet. Her course was meandering but it took her closer and closer to the thugs. As she reached their location, she deliberately took a turn in their direction, tablet in front of her face.

The collision caught everyone's attention, mostly due to her high-pitched squeak from the collision. Cassie began babbling her apologies for not looking where she was going. The two thugs were confused, not expecting anyone to deliberately approach them as they tried to untangle themselves from this situation. As she expected, one of them growled at her, "Watch where you're going, girl."

She pressed the knife into that one's hand and then let out a scream. "He's got a knife! Oh my God, he's got a knife!"

As she backed away with remarkable new-found dexterity, the rest of the people around got a good look at the thug, now holding Cassie's knife. His confused look rapidly changed to 'oh shit' as he realized what he was holding. He released the handle and it fell to the deck with a resounding clatter, which only highlighted to everyone what he had been holding. All eyes turned to the security officers at their booth.

Both of them looked at each other and then sighed. They approached the two thugs, calming gestures with their hands. As the four of them went into a rapid, hushed conversation Cassie took the opportunity to slip into the Justice offices.

A very alert man in body armor, carrying a shotgun greeted her from behind ballistic glass. "Please state your business with the Justice Ministry."

She stood up straight and smoothed her bright jumpsuit down. Smiling, she said in her best corporate tone, "I'm here to see Agent Drusk. We talked previously and I believe she's expecting me?"

Minutes later, she and Drusk were sitting down in her office. The agent shook her head as Cassie relayed her method for getting in undetected. "Lady, you got some real *chuss*. Just what is it with you and the 76th? Or with you and Captain McMannus?"

"My business with them is strictly professional. They're going to help me get the bastards who took out my team and ruined my career." That pronouncement required another tale, which Cassie edited for the sake of time.

Drusk shook her head again, this time in disbelief. "You've been on this station, what a week? Ten days? And you got into ALL this trouble in that amount of time?"

She shrugged helplessly. "What can I say? I'm an overachiever. Now, can you help?"

Sighing, the Justice agent waved at the locker on her wall. Her body armor was on a stand inside the locker and a Remberg shotgun hung on the wall. "I can help. I WANT to help. I can get another two agents who know what to do with a gun and are not afraid to go up against these crooks. The rest are more for customs and immigration. I wouldn't trust them not to cut and run. Plus, they live here with their families. The rest of us are only here on rotation. If we don't get all the Hoffmans then they would be screwed."

"What about station security?"

"Penetrated completely. Hoffman owns most of them. You saw how it was outside this office."

"Will they stop us from going to help?"

Drusk waggled her head from side to side. "Some might try. I think we can put them in their place without resorting to violence."

"What about communications? The 76th is cut off from everyone. I had to run a pirate tap from outside to talk to the Captain but I couldn't get through to you covertly."

"There we can definitely help. We have several cutters here. I can dispatch one to serve as a communication relay. Provided we can put in an antenna for the Marines to use."

"If you have a portable antenna, I can do that. Then we can coordinate our actions. The rest of the 76th will be here in," she looked at her watch, "less than four hours. If we can keep the Hoffmans stalled or distracted until they arrive, then the whole game changes."

Drusk sat back on her four legs, thinking. "Ever hear the old adage, 'enemy of my enemy is my friend'?"

"Yes and it rarely works out that way. What do you have in mind?"

"The Hoffmans have competitors. No one near their size but they keep a close eye out for any weakness. Would you say that they have committed a lot of people to this attack?"

"Yeah. It sure seems that way."

"Good." Drusk stood and headed for her body armor. "Then I'm taking my people out to have a chat with some other people about seizing opportunities. I may not be able to directly affect the Hoffman attack but I'm pretty sure I can divide their attention. As you said, we need to buy time."

Cassie left via a back corridor, headed to the government ship docks with the crew of the cutter. She carried a portable antenna and radio on her back. The cutter would drop her off at the hole near the 76th so she could set up the relay. For the first time today, she began to feel hopeful.

*****

Lieutenant Kan stood alone in the briefing room. His sole contact with the outside world was through a series of relays to the portable radio on the station hull, manned by a civilian and then to a Justice cutter. Without Sparks here, they'd had to jury-rig a patch and the briefing room was the only place with the right equipment. All the while, they'd seen the metal on the Back Gate blast door turn yellow and then white in two separate places. The enemy was going to burn their way through, no doubt.

Sergeant Valenti and his sole remaining fire team member were guarding the Front Gate. They had reported an initial burning metal smell but that had ended after the Back Gate was locked down. It appeared that entrance was going to be the main focus, so Sergeant Baines and his fire team had set up a free fire zone in the corridor beyond. The entrance to the 76th compound was just behind the blast door and they'd placed a makeshift barrier about chest height just past their hatch. Anyone attempting to get past the open hatch would have to pause at the barrier and the defenders in the compound had a clear line of fire at them. The idea was to force the attackers to waste time clearing out the defenders before proceeding any further.

Once the enemy forced their way into the compound, they had several surprises waiting for them. The Captain had authorized the defenders to 'use all available means' and Lieutenant Kan had his people get creative on their defenses. They may not have had any frag grenades but they had their breaching charges. Placed against an interior wall or door, the shaped charge created a one and half meter hole. If you flipped it around, with the blast cone facing out into the hallway, it made for a very unpleasant time.

And Corporal DeMarco and his team are providing a second line of defense in the dependent area. If we do our job right, anyone who reaches him will be unsupported and disorganized.

He looked at the time in HUD. "Less than three hours until the Captain gets here, Klowns. Plenty of time for us to see off these unwanted guests. VIS, Marines."

A chorus of 'Oo-rah!' and growls came across the channel. Lieutenant Kan nodded, chest tight as he left the room. The radio would rebroadcast any response it received, although he would have to come back here to manually key in the response.

*****

Thirty minutes later, the cut-away section of the blast door fell back into the hall, leaving the entrance filled with acrid smoke. The Hoffman teams operating the plasma torches also fell back, clearing the way for the attack groups. They had spent the last hour drinking the booze and smoking the dope their bosses had sent forward. Rarely did they get a chance at free stuff like this and all of them took advantage of it, not thinking about why it was being made available to them.

The first half dozen, emboldened by their intoxication, came through the slowly dissipating smoke and saw the barrier, with nothing beyond it to stop them. Whooping with joy, they rushed the barrier. A few even tossed their weapons over the other side so they could climb with both hands.

Four shotguns fired from the open hatch, aimed shots that took down their targets one by one. None of the first wave knew what hit them but the element of surprise was gone now. The rest of the attackers saw where the danger was now and they approached the hatch with caution.

In addition to bringing up the solvent for the tangler grenades, they had brought up their own tangler and smoke grenades. These were used when going after the merchies, since it wouldn't damage the cargo they were going to steal. Now, under the covering guns, two Hoffman goons ran up to the hatch and tossed in a tangler grenade each. When those went off, they then tossed in a smoke grenade. The second goon lingered too long in the exposed space and took two shotgun blasts to the face and chest, dropping him where he stood.

The attackers rushed the door, anxious to use the cover from the smoke before it dissipated. Their only experience in using smoke to cover an attack was against spacers who were even less eager to damage their ship. The Marines had no such qualms and besides, the hatch and corridor were a known quantity. Smoke or no smoke, there was only one way to come at them.

The remnants of the attackers stumbled back out into the main corridor, coughing and firing blind over their shoulders to cover their retreat. One of Ana's lieutenants, a big blond man with a battle rifle supplied by Oliver, realized that the smoke also prevented the Marines from seeing what was happening at the barrier. He led a small group over the barriers before the smoke had cleared.

"Whisper One to Blocking Force. Some leakers got through. Be ready. VIS"

*****

There was a garbled message over the platoon channel. He was pretty sure it was from the lieutenant and that had company on the way. Jordan clicked his transmit button twice, hoping the acknowledgement got through the jamming. To his team, he said, "Our turn, Marines. VIS."

The housing area the station had allocated for the use of the 76th families was modular. Walls could be opened up to create larger apartments and Jordan's team had used this to create a maze of winding paths through the first two dozen or so units. They hadn't had time to create more but with only four of them, he thought it would be enough. They were to operate in teams, Hassan and Santis and Bennings and himself. They would be able to move forward and back across the maze, hoping to confuse their attackers as to how many defenders they faced.

The lack of explosives was a disappointment but since they were in their own spaces, it was probably best. All the lights were off and most of the overhead fixtures smashed, plunging the whole area into blackness. Their MACEs had low-light gear, which he doubted the Hoffman goons had. Another plus on his side.

The faint sound of gunfire from further back let him know the rest of the platoon was still fighting it out. *Our turn. Stop these fuckers and anyone else they let in the door.* He could see the back of Benning's MACE out of the corner of his eye. She was slightly ahead of him but around a corner. He would get the first shot, then displace. Anyone who followed him too closely would get shot from behind.

The scuff of shoes on the cheap carpeting reached his audio pickups. Several seconds later, there were soft clicks as they tried the light switches. A muttered 'Scheiss' and then whispered commands. *At least three of them.* He clicked his transmit button twice to get his team's attention and then three more times.

The first goon came around the corner less than three meters away, old style subgun held at waist level. *What's he going to do, spray and pray? He can't aim like that.* Jordan let him get a few more steps and then fired his Remberg once. The triple ought blast caught the man full in the chest, dropping him in his tracks. Without waiting to see what the others did, Jordan slid back out of his hiding spot and started back along the path. Just to fuck with them, he deliberately knocked a heavy lamp over. It landed with a thud and he heard excited shouts from behind him. Then two blasts from a Remberg.

"Two to your one, Jordan."

A few minutes later, Santis reported taking down two on his side. *"But there's still some out in the corridor. We can hear them talking. I think they've got comms with their own leadership. Might be calling for support."*

"I copy. Go to secondary positions and be ready. We let them come to us. This is our ground." He put in a call to the lieutenant but all he got was static. That information he kept to himself.

*****

Cassie sat on the station hull, watching the telltales from the radio. So far nothing new from the returning mercenaries. Their pilot had provided an update after their break and turnover point but nothing since then. It was very possible that the Hoffmans were monitoring the radio transmissions so she'd said nothing more than a brief acknowledgement. It seemed to be working, because she hadn't seen anyone else outside in this area.

Kan had warned her that the Marines would be dropping right on top of her. "Find cover and stay there. Don't go inside the breach. They're likely to shoot first when they enter. Just stay out of the way the best you can."

Which was no problem for her. She wasn't armed and she wasn't really trained for microgravity combat. Oh, she'd done some combatives but that was mainly for inside a ship that was in freefall. Losing her connection to the station hull was not appealing at all.

So she sat and waited for someone to show up. She had her hiding places already picked out.

*****

Ana and Oliver were around the corner from the former 76th gate, watching a load of mining explosive trundle by. Oliver shook his head. "Your guy gets his math wrong and you're going to wish you were wearing a suit."

"Viktor is very good at this. Bigger scale than he is used to but he is precise. It's a German thing, ja? We blew their barrier down and seal them at the same time. Two for one."

"You're trying to get cute again. Don't go for elegance, just get the job done. Forget the guys holed up in their compound. Put a blocking force at the hatch and then move against their dependents. You can't get in but that means they can't get out to stop you."

"And leave them at our backs? Nein. Besides, you forget they have information about us. This will work."

Sighing, he stepped back to look at the terminals of the two hackers with them. One was working the exterior indications, keeping random people away from this section of the station. The other was monitoring Justice and station security, along with the external communications. They wanted the earliest possible notification that either of the law enforcement agencies were moving out or that the 76th was arriving.

So when Agent Drusk left her office with two other agents, all armed and armored, Ana was watching. "Where does she think she goes? Only three of them? I know Justice has an inflated opinion of themselves but three against us? Bah. Watch her and tell me where she goes."

Minutes laters, as she watched Viktor carefully place explosives on a wheeled cart, they found out where the Justice agents were going. They had marched right into Black Sun territory and were now meeting with the leadership. Ana slammed her fist into the wall. "Gotverdammt! I told you this happens. Now the Black Suns and maybe even Ghost Dragons will be moving on our operations."

She turned away, issuing orders that pulled away over half the remaining force she had. Oliver watched and said nothing, suppressing his professional opinion. He had a larger goal and the Hoffman leader was moving quite nicely in that direction. And while she was distracted, he keyed a message to Flatley.

*****

Viktor, true to his skill, placed the explosives right where they needed to be. The intent was to widen the entrance and expose the rooms on either side to assault, while knocking down the barrier. He just hadn't counted on the 76th creativity. When the charges went off, the hatch was blown down the corridor, taking out the barrier. The walls were peeled back, briefly exposing the offices on the other side. Then the breaching charges went off, triggered in a sympathetic explosion. The six of them just inside the entrance, three on either side of the hatch, blew the walls of the corridor to shreds, collapsing them on themselves and bringing the ceiling down.

Lieutenant Kan peered through the haze, his MACE filtering out the noxious smoke and fumes. Wires sparked and metal creaked in the tangle of debris and small fires here and there added to the smoky conditions. Almost five meters of hallway were destroyed and the offices on either side were blasted open, their furniture thrown back and computers smashed. Anyone coming through that mess was going to have a hard time.

Baines leaned around the corner to take a look. On the platoon channel, he said, "Sir, Gunny is going to go apeshit when he sees that mess."

"You think that's bad? The Captain told me to defend this place. I don't think he meant I should destroy it in the process."

"You think we're going to lose our security deposit?"

"We might even be blackballed from renting on this station again. Okay, Klowns, here's the story. We didn't have any explosives. We certainly didn't know the Hoffmans were going to blast the place open. We were just sitting here, when all of a sudden the whole place blew in on us."

He very carefully did not say that their line of fire to the barricade and indeed the barricade itself was gone.

*****

Jordan crouched, hidden in a tangle of furniture. They had several backup positions like these prepared and it looked like they were going to need every one of them now. Now, they just waited for the enemy to show up. It was anxiety and boredom at the same time. Over the team channel, Santis made a squelching sound.

"Hear that, people? That's the Suck pulling your soul out."

Jordan was about to tell him to shut it when Bennings called out. *"Fuck, Santis, I didn't know you had a soul? And how do you know what sucking feels like, anyway?"*

Hassan weighed in with his opinion and they were off. He let it go for a few minutes before quieting them down. "Okay, team. Got it out of your system? I hope you saved some attitude for those tangoes outside."

"Hey boy! You got a pretty mouth! Come suck start my Remberg!" Santis' laugh was infectious and they all joined in, until Hassan spoke up.

"Heads up. Target spotted."

*****

Ana beckoned Oliver over to their monitors. "Traffic Control spotted the mercenary ship on their scopes. It'll be here in less than thirty minutes."

"Well, that's a plus for us."

"What? How so? They are here sooner than we planned."

"They had to burn at high gees to get here that quick. Means they've been pinned to their seats for hours. Muscle fatigue and other problems set in. It'll slow down their reflexes and they'll get tired quicker. Trust me, I've done that kind of assault before. You feel like shit when the burn's over."

"Fine. So go up there with Klaus and take them out."

He wheeled on her. "You still don't get it, do you? A MISTer at his worst is still five times better than an untrained person out there. We don't have enough people outside to stop them. We can slow them down, thin their numbers some. But make no mistake, they will come through those airlocks. Hell, they'll even blow their way through the hull just to get at you. You had better have their families all locked up or you're toast."

Chapter 41

Onboard the Calypso

It hurt to breathe. The high gee burn left you feeling tired all over, like you'd been working out for hours. Muscles ached and burned, as you tried not to move or fidget under three times your body weight. Training helped you endure it but pain was pain.

"Ten minutes to release point. Cutting engines in 3, 2, 1."

People sat up, groaning and shaking their heads. Gunny Mulongo was on his feet before everyone else, stalking through the sitting troops. "Alright, what're you waiting for? An invitation to tea with the Emperor? On your feet, Marines! Form up in drop sequence. Weapons and equipment check in five. Move it!"

McMannus left the organization of the drop to the Gunny. He moved up to the cockpit and looked at the screens. "Any news?"

Eisen looked like he felt and he'd been in a gee couch the whole time. "Nothing yet. Funny thing: Traffic Control hasn't pinged us for an approach request yet. Think someone's trying to surprise us?"

"It's not like we're going to surprise them. What about word from Lieutenant Kan?"

"Trying to reestablish with Ms. Vickers. We had comms until about ten minutes ago when she said there were people coming out the airlocks and she was going to hide."

"Smart lady. So we got a welcoming committee. What're we looking at for delta-vee once we leave your fine ship?"

Neil tapped on the navcomp, displaying his current velocity. "Bit higher than what you gave me. I can do another burn–"

"No. That's fine. There's always a difference between what the book says and what the equipment can really do. Besides, faster down means less time being shot at."

The pilot shook his head. "Good luck to you. I'll loop back around the station and be on station fifteen minutes or so after release."

"This thing will be over in ten, one way or the other."

*****

Klaus was as good as advertised in micro, Oliver noted. He was shit for combat, though. He had his troops clustered in groups of five and six and they were spread too far apart for mutual support. Unfortunately, Ana had spread his own team among Klaus'. Still, he'd managed a covert message to them, setting a rally point some distance away. Once the mercs got down, he didn't want to be anywhere near them, both to stay alive and prevent any association of Galactocity with this clusterfuck.

"Ja, ja, I see them!" Klaus was standing atop an equipment housing, a good three meters above the hull, pointing his rifle at the approaching ship. "Hey Marines! Du kannst mich mal!"

The rest of the goons around him were craning their heads and weapons upwards, tracking on the merc ship. Oliver slowly started to edge his way back, taking slow careful steps to not attract attention.

*****

The *Calypso* was again approaching the target rear first, the cargo hatch open, this time canted at a 'down' angle to the station. McMannus stood at the edge of the hatch facing outwards, Mulongo and Harry on either side of him, with the bulk of the station passing in front of him. He opened the general channel and pointed down.

"Marines, this is it. We're just about home. It's been a long, hard trip. You're sore and tired but every one of you is still better than ten of them. This time, we're dropping not to grab a prize for some admiral or fight over nameless territory. We're dropping to rescue our families and 1st Platoon. So remember who and what you are. I expect every one of you to do your job, on the bounce and by the numbers. 76th, follow me."

With that, he unmagged, triggered his suit jets and dropped off the ramp towards Colon. Mulongo and Webb were a step behind him. The rest followed in four columns, thrusters bright against the black background. They fell towards the station, feet first with jets burning hard to shed the velocity from the long trip.

All the Hoffmans saw were fifty plus points of light in space. The distance was long and they soon found out that aiming at that range was difficult. The MISTers were able to sideslip with their attitude control thrusters, causing them to dance about in the Hoffman scopes. Bullets that were aimed at a suit found empty space by the time they got there.

The mercenaries held their fire, knowing from training and experience that it was next to useless. Instead, they concentrated on getting down as quickly as possible. Their objectives were the two airlocks closest to the 76th compound and the hole in the hull that had Cassandra's radio. Webb's platoon was tasked with the airlocks and the rest of them headed for the breach. Their suit thrusters burned red hot, reversing the velocity accumulated on the burn from Metzli. It made for a bouncy ride and they watched their thruster pack temperatures spike into the red.

For a brief moment, it didn't look like there would be a response from the hull, Then three brilliant azure bolts flew from the Hoffman positions. A second later a suit exploded in mid-air. One of the three Barrett's firing from below had just gotten lucky. McMannus gritted his teeth, eyes focused on the drop zone. There was nothing they could do about the surface fire, just weather it and get down.

The incoming fire wasn't all plasma. There were bullets flying through space but none were coming close to the dropping Marines yet. Some of the Hoffmans were now trying to reload their rifles, after futilely emptying their magazines. If the situation hadn't been so dire, it would have been comical to watch them fumbling their way through the process. The ones who held their fire, though; those were going to be the problems. They figured out it was better to wait for the target to stop bouncing all over the place.

The dropping formation split into three groups as each squad headed for their target. The Hoffmans were starting to move as well, pulling back into tight clusters near the two airlocks. They realized that the party that controlled the airlocks had the only guaranteed way back inside. Klaus was directing them to find cover among the various protrusions and low places in the station hull.

Oliver was a good hundred meters now from the airlock. His minder had apparently forgotten about him, more intent on shooting the arriving mercenaries. He checked his display, nodding in satisfaction as he saw his men also a good distance away and headed for the rally point. The Hoffmans would be shredded in short order and it was time to get out.

The 76th was less than a hundred meters now from the hull. Two more suits had been taken out by plasma fire and several more were damaged from lucky small arms shots. A few of the Marines were firing back, single shots aimed at a cluster of enemies in the hopes of hitting one. The difference in training was telling; a few Hoffman goons hung limp, lifeless bodies with boots still magged to the station hull.

McMannus watched the range to the hull drop with one eye, the other monitoring the developing tactical situation. The criminals had made things easier by clustering around the air locks. None seemed to have detected the breach in the hull, so his group was going to have an easier time of things.

"Sparks, first thing on touchdown; get me comms with Whisper One. Whisper Seven, take the command squad through the breach and ensure the other side is clear. Whisper

Two, I'll stand by with the reserve force until you've either secured your objectives or pivot them to flank. Everyone copy?"

A round of acknowledgements came through as he hit the hull. He still had enough velocity that his landing was a stagger, even with his boots active. Several others in his vicinity weren't so lucky. One Marine hit faster than the others, stumbling forward in a fast stagger and then lost contact with both boots. He continued sailing across the hull at a meter height, until he was able to fire his magnetic lines and arrest his motion long enough to get down to the deck.

Elsewhere, Webb's platoon was falling into a firefight at both airlocks. The Hoffmans had grabbed whatever cover they could, which wasn't much while the Marines were above them. Once on the deck, however, it became a deadly game of cat and mouse on the expansive station exterior. Suited figures bounced from cover to cover or crouched in ambush in shadowed spaces.

The greater tactical knowledge and training of the Marines soon became apparent. Moving in two-man teams, they flanked their stationary opponents in several directions. The amateur soldiers found themselves taking fire from all around them and cover from one side became a dangerous surface from which rounds richoted into unarmored suits. That was another advantage the Marines had, as the Hoffmans soon found that even a glancing hit or ricochet opened up a breach in their suit's integrity, taking them out of the fight while they desperately tried to patch the hole.

Sparks hooked his rig into the portable radio with quick efficiency and brought Lieutenant Kan up immediately.

"Whisper One, Whisper Six. We're on the roof and ready to come on down. Gimme a sitrep."

"Whisper Six, thank God you're here. What's left of us is holed up by the Front Gate. They breached the Back Gate several minutes ago and put up a blocking force. There's only a fire team to cover the dependents. We're pinned down

pretty good by debris and enemy fire. Recommend not pushing through here."

"Copy, Whisper One. Be ready to move once we pull the pressure off you. Do you have contact with the fire team with the dependents? Where are they sheltering?"

"Whisper Six, negative contact. The emergency shelter location was the school and community center. But I can't confirm they're all there."

"Good copy, Whisper One. Whisper Seven, exfil the breach and be prepared to move to either airlock. Whisper Two, status?"

"Whisper Six, they're going down easier than the general's aide. Some already broke and headed inside. Should be wrapped up here in the next few mikes."

"Copy, Whisper Two. I want to use the airlocks to flank the enemy assault force. Maximum effort to secure and get a strike force on the other side. You're at Objective Tango; I'm sending you one squad from 1st to support. Whisper Seven and I will push through Objective Sierra." Both airlocks were the standard size, meaning the MISTers could only fit three at a time. *Here's hoping the enemy kept running when they made it inside.*

*****

Jordan leaned around the door frame and fired twice at the heat blob in the hall, ducking back without waiting to see if he hit. The scream of pain was all the confirmation he needed. Bennings had already displaced further back in the room and he passed her position without a second glance.

There wasn't any activity from their side of the hall for several minutes after that and Santis confirmed their side was quiet too. *"Think they gave up and went home?"*

"We can hope."

Bennings spoke up. *"Voices in the hall. They're speaking German or whatever, can't tell what they're saying. But I think they're forming up for another attack."*

"Right. Two shots and displace. Got you covered."

A machine pistol poked around the door frame and fired on full auto. Bullets splattered all over the room, tearing into stacked furniture and the walls. None came even close to hitting either one of them. They ducked anyway, training kicking in. Which meant they were just poking their heads up when the Hoffman goon stepped into the doorway, one arm cocked back. Avery shot him twice as his arm came forward.

The grenade, instead of being propelled to the back of the room, flew a bare seven feet before hitting the floor and rolling. Which put it right at Avery's barrier when it went off. The explosion shook the room, shrapnel making a further mess of the contents and walls. There was a scream from the hall outside as some of the shrapnel found a home.

Jordan popped his weapon back around his hiding spot, trained at the door. "Bennings, you okay?" He didn't have the medical feed the lieutenant or gunny would have but her position was a mess. The carpet was scorched and only a little bit on fire but her barrier was in pieces. Before he got a response, two of the enemy came through the doorway at a rush, shotguns blazing.

He got one but the other dove into cover and started peppering his position. Continuing his calls to Avery, he tried to return fire but two more goons were firing from high and low around the door. It was impossible to put his head up and the Rembergs didn't have the integrated sight that would feed the visuals into his HUD.

A shotgun fired twice from Avery's direction, causing the fire on his position to temporarily slacken. Her voice came over the channel, weak and slurred. *"Hit my helmet. Can't see so good. Can't move one leg either."*

"Can you give me some more covering fire? I'll get to you and–"

"Fuck it, Jordan. I can see them in the doorway. Go." She started firing in a slow, controlled manner.

Gritting his teeth, he backed out of his hide and made his way to the next position. "Guys, we've lost Avery."

*****

Oliver met up with his team around the curve of the station hull. Whatever was happening back there no longer concerned them. It was time to get back inside and get control of the new developments. Flatley would be able to use the destruction of the Hoffmans to good effect and he had to locate Cassandra Vickers and whatever information she had.

They made their way to a public airlock near the ship docks. Along the way they stashed their weapons, marking it with a beacon that would only respond to the correct code. Oliver had contacted Flatley to come meet them at the airlock with changes of clothes, something more tourist-like so they could blend into the crowds.

So confident was he that they had left the firefight and its results behind and so intent was he on the work to be done that he failed to notice a slim figure in a blue and orange vacc suit emerge from the shadows of a heat vent. It followed them at a distance, keeping to shadows and cover.

Cassandra watched as they entered the airlock. This one, like many of the public locks, had large, windowed areas where the visitors who didn't want to go outside could watch those who did. She found a good spot to look through the windows, not too close and saw the man she knew as Mr. Smith meet up with another man. This one she realized she knew, although it took her a few minutes to come up with a name. Thomas Flatley, with the Galactocity team. He seemed very familiar with Smith and handed him and his men some clothes as they talked. All of this she caught on her suit camera, recording everything she could until they disappeared further into the station.

Well, now what to do with that information? I think maybe Agent Drusk might be interested to learn who was behind the Hoffman pirate scheme, or at least who might have been calling the shots. And now that I have images of 'Smith', maybe we can identify him as well.

She waited for several more minutes to be sure before entering the airlock herself. Now she had to find Drusk.

Chapter 42

The MISTers took the airlocks away from the surviving Hoffmans with ease. The few that had returned inside were already scared, having seen their comrades torn to ribbons outside. Some ran clumsily deeper into the station, still clad in their vacc suits. Others took up defensive positions at doorways and corners, nervously waiting for the attack.

What came was something outside their experience. An airlock had two doors but usually only one opened at a time. Both open equaled depressurization, a danger that all spacers feared.

For the MIST, depressurization was an opportunity, a tool, just like any other weapon.

The defenders could see the lights on the control panel come on, signaling the outer door was open. It took a couple of minutes for the air to cycle, a fact they all knew. So they thought they had time.

The inner door flew open, courtesy of the Marine-issue electronic lockpicks. Air rushed out, alarms screamed and armored figures came clumping through the airlock, guns blazing. The Hoffmans were too stunned to fire right away and the MIST picked off the defenders they could see with short bursts. That broke the remaining defenders, who turned to run. They died with 4mm needles in their backs, mag boots keeping them stuck to the floor and waving like grass in the outrushing wind.

It was a calculated risk. A station like Colon had multiple interior pressure doors to minimize the risk of a depressurization situation and they would slam close the instant the sensors detected a severe enough drop in air pressure. Captain McMannus was betting his electronic lockpicks would be able to override them, just like he'd do on a Grausian ship.

Both airlocks went down the same way and the MIST poured in, including the wounded. Once the airlocks were sealed again, temporary aid stations were established as the assault forces pushed on towards their home base.

"Whisper One, Whisper Six. We're inside and pushing forward. Status?"

"Whisper Six, we're holding on but we cannot advance. I can keep their attention while you flank them."

"Copy, Whisper One. Whisper Two, maximum effort. What you can't force right away, go around. Watch out for civilians."

Gunny Mulongo already had their force moving down the corridors, after making sure of the dead Hoffmans. Soon, the only Marines left at the airlock were those whose suits or bodies were too damaged to be forced into action. No one wanted to miss out on the relief force but damaged servos, destroyed weapons and leaking bodies held them back.

Ana was busy trying to coordinate a battle that spread across multiple compartments. She had a blocking force in place to contain the Marines in the headquarters, there were several groups who had forced their way through to the dependent quarters and she had to contend with those she'd sent back to prevent the other gangs from taking over. She was also learning that coordinating logistics was a specialty in and of itself, as the attacking forces constantly sent back requests for ammunition and a steady trickle of wounded came back.

Thus it was several minutes before she learned of the defeat of the outside force. This came from scared gang members who finally made it back to her command post, still clad in their vacc suits. Her cyber operators pulled up video footage of armored Marines pouring through the corridors. The relentless advance was unopposed, even by the station blast doors.

"*Scheiss, scheiss, schiess*! Put something in their way! Close all the blast doors between here and there! Turn out the lights! Anything!" She looked around the compartment, now right across from the Marines back gate. They would come through here, so she could not be here. The best place would be among the dependents.

"Hans! Claudi! Get these *idioten* organized! The Marines will be here soon and we must give them a proper greeting, ja?"

As her lieutenants set about their task, she grabbed the two cyber operators and dragged them with her towards the dependent quarters.

*****

A few more closed doors made no difference. McMannus was wondering just where exactly the enemy was and when they were going to fight. The initial attack on the garrison and the battle outside the station hinted at a more determined enemy. So why hadn't they seen anyone since the airlocks?

"Contact front! Whisper Six, Whisper Seven. I have an enemy force just outside the Back Gate. They're fighting hard but no serious defenses."

"Whisper Seven, copy. Clear them out quick-like. Use grenades and dirks if you need to. I want to relieve Whisper One ASAP."

"Whisper Seven copies."

"Whisper Two, status?"

"Whisper Six, almost to the Front Gate now. I expect, yes, there they are. Enemy contact, sir. Same orders?"

"Same orders, Mr. Webb. Let's get Mr. Kan out so he can get a breath of fresh air." He motioned to Sparks to set up the battlecomp display as he listened to the sounds of gunfire and explosions up ahead. The 3D holo map filled in with data rapidly, although he had no idea what was happening past the two gates. There was still some jamming in the area, hampering information gathering.

Mulongo reported the compartment up ahead as clear and was redeploying to assault the identified blocking force at the headquarters. Harry's action to clear the front gate was short, there being very few defenders. It would take too long to go around, so McMannus ordered him to make contact with Ishido and head through that way.

Too long. We're taking too long. I have no idea what's happening with our families. The only good news is that the enemy commander hasn't contacted me to negotiate for their safety. That means they're still free, right?

*****

Hassan went down next, his weapon jamming in the face of a determined assault. "Is it just me, Brian, or do they seem more desperate?"

They were together now, at their third-to-last fallback position. Both had small amounts of damage to their suits, courtesy of the large volumes of fire encountered. Both had their visors up to talk. The jamming was making even their suit-to-suit comms difficult.

"Desperate like a private with his first stripper. Shit, they want to get with us so bad it's like we're the strippers."

"That's an image I don't need. Besides, you couldn't swing on a pole if your life depended on it."

"Daddy's little moneymaker can pull in the credits, man. I'll show you when we're done here."

Jordan turned to look at him, a smile beginning on his face. "You know what? I'll take you up on that. But I am NOT stuffing credits in your thong."

The harsh voices in the next compartment forestalled any further conversation. As before the attack was preceded by a thrown IED, in this case mining explosive with a wristcomp taped to it. They hit the deck and waited for the explosion to clear, then popped up to fire. Bodies fell in the doorway, some crawling backward with painful moans while others lay still.

"Dammit, Jordan, I'm down to my last mag. Then it's dirk work for me."

"I've the rest of this mag and one more. I'll hold here while you head back to the lieutenant. They might have more ammo."

"Might? Fuck it, man. I'm staying. This is the best fight we've been in. Besides, if you go down, who'll see my show on the stripper pole?"

Jordan sighed.

*****

Alanna watched the fuzzy signals on her HUD. The jamming was getting stronger, or maybe closer. She popped her visor open. "Dad, I'm going to lose the team signals real soon. The jamming is bad now."

They waited behind a barricade of tables and doors removed from the other side of the room. Her father crouched next to her, shotgun in hand. She was surprised to see his normally calm face beaded with sweat. He saw her staring and gave a crooked grin.

"Yes, I'm scared. More for you than for me but I'd be a fool not to be scared."

She watched him for a moment, then stood. "Dad, I'm going out there. The more we can delay them there, the more likely the Captain will come."

He sighed and shook his head. "Your mom said your stubbornness came from me but I think it comes from her. Just… be careful, okay?"

She smiled as she leaped the barricade. "Marines aren't careful. They're dangerous."

*****

Sure enough, the next attack saw Santis using his vibrodirk to cut down the last of the wave. It also saw more damage to their suits. This group had battle rifles and subguns, although they tended to spray and pray rather than use aimed fire.

Alanna found the two of them setting up in their last fighting position, in the compartment just across the way from the safe room. She slid into the position with a smooth, quick motion, avoiding fire from any spotters.

"What's the sitrep, boys?" She popped her face shield and they did the same. The radios were useless now.

"Fuck me, LT, it's good to see a friendly face. Don't suppose you've got any extra mags? Lance Corporal Santis is out and I'm down to half a mag."

She distributed her extra magazines while Jordan gave her the download on their position and the enemy forces. "Any word from the Captain or Lieutenant Kan?"

"Negative on both. But the jamming's got everything blanketed. Might not hear anything until someone takes it out."

A voice called out from the enemy side, a woman. "Hello, Marines! We talk, ja?"

Alanna put her finger to her lips, looking at the other two. "We'll talk to you. This is Lieutenant Vestry of the 76th MIST. Who are you?"

"Ah, the daughter of the spy. Your first fight, ja? What do you think? Not like your war stories in training, nein?"

His eyes wide, Santis whispered. "How the fuck does she know about you?"

Her glare back shut him down hard. "From what the rest of the unit is saying, you're not much compared to the Grausians. So I guess this is a letdown. What about you? How do you like fighting someone who can really fight back? Ready to surrender yet?"

A harsh laugh came back. "Oh, I like you. Sie haben Mut, kleines Mädchen. But all good things must come to an end. It's all over now. You have nowhere else to go and no rescue in sight. Surrender and nobody else has to get hurt. When your Captain McMannus finally gets back, he and I have a little chat and then everyone leaves Colon. Simple as that."

Alanna looked at the two enlisted men. "The Captain will be here soon. I know it."

They both looked back at her and nodded. Jordan pointed at the deck. "Cap'n would never let us down, ma'am. He said he'll be here, then he'll be here. Keep this lady talking; longer she talks, less they're attacking."

Eyes bright, she nodded back. "Who are you? You never answered my question?"

"Ana Hoffman. Maybe you heard of my family, ja? We own this station. And we say it is time for you to go."

Santis reported the enemy were definitely stacking for an attack but Jordan wondered why they were talking now. "LT, why talk now? All along, they've been pushing hard. Now they want to talk about surrender?"

"It could be that they've lost too many people. Maybe they want to minimize any losses in the final attack? Besides, they have to know if they kill any of the civilians, it's over for them. The Captain will never let them get away."

"Maybe. I guess it doesn't really matter. We're going to fight, right?"

She winked at him. "Damned straight. As my dad would say, 'Never give up, never surrender.'"

He considered the phrase. "That's... dumb. Where the hell did he get that from?"

"Old Earth thing he says. Keeps promising to show me when I'm old enough to appreciate it." She turned back to Ana. "We say we're staying. Maybe you should be the ones to go. Especially when the rest of the unit gets here. They're going to fuck you up for this."

"Ah yes, your precious force coming from Metzli. They will not get here in time. You will be dead and your families will be ours to control. So why not save yourselves and surrender now? No more dying."

Alanna smiled coldly. "She wants us to surrender real bad. That means not surrendering screws up her plan. So let's do what we do best and screw up the enemy's plans. Be ready, boys." She pitched her voice back over the barricade. "Enough talking, lady. Fight or leave. I don't care which."

There was no response but they heard hoarse whispers coming from across the room. As Alanna closed her visor, Jordan noticed her hand was shaking.

*****

Ana pushed and shoved her people into a line at the door. Most were reluctant, now that most of the booze and drugs were wearing off. Plus they'd seen a lot of their friends and other members dead or wounded. They were no strangers to blood and injuries but this slow crawl, foot by foot to gain ground was a concept they were unfamiliar with.

Her cyber operators were working to regain control of the tech in these spaces. The attack and the Marines themselves had done a lot of damage. Relays were severed in multiple places, power couplers were blown and lots of things were broken. They couldn't even get the lights back on in many places. *Oliver was right; these Marines are thorough when breaking things. No matter. We will have them soon.* Her eyes lingered on the one section of screen showing the camera feed they'd established early on. The Marines were streaming through, her rear guard at the gate destroyed. *We can delay them, like they delayed us. Make them fight for every centimeter. I just need a bit more time to finish this.*

She slapped the shoulder of the man next to her and he armed the explosive pack. Viktor built this small enough that it wouldn't breach the hull. He was pretty sure that wouldn't happen. The bomb man stepped up to the door, going low and lobbed the pack in with a strong sideways through. Everyone turned away, putting their fingers over their ears.

*****

The explosive pack was unbalanced, courtesy of the jury-rigged build. The thrower was understandably concerned about not exposing himself too much, so he released early.

As a result, the pack flew to a far corner of the room before detonating.

Santis called out the throw as it happened and they all ducked behind their barricade, backs to the blast. When it came, it shook the deck like an earthquake. The walls next to where the pack landed were blown to pieces for ten meters and a holed opened up in the floor nearly five meters across. Beyond the walls were more rooms but the floor contained the pipes for water, cooling fluid and sewage. Fountains of various fluids spouted up into their room, coating everything.

The Marine barricade, makeshift as it was, didn't stand a chance against that blast. The three of them were pelted with bits of barricade as it blew apart. Jordan, farthest from the blast, was nearly buried in debris.

Several seconds passed in stunned silence and then the Hoffman goons poured into the room, firing from the hip. Some slipped and flew on the liquids that were now everywhere, rounds impacting the already damaged ceiling. Santis was the first to recover, pushing off against the deck with a blast from his suit jets. He didn't get the same effect in gravity but he got in among the leading wave, slashing back and forth with his vibrodirk. Blood began to join the other fluids on the ground.

Alanna was next, firing from one knee. She got off five shots before a slug from a battle rifle took her full in the chest. Her armor absorbed the hit but the energy transfer knocked her onto her back. She hadn't been magged to the deck, Jordan saw from under his pile of debris. He was still struggling to shift the pieces, at least enough to get his Remberg out.

Santis took a full shotgun blast to his right leg, collapsing it. He went down to one knee, still swinging, although all his close targets were either down or retreated.

Jordan got his shotgun up finally. It was a bad angle but he started firing anyway. Alanna was struggling to right herself, a tricky maneuver since her thruster and life support pack made her position like a turtle on its back.

People were pouring into the room now, firing as they came. Most of it was directed at waist level or higher but there were so many of them. Jordan was sure he hit a few of them but when his magazine was empty he couldn't reload because of his position. A muzzle rapped on his visor and he let his hands fall to the deck.

Santis was also on his back, with two men holding his arms down by the simple means of standing on his forearms. He could have thrown them off, given his suit's exoskeleton strength but a third pointed a battle rifle at his face. Lieutenant Vestry was sitting up but she had three guns trained on her.

A tall blonde woman strode into the room, wearing a ballistic vest and a PW-93C at her hip. She stopped in front of Alanna, a sneer on her face. "Pop your visor, kleines Mädchen. Let us talk like civilized people."

"Civilized." The young lieutenant waved a hand at the room, her voice an electronic buzz from behind the helmet. "Right. You call this civilized."

Ana tapped the muzzle against the visor. "I will not tell you again. You are a bonus hostage but I don't need you. And I think your men will be much more motivated to cooperate if you are alive. With you dead, I don't need them either."

Alanna's visor popped open, her face red and eyes blazing. "You will not touch my men! They surren–"

Her voice cut off as Ana reversed her weapon and smashed the butt into Alanna's face. The Marine toppled backward, blood streaming from her nose.

"Shut. Your. Mouth." Ana leaned over her captive and spit on her. "There. That's for your rules of war. This is my rule; there are no rules. Kill or be killed. One more word and I kill one of yours."

The earphones in the MACEs let out a piercing squeal, loud enough to nearly deafen their wearers and cause the Hoffmans to wince. A man came running into the room, carrying a computer in his hands. "Bossin! Bossin, the jammer is down! We have lost the cameras, too!"

The wall speaker, one usually only for station use came to life. *"Attention, members of the Hoffman gang. This is Captain Fremont McMannus of the 76th MIST. I am ordering you to surrender and lay down your arms. Failure to comply will result in your complete destruction. You have one minute."*

Ana slapped her cyber operator on the side of the head. "Dummkopf! Why do you let him talk! Shut him down!"

"We can't! There is something controlling the networks now. I haven't seen it before!"

McMannus' voice came through the speaker again. *"We control the comm networks now. I'm sure your people are good but they aren't as good as Terran Union Security Agency algorithms. You now have forty-five seconds."*

Ana swung back to Alanna, weapon pointed at her head. "Try anything and she dies. They all die!"

"Then you die next to them. I'll burn your organization to ash before I'm done. The Hoffman name will be a lesson to anyone in known space about fucking with the Marines."

The Hoffman goons were looking at each other, at Ana and at the exit. She screamed at them. "Don't listen to him! He is nothing! We own this station!"

"Time's up. On your head be it, then. Execute entry protocol." The room went quiet and the Hoffmans looked around wildly. Weapons came up, pointing at the exits. Even Ana was caught up, pivoting in place and trying to watch both doorways at once. Unnoticed, Alanna shut her visor and turned her head to the side, as did Brian and Jordan. After several seconds, when nothing happened, the crime boss laughed.

"Oh ja, gut trick! Very good. See! They are not here. We own this station! They are bluf–"

The multiple explosions cut her off. Four large holes opened up, two on each wall. Armored figures stormed into the room, weapons firing. Hoffman soldiers were caught in a crossfire, their bodies riddled with 4mm needles. Ana was hit as well, going down in a spray of blood as the neecle shredded her vest and ripped open her chest.

Captain McMannus followed the assault teams into the room. He walked past the Marines disarming the survivors to where Ana lay. She was gasping for breath, a froth of blood in her mouth. He popped his visor and looked down at her.

"You don't own anything anymore."

Chapter 43

Oliver walked with his team to the departure lounge. They were all on the same transport out but that couldn't be helped. Speed was of the utmost importance now, because once McManns figured out who was behind the Hoffmans he would tear the station apart looking for them. Everything that could implicate them, weapons, data, even clothing was cleaned up and spaced. Someone would find it but they'd be long gone by them.

Clearing the security checkpoint took time but he didn't see anything amiss. Station security was finally doing their job and not hiding away. He wasn't sure if this was a good sign or not. But as long as there weren't any armored Marines waiting for them, everything should be good to go.

The lounge was mostly empty, with maybe a dozen people waiting there. The four of them took seats together, all with good views of the entrance. There was still more than an hour until departure and he wouldn't relax until he was on that ship.

A woman entered the lounge, dressed in a shirt that read, 'Colon High Station. Fun Above All!' She dragged a large suitcase behind her and was speaking loudly to someone about her vacation. Her path took her to a seat across from them.

Sighing, Oliver gave his men the 'stand down' signal and walked over to sit next to her. "Cut the act, Cassandra. You don't fool me."

She cut off in mid-sentence. "Damn. I thought that was a pretty good look. What gave it away?"

"What are you doing here? Come to get revenge on me?"

"Yes and no. Yes, I want revenge. No, I'm not the one doing the revenge."

"Then why are you here?"

"I'm the distraction."

He looked up suddenly as the dozen people in the lounge stood and pulled weapons out, shouting, "Justice Ministry! Don't move!"

Cassie stepped quickly out of his reach, smiling. "Consider this some corporate goodwill. Now you don't have to worry about Captain McMannus killing you."

Chapter 44

Captain McMannus sat at his desk, working steadily through the files on his computer. Writing letters to the families of the deceased came first. There were far too many of those, more than he thought he'd need as a mercenary captain. Then came the loss reports, of ammunition expended, weapons damaged or destroyed and other gear. Then the reports to his employers on their actions, to include details of the damage to Colon High Station as a result of the Hoffman attack. Finally, there were the after-action reports, an internal look at their own actions and how they responded to the enemy. These would be further discussed among themselves, with an eye towards improving their own skillset.

There was a bright side to all the paperwork. He saw the messages as they came in, both kinds. There were congratulations from several of his former TUMC comrades, to include one from Colonel Garza, now Chief of Security Garza at the Hirano colony. *"People said you were crazy to jump ship but I knew you'd land on your feet. I've had word from some old friends that your name is being passed on to more of those getting pushed out. Looks like you might get that battalion command anyway."*

Col Meagher also sent his own kudos, along with a note that he had referred a few dozen micro-trained former Marines his way. *"I can't use them the way you can, Free. Do good things with them."*

Also welcome were the inquiries into the 76th availability for hire. Security, training, anti-piracy, the list went on. *We've gone from taking the only contract to come our way to having a plethora of choices. Success breeds success.* All of those he forwarded on to Ezekiel and Alanna for their review and recommendation.

Towards the end of the day, as he was closing down his terminal, his intelligence officer walked in and flopped down on the chair across from his desk. Free gave him the side eye; the dapper former Naval captain never flopped. "Is there something you wanted, Mr. Vestry?"

"Just a report from Justice. They caught the guy behind the piracy before he left the station. He's not talking but word is he was associated with one of the big corporations."

"Given Justice's methods, is he going to be taking a short walk out of an airlock soon?"

"That one's more complicated. I suspect whichever corporation he works for is going to pay off the government to keep things quiet."

Free sighed and looked up at the ceiling. "So he gets off, despite all the damage he did."

"Well, look at it this way. He screwed up and got caught doing illegal things for a corporation. They're not likely to be in a forgiving mood." The older man closed his eyes and rubbed the bridge of his nose. "I wouldn't worry about him. Save that for your own people."

"Like you? I take it there's something wrong?"

"As a matter of fact, there is, sir. I'd like to lodge a formal complaint and a request."

"Complaint? Against whom?"

"You. How many inquiries and job offers did you forward to me? Ten or twelve, I think. That's a lot of work for an old man."

Free leaned back in his chair, steepling his fingers. "And the request?"

The other man sat up, face eager and all tiredness banished. "I need more people in the intel shop."

"You are about as subtle as a plasma thrower."

"I have a candidate in mind. Fits the job skills list down to a tee. Be the perfect assistant S-2."

"Oh, this I've got to hear. Who is it that meets your exacting standards?"

"Check your messages. I just sent you the name and what we should offer."

Free sighed and opened up the new message, which had a name and attached file. The name wasn't a surprise, now that he thought about it. The attachment was an award decoration for the Navy and Marine Corps Commendation Medal. As he read through it, he nodded. "I heartily endorse your suggestion, Mr. Vestry. Think you can get this person to sign on?"

"No doubt about it, sir."

*****

Cassie sat in the outbound lounge, staring out the plexisteel windows at the busy docks beyond. Her ticket took her back to Tau Ceti, courtesy of StellarMart. What awaited her there was an unknown, although she suspected the worst. Oscar had only sent one reply to her report, a bare-bones communique that hinted she would be finding a new career soon. *I can't even feel sorry for myself. Selena, Vera and Janik are gone. They died and I survived because of corporate politics. Do I even want to go back to that world?*

Her musings were interrupted by the arrival of two people in 76th undress grays. Ezekiel and Alanna Vestry stood in front of her. The young Marine's face was still swollen from the broken nose and cheekbone. Her father smiled, waving at the departure lounge.

"Cassie, I had hoped you would say goodbye to us before you left."

"I'm not much at goodbyes, Ezekiel. Most of the time, leaving a job meant leaving in quiet and secrecy anyway."

"I'm too familiar with that. But before you go, we have something for you. The 'we' in this case being the 76th." He motioned to his daughter, who was holding a blue folder and small case.

She opened the small case, displaying a medal with an eagle over a fouled anchor. A black, gold and red ribbon was attached to it. Smiling, she held it forward and recited from memory. "For heroic conduct during an attack on the 76th

Microgravity Strike Team garrison. When communications were lost with the relief force, Cassandra Vickers, with cool courage and alert presence of mind, unhesitatingly volunteered to re-establish communications by extra-vehicular activity. She also, at great risk to her own life. carried a message to the Pavo Real Justice Ministry to enlist their aid in relieving the siege of the garrison. Her gallant conduct in risking her life to bring aid to the beleaguered garrison was in keeping with the highest traditions of the Terran Union Marine Corps."

Cassie sat, open-mouthed at the display. A lump formed in her chest, making it hard to breathe. "I... I didn't do that much. Really, it was…," her brain failed her at that point, her voice trailing off.

Ezekiel shook his head. "Without you, the garrison surely would have been overrun and the dependents taken hostage. Your radio link gave the relief force the ability to get the information it needed to relieve the siege and save the civilians. You earned this, Cassie. I think your brother would be proud of you."

He then reached over and put one hand over the medal. "There's just one problem. In order to accept this medal, you have to be part of the 76th. Can't just give medals to random civilians, you know. Captain McMannus himself endorses this offer. So, Cassandra Vickers, would you like to sign on with the 76th and become a mercenary? The unit really needs your unique set of skills. And I could really use an assistant who knows the business."

The future, previously uncertain, now looked brighter. One door closed but another one opened. She nodded at their uniforms. "I think gray is going to look good on me."
To be continued!

If you'd like to see more of the 76th MIST, they also appear in the Fallen Empire anthology "Overrun", helping The Irish Brigade take out a space station that's homebase to a thriving slave trade.

For these and other great works of Military Science Fiction, go to www.cannonpublishing.us

And make sure you follow Michael Morton on Amazon!